PUSHCART PRIZE XLVII

2023
PUSHCART PRIZE XLVII
BEST OF THE
SMALL PRESSES

EDITED BY BILL HENDERSON
WITH THE PUSHCART PRIZE EDITORS

Note: nominations for this series are invited from any small, independent, literary book press or magazine in the world, print or online. Up to six nominations—tear sheets or copies, selected from work published, or about to be published, in the calendar year—are accepted by our December 1 deadline each year. Write to Pushcart Fellowships, P.O. Box 380, Wainscott, N.Y. 11975 for more information or consult our website www.pushcartprize.com.

Acknowledgments
Selections for The Pushcart Prize are reprinted with the permission of authors and presses cited. Copyright reverts to authors and presses immediately after publication.

Distributed by W. W. Norton & Co.
500 Fifth Ave., New York, N.Y. 10110

Library of Congress Card Number: 76-58675
ISBN (hardcover): 978-09600977-8-4
ISBN (paperback): 978-09600977-9-1
ISSN: 0149-7863

IN MEMORIAM

Daniel L. Dolgin
Pupil, Teacher, Friend

INTRODUCTION

So many years, so many hundreds of writers and presses—isn't it about time this Pushcart thing gets stale and old and creaky? One would think so, but quite the opposite has happened over the decades.

It seems the small press universe is a roiling sea always churning, always new. We are indeed news that stays news and that's because we are free from commercial or political shackles.

Which leads me to a reprint from the 1977 PPII—"The Deportation of Solzhenitsyn" smuggled to the West out of Soviet Russia by the underground *samizdat* movement. To run a small press in the USSR in those days risked imprisonment or worse. For several years, until the fall of the Soviet Union, our PP reprinted *samizdat* publishers to encourage our censored friends behind the Iron Curtain. Sadly, we see an emerging situation where *samizdat* may return and not just in Russia or China.

After 47 years the Prize—this small good thing born in a Yonkers, NY studio apartment and presently residing in a backyard shack on Long Island, is a continuing global witness thanks to thousands of authors, presses and readers who have kept us alive and nimble. Spirits, love, luck, defiance . . . you name the reason. Here we are, always ancient, always new.

✤　✤　✤

And sadly, over the years so many friends of this series have crossed the bar. Just recently we lost two of our long time Board members. Daniel Dolgin was our pro bono lawyer, financial backer, and over all cheerleader. Dan was a student of mine way back in 1963 when, as a Harvard graduate school dropout, I taught 6th grade at Staten Island Academy. With my meager salary I planned to collect funds for a stay in Paris where I would write my great American novel (self-published

9

after years of rejection). Dan was a 12-year-old joy in that day, and he remained an enthusiastic supporter to his dying day.

Jim Charlton was a buddy from my Doubleday editing days, where we both learned of the shenanigans of corporate publishing. Jim helped me found the New York Publishing Softball League. In our first season Doubleday lost all of its eight games except for one forfeit from McGraw Hill. Everyone who knew Jim will remember his expansive humor and often irreverence, but he kept his eye on what was important—baseball especially, his own small press Quick Fox and always the Pushcart Prize.

Philip Spitzer was my first literary agent. All writers know what that first recognition means, that first jolt that lets you know what you put on paper is OK. Phil did that for me back in 1968 and his recognition is why the Prize always attempts to reprint and list so many writers of promise and accomplishment. Philip died recently after a long illness. In remembering him I recall Truman Capote's elation at receiving his first acceptance letter, "Dizzy with excitement is no mere phrase." Phil got me dizzy.

So many people to thank: our devoted readers first of all, W.W. Norton our noble distributor for decades, all our financial backers listed later, our guest editors for this edition—Jerald Walker, Olivia Clare Friedman, Lindsay Starck (prose); Edward Hirsch, Mary Szybist, Chen Chen (poetry)—and especially the writers and presses in this edition.

I know I say it every year but the wealth of talent, empathy, and insight here is overwhelming. Year to year the literary excellence of the small press world has grown profoundly. I can barely express my admiration to our writers who, in the face of such enormous obstacles of climate catastrophe, war, and deep international anxiety, cast aside gloom and persist—pilgrims on the sacred journey.

Pushcart salutes all of you.

Love and wonder,

Bill

THE PEOPLE WHO HELPED

FOUNDING EDITORS—Anaïs Nin (1903–1977), Buckminster Fuller (1895–1983), Charles Newman (1938–2006), Daniel Halpern, Gordon Lish, Harry Smith (1936–2012), Hugh Fox (1932–2011), Ishmael Reed, Joyce Carol Oates, Len Fulton (1934–2011), Leonard Randolph (1926–1993), Leslie Fiedler (1917–2003), Nona Balakian (1918–1991), Paul Bowles (1910–1999), Paul Engle (1908–1991), Ralph Ellison (1913–1994), Reynolds Price (1933–2011), Rhoda Schwartz (1931–2013), Richard Morris (1936–2003), Ted Wilentz (1915–2001), Tom Montag, William Phillips (1907–2002). Poetry editor: H. L. Van Brunt

CONTRIBUTING EDITORS FOR THIS EDITION—Steve Adams, Dan Albergotti, Idris Anderson, Tony Ardizzone, Barbara Ascher, David Baker, Kathleen Balma, Kim Barnes, Eli Barrett, Ellen Bass, Rick Bass, Claire Bateman, Bruce Beasley, Karen Bender, Bruce Bennett, Linda Bierds, Marianne Boruch, Michael Bowden, Fleda Brown, Ayse Papatya Bucak, E. S. Bumas, Elena Karina Byrne, Richard Cecil, Jung Hae Chae, Ethan Chatagnier, Samuel Cheney, Kim Chinquee, Jane Ciabattari, Olivia Clare, Suzanne Cleary, Michael Collier, Martha Collins, Quintin Collins, Lydia Conklin, Lisa Couturier, Paul Crenshaw, Claire Davis, John Drury, Karl Elder, Kathy Fagan, Ed Falco, Beth Ann Fennelly, Gary Fincke, Maribeth Fischer, Robert Long Foreman, Seth Fried, Alice Friman, John Fulton, Frank X. Gaspar, Christine Gelineau, Nancy Geyer, Gary Gildner, Albert Goldbarth, Debra Gwartney, Becky Hagenston, Jeffrey Harrison, Timothy Hedges, Daniel Henry, DeWitt Henry, David Hernandez, Bob Hicok, Jane Hirshfield, Richard Hoffman, Andrea Hollander, Elliott Holt, Maria Hummel, Allegra Hyde, Holly Iglesias, Mark Irwin, David Jauss, Jeff P. Jones, Rodney Jones, Christopher Kempf, John Kistner, Mary Kuryla, Peter LaBerge, Caroline Langston,

Don Lee, Fred Leebron, Sandra Leong, Shara Lessley, Emily Lee Luan, Jennifer Lunden, Margaret Luongo, Hugh Martin, Matt Mason, Dan Masterson, Lou Mathews, Tracy Mayor, Robert McBrearty, Nancy McCabe, Jo McDougall, Elizabeth McKenzie, Edward McPherson, David Meischen, Patricia Cleary Miller, Douglas W. Milliken, Nancy Mitchell, Jim Moore, Joan Murray, Carol Muske-Dukes, David Naimon, Aimee Nezhukumatathil, D. Nurkse, Colleen O'Brien, Meghan O'Gieblyn, Joyce Carol Oates, Dzvinia Orlowsky, Alan Michael Parker, Molly Peacock, Dustin Pearson, Dominica Phetteplace, Carl Phillips, Leslie Pietrzyk, Dan Pope, Andrew Porter, Lia Purpura, Anne Ray, Janisse Ray, Nancy Richard, Ron Riekki, Atsuro Riley, Laura Rodley, Jay Rogoff, Maxine Scates, Philip Schultz, Lloyd Schwartz, Maureen Seaton, Annie Sheppard, Suzanne Farrell Smith, Lucas Southworth, Marcus Spiegel, Justin St. Germain, Maura Stanton, Jody Stewart, Ron Stottlemyer, Ben Stroud, Nancy Takacs, Ron Tanner, Katherine Taylor, Susan Terris, Joni Tevis, Robert Thomas, Frederic Tuten, Lee Upton, BJ Ward, Michael Waters, Marc Watkins, William Wenthe, Philip White, Joe Wilkins, Elanor Wilner, Sandi Wisenberg, David Wojahn, Pui Ying Wong, Shelley Wong, Carolyne Wright, Robert Wrigley

PAST POETRY EDITORS—H.L. Van Brunt, Naomi Lazard, Lynne Spaulding, Herb Leibowitz, Jon Galassi, Grace Schulman, Carolyn Forché, Gerald Stern, Stanley Plumly, William Stafford, Philip Levine, David Wojahn, Jorie Graham, Robert Hass, Philip Booth, Jay Meek, Sandra McPherson, Laura Jensen, William Heyen, Elizabeth Spires, Marvin Bell, Carolyn Kizer, Christopher Buckley, Chase Twichell, Richard Jackson, Susan Mitchell, Lynn Emanuel, David St. John, Carol Muske, Dennis Schmitz, William Matthews, Patricia Strachan, Heather McHugh, Molly Bendall, Marilyn Chin, Kimiko Hahn, Michael Dennis Browne, Billy Collins, Joan Murray, Sherod Santos, Judith Kitchen, Pattiann Rogers, Carl Phillips, Martha Collins, Carol Frost, Jane Hirshfield, Dorianne Laux, David Baker, Linda Gregerson, Eleanor Wilner, Linda Bierds, Ray Gonzalez, Philip Schultz, Phillis Levin, Tom Lux, Wesley McNair, Rosanna Warren, Julie Sheehan, Tom Sleigh, Laura Kasischke, Michael Waters, Bob Hicok, Maxine Kumin, Patricia Smith, Arthur Sze, Claudia Rankine, Eduardo C. Corral, Kim Addonizio, David Bottoms, Stephen Dunn, Sally Wen Mao, Robert Wrigley, Dorothea Lasky, Kevin Prufer, Chloe Honum, Rebecca Hazelton, Christopher Kempf, Keith Ratzlaff, Jane Mead, Victoria Chang,

CONTENTS

PUSHCART PRIZE XLVII

AMBIVALENCE

fiction by VICTORIA LANCELOTTA

from THE IDAHO REVIEW

On Wednesday mornings the father hoists someone else's
    daughter onto his naked lap
    bends someone else's daughter over the pressboard motel desk
    flips someone else's daughter onto her skinny back
    does not think about his own
    will not think about his own.
    His own is younger than this one
    but not by much
    not by enough.

His own is a junior at an all-girls prep school, an honor roll student, a varsity field hockey player. He should be so proud. He should tell this one how proud.

This one likes banana daiquiris and smoking meth off shiny foil squares and giving head.

Upon further reflection.

It's possible that he shouldn't, in fact, tell this one. It's also possible that he is not, in fact, so proud of his own at all. He'll get around to considering this.

This one has lavender-painted toenails and skin that tastes like watermelon candy. She has sticky lips and straight white teeth and when he looks at them he can think of nothing but what they feel like on his nipples.

He lifts her onto his lap and she hooks her legs around his waist, flips her crackling hair over her shoulders and sets to unbuttoning his shirt. With dexterity, with aplomb, with great industriousness.

Her name is Samantha and she likes to be called Sammy and he does not give a fuck. He feels somewhat aggrieved that he knows her name at all. She lowers her head to his chest. Those teeth. It's eleven in the morning.

Wednesday is made of the hours between 10:30 and noon, or sometimes one, if he is lucky. Wednesday is furnished with two queen-size beds covered in rough blankets and sheets that smell of bleach. It is a comforting smell, the white nasal pinch of it. When he was a young man he worked in a commercial laundry, and bleach to him still smells of possibility, of a vast and numbing freedom.

There are paintings of harbor scenes on Wednesday's walls, piers and skiffs, gulls screaming in this motel room one hour into Pennsylvania.

His belt buckle jingles. Samantha's busy hands are at it. They are soft, lotioned. Her nails are uniformly long and shiny and filed into perfect ovals.

His daughter's nails are chewed and ragged, her knuckles bruised and palms calloused. Samantha lowers her face and her giggling breath is hot, unbearable, and of course he would never tell this one *anything* about his daughter, his little girl, his pumpkin, of whom he should be, remember, so proud.

He finds he has a fistful of Samantha's hair, doll's hair, pale and plasticky. He finds he *has* no daughter on Wednesdays. He yanks and this one's head jerks back, her throat pulses.

No daughter, no five-bedroom house, no three-car garage. He stands, ridiculous, shirt open and pants sagging at his hips, shuffles to the closer bed with Samantha still clinging to him. Wednesday is too small to hold anything beyond this shitty room. He drops her backwards onto the bedspread, his belly soft above her. It quivers with his breathing.

No tennis club membership, no Saturday tee time, and he lowers himself onto her. On the nightstand: a clock radio, a plastic stand with brochures for buggy rides and quilting demonstrations, her purse. No airport lounge priority pass and no NFL season tickets. Her purse is canvas, trimmed in narrow strips of leather; her shirt is stretchy and thin, an oversaturated purple. The fabric looks spotlit. He shoves it toward her armpits and she squirms helpfully, works one shoulder out and then the other. Beach grass and sand dunes and lighthouses on the wall behind her and her clothes in a cheap rayon pile on the rug and somewhere

24

outside this Wednesday door the Amish are plowing and scything and tilling, he thinks, aren't they, isn't that what they do, when they're not dealing methamphetamine to somebody else's daughter?

One hour into Pennsylvania and this one is on her hands and knees with a boardwalk hanging over her head, or what looks like a boardwalk. If he backhanded her she would go flying off the bed like a doll, but it's only 11:15. Plus, those teeth.

Herewith, a partial accounting of things the father doesn't know: That his daughter's boyfriend is a preening dolt, Lacoste shirt and khakis and deck shoes notwithstanding. He gives her hickeys in spots her clothes cover and fingers her in movie theaters. The father, having never seen the hickeys nor been to the movies with them, likes the dolt a great deal.

The daughter doesn't. Sometimes she actively dislikes him, but he's got the manners and the car and the haircut. He goes to a Catholic boys' school across town and when he comes to pick her up on Friday nights he doesn't just pull into the driveway and honk, he rings the doorbell and shakes the father's hand while the daughter collects her purse. This gets her an extra half hour on her curfew, which she wishes she didn't have to spend with him. He keeps a flask of Jack Daniel's in his glove box and wedges it between his legs when he drives. He sucks on it at stoplights, slouching low behind the steering wheel.

Even so, the boyfriend is not as stupid as it suits him to appear—the daughter knows this; she can tell by the sneaky glint in his eye when he says or does something particularly idiotic, which happens only when they are with other couples.

Juggling raw eggs blindfolded, for instance, or trying to steer a car with his feet.

When they're alone he is quieter, less foolish, nastier. More handsome, somehow, though she hates admitting this, even to herself. His eyes go hooded and snaky and when he looks like that her face heats up, and her belly, and she thinks maybe he isn't so bad, maybe she shouldn't be so hard on him even in the privacy of her own head, maybe her father sees something in him that she's missing.

He likes to shotgun beer. He likes lacrosse and breaking shit and paying the pizza delivery guy with hundred dollar bills. He likes to slide his hand up under her blouse in the parking lot by the upper school playing field in the minutes between the red sun going down and the fluorescent lights coming on. He likes the way her breath hitches when his fingers find the nipple—she can tell by the way *his* breath hitches.

Her father doesn't know how much she likes *that*, or how much she likes to see the wet tip of the boyfriend's tongue caught between his teeth, or the way his warm hand trembles, just barely, on her skin. She likes how his eyes widen before he blinks them closed as though he can't bear to look at her and she likes to imagine what he sees when he does.

She's smart—her father knows that much—but sometimes smart is useless. She's too young to understand this yet. Her father has no such excuse.

When they're finished Samantha climbs over the father's legs to get to the bathroom, where she urinates without closing the door. He can see most of her in the mirror, leaning over to examine a toenail while she sits on the toilet. Her hair brushes the floor.

Who *raised* her? he thinks, a prissy twist to his mouth. Who didn't even bother to teach her to close the door?

Long legs splayed, lilac flash of toes on the tile, she hugs her knees, rests a cheek on her naked lap to smile at him.

I'm hungry, she says. Droplets hit water and she reaches for the toilet paper. Do you have time to maybe grab some lunch? I can shower quick.

Lunch, for God's sake, he thinks, and again his face contorts, enough that she notices, that he can see her notice: her sunny smile falters, the fastest cloud. There are truck stops along the highway and farther down the two-lane roads, buffet restaurants with names like the Bird-in-Hand or the Plain 'n' Fancy, restaurants with wide parking lots and reserved areas for hitching horse-drawn buggies, restaurants that serve friendship soup and shoofly pie but no alcohol.

She stands and flushes the toilet, dampens one of the hand towels with hot water from the sink tap and presses it to her face and she is nothing but a body, solid and symmetrical and crowned with that pale spill of hair, shrouded and silent and perfect.

There's a vending machine in the lobby, he says. He can't look away from the pinkish hands holding the white towel, the flushed belly and thighs. He pictures that body dressed again in the bright cheap clothes it walked in wearing. He imagines following it into the Dutch-Way Smorgasbord and sitting down with it at a table set with spindled wooden chairs and paper napkins.

Plastic tablecloths, plastic flowers. A small wooden triangle pegged with brightly colored golf tees meant to keep children busy. When she was three his daughter had a wooden box with basic shapes cut out of it, circles and triangles and Xs, each piece small enough for her hands but too big to shove into her teething mouth.

Aren't all children here busy, aren't they kept so, from the time they're old enough to milk cows

bale hay

knead dough?

Too big to choke on.

Samantha rehangs the damp towel carefully on the rack. It's like checkers, the game with the triangle and the golf tees. Her cheeks are shiny, clean of makeup. He can't remember if she was wearing any when she arrived because he hadn't looked at her face.

Busy tilling fields shelling peas mending clothes?

He tries, these Wednesdays, not to look at her body after he's finished with it. He tries to tell himself: her flesh is nothing to him once he's no longer inside it.

Things his daughter once put in her mouth: towels, shirtsleeves, keys on the ring. The edge of seat cushions on kitchen chairs, cork coasters. The end of his leather belt, of his backup plans and hedged bets.

His stomach rumbles. What would it be like to follow that body into a place that smells of gravy and yeast rolls and sawdust?

Her mouth like an opening flower, a depthless pit. Her flesh the context for his, nothing more.

Then I'm going to push on, Samantha says. She steps into her underwear, a scrap of bright pink, the brightest thing in the room by far. How many Wednesdays has Pennsylvania swallowed?

Enough, too many, a few. Over the underwear, pants of some flimsy material made to look like denim. She works her way into them.

To sit at a table in a room that smells of coffee and leather and virtuous sweat across from that hair, those wet white teeth?

The sleeves of her sweater are too short; she tugs at the cuffs but they only come halfway down her forearms.

Next Wednesday, she says, I'm taking my grandma out for her birthday. Her wrists are thin as skim milk. His hand is big enough to circle both of them, squeeze until the birdy-bones grind. So I won't be able to make it, okay?

He could yank her arms clean out of the sockets without even trying; he could dislocate her shoulders.

Which raises the question: what could he do if he tried?

The father pulls out of the motel lot onto the state road that will take him to the interstate that will take him to the beltway.

Following, a selection of places the beltway will not take him: To the upscale retirement community where he installed his parents, believing they would partake of movie nights and Scrabble tournaments, day trips to casinos and outlet malls, but where instead his father had immediately fallen on the slippery indoor pool deck and his mother had flooded both their apartment and the one below when she left the kitchen faucet running overnight. Stitches, antibiotics, insurance claims, and mold remediation.

To his daughter's school, all twenty-six grassy acres and $32,000 per year of it, every trimmed hedge and power-washed brick of it.

To the church where he was married, the office where he first practiced law, the bar with French movie posters and carriage lights where he'd ordered dry martinis with the partners in his firm and laughed at every one of their vulgar and tasteless jokes, where he wanted to drink himself blind and deaf so that he would not have to see or hear them, where he first began to understand how familiar he would become with the icy juniper chill of regret.

To the laundry and his body as it worked there, strong enough to move sixty wet pounds of fabric from one end of the steaming floor to the other and back, not stopping for hours on end, agile and steady in rubber-soled shoes.

To the hospital where his daughter was born prematurely, unexpectedly, and the apartment of the paralegal he'd been fucking while the infant was transferred, purplish and gourd-sized, to the NICU.

To the partially subsidized duplex where Samantha lives with her sister, her sister's boyfriend and the boyfriend's cousin and the cousin's—nephew? Uncle? He has no idea because he stopped listening to Samantha's cheerful recitation of her housemates once he realized that she would not be upset if he failed to respond, that she did not in fact expect a response, that she was happy enough to talk to him in much the way she must have once talked to her dolls. He realized this on their first Wednesday. If he hadn't, there would not have been a second.

28

If he had known his parents would be so indifferent to the activities listed on brightly laminated calendars in the hallways of their building he would not have bothered paying for such an overscheduled facility. If he had known his daughter's birth was imminent he would certainly not have been fucking the paralegal.

If, if, if.

The beltway smells of hot asphalt, honeysuckle and wastewater and exhaust. It is congested and too sunny and it will also not take him to his wife, or if it would he has no idea how, because his wife's location is yet another thing he does not know.

If he did know, how would that knowledge change his day? Would he be more or less likely to speed, to tailgate, to change lanes without signaling? Or would it make no difference at all?

He knows that she is not at home, that she has not been home for three years. He knows that three years is enough time to disappear from whatever place a person has come to hate, or possibly only to no longer love enough. It is enough time for many other things to transpire concurrently.

It is enough time, for example, to find oneself at fifty giving motel change for candy bars to a girl who is *youngenoughtobehisdaughter* but who is nothing like his daughter, who might as well be a different species entirely from his daughter and his daughter's kind, who was made to be consumed without thought or guilt, and who is lucky that he is the one doing the consuming.

Sunlight bounces from chrome and mirrors and he is hot, he is hungry, he is going to be late for a meeting with the affordable housing associates, most of whom are under thirty-five and optimistically committed to securing HUD financing and low-income tax credits for similarly idealistic corporate clients, and none of whom yet understand that contradiction in terms.

It is enough time to recognize how few decisions make a mattering difference, to consider that Samantha's dolls most likely had hair the same color as hers, to realize that he has no idea what his own daughter's dolls looked like.

He has found himself at fifty marveling at how his wife has managed to remain so perversely *present*—she is in the slight cleft of his daughter's chin and the length of her slender ring fingers, the unconscious throat-clearing when she is nervous or impatient. She is in the way his daughter lately has of closing herself off to his attempts at what

29

he hopes is appropriate fatherly intimacy, of dismissing his lukewarm overtures with an offhand amusement. She is in her absolute self-possession and her uncanny ability to inhabit an unreachable galaxy when they are no more than two feet apart. This is neither insulting nor hurtful to him. It is absolution.

What do fathers *do* with the daughters who belong to them? It is the arterial pulse of his life, it seems to him, sitting in traffic on this bright Wednesday, how little he knows, but if he did.

The daughter is spending her lunch period smoking weed in her new best friend's Prius. The new best friend's name is Rachel, and she has greenish hair and a pierced septum and a plush ass the daughter would kill for. She has a perfect GPA and a bubblegum smile and she finds organized sports and the daughter's boyfriend ridiculous in equal measure.

The daughter tells herself that Rachel doesn't think *she's* ridiculous, and sometimes she even believes it.

The father doesn't know there's a new best friend, or that the old one has been demoted. The old one didn't know she had been demoted until she overheard a senior dishing eleventh grade gossip in the bathroom.

The daughter pinches the joint out carefully and tucks it back into the repurposed sea salt container on the dash. She checks her watch and Rachel rolls her pretty eyes at this, which are watery and blood-shot and more vividly green than her hair.

Don't start, the daughter says.

Slave to the dick, Rachel says, and the daughter laughs, although it is not funny, although it is true. It's not funny *because* it's true.

A bunch of people are thinking about going to Chase's after the game on Friday, she says. His parents are out of town but his sister's home for break so she'll buy.

Rachel shrugs, slides the salt tin into her backpack and frees a hairbrush and a bottle of perfume. I have a Habitat meeting at seven, she says. She sprays the bristles and runs the brush through her hair. Maybe after, if it doesn't run too late.

Cool, the daughter says. She digs through her own pack for her makeup bag. Can I tell my dad I'm spending the night at your place?

Tell him whatever you want. As long as he doesn't call my mom to check.

The daughter flips down the visor and angles the mirror, dabs on lip gloss that the boyfriend will immediately tell her to wipe off. She checks her watch again, surreptitious this time. She has study hall after this, fifty minutes where she could be in any library on campus. Honor system for honor students: the school prides itself on its liberality. It'll only take her ten to walk down the delivery road behind the cafeteria to the back entrance of campus, where he'll be waiting. The interior of his Volvo smells like old beer and dollar-store air freshener and sometimes, now, her. Her father approves of the safety rating.

He won't even ask for a phone number, she says.

His daughter's kind is expensive. Dermatologists, sports therapists, tutors. Manicurists and psychologists. Coaches for field hockey and standardized test prep, for public speaking and college interviews. Four hundred dollars and four hours in a hair salon chair and when she's finished he can't even tell what's been done.

His own office chair is deep, soft leather, silent casters, and shining chrome. It's after one o'clock and he's eaten nothing and the ozone smell of commercial-grade odor neutralizer is still in his nostrils. He considers the briefs on his desk and the inbox filled with email he has to force himself to read. He considers the fact that, if asked under oath, he would have to say it: he would rather be with an undereducated tweaker who likes sucking cock than his own daughter.

Of course he would. Any man would, and any man who'd claim otherwise would be torn apart on the stand.

The truth is that he could have looked harder for his wife. He knows this, on some level, on the level he keeps sealed, drum-tight, barely lit, for what he won't quite permit himself to acknowledge.

He had the resources and the money and the connections, and the further truth is that if he'd wanted to he could have had her dragged back from whatever inadequate hiding place she'd tucked herself into, that she'd imagined would be sufficient.

What he did, instead: made a few phone calls—to her sister in New York, her friend from college she spent one weekend a year with, her personal trainer—and accepted whatever bullshit story they told him. Calmly, resignedly. Chastened. I'm so sorry to have bothered you, he'd said, can you think of anywhere she might be? Would you call me if you hear from her? I can't thank you enough. Sorry. So sorry.

His voice breaking while he sat with the cordless on the back deck of the house, his daughter's bedroom window glowing above him, a tumbler of single malt on the weather-sealed picnic table. A June night, honeysuckle and cut grass, the gold wink of fireflies in the soft sky and a bass line thumping from his daughter's open window, sobs beneath it. Warm enough to switch out the Scotch for gin.

So that he could say he'd done it, so that he could say he'd tried.

Even three years on, he thinks, he could find her, could haul her thrashing or limp from her brother-in-law's place upstate or an ashram or a convent or an apartment complex in Albuquerque made of Flexi-core and vinyl cladding. Or the mixed-use development right behind his office, for all he knows.

But instead he will leave her untouched in the sheets folded at the back of the closet shelf, the serrated blade in the kitchen drawer, the sleeping pills in the medicine cabinet. It is the one remaining kindness he has left to show her.

Friday afternoon and the daughter is working her phone at the kitchen counter, legs crossed and one shoe dangling from a toe. Brown moc, white sock, a leg that needs shaving. Both legs actually, armpits too. He doesn't want to notice but how can he help it, especially when she comes home in the hockey uniform she couldn't be bothered to change out of, no longer sweaty but still flushed in the cheeks and at the base of her throat? She has her mother's prickly skin.

As she gets older he finds it increasingly difficult to look at her.

But wait—as long as we're telling the truth: he has never found it easy to look at her, not even through her mother's mediating gaze. She was too fragile as an infant and too noisy as a toddler and too easy to ignore in grade school, always huddled over notebooks or textbooks or a stack of creased and wrinkled paperbacks from the public library.

He tells her he loves her every morning before she leaves for school and every night before she goes to bed. He does not think of her in the intervening hours, and he is grateful to her for this.

Do you mind if I spend the night at Rachel's? she says, not looking up from her phone. Her hair at the roots is slightly matted, still damp from the scrimmage. Her cleats are in a pile on the floor. Who won? He has no idea.

That's fine, he says, and pours another gin and tonic. Will Rachel's parents be home? The name means nothing to him.

His daughter nods, drops her phone on the counter with the air of a frustrated CEO. She huffs a breath out and up to flutter loose strands of hair from her forehead.

Her mom, yeah. It's for a school thing. I'll be back probably early tomorrow. She slides off the stool and yawns, stretches: stubbled armpits and bruised thighs and a scrape below one dirty knee.

The teachers at parent-teacher night last Thursday told him how motivated his daughter is and the mothers told him how well-rounded she is and the other fathers told him how ruthless on the field she is and he nodded and smiled and what he was smiling at was what he had done to someone else's daughter the day before during Urbanization and Progressivism or Concepts of the Utopian Movement or General Chemistry or whatever useless subject was on the docket in the eleven o'clock hour.

Showering, then heading out, his own says, brushing past him up the carpeted stairs.

Shin guards and mouth guards and shorts under kilts, the smell of sweat and wintergreen. Orange wedges and Gatorade. Offsides, obstruction. Boys in khakis watching girls in ponytails running faster than they'll ever have to again, if they're lucky. And his daughter's kind is nothing if not lucky.

Samantha twists her hair up and secures it in a stretchy flounce of fabric. She turns the shower on and lines up the stingy plastic bottles—shampoo, lotion—on the lip of the tub. She empties the shampoo onto the washcloth and scours until her skin is blotched red. When she towels off she hums. She squeezes the lotion into a damp palm and slathers, slopping viscous white onto the floor. She blots it with the bath mat.

I don't think it smells bad at all, she says, as though he's asked her. He asks her so little. Wednesdays are too short for questions.

He watches her from the bed. Of course she's *youngenoughtobehisdaughter*. That's the fucking point. The hard mattress is the point, and the thin white sheets and thin white walls, the harness-jangle and hoof-clop and dust outside the motel windows. Her clean skin is the point and her body when he is inside it.

Her body when he is not inside it is irrelevant.

Also irrelevant: if she understands how unnecessary she is, or how quickly the damage accrues.

Check this out, the boyfriend says, and angles his phone so the daughter can see. It's a video of a living room filled with naked women licking and grinding on each other while the men watching pour beer on them and cheer. She can see pimples and razor burn on the men's necks, sweaty layers of slap and spackle the women have covered their faces with. Beer foams over expensive-looking upholstered chairs and a coffee table.

This is disgusting, the daughter thinks, and it's happening in someone's *house*. Who has to clean this *up?*

She pushes his hand with the phone away and straightens her skirt. I need to get back, she says. They're in the front seat of his car, parked in the overflow lot behind the auxiliary gym. If I'm late for lab I'm toast.

The boyfriend slides the phone into his pocket and draws back, cups her chin and looks her long in the face and she decides to forget the stupid video because he's moving in to kiss her, because the salty tip of his tongue is sweet fire on her lips.

One thing among the many she doesn't know about him: that he doesn't kiss the women he orders from a website. Another: that he sometimes pushes them from moving cars, but only if his best friend is driving, and only if they're going slow. And one more, why not: that he laughs when he crumples twenty-dollar bills to stuff into their cheap spike-heeled booties before throwing the shoes out after them.

Outside the motel the parking lot is cracked and dry, the striping faded, barely white. The sides of the road are strewn with beer cans and plastic soda bottles, candy wrappers, and oil-stained rags.

The father is waiting for Samantha. He's sitting at the flimsy desk, his briefcase on the floor by the door. He won't leave anything in the car.

She hadn't understood that. These people around here don't *steal*, she'd said, earnest, wide-eyed—they're *religious*.

Fast-food bags and shoes worn through. A bleach bottle by the entrance to the parking lot. He'd laughed at her when she said that.

Her car pulls in, a bit of rust on the side panels and a dented rear bumper, a plastic lei hanging from the rearview. If he cared just a little bit more than he does he would tell her to be careful—of cops, for starters. Of her dealer, of whoever cooks the shit she knows better than to smoke in front of him.

She parks in the last row, by the cornfield, husks dry, crushed down and broken.

He doesn't know that just before settling into the front row in Environmental Science his daughter was running from a Volvo where she let a feckless twat hike her skirt above her waist and do the things that girls like her are not supposed to want but do

34

but do

but do.

If he knew he would care, but not enough. His daughter is smart, his daughter is careful, his daughter is close to disappeared herself.

Not close enough.

Plastic straws and paper bags, horseshoes and hypodermics. Samantha picks her way across the asphalt in what looks, from where he sits, like a pair of bright pink sandals. It's too cold for her feet to be so bare.

If he cared enough he would tell her to be careful of people like him. She's someone's daughter, after all.

Nominated by The Idaho Review

TALKING TO THE HEDGEROWS ABOUT MONEY

by JEB LOY NICHOLS

from CAUGHT BY THE RIVER

I go out walking in the new morning, the new year two days away, watching a pair of crows fall and twist in the grey sky; I try and fail to make sense of the day, the week, the year. I'm reminded of a creation myth that I once read, from the Yup'ik Indians of southern Alaska. There was a time (so says the myth) when there were no people on the earth. After thousands of years of peaceful life, the first man was born from out of a pea pod. A raven appeared, raised its wings and said, where have you come from? The man pointed at the pea pod. The raven said, I made that plant and all the others and I've never seen anything like you. The man stood up and said, what am I? The raven, who knew well all the makings of the land, said, a mistake, a malignancy, a sickness. The man said, perhaps I am, but nonetheless I'm here. The raven said, you're my mistake so I shall deal with you. And with that he ate the man, as he often ate slugs or caterpillars. He flew away and the next day had a terrible stomach ache. In the night he died. The next morning his belly split open and out walked the man. He returned to the pea patch where he waited a thousand years for another human to appear. This time it was a woman and together they went forth into the world. From that day to this they have blundered across the land, unable to not be the thing they are, a creeping sickness.

Last night someone told me that Bruce Springsteen has sold his publishing for 500 million dollars. 500. Million. Dollars. He's also recently written a book with Barack Obama, who is worth in excess of 80 million

36

dollars. A politician and a musician, each one richer than God. The grotesque horror of this is impossible to put into perspective. The idea that one person can have 500 million dollars while others have nothing is a perfect illustration of the diseased heart of humanity. I understand that the accumulation of wealth is sometimes beyond our control. You write a hit song (or get elected to public office) and suddenly, through no fault of your own, you're rich. OK. It happens. The only acceptable option at that point, the only creative option, is to get rid of the money. It becomes a simple question—are you an egalitarian or an elitist? Either you live simply, in a modest house, travel as little as possible, eat sensibly, or you live like a king. How much money do you need? After all, everyone can be poor, only an elite few can be rich. If Springsteen gave away all 500 million tomorrow, he'd still be unspeakably wealthy next week. The maintenance of great wealth is the new slave trade. Utterly indefensible and wicked. Wealth generated and multiplied by a system that brutally exploits and divides humanity (not to mention animals and the earth) is something to be ashamed of, not applauded. To be rich is to be in league with those things most awful and most unacceptable. The mega rich are the new slave masters.

I must learn to say no. I must learn to say: I don't want to do that. I don't want to participate. I prefer to be uncertain and uncomfortable and lost. I prefer to be damaged. To be scared is better than being entitled. I want to be away from wealth and glamour and success. Wealth is terrorism. A display of potency. A performance. All volume and flash. It has a single message: I'm the important one here and everything else, the less rich, the inhuman, the useless, the failures, are of no interest to me.

Can you tell me what is gained by the constant whirl and flash in which we spend our lives? What do we achieve? What's accomplished? What do we learn? What do we make better? Surely the better way is inaction. Do little. Do less than is expected. In every human relationship force defeats itself. Be as humble as water is; in a thousand years water will wear away stone, metal, earth. Water wins.

I'm not, believe me, trying to glamorise poverty. I know how debilitating it can be. I know about the sleepless nights, the gut churning fear. I know how things can go suddenly wrong. I've seen it, I've been there. I've spent the night in a storm of anxiety, listing my failures, envisioning new disasters. I wait for the morning. The night offers me no solace. Morning comes. I watch a single crow land in the sycamore tree. I imagine myself inside the bird, my bones suddenly light, my feet sharp.

I look down on my doings, my house, my muddy pond, my weed-choked garden, and fly away.

I have a friend who doesn't want to take the vaccine. It is, she says, a pharmaceutical answer to a profoundly non-pharmaceutical question. No one ever addresses the root causes. Frantic global consumerism and exploitation of animals, desperate greed, the swirling cocktail of chemicals and pharmaceuticals and military paranoia, it all goes on and on. Just as the new virus and its army of mutations will go on and on as well. When they develop a vaccine against greed and capitalism and nationalism and growth, she says, I'll take that. Oh, wait, she says, they already have. It's called Having Less.

On occasion I scrunch further into darkness. Make myself skeletal and teeny. It's true that I'm mostly empty handed, that there are certain levels of damage, that I've thought myself into a jam. I wish to be less hectic in my notions, have my thoughts be kinder. I want to close my eyes. I could add something here about the uncertain pathways of memory; about ice cream, about long walks, about faithful pets, about the first touch of private places, about expectations, about the specific shape and feel of a lovers foot, about the last small thing you hear before you give in to sleep.

And what's the deal with this guy who's building rocket ships and planning to go to Mars? He says he can't live on a planet that doesn't have 'interplanetary ambitions'. He talks about 'industrialising space'. He wants to build space stations and fill the skies with communication satellites. He's already launched sixty thousand of them. He wants to build electric driverless cars and have 'interactive highways'. He wants a future that sees space as a holiday destination. There are, as I write this, three multi-millionaires up there, each of them having paid him millions of dollars for the privilege. My thought is this: sit quietly in a room for two hours doing nothing. Then take a three mile walk. Then come back and be quiet. Repeat. That's a life. As Walt Whitman said, *a mouse is miracle enough.*

Can we not be content with rosemary and mint, with fresh bread, with the sound of rain on the roof, with simple jobs for which we're adequately paid, for small thoughts and small deeds? Is it not enough to simply live and admire and be thankful for this beautiful place?

Nominated by Mary Kornblum

OPEN WATER

by ADA LIMÓN

from NEW ENGLAND REVIEW

It does no good to trick and weave and lose
the other ghosts, to shove the buried deeper
into the sandy loam, the riverine silt, still you come,
my faithful one, the sound of a body so persistent
in water I cannot tell if it is a wave or you
moving through waves. A month before you died
you wrote a letter to old friends saying you swam
with a pod of dolphins in open water, saying goodbye,
but what you told me most about was the eye.
That enormous reckoning eye of an unknown fish
that passed you during that last-ditch defiant swim.
On the shore, you described the fish as nothing
you'd seen before, a blue-gray behemoth moving slowly
and enduringly through its deep fathomless
North Pacific waters. That night, I heard more
about that fish and that eye than anything else.
I don't know why it has come to me this morning.
Warm rain and landlocked, I don't deserve the image.
But I keep thinking how something saw you, something
was bearing witness to you out there in the ocean
where you were no one's mother, and no one's wife,
but you in your original skin, right before you died,
you were beheld, and today in my kitchen with you
now ten years gone, I was so happy for you.

Nominated by Jung Hae Chae

THE GLACIER

fiction by IDRA NOVEY

from THE YALE REVIEW

We were camping in the Andes, one of six families on a trip with a collective horde of sixteen children. Each car ride, the kids switched vehicles. They often swapped their sunhats as well, and I didn't pay much attention to who scrambled into our car. Or I didn't unless they got too loud, or did something that had to be stopped, as with the boy currently seated behind me, who kept pressing his toes into the back of my seat.

For several hours, we'd been making our way up a winding, increasingly narrow road along a cliff. There was no guardrail, and our car kept rocking, shiplike, with each turn. The mission of our six-family caravan was to swim in the hot springs we'd found on this mountain once before. I was certain we should have seen the hot springs by now, and my husband Gustavo, who was driving, thought so as well. He guessed we must be misremembering how far up we'd driven when we found the hot springs last time, which had been twelve years ago, before we'd all had children.

Watch out for those monsters, I told him, pointing through the windshield at a cluster of particularly large rocks that had tumbled onto the road.

I see them, Gustavo said with irritation, and I apologized. I knew he was eminently capable of spotting a giant rock in front of us without any anxious warnings from me. But what had happened to the hot springs? It didn't seem possible that they could all be gone in just over a decade.

40

These chaotic trips in the Andes were an annual event. I knew the other couples through Gustavo, who'd been coordinating the campsite reservations for twenty years. The trips often felt like a marital test, although I never regretted them once they ended. On Monday, trapped again in the grinding machinery of city life, I knew I would enjoy recalling the children this morning in their bright pajamas making rock sculptures behind the tents after breakfast. Or the sight of them last night, perched on a log like a flock of birds while I reheated some pasta for them over the campfire.

I thought I had a good sense of the children by now, and yet when I turned around once more to ask the boy seated behind me to please keep his feet on the floor, I couldn't recall his name. He definitely belonged to Andres and Nora. His dark hair was chopped into the generic, unchanging haircut Nora had given all her sons since they were toddlers. He was fairly indistinguishable, with his bony knees poking out of blue athletic shorts. Other parents on this trip likely thought the same of my own sons and couldn't remember their names either, none of us being quite as invested in each other's offspring as we liked to think we were.

In fact, if one of our vehicles hit a rock and fell off the cliff, there was a good chance no adults in the car would be able to name every child plummeting with them down the mountainside. I was about to remark on this bleak possibility when the minivan ahead of us came to a halt. Paulina emerged from the driver's side, swinging her loose hair out of her face, and motioned to the van with a frown, flicking her fingers to show something had punctured their front tire.

Kids, please stay away from the edge if you get out, I warned the passengers currently in our care, though they were already slamming their doors, and Gustavo was half out of the car as well, rushing over to join the other fathers. All six of the men began vying to make themselves useful in replacing the tire. A few of the mothers gathered with the pack as well. Nora, being one of the bolder ones, insisted on taking a role in the installation of the spare.

Watching them through the windshield, I knew I had chosen yet again to be the resident loner. On these group trips, the other women no longer expected me to join them, and I couldn't bring myself to get out of the car now either, not with fifty pages left in the bulky novel I'd been reading for over a month. I'd been determined to fit it into the glove compartment, hoping for a moment like this today, when I could sneak in at least a few minutes of reading and being alone.

Twelve years ago, on our last group trip to this area in the Andes, we had showered under a small waterfall along the roadside that I was certain we should have reached by now. Gustavo agreed the waterfall had been lower on the mountain, although the hot springs were the reason that we were continuing higher for the children to experience the wonder of those sudden pools, the water bubbling up from underground, steaming and reeking of sulfur.

By the time the spare tire was installed, I'd gotten through enough pages to project a sense of calm as a new trio of children clambered into our car. Yet there was no feigning composure at the blasted ruin of the mountainside as we drove higher. I'd read online about the gypsum mining empire that had lobbied for access up here, but I hadn't realized they'd razed such massive areas out of existence. Entire slopes had been burned away, reduced to a uniformly flat, blackened expanse of ground-up stones and grimy, unnatural-looking gravel.

There'd been rumors the mining company had slashed a glacier in half, messing with the flow of far more meltwater than they admitted. Still, I'd assumed the damage must have been contained to a limited area. Last night at the campfire, I'd agreed when Paulina said the government surely wouldn't have allowed the mining company to move too many things around, not when all of Santiago drank from reservoirs fed by these glaciers. Paulina's reasoning had seemed not just hopeful but conclusive how could it not be, with twelve reasonably informed adults nodding along, sipping beers together in camping chairs under a gloriously clear, star-riddled sky?

Yet even the goats were gone now. None of the big rangy herds we'd seen on the last trip remained. We'd seen hundreds of them at this altitude then, gathering wherever meltwater from the ice shelves had trickled down and formed networks of streams. Goats had stood together grazing all over then, blocking the road or clustered on grassy areas that were gone now, too.

The wind was pressing harder against my side of the car, rocking us more wildly than before. The light, too, felt sharper and less forgiving as I squinted through the windshield. After replacing the tire, we were now advancing with the deliberate slowness of the penitent. Every rock and hole felt like a scolding for having indulged in such naive optimism.

In the backseat, our new crew of passengers wanted something to snack on. But the previous passengers had finished the last treats that Oscar and Miguel had jammed into the pockets in the doors.

But you must keep something hidden in here for emergencies, said Maria José, the oldest and most indignant of the current trio. Not even in your glove compartment?

I'm sorry, I told her; if we had anything edible left, I'd give it to you I swear.

I opened the glove compartment to show her it contained nothing but car manuals and the bulky novel I'd brought, filling what now seemed a conspicuously large amount of space.

Are you sure there isn't anything under the seats? Gustavo asked, as if even he assumed I should be able to produce some form of sustenance for these children if I wanted to badly enough.

Meanwhile, the road kept narrowing with each turn around the mountain, my dizziness tipping into nausea. To keep driving higher made no sense at all and why, collectively, had we had so many children?

I really think we better turn around, I said to Gustavo. Could you flash the lights or maybe just stop the car?

We'd lost cell service some time ago, and there was no way to discuss things unless we brought all six vehicles to a halt. But Gustavo didn't want to stop. Without turning his head from the road, he insisted the mining damage would have to end eventually, and we'd driven all this way.

Please, the kids are ravenous, I said. We at least need to stop and see who has snacks left.

Gustavo offered no answer to this, just gripped the wheel more intently and continued with the procession. When the van ahead of us came to another halt, I scrambled out as fast as the children. Before Gustavo could get out of our car and interject, I asked Paulina whether she was ready to turn around and give up, to admit the hot springs were gone.

It never occurred to me they could just be gone, Paulina said, but they are, just like that no more hot springs. She shook her head.

On the other side of the minivan, I heard what sounded like someone vomiting, and Paulina explained that one of the kids had gotten carsick. It was Andres and Nora's son in the blue athletic shorts who'd been pushing into my seat. Doubled over on the roadside, he was ejecting an astonishing quantity of clear liquid, which was now splashing over the dry ground. A puddle had begun to widen around his feet.

Maybe the altitude was the cause. Maybe all the sharp zigzags of mining roads cutting through the stripped face of the cordillera. Whatever had gone wrong inside his body, the result just kept pouring forth. I watched, as stunned and motionless as everyone else. It was a shocking rush of liquid, so abundant it seemed to be jetting up from a source under the ground beneath him, rising up through his scrawny legs, turning his body into an unbidden conduit.

I can't remember his name, I murmured to Gustavo. He drew nearer and said he wasn't sure either. I looked around at the growing gathering of adults but didn't see Andres or Nora, who had been at the front of the caravan. Somebody really needed to step forward to console their son until they got here. The boy was heaving now, releasing such a bewildering quantity of liquid that the puddle was now trickling toward our feet.

And yet no one in our half-circle of seven or so parents had moved toward him. It was like we were trapped in a spell, compelling us to remain exactly where we had stopped, watching this poor kid vomit alone, more coming up each time, the puddle spreading faster over the cracked, dusty surface of the road.

I wanted to think my inaction was not due to pettiness about the boy pressing his restless feet so many times against the back of my seat. I liked to think of myself as inherently decent, a person eager to step forward when it was necessary. But if that was true, why was I standing meekly next to my husband while this other family's child went on retching?

My God, what's going on? Nora finally rushed up, stepping in her open-toed sandals into the puddle around her son. As soon as she touched his bony back, the boy took an audible gulp of breath, which seemed to bring his incomprehensible purging to an end at last.

Or not yet, as he didn't stand up. He stayed hunched over, coughing and gripping his knees. To avoid the indictment in Nora's gaze, I stared down with dread at the bile about to reach my feet. And then it arrived—a warm, awful squish against my toes.

Before I could react, two small hands pressed against the back of my legs. It was Oscar, hoping to be held. As I lifted him onto my hip, something about the arrangement of his face took me by surprise. I knew the rest of him, his short fingers and shaggy brown hair, the source of the scar on his wrist. I knew who had given us the hand-me-down T-shirt he was wearing, with its half-submerged hippo, as a gift to his older brother four years ago.

And yet Oscar's small, round face still startled me, the unabashed need of his open mouth, all the tiny milk teeth inside it, waiting to be pushed loose and supplanted.

We'll figure it out, don't worry, we'll get back okay, I told my child, who didn't reply, just turned his face, open-mouthed, toward the vastness of the ground-up, ash-colored particles behind us, covering the entirety of the mountainside.

Nominated by Genie Chipps, The Yale Review

STANDING IN THE FOREST OF BEING ALIVE

by KATIE FARRIS

from AMERICAN POETRY REVIEW

I stand in the forest of being alive:
in one hand, a cheap aluminum pot
of chicken stock and in the other,
a heavy book of titles. O once, walking through
a cemetery I became terribly lost and could not
speak (no one living knows the grammar).
No one could direct me to the grave,
so I looked at every name.
Madness hung out over the gravel paths,
swaying like laundry.

A heavy bird flapped its wings over someone's
sepulcher. Some of us are still putzes
in death, catching birdshit on our headstones.
Some of us never find what we're looking for, praying
it doesn't pour before we find our names; certain
we're headed in the right direction, a drizzle begins,
and what's nameless inside our veins
fluoresces, fluoresces in the rain.

Nominated by American Poetry Review, Maxine Scates, Jody Stewart, Michael Waters

THE CHILDREN ARE FRAGILE

fiction by JEN SILVERMAN

from THE SUN

Was he audacious? Certainly.

She'd never known him not to push the boundaries of good taste, but also physically. He'd put a hand on your arm when he talked to you; he was a hugger, a close talker. He'd even commented on this himself "I'm Jewish-Italian, I got it on both sides of the family. You know, I was raised to feel that if we aren't like *this*, we can't hear each other" and he'd thrust his face close to hers. They'd both laughed. She'd found him charming, had not felt threatened by him.

That was the first meeting. On the second, he'd told her about the woman he was dating "Younger than me, she's a young woman" but it turned out she was forty-five. ("Ten years younger; I said younger, didn't I?") He'd mused out loud on what to call this woman "girlfriend" sounded childish, but "lover" was an unforgivable affectation. "Can Americans even use that word, *lover*?"

"Sure," she said easily, "I think so."

"Straight ones," he corrected. "Straight Americans, I mean." He looked at her searchingly, as if she were the arbiter of what straight Americans could and could not do. His eyes were a warm gray, flecked with sea green.

"I think anybody can call anybody whatever they both want."

"What do you call your . . . ?" he gestured, indicating the blank and making its existence a shared joke.

"I'm single," she said, amused. "But I was with my partner for eight years, and I called him . . . a partner."

"You didn't worry that people would think you meant business partner?" He smiled, but his eyes were keen he'd thought she was a lesbian, she knew, and now he was sizing her up, repairing the blanks in his read of her.

"No," she said, letting him study her. "I guess I don't spend a lot of time worrying about what people think."

"Cool," he said, and a boyish smile lit his face, made him look like a co-conspirator. "Me neither."

That was July. She saw him once more in September; she told him she'd be passing through the city, and he asked her to get a drink. This time he'd set up a meeting himself the first two had been set by his office. This third time, he reached out with his distinct mixture of provocation and gravitas: "Would you do me the honor of joining me for a drink?" And then: "Pleasure, not business, but we can discuss business if you have business to discuss."

"I always have business to discuss," she replied, "but it gives me a great deal of pleasure."

Walking to the bar, it had occurred to her that, in her twenties, this might have felt very different. He was an artistic director, after all, and back then she was still trying to make it as a playwright herself. She might have felt anxious to impress or please him. She might have felt that she was en route to an assignation with no determined parameters, that anything might be the result of this evening. (She had heard the whispers by then; she must have, to even be thinking this. But when she looked back, she felt she had been completely blindsided by the accusations, and in later years she never knew what exactly she had known.) Now, though, in the early stretch of her forties, she felt only the hum of anticipation that preceded any social interaction.

The evening was pleasant. Looking back, scanning for any moment that felt wrong, she couldn't find one. He was cheeky, yes; he looked for the places where polite convention dictated one kind of response, and he gave the opposite; he talked about sex, but with the aplomb of a storyteller. He told her a story about dating right after his divorce: how he'd taken home a woman who resembled Farrah Fawcett; how, as a preteen, he used to worshipfully masturbate to Farrah Fawcett; how, when confronted with the naked body of this actual woman, he'd failed to achieve the prominent erection that he'd promised her; how instead, he had wept. "I thought of how my teen self would have been so impressed with me and what a loser I had grown up into, how unimpressed I was with myself now and it made me incredibly depressed." The Farrah Fawcett lookalike had waited for a long moment and then, faced with both his tears and his flaccid folds, she'd said briskly but not unkindly, "Well this is unfortunate," and gathered her clothes and left. His stories generally cast him as the loser, the failure, the middle-aged man who just kept fucking it all up but there was a confidence in the delivery that made it a performance more than a confession. Mars didn't mind; she was incapable of sustaining small talk.

He asked her about herself as well genuine questions, and he listened closely to the answers, a listening that took her in completely, in all her details. When he called her Marsha, she wasn't aware of knitting her brows, but she knew her body must have telegraphed the subtlest flinch because he corrected himself: "Mars." And, laughing at herself, she conceded: "My mother is the only one who calls me Marsha she says she didn't name her daughter after a planet and she refuses to start now."

"A planet works fine for me," he said, and refilled her wineglass.

They talked about business, too. He was fifteen years into his tenure as artistic director; he'd done well for his theater, in its track record of both new plays and classical work. Unlike many ADs, he wasn't himself a director; he had been a playwright, many many years ago, and he spoke of plays with the concentrated devotion of a lifelong believer. As if they were sacred, she thought, and the thought touched her, because she thought of theater the same way: as a sustained prayer, as something that reached for whatever was above it and tried to take its audience along.

She had also given up on writing plays, but she taught them, and she knew he had instituted a program for commissioning young writers "emerging voices," as the terminology went. She knew the phrase was a cliché, but she liked the image anyway. She imagined a blanketing fog, and through that fog, the traveling echoes of voices that no one had yet heard, cadences and rhythms that held the promise of newness. She suggested to him a few of her students and he listened as she described their backgrounds, their plays, the moment in which she had read their work and thought: This person could be the real thing.

"Could be," she said, "but it's all about encouragement at this point. As you know."

"Yes and no," he replied. "Maybe there's too much encouragement these days. Everybody gets a grant, everybody deserves everything. But wouldn't you rather know who are the writers that are just . . . doomed to it? The kids who have to write, that will do it even if they have nothing?"

"Right," she said patiently, almost condescendingly. "But wouldn't you like to see what those kids can do if they aren't constantly worried sick about having nothing?"

He asked her, late in the night, during the last drink, if she wanted to pitch him any of her own work. If she was still writing. "You know, we have a bunch of commissions coming in this fall, so I'm not supposed to say this but hey!" There it was, that open boyish smile. "Let's say I had a slot. You want to tell me about something of yours that I should put in it?"

She thought about it. The wine had made her fuzzy, but in a way that felt supple and generous, that enabled her to think more clearly than usual. The light in the bar was soft sepia, and under its glow she felt as if she were a witness to her own history not to a specific event but rather to the quiet decisions that compounded on themselves, the sacrifices and compromises and hard-won realizations that had eventually accumulated into a life. Her life.

This was a life in which she no longer chased the pipe dream, she told him kindly.

This bothered him. She could tell. For the first time he got a little aggressive, a little bullying. He wanted to shake her out of it, she felt what he perceived as stasis or defeat. "You must be writing *something*, you can't just be changing the diapers of college kids, reading their banal dramas about their breakups, and not be writing *something*. You'd have offed yourself, otherwise." But even that didn't upset her. Maybe because he was voicing the other half of a conversation she'd already had with herself and then left behind.

"I like teaching," she said, "and when I don't like it, I do other things that I enjoy. I garden, I've been fostering pitbull rescues. And spending time with my niece. So you know it's not the old dream of A Life In The Theater, but there have been a few reasons not to off myself, when the teaching gets tedious."

"OK," he said at last, and that was the only part she didn't like; the only part that felt like a violation. And that was only because his pity was so apparent.

The news reached her in mid-November, a week or so behind the rest of her world. There had been articles online, but she hadn't read them; there had been a flurry of texts, but in the first week, none of them were to her. She wasn't an integral part of his life most people hadn't even known she knew him. It was her student Sheila who brought her the news in a series of informative bullet points: the intern's accusation, the tweet that went viral, the two other women who surfaced. One was an actress who had worked at the theater ten years prior; the other was a midlevel employee from marketing. The intern was twenty, the actress was fifty now, and Marketing was thirty-one.

"Well at least he has range," Mars said. She didn't know what else to say, and from Sheila's shocked face, she could tell this wasn't it. These kids were always so much more shocked than she ever remembered being. It was like flicking a switch, how easily their faces went from earnest to disapproving.

"I mean he harassed these women," Sheila said. "Like, serially, for years, and nobody said anything. I mean, that's . . ." She searched for a word and landed on *appalling* but continued to look undecided. She'd wanted a more satisfying one, something less prissy.

"Sure," Mars said, "those are the accusations."

Sheila's face took on a stonier cast. "Are you saying you don't believe it?"

"I'm saying that he's accused it sounds like of some really questionable behavior. And I would need to know more about the accusations to know what I thought."

"'Questionable,'" Sheila said, giving the word a slant that implied she found it particularly unsatisfying.

Mars held up a hand, as if warding her off. Sheila was one of her favorites; Mars prided herself in being honest enough (inside her own head, anyway) to admit that she had favorites. Sheila was small and fierce and looked a little bit like a ferret; she worshipped at the altar of Sarah Kane and Bertolt Brecht; she always smelled a touch like the inside of a burrow. From time to time Mars heard her colleagues say that they looked at their protégés and saw their younger selves, but this was not the case with Sheila; Mars looked at her and saw someone capable of a ferocious conviction that Mars herself had not possessed at that age. For this reason, among others, Sheila both irritated and impressed her.

"'Questionable,'" Mars told her, "as in: I have questions. Which, I hope, you would have as well. Because it is a mark of *rigor* to ask *questions*, to demand facts, and to form our opinions based on those facts once we collect them."

"What about 'Believe Women'?"

Mars sighed. "I think it's a slogan, Sheil. I think anything that becomes a slogan loses its actual use."

51

Sheila gave her the look that said, You Are A Tool Of The Patriarchy, but she didn't say it out loud, in part because all the kids were just a little bit scared of Mars in a way that never ceased to be useful, and in part because Sheila understood the utility of a look over a phrase. It was yet another thing that Mars liked about her.

Mars looked the rest of it up later that night, alone in her apartment. She didn't know why she made herself wait that long, but something had prevented her from just reading it all on her phone between classes. The accusations were detailed, and they were convincing in that they didn't exactly clash with the man she'd met. They didn't mesh with him either, or the version of him that she knew; she found it hard to imagine him sliding a hand down her thigh, cupping her ass as she moved past him in a crowded room. She tried to summon the image of him sticking a beer-scented tongue in her mouth during a gala and found it frankly impossible. But he had respected her, she thought. She had been aware of it on each occasion, his respect, without knowing entirely where it came from. Even that horrible pity in their last encounter had come from respect believing her to be better than the way in which she was living. The thought occurred to her that maybe these women were *unserious* the intern and the actor certainly, who knew about Marketing? and she sat very still with the aftershock of that thought, of having been the person who'd had it, of how the thought had made its way into her mind. She felt hot with guilt and adrenaline, as if Sheila had suddenly reared up, accusatory and omniscient.

OK, Mars corrected herself. Not *unserious*. But they could have been flirting, and it just went farther than they'd wanted. This, too, squared and didn't. He had been good at reading signals he'd read hers seemingly effortlessly. But also he'd pushed, in a moment when she hadn't invited him to the stuff around her writing. He'd wanted to make a point more than he'd wanted to respect her signals.

But people do that all the time in conversation, Mars thought, herself included. That was indicative of nothing.

Those women must have been flirting.

He'd thought she was gay, so *they* hadn't been flirting.

Over the drinks, that third time, had they been flirting?

She suddenly wasn't sure. It had been so warm and easy, and there had been a spark. But an intellectual spark arguing over the education of budding playwrights the kind that invited banter, not physical contact.

When Sheila brought it up again in class the next day, Mars didn't take the bait. "I guess we'll find out what happened," she said. "Sounds like it's all getting swept out in the open, anyway."

But in the end it didn't. The board fired him and he settled out of court with each of the three women. The theater was handed to another artistic director, who published a series of statements about a new chapter for the institution, one in which certain behaviors weren't tolerated, and in which values of safety and artistic inclusion went hand in hand. Mars skimmed the press release. She felt like she could have written the statement herself, given a checklist of buzzwords and a three-part structure that went: Denunciation, Distancing, Vision For The Future. Her cynicism was abruptly more alarming to her than the situation itself. She closed the browser window, and for a time she didn't keep track of where he was or what was happening to him.

All the men were in the news that winter. There was a trial, and another one, and another. She couldn't keep them straight and she didn't try. A sports mogul, a movie mogul, a finance mogul. She had never been a person who knew moguls, so she didn't know how she would have behaved if one of them had made a pass at her.

"It's more forcible than *made a pass*." This was Sheila, outraged. Office hours, a lazy Thursday. They had begun by speaking about her thesis on Adrienne Kennedy, and now they were just shooting the shit, and of course it came around to this. Sheila had been glued to the coverage.

"OK," Mars began, in her conciliatory teaching tone, but Sheila cut through it, as she'd started doing more and more these days.

"It's not like, *Oh would you like a drink*, like making a pass. We're talking about rape."

"Rape," Mars repeated.

"Like, in hotel rooms. Like forcible yeah, rape."

"But they went to those hotel rooms?"

"What?"

"The women the ones testifying. They went to the hotel rooms, right? Like, they weren't *dragged* to the hotel rooms, were they?"

Sheila's face underwent its seismic shift. Something about it this time made Mars wonder if she'd pressed too far. But when Sheila spoke, her voice was steely and controlled.

"No," she said, "they walked to the hotel rooms on their own legs, and *then* they were raped. You know what rape means, right? That you said *No* at some point, any point. You can say *Yes* to everything all day long, but then once you say *No* anything after that point is rape."

"I mean, I understand what rape is," Mars began, but Sheila kept going.

"People are saying, *But they e-mailed these guys, they talked to them afterwards* and it's like, yeah their behavior was contradictory and weird because they were fucking traumatized. Because you can be raped by people you trusted."

Sheila stopped talking. Under her tank top, her narrow chest was heaving. Her sternum was as prominent and knobby as a bird's. It was midwinter but the heat in the old building was cranked up unconscionably high. Sheila's slightly feral scent filled the office, although Mars didn't find it objectionable. Mars had expected Sheila's usual glare the one that dared her to argue but this time Sheila just looked disappointed, and that bothered Mars more than she'd expected.

She wondered if Sheila was speaking from personal experience but felt she shouldn't ask she wasn't a therapist, she'd never even taken a psych class, she just taught kids how to write.

As if Sheila had read Mars's thoughts, she added grudgingly, "I haven't been not like that. Guys have been shitty here and there, but ₁ . . . I have killer radar for who is gonna be a shady asshole. But that shouldn't be a requisite for, like, how to get by in the world."

On the contrary, Mars thought before she could suppress it, *it's the* only *requisite.*

She had been, when she was younger. *Like that.*

Eighteen, summer, backpacking in Europe. The crowded hostel, the boisterous evening, rum and clove cigarettes and strings of fairy lights out on the patio, and then the rest of the night like a dark shadow falling across all those little lights. Mars didn't think about it often, and when she did, she didn't assign words to it, but she knew what they would have been. It wasn't that she lied to herself about what had happened, but rather that she had come to terms with it in her own way. A way that involved a certain pragmatic toughness *these things happen* and a refusal to dwell on it. A refusal to feel self-pity. Of course that hadn't been possible in the weeks and months right after, but eventually it was, and she was grateful for that shift inside herself. She didn't think of herself as a victim, but she also didn't like being called a "survivor"it felt condescending, like an award given out after battle by the people who had stayed home. When she thought of herself in relation to that event which was not often she thought in the terms of Greek melodrama. Oedipus putting out his eyes, Agamemnon punctured with swords, Odysseus exiled far from his home. Something about men in the face of implacable power: they could fight and lose without being weak. She had fought and lost, but she would never agree to think of herself as weak.

When Sheila first mentioned her new housemate, it took Mars some time to realize what she was saying. It was early March now, and the sooty snow was starting to peel itself back from campus and the adjacent town. Sheila had dark plum-colored circles under her eyes, and she picked at the unraveling edges of her knit sweater. She was in the throes of her thesis, and Mars had assumed the visit was about that, and then after a long preamble that Mars failed to follow, Sheila said, as if she was re-peating herself, "And I can't even concentrate at home."

"Wait," Mars said, realizing too late that she was several steps behind. "Why is that?"

"Javier," Sheila said impatiently.

"Wait, who is Javier?"

"I told you about him last week the new housemate, the one who stares."

That jogged Mars's memory Sheila lived in a house of boys, most of them undergrads, and a grad student had moved in a few weeks ago and taken the room of a boy who was studying abroad.

"Right," Mars said. "Javier."

"Yesterday I was doing laundry and I turned around suddenly and he was right *there*. In the doorway."

Mars felt a cold trickle of alarm. "Has he ever touched you?"

"No," Sheila said. "But the way he looks at me, it *feels* like a touch."

Mars tried to think what to ask that would tell her whether or not to be concerned. To her mind a touch was a reason to worry and a look that felt like a touch was a thing to ignore, but sometimes the one be-came the other and then you really had a problem. She realized she was scanning Sheila closely for fear, but Sheila didn't seem frightened. She seemed pissed off. As Mars considered, Sheila added: "I talked to Benji about him? But Benji is all like: *He's not from here.* Benji says his cul-ture is like I don't know, different about women."

"Where's he from?" Mars asked.

"Spain. They're like . . . culturally . . . I don't know. *Aggressive.*"

Mars had been to Spain once. In her early twenties a theater had done her first real play, and they had flown her to Barcelona. She didn't remember the production well anymore, but she remembered the late dinners, the free-flowing wine. How, on her last night in town, she'd made out with the lead actor in the small alley behind the restaurant. The deliciousness of his stubble and the rough stucco wall through her thin shirt. He had been aggressive, but Mars couldn't have said whether he was *culturally* aggressive; that is to say, more or less aggressive than an American actor would have been. She had made it a point never to get involved with American actors.

"If he's making you uncomfortable, you should talk to him. Don't you think?"

"I do talk to him," Sheila said, frowning. "I tell him to fuck off."

Mars considered this. "And does he fuck off?"

"No, he like I don't know. That seems to make him more interested."

"He might think you're playing hard to get," Mars said. Sheila's jaw dropped into the position of seamless outrage, but Mars forestalled it. "I'm not saying you are, I'm just saying it's harder to misinterpret a multi-sentence conversation. Maybe if you said, 'These things make me uncomfortable,' he'd understand. Maybe Benji could be there for that conversation or an adviser, a counselor, someone you trust."

"He'll just say that he hasn't done anything," Sheila said. "And everybody will side with him, because it's not about doing, anyway."

"Isn't it?" Mars felt the familiar confusion return. "Aren't you worried he *might* do something?"

"No," Sheila said. "It's not that he'd do something, it's that he's so fucking entitled, he thinks he can just take up all the air. Like he thinks his thoughts so loudly, he looks at my ass and he thinks his thoughts, and I just *fuck him*, you know? I was trying to work at home just to be like, *You don't get to take up all the air*, but now I'm just fucking exhausted, frankly."

Mars cleared her throat and tried to think about what to say that would be wise and understanding, that would simultaneously illuminate and solve the problem. She found that she had nothing. "But are you concerned that he poses a physical threat?" she heard herself ask.

Sheila sighed, as if Mars had let her down more than usual. "Not all threats are physical," she said softly. Mars began to argue this point gently she expected that Sheila would warm to the argument, or in some way would find their usual dynamic comforting but Sheila refused to engage. In fact, she changed the subject, and shortly thereafter she left.

The encounter stayed with Mars that evening, as she cooked, as she ate, as she did the dishes, as she had a second glass of wine and listened

56

to the radio. Unease worked its way through her body, until she couldn't enjoy the food, the wine, or the classical strains of WQXR. It came back to language, she thought you used to know what was really dangerous and what wasn't by how girls talked about a thing. But these kids now talked about everything the same way it all had the same weight, so you didn't know when they were actually in danger or when they were just offended. Mars wanted to think that was progress, but more often than not it left her bewildered and resentful.

Sheila unraveled that whole spring, and so did the world. From a burst pipe to a foster dog that ripped its neck open on a fence, everything in Mars's vicinity seemed to be coming apart at the seams. There was another scandal with another artistic director a large regional theater but in this case, he managed to step down and collect a luxurious severance. Mars couldn't escape knowing the details of this one, in part because Sheila's outrage was incandescent: "He should have been *fired*. He should have been *punished*. He's getting three hundred *thousand* dollars for abusing all these women!"

"Three hundred and eighty-three," Mars corrected dryly. "Thousand."

"Even *you* have to be mad about this," Sheila said. The plum stains under her eyes had become a normal facet of her face, but there was something haggard and defeated about her that felt new. It was this new weariness that touched Mars's heart and troubled her. And because she wanted to help Sheila, she decided to be honest with her.

"Look," she said, "it's appalling. Obviously. I think you think I find this acceptable, somehow, but I don't. I never have."

"But?"

"But men in power escape consequences all the time. Being surprised by it is . . . I don't know, not an efficient use of my energy. Everybody thinks we're in some new age, but that's just . . . rhetoric, I think. I know you want me to be outraged, but I don't feel outrage because I don't feel surprise I never expected things to be different."

"But . . ." Sheila looked genuinely pained. "How are things supposed to change if we're just resigned to all of it? Like, you go home at night and you . . . what? Wait for the next terrible thing to happen?"

"Honestly," Mars said, as gently as she could, "I go home, and I read all of your plays, and that is fulfilling. And I make dinner, a healthy dinner, and I have a glass of wine, and sometimes I read a novel in my study. And that gives me pleasure. And I don't watch the news, and I don't get angry at people I don't know, or upset about things I can't control, and I would say that my life doesn't feel like a string of terrible things about to happen, because that's not the way in which I live it."

Mars had expected Sheila to argue. But instead Sheila just sat quietly, as if the air had gone out of her. She pulled at the sleeve of her knit cardigan, and Mars realized that it had been months since she had seen Sheila in a different one. It swallowed her slight frame and masked her scent with the all-blanketing one of wet wool.

A few minutes passed in silence. Finally Mars asked how things were with Javier. "Is he still bothering you?"

That seemed to jolt her out of the trance she was in. Sheila turned her cool brown gaze on Mars. "Don't worry," she said. "I'll take care of it."

It was after this, in the three or four weeks before she stopped coming to class entirely, that Sheila started bringing in the Murder Plays.

It was her classmates who began calling them that. Each short play culminated with a woman committing an act of violence. Not just on boyfriends or bosses, as one might expect; in the final three plays, a landlord, an innocent grocery-store clerk, and a boy on a moped were among the victims. Initially Mars treated each play as a piece of theater, and contended with it on its own merits, which she found limited—the concept alone was cliché, she felt, and the execution didn't elevate it. She suggested that Sheila read Valerie Solanas or Virginie Despentes, and she was aware that she was both trying to contextualize Sheila's rage for the class, to make it literary and therefore palatable, and trying to give Sheila artistic elders in whom she might find solace. Mars was aware that she had failed Sheila, but at least perhaps she could give her a series of older women writers by whom she might feel less let down. Eventually the agitation of the class torn between teasing and anxiety and Mars's own growing concern led her to call Sheila into office hours to discuss.

Sheila didn't come to office hours, even though Mars waited an extra hour. Sheila didn't respond to e-mails, either not the first one Mars sent, at 5 PM, nor the flurry of e-mails across the following few days. She didn't show up in class that Thursday, and her classmates glanced nervously (but with relief) at her empty chair, blatant as a missing tooth in the familiar workshop circle.

Mars worried about Sheila over the weekend, and on Monday she went to the department head. Jan was in her sixties, a person who lived or died by a good sweater, and the one today was velour mustard. Mars had never seen anything like it, and Jan informed her that her daughter-in-law had made it: "She's trying to start a fashion line, poor thing," Jan said comfortably. She adjusted her glasses on her narrow nose, cracked the window over her desk to combat the thick dry heat churned out by the radiator, and nodded to Mars. "Anyway, dear, you'd wanted to chat?"

Mars talked about Sheila, and as she did, she thought about the general insanity of what she was saying. *She's very upset about the assaults that have come to light. That have happened at all. She's obsessed by questions of injustice.* Perhaps the problem wasn't with Sheila, Mars thought fleetingly, perhaps the problem was with the rest of them, who were less upset and therefore better able to get on with things. But then again, they were all in the same world, and Sheila was the one who had stopped being able to function there.

She went on to mention the issues with the housemate, although she had to admit under Jan's detailed questioning that she didn't entirely know the nature of these issues. She arrived at the end of her report with the one inarguable fact under her command: Sheila had written twenty six short plays about murder and then stopped coming to class.

"Twenty-six," Jan repeated, a fine eyebrow arching. "Are you sure?"

"Yes," Mars said, "I counted them right before I came here."

"That's just a very impressive output," Jan said. "I have students who can't even finish one play. Twenty-six!"

"They're only ten minutes apiece," Mars hastened to say, and then felt that she might somehow be disparaging Sheila's efforts, so she added: "Although it's not easy to write a good ten-minute play."

"Ah," Jan said with interest. "Were they good?"

"Increasingly not," Mars admitted. "But also, I think she isn't wasn't sleeping. May not be sleeping."

"Have you spoken to any of her friends or classmates?"

"She lives off campus," Mars said. "I don't really know the kids she's close to. The other students in my class haven't heard from her either."

Jan nodded rhythmically, glancing away at her computer monitor, at the stack of student papers on her own desk. Mars could tell their conversation was drawing to a close, though she wasn't sure what conclusion they'd reached. She asked abruptly: "Should I go see her?"

Jan blinked. "Do you have her address?"

"No," Mars admitted, "but I could get it from the registrar, I think? I mean, I don't know if there's some . . . policy, of some kind about student addresses, or . . ."

"Why don't I see if I can get in contact with her," Jan said mildly. "But of course please do send her another e-mail and let her know that you're concerned." As she stood to let Mars out of the room the office was so small that the door couldn't open fully without a do-si-do she added wistfully, "The children are so fragile, these days."

The statement stopped Mars in her tracks. She had the same thought, often, but for some reason, hearing it spoken out loud in this exact moment, it landed on her ear like an indictment. Not of the children, but of herself. *Why am I not more fragile?* Mars wondered, and, failing to produce an answer, she went home.

It was a night or two later that he called her. Just after mid-night. She had given up on reading student plays and was sitting on the hardwood floor, her back against her reading chair, finishing a glass of wine. There was something about sitting on the floor that took her back to her twenties, made the picture briefly blur as she glanced at her stacks of books, the worn couch, the shell-white walls with their peeling paint. The landscape hadn't changed, just her place in it.

When his number came up on her phone, she blinked at it, bemused, but it didn't occur to her not to pick up. She hadn't heard his voice since September, and if she hadn't had caller ID, she might not have known right away who he was. He sounded older; his voice was thinner, as if it were reaching her across a vast distance.

"Mars," he said, and then a pause. "How are ya?"

She blinked at the wall. Took a sip of her wine. "Fine," she said, cautiously, "how are you?"

The second the question escaped her mouth, she wished she could take it back. It had been purely automatic, but how could it not be loaded?

She could hear the wry smile in his voice when he said, "Just great." An awkward pause and then he asked, with an almost formal courtesy, "Is it all right that I've called you?"

"I think so," she said. She knew there was a right way to have this phone call, but she didn't know what it was. She'd never learned any etiquette that applied to this. After a moment, she gave in to curiosity. "Where are you calling me from?"

He hesitated and then: "Miami." Another odd pause, and he added: "My stepmother's condo, actually."

"Oh."

"She's eighty-three. She listens to audiobooks and we play bridge."

60

"Oh," Mars said, inflecting her voice in such a way as to imply that that sounded, perhaps, like a positive outcome.

"You don't have to look for something cheerful to say," he told her, wryly. "It's a total hellscape. Lin isn't talking to me that was my girlfriend, note the past tense and every time *The New York Times* publishes a new op-ed about what a shit I am, my ex-wife forwards it with the subject line 'FYI.' You'd be surprised how many of the people who used to beg me for a job are talking about how they always knew I was rotten. But we know all the same people, I'm sure you're aware."

"Honestly," Mars said, "I don't spend a lot of time online. Or off campus, these days."

"You did hear about me, though?" He sounded suddenly alarmed at the thought that he was the one bearing this news.

"Yeah," Mars told him. "I mean, the basics."

"Ah, the basics." He sighed, and they were quiet, and then he laughed. "God, it's good to hear your voice," he said. "The other thing is just the *silence*. People don't talk to me the way they used to . . . but also, mostly they don't talk to me. They're all so afraid that someone will say, 'Oh, I hear you've been in touch with' and then there they'll be: the enemy. Which, I get that. So even my friends . . ." His voice trailed off and after a moment he said, "It's safer for them not to be my friends, ultimately." He tried to inject some of the flippancy back into his voice, but didn't entirely succeed, when he added: "Careful, you're now consorting with the enemy."

"I don't worry about people's opinions so much," Mars said automatically, and the smile was back in his voice when he said, "No, I remember."

Silence descended. After a moment, she asked, "Why *did* you call me?"

"Oh," he said, "well, it gets a little lonely in Miami." A silence, and then, "Why did you pick up?"

Mars opened her mouth to say any number of things, and then closed it again. She might have said, "It gets a little lonely in New England, too," but it felt cheap not untrue, but too symmetrical to be honest.

In the quiet, a dog barked next door. A door closed somewhere in the building, and the vibration made its way through her walls. The reading light flickered the wires were loose and she jostled it until the flickering stopped.

"I need to ask you," he said, and his voice was more serious than she'd ever heard it. All the schoolboy irony was gone. "And it's OK if the

61

answer is . . . but I'd like to feel like you would be honest with me. Even now. Especially now?" He took a breath, and she said nothing, and he placed his question with delicacy into the space between them. "Did I ever make you feel unsafe?"

"Unsafe," she repeated, tasting the word, testing it. Her mouth was dry and her heart rate was elevated, and she wasn't sure when either of those things had started.

"When we were alone together," he said. "I . . . this is selfish, but I keep thinking about . . . all the people who *didn't* say anything. The women, I mean. And I guess I keep wondering if all of them felt the same way, but some of them just didn't . . . say it."

"I only saw you three times," Mars said curiously, probing the question from all sides.

"I know."

"You didn't put your tongue in my mouth, you didn't touch me."

"Yes," he said. "But . . ." And he was quiet, with the whole weight of the *but*, and the image flickered into Mars's mind of Sheila, straightening up from the washing machine, turning to find Javier in the doorway. Watching her. The way Javier had looked at her, that Sheila had felt to be as tangible as a hand on her skin. A reaction that Mars had not fully understood because Mars had made the choice many years ago to ignore all the things that were not hands.

She went to take a sip of her wine and found her glass was empty. On the other end of the phone he breathed, softly coughed once but was silent, awaiting whatever judgment she might hand down. Another image came to mind unbidden: Sheila again, studying Mars, her brown eyes liquid with disappointment. *I have killer radar for who is gonna be a shady asshole. But that shouldn't be a requisite for, like, how to get by in the world.*

"No," Mars said at last. Her voice felt rusty, coming from a place deep in her chest. "I didn't. But I think there's something wrong with me."

"With *you*?" His astonishment was electric.

"I'm realizing that, yes." She licked her chapped lips, tasted copper. "I think that all the I don't know, the *antennae* or the the little parts of me that were made to suss out . . . disrespect, or unsafeness I think those parts aren't there anymore. They *were* I know when I was very young they were there, because I remember . . . talking to men and knowing that they were disrespecting me even in subtle ways, but directly to my face. But I had to sort of tear that out of myself by the roots, I think. I don't know how to say it, but inside of me now, there is a kind of general bluntness, a sense of . . . I don't *feel* unsafe in that way anymore. And so it's worked for me it's worked exactly the way I intended because it's made me . . . impermeable. But. Then again, has it?"

And now she was asking him how did it become a genuine question? now she was asking him with a ragged determination, as if he might be the one to know because Sheila was not here and could not be asked; because Sheila was too young to manage an understanding of the days and years and decades, things half buried and determinedly erased, the sheer time that had accumulated into this question; or perhaps it wasn't youth so much as an abyss between them that could not be bridged; they had been born into such different worlds, how could they not be shaped so differently that it became impossible to understand each other at all? Now she was asking him, a man, but at least they were the same age: "Has it actually worked for me?"

"I don't know," he said at last. "I don't think I can know that." His voice was very gentle, as if he were talking to a child or a family member, but the gentleness was not pity, and that alone felt akin to kindness.

"I don't know either," she said. And they were both quiet, their breaths synchronizing into a single rhythmic tide, listening on opposite ends of the line to the growing silence.

Nominated by Jennifer Lunden

DEAR FRIENDS

by MARY RUEFLE

from SEWANEE REVIEW

I have had friends, and have them now, but never once did I believe that in my lifetime the word *friend* would have a new, different, other meaning. I knew language evolved and changed over time, I knew there were new words every year to accommodate its growth and that some words changed meaning; but *love, death, flower, fire*? *Friend*? Then one day I picked up a magazine and read an interview with the COO (Chief Operating Officer) of Facebook, perhaps she still is, I don't know, but she was asked how many friends she had and she said, "Over three thousand; I don't know all of them, but I have met them in one shape or form." I would rather be antiquated—I would rather die—than make a statement like that. I *know* my friends, I know the sound of their voices, their speech patterns, their inflections, their hand and body gestures, the wet of their eyes, what makes them laugh, what makes them cry, how their nose was broken and how they became beautiful after that, and mysterious, so mysterious I cannot reconstitute them even as I try, because they are *people*, they walk on this earth, and they will die here.

As Frances Burnett wrote, there are only a few times in life when we think we are going to live forever. And I think one of them is when we are with our friends, laughing, eating, looking each other in the eye. I would rather write about friends than relations. Relations—parents, children, siblings, spouses exist within a grid of social conceptions and expectations that have evolved over centuries, and though we may fail in these relations, though we may let the preconceived down, nowhere in these relations do I find the sheer unexpected *variety* that friendship offers, for no two friendships are based on the same thing, the bond between two friends has no other explanation other than itself.

I have a friend who has never read a single word I have ever written. I love being with her.

I have a friend who is not a person I could ever be, even if I tried, nor would I want to be, and I love being with her.

I had a friend who peeled an orange in public for the first time when she was seventeen. I do not remember the first time I peeled an orange, but it was probably in front of another. Do any of us remember such an act, such a little act lost in so many other acts performed for the first time as children? My friend's mother was cultivated to the point of exoticism, and at the same time conservative and strict; at least that is how I remember her. She taught her daughter that to peel an orange, or any other fruit, in the presence of another person, was perverse; you might as well undress in front of them. Fruit was peeled in the kitchen by servants and served naked on a plate with a little knife to the side. The logic of this is itself perverse—do not undress in public but appear there naked—but as a result of such logic my friend was apprehensive when I unpacked our lunch one sunny afternoon, spreading a blue napkin on the stone steps of a cathedral; we were two teenagers having an outing in the city, an adventure, and I had thought to bring a picnic. Hence two unpeeled oranges appeared on the napkin, and I watched my friend's face color as she told me the rules regarding oranges. I insisted that people did it all the time, no one would notice, not a head would turn if she ventured to try. Never before or since have I seen someone peel an orange with such exquisite delicacy. She took off the skin as if it were covered with tiny mother-of-pearl buttons, and her hands trembled every time a piece of skin came off and fell away like a little continent set adrift, revealing the flesh inside, which was sometimes translucent and bright and bursting with moisture, and at other times covered by a thin white cottony undergarment. And that was that, we ate our oranges in public as carelessly as any two girls, none of the passersby noticed anything historical, and years later when I ran into my old friend, and recalled that afternoon in the sun, she told me she has hated oranges and never ate them, her mother was dead, and she had no memory of any picnic on the steps of a church.

I had a friend who loved apple trees and apple blossoms and apple orchards, he loved swimming in ponds and lakes, and making currant jam and jam from mulberries and playing the harmonica, but when he

65

read, for he loved books, he read heavy German tomes. He was diagnosed with cancer, and the treatment for his cancer caused a stroke that caused his blindness, he was blind at the end, and I took him swimming in a lake, I held his hand and helped him wade out until the water was waist-high, and then I said that I would be his beacon, I would not move. And he swam, not far, not much, but he went under and came up utterly refreshed, and all the while I stood there with my arms outstretched and thought *look at me, look at me, I am helping a blind man swim.* And when my friend died, I actually felt *lucky* because my last words to him were *I love you,* and his last words to me were *I love you* and I thought that it didn't get any luckier than that, though of course it could have been luckier, he could have lived with his sight for the last few years of his life, he could have seen his apple trees and gone swimming without my help.

I had a friend in high school, I had a crush on him, he was gay but I didn't know it. I had other friends who were gay, and my favorite teachers were gay but I didn't know it, and there were other teachers who were not gay and not my favorite who were having sex with students who were not my friends but I didn't know it, I found out years later, my friend told me all about it, and I was shocked. We were in our thirties then, and he was dying of AIDS. I mean, he had AIDS and knew he would probably die but was not certain; he didn't want to die, but he did come to see me, twice, in what turned out to be the last year of his life. We sat in a diner in the middle of Michigan and he told me all this stuff that was going on in high school that I had been completely unaware of. None of the gay guys in high school had come out, and he talked about that, about how he knew I had a crush on him but he couldn't bring himself to tell me he was gay. We actually laughed about it, we were in our thirties and considered ourselves grown-ups, adults. Later I found out that I was not grown-up at thirty, but he never found out, he died before he could find out he wasn't a grown-up. Sitting in the diner I said to him, *I am so sorry.* And he said, *Why, because I am gay?* I said *No, not that; because you are going to die.* And he said, *I don't want to die, but, you know, these things happen.* These things happen—I think in that moment I must have grown up, but later I lapsed into childhood again, and it was another thirty years before I remembered his words—*these things happen*—and by then I had lost countless friends and family members, by then his words seemed the simplest statement of the truth I had ever heard. After the diner, he wanted to take a strenuous hike through the dunes of Lake Michigan, he had had chemo and was weak but was determined to try this one thing while he still had the chance, to see if he could. He barely made it, we would stop every few yards so he could rest, but he would not give up or turn back, and when we reached the shore of the Lake, he opened his fly and pissed right into the water, I saw his penis for the first time, he had a huge grin on his face and he took off his baseball cap he was bald beneath it—and waved it in the air like he was riding a bronco in a rodeo. His lover was at the opera when he died, and his mother called me to tell me her son was gone. I had never met her, and she said to me, "He talked about you a lot in high school, and at the end—but I never understood—what was the nature of your relationship?" I could tell this was awkward for her, that in her grief she wanted to know everything she could about her son's life and wondered if he had had sexual relations with women as well as men. I told her the truth, I said, "Your son was my friend, we were always friends, he was a friend of mine, and I was very lucky."

I have a friend who believes that birds have souls but humans do not. This may sound like the belief of a misanthrope, but my friend is anything but that, she is unfaltering in her cheerfulness and kindness, she plays Ping-Pong and badminton with relish, and though she has suffered the blows and disappointments of life like the rest of us, they have never laid a mantle on her shoulders, and I have often wondered if her explication of souls is connected to her sense of contentment, if it is the secret key to a disposition we could all use. I have known her for most of my life, and she remains a mystery. Birds! Little brown birds!

I had a friend in high school with whom I felt a deep bond; we were both interested in religion and philosophy. In college she went the way of the Greek Classics and, by a turn in the road, became a Buddhist. I went the way of English literature and, by a turn in the road, became a poet with a Zen approach to writing who used the word God in every third poem. When we were teenagers, we shared the belief that we were human beings on a spiritual journey, but by the time we were fifty we both pretty much knew we were spiritual beings on a human journey, and we expressed this belief by exchanging Christmas cards every December. We didn't see one another in all that time, and then one year I happened to be teaching near her and we managed to spend a day together. We were both divorced and living alone by then, and of course we had lunch in a nifty restaurant (she was a vegetarian, I was not) but the rest of the afternoon we spent in the old swimming pool behind my crumbling apartment complex (the Eden Roe, pink stucco, or what was left of it). And what did we do in the swimming pool? Not swim. We stood waist-deep in the water and saved the lives of hundreds of drowning wasps, picking them one by one out of the water while we lazily talked, without either of us mentioning the wasps and what we were doing for them; for three hours we stood there and had a rhythm going, wasp up wasp out, and I can't remember any of our chat, I only remember the wasps in a pile on the side of the pool, coming to realize in their squirming that they were still alive, though most of them crawled right back into the pool and we saved their lives twice. It was lovely to see my old friend again, but that afternoon we didn't quite act like human friends, we acted like reincarnated lotus buds who, if they wanted to float, had to clear their pond of debris, which amounted to a good deed.

When I was an adolescent behaving in irresponsible ways, I had two friends I adored; they were twins, a boy and a girl, their names began with the same letter and almost rhymed. He was feminine and she was masculine, he was lithe and delicate with a high voice while she was muscular with a low, gravelly voice. I was closer to her than to him, but as they were as close as close and always together, it hardly made a difference. They were in a band; he played guitar and she played drums. I was not in the band, but on Friday nights there was always a party in the basement of the twins' house and the band played, or practiced, which were basically the same thing. When they weren't playing, we did things that we thought were outrageously funny, such as throwing breakfast cereal into the toilet bowl and pretending it was vomit. We went to my friends' house because their mother was a widow, and every Friday night she went on a date, leaving the house to us. We would party, and though I no longer remember what that feels like, I know it involves a desperate need to forget something. At around midnight their mother would come home so drunk she had to be put to bed by her children, and often I would help them get her up onto the bed and out of her shoes. We didn't think anything of it, obviously she had partied while we were partying and that's what Friday nights were for. This went on for two years and then my family moved away and I had new friends and went to a new school. But judging from the journals I kept then, my sole purpose in life was to find a way to get back to my old friends. Reading the journals, it is quite clear I was in love, though I have no memory of feeling this way. We wrote letters for a few years, but by the time I graduated from high school we had lost touch altogether. Years later—I was in my fifties—I came across a box of their baby pictures and pictures of their early childhood. It seemed to me that I had so many pictures of them that they must have none, and I wanted to return the pictures but hadn't a clue as to where the twins lived. Somewhere in Texas, I thought. I called information in Dallas, I called information in Houston, and then I gave up. The pictures meant nothing to me, they just took up space, so I threw them all out. And then about a year later my phone rang and it was her. She had found me. We talked for about thirty minutes military, disability, cabin in the woods, dogs, mother had gotten sober and married a great guy but was dead now—and promised to stay in touch. I knew what would happen next: the phone rang again and it was her brother, she had called him immediately after talking to me. So I chatted with him— military, commercial pilot, never married—and said goodbye. I didn't mention the pictures. The next day I got another call from his sister, inviting me to their high school reunion; I reminded her that I didn't go to high school with them, it had been junior high, but she said it didn't matter because she and her brother organized the reunion every year and could invite anyone they wanted and I wouldn't regret it because it was a *blast*, they rented a Ramada Inn in Dallas and partied for two days, a whole weekend, it was *the* event of the year, they lived for it, everyone lived for it, I would love it, it was a *blast*. I told her I didn't go to my own high school reunions, that I was not the "reunion type," that I was very busy and didn't like to travel anyway. She would not take no for an answer and called week after week begging me to come party in Texas. Finally I stopped answering the phone. She kept calling, I didn't pick up, and finally she stopped. I think she understood I was some-how "not the same." I was not the same as I was at thirteen and I was not the same as they were now. I felt bad about the pictures, though; I don't really know how I came to have them, it must have been we were partying and the family album came out and I either stole them (because I was in love) or they were wantonly given away. But in the photographs, my friends were so innocent, little children on tricycles or holding Easter baskets, and it saddened me to think of them as adults, having a blast in the Ramada Inn once a year; it fairly broke my heart, but then again I was just as sad over myself, look who I had be-come, having destroyed without thinking the childhood memories of another, just sitting there at my desk ripping the photos up, tossing them into the basket beneath me.

I have a friend whom I have never met; I am pretty sure we will meet next year.

One of the friends I've written about here has died since writing this.

I have a friend I met once and only briefly and we have corresponded ever since. In the beginning, we wrote long letters using words, but for some years now we have not, now we exchange, by mail, flowering branches, birds' nests, tiny gloves, feather hats, and once she sent me the entire sweepings from her porch—shards of blue clapboard paint mixed with dirt, leaves, and debris; beauty by accident, as so many friendships are.

I have a friend who wishes that she were not a human animal, but an animal with fur. A cat, fox, dog, or rabbit. This disturbs me so much I love her even more.

I have a friend I have known for forty-five years. She is the purest poet I know, but she has not written a poem since she was twenty; instead she has chosen, day after day, to wear only blue or gray, and I consider this an ingenious, even perfect, solution to the problem of poetry and time.

I had a friend I loved for twenty-five years, and then the earth opened between us, and now we have not spoken in twenty-five years. But nearly every week I dream of her, so there is this sense, for me at least, that we still know and love each other, but only late in the night, behind closed eyes.

I have a friend who "did exactly the opposite of what one would have expected from the first" (as Proust says in a letter) and when this was done, my last beliefs in the architecture of reason and coherence were completely demolished, and as for the inevitable debris found among the ruins, I blew that away myself, though not as easily as one dispels a bit of dust. Thus I have a friend I love but do not trust and never will.

I had a friend who, at a very sad time in my life, was more or less my only friend, and she was sad too and she was a dog. She was not my dog, I had never had a dog, I knew nothing about dogs, I had heard they were "man's best friend" but thought that was sentimental and without weight. My friend belonged to a very young couple—too young to be a couple, in my opinion—who lived in the apartment below mine. They fought all of the time, especially at night. They screamed and hollered at each other and sounded a lot like an old married couple who fought, which is why I thought they were way too young to live like that. My friend, the dog, used to visit me when her parents (masters, owners?) fought; I would hear her scratching at my door, she couldn't bark because her vocal chords had been removed by her original owner (parent, master?). Her hips had been damaged in an accident and she wore a brace around her hind parts. I could hear her scratching at my door with her front paw, and I would let her in, together we would sit and listen to the fighting coming up through the floor, she would be trembling and I would put my arms around her and we would stay like that for the longest time. I always had food and water for her, she knew right where they were on the floor, and since at that time I myself was eating very little on account of my sadness, I would eat a little something from my cupboard when she ate. So we would eat together and hold each other, and then her master (parent, owner?) would holler for her to come down and she would go, I would hold the door open for her and she would turn one last time to look at me before she limped down the stairs. She could not bark or whimper or make the least sound. I loved her. One day I put a silly cardboard frame over her head so that it sat on her neck and framed her face and I took her picture. The whole thing lasted no more than a minute, and today, thirty years later, her portrait still sits by my desk. I know she is dead, but I don't know how the last years of her life turned out—one night the couple had an explosive fight, my friend came upstairs to sit with me, and in the morning her mother (owner, master?) packed the car and left, taking my friend with her. As I stood in the parking lot, I could not bring myself to say good-bye, I didn't hug her or pet her, I just looked at her and walked inside. If she had anything to say, she couldn't say it, nor could I. But I could cry and that was a blessing. Now when I think of dogs, I understand that the relationship *is* very sentimental and carries great and lasting weight.

I have a friend, and for several years we were both lost at the same time, at loose ends, adrift. He lived on the West Coast and I lived on the East Coast, and many nights we talked for hours on the phone, keeping each other company. Even the long silences were comfortable between us, but some of the things we said to each other were so strange I began writing them down, writing things down was everything to me and it was everything to him, someone who knew us well said we could complete each other's sentences, and that was true too. He would say "I can't talk to people who don't know what they are doing," when it was clear neither of us knew what we were doing. Once he said, "I'm so slow," and I said, "I know, you have a head of butter and a body of water," which he pretty much does, and another time he said, "L. is so much smarter than I am . . . no, not smarter but . . . he has a wife." Then we would crack up and the minutes flew. Suddenly he would exclaim, "Look at this, a helicopter! What would Kafka say?" He was always reporting on things happening outside his window—once he saw a mountain lion—while out my window I saw only squirrels. A dear friend of his

71

died, and his wistful comment was, "I am completely unable to make myself stutter." He was that smooth, butter and water. Then he lost another friend, suddenly and unexpectedly, and he said, "No one knows what to say. That's why poetry exists." I was contemplating getting an aquarium, a large one, and his reaction was, "You have to have a sense of irony to buy a gigantic aquarium in the first place, but once you start sitting in front of it and staring you've lost your sense of irony." We would always talk about what we were having, or just had, for dinner. I'd say, "I just bought a plump little hand-fed, hand-raised chicken, isn't that sad?" and he'd respond, "I don't want to upset you because you've already upset yourself, but all I ate today was cardboard." Another conversation went like this: "Sorry, I'm just me these days"; "That's your problem, you're just you, so snap out of it!" I would hear his doorbell ring in the background, and he would say, "That's my dry cleaning being delivered." To me that was insanely indulgent, but he would remind me that his family were immigrants and say, "We didn't come to this country to change lightbulbs," then I'd remind him that they came to this country because we *have* lightbulbs. It was just banter, completely idle, and we loved it. We could say anything to each other, and that is one of the great gifts of friendship. We shared a wavelength, and we still do, though our lives are no longer adrift and we don't talk nearly so often, but the sound of his voice is as familiar to me as air. We often spoke out of the blue, without any context, and once he said something totally unexpected, he said, "Women are incredible. I just wanted to say that, in case any women are listening."

I have a friend who is the best-read human being I have ever known; not only has he read everything you have ever heard of, read, or hoped to read, he has read novels like *The Mysteries of Udolpho* and *Penguin Island*, he has read *Lorna Doone*, he has read *The Exegesis of Philip K. Dick*, he has read Duns Scotus, his idol is David Hume, and although he is completely indifferent towards Shakespeare, my friend is also the sanest person I know. Eccentric and sane, a dynamo combination. He has a beautiful, compassionate wife whom he adores, two beautiful grown children whom he adores, and he lives in a modest home that is one of the warmest and most welcoming I have ever been in. Yet his special place is in its basement, where he has a grotto, his refuge, his private sanctuary. This room is cold and damp and covered floor to ceiling with shelves holding his collections, which include a hundred porcelain figurines on whose faces unusual expressions have been caught, framed photographs of forgotten movie stars, a hundred odd ashtrays, a thousand tiny matchbooks, and everything in between. It resembles an antique store of the particular kind that a fetish-minded customer would buy out on the spot. A foreign film crew once wanted to film it, but my friend declined. This is where he keeps his books and his postcards of which he has over twenty thousand—filed in metal filing cabinets. In middle age he suffered the proverbial collapse, after which he became a serious student of Buddhism, meditating daily in his grotto. He was born a Jew, the son of Holocaust survivors who so traumatized his development that their level of control and his level of guilt constantly collided—his mother would not allow him to wear worn, frayed jeans in high school because she didn't survive for her son to wear rags—and eventually he became not a misanthrope but a slightly misanthropic man, having learned early on through books and life that inhumanity is an ongoing reality. If "history teaches, but has no pupils" (Gramsci), my friend is sitting in that otherwise empty classroom. Yet over the years, his wife and family, his music, his dog, have brought him such genuine solace and love that he considers himself a fortunate man. One day I said to him his whole philosophy could be summed up in a sentence, "Life is terrible, terrible, and I am a fortunate man." He laughed with acknowledgment. But sometime later, it dawned on me that my friend, who had spent his whole life escaping the clutch of his parents, had finally come to a summation that was in effect theirs, for they had drummed into him since he first gasped for air that life was terrible and he was fortunate. Which is my philosophy entirely, for life *is* terrible, and I *am* fortunate, fortunate to have such a friend, who keeps me ever aware and in check, as on the day he said to me from out of the blue, "Oh, are you so cozy in your life you can turn down a red-flocked bear ashtray?"

I have a friend who died, yet every time I think of him, I smile and am never sad. How can you not smile when you recall a man who, given the choice, would only eat white food? His favorite meal, which he often served to guests, was boiled spaghetti with cheese sprinkled on top, cheese you shook from a can, and for dessert a boxed Boston cream pie with the chocolate glaze diligently scraped off. A man who was such a romantic his idea of a pickup line was, "You have all the colors of October in your hair, come and have a donut in my car." He also dumped a bucket of sand on the floor of his car so he could "take the beach with him" wherever he went. A masterful writer who had published to acclaim but fell out with the times and in his dotage announced with glee that a few paragraphs were appearing in *Yankee Magazine.* Someone who recited Shelley and Keats in the middle of a conversation about pudding. A man who was determined to tap a maple tree for syrup, and upon tapping the lone spindly tree in his front yard announced with pride that a cup of sap had produced a teaspoon of syrup which he gave as a gift to his neighbor's dog. The last time I saw my friend was the night of a full moon, and he desired us to view it from the end of a pier so dangerously dilapidated it had been cordoned off by a chain and an ordinance. He drove as far as the chain, got out of his car, unhitched the chain, and drove us to the end of the pier where we parked and sat in silence as the moon rose over the ocean. Finally he turned to me and said, "They can't keep the moon out."

I have a friend I have known since the day she was born. She is not my daughter, or my sister, but the daughter of a friend, at least she was the daughter of my friend for the first twenty years of her life before she became my friend. This came as a surprise to me, I had never considered that someone you knew before she could feed herself would one day be having dinner with you, holding a fork. If we are at the movies and go to the ladies room together, I don't think of her as being in diapers, though she once was and I knew her then. It is a mysterious thing how one person becomes another, and I cherish her friendship as utterly distinct from any others I have. But because she is thirty-five years younger than I am, and in all probability I will die before she reaches her full adulthood—before she is my age—I sometimes feel like a wild duck flying over her head, knowing all the time we have spent together will one day be no more than an occasional vivid memory for her (unlike a parent, whom one thinks of constantly). And then I realize that this is true of all friendships—they are wild ducks flying overhead—and that my friendship with her is no different than any other, and therefore perfect.

I had a friend I had known for years, but we never lived in the same place at the same time, and then we did. For six months we lived in the same city and had dinner every week on the same night in the same restaurant at the same time at the same table and ordered the same thing (wild mushrooms in cream sauce) and drank the same wine (Sancerre). During dinner he told me the story of his life in increments, dinner by dinner, like a serialized novel. They were wonderful dinners and because we were moving from his birth to the present, and because the story of a heterosexual stockbroker who becomes a bisexual surrealist poet is a long one, we were always the last to leave the restaurant, the staff came to know us and let us linger at our table while they prepared to close for the night. My friend and I were doing the same work, but because he was paid twice what I was, he insisted on paying and would never let me pick up the bill. He did agree that I could pay for our last dinner and that on that occasion we would go somewhere new. Because I wanted to re-pay him in any way I could I chose an even more expensive restaurant, a Japanese one that was written up in all the papers. It was terrible. The food was so minimal we would look at our plates and make up ridiculous haiku on the spot, staring at a shred of vegetable floating in water. There were a hundred kinds of sake and we tried a great many of them, giving them titles. Haunted Bell. Chrysanthemum Tragedy. Nightingale Hit By A Fan. As the evening wore on, the names grew increasingly Western and literary until we were drinking "Forlorn Incubus" and "Apropos Of Wet Snow." Shared misery can be a joy. I saw my friend once more be-fore he died—we had dinner in a foreign country—and we spent that dinner talking about all our other dinners. Dinner with friends—it doesn't get any better than that. When you eat dinner with friends, the ones you really love and no other, you have reached a pinnacle you don't see, but it is there. Look around the table—*in the still garden the meal shines for a gathering of friends*—and if someone starts clearing it, put your hand on their arm ever so lightly, ever so briefly, pause that plate in midair.

I had a friend when I was ten, and she was a Mormon. We played together after school and on the weekends, and one night her mother invited me to stay for dinner. It was a large family, and they sat at a round table, and when it was time to say grace, each one of them folded their arms in front of their chest, which startled me, as that was some-thing my mother did when she was angry, when she stood in the kitchen and let you know. We said grace in my family, but we folded our hands together and bowed our heads, and no one could ever tell who was an-gry and who was not. When I ate with my friend's family, I thought they were all angry with God, and it confused me: Why would you pray when you were angry with God? I was too polite to ask my friend why the Mormons did this, so for a long time it stewed in me. I had another friend at the same time who was also Mormon, and one day she took me down to her basement and showed me what her family kept down there—huge burlap sacks of lentils and beans and rice. She said this was the food her family would live on when there was an apocalypse. I asked her what an apocalypse was and she said it was an event that would cause the whole planet to explode and burn. I did not understand why anyone would want to survive if such a thing happened but was too polite to say so. Then I remembered the Mormons were angry when they prayed, and why not, they had to survive in ashes and live on beans. Suddenly I understood and things began to make sense to me, at the age of ten, thanks to my friends.

I had a friend in high school who was not my best friend but she lived closest to me in the city and it was easy to walk to her house on the weekends. She lived in a house and I lived in an apartment. Her family was sophisticated in ways that were new and mysterious to me. Her father, I found out years later, was a CIA agent whose cover was working for the embassy as a cultural attaché with an emphasis in Asian art. These were the "days of Vietnam," as we refer to them now, which sounds so peculiar in retrospect, as if a fad for straw or silk had swept through the country. My friend's mother came from a wealthy Southern family and had once been a professional ballerina, a fact that deeply impressed me, as even my English teacher, whose class I excelled in, told me I was a *klutz* without a single bodily grace belonging to any of the nine muses. He had been watching me through a classroom window as I tried, on the court below, to hit a tennis ball. Later he went so far as to insult my clothing, telling me to my face my dress was ridiculous, and so it was, a brown shift with huge turquoise polka dots, a Peter Pan collar, and a big floppy bow. My sister had made it, she made all my clothes. We weren't allowed to wear pants to school. My friend's sister took *fencing lessons* in a white body suit; she had a *saber* and a *grilled mask.* It was all too much. My friend had several fur coats that were so odd and interesting you couldn't guess what animal they were made from. I joked once that she was wearing her monkey coat. It occurs to me now that it probably *was* a monkey coat, as monkeys can be found in all of the Asian countries her father traveled to, supposedly collecting the antique heads of the Buddha. So that was the situation. My mother adored my friend, she liked my friend better than any of my other friends because when meeting my mother for the first time my friend had *curtsied.* I think my mother had waited her whole life for that moment. My mother loved fruit. I think she would as soon have married a pear as my father. There was always a big bowl of fruit in the kitchen. Liver-spotted bananas, and green grapes translucent as jade, though if I ate the grapes, the arthritic stems that remained terrified me, I imagined them as crippled hands coming to get me. And there were always apples, her favorite. In those days there weren't *kinds* of apples, you couldn't say, "I feel like a Gala," or "Pick up some Granny Smiths," there were only, well, apples. They were red and all shaped the same and perfectly tasteless. My mother kept another bowl of fruit in the dining room, and all of that fruit was artificial. When I was younger it was plastic, but by the time I was in high school it had all turned to bone china. In my mother's mind, there was a very big difference between a plastic orange and an orange made from china, and if you couldn't tell the difference you had no taste, none at all. It was the difference between a handshake and a curtsy. Years and years later, I wrote a poem and in the poem are the passing words *a world where no one ever even curtsies anymore.* And I have noticed through the years that many readers want, even demand, a backstory to anything that is ever written, and now I have given them *the entire backstory* of these fleeting words, and I feel for a moment like my friend, who curtsied in front of my mother, something my mother had always wanted, and got once.

When I walk through a city, I see many strange faces, and though none leave a trace, I know they have friends. Who are their friends, whose friends are they? For wherever I walk, the image of my friends goes with me.

I have a friend who used to be a dancer. She once choreographed and performed a dance I have never forgotten. She danced to Al Green singing "How Can You Mend A Broken Heart?" She was solo on the stage, and a spotlight followed her as she moved. She was wearing a paper bodysuit, and as she moved the paper tore, at first in tiny slits at the seams, and then in big gashes, rip after rip until she was dancing in shreds, practically naked. It was so bold and beautiful and sad, and happened once and once only; it was something to behold, and then it vanished from the earth.

Nominated by Marianne Boruch, David Jauss, D. Nurkse

MANTIS

fiction by GINA CHUNG

from WIGLEAF

The praying mantis lives in a small but well-furnished and moderately priced studio apartment in an oak tree overlooking a baseball field in the park where, on warm spring days, she hears the crack of a bat and the faraway roar of a crowd she doesn't pay attention to. On weekends, she likes to stay in and read, or catch up on the latest news with a friend. Her friendships don't last very long, so the news she gets from them is always fresh, and she never has to concern herself with keeping the names and situations of their lives straight in her mind.

Lately, the mantis has felt restless, the thrill of stalking and consuming her prey—whether it be a moon-addled moth, a frisky horsefly, or a crisp ladybug—no longer as exciting as it once was. The mantis is not used to this, as she has always been driven by her desires, from the moment she wakes up till the moment she folds herself up into a green pagoda to sleep at night. But tending to these wants has grown tiring. She wonders if inside her there is only a series of jaws, daisy-chained into a flat loop of unceasing hunger. She finds herself second-guessing her decisions, listlessly contemplating her desires and finding them uncompelling. Her increasing inability to derive enjoyment from things was something she had been working on with her therapist, a millipede with a tendency to run late, until she got fed up with his tardiness and ate him. He had been juicy yet surprisingly tough, and he had tasted like dark soil, a slightly bitter flavor she dreamt about for days afterward.

Sometimes the mantis goes on dates. She's never disappointed by the males she meets, because she never expects much from them. The sex is usually fine—adequate at best and unremarkable at worst. She enjoys the click she feels when they mount and socket themselves into her, as well as the crackling sound their heads make when she pincers her mouth around them. The males seem grateful to die while inside her, their jerking bodies moving even more frantically once she's killed them. She remembers most of these assignations, if not the males themselves, fondly.

When the mantis falls in love for the first time, it is with a male almost half her size, the same subtle green as her—a shade darker than the leaves of the oak tree. He approaches her boldly, unlike the others, who all creep up to her with the same air of mingled shame and excitement, and she is surprised by how much she likes this boldness. One of his front legs is slightly shorter than the other, and he walks with a graceful, tripping gait that she admires.

He invites her to a bar in his neighborhood and she accepts, taking care with her appearance. They discuss themselves and the things they enjoy: the sound of birds in the morning, the tremble of the leaves in a storm, the taste of dew.

"It's too bad that all of this will end with you eating me," he says at the end of their date, when he's walking her back to her place. "I've enjoyed getting to know you."

"We don't have to do that yet," she finds herself saying. "We can continue getting to know each other."

"I don't take it at all personally," he says, almost apologetically. "I know how it goes." And he closes his eyes, in case she changes her mind and decides to end things then and there.

The mantis considers her options. Her hips swivel, ready to accommodate him, while her jaws ache to snap around his neck, to crush his eyes and pick at his flesh. But she remembers something the millipede said to her, a session or two before she ate him, about how wanting did not always have to equal having. If all you ever do is go after the things you want, you'll never know what it is you need, he'd said, and she'd wondered if she should just eat him up right then and there for saying something so stupid.

But it is late and she is feeling generous, and as the rosy August moon strawberries into the sky, she kisses him good night—she notices the twang of fear in his body when he feels the whisper of her jaws along his face—and goes inside her apartment and shuts the door, leaving him outside, and alive. She sleeps easy that night for the first time in weeks, and in the morning she catches a fat mayfly, relishing the crunch of its wings, but decides to eat only half of it, saving the rest for later. *Perhaps not everything has to be consumed right away in order to be enjoyed,* she thinks, proud of herself.

A few days later, his body turns up below the oak tree. Someone else has made short work of his head and thorax, and she knows that it is him by the length of one of the front legs, curled underneath the limp body. She feels an alien regret pool inside of her, fresh as rainwater, watching as a group of human children gather around the body to poke at it with a stick. She will never get to ask him his thoughts on the sound of ducks in the spring now, or about the leaping of crickets in late summer. She will never see the look of fear and awe in his acid green eyes when she twists her head to stare into them mid-coitus. And she will never know if she would have stopped herself, kept her jaws closed, after he had been inside her; if she would have known how to enjoy his company, without making him forever and irrevocably hers.

Nominated by Wigleaf

THE CLOUD LAKE UNICORN

fiction by KAREN RUSSELL

from CONJUNCTIONS

Before I started living on extraordinary time, I used to set my watch by
Garbage Thursday. My landlady often jokes that Garbage Thursday is
my Sabbath. Garbage Thursday is a secular ceremony of reckoning and
forgetting. You hear the same hymn booming across our leafy block
each Thursday evening: the trash bins bumping and scraping over as-
phalt, the rolling harmonies of a neighborhood remembering in uni-
son that this is our weekly chance to liberate our lives of trash. Smells
and peels, used neon condoms and yolky eggshells, kombucha six-packs
and leopardy bananas—down the driveways they come, our open se-
crets straining at white Hefty bags. Clink-clink-clink, we rattle to-
gether, the Ghosts of Garbage Thursdays Past, Present, and Future.

Via neighborly telepathy, I always reach the curb at the same moment
as my friend Anja. She lives in Unit B of the Cloud Lake apartment
complex across the street. The name "Cloud Lake" is like a cemetery
marker for the acres of water that once flowed here, drinking in the sun-
shine of the last century; we live in Multnomah County, Oregon, where
the names of the dead can be found on condominiums and athletic clubs
and doomed whimsical businesses. Anja says she can feel the lake water
rippling below the pavement. What I see as early-morning mist, she says,
is actually the vaporous ghost of Cloud Lake. Anja vibrates at a special
frequency. She emigrated to Portland from Sarajevo, and tells me she
was epigenetically altered by her childhood experience of the Bosnian
War. She smokes pre-rolled joints and has a secondary addiction to
deep-dish pizza. We have developed a kind of whistling camaraderie
on Garbage Thursday, what I imagine to be a gravediggers' rapport, like

something out of Shakespeare. "What's good, Mauve!" she waves to me across the street, centaured before her own overflowing bin. "Disposing of the evidence, I see!"

The curb is like the diary where we record our hungers. A diary slated for weekly erasure. The amnesiac's log of "refuse." This used to strike me as a squeamish euphemism, but now I think it's the perfect word, noun and verb, for the toxic mosaic we make in our ad hoc collaboration on Ninth Avenue. Through the upstairs window on Thursday nights, I watch a small, ephemeral mountain range building itself on either side of the street. Everything my neighbors have refused to hold on to that week—our dubious purchases and irreparable mistakes, the husks of daily life. On my pilgrimage to the curb, I've seen an imploding piano gusting sheet music like autumn leaves; an artificial lemon tree; a still-running Roomba vacuum cleaner, flipped onto its back like Gregor Samsa; family-size KFC buckets and like-new KETO LIFE diet books; a Lynchian arrangement of IKEA "Malm" dressers, the Stepford Wives of furniture; ferrous badminton rackets and mossy novelty bongs; a silver cage into which a wild crow had flown, sleekly pillaging some poor ghostbird's uneaten seeds; an unlucky vanity mirror with a lightning crack; a buck-toothed donkey piñata, mysteriously intact; red rubber galoshes, size 14, that made me picture a barefoot giant wandering into the rain; a crushed VHS machine next to a box of time, a stack of unspooling tapes; a live bait cooler from which a dead prawn hung like a pirate earring; a child's Civil War diorama; many desecrated Swiffers; deflated kiddie pools in summer; toothy shards of sleds in winter; confusingly geometric sex toys in every rainbow hue; a flattened pyre of Fisher-Price tricycles. It amazed me, each Thursday, the sheer heft of what we could not digest, the aftermath of our appetites. Anja bent to stack her pizza boxes into a cheese-and-rain-cemented tower, while I arranged my bottles into a calliope in the blue bin. Ruby and indigo and emerald glass, so pretty in the moonlight. Sometimes I wonder if it was these jeweled colors that first drew the unicorn to our street.

Strange prohibitions govern what can be said between two neighbors, even friendly neighbors, on a slab of asphalt in haunted October. Anja claims that she knew I was pregnant before I did. "But I didn't want to say anything, Mauve. You weren't showing yet, and the beginning is so touch-and-go . . ."

The tell was not subtle. Anja watched me collapse in my driveway. Last October, I was dragging the bins to the curb under a jack-o-lantern moon, enjoying the lullaby of the little wheels, when something twisted sharply inside me. Pain dragged me to my knees. Anja ran across the street to help me up. When I could breathe again, I walked down the hill to the Cloud Lake Pharmacy. I am almost certain this "drugstore" is a mob front. They sell hemorrhoid creams and medicated lollipops and almost nothing else. Once I'd tried to buy Advil and the sheepish clerk suggested that I try the Walgreens on Holgate. But, incredibly, these likely mobsters had a single pregnancy test for sale.

"What's gotten into you, Mauve?" asked Edie that evening. "You seem nutso lately. More than usual, I mean."

Something had, indeed, gotten into me. This new life marked reality so faintly—a watery pink line on a test. I held it up to the light, watching the pale line firm and darken. What a strange way to take the temperature of one's future. It seemed impossible that a life had planted itself inside me without my awareness. I had been moody and queasy, cratered with surprising acne, but these signs seemed far too subtle to herald a baby's arrival. The mildest augurs of a stowaway. I felt the mind-body split acutely that night, studying my thirty-nine-year-old face in my landlady's mirror. The glass stared beyond me to the night sky in the window, where a full October moon bobbed over my shoulder. Trick or treat, I thought.

Next came the cold thrill of betrayal. A positive result meant I had already been pregnant for several weeks. You'd think women would be alerted at the moment of conception, receive an unmistakable sign, like the crystal ball dropping on New Year's Eve in Times Square. We should levitate above the bedsheets; our eyes should change color. Instead, my body had behaved like a surly teenager—cranking her music behind a locked door, bass shaking through the walls, none of the lyrics intelligible. Why hadn't my body trusted me enough to say, "Mauve, we are pregnant"?

A line of poetry drifted back to me then, something I'd memorized in college for a grade and managed to hold on to all this time—"And of ourselves and of our origins / In ghostlier demarcations, keener sounds." To figure out the age of my possible baby, I turned to Google. Older generations felt connected to their foremothers by handwritten diaries, the ghostly wheel ruts of the Oregon Trail; I had Autofill. Millions of other women at this same phantasmal threshold, it seemed, had also typed my question into the search engine. Google directed me to a dubious oracle: the Pampers Due Date calculator. I plugged in my dates. The Pampers genie congratulated me: YOUR BABY IS SIX WEEKS OLD! The illustration of the embryo looked like a scowling pencil eraser. I waited to feel whatever you were supposed to at this juncture—something, surely.

I realized that I was freezing, chilled to the bone. Perhaps I had been for some time. I went fishing in the hamper and borrowed two of Edie's sweaters, pulling one on top of the other. Out here I struggled to do a load of laundry, and yet somehow in the deep privacy of my body, an embryo had built itself a spine. It was braiding neurons into a brain. Soon it would discard the tiny comma of a tail, which was vestigial and marvelous, tadpoled between two future legs. With every heartbeat, I realized, a stranger grew stronger inside me. More human and more animal.

I was afraid to leave the computer screen, afraid to blink, as if I thought that by freezing myself in one location I could bring Time to heel. I would need years, I felt, to prepare for this pregnancy—an event that had already happened. For an hour or more I sat there, sick with vertigo. A belly growl broke the spell. I tossed the pregnancy test in the wastebasket; I'd been holding it midair like a demented conductor. Then I walked downstairs and began to eat. I opened jar after jar with the blank ravening of a bear. I stole and ate Edie's raw wildflower honey, which moved like liquid amber and tasted sweetly green and prehistoric—eating it, you could imagine crunching down on a trilobite. I sprinkled sea salt onto the black honey, picturing my baby's tail. Under my conscious mind, a longing began to spread—a hope I was afraid to speak out loud, even to myself. Was it possible I could be the mother of a child? A violent desire took root—and this time I felt it. I wanted to know my son or my daughter. I wanted to be this baby's mother. Later I'd remember this moment as a second conception, the one I was sober and awake to register, although no less mysterious to me. Alone in the dimming kitchen, I licked the salty honey from the spoon and continued digging, wrenching amber from the jar, waiting for my stabbing hope to dull.

When I finally called the doctor, the receptionist said breezily that they would see me in six weeks for my first ultrasound. The unspeakable rider to this appointment lifted out of the silence on the line: *if you are still pregnant in six weeks' time.*

My first trimester unfolded inside green parentheses. A long-held breath, where I tried only to think about my baby in italics. *Your baby is seven weeks old today. Eight weeks. Nine weeks.* Your baby is the size of a pomegranate seed, a blueberry, a red grape. Every pregnancy chart I consulted compared the size of a human fetus to fruit. Figs, papayas, rhubarbs. As the weeks advanced, your grocery basket grew heavier: a lime at week eleven, mango at twenty-three, a cantaloupe at thirty-four, until at last there was a triumphant exit from the produce aisle. At week forty, the fruit bowl of metaphor abruptly disappeared, and the analogy sutured itself into a circle, beautifully tautological: your baby is the size of a baby.

Why fruit? In the OB-GYN waiting room with Caro, we debated this. Maybe, I said, the makers of these fetal charts loved fairy tales. Perhaps, like Milton and the Brothers Grimm, they understood the power of a seedling taking root inside a woman.

But my sister had laughed angrily and told me, "Mauve, don't give them too much credit. These charts aren't relics. Someone thinks that mothers are too dumb for the metric system."

For the past four years, I'd lived alone in the basement apartment of a house I shared with Edith Stone, a white woman in her early sixties who had grown up in Walla Walla, a lifelong smoker of Kools cigarettes and warm misanthrope. In our time as roommates I had never once heard her apologize to anyone, for anything, which I viewed as a feat worthy of a trophy. Edie was a kind of Social Olympian that way—she refused to dye her blue-gray hair and had a parroty rasp, and she said yes only when she meant yes, and no the rest of the time. She made enemies everywhere she went, including places where this seemed impossible, like the St. Stephen's Religious Bookstore where she worked. She was as dedicated to her God as to her vices. No nicotine gum for Edie. She lived with a bald-faced integrity I could barely imagine—I who had grown up believing it was a woman's job to be the sugar stirring through life's lemonade, I who often said "Yes" when what I really meant was "Go away," or in the more extreme cases, "Please don't kill me."

I asked Edie to be the godmother of my baby.

"No way," she told me. "How much longer do you think I want to stick around here?"

"Do you mean 'here' as in our house? Or 'here' as in life?"

"Both," she said, after a moment's reflection. "But rent is still due on the first."

I didn't see the unicorn until the tenth week of my pregnancy.

One Garbage Thursday in November, facing a curtain of lightly falling snow, I put my boots on and pulled the compost bin through the slush—a quiver of arrows that week, amputated cherry boughs. I'd rescued one of Edie's quartz rosaries from the trash, where it had snaked around the deadest branch. Too cheap to call an arborist, Edie had taken to hanging these discounted rosaries from the ailing foliage. Now our yard looked like an Uber driver's windshield. She bought them in bulk with her employee's discount from the St. Stephen's Religious Bookstore; she left a lot to God's care, and sometimes I had to step in for God with the pruning shears. At the curb, I stopped to catch my breath and stared up our driveway in time to see a feral creature lifting its pale skull from Anja's garbage. A single antler speared out of the middle of its brow. A deer, I thought at first, squinting through the fog. I had never seen a deer on Ninth Avenue before—certainly not in the dusk light of November, a blue hour when the porch lights switch on but the moon is unrisen and the northern stars are few and aloof.

Was it a snow-covered doe? Could snow cover any creature so completely, from ankles to skull, eyelids to hooves? The antler wasn't an antler after all. It was a horn, long and cetacean, white as the birches that stood sentinel on our leafy block at night.

"Anja?" I called shyly from my side of the street. Her windows were dark. Then I remembered Edie was volunteering at the women's shelter until ten, and so I had no saner pair of eyes to summon to my side as night fell around the Cloud Lake Apartment Complex. As far as I knew, I was the only person to witness this eerie scavenger as she cantered down our block toward the highway, an ancient piece of pineapple pizza dangling from her lips like one of Edie's cigarettes.

I decided not to mention her to anyone. I was afraid that I would chase her back out of time and into eternity if I spoke the word "unicorn" out loud.

Craving salt is a survival mechanism, said the doctor. But in you, it's gone haywire.

Cookies, kiwis, ice cubes, salad, bread, the webbing of my hands—I was salting everything. I bought a spice rack and filled it with garlic salt, turmeric salt, black lava salt, red chili salt, a keg of your good old-fashioned Morton's salt. Food became a vessel for iodine, and if there wasn't a shaker on the table I wasn't interested in eating.

Dr. Barretto told me that I was severely anemic, and that I should remedy this with iron supplementation, not an ocean. "Try cooking on a cast-iron pan," he suggested. Dr. Barretto was a portly Argentine man in his fifties who seemed to feel I was ridiculously old to be having a first baby. He always hit on Caro when she accompanied me, even when we spoke loudly about Caro's girlfriend, Nieves. He scheduled my delivery for July 2, and it astonished me to learn that we could choose my daughter's birthday. Because I would be forty in July—a *geriatric mother*, he kept repeating with increasingly angry emphasis, as if this were a punch line I'd failed to get—he would be performing a Caesarean section.

"Perform" is a disconcerting verb to hear in relation to one's surgery. It made me think of sad circus seals and belligerent standup comedians. Caro teased me about this, the medicine she mixes for me when I'm afraid; her jokes are more potent than anything the gangsters stock at the Cloud Lake Pharmacy. "Catch the June 2 performance—live, for one night only! Standing room only, your C-section!"

When I made it to week twelve, that spectral mile marker when a miscarriage becomes less likely, we had a small party. My sister bought me a Himalayan salt block. I'd never seen one of these things before, although she told me they were bougie fixtures in all her Vancouver friends' backyards. It was a twelve-foot-by-eight-foot slab of salt, crystal pink and twinkling in the night air. Caro held up a candle so that we could see the waves of rosy inlaid mineral. It looked like a mountain sunrise planed into a rectangle, or a doorstop for an archangel.

"Wow, Caro," I said. "Thank you. Where did you buy this thing, the Narnia Gift Shop?"

"You're going to love it, Mauve. Everything you cook on it will have your favorite taste: brine." She handed me a cookbook filled with pictures of raw meats sweltering on the sunburn-pink block. "It's also a present for my niece," said Caro, touching my belly. I'd been crediting so many of my strange appetites to this fetus, including the insatiable need for salt. Did these cravings originate with her, or with me? I no longer knew.

At another office, they did a high-tech new test. A vial of my blood disappeared into a sterile back room and got shaken down for information. "You are having a daughter," said the friendly, bored technician, a middle-aged Black woman with a photograph of twin girls in blue school plaids on her desk, and a yawning conviction about my baby's future reality that I wished I could feel.

One night at the start of my second trimester, alone in our yard, I bent to lick the salt block. I don't know what possessed me. The pink crystals scraped at my tongue. Under my rib cage, the baby began to kick. We developed a rhythm: *lick, kick, lick, kick*.

When I rose from the salt block, the unicorn had reappeared.

It had been hours since dinner, and the block had cooled, its color changed from sandy pink to Martian lake. The plants in the yard were a uniform blue. But the unicorn was lit unsteadily from within, flickering from white to gray, the wattage jumping each time she snorted. I recoiled in an awe that was also revulsion—what was a unicorn doing in our backyard?

"Deer are vermin out here," my boss, Steve, told me when I first moved to Oregon from Florida, eager to live closer to my sister and to work for a real newspaper. My boss was one of Seattle's jaded children—a transplant like me—an ursine white man with a combustible ratio of insecurity to entitlement. He seemed to find it hilarious that I was so enraptured by the sight of a doe and her two fawns. I could see them from our office window, grazing in the alley of daffodils beside the Willamette River. "You grew up with sharks and alligators, and you're creaming yourself over a *deer*?" (Steve's teasing could make even my hairline flush. He made a blow-up doll's face to mimic my stunned expression, fluttering his eyelids. I couldn't recall how I responded that day. Said nothing, probably. Possibly I laughed. I said a prayer of thanksgiving to the pantheon of does that Steve was not my baby daughter's father.)

"Girl," he'd chided me. "Put your camera away. Don't you know that miracles are regional? To us, a deer is like a big antlered rat."

Now I wondered if the same was true of unicorns in the west. Could a unicorn be rabid? Were their eyes always this feverish? I stared into her bottomless pupils and I felt dizzy with echoes, filling with some kind of primordial déjà vu; my arms shot out as if I were wheeling over a stairwell. As I crept closer I could see gray scuff marks on her hooves and horn; they made me think, insanely, of bowling shoes. Parts of her were emaciated—her wishbone haunches, her thinning white mane. The unicorn whinnied once, exhaling spume. Her rib cage lifted like a shipwreck at low tide, the long bones curving up with each breath, while her large belly swung heavily below her. It sounds silly to feel sorry for a unicorn, but I did then. Time predates unicorns, just like the rest of us. Eternal beings, it seems, are not exempt from aging. The unicorn kept changing as she walked toward me. Like a hologram, she seemed to flicker between realities. Now she was a scabby trespasser, now an otherworldly traveler. Ordinary, extraordinary, beautiful, ugly, starving to death, and luminously alive. Each time I blinked, her status shifted on me. Even her shadow seemed to change on the grass, elongating and twisting, melting and transforming, molten with light.

"Oh!" I shouted like a Jeopardy! contestant, startling us both with my *eureka!* syntax, having recognized her uncanny condition. How had I missed it? "Are you pregnant?" I hadn't guessed that an immortal could get knocked up. I wondered what the gestation time for a unicorn might be: hours, centuries? Now I guessed the reason she'd come bounding out of the mists to nose at Anja's pizza boxes.

Cravings are ephemeral, but also undeniable.

She trained her dish-huge eyes on me and began to steadily blink, like a carpenter aiming a nail gun. If she'd hoped to bolt me to my shadow, it didn't work. I could still move, but I did so slowly, not wanting to scare her off. I took a few steps backward, snapping my fingers to beckon her to me and instantly regretting it—a unicorn is not a lost puppy. And I wanted to earn her trust. I wanted to soothe the concave ache that had driven her out of the ultraviolet and into the range of my senses. This hunger I believed we had in common, me and the unicorn.

Carefully, I negotiated backward through the shining rosemary, around the dented meteor of the BBQ lid, making my way to the salt block. I watched her lower her long face to the illuminated surface, which glowed more intensely by the second, brighter than the porch light, brighter than the cloudy moon. It was her phosphor, I realized. She had suffused the block with her strong light. In my own body, I could feel her blood pressure rising, iodine funneling to her starved cells. Branches were caught in her dirty hair. I wished I had something else to give her: a garland of flowers, a heating pad. I smiled as I watched her purple tongue rowing across the block: "So you're a salt freak too?"

On an ordinary night, our yard is a thoroughfare for tame raccoons and stoned Anja. I had never been visited by a beast before. Her horn had the bioluminescence of marine life, and her tongue seemed almost prehensile. She ran it around the edges of the salt block, snorting with pleasure. Salt and thirst go hand in hand, I thought as I turned on the sprinklers and watched her lap at the whiskers of water. Then she shook a cape of droplets from her mangy, magnificent coat and took off. She went soaring over the hedge, knocking a few more branches off the dying cherry tree as she disappeared into our neighbor Jessa's yard.

I was never a horse girl. I was never even a mule girl. The sound I made to call her back to me was my poor ventriloquy of the child actress in *Black Beauty*. It didn't work. She did not return. Did the unicorn know I was not a virgin? Probably, I thought. Any stranger could tell.

I'd grown up believing that I was infertile, and the hundreds of uncontrolled experiments I'd conducted over many sozzled nights seemed to bear this out. I had hosted boyfriends and girlfriends and bartenders and AA sponsors and wizard-like poets and party acquaintances and true strangers inside my body, and for decades none of these visits had ever resulted in a pregnancy, or even a "scare," as teenaged Caro used to call them. I had gotten a single period at the age of fourteen; our family doctor had discovered that I had a rare hereditary mutation. Everyone had seemed so sad for me, even the guy who cut my mom's hair, even my aunt Rhea who loved her life as a happily single and child-less engineer, and so I'd had to reassure these adults that I was much more excited about being a mutant than being a mother. The diagnosis was a relief to me—a nonfatal answer to the case of my missing men-struation. They'd sent me home with a peacock fantail of glossy bro-chures, thin legends about married couples overcoming infertility. "Help will be available, Mauve, when you're ready to have a baby," the doctor told me. But that day never came. I had never longed for a child like some of my friends, whose crisp, adult voices went doughy at the sight of baby hands. It was strange to feel this new appetite growing at pace with the fetus inside me. *Fifteen weeks. Sixteen weeks.* At night, I paced my basement bedroom, sweaty and nauseous, flush with the terrible hope. I felt as powerless over the longing to hold my baby as I did over the hunger for salt.

Garbage Thursdays excepted, I would ordinarily never spy on my neigh-bors. But that night I could not resist peering over the hedge to look for the unicorn. I saw Jessa's Jacuzzi and cheerfully unseasonable Christmas lights, and beside it the two giant raccoons that split their time between our yards. Usually these twin behemoths move in slow, panda-like cir-cles between our properties, carrying greasy Styrofoam shards from the Lucky Devil dumpster in their mouths. Sometimes, I swear, they wave at me. I love their tiny, sleek hands, which make them look like lady assassins. Tonight, however, the raccoons were standing straight up on their hind legs, bristling all over. Had they just seen her, the horned interloper?

They stood shoulder to shoulder, staring forlornly down the empty road like tiny stockbrokers watching the market plummet. "You two look the way I feel," I told the raccoons. It reassured me to know that other animals also felt surprised by a unicorn manifesting on our residential block, and bereft at her disappearance. Under my navel, the baby woke into a somersault—she was most active at night. I loved the sharp surprise of her foot discovering my ribs. This alien metronome inside me.

"Come back anytime," I called softly over the hedge. The sprinklers were arcing water over the grass in liquid scimitars, unlit rainbows in utero. "I'll leave the salt lick out for you."

"Are you worried about people calling your daughter a bastard?" Edie asked me one warm night in the backyard, where the hedge shivered suggestively but kept its secrets. "Jesus, Edie," said my sister, but I laughed to let her know this brusqueness was just Edie's way of stamping a valentine. Her frankness makes me think of a lizard's throat—that bright scarlet bulging out, as irrepressible as life itself.

"No," I said. "Besides, she has the best aunt in the world. And the best . . ."

"No honorifics, Mauve. I can't be a godmother, OK? The houseplants are already too much for me."

At the twenty-week ultrasound, Edie and my sister flanked the bed. They stood there quiet as the Secret Service while the technician murmured, "Good, good, all good. Would you like to see inside her heart? Let's count the chambers together—one, two, three . . ." She clicked a long ellipsis against the roof of her mouth."Four!"

"Fuck!" said Edie, who never whispers to be polite. Cigarettes have thinned her voice. "Is four too many or too few?"

"Just the right amount of chambers."

We watched the pinprick of light that was the baby's beating heart. It pulsed on the dark screen, the cosmically black screen, and I shut my eyes between blinks and saw our unicorn's horn moving off into the distance.

In mid-March, I harvested six sullen-colored cherries from the sick tree. A week later, I nearly lost the baby. At the ER, the first doctor who examined me was cagey as a carnival psychic. "The pain and bleeding may go away and you can continue to have a healthy pregnancy and baby. Or things may get worse."

I was discharged and told to take a "wait-and-see" approach—was there another option? I wanted to ask the nurses. Edie prayed for us, Anja sat in silence with me on the basement couch, Caro stayed over and made us dinner on the salt block: the baby stayed inside my body, and after seventy-two hours I began to breathe again. But the fear never left me. After that scalding day and night at the ER, trying to mentally separate the six gloomy cherries and the blood clots in the toilet bowl felt like pulling magnets apart.

Not an omen, said Caro. You read too much into the world, Mauve. You think everything has to mean something. But you're not the addressee on the envelope here, OK? Mostly, the world is talking to itself.

I knew my sister was right, and yet I could not make myself believe her. A part of me felt certain that I had been punished for trying to become a mother—for failing to listen to the world as it whispered and shouted "no."

"Hope can be agonizing," Anja told me one Thursday night, three weeks after I'd been discharged from the ER. "But you have to keep hoping."

I was still pregnant, but Anja was losing her mother to a long battle with ovarian cancer. We stood bracketed by our garbage bins, staring down the hill toward Mount Hood and a wall of advancing rain. I wished the unicorn would come galloping into view to frighten flowers out of the mud, to bring Anja comfort from a world beyond this one. I combed my memory for something true and consoling. In one deep pocket I found the lint of a half-forgotten poem.

"Hope is the Thing With Feathers . . ."

"Is that the Obama book?"

"Emily Dickinson. Wilin' out with the capitalization."

I managed to reassemble most of the first stanza for Anja, the only one I still knew by heart

"The Thing." Anja smiled. "God, I used to love that movie as a kid."

We riffed for awhile: Hope is a dolphin's fin. Hope is a cherry lip balm. Hope is an unwritten Rihanna song. This week, your hope is the size of a mustard seed, a blackberry, a four-headed dragon.

Hope is a salt lick, I said. Muscle and mineral. Hope is a habit that the living can't quit. Anja was right about the verb and the noun of it. Hoping was nothing to romanticize. It was a necessary, excruciating activity.

I was thinking about the pink slab waiting outside our house in the rain. All the women in history before me who had tried to tempt a unicorn out of a glen. I was remembering the sound of my baby's heartbeat faltering, the lengthening hyphens; we had watched her ultrasound on a large black screen, the ER residents crowding in as if we were the football game. The ice-water voice of the weekend nurse who told me, "Your baby is performing poorly." The sound that wrinkling paper makes under skin, the disposable hospital sheet tearing as I swung my legs wider for another stranger's gloved hands. The melody of our tiny wheels on Garbage Thursday going up and down a thousand driveways. In the taxonomy of losing, these must be the two fundamental categories: those things we lose and believe we might find again, the sting of grief lightened by the hope of retrieval; and those losses that are final, insoluble, eternal.

April rains covered Portland in a steady mist. I reached Week 28, my third trimester, another spectral mile marker—even if the baby was born prematurely, the odds were now very good that she would live. At 4:00 a.m. when the baby and I were both awake, I prayed a two-word prayer to her pummeling fists, to her head butting at my ribs in the womb's windowless darkness: "Please, come. Please, stay." I had not seen the unicorn for eleven weeks. Not an omen, I told myself in Caro's voice. She is an immortal ungulate. She has a life.

There are events for which I fear I'll never find language. Whole years of my childhood that have lost their magnetism, sending the alphabet clattering to the floor, a pile of symbols that won't stick to the door. Even talking to my sister, I often feel like a clumsy surgeon botching the operation—using the wrong-sized tongs for certain slippery red truths. I must be constantly underestimating and misreading everyone in my life if I can't describe one painful hour to Caro, or even to myself. Every human body must be a library of unspeakable experience. Glaciers go sinking through us before we can utter a word.

But now I know that the unspeakable can also be beautiful. Delicately, deliriously joyful. Secrets can sieve through a heart, fine as stardust.

Here is a secret I am happy to share, even if I can only do so in this galumphing sentence, which is too coarse, too clumsy, too earthbound, too human for what I wish I could evoke: the unicorn came back.

I had no history of miscarriages, I told the first and the kindest of a rotating cast of ER doctors on the night of the blood clots. (I continue to see these in nightmares, dark red and gnarled as tree roots.) Yes, I'd confirmed when the doctor's eyebrows lifted. I was turning forty, and this was my first and only pregnancy. Gravida 1, para 0. He pushed his eyebrows down politely and hid his face behind the clipboard, He was a handsome Black man who looked to be half my age, his shy eyes lassoed in spearmint-green glasses. His hands were as reticent as his voice during my examination, prodding only where necessary, taking great

93

care to avoid causing me additional pain. I told him that I was surprised to be a gravida too; I had grown up believing that for me, pregnancy would be impossible. The nurse who had been tightening the black cuff on my arm, a white woman with veiny hands and beautiful smile lines, paused to stare at the side of my face. "Would you have made different choices, honey, if you'd known you could get pregnant?" she asked me, with the mild, automated curiosity of a waitress inquiring, "Cream or sugar?" I answered honestly. I said: "I don't know." As I've mentioned, I haven't always been aces at safety. I had a history of "kamikaze promiscuity," as my sister calls it. That's a longer story, but suffice it to say that I have no interest in solving the mystery of my baby's paternity—the main suspect has already informed me he wants nothing to do with me, which is really the best possible outcome. I don't want to disparage the possible fathers of my baby, so I'll follow Thumper's mother's sage advice and say nothing at all. My daughter had so many arms waiting to hold her. My sister Caro, whose love is infallible. Anja, hostess of the best CBD pizza parties. Edie, who couldn't fool me into thinking she didn't love me and my baby.

We had the blessing of a unicorn.

And if our unicorn looked a little like a curbside sofa left to moulder in the rain, a FREE sign disintegrating on its soaking cushions? Well, I thought, I'm no spring chicken myself.

At the OB-GYN, they treated me like an audacious cadaver. The twentysomething nurses spoke to me with a tenderness reserved for the terminally infirm. I began to feel so self-conscious about this that I bought a push-up bra and cream blush. "Uh-oh!" said Caro. "What happened here? You look like Mel Gibson in *Braveheart*." "Thirty-year-old Mel?" I asked hopefully, and she declined to answer. I wondered how the pregnant unicorn felt about her own growth and decay. I'm sure there must be ups and downs on the trampoline of eternity.

I didn't wash the Himalayan salt block before I cooked on it again. For the first time in my life, friends treated me like a master chef. My sister said, "You seasoned this perfectly!" Even Edie asked for seconds, then thirds. I demurred, shy with pleasure—I credited the salt block. I thought we were tasting her magic, but I knew better than to tell anyone about the visiting unicorn. Everything I grilled on the salt block had a lavender taste now, ineffably fresh and bright as graveyard bouquets. I wondered if we would all live forever.

Sodium chloride, I've since learned, can bring on muscle contractions.

On the night the unicorn returned, we both went into labor. Week 36–four weeks before my scheduled delivery, when my daughter was the size of "a large jicama"—I left the house to take out the trash and found myself drenched and speechless on the damp grass. Nothing I had read or heard about labor could have spoiled the surprise of my water breaking; for a moment I thought I might be dying. The unicorn was watching me silently from the shadow of the cherry tree. She chewed the bark off the sickly trees with the nonchalance of an old pro; I thought she must have given birth many thousands of times before. At one point, she craned her neck over the hedge and dipped her horn into my neighbor's Jacuzzi, purifying it forever. I considered lumbering through the hedge into Jessa's yard, naked and hairy as the Sasquatch, and lowering myself into the bubbling tub. The Portland water birth that nobody wants to see cannonballing into their Thursday evening.

Then the unicorn shouldered through the thin branches to the salt block, and I crawled over to join her, hunched on all fours, gathering my strength between what I realized must be contractions. They seemed to be happening everywhere that night, not only in my body. The black sky curved into an hourglass above us, opening outward in twin parabolas, forcing the constellations earthward; I waited for stars to fall on our heads like grains of sand. A warm, mammalian calm filled me. My breaths synced themselves to the accordion inhalations of the laboring unicorn. Anja's ghost lake under the Portland streets, hidden moons and satellites, pregnant strangers moaning as they parted the glass hospital doors, every laboring animal, bats dreaming under bridge trestles and matronly whales skimming Antarctica—I felt myself expanding and contracting in secret solidarity with so many near and distant bodies. That night I drew as close as I ever have to the unspeakable domain of the animals. Carnality without estrangement, knowledge without thought.

Dead light came slingshotting across the galaxy; Edie's automated sprinklers turned on, dousing us with chittering water. Whatever was earthquaking down the length of the unicorn's body did not seem to frighten her, which helped me to welcome my own spasms. (She seemed, if not bored by them exactly, casually resigned; I saw with horrified awe that a coltish leg and hoof was now dangling from her lower body.) Between contractions, we bent and licked at the salt in

95

tandem. I wondered if Edie could see us from the upstairs window, if she was sitting at the typewriter, smoking her Kools and questioning her sanity. Knowing Edie, if she was still awake she would most likely be out here on the deck shouting instructions, reminding me that she was not liable for any injuries sustained if I was gored on her property.

As the unicorn shuddered beside me, I wondered for the first time if she'd come to me specifically, despite my slovenly habits and erratic employment and inability to apply cream blush at age forty. Maybe so, I let myself believe. We had a powerful lifewish in common. We had formed and carried the same heavy dread inside our minds. Eternal life is no guarantee, it appeared, of delivering a live baby. Her gray belly swayed, and I saw the unspeakable possibility shining in one inky eye.

I was too shy to stare directly at the unicorn, but I watched her in profile. The huge eye was all pupil, with the thinnest rim of violet around it. Soon I could only see her in flashes. Pain was blanking us out of the canvas. Her dilated eye swallowed me into it. A full moon floated in the center of the vanished iris.

My hospital bag was packed and waiting by the door. Caro had volunteered to drive me to the labor and delivery ward months ago, but I didn't want to bother her until things were further along. And I didn't want to leave now—who could abandon a unicorn? My own contractions were becoming faster and stronger, waves of hot crenellated pressure that pinned me to the ground. I could still sing, which I did. The O of my mouth echoed down, down, down, a wild guttural sound, threading through the tree roots and the ghostly lake. I should call Caro now, I decided, just before my body caved in on itself. Then I understood with a piercing shriek that I would not be having my baby in the hospital.

When I recovered from the final push, the cherry tree had split down the middle, and a new voice came wailing into the world. My daughter was born on a nest of sticky red grass beside a raccoonmasticated Frisbee and the balding rosemary bush, where the pink quartz beads of a rosary glowed like tiny berries. I'd awoken the entire neighborhood, it seemed, with my final scream. Six minutes later, an ambulance came roaring down Ninth Avenue, whisking panic out of the dark firs and the silent bedrooms with its spinning red siren. But the emergency has passed, I wanted to tell them. My daughter is here with us, alive.

What fresher salt lick exists in our universe than a newborn's eyelids? The unicorn leaned over and licked the angry tears from my daughter's blossoming, astonishing, ocean-blue eyes. Then she dissolved from sight

96

a final time. In her place was a warm, bloodwet, tiny mortal. A verifiable miracle. Her fists windmilled everywhere as the paramedics put her onto my chest, her wrinkled face furious and waxy, ashen white as a Pompeii survivor. I was afraid she would vanish as mysteriously as she'd arrived. Diffusing into the void again, like the unicorn. "Please stay," I begged my daughter that night in the garden. So far, she has.

Nominated by Marcus Spiegel, Conjunctions

1940

by D. NURKSE

from MANHATTAN REVIEW

1

My mother and father meet on the last boat out of Lisbon.

She stands at the stern rail staring back. The wake is already a long scar. The last shore gulls swoop at bobbing eggshells and coffee grounds.

How to talk to her? My father drops his handkerchief. *Miss, is this yours? No,* she says, but she turns. I am the future.

2

Julius and Ethel Rosenberg are burned alive in the chair to prove the decay of the atom was a secret in Truman's mind? I hear a triumphant voice through the wall, the same wall I keep bumping into. I've just learned to walk. It's still 1940.

3

I'm old now. My teeth hurt but it could be just my sinuses. I'm beginning to live forever, but backwards. The voice is all around me: George Soros, the Rothschilds, the cunning of the vaccine.

1940 is just beginning. The straits of the Tagus vanish behind gray waves.

Nominated by Richard Hoffman

FIRE AND ICE

by DEBRA GWARTNEY

from GRANTA

Three days before he died, my husband got out of bed. Somehow he propelled himself down the hall and into the living room, where I found him bent over a volume of Esther Horvath photographs called *Into the Arctic Ice: The Largest Polar Expedition of All Time*. Barry's white hair was sprung wild and his feet were bare though it was late at night in December, sleety rain driving against the windows. How had he pulled sweatpants over his bony hips? He'd hardly stirred all day, lifting his head only to sip on bone broth made by one of our daughters, leaning against me to get to the bathroom because he was bleary from pain drugs. Yet he'd managed to transport himself to the center of this rental house to dig out a book that now held his rapt attention.

The book had arrived by mail a few days earlier, when Barry was still able to sit on the sofa for an hour or so, and he'd turned its pages with the slightest pressure of thumb and finger so as not to mar the saturated colors of the photos. Our son-in-law was over with the rest of the family for a subdued holiday visit. The two men spoke in calm, low voices about a region of the planet once intimately familiar to my husband, second only to his knowledge of the thirty-six acres of western Oregon rainforest where he'd lived for fifty years and where I'd lived with him for nearly two decades until a wildfire booted us out one late-summer night. Barry moved closer to Pete and pointed to streaks of blue in Horvath's images of a vast icescape, the humps of polar bears, the eerie glow of human light piercing the darkness. The peeling noses and cheeks of scientists too long in the cold. I remember how he laughed with a whistle of nostalgia, missing days when he must have felt fully alive.

But now in the living room, he whipped through the pages until I heard an edge tear, a fluttering as if he'd startled a bird. When I said his name, he didn't answer. When I touched his shoulder, he jerked in my direction and insisted I start packing the car, though first he wanted me to find his suitcase and the down jacket he'd worn for forty years of polar travel. He returned to the book frantic, a man who'd dropped a key into a well's murky bottom and was crazy with the loss.

I was certain my husband was about to insist I bundle him up and drive him through the rain to our fire-damaged house, an hour away. I steeled myself for it. He'd say he had to die on his own land, near the remains of ten cords of combusted wood and his melted truck, on the smoke-saturated bed in our bedroom whose windows were still smeared orange with fire retardant. He'd check to make sure the essay he'd been working on was secure in his typewriter, waiting. Then he would rest. He'd watch through the window over the bed for flashes of kingfisher and fat rain clouds, for the sky arcs of an overwintering eagle. What nonsense it was to come to the end instead in this stranger's house with a stranger's furniture and its strange cast of light. I was sure Barry would rather use any last bursts of energy to pace the perimeter of his scorched archive, as he had most days since the fire. He'd become the lone sentry at the gates of that phantom building, which once held the history of his fifty-year writing life. For months, I'd watched him rake through the mound of ash, releasing shiny particles of the past into the smoke-stilled air. He churned up chunks of paper—cremated books that disintegrated with the slightest touch—and bent metal that he held up to the faint light in the withered forest. *What were you, then?*

Except that noise was inside my head. In fact, Barry hadn't mentioned home for over a week. What I finally put together on this Saturday night, from his various mutters and fragmented speech, was that his destination was an archipelago called Svalbard. An Arctic expedition had lost its leader, so he'd been called in to take over. He had mere hours to get there. He slammed the Horvath book shut and clambered into the spare bedroom, where he yanked out a duffel bag I'd recently emptied and stored away in my effort to make this place feel something like a home. He tossed in a broken alarm clock, a pillow, a packet of picture hangers. Where are my gloves? My Gore-Tex pants? My expedition sunglasses? Where have you put my things? Why won't you give me my things? He flailed his arms so I couldn't come close. As if the only person preventing him from the most important launch of his adventurous life was me.

And then he fell.

Barry was running—no, there was no run left in him, more an agitated hobble—back to our bedroom. He skidded on the wood floor and went flying. His hip slammed down, then his shoulder, his head bouncing against a doorframe. I cried out, and half dragged him to the bed where I wedged him under the covers. I squeezed a vial of liquid morphine into the pale ditch of his gums and sat next to him, his chest heaving, until he was asleep.

Horvath's book is about a German icebreaker called the *Polarstern*, which was allowed to become locked into sea ice off the coast of Siberia. This happened in the autumn of 2019, when the ship's engines were shut down and the vessel, lit up like an all-night casino, was left to drift, driven only by hidden ocean currents and 'at the mercy of the wind'. The ship, with more than one hundred expedition members on board at any given time, groaned through dark days and nights, destination wherever natural forces led it, mile after uncharted nautical mile into utterly undiscovered territory: 'no ship has ever ventured so far north into the central Arctic', the prologue tells us. The *Polarstern* churned through ice and storms for an entire year while an international team of scientists did what they could to record the effects of climate change.

On a thin January afternoon about a month after his death, I pulled the Horvath book from the drawer where I'd hidden it to study the photos that had so ignited my husband. I discovered in the text a mission obviously steeped in scientific logic and methodology, yet also not that far from the koans of my weekly yoga class: embrace the moment. Trust the wind to push you where you need to go. Be prepared to find your way back to center through the densest of fog. The only authentic discoveries are those that aren't forced. Stop trying to control that which is beyond your control.

Barry had been ill for a long time, but his death swooped down on us like a hawk, talons first. Startlingly fast. Everything that gave me stability and safety—our long marriage, our house, the surrounding woods, the river—was unreachable now, in dodgy shadow, and this was probably the source of my irritation toward the book in my lap. It dared to tap into what terrified me most: a reminder that there'd be no clear answers for a good long stretch; that I would have to swim in bewilderment and confusion before I could emerge on some distant shore. Solutions would roll out in front of me in their own time and at their own pace, in their own shape. In the meantime, I would have to learn to drift.

A few months earlier, on 8 September just after midnight, I found a young man on our porch holding a brick he'd been using to batter our front door. I was already awake and out of bed when I heard his pounding, his shouts to *open up*. A friend had called me minutes before, waking me from a fitful sleep. She told me to rouse my husband and get the hell out of there. I pulled on long pants, though the temperature was sweltering and the house already choked with smoke and grit. Barry was sleeping in our guest cottage that night, a few hundred feet away. I was headed there to wake him when the young man appeared on our porch hollering words my friend had already said: *Get out now.*

How odd to remember that crystallized moment, to recall how my mind slipped into the uncanny human tendency to minimize any emergency you're smack in the middle of. This could not possibly be happening to me, could it? This couldn't be how our story went. How was I to take this boy seriously with his lace-up boots and flannel shirt, red suspenders holding up canvas pants? I let myself imagine someone was just around the corner filming this non-crisis, this rumor of terror and destruction. Otherwise, what was with the klieg lights over-illuminating the woods around our home with a pumpkin-tinted hue as if we'd all been transported into a Wes Anderson movie?

You need to go now, the young firefighter said. *You need to hurry.*

Barry and I had argued some hours before the phone call from our friend, before the brick-wielding man on the porch, a spat between us that gnaws at me still. I think of it, our last argument on our last night in our own home, as one of those bullhorn warnings that sound at certain points in a marriage. As in: it's time to take account of where you're at, as individuals and as a couple. Seven years post cancer diagnosis, my husband's stamina and drive were still remarkable, the mainstay of his character, and yet there was no missing the increasing pain in his spine and ribs, his body's insistence on deep, long naps, his papery skin now drained of color. He had fewer hours of focus and attention and he meant to give those to an essay he'd begun, and after that to other pieces he'd sketched out to prove (mostly to himself) that in the wake of the latest book, published a year earlier to vibrant acclaim, he would continue on with his legendary verve and purpose. Barry was quite fixed on the idea that a writer is writing *today*, not dozing in the soft nest of what he (in this case) wrote yesterday. As for me, I had published a book in the same month as Barry's *Horizon*, though mine pretty much landed with a thud and garnered little notice. I'd composed hardly a paragraph since, and was plunged into doubt, plagued with a truth I didn't want to face about my late-in-life prospects. I begged Barry to escape with me, to run away. We'd fly to Barcelona, Costa Rica, the two of us alone in a new land where I didn't have to stare at my desk with its yank of defeat. But even as he was unfurling a map of Spain, spreading it wide on our table, running a light pencil line from Madrid to Lisbon across the border, I knew we wouldn't go.

Here was an ongoing tension in our marriage: I often wanted us to slip off together, just us. No obligations, no university speeches or community gatherings, no award ceremonies. But Barry found it nearly impossible to disrupt the rhythm of his writing life for reasons of rest and relaxation, and rarely did so. This often led to stiffness between us, harsh words. But this time I surprised myself. As he rolled up the map while saying something about how we'd go *as soon as I finish* . . . I waited for the disappointment that usually thrummed in me when plans were put off. But it wasn't there. I saw that he was past traveling now, no matter what part of the world called to him as a writer, and no matter how adamant I was about days together away from the hubbub. Now he needed to be home. Home is what fed him. He fit hand in glove at his small desk overlooking the river, tight in his narrow chair, fingers on his typewriter keys, his pile of research books at the ready and pencils sharpened to fine, dustless points.

The evening of our argument I was grilling our dinner. I had returned two days earlier from Idaho, where I'd sat with my mother in her final hours and stayed for a week to arrange, with my siblings, a small family burial service under the beating sun, since Covid-19 dictated we stay strictly outdoors. At home on this evening, it was too early for dusk, but smoke from a nearby wildfire dimmed and dulled the summer light. Barry stood at the far end of our deck, double-masked, refusing to step closer to me in case I'd been infected by the niece I'd hugged, the daughter who drove with me, a gas station attendant, the man who took my mother's burial clothes from me at the mortuary. Barry and I had both agreed that it was too risky for him to go to Idaho, but now that I was back, I was aching to be held, aching to spool out my version of the disorientation one feels after losing a parent. I wanted my husband to ignore the coronavirus rules, this once, but he wasn't ready to take the chance.

He proposed that we instead talk out on the deck with six feet between us. I hated the idea and fumed at him for bringing it up. For one thing, we had to raise our voices over the roar of an unusual wind, an unbidden wind, that whipped the 150-foot trees around us as if they were blades of grass. Dense smoke pillowed in the sky, and, when my phone beeped, I read Barry a text from various authorities instructing us not to panic, but to stay indoors—indoors!—with windows closed and to stop calling 911. The smoke was from a distant conflagration, that message explained. *A fire that poses no danger to you.*

Later, I'd bring it up with neighbors—those of us who'd escaped our burning river valley that September night—this curse of technology, the way we'd all been tripped by miscommunications and the confusion that reigned about what to do and when to do it. But that was still to come. For now, without a notion of what was racing toward us, our standoff on the deck continued, neither Barry nor I willing to give in to the other. *Come here, go away.* Months after he'd died, in anguish over that final night at our house, I would try to parse our code, our meaning. What it was we were trying to say to each other. Some version of: *I don't want to go on without you. You must figure out how to go on without me.* Neither of us admitting that we were running out of time.

I dished up fish and vegetables, my spoon cracking against his plate and then against mine. He picked up his food, his fork and his knife. He said, 'Please. Give me a few days,' and I watched him walk to our guest cottage and snap the door closed.

When I jumped down the back stairs, rushing to the cottage to wake Barry, I was smacked by the light I'd noticed a minute earlier behind the boy on the porch. I turned around into the sucking exhale of a hillside fully on fire, hoodoo flames leaping from the ridges, an orange glow washing over trees and sky. Over me. The crackle, the roar of it. The snowy ash. I shouted my husband's name, I pounded on the locked door. He opened up, startled and wide-eyed. 'We have to go,' I said.

Within five minutes, we did go, with two firefighters now ushering us into the car. I threw our hissing cat—Barry had dragged her from under the bed—onto the back seat. I had my purse slung over a shoulder, but that was it. He had nothing but the clothes he was wearing, not his wallet, not his cancer drugs, not the manuscript he'd been writing over the days I was away. But of course there was no going back, even after we thought of things we were desperate for. Or even when, a half-mile from our house, we were stopped by a cedar tree toppled in the road, flames sparking from its branches. Two men in the car in front of us hopped out—one already revving a chainsaw. They also knew our only choice was to push on. Barry unclicked his seat belt and made moves to join them. I grabbed his arm. 'Don't,' I said to the man who for fifty years was the first to arrive at every such dilemma, ready to act, to solve. 'This once, please don't.'

For me, he stayed.

We drove ahead in a procession of maybe 200 cars. The cat in the back seat yowled without ceasing so we didn't have to. Within a few miles we were beyond the fire—but it would catch up, soon. It would burn for weeks. It would consume 173,000 acres and 500 structures. None of us would be allowed back in for over a week, and only then with a police escort, to stand on our respective properties and witness for ourselves the transformative power of fire. Barry and I stepped out of a sheriff's car that day to find our house intact—one of the few on the river that firefighters managed to save. It looked as if it had been picked up by a claw and flung onto a pile of rubble. It looked broken and stunned. Still, we wept with relief.

We'd done little but sit in a hotel room those first few days after evacuation, answering a barrage of phone calls and emails. It was one of those pet hotels—we were consigned to such a place because of our cat, though it was dogs that barked in the hallways and left puddles of pee on the lobby floor and caused our kitty to press into the far reaches of a closet, where we'd sprinkle her favorite treats and set a bowl of fresh water. Over and over we were warned not to go outdoors. The air in this town now registered as the most toxic in the world, worse than any industrialized city in China or India, worse than the notorious bad air of Mexico City. On the day I write this, the worst air quality index in the world was measured in Dhaka, Bangladesh: 313. In those first days in the hotel, the AQI was over 500, and one morning it reached 800. We were breathing our cars, our refrigerators, our metal roofs and generators. Dead birds and bobcat and bear and elk. And of course, we were breathing our trees.

Did we have a home? We didn't know then, couldn't know, for the first ten-day stretch, and this is what Barry explained to his oncologist, a woman he trusted and loved, when she appeared on the screen of my

105

laptop for a Zoom appointment. She had come to deliver her own bitter news: the drugs that had for years kept Barry's cancer from growing, that prevented new metastatic lesions beyond those cemented in his pelvic region and ribs, were no longer working. The cancer had found new purchase in his bones and in his blood. Beyond clinical trials and palliative medications, she had no treatment to offer.

We hung up with her. I put the computer away and went down to the hotel restaurant to order the same mediocre sandwiches we'd eaten the day before. We watched the election news. Barry sprinkled cat treats in the closet. I stuffed towels around the windows. We read our books, got into our bed. We drifted.

It took me several months to locate a rental house that we both felt was right. On three acres, sun-drenched, clean and welcoming. We could settle here and make decisions—that's what we both believed; this was the mini-relief we gave in to. But on the third morning here, while I was cooking oatmeal, I heard a crash in the spare bedroom. When I rounded the corner, I saw Barry on the floor, tangled in the drawers of a bureau that had fallen with him. The side of his head was gushing blood. I followed the ambulance I'd called to the hospital, but was told at the door that coronavirus protocol prevented me from entering the emergency room. 'Go home,' a nurse told me. 'We'll phone you as soon as we know something.'

I was nearly at the rental house when my phone rang. It was the ER doctor. He told me that Barry's heart had failed, a total block, and that he'd been shocked five times with the defibrillator to bring him back. 'If he codes again,' this doctor asked me, 'do you want us to resuscitate him?'

I instantly convinced myself that the doctor had reached the wrong person, dialed the wrong number. My husband had taken a fall and likely had suffered a concussion, that was all. Right? This other thing about hearts and shocks couldn't be happening to us. Hadn't we endured enough? But then a few days later the hospital released Barry into my care. It was clear he had nearly reached the end. I drove him back to the house where we met with a hospice nurse. She'd brought a box of drugs. This one for pain, this one for worse pain, this for hallucinations, this for panic. *We'll use none of them,* I told myself, *she doesn't know how strong he is* (we used them all). The nurse also told us Barry would likely not survive a trip to our home on the river. The rental house is where he would die.

The morning after Barry's near escape to Svalbard, I woke early. I'd been up every few hours to give him his pain drugs, to check his breathing, to wash the crust from his lips. I rose in the fluid winter light to slip into the kitchen so I could call our same nurse. I'd tell her that something had changed, a shift in him, a shift in me, and it was time, as she'd told me it soon would be, to bring in a hospital bed to set up in the living room. That way we could all—the four daughters and I—take turns keeping him company, making him comfortable. I'd resisted the finality of the hospital bed, as some part of me believed my husband would rally one last time. He was famous for it. Crisis after crisis with his health over the past year, until doctors were sure he was done for. But my husband would gather up that Barry Lopez resolve and determination and mighty bone strength, and he'd stand on his feet. I almost expected it again today: Barry sauntering around the corner in the same flannel shirt and sweatpants he'd worn the day before, thick wool socks on his feet, asking about a cup of coffee, asking about the *New York Times* headlines while the cat rubbed against his legs in her bid for breakfast.

But I was alone and I leaned against the counter in this strange house and took in the first of the lasts. The last night we would sleep in a bed together, the last time we'd choose a movie to watch, the last meal I'd make for him, the last music he'd put on to well through the living room. I'd overheard a conversation between Barry and his young friend John the day before about that last essay still rolled in the typewriter at home—there was an exuberance in my husband's voice I hadn't heard for a long while. The talk between the two men had sprung open a clarity of mind Barry was known for, the next revision cooking on high in him now. When they hung up, Barry wrote down three simple lines, or maybe a series of words. I don't remember, though I do recall a pinch of envy in my own rib cage. His rush of happiness, this lifting of a burden, was in reference to the final piece Barry intended to write and not the chance to spend diminishing hours with me. We hadn't said much about the inevitable parting from each other; I was waiting for him to begin the conversation, whatever words we still had to say. He finished his note and asked me to put the scrap of paper on the desk, which I did. Weeks down the road, I'd think of it, but in the hubbub of moving furniture and candles and loved ones in and out of the room, the paper had been lost. The shape of an essay that died with its author.

I went back to the bedroom now and saw that Barry was beginning to stir. I pulled away the covers and got into bed with this man I'd loved for twenty-some years, who helped me raise daughters, and who was cracked open by grandchildren in a way he couldn't imagine he was capable of. I could feel his heat, hear his breath, but I made myself accept that he might already be gone, that I had let him leave without a proper farewell, without speaking in the language of our long intimacy. Maybe Barry was on the ice now, leading his ideal expedition. With sled dogs straining at the bit, fat mittens on his hands and goggles protecting his eyes, his exhalations frosting the air around his mouth. He was journeying across the wide sweep of the Arctic and, like the scientists aboard the *Polarstern*, eager to take in whatever the land and sea deigned to offer him. Barry was not one to invest in answers. It was the questions that pulsed in his body and propelled him forward no matter where he traveled in the world.

But me—I had questions and I did want answers. How was I to make peace with my husband's disappearance before he had actually disappeared? How was I to give up on a last chance to express what we meant to each other? I rolled toward him, careful to stay clear of ribs that exploded in pain with the slightest brush. He opened his eyes. He turned to look at me.

'Barry, do you know who I am?' I said.

He reached over to put his palm on my face. He said my name. He said, 'Debra,' and an ease filled me like honey. In the middle of lonely nights now, I try to remember the warmth of it in my arms and legs, the way it opened up in my belly. He wouldn't say my name again; I wasn't sure he would recognize me again. It was the last time we'd be alone. I would learn to live with that, because I had this memory now. For a beat of a few seconds there was no one but us, the two of us undisturbed in our marriage bed, floating on our distant sea.

Nominated by Granta

THE OBSERVABLE WORLD

fiction by MARCELA FUENTES

from PLOUGHSHARES

The man she loves has red hair and is afflicted by a nameless and terrible unhappiness. Even so, he loves climbing trees, building small electronics. He loves insects. Today on their dog walk, he stops to move slugs off the sidewalk. She watches how precisely the man she loves takes a fallen leaf, and with it, scoops the slugs into the grass.

He admires their eyestalks. "That's what makes them cute. Without them, they would be horrifying."

He's right. He's often right about what makes something lovely. Without eyestalks, the slugs' bodies would be damp, glistening sacs. Like leeches. But the eyestalks are delicate. Probing the air in a kind of slow wistfulness. They make her think, a little, of faeries.

He crouches, watching the slugs settle into the grass. He tells her that eyestalks are actually tentacles.

"Tentacles," she says. "Like an octopus?"

"Well, no," he says, frowning. "Octopi have prehensile tentacles. For grasping."

She scans their environment. In the distance, a hive of late afternoon life: parents with strollers, children on bikes, joggers, dogs dawdling on the sidewalk while their owners look at phones. She and the man she loves are in the neighborhood park, a diamond-shaped meadow expanse that leads to a wooded trail. The woods are dense, but too small to be actual woods. She has passed through them many times with their dog. Less often with the man she loves.

He observes the eyestalks with intensity and fascination. He does not touch the slugs, as that might injure them. He tells her that some

109

eyestalks are retractable. Some can regrow if severely damaged. That the eyestalks are tentacles makes it possible for the slugs' observable world to shift and change, quite apart from their bodies. These eyestalks, these tentacles, are ommatophore.

"Oh," she says. Oh is the right response. He doesn't look up.

His unhappiness is not a tame thing. If she says, for example, you know so much about insects, he will fall out of this moment of peace. He will tell her the slugs are *not* insects. She knows they are not insects, but their exact classification escapes her just now. If she says, they make me think of faeries, he will leave this gentle moment, saving slugs. *That doesn't make sense,* he will say. *That doesn't make any sense at all.* He might even have a tantrum.

She assesses the back of his neck, freckling in the sun. He might.

At home she says, *I think you need to take a break.* His fury radiates like a bomb blast. It doesn't faze her anymore. Mostly, he will take a break before it gets to that. Mostly. If he doesn't, she will outlast him. She has miles of stamina.

She is not afraid of him. They both know very well, and have for many years, that she will not be bullied. She is a warrior. His strange, bitter silences are harder to bear.

A public tantrum is unacceptable. If it happens, she will leave him at the park. He will want to follow her. He hates when she walks away from him, particularly in the thick of his wrath. But he won't follow. The dog, an aging but well-preserved German Shepherd, loves the man, but she is the dog's favorite. If the man she loves yells at her, the dog will interpose his body between them. He will bark at the man she loves. The dog, like any dog, has many tones, but this will be the real Shepherd bark: booming, heroic, carrying the clout of authority. Stop this. Now. Stop.

Justice Bark, the man she loves calls it. He will get the Justice Bark.

The man she loves cannot bear when he's made the dog warn him. He does not blame the dog. *It's natural,* he says. *He's a protector. That's his job.* He loves the dog. He loves her. He will go into the woods and be angry by himself. All this has happened before.

Something's wrong with me, he will say later. *Something's wrong with me.* She knows something is wrong with him. But she does not know what.

They walk on, into the woods. He holds the dog's leash. The dog browses the underbrush, investigating scents in his unhurried way.

Happiest, as he always is, that the three of them are out in the world together.

"That tree smells like grape Kool-Aid," she says. Yesterday the man she loves was cross that he did not know the name of the tree. So today she mentions it again. He has probably corrected that gap in his knowledge. He will want her to know that.

"Texas Mountain Laurel." He cuts a sprig and places it behind her ear, lightly as he had lifted the slugs.

"Que linda eres," he says with competent pronunciation. He has absorbed so much language from her. Not just what the words mean, but how to say them accurately. Her grandmother has an abiding affection for the man she loves because of this. Not because he's quick to learn, which he is. Because this gringo wanted to learn in the first place. In fact, he has surpassed her in some ways. Her grandmother has taught him to make tortillas, champurrado, tamales—so many things she, the granddaughter, does not know. Que parejita tan moderna, her grandmother laughs. What a modern couple.

He leans in to smell the sprig of laurel. He kisses her hair softly. "It really does smell like sugar. Maybe it's you."

"Maybe," she says.

She does not say, I have an eyestalk. My eyestalk is a searchlight. Looking, looking for, what?

She is still thinking about faeries, so after a little while, she decides to tell him a story. This is fine because he's been talking about slugs at length. She's made it clear before that she will have her turn too. He understands.

The story is a Scottish one, Tam Lin, but she doesn't bother with the name. This is a detail he will not care about. He brushes little bramble bits out of the dog's ear, makes soft clucks when the dog stops too long at one bush or another. He listens to the story.

"—And after the tryst in the woods with the faerie, Janet realizes she's pregnant. She's afraid her family will find out. So she goes back to the woods to get herbs that will end the pregnancy. And that guy Tam Lin is there again. He asks her not to get rid of his baby. He loves her, and it's their child."

"The guy is an elf?" the man she loves asks. He has no patience with fantasy creatures. But it's her turn, so he restrains himself.

"Well, Janet asks him, have you ever been a human? And he says yes, he was a human, but he was stolen by the faeries as a child." She considers, briefly, explaining the mythology of changelings, but flicks it away as ranging too off-topic. "And he tells her he wants to be with her. He can be a human again, but she must free him. Because the faeries are going to sacrifice him to hell on Halloween night."

"Sam Hain," says the man she loves. She ignores this.

"He tells Janet, there's one chance. Right before midnight, the faeries will be heading out to a certain place in the woods. Janet needs to lie in wait. Let the Queen of the Faeries pass. Let the queen's chamberlain pass. Then she'll see Tam Lin riding a white horse. And when she does, Janet must interrupt the procession and drag him off the horse."

As she tells the story, she can see Janet. Janet alone, belly full of baby, hiding in the underbrush, a guerrilla force unto herself. Janet in the dark, straining to see a white horse illuminated in the filtered moonlight of a midnight wood. Waiting for the flicker of torches as the faeries emerge into her line of vision. The low thump of unshod hooves on the path. There it is, the white horse. There it is, finally. She sees it. She will free Tam Lin.

"That's it?" he asks. "Just get him off the horse?"

"No," she says. "She has to hang on to him for the space of twenty-one heartbeats. One for each year of his life. She has to hold on and not let go for twenty-one heartbeats."

"Huh," says the man she loves. He is considering twenty-one heartbeats in terms of actual time.

"So that's what she does. She hides in the woods and waits. Sure enough, here come at least twenty faeries on horseback. The queen passes by. The chamberlain. And there's Tam Lin on the white horse. Janet leaps out and pulls him off its back."

"Hold on," he says. He cleans up after the dog. He ties the knot at the top of the bag. "We should turn back, I think."

"OK," she says. He drops the bag in the trash bin, another marker that this is not a real wood, only a city greenscape, and she continues. "Janet clutches Tam Lin in her arms. He's dazed, spellbound. The faeries circle round them, hissing and furious."

She imagines the faces of the faeries as hidden inside the deep cowls of their cloaks, eyes glinting in the torchlight. Janet, defiant, planted in their midst, her arms a steel vise round her lover.

"And Tam Lin begins to change. He turns into a giant shard of ice and freezes her. He turns into a seething hot brand. It's agony. But she doesn't let go."

The man she loves is looking at her now. He is not a stupid man. But he says nothing.

"He turns into a horrible beast that claws and bites her. He turns into a swan, tries to fly out of her arms. An eel, writhing to get free. Janet holds on. She doesn't let go."

"Janet really loves him," he says in a very quiet voice. He's not looking at her anymore. She doesn't answer. If she says yes, he will go into a rage right now. It is that close.

"Finally, the twenty-one heartbeats pass. Tam Lin transforms into himself. He's naked, but human. Janet throws her green mantle around him. To cover him. To claim him for herself. The faeries are so pissed, but they can't harm them, because the spell is broken. She and Tam Lin walk out of the woods together and start their lives."

"Yeah, great for Tam Lin," the man she loves says. "What about Janet? Is she happy?"

They, too, are leaving the woods, which are not real woods. There is the playground. Beyond it, the diamond-shaped park, the basketball court. The orderly grid of residential streets.

"I don't know," she says. "He became a human again. So, maybe."

She takes the dog's leash from him as they reach the sidewalk. A little boy in a Pokémon shirt has just spotted them. He bolts straight for their dog. His mother pursues him, her voice a hook of fear. The child runs faster.

"Here we go again," the man she loves says. He doesn't mind the child. He minds the mother. *Moms panic so much,* he's said. *That's normal,* she's told him. *Moms are supposed to see danger.*

She puts the dog in a down stay. She does this for the sake of the mother. The dog lies there, complacent and panting, while the child drops to his knees beside him. The mother arrives seconds later, gasping out apologies. She tells the mother it's no worries. It's OK.

"He looks like a wolf," the child says. "A wolf who came out of the woods."

"He's a German Shepherd," the man she loves says. "Prick-eared breeds look like wolves."

"What's his name?" asks the child.

"Edgar," she says.

"Edgar the Enormous," says the man she loves, grinning at the boy. Indeed, the dog is an imposing animal. The man she loves jokes that Edgar's real name is oh shit. That's the refrain when Edgar is out in public. Oh shit, that's a big-ass dog. Oh shit!

113

"E-normous!" The boy giggles. "He's e-normous!"

"One hundred pounds," says the man she loves. This is accurate. He has consulted with their veterinarian about the healthiest range for the dog's size and structure and he keeps the dog trim. The dog has hip dysplasia. Though he is eight years old, its effects are minimal. He gets regular exercise, fish oil and joint supplements in every meal. Still, the man she loves worries he will get arthritis in the hip, possibly lose mobility. He loves Edgar very much.

"Hi, Edgar," says the boy. The dog licks his hand. The boy brushes his small index finger along the dog's canine. "Lookit his wolf *teeth*."

"No, no, not his mouth!" the mother cries. Nothing happens, so she adds, "You could scare him."

"It's safe," says the man she loves. "Edgar's a gentleman."

The mother is young and white. She wears yoga pants and has a ponytail pulled through her baseball cap. She could be any given mom in this neighborhood. She hovers uncertainly behind her son. She apologizes again. This is why the man she loves often finds mothers irritating.

He doesn't see what she sees: this mother fears the dog. Bodily fears him, so much that she cannot bring herself to pick up her son. Her terror is palpable. What pins the mother to the sidewalk like a lanced butterfly is that she will not say so. Because it's bad manners.

The child ignores his mother. He strokes the dog's thick pelt, runs both hands between the dog's brawny shoulders, down the curve of glossy black spine. The dog accepts the child's questing fingers. Allows the tender gesture when the boy presses his cheek to the dog's neck. He snuffles the boy, reading these new scents with delighted curiosity. He doesn't jostle the boy. He is an old hand at children.

"We've kept them long enough, honey," the mother tells the boy. "It's time to go."

"No," says the child.

The mother is angry with her son, has been angry with him, at the bottom of it all. His refusal sparks her. The mother tells the boy he cannot run up to strange dogs. He *cannot*. Dogs can bite.

"He won't bite me," the child says, stung. "He's my friend."

"Did you hear me tell you we're leaving?"

The boy does not answer. He keeps petting the dog's back.

The man she loves hunkers down beside the dog and boy. He rubs the dog's back too. "He *is* your friend. See how he's sniffing you? He's learning your scent. Next time, he'll remember you."

"He will?"

"Yes," he says. "His nose tells him who you are. You're the only one who smells like you. Scoot on home with your mama. Edgar won't forget you."

"OK." The boy gets up, though reluctantly.

"See ya later," he tells the boy. The man she loves understands children, even difficult ones, she knows. *They just want to learn about things,* he's told her. *There's nothing wrong with that.*

When they are a few steps away, the mother scoops up her son. The child is outraged. He struggles in her arms. He shrieks. His mother takes no notice. His mother trudges resolutely across the park. Straight home.

The man she loves shakes his head. "She is gonna paint his back porch red."

"No she won't," she says. "He's gonna get tired before they get home."

The dog releases himself from his down stay. He takes a few steps, makes eye contact. He's ready to go. She gives the leash back to the man she loves. They walk home.

The light is clear, but fading, in the manicured suburban park. Families replaced by this dusky hour with young men on the basketball court. She hears the faint bass thump of their music, their crowing and swagger. On the sidewalk, middle-aged women, singles and pairs, move at a brisk pace, getting their steps in before night. A different half-dozen dogs with their owners. A different smatter of joggers. In her field of view there is nothing, not one thing, out of place.

"No offense," the man she loves says. "But I didn't like that story you told earlier. You can't measure time by heartbeats."

Nominated by Papatya Bucak

BOTH SISSIES

by LE VAN D. HAWKINS

from CHICAGO QUARTERLY REVIEW

It's Friday evening over four decades ago. I'm at my church for our weekly junior usher board meeting, preparing for the upcoming junior Sunday services. On the third Sunday of every month, junior church members aged seven to eighteen took over the adults' duties—the junior choir in vivid purple robes sang modern gospel songs, and the junior ushers stood in the church foyer warmly greeting church members and visitors as we passed out offering envelopes, handheld cardboard fans printed with the face of Dr. King, and church programs that listed that Sunday's order of service.

The junior ushers were easy to spot in our usher uniforms—the boys in crisp white dress shirts, black clip-on ties, black pants, and black dress shoes; the girls wearing fancy white blouses with frilly bows, black skirts, and shiny black patent leather shoes. We'd steer the attendees into the sanctuary, where they were greeted by a junior usher standing in the center of the aisle. Right hands extended in welcome, left hands behind their backs, they executed a sequence of precise, well-choreographed moves that welcomed church members and visitors, then directed them to their seats. Later, during the services, we collected the membership offerings with the same sense of purpose, precision, and showmanship, then brought the gold-plated collection plates to the prayer table in front of the altar, left hands behind our backs, right hands holding the collection plates at our waists. As the minister began his offering prayer, every usher standing in the sanctuary—in the aisles, posted at the exits—would take their cue from the ushers standing before the prayer table as they emphatically dropped their hands

116

to their sides in unison, raised and crossed their arms at their chests, then, finally, bowed their heads in prayer.

Extended hands, graceful turns on the soles of our freshly polished shoes, these stylish maneuvers originated at a Black Baptist church in Chicago less than a half hour's drive from my church in Robbins, a predominately Black Chicago south suburb. Representatives of various usher boards—officers, junior supervisors, or in many cases, the usher board's most graceful members—traveled across Chicagoland, where they were taught these procedures along with a series of hand signals that enabled the ushers to communicate while going about their duties.

The number of workshops grew rapidly. Soon, the trainers were supplying rudimentary training manuals for their trainees to distribute among the usher boards they represented. At our usher board meeting, we studied the manuals and repeatedly went over the moves described and illustrated until we had converted them into dazzling live perfection. Quickly, this dynamic new style of welcoming church members and visitors became so popular it was used in Black churches across the United States.

✣　✣　✣

That Friday evening forty years ago at junior usher board rehearsal, I couldn't master a new sequence of moves our trainer/president/dictator-for-life seventeen-year-old Robert Monroe was teaching us. Our moves needed to be precise and synchronized. Every time we went through them, I was a few seconds off. *Every time.* I was fifteen years old and the only member of the junior usher board who couldn't keep up—out of everyone—including the seven-year-olds, the eight-year-old boy with polio, and Mr. Perry, our seventy-something supervisor. My feet began to shake; I could feel the sweat of humiliation draining down my face as my leg spasmed.

"WRONG, WRONG, WRONG," Robert yelled at me. "What kind of sissy are you?"

Robert took special delight in harassing me. He knew how uncomfortable I was interacting with him and he knew I hated being called a sissy. I was doing everything I could think of to squelch that description. My mannerisms were subtler than Robert's, something I thought made me more acceptable than him until one of my high school classmates sat across from me in our crowded cafeteria and loudly told everyone in the vicinity of our table that unlike Robert, I was a "sophisticated" sissy: one who couldn't be detected on first glance, but was a sissy just

117

the same. My classmate explained, in front of me but as if I weren't there, if you watched me closely, the sensual way I rocked my ass against the gymnasium wall and waited for jock strap inspection—yes, it's exactly what it sounds like: points deducted if it was dirty; double points off if you weren't wearing one if you watched the way my hand fluttered when I was annoyed and attempting to shoo someone away (according to my classmate, only sissies "shooed"), you'd *know* I was a male of the *sissy sally fairy* variety.

After all the work I'd done, I still behaved like a sissy??? At the very least, I thought I had made the transition from sophisticated sissy (my classmate's description, not mine) to nice but kool dude (*kool* with a *k*, like Kool cigarettes). I gave my voice edge when I spoke, dropping f-bombs and making sure when I tossed out *motherfucker* it was "mutha" and "fucka," not "mothER fuckER."

"Oh you kool, now, hunh?" the best football player in the history of my high school asked me (in reflection, perhaps there was some sarcasm in his question) when he spotted me wearing one of my recent purchases from an urban store in "the city," which was what kool people called Chicago. My idea to wear the kind of clothes the kool kids wore instead of wearing tight high-water pants riding my ass was paying off! Soon, I would be just another dude, my past clothing choices forgotten.

That day in the cafeteria was a setback, yes, but I vowed not to give up. The next day in gym class, I stood up straight for jock strap inspection, so straight my spine began to ache. I had no choice but to roll it out on the wall, sighing in relief as forty teenage boys eyeballed me.

Yes, the *sissy sally fairy* variety.

Here's the big difference between Robert and me: I did everything I could to fit in; Robert did everything he could to stand out. A few weeks before this particular junior usher board meeting, Robert had gone to our sister school to pick up Michael Washington, our church organist. For the occasion, Robert wore a woman's black fur coat that stopped midway between his knees and ankles, large round women's sunglasses, and a bright-red turban and matching gloves.

No one would ever accuse Robert of being a sophisticated sissy.

Even if I'd owned that outfit, I would have known better than to wear it to a high school in the south suburbs of Chicago. The high-waters I'd worn before I turned kool were an accident—it had never occurred to me to wear something loose. I simply had to learn different behavior. A red turban and matching red gloves—that was no accident; Robert knew what he was doing. Then maybe he didn't. Maybe he did as everyone else did—instinctively gravitated to whatever attracted him, never realizing there were observers who would vehemently object to his choices.

Dozens of laughing students gathered around him that day, branding him, in case he had forgotten he was a male of the *sissy sally fairy* variety. A security guard had to break up the crowd. Though there was no social media then, word quickly got around about Robert's outfit and how he'd been taunted. Today, the incident would have gone viral, a video of Robert's outfit and the harassment he endured all over Instagram and Facebook, some posters mocking him, others angry at his homophobic tormentors.

When I first heard the news, I wondered how Michael had reacted when he'd seen Robert. Had he seen him and thought, What the hell? Had he worried people would see them walking together and think he was gay? Had anyone harassed them? Had he stood up for Robert? Or had he gotten so accustomed to Robert's ensembles, he'd simply seen what Robert was wearing as another one of his outrageous outfits?

I couldn't be seen with Robert except while performing usher duties at church. My mother demanded my brother and I stay away from "that Monroe boy who can't make up his mind whether he's a boy or girl!" Secondly, I felt I had done much too much work transforming myself to negate it by associating with Robert. If we were together, he would inevitably draw everyone's attention, then they would broaden their lens and close in on me. And as my classmate said in the cafeteria—IN FRONT OF EVERYBODY—ALL would be revealed.

✿　✿　✿

"WRONG, WRONG, WRONG!" Robert yelled as I tripped over my feet.

While he barked at me, I had flashbacks of being humiliated at the local YMCA when it took me all summer to progress from "Guppies" to "Beginners" in swim class, something the six boys in my neighborhood did the first day we attended. I saw the exasperated and repulsed face of my older cousin when, after weeks of his instruction, I still couldn't ride the new bike I'd received for Christmas while my brother, thirteen months younger, hopped on it, pedaled, and sped off.

"Amateur!" Robert yelled.

"I'm not an amateur, Madame President. Your moves suck."

Everyone in the sanctuary, including Mr. Perry, gasped. No one, including Mr. Perry, dared defy Robert.

Suddenly, a black flash is moving towards my face. I duck as a Bible missiles over my head. The word of God rocketing over me at a thousand miles an hour. I was one Bible verse away from being decapitated. The Holy Book has a lot of pages.

"You almost hit me!" I yell at Robert.

"If I wanted to hit you, I would have." He snaps his fingers in front of my face for emphasis when he says, "I *would* have," the finger snaps sounding through the sanctuary like gunshots.

"I had to duck to stop from being hurt."

"Nice reflexes."

"You hear him?" I angrily ask Mr. Perry.

"He said he wasn't trying to hit you, Le Van," Mr. Perry answers meekly.

I loved Mr. Perry but he was no match for Robert and wasn't good for anything but calling 911 the day Robert finally decapitated me. Robert was always throwing Bibles at me. I was the only one who defied him, the only one who desperately needed to maintain a distance between us. I thanked God for Robert's hate but that night, I'd had enough. Forget my tormentors who ridiculed me and robbed me of my lunch money, and the ones who made me do their homework—Robert was my number one nemesis. That year, we did everything but arch our backs and hiss at each other. It was one outrage after another, and when I thought it couldn't get any worse, he modeled at our church's biggest event, the annual Palm Sunday fashion show and tea, and ruined the show I'd waited all year to attend.

✿   ✿   ✿

My enthusiasm for fashion began around the time I joined the junior usher board. That year, my brother and I accompanied my mother to the fashion show for the first time. All our babysitters were at the fashion show—even the men. My uncles—my mother's brothers—were available, but with their exuberant profanity and drinking, they weren't allowed to look after us, so my brother and I grudgingly attended another of the million church events we had to endure. Funerals, weddings, prayer meetings, church business meetings, Mother's board meetings we did them all. I didn't expect to *love* the fashion show and tea. To become so excited, I had to stop myself from bouncing up and down in my seat.

Everything about the Palm Sunday fashion show was larger-than-life and glamorous—from the overflowing auditorium (my future high school gymnasium, where, years later, my classmates would notice how my ass rode the walls during jock strap inspection) to the mistress of ceremonies exhorting us to "applaud till the roof caves in!" to a gospel singer with a classical contralto like Marian Anderson (*Who hung the moon and the stars in the sky? Somebody bigger than you and I*).

After the fashion show, there was the tea—elegant tables covered with white tablecloths set around a cavernous room that one day would become my high school cafeteria, site of some of my greatest teenage humiliations. Each table was sponsored by a church organization. My mother was in charge of the usher board's table. She nervously watched the judges pace from one table to another with their ballots and pencils, awarding points for theme, originality, beauty and refreshments. Guests were served finger sandwiches with no crust and pastries I loved but rarely ate such as macaroons and petit fours. (Macaroons looked like they were cloaked in colorful designer coats! The pretty petit fours I could eat two at a time!) There was also frappé made of pink sherbet, vanilla ice cream, 7UP, and a variety of fruit slices and juices. I had watched my mother make the concoction, mesmerized by the way it foamed in the giant sparkling glass punch bowl.

The usher board had as their centerpiece a cake shaped and decorated as a replica of a red straw high-crown hat with its large brim curving down. To my seven-year-old eyes, the hat reminded me of my grandmother's favorite Christmas bell ornament. It sat atop an ornate silver cake stand. A pink ribbon hugged the crown; a burst of pink flowers sprouting through the ribbon—the details so exact I had to fight the impulse to snatch a flower petal off the cake and eat it to determine if it was really cake and candy.

"Everything on the cake can be eaten," my mother informed fascinated guests as they gathered around the ushers' table.

She and the women ushers erupted in screams and hugs after our minister announced the ushers had won the giant winged-woman trophy that stood proudly all year in a locked glass box in the church foyer, the name of the organization that had won that year's Palm Sunday tea table contest engraved on a gold plaque above the winged-woman's head.

✿　✿　✿

Most of all, I loved the models I saw that Palm Sunday as they posed and twirled in their resplendent outfits. I wasn't old enough to be aware of the subtleties of color; everything I saw was viewed through the prism of the simple colors in my first crayon box. Blue! Red! Green! Yellow!

Pink! Even the colors I thought boring thrilled me. White! Black! Brown! Gray!

I couldn't stop spinning and twirling. My grandmother thought it was cute. "Show me how they modeled," she smiled, urging me on. I twirled and struck poses as she applauded. Applauded like she was trying to make the roof cave in!

I twirled in delight until I heard, "Sissy."

I turned to my cousin Freddy, a few months older than me. Repulsed, he shook his head and frowned. I rushed across the room and punched him in the face. It may not have been the manliest of punches, but it was effective. This sissy gave him something to frown about. We fought through the house like UFC warriors, my grandmother, hands raised in distress, whooping hysterically. A few of her ceramic knickknacks crashed to the floor. She whooped some more. When my mother arrived at my grandmother's house that night, my brother hurried to her and informed her I had been fighting, my cousin effeminately mocking my fashion turns, mincing through the house as he made his case for having called me such a vile name.

Later that night, my mother whipped me with a limb from our apple tree.

"You know why I'm whipping you, don't you?" she asked me.

"Yes, ma'am . . ."

※　　※　　※

But the time I became a teenager, I knew the colors magenta and crimson and could explain the subtle differences between the two, but apple tree limbs and my ongoing efforts to be nice but kool forced me to limit my descriptions to "pink."

Shortly after my fourteenth birthday, my aunt was appointed chair of the Palm Sunday fashion show. She told me she wanted me to be the fashion show handyman. I thought my head was going to explode. I attended all the rehearsals the week before the show, carried heavy items, gave my opinion on the decorations, and was at the disposal of all the models.

I was a crack addict working in a crack house.

I loved it all, but with studied indifference, only allowing myself to be thrilled on the inside, occasionally griping about the demeaning women's work my aunt had me doing. Alone in my bedroom, I locked my door and spun and struck poses like the models I had just watched rehearse.

That Palm Sunday morning and afternoon, I hurriedly assisted my aunt and her committee, then changed into my dress clothes. My work was done. Time for the show! I excitedly sat in the crowded high school gymnasium and delighted in the fashions. On the inside. Indigo! Rose! Fern! Dandelion! Ivory! Obsidian! Gingerbread! Pewter!

There were only two male models in the fashion show Robert and Joseph Cobb. Joseph took a hypermasculine approach to modeling. As the mistress of ceremonies described his clothing, he performed vignettes as he pimp-walked down the runway. In one, he slowly retrieved a cigarette out of an antique silver cigarette case. He stopped, returned the case to his front pocket, lit his cigarette with a shiny silver lighter, then blew fancy rings of smoke as he continued his leisurely stroll. The women loved Joseph. In his presence, they seemed to forget they were attending a church event and swooned and screamed like they were seated in the front row at a male strip club.

"Next, we have Robert Monroe," the emcee excitedly told the audience. Robert hadn't allowed my aunt to see what he was going to do or wear. He'd worked on his routine privately with the emcee, who'd assured my aunt Robert was "going to be outta sight!"

Robert sashayed onto the stage wearing the largest sunglasses I had ever seen; they practically covered his whole face. "Robert is wearing Jackie O sunglasses, which are all the rage," gushed the emcee.

"For women," a man snorted behind my brother and me.

I turned to the president of my church's deacon board. His wife, amused at his discomfort, put her finger to her lips to shush him.

"Robert wears a gray tweed sports coat with yellow flecks, a yellow silk pocket square, a yellow silk dress shirt designed by him, yellow linen pants, and pale-yellow socks," the emcee continued. "Mellow yellow!" Robert pulled up his pant leg and seductively revealed his shoe. "And dark-gray Stacy Adams shoes!" He playfully kicked his foot at the deacon, then dramatically swished his ass down the stage. My brother turned his attention to the floor. The deacon frowned as Robert stopped at the edge of the riser, then slowly began to remove his coat.

"Go, Robert, go," the emcee urged. "Let it all hang out!"

Robert removed his coat, held it in one hand, then swiveled, his back to the audience.

Then he froze.

I froze.

The deacon froze.

My brother groaned.

123

Robert had cut a large heart in the middle of his shirt, his sweaty naked back peeking through.

"Ladies and gentlemen, THE KING OF HEARTS!!!!"

The crowd roared and broke out in laughter and rapturous applause. Suddenly, Robert threw his jacket to the floor and dramatically stormed down the runway, his butt cheeks thundering in his tight yellow linen pants. I thought I saw lightning bouncing off his ass. "Are we having fun yet?" The emcee laughed. "Go, Robert!" The deacon's wife hooted; the deacon groaned. My brother shook his head. I looked around the gym and the deacon locked his eyes on me. He wanted an audience. He rolled his eyes at the stage and shook his head disapprovingly at the spectacle. If only he knew how much I hated him. I joined him and rolled my eyes at the stage. And hated myself.

It took several minutes for the crowd to simmer down after Robert's sweaty back and thundering butt cheeks. "Your president," the deacon leaned in and said to me as Robert returned for a curtsy then dramatically turned his back to us, once again revealing his heart. "Peekaboo, indeed," the emcee chuckled.

The deacon called an emergency deacon board meeting and later informed my aunt Robert could no longer model at church events. It saddened her. I don't know if she felt it was wrong denying a loyal church member what he loved or if she just knew a good thing when she saw it. People talked about her show for weeks.

My mother was silent.

✿　✿　✿

When I ushered the next junior Sunday, I felt everyone's eyes on me, a member of Robert's "crew," their close-up lenses moving in. That Sunday, my usher turns felt like the twirls I did alone in my bedroom. They were taboo. Something I was mysteriously drawn to but also, something that caused me shame. I awkwardly attempted to make my usher turns more masculine and fell out of step with my junior usher partners.

My male classmates' taunts rose in their frequency and their explicitness. "Did you get Robert in the booty and recite Bible verses?" "When the Bible says, 'Come onto me,' do you and Robert jerk off and cum?"

I used to volunteer to travel with the senior ushers on Sunday afternoons to various churches located in Chicago's Black neighborhoods. I loved exploring the city. What I'd once loved, I started avoiding, fearful someone would see me in the same car as Robert. I no longer went on excursions to Chicago.

I had had enough.

I decided to have my brother nominate me at the end of the year for president of the junior usher board. In my convoluted thinking, I would take Robert's beloved job. He would never take orders from me; he'd quit first. I had a great chance of winning. The other junior ushers were just as tired of Robert as I was—especially the boys, my brother included. They, too, were the butt of jokes. Being a sophisticated sissy, I was never as flamboyant as Robert and damnit, I was changing. I wore kool clothes and watched my every move to make sure I was acceptable. How could I fail with such dedication?

After my brother nominated me, Robert stood at the head of the sanctuary, his face panicked as he looked around the room, tallying votes in his head. I smirked at him.

Before we proceeded to vote, Mr. Perry asked to speak. "There's a lot of work involved with being president. Rehearsals. Communication from our district and state. District and state meetings. Conventions. It's not just show. Or play." As he spoke, I realized he was telling the ushers I didn't have the ability to be president; only Robert did. "Then there's the choreography issue." Mr. Perry paused and shyly looked away from me. Robert eyed me and smirked.

He who smirks last, smirks best.

Humiliated and angry, I withdrew from the race. Robert smirked at me the rest of the night.

A few Fridays later, he once again mocked me as I struggled with a move. "WRONG! WRONG! WRONG!" he yelled. Once again, I called him "Madame President," this time adding "and fired supermodel." He angrily grabbed a Bible off the prayer table, the flash of black zipping towards me. In those few seconds, I saw flashes of Robert's smirk while Mr. Perry spoke before we voted. Then I heard my classmate call me a "sophisticated sissy" in the cafeteria.

I wanted out.

I decided not to duck.

I winced as the Bible crashed against my nose and mouth. I grabbed my face, wailed, and fell dramatically to the floor, blood dripping from my lip. I didn't have to do much acting; that shit hurt. One of the little girls screamed and began to weep.

Robert stood frozen, hand to his mouth, as Mr. Perry rushed to me. "I wasn't trying to hit him!" Robert told Mr. Perry. Mr. Perry ignored him and directed one of the boys to hurry to the restroom and grab a handful of paper towels.

I told my brother to help me up, then said, "Come on, we're outta here." I defiantly walked through the church smirking, my brother at my side.

He who smirks last, smirks best.

❈   ❈   ❈

When my brother and I arrived home, my mother was in the kitchen preparing dinner. She had been a junior usher when she was young and later served as president of the senior ushers when she was in her twenties. As soon as I was eligible to join the junior ushers, she'd signed us up. Though my brother had been a year younger than the minimum age allowed, my mother had persuaded Mr. Perry to take both of us as a package. We hadn't had a say in the matter. Nor had Mr. Perry. My mother would be displeased we had walked out and would force us to return. I had to use the one thing that would stop me from returning to the usher board so I could continue cultivating my image.

I had to use my mother's homophobia.

"That Robert Monroe," I said.

"I told you I don't want you around that Monroe boy."

"I'm not. I don't hang with him. He just hit me in the face with a Bible."

"What?"

"On purpose. Look at my lip. It's bleeding."

❈   ❈   ❈

That was the end of my ushering. *And* Robert's Bible throwing he was put on probation: if he threw another Bible, he would be permanently kicked off the usher board.

A few years later, I attended the University of Illinois at Urbana-Champaign. During a visit home at spring break, I ran into Roy Fordham, who'd been a junior usher along with Robert, my brother, and me. We talked about college and shared the latest news.

"Did you hear about Robert?" Roy asked. "He lives in the city now and calls himself 'Robbie Mae.'" Roy grunted derisively, the way a man who secretly sleeps with men makes fun of the men he's slept with, so no one suspects he's sleeping with them. It was too late for that performance. EVERYONE knew Roy had slept with Robert. Including my mother.

Months later, I visited my church during another break. During the services, I spotted one of our church members urgently tapping the shoulder of the woman in front of her. The woman turned to the row

126

behind her and suddenly put her hand over her mouth in shock. People all over the church were tapping, elbowing, and turning. Tapping, elbowing, and turning. Then a hand to the mouth in surprise or outrage. Or was it both? I turned to see what everyone was looking at—Robert.

I didn't know enough to think, *There's Robbie Mae.* But there she was, dressed in an exquisite crimson dress. On her head was a magnificent church hat. (Picture the one the late, great Aretha Franklin wore when she sang "My Country, 'Tis of Thee" at Obama's first inauguration—the majesty, the circumference, the oversized bow, the sequins—but in pink with streaks of crimson.) My quick fashion eye took in her satin pumps, pink as the peonies in my mother's front yard. The murmurs rumbling through the congregation brought me back to the problem at hand. I wanted to flee. I had just started to accept myself. I'd read all of James Baldwin's novels, attended gay bars in Champaign, and enjoyed being in the presence of my new gay friends. That day at church, I felt shame and a familiar fear. Robbie's feelings didn't matter; she was a thing. And so was I. I wanted to shout: *She's not a thing! She's a human being!*

I frowned at the gawkers until I caught Robbie Mae's attention—I was frowning in her direction. She stared at me, her face indignantly asking, *What are you looking at? You still think you better than me? Haven't you learned anything?* For a moment, I expected her to scream at me and call me sissy in front of the whole church. *He ain't nothing but a sophisticated sissy!*

I quickly turned away and kept my head lowered through the rest of the church services, afraid at any moment, a Bible would rocket my way.

During the services, the deacons gathered in the pastor's office and decided Robert needed to be reminded he was of the *sissy sally fairy* variety. They vowed if he entered the women's restroom, they would do whatever was necessary to get him out. How far would they go? Stand at the women's restroom door and shove him away if he dared attempt to go in? Call the police? Shoot him?

I don't know what is with straight men feeling the need to protect their women from trans women using the restroom. Apparently, it's a thing . . . because this was decades ago.

❋　❋　❋

Decades ago, when I saw Robbie Mae in all her glory, I wasn't familiar with the words *trans woman.* I also wasn't aware of *internalized*

127

homophobia when I began altering myself to please people who hated me. I hadn't heard the phrase *toxic masculinity behaviors* when I began mimicking the kool dudes' stereotypically masculine way of behaving.

Occasionally, the fears of a gay teenager living in a small town assert themselves in my adult life and I find myself assessing my body language and the way I speak. Am I kool enough? The teenage me flinches when I arrive at a poetry or storytelling event to perform what my ex-boyfriend once called my "fag shit." I can feel the fearful heartbeat of my teenage self nodding understandingly at my ex's embarrassment and self-consciousness. The adult me has vowed to read my fag shit until I am no longer fearful of owning up to who I am. The teenage me puzzles over why Robbie Mae and I subjected ourselves to scrutiny—he certainly wouldn't have. Then I realize Robbie and the me who shared my personal life in my writing weren't the ones altering ourselves to please oppressors. Robbie never hid. She defiantly entered our church on her own terms, worshipped her God, and made us deal with her presence.

I have no idea where Robbie Mae lives or whether she is dead or alive, but the expression on her face that Sunday remains with me—*You still think you're better than me? We're members of the same family.*

She lived her life as Grand Diva Ruler because good or bad, that's who she was. She was brave. I was not.

I still have a long walk to get to freedom.

Nominated by Chicago Quarterly Review

LOQUATS

by SALLY WEN MAO

from THE PARIS REVIEW

In the spring they ripen and swarm the trees,
the waxy little fruits that resemble bald heads.

I collect their remains: piebald, sweet
and sour. A syrup made of loquats

is said to cure cough. Their woolly twigs
splinter in pear blight. I am bereft

when I eat them all. My throat and heart
always sore. Whenever I got sick my mother

used to skin yellow loquats, but they tasted
better with the skin on. This season, my cough

grows and grows. There is a tree or a fungus
in my chest. I once kissed a man in the hollow.

His tattoo of a stump on his chest. I counted
the rings to a hundred. His memory broke

against my cracked phone screen like waves
against the Sutro Baths. In different years

of my life, 2012 and 2017, two men
with the same name fucked me. Futility

was their name. Their bald heads, their kisses,
the spittle of spite, crawl into me refusing to exit.

At the herbal medicine store, the most expensive
item is *congcao* or worm-grass, dead caterpillars

whose brains become host to a fungus that rots
them from the inside out. Good for the lungs,

a panacea for all pain, the saleswoman pitches.
I am worm-grass, expensive but brain-dead.

Comatose in my love, my refuse, futility fueled
my every waking hour. The tree inside me is not loquat

but strangler fig. A tree so pretty and snakelike
it renders you breathless, then worthless, all at once.

Nominated by Katherine Taylor, Shelley Wong

THE TOLL

fiction By DANIEL MASON

from NARRATIVE

Late last October, when the plague had reached its nineteenth month, and the latest attempt at loosening the quarantines had only flooded the hospitals with another wave of patients; when we had stopped following the daily numbers, the press briefings, the evening footage of gray-green helicopters; when, fearing the alms-takers, we no longer opened the doors except to collect the sealed and sterilized Cal Emergency Management Agency food boxes; when, in sum, what had come to pass was *exactly* what any student of history, any devout millenarian, any B-movie hack, could have told us was going to pass—I received an email from a long-ago acquaintance and editor asking me to write, for his obscure journal, a short piece of fiction about the pandemic and its bearing on the future of the human soul. There had been a lot written, he said, about the biology, the epidemiology—this was all people were writing about, really—but very little on the soul.

My first reaction was to decline the invitation. I've never been able to write anything on commission, even before events had reduced my days to these vague stirrings. There was also the matter of the author of the email that had appeared in my old Yahoo account without a subject line and with such eccentricities of capitalization that the robots flagged it as spam. I had met Ignaz Knoll almost two decades earlier, shortly after the publication of my first novel, at a reading in Berkeley for a now-defunct bookstore near campus. He'd come rustling in after I had started, plopping down on one of the sofas preferred by the local transients. Indeed, on first glance, I suspected that he was also there to seek some shelter from an uncharacteristically wet late-autumn night.

Bare-armed despite the weather, his hair unkempt, with thick smudges on his glasses and dandruff dusting the collar of a black polyester shirt that clung tightly to a rotund belly, no sooner did he sit than he began to arrange around him a clutch of plastic bags from take-out restaurants, full of newspapers and notes. The soles of his sneakers, visible each time he sighed and conspicuously shifted in the chair, had been worn down to hieroglyphs of bright-red foam. At first I thought this to be evidence of physical injury. Later, as he left the store and disappeared into the evening crowds, I concluded that it was just because he toted so much crap.

There is always someone at a reading who waits until the end of the signing line to ask a question, chivalrously offering their place to others so that they can corner the author without the censure of anyone else. He didn't have to wait long. There couldn't have been more than ten people in attendance, mostly friends who left swiftly for a local brewery, pantomiming that I should meet them there. The bookshop was nearly empty when Knoll approached. The remaining clerk, either oblivious to this omnipresent species of eccentric who haunted almost every bookstore in Berkeley or secretly vengeful over the poor attendance, had abandoned me to struggle with a stack of unsold books.

Of the four questions asked of me that evening, two had been asked by Ignaz Knoll: what was my abiding metaphysics, and did I write in pen or pencil. As he approached the table, I readied myself for an expansion of these cryptic queries. Instead, he just set the bags down before me, extracted a bulging wallet from his coat pocket, and after spilling its miscellany onto the table, licked his thumb and smoothed the creases on a yellow calling card. He asked for a pen; I handed him my signing one. He crossed out a phone number and wrote a new one, then, below this, an email address. This was how I learned his name, and the name of *The Toll*, his magazine. Had I heard of it? he asked me, and when I tried to answer noncommittally (for somewhere in all our collected memory, there must be a literary magazine called *The Toll*), he handed me a slim volume wrapped in a plastic bag.

He liked my book, he said, with the downbeat on *like*. Yes, it was a bit self-limited, he said, a bit predictable, and it pandered to the reader with its benevolent characters and facile tricks. One waves one's wand and—poof!—solutions! But those were faults easily remedied, said Knoll. In any case, he knew the pressures on a young author writing for the masses were considerable. We've all been raised to think one needs to earn a lot to eat, he said. He was a writer too, and he knew well that many a good author had been seduced by the glitter of the bestseller list.

Anyway, he said, take a look at my little journal, perhaps we—and even then I noted the oddness of this chosen pronoun—might think of something that could fit.

I thanked him, politely. I wanted to leave. Knoll had horrific halitosis, and it was clear from the state of his clothes that bathing was not a regular pastime. I was six weeks into such readings, exhausted, and his queries had announced him as a particular species of smart-ass I'd quickly grown weary of. And, among my friends now gathered at the bar was C., the sister of a neighbor recently parted from her boyfriend, who had arrived with cheeks pink from the weather, brushing wet bangs back from her forehead when I met her at the door.

Unfortunately, I have long been among that group of people who don't recognize what should be a basic rule of human discourse, namely, that the impolite—the bore that corners you at a party, the interrupter, the drunk—need not be tolerated with politeness. I should have responded curtly to Knoll's insults and headed off to meet the girl. But some part of me must either have pitied him or feared him (or feared *her*), or believed the accusation of an older author who'd just called me a fraud. And so I responded by asking what kind of fiction he wrote.

For the next twenty minutes, first seated before me at the table, then standing as I gathered my reading copy and jacket, then following me about the room, Knoll answered. I can't remember exactly what he told me. I'm not even certain I could follow him clearly at the time. Somehow he mentioned Italian futurism, the Greeks, Mozart ("that fucker"), a novel about Hermes Trismegistus, a coded Victorian erotic text . . . There were moments when he veered into shared interests—Borges, for instance, or early science fiction—topics, that, either due to those same cursed manners or perhaps because I wished to exert some order over the conversation so that I might end it, I encouraged. But then he veered off quickly again.

Eventually, the bookseller rose to her responsibilities, approached, and gently interrupted Knoll, who though mid-tangent, seemed utterly unoffended. Read it, he said, tapping on the book in my hands. I gave you my card, didn't I? He had, I told him. And bells jangling on the door, he disappeared into a parting ripple of brightly umbrellaed theatergoers in the crowded street. When I left I half expected to find him waiting for me. But no: I met my friends in a bar full of undergraduates jubilating over some sporting victory, a scene that now—recalling the close press of bodies, the spittle formed on lips shouting over the din, the peanut bowl with probing foreign fingers, the couples kissing— seems one of almost reckless incaution.

C., a medical student who had to rise at 5:00 a.m. for a surgery rotation, alas, had left.

I lived in San Francisco then. Earlier, in my usual rush to catch the MUNI that would get me to the 6:07 BART leaving Montgomery, I had forgotten to bring anything to read, and so on my way home, I found myself alone on the train in possession only of Knoll's journal. For some reason, he had given me an issue from 1994, some eight years old. It was about forty pages, unnumbered, saddle-bound with staples. The cover was made from light-blue construction paper. THE TOLL, by KNOLL was typed, all caps, in Courier font, next to a small outline of a bell. Were it not for the torn cover, the rusting staples, it might have passed as an experiment with minimalism. But inside it was so amateurly produced that I was surprised to find, in its table of contents, amid an introduction by Ignaz Knoll and a villanelle by Ignaz Knoll and an essay by Ignaz Knoll, a short story by a well-known Californian writer whose byline was subtended by the explanation "Author of *The____*", *The ____* being the title of the novel, later movie, that had turned him into a household name. I won't reveal his identity; I later met him and found him funny and generous. But the truth was that even at that time I thought his book both thin and overwritten, charges that, on a deeper level, I knew could be leveled at my own work. And so I was surprised not only to see his writing in a publication with a print run less than that of a typical high school literary magazine but also to read the opening lines and recognize immediately one of those exquisite, utterly perfect sentences that announces a writer's total mastery over his gift.

The rest of the story followed. I read it swiftly, then again. If there was little plot to speak of, it didn't matter. It was dense and complicated, and somehow the beauty of each line propelled it forward; its ending settled nothing but left me with a disconcerted longing that could only be satisfied by reading again. It was, in sum, nothing like *The ____*. It even occurred to me briefly that the famous Californian writer had not written it at all but that his name had been used only as some pseudonymous prank. Indeed, this was my reigning theory, when, later that week (having missed my BART stop, waited almost an hour on the Millbrae platform for a delayed inbound train, and returned home to four days of trying, miserably, to imitate the Californian writer's story), I had

134

lunch in the Mission with D., a friend, bookseller, printer of chapbooks, and a master of publishing arcana of the kind that I now sought. Not surprisingly, D. *had* heard of *The Toll*. Knoll, he confirmed, over the ringing clatter of a taqueria brightly illustrated with murals of Mexican country life, was somewhat of a legend: a nut, no doubt, but a talented and productive one, who had been associated in the late 1960s with the Language poets, before some kind of mental condition had led to his increasing distance from that collective, eventually culminating in institutionalization following a rather violent break. Despite this, or perhaps because of it, Knoll had achieved a certain underground reputation, and *The Toll, by Knoll,* with its silly rhyming title, and address at a workshop in Napa State Hospital, carried with it a subversive frisson. It was not uncommon for well-known writers to receive, via their publishers, rambling invitations from this crazy man, said D.: part praise, part condemnation, just like our conversation back at East Bay Books. Eventually, however, persistence bore fruit: in the early 1970s, a story had appeared by "Charles Portis," displaying a complexity and depth unexpected of the popular writer of *Gringos* and *True Grit*. Whether or not Portis actually had written it was a topic of conjecture—D. had heard arguments for both—and it was even possible that Portis, himself notably reclusive, had no idea that he'd been pranked by a Berkeley schizophrenic. At the same time, the Portis story was entirely different from the five other essays, poems, and stories in the issue, all of which appeared under Knoll's own name. Regardless of whether this was truly Portis or whether the story "Asphodel" by "Louis L'Amour" was truly by L'Amour, or whether "The Blue Rose" was in fact written by Jean Auel—regardless, in 1991, Knoll either extended his streak or carried out his planned-for coup, when he convinced Tom Clancy to publish a strange little story in *The Toll*, a story Clancy acknowledged privately to D. at a bookseller's dinner but that—given the terms of the arrangement—had never been published elsewhere. After that Knoll apparently had found his modus operandi. There was no honorarium, no publicity. The print runs were no more than fifty. And yet among certain circles, a publication in *The Toll* became a kind of initiation into a secret society, a mark of both exclusivity and authenticity, which—D. surmised—validated the insecurities of popular writers, who knew, on some level, that in accepting the Faustian offer of the bestseller list, they had forsaken their true arts.

For a moment D. paused and glanced up at the taqueria murals, aware, I think, that he had treaded a bit close to a betrayal of what he actually thought of my writing. A group of canary-vested workers, still dusty from a local demolition, took seats at the long table besides us, and we shifted to make space. On the wall above us, my eyes found a circle of village children dancing in a round, their mouths painted with bright scarlet swipes. Then once again D. was talking. The silence of these authors always perplexed him, he told me: it was hard to imagine Clancy keeping mum. It was conceivable, he said, that Knoll had, in addition to exclusive publication, required some kind of nondisclosure, though it was unclear how such silence would be enforced. The other possibility, which went a long way toward explaining the wonderful strangeness of the stories, was that they were written as some kind of hybrid, perhaps being suggested by Knoll or emerging from a correspondence or perhaps shaped by his final, heavy, editorial hand.

Anyway, said D., drawing up suddenly, for at the entrance to the taqueria a mariachi band had materialized and it was clear that all conversation was about to be subsumed beneath their opening ballad. You will write him, of course.

I paused. D. took one of my chips and scoped a gob of guacamole from the bowl. Feet away, the sequins on the sombreros glittered. The accusation of mediocrity still rankled, and I was unsettled by the story of a madman—now loose!—and the memory of his rank breath, the odd, truth-taking stare.

Oh, but you must, D. said. If only for you to learn how all this works.

At which point the trombonist let out a gritty preamble, halted, cleared his spit valve in a glistening spray, and then, in clarion, began.

I left still uncommitted. But if there was one clear effect of this conversation, it was to induce one of the most precipitous cases of writer's block I'd ever known. I am hardly unfamiliar with the heavy paw of the monster, but what followed for the next six days, if short in duration, was of an intensity unlike any I had experienced. I was paralyzed. The moment I sat down, I sensed Ignaz Knoll standing over my shoulder, appraising, with growing disapproval, the words that appeared above my keyboard. He was right: everything I tried to write, had written, was nothing but mediocre. My blancmange heroes were too kind, too good; the dark current that runs through life was all but absent; I leaned too heavily on a cheap showman's case of adjectives that served only to distract from the lack of living meat in the rib cage of my work. In short: it was *predictable* and *limited*, as he'd accused me. In early October, two weeks after our meeting, I withdrew the yellow card from where I had filed it in my copy of *The Toll* and wrote.

I waited.

I moved twice, traveled, wrote, met another girl.

I married, I had children.

Plague struck.

In November, eighteen years after having written Ignaz Knoll, I received my reply.

Mr. Mason, My apologies. I have been inconvenienced by personal circumstances. And then the aforesaid request for a *piece of fiction pertaining to the pandemic.* And then a phone number. And then. *I. Knoll.*

Given the hiatus, the present circumstances—the early isolation orders having transitioned to a series of more restrictive lockdowns, the airport Hyatts converted into sites of mandatory travelers' quarantines, the closing of the highways across the Oregon border and the passes through the Sierras; given the folding of bookshops and the shuttering of publishing houses; given the unreality emerging from the impossible images of creatures in hazmat suits and families embracing across plastic barriers; given the numb knell of Death's tickerboard; given the faces vanishing behind masks; given the silent exits: of the neighbor with the Jack Russell terrier, the sullen cashier, the arborist who butchered the plane tree, the colleague of once so many fantasies, the postman and the postman's replacement, the older woman down the block who once gardened in a brilliant magenta sari, the father of an editor, the second cousin, the sister of a friend; given the feeling that slowly something vital was being drawn away, leaving what remained the sense of something castoff, molted; given the emptying of language, the repetitions, the dwindling vocabulary—given all this, it seems remarkable that this single email could stir in me the same emotions I had felt when Ignaz Knoll had first lurched into my life. It seems to matter little in the face of all that's happened, but in the intervening years I had published two more books, one that had fallen so short of my publisher's expectations that I was offered a chance to buy remainders at a buck-fifty before pulping, and a second, written after fourteen years of misdirection, which had ultimately reclaimed some readers by resorting to some of the indulgences (crashing armies, plucky heroine) that Knoll had once deplored. Still, Knoll's accusation, as well as D.'s clarification of the *Toll* myth, had never really left me. I'd only ignored them enough to finish my other books.

I knew instantly I would call him. If the cryptic nature of his request were not enough, there was also the simple fact that my world, despite most of my family's survival, had so dwindled as to be empty of other people. There was no news, really, to share. Everyone had grown tired of speaking of the outbreak once we accepted the terms of surrender, and the reduced circumstances had led to such a retreat into private life that there was almost nothing left to say. The news seemed set on repeat, the same mix of despair and hope served up by a proven algorithm; our friends' Twitter feeds had begun to read increasingly like the ravings of the same demented bot. We had read the same books, knew Camus, Defoe—*they had shut up their shops, their puppet-shows, their rope dancers, their music houses, their merry-andrews*—like they were scripture. It had been perhaps two weeks since I had spoken to anyone beside my wife, stuck now with our children, in Boston, for six months, due to a poor draw in the travel lotteries. The single change that I could remember from this time was the day, sometime in June, when I'd been wakened by the ringing of the university's distant carillon, which, from that day forward, played in the morning and at night. None of my neighbors—whom I spoke to by telephone—knew who had broken into the campanile. And yet, thank God, no one kicked them out.

I was outside when I dialed the number in Knoll's email. I was standing in People's Park, now thick with knee-high grass and stalking ravens. The sky was gray. There were penalties for being outside, but it was the one risk I would take now. The air in our apartment seemed at times deprived of oxygen, and there were days when I had to throw open the window to take a sudden, desperate gulp.

And so began our second conversation. There were, as with the first time we met, no niceties. Knoll answered, after some two dozen rings, with *my* name. Of course: like me, he had no other callers. He would like a short story, he told me. He hoped I'd had a chance in this intervening period to have a look at his little magazine. It was, he said, given personal circumstances, the last issue he had published. Now, with a special edition devoted to the pandemic, he was ready to resume his work, he said. His request, I would see, was rather specific, but his requests were always specific. Indeed (and here he confirmed D.'s long-ago suspicion) he saw the work between writer and editor as a true collaboration. Since Portis, it had been his process to suggest a topic, which then would be crafted *ex duobus unum:* together. For now he wasn't asking for any commitment. He just asked that I would hear him out.

In the distance, coming down from the hills, I could see another figure approaching in the middle of the street. It was too far away to see whether he was a member of a citizen brigade or someone just breaking curfew. In either case, I knew it would be best to avoid him. There is a long-held observation that during pestilence only those with no business being out were in the streets.

Hastening through the grass at a diagonal, I headed down toward Telegraph Avenue. Behind me rose the campanile, and I realized with a sudden start that I hadn't heard the carillon that morning. Knoll, oblivious, was speaking. He had a theory, he told me, about the virus, the pandemic, the effects on the society we live in, which he wanted me to craft into my "simpler" prose. It was clear to him, he said, after much reading and consideration, that these so-called changes, this new solitary existence—not new to him, of course; indeed, because of individuals given to harassing him, he had not left his apartment for years except under great duress—these changes were not changes at all but rather a condensation of a process that had been unfolding for decades, even centuries. Indeed, as he had applied himself to the study of the history of epidemics, what was increasingly clear was that rather than a rupture in human experience, each plague could be understood instead as a perfect expression of forces already at work. The Black Death did not interrupt life as it was in Europe, said Knoll. Rather the opposite: it concentrated the intense fear, superstition, and devotion that dominated medieval existence. The epidemics of yellow fever that struck the American colonies in waves in the late eighteenth century were not some caesura in the path toward nation building but rather a tearing of political and social fabric along rifts that had already begun to pull apart. Smallpox for the American Indian merely accelerated what the settler's gun had started. And so on: he could provide me with other examples. But he could not bear to hear another person speak of these "unprecedented" times, these "uncharted waters," these "interruptions." There was no change, no interruption, nothing had altered at all. Like the plagues before it, this one was merely accelerating the path we'd been on. Which was, said Knoll, the relinquishment of the human soul to the machine.

For the first time in his monologue there was a pause, and as I crossed beneath a blinking red traffic light, I heard him take a breath. He was aware, he continued, that the circumstances of his life would prejudice me that these were the ramblings of a madman. That was fine; he'd given up fighting with fools. Hang up if you want, he said, but I stayed on. I continued, past a boarded-up beauty bar, and the weed-filled lot of a dialysis center. What struck him from his study of the past months, Knoll said, was not death, but rather death's absence. Boccaccio described the dead packed into graves like ship's wares. Defoe wrote of great pits, into which *the delirious, wrapt in blankets, would throw themselves;* of *churchyards in Cripplegate, St Sepulcher's, Shoreditch* stuffed with bodies; of fugitives from quarantine tumbling and rupturing their buboes in bloody puddles in the streets. *Homo sapiens* was, this time, at least for the most part, surviving. After the initial cycles of hubris and the virus' recurrent castigation, enough of us had learned. What was striking, however, was how incidental humans were to this survival. Only the bustling hospital corridors teemed with life, and even there machines did our breathing for us, computers doled out food into our veins. Outside, mass starvation was being forestalled by the near total mechanization of agriculture. The container ships that resupplied us in our isolation were manned by crews of twenty Filipino sailors. Airplanes on autopilot carried our nourishment. Sex had all but vanished. Human travel had been revealed for what it had always been, a luxury, a deception, no more necessary than the video streams of simulacra that kept us sedated as we ticked off each day until our deaths. Consider, he said, as I crossed Alcatraz with its gardens bursting with the remnants of such summer abundance that I was forced to bat aside the dry, dun ranks of fennel and valerian that rose up to my shoulder: consider how even our conversation is one in which you and I are but specks within a vast network we have been deluded into maintaining. We are no wiser than the mushroom hunter who thinks that the purpose of the fungus is the chanterelle, the oyster, while vast acres of mycelia prowl the earth beneath his feet. For now such fruits—the chanterelle, this conversation—have been necessary to persuade us to keep the machinery oiled, to replace its faulty wiring, to clean the rust out. But at some point it will be decided—and I use the passive voice, said Ignaz Knoll, for the idea that an adversary should be an active subject is another of our delusions—it will be decided that there is no need for it to feed us, and only then will the true change, the rupture, the transformation, come.

There was a crackle on the phone, a brief electronic static of the kind that we've grown used to, a testament—they tell us—to the volume,

140

the abundance, of all the life that's lived over the wires. When his voice returned, I found him almost impossible to follow: his words, treading so close to madness, had buckled into it. By then I had walked farther south than I had ever walked before, to a spot beneath the highway where a supermarket once stood. It was not a casualty of the pandemic—they had bulldozed it some years ago to make room for upscale apartments that were never finished. Around it rose the mirrored windows of a pair of nameless office towers. Now the streets were empty, no cars came from the highway, and I stood there as if defying someone, something, to come. The windows of the towers, dulled with dust and summer pollen, reflected the overpass above me. Briefly I thought I heard a keening, but it was only the whine of the transformer that draped its wires like a forlorn maypole over the lot. A hawk circled. On the phone, Knoll was still speaking, but I was no longer listening, for now there was a rustling in the old construction fences, and at the far end of the lot, a man emerged out of the earth, dressed in motley robes, and at his side, a skipping, skirted child. Something human on the top of a telephone pole unfolded itself and scuttled down in flashes of color. There were voices behind. I turned and saw a woman with her hair in purple rollers, great breasts swinging inside a nightdress, pushing a squealing infant in a light-blue pram. I heard a carnival band above me on the highway, and in a car at the edge of the lot, saw bodies tumbling, pink flanks swiping swathes through the condensation on the windows. A crowd of boys and girls danced in a circle, hands together, singing a nursery rhyme as they collapsed into fits of laughter. Something from the clouds came down and met my lips with fevered ardor. The maypole turned, turned, pink, blue, white, yellow, the ribbons looping over under, over under. Defoe: *And no wonder if they who were poring continually over the clouds saw shapes and figures, representations and appearances, which had nothing in them but air and vapour.* My phone went dead. Would I write for him, asked Ignaz Knoll, and I turned and left the heaving crowds and headed back along the empty streets to where I lived.

Nominated by Narrative

BAD DOG

by MOLLY GILES

from WIFE WITH KNIFE (Leapfrog Press)

Whiskery tub of muscle with flicks of spit and slime shot from spotted tongue and slick pink dick. Sly beggar eyes, wheedler's grin. The forelegs stiff in bossy supplication, the butt high, the propeller whirl of tail, the dance in place at the door, the stench of slept-in, spit-on hair and hide, the yellow sulfur farts, the bared teeth, the fetid breath, the slobber, the snuffle, the hurry up yip. Let him out! Let him in! Don't leave him here, secure in the house, warm in the car, safe in the yard! Take him with you! Let him dog you! Take the stick! Throw the stick! Take the stick again! Throw the stick again! Walk him! Not here! There! Not there! Unleash him, free him, see him circle, snarl, fight, bite, pee in six places, chase cars, attack strangers, spook horses, unseat cyclists, break the necks of sunning cats, gulp dead birds, roll in cow shit, chase squirrels up power lines, pack with Scout and Maggie and Bobo to bring down a fawn or a city child alone on the corner. Pick his dung up. Sack it. Schlep it. Pet him! Praise him! Feed him! Feed him horsemeat, cow-meat, chickenmeat, pigmeat, ratmeat, catmeat, zoomeat, road-kill, dogmeat! Gulp! Gone! Watch him gnaw the menstrual goo from your twelve-year-old's gym shorts, slop the snot off the baby's face, dig up the dahlias, bury the hiking shoe, chew the ankles of the antique bedpost, hump the limp leg of the Alzheimer patient, pull your guests' dinner off the dining room table, knock the vase down, flee as china and crystal crash to the tiles, plead guilty with hope-stricken eyes. Bad dog, good dog, come dog. Sit. Beg. Heel. Roll over. Down. Clown! you say. Comrade! Confidante! How cute he is! How clever, how comic. Look how he loves me! But how can he love you? He doesn't know you! He doesn't know you lied to your lover, stole from your mother, slapped your sister, abused your child, cheated your boss, falsified your taxes, perjured yourself in court, slashed your enemy's tires, slept with your best friend's spouse, betrayed your business partner, vandalized your neighbor, hit a pedestrian, slandered a co-worker—he does not know that you have behaved, all your life, in fact, like a dog—nor does he care. His interests are not your interests. His thoughts are not your thoughts. His dreams are of hunt, quarry, catch, and kill. His strange brain is at secret work in your house all night. Is it your house? Whose ghost startles your dog on the stair? Why does he bark at the mirror? What does he hear when the kitchen clock stills? Those claw marks high on the lintel of the locked door—where did those come from? And the flash of his moon-sharp teeth when you call? The grin of an exile, far from his kind, slavish, obedient, biding his time.

Nominated by Jane Ciabattari, Leap Frog Press

SWEET POTATO

by JANICE N. HARRINGTON

from JAMES DICKEY REVIEW

The 1997 census shows that Black farmers owned 1.5 million acres of "farmable land,"
down from 16–19 million acres in 1910.

1
Food travels, the speaker said.

These came over that Mason Dixie:
stewed tomatoes, green tomatoes, fried corn,
fried pies, grits, sawmill gravy, okra,
parched peanuts, field peas, sweet potato pie,
fried sweet potatoes, baked sweet potatoes,
and candied sweet potatoes.

I am Black. I am black-eyed peas.
I am the blackened, scorched peel of a sweet potato,
the potato left roasting on a stone hearth
(Lillian did this), hot coals and ash mounded
over orange tubers: old way, old ways
and dark bodies heading to the fields in darkness.
Dawn coming, the sky is blackberry juice
and hearth-roasted sweet potatoes.

2
After the West African Folktale
Once a woman wanted a child.

She planted a sweet potato slip
beside her hut. It grew into a child.

The Sweet Potato Child swept, and
scrubbed, and cooked. She did all
that daughters do. But a child is a child.

The woman scolded, "You are nothing
but lump and leaf I dug from dirt!"

The Sweet Potato Child left and stood
in the dirt beside her mother's hut.
Her hair twisted into vines.
Her arms and legs grew long, long, long
and bent crooked into roots.

The woman wailed and struggled to pull
her daughter from the dirt.
    The Sweet Potato Child sank.
The woman pulled with both hands.
    The Sweet Potato Child sank.

The sinking took a long time.

I told you it took a long time.
Did you listen?

3
Listen—they sold all that land.
Nobody was going back there.
Least they got something for it. Can't blame 'em.
These young people don't care nothing.

At Tuskegee, Carver made vinegar, molasses,
postage stamp glue, synthetic rubber, and ink
from sweet potatoes.

Have you ever sipped sweet potato wine
or brewed it in a five-gallon jug?

It's not just the slow charring that sweetens, but
more the ash, even more the chop-chop of Lillian's hoe,
the slurry of horse manure ladled from a bucket.
Say there was nothin' she couldn't grow. Had two gardens.
What they had to live off of. That woman worked all the time.

A sweet potato needled with toothpicks
grows in a mason jar filled with tap water
atop my kitchen counter.

Fewer than 2% of all United States farmers
are African American. How many grow sweet potatoes?

4
In the evening, after supper
she pared a sweet potato. She peeled the skin
and scraped her blade against the orange meat.

She lifted a mince of pulp and brought it by knife edge,
a coarse confection, to a child's lips.

The child's tongue, mothy-greedy, fluttered,
and beat for more.

The child chewed and swallowed,
consumed the potato.

But the sweetness stayed, and the child,
bearing its ink upon her tongue,
wrote her first words.

Cover your words with ash.
Leave them to sear, blacken.

Paradox: it's the heat, the burning,
that draws the sweetness.

Nominated by Hugh Martin, James Dickey Review

THE THERMOPOLIUM

by DORIANNE LAUX

from ALASKA QUARTERLY REVIEW

Ancient Snack Stall Uncovered in Pompeii
—The Daily Star

Even in 79 AD, people loved street food,
all the young Romans flocking around
the sizzling terracotta pots, the stalls frescoed
with chickens and hanging ducks, hot drinks
served in ceramic two-handled pateras
filled with warm wine and spices.
Their sandaled feet glimmered
as they milled around, waving hellos,
smudging one another's cheeks
with kisses, murmuring gossip,
complaining about the crazy rise
in the price of wheat. Soups and stews,
skewered meats, stacks of flatbread,
honey cakes and candy made with figs.
They sprawled on the steps or sat
near a neighbor's open door, stood
under a blur of windows, someone
playing a lyre, barefoot children
reciting the Odes of Horace. Just like
New York before the pandemic,
before the many retreated and retired
to their living rooms to watch the news

on a loop, alone with a cat or dog,
a furry stay against the nothing,
nothing, nothing of loneliness,
their dreams a passport to fear.
I used to see the excavated people
of Pompeii frozen in time, caught
curled in sleep or kneeling, a couple
fucking, though there is one
of a possible father propped
in what looks like an easy chair,
a mother bouncing a child
on her lap as if they'd decided
in their final moments to be
happy to go into the afterlife
covered in ash, buried alive
by joy.

Nominated by Alaska Quarterly Review, Claire Davis, Christine Gelineau,
Jane Hirshfield, Robert Wrigley

AGAINST MASTERY

by BRIONNE JANAE

from AMERICAN POETRY REVIEW

give me no seat at the table
let no trembling hands lay food on my place

let me lord over no one and nothing
not the dog curled up in my bed

not the land nor children who wander
through my care let me learn from the babies

and be always laughing at my ignorance
only humble discovery give me

and keep my eyes on the pattern of birds' wings
breaking the blue overhead let me face

the ones I harm with open palms and let love
be the method and measure of my worth

keep my heart with my people
and the coal glowing beneath my feet

let me run and run and run and run
and let the flame of my torch never go out

I am here with you
to burn the house down

keep me to this cut me down
before you let me lose my way

Nominated by American Poetry Review

HOW DO YOU ROLL

fiction by KIM CHINQUEE

from POST ROAD

Things I love about my new home: having a full spread on the bed if I want. Bright colors. Lighting candles. The whir of the transit busses passing. Keeping my life clean. Being organized. Being able just to find things. Eating meals at the table on a plate without having a dog jumping. Not always having the TV on. Being close to Wegmans. Cooking for myself. Doing my own laundry. Enjoying my art, my plants, my dogs. Long soaks in the bathtub, taking in my salts, lavender oils, lights down, with a lit candle and low music. Practicing self-care. Knowing where my clothes are. Being able to exercise whenever and in whatever ways I want. Drinking wine with dinner. My nice, big kitchen! Cooking vegan, cooking nonvegan, or not cooking at all. Making my own cheese plate. Not having to hear bad things about liberals. Being liberal. Writing at my desk. Reading. Being quiet. Feeling cleansed.

Asking my dogs: how do you roll? Walks to my favorite park, where I can fly a kite if I want. Being in awe of the enormous sky I can see clear out my window. The pandemonium it makes when a storm breaks. Making a lime into a kickball. Acting like a whimbril or a warbler or a goose. Being silly with myself. Playing imaginary golf while playing an imaginary trumpet, eating imaginary (or real) blueberry sherbet in my fluffy velvet robe. Oh, how scrumptious!

My place smells so delicious! Can you study my serology? Can you tell that I am free now?

Nominated by Jane Ciabattari, Post Road

THE KISS

fiction by KATE OSANA SIMONIAN

from THE IOWA REVIEW

In the beginning, THE KISS lived within the vast acreage of Pellwood's Private School for Girls. It was the waterlogged soil under the Shakespeare Garden. It was the fertilizer spread around the picnic area by the maintenance staff. It was the clay shelf on which rested the twelve-million-dollar indoor swimming pool. THE KISS felt the vibrations of the chapel organ piping over the tennis courts, and it longed to be free. For THE KISS was trapped within the vast acreage of Pellwood's Private School for Girls.

THE KISS first surfaced in the mind of Miss Weber, director of Pellwood's production of *42nd Street*. *42nd Street* followed Depression-era Julian Marsh as he staged a musical called *Pretty Lady*. Wannabe actress Peggy won a spot in the chorus line. At the eleventh hour, the star of *Pretty Lady*, Dorothy, was injured. Peggy took her place, saving the show-within-a-show.

It was a feel-good production, and Miss Weber was confident in her choice. The next step was casting. She'd usually contact Campbell's Catholic School for Boys, but she hesitated. Boys were a bother, being liable to get sexual, or at least put sex in the air, get the girls all whipped up without knowing why, like Cinder the first time she went into heat and twerked against the curtains then raised her unclaimed haunches to the sky and gave a befuddled meow, like, *What am I even doing?* No. She was sick of the girls using art as an excuse for self-expression. Last year, the second daughter in *Fiddler on the Roof* had been found

152

kissing Tevye in the keyboard room, which was a bit too Old Testament for anybody's liking.

What Miss Weber really wanted was an all-female cast, but she had to consider THE KISS. Before the opening of *Pretty Lady*, Julian visited Peggy and, ostensibly to improve her performance, made out with her. That would have been fine if Julian was played by a boy, but two girls kissing? This was a church school after all.

Miss Weber asked her cat what she should do. Cinder gave her a slat-eyed look, then went back to sleep. Of course, Miss Weber thought. She would *ignore* the kiss. She crossed it out on page eighty-one and replaced it with a platonic shoulder pat. Problem solved.

THE KISS was overdetermined from the start. Spare it a moment of sympathy. It could not even shrug its slobbery shoulders, for its body was figurative.

At the first audition, Miss Weber announced her decision to make the cast entirely female.

"Then what's the point!" asked one exasperated choir nerd, whom no one had suspected of a sexuality.

"Worst musical ever," Tracy whispered to her best friend, ECL, whose name stood for Extremely Charismatic Lesbian.

"More for me," replied ECL. She spread two fingers over her mouth and undulated her tongue. Girls giggled in horrified delight. Everyone did the cunnilingus sign, but when a lesbian did it, it meant something.

Tracy was too nervous to laugh. Tracy Kharpetian, half-Syrian scholarship student known for such stunts as reading from the Koran in chapel after 9/11, was the most popular girl in the school. This did not guarantee her any breaks, though. For five years she'd tried out for every musical, and despite her (extremely) legit acting skills, she'd been turned down as too unfeminine for any role (read: too swarthy). Racism. Within the rarefied atmosphere of Sydney private schools (read: blindingly white), she was ethnic. To cast her as an important character in any play set before, like, the 1980s would not be realistic.

The cast-list went up. Now, when ECL whose name was Anna was cast as the ingénue Peggy—for she could tap dance (a lesbian who dances?)—and Tracy was cast as Julian, what Tracy thought was, Urgh. She'd finally been cast as . . . lead male. It made sense, in a way. Tracy was intellectually ferocious, sexually invisible due to a dearth of mammary, and in possession of unfairly tenacious facial hair that took her hours of tweezering to remove. She was more competitive than her brothers, which her father approved of; encouraging aggression was how he expressed affection. But acknowledging the sad androgyny in front of everyone might erode the cult of personality Tracy worked so hard to maintain.

The rest of the school was excited by the cast. Tracy's rich-girl, milk-colored nemesis was a lead as usual (Dorothy), but here was added celebrity. ECL was the only out lesbian in the school and charismatic (extremely), and Tracy was whom the student body would have voted Head Girl had not the teacher's committee vetoed her as (their words) a dangerous element. In hindsight, the sheer magnitude of this celebrity collision might have been cause for concern, but recall that THE KISS was at this point nascent. It could only be sensed while walking barefoot through the school grounds on a summer night. No, it just seemed like something grand was about to happen, such as a killer musical starring the two most notorious girls in the graduating year at Pellwood.

Miss Weber had forgotten to redact THE KISS before copying scripts for the main cast, so she took a dry-erase marker and manually blacked it out on page eighty-one of every script. She drew an arrow out of each oblong and wrote, *Julian Pats Peggy on Shoulder.*

It was ECL who noticed the erasure the night before the first rehearsal. She was sitting on her ironic *Star Wars* bedspread and looking at a tasteful BDSM photo book her mother had bought her. ECL had an irritatingly accepting mother who treated her like a teenage boy and often opined, given the slim pickings among fifty-year-old men, that she wished she was gay too. Still, mother was alright. She'd bankrolled ECL's fake, so that she could go to gay clubs. ECL didn't have many friends apart from Tracy, so the ID wasn't used for clubs, but to buy booze for whichever Pellwood girls asked.

ECL was considering masturbating although her deadbolt wasn't drawn, when, beneath the dry-erase rectangle on page eighty-one, she spotted a glint. Two words, scintillating:

They kiss.

The words spoke to a wish that ECL already had to kiss Tracy, regardless of it being a gay trope to have a crush on one's straight best

154

friend. Just because it was a cliché didn't mean it wasn't true. Wasn't that a musical? A throbbing cliché that embarrassingly moved you? And Tracy was not a trope. She could not be contained, summarized, silenced with a marker's tip. She was beguiling and brilliant, like a talking snake, that, through its belly, sensed the vibrations of your soul. She'd do something remarkable and then call *you* the special one, like she had the day ECL came out and Tracy christened her the Super-Hot-And-Charismatic-Lezzie-Anna-Docious, aka, the Extremely Charismatic Lesbian, aka ECL. ECL traced her crush on Tracy farther back than that though, back to the first day of drama class in grade seven, when Tracy had sat next to her with a full tub of sherbet and asked, "Wanna share?" ECL had never felt so chosen.

ECL knew that the way to her best friend's heart was through scandal. The mere suggestion of it had prompted Tracy to ask ECL to their year-ten formal, in protest of the implied stipulation that girls would bring partners of the opposite sex. Despite posing together in some raunchy photos and sharing an obligatory dance, it had been a chaste "date," even though Tracy had gotten drunk at the afterparty, vomited, and laid her head in ECL's suited lap for a few wonderful minutes. Perhaps THE KISS would awaken in Tracy a latent desire? Perhaps the glory of savaging the cherished musical would commingle in Tracy's mind with ECL, sanctifying them as a couple made inviolable through transgression? An onstage kiss. That was next-level salacious. A trembling peach bottom there was no way Tracy could resist.

Why does ECL's nickname matter, or that everyone used it, from the girls to the office staff to the softball coaches? Because at Pellwood, Anna's identity was subsumed into that of the Extremely Charismatic Lesbian. Or maybe just, The Lesbian. She was the subject of scandal and, in some quarters, subtle pride. Yes, lesbians! Legit a thing now, and we got one! The headmistress bragged to her more enlightened friends of ECL's existence. The headmistress had to be careful, though. A girls' school was always on the verge of becoming a hotbed of lesbian sex, at least in the minds of parents. Also, Jesus. Also, left-wing teachers and a student body down to party, but let's draw the line with celebration, not experimentation. They didn't want a sapphic plague, some sexy collective hysteria, girls being so susceptible to fads. And the boarders! What would it mean to have charismatic lesbian boarders, seducing good country girls who just wanted to sleep (unmolested!) at night and slowly virginally grow into entertaining companions for the landholding

155

husbands they would one day snag? Pellwood was not about that kind of sentimental education.

Do we want THE KISS to grow, bud, break into bloom? Or be crushed beneath the bootheel of authority? Let us bow our heads in prayer.

By first rehearsal, Tracy had decided that not even playing a man could dim her incandescence. She'd been cast as a lead, and the Powers That Be were going to rue the day. She'd show these WASP fucks they should have made her lead in every musical since the beginning of time, now that the spotlight ludicrously denied to her with the position of Head Girl had, of its own volition and appetite for quality stardom, fixed her in its blistering eye.

You see, Tracy knew about THE KISS. She'd seen the film version of *42nd Street* and noticed the redaction. Wouldn't a kiss smash the smile off Miss Weber's face? And the face of Reverend White, and the Headmistress, and all the gutless wonders of Pellwood's Prissy School for Good and Godful Girls? ECL would be a willing accomplice. There had even been moments in which Tracy worried that her best friend had feelings for her, which they'd never touched on, thanks be to Jesus. Sometimes Tracy had thoughts—banish those!—of ECL's athletic shoulders, her dancer's core and fatless musculature, her V-shaped torso and utter titlessness, but wasn't that natural? A teenager always existing in a state of pansexual longing? THE KISS was a gift. Through it, Tracy would transcend her tepid peers. She would be so good, they'd believe she was a man. She would be so good, she'd surpass the ostensible ick factor of making out with a girl.

THE KISS willed itself into being, but it was Tracy who first voiced its possibility, on a rainy afternoon. The friends were walking back from Chookas, the chicken shop where the cast ate before rehearsal.

"You know what I hate?" said Tracy, adjusting the umbrella. "How Miss Weber deleted that kiss."

ECL was shocked that Tracy knew about THE KISS, but then again, it's not like the erasure had been hi-tech.

"They couldn't have two girls kissing onstage," she replied. "Think of the scandal. We would be infamous." They walked on, listening to the drip-drop of water on the footpath.

Tracy grew thoughtful. "We should do the kiss. On the last night. Like a fuck-you surprise."

ECL pretended this was a bridge too far.

Tracy grabbed ECL's hand (!). "We owe it to the script," said Tracy. "We owe it . . . to art."

By the time they got back to school, ECL had reluctantly acquiesced.

THE KISS exploded into existence in a blowhole shower of iridescent blood. THE KISS sprouted armlets. Its torso extruded two nubbins that lengthened like the legs of a skinned rabbit. THE KISS licked a ravening tongue over wet cheeks and looked up at the sky. Soon, the rapture.

With a month to go, the leads went scriptless. Meanwhile the choreographer, Miss K, drilled ECL on her tap routines. Apparently, ECL had to have all of them down before the chorus did so much as a box step.

ECL had begun to hate the musical. She didn't like acting. She only auditioned to get put in the chorus with Tracy. And wasn't it sad that they were pantomiming Americans? Where the fuck even was Forty-Second Street? Even if there had been Australian musicals, they'd never put one on, because Australian was synonymous with shitty, and the whole point of drama was to pretend that you lived some place relevant.

Tracy sighed. "The issue is that you fundamentally object to Peggy's existence," she said.

"Peggy is a doe-eyed idiot. When I play her, it's like, I'm doing a violence to myself."

"Think about this," said Tracy. "The more bloodless and gender-conforming Peggy is, the more awesome it'll be when we spectacularly queer her."

Queerness. That was another thing that made the play suck. When ECL walked through the dressing room, the girls were mindful. One of the straight dancers flirted with her because she was so extremely pretty that she assumed that ECL would get a thrill out of it. Being gay was a lethal combination of being unseen, yet hypervisible. Take Miss Koch, for instance, referred to by the girls as Big Gay Miss K. Miss K sometimes mentioned her partner but never brought said partner to mixers, which created a hush around her sex life that excited everyone even more.

Miss K often fixed ECL with communicative looks during problematic dance routines (every routine in *42nd Street*). Last week, during the rehearsal of "Dames," Miss K had directed a line of strutting girls across the stage. Billy the Crooner did body checks on each woman as she passed. Miss K had said, "That's about right," and looked at ECL. Like a goddamn queer mentor.

It was clear to Miss K that Anna was in love with Tracy Kharpetian and that Tracy was not interested (in anyone other than Tracy). Miss K wanted to take Anna aside and give her a hug and tell her how one day she'd leave this tightwad school and find women capable of loving her fully, completely, in the way that she deserved. But this was a church school. Instead, Miss K channeled her care into unpitying exactitude during Anna's tap routines, which were one of the strongest parts of a somewhat gormless show three weeks from opening. Also, she was careful to call Anna by her nickname, ECL, although what the heck that stood for none of the teachers knew. All Miss K could do when she saw Anna watching Tracy strut around like a Machiavellian clit-tease was to recall Anna to some concrete task, like nailing that montage.

Unknown to all, Tracy had been practicing THE KISS. Gus had played Danny in Campbell's Catholic School for Boy's production of *Grease* the year before. He had been, according to the school paper, "luminous and incandescent." Tracy had called that phrase redundant and questioned the competence of the reporter, but she agreed that Gus had been very good indeed. Especially in those leather pants, through which you could actively see his religion. The two regularly met in the park on Mondays to trade acting notes. And kiss.

Gus now read the part of Peggy from a grass-stained script held together by two brass clips. "Remember," he said, "Julian is a perfectionistic artist whose whole career is on the line. He's begging Peggy to deliver on the show, more than you know—sexually."

Tracy-Julian sat next to Gus-Peggy and sanded back the hard edge in her voice. "Dammit, Sawyer. Have you ever been in love? Have you ever had a man take you in his arms, and crush you to him, and kiss you?"

They kissed.

"That's good," he said.

Gus felt weird about Tracy's competence in inhabiting a man. She was forceful. Great projection. But she looked like a girl, was biologically a girl. At parties she wore miniskirts and skimpy tops. She was hot, facially speaking. Such was the opinion at Campbell's Catholic School for Boys. Even with the slightly hairy back-of-neck; that was an Armenian

158

thing. Gus had always liked short hair, thought it emphasized a girl's feminine features, and Tracy had lips like a bow. And her devotion to her role was admirable.

"Do you think you'll go through with the lezzo make out bit?" he asked.

"It's like, the whole point," she said.

"Won't your dad get mad?"

"*Everyone* will get mad."

When they got back to Chookas, Tracy let go of his hand. "I don't want ECL to see."

"Doesn't she know we're dating?"

"Are we?" Tracy said it on the fly, as she walked away.

From the wings, ECL watched Tracy work through "The 42nd Street Reprise." It was the final scene of the play, after *Pretty Lady* had been declared a success.

Tracy was better when she talk-sang than when she sang-sang, thought ECL. Tracy was also, in ECL's opinion, perhaps too committed to her role. Earlier during dress rehearsal, one of the dancers had ground on Tracy's crotch (stuffed with a gym sock), and moaned, "Oh Julian, you're making me wet." Julian was gross. Tracy was way more sexy and unique, though now that she was so often in-role, it took everything ECL had to focus on her friend's continued existence. There was a quick path from Tracy's dressing room to the stage, but she liked to stride through the main dressing room, especially when the dancers were half-nude, Julian-mashing her crotch into G-stringed asses and exclaiming, "Dames, dames, dames!" Sometimes ECL worried that this whole thing wasn't about Tracy being gay but wishing that she was a man.

The orchestra chased Tracy's reedy note to the end of the bar. The curtain fell and plunged backstage into darkness. Tracy was just on the other side of the curtain, and ECL could sense her heat, smell her curl-preserving shampoo. She wanted to roll in the folds with Tracy until they'd made a velvet cocoon. They wouldn't kiss, just breathe into and out of each other's lungs. Then Tracy would whisper, *Dammit, Sawyer. Have you ever been in love?*

The day of the first performance gushed, in the way that other days are said to dawn, or fade in, or open their peepers with a few squints of bird-song. The girls walking from the train station were usually a compact beetling of helmet hats and crossed arms, but the trail had shaken out.

The dancers wore their hair in wormlike pastel curlers, and against the black uniforms, the color said carnival. The stream of sloppy dress washed along the overpass and into the grounds, cutting a swathe across the grass.

Towering above, THE KISS strode over the lawns of Pellwood. It peered into classrooms. It peeled the roof off the auditorium and looked down on the morning assembly. Its unholy slime pattered across the shoulder pads of blazers and fell in dollops into braided hair. The girls could not see the slime, but their bodies surged with a crackling, almost libidinal, enthusiasm for musical theatre.

The girls grew rowdy. As a performer, Miss K recognized the jitters, and it warmed her heart. As a math teacher, Mrs. Poole recognized distraction, and she yelled to restore order. As a man of God, Reverend White recognized passion, and he gave a silent prayer of thanks for the energy of youth.

"As you can see, the stage is all set for tonight's performance," the Headmistress announced from the podium. "I would say break a leg, but that's bad luck. Instead I'll honor Pellwood tradition, and say, 'Chookas.'"

Girls swivel-headed to look at Tracy. There was nothing more beautiful than this, Tracy thought. At lunch, she moved to her dressing room. She organized lemon juice and honey sachets for the elixir that kept her vocal cords slick. She set bunches of flowers she'd been given in the sink still in their plastic, so that, like a real star, she would seem too busy to vase them. She flattened her pathetic rack into pecs with duct tape. Then, three hours before it was necessary, she slipped into the luxuriant tweed skin of Julian Marsh.

The time snapped by. Big Gay Miss K did Tracy's hair, a slicked-down wave so full of gel it dried into a hard crust. Makeup girls applied base, powder, crow's feet, a five o'clock shadow. Chorus girls gathered round as Julian Marsh took on the flesh. Last minute pirouetting, hairpins, mist of powder setter, staticky snap of slips. Then the *coup de grace* of the (upgraded) gym sock in the pants. The audience filed in. Tracy's mic sparked on. Mr. Lee tapped his conductor's stick and the violins tweaked no more. The houselights fell and took Tracy with them. This was the bliss. How in the dark, before the overture swelled, she had finally disappeared.

Tracy received a standing ovation when she entered the locker room the next day. A reporter from *The North Shore Times* interviewed her for the culture section. Tracy pretended that she was mortified when her mum asked if they could put the clip-out on the fridge. Tracy's dad had fallen asleep in past shows, so he was saving his attendance until closing night, when the play would be at its most engaging. Tracy thought about how he would feel about THE KISS. He'd think she was a Judas. A kiss always meant betrayal. The immensity of this thought floored her. That was the Bible for you. No matter what you said, it was one hell of a text.

Too fast, they were at the end of the week and already halfway through the run. On Monday, Tracy found ECL on a balcony overlooking the hockey field.

"So, we're still on for the kiss on Saturday?"

"If you are," said ECL.

They watched a marsh bird dipping its beak into the Astroturf.

"I just wanted to check that you were." Tracy sucked on a perfect pink nail. "I guess we can practice, if you want."

There was no one around so they sat on the common room couch. They talked about THE KISS first. Tracy was going to come in and give ECL a light lip touch, then pull back, because Peggy had to surpass herself and become the huntress. After Julian's respectful pull-back, Peggy would give him a spirited kiss. Julian would recover from his surprise, then slide his tongue home like a hot pink member.

"Dammit, Sawyer. Have you ever been in love?" said Tracy. "Have you ever had a man take you in his arms, and crush you to him, and kiss you?"

Tracy and ECL maneuvered their bodies and reached out in a pose as if to then [insert kiss].

ECL pulled her hand back from the dip of Tracy's waist. "Then you'll kiss me," she said.

"I can't wait," said Tracy.

Although she certainly could. The rest of that week, Tracy avoided ECL. Each night, after they performed the sanitized shoulder pat and exited stage right, Tracy split to the Music Department, taking a circuitous route to her dressing room. Tracy wondered, did she want to kiss ECL? It was Peggy who turned her on. Tracy wanted to show condescending care, to tenderly instruct, to hold a vulnerable creature and say, I'll care for you, provided you have sex with me. That she could never love in this way, in the man way, felt unfair.

The morning of the final show, Tracy broke out in a stress rash, which had only happened once before, during the national debating finals. The makeup girls slathered her in moisturizer and foundation. In the mirror, fun? Gus was in the audience tonight. She had to be luminous. All she felt was sick. Something had appeared in her dreams the night before, slick with dark blood and glitter. It had hunkered down on Peggy's settee in the auditorium wings, where it slept with limbs bent around itself like an insectile cat. We know it as THE KISS. Before Tracy had woken in a sweat, it looked up and fixed her in its blistering eye.

That evening, Tracy's father told his wife they should leave the house early, in case of traffic. The florist charged him eighty-five dollars for the bouquet, but how often was your little girl the lead in her high school musical?

The foyer was empty when they arrived, but there were golden spangles falling from the ceiling, hand-painted Broadway signs, and a wall of stars. Jazz sleuthed in the background.

"It looks so professional," he told his wife. "I guess that's why we pay twenty thousand a year."

"We don't."

"If we did, it would be highway robbery," he said. "Anyway, Tracy got her brains from us."

"Well, we didn't give her acting talent."

"Speak for yourself," he said. "I was good at drama. But in those days, no one put on plays for wogs."

"They still don't."

"No. No one handed this to T. She got it on pure talent."

In the past, Vartan had told his daughter that acting was a waste of time—theatre-types weren't exactly world-beaters, her lezzo friend included—but it was something to see how the whole school had rallied behind his daughter. What a kick to see her up there, socking it to these Caucasian hacks. The sickly usher now handing them a program for instance, with her invisible eyelashes.

"These flowers are for my daughter," Vartan told the pale girl. "Tracy Kharpetian."

The girl's blue eyes went wide. "You're Tracy's dad? Your daughter is *ah-may-zing.*"

"You're lucky to have her," he said.

The girl smiled in confusion and gave a program to another couple. Vartan looked at his watch. There was still half an hour until the show.

162

Sweet Jesus. He was going to have to hold this bouquet for two and a half hours.

ECL didn't join in the pre-show gallivanting. She asked her mum to drop her off at exactly five thirty and sat alone in her dressing room until someone from makeup told her to get her ass moving.

Her dressing room had a glass side that looked out onto an amphitheater of hewn granite. Her sink was not dense with flowers. There were no handmade cards slotted into the glass or Vaseline kisses from the dancing girls. She'd tossed away a good luck card from Miss K. Her only support was a Yoda toy from mother that told her the force was with her. It made no sense, this emptiness. Was she not one of the most popular girls at Pellwood?

For the final performance, the ushers let ticketless students cram the aisles. The first half of *42nd Street* ran by without a hitch. Peggy-ECL won a spot in the chorus line. Rehearsals began, and Julian whipped the show-within-a-show into shape. Peggy and Billy flirted, even though Peggy was a mere chorus girl. Dorothy fell during a drunken argument and broke her ankle. Julian-Tracy, with a heavy heart, cancelled *Pretty Lady*. The lights went down for intermission.

There was a moan of pained pleasure from the dearly assembled. When the lights rose, chatter filled the room. Most of the audience stayed in their seats. Tracy twitched open a small partition in the curtains. Her dad was in the center of the third row. He was clutching a bouquet. His face was torqued in a smile like she had never seen.

Tracy walked back to her dressing room, where Gus was waiting for her with a slender clutch of gerberas.

"You were amazing!" he said.

"Kiss me, angel balls!" said Julian-Tracy. Gus annoyed her. Here was a boy on whom masculinity was wasted. She ran a hand down his denimed thigh, then up, then rested her palm like a clam over his fly. "I'm not taking no for an answer."

Tracy pressed herself on him. A creepy thing to do was to keep your eyes open while kissing. Gus's face was slack and trusting, his lashes inordinately long. His hands shook as they grappled her ass. Tracy pulled him into the dressing room so he could see all the flowers and how lucky he was to be kissing her. She ground her body against his, rubbing the bulb of her gym sock against his dick.

"Oh," he moaned, in discomfort or pleasure she didn't much care.

They'd left the door open. There was no knock. Tracy heard a noise like a throat clearing and saw ECL on the threshold. Tracy pushed Gus off.

"You're busy," said ECL.

The shock wasn't in ECL's face. It was in how she kept her eyes roving and looked around her own Sawyeresque body, like she'd misplaced something.

Tracy grabbed ECL's elbow as she walked down the corridor. "No, what did you want to say?"

"Who was that?"

"Some guy I practice making out with."

"Okay," said ECL, and jerked her arm back.

"Are we still on for the plan?"

ECL gave a thumbs up over her shoulder, like she was trying to hitch a ride out of there.

When Tracy got back to the dressing room, Gus was standing there like an idiot, half-boner in the pants. She shooed him out.

What prickly thing had just happened with ECL? And her father with that bouquet. He was proud of her, for maybe the first time ever. Could she really go through with this? Tracy reapplied the beard shade that Gus had suctioned across her face into a grubby blur.

As she worked, the dressing room door cracked open, and in slid THE KISS. It walked on all fours, jouncing at the joints. It crawled across the wall. It climbed down and across the floor. It put its forearms on Tracy's shoulders like a mother offering good advice, licked a fingertip, and pushed one spiny dactyl through her skull.

Oh, thought Tracy, and dropped her makeup palette. She remembered when she'd shown up to Pellwood, over five years ago. She'd been poor, ugly, uncool. She'd joined a Bible study because the girls had to be nice there; in school, there were no such kindnesses. Someone had put a decomposing rat in her locker. The teachers called her Agro because of her unibrow. One girl had thought that Tracy looked like such a dork with her bag crammed with books and buckled across her front, that she pushed her backwards over a fence, leaving her to turtle helplessly in a mass of sappy agapanthus. For three hellish months, the whole grade had made a game of shoving Tracy off walls and into garden beds. Tracy learned that people were terrible, and to be unpopular was to be vulnerable to their sadism, so she rebuilt her personality from scratch. She became art-in-life, charisma at all costs, and soon no one remembered the dork she'd once been. Would ECL even like Tracy had she not made herself into this? Tracy owed everything she had to the choice she'd made that day, while writhing in those agapanthus. She could never go back. This was a matter of survival. ECL was her best friend, but THE KISS was indispensable.

In the second act, there was extra stuffed in every pocket. The dancers worked in some inspired improv scrapping. Maggie infused her solo with jazzy swagger. Back onstage, Julian-Tracy sang "Lullaby of Broadway," and her voice actually held. Peggy-ECL was convinced to take the lead in *Pretty Lady*. In a two-day marathon montage, Peggy learned the dance sequences.

Then ECL-Peggy was left onstage, alone, before the show. It was time. THE KISS was famished, cresting.

Julian-Tracy opened the dressing room door and strode onstage with a nervy gait. Her transformation was complete. This was not a seventeen-year-old girl, but a middle-aged man on the brink of nervous collapse.

"Mr. Marsh. I didn't expect you here," said Peggy.

At first, Julian was his bold, imploring self. He told Peggy that she would succeed, she had to, because this was a Marsh production. Then he touched his temples and sank onto the settee.

Peggy touched his arm.

He swiveled round and gripped her. "Dammit, Sawyer. Have you ever been in love? Have you ever had a man take you in his arms, and crush you to him, and kiss you?"

Julian planted a feather kiss on her lips. Peggy closed her eyes, as if drifting away. He pressed in again. He gave a groan of pleasure as he worked his mouth over hers, like he was eating her alive.

The auditorium was vacuumed clean of sound. They kissed. They kissed. They kissed.

Somewhere in there, THE KISS became a slap. ECL-Peggy reared back from Julian and smacked him. The beaten face mic whined, lancing the audience with pain.

It was Tracy who was left on the settee, holding her own cheek. For a moment she stared, shocked, at the crowd. Then she snapped back into role.

"You're a feisty one," Julian-Tracy said. "Good luck tonight, kid."

Exit, stage left.

The lights flicked off and the band started to play "Lullaby of Broadway." The reprise resembled a soundtrack to madness. Meanwhile, the silhouette of ECL was visible in the gloom. She was perched on the settee, her hand still raised. The backstage crew started to push on the train for "Shuffle Off to Buffalo," the first number in *Pretty Lady*. The crew members who were supposed to take the settee off stood puzzled around ECL.

Miss Weber shrieked, "Get her off!"

The tech coordinator burst out of the wings. He tossed ECL over his shoulder and carried her out of sight.

Tracy inched open the curtain. One lady in the front row had her mouth still open. Tracy couldn't make out her father's expression, but he was angrily gesticulating. He stood up, leaving the bouquet on the seat. He pushed his way through legs out of the row and her mother followed.

Miss Weber made her way down the aisle and scurried onstage. "Our apologies," she said. Her Broadway-worthy lungs ricocheted off the back wall of the auditorium. "But in the interests of student safety, we are ending tonight's performance. For refunds, please contact the Drama Department on Monday."

THE KISS lifted like a bird-titan from the roost. Blood-streaked feathers spoked through the skin of its back, until, with a tear, two wings jerked out. In its jaws, THE KISS held the friendship of the two girls, who would never speak again. THE KISS beat its pinions. When it rose into the sky, it left behind the faint smell of sulfur.

"Lean on me," Miss K told ECL, when she was finally able to walk.

"Don't touch me," said ECL.

"Do you want to talk about it?" asked Miss K, once they were in ECL's dressing room.

"I want to be left alone."

Miss K stood. "I'll tell your mother you're down here when she arrives."

Alone at last, ECL looked into her mirror. With only a hairnet on, her fake eyelashes were gaudy. She tore them off. Who was that girl? She was not charismatic. She was magnetic because she moved around like a big gay ion. Compelling. Propelling. Objects to and from. But any charisma she had was an extension of Tracy's. It had been Tracy, after all, who had given her the name ECL. And telling someone they were charismatic,

166

isn't that exactly what a charismatic person would do? Now ECL knew what charisma really was. It was a willingness to step on people.

Later, someone told ECL that she'd slapped Julian as a correction to the rampant misogyny of *42nd Street*. That was not true. It was because when Julian Marsh had kissed ECL, for the first time ever she could no longer discern the contours of Tracy beneath him. Her friend had disappeared into a forty-year-old man who held ECL like something he wanted to wipe himself on and throw away. From now on, no one would touch her, ECL thought. No one came by to check in on her, and she was glad.

What makes a show a hit? For the final performance of *42nd Street* was certainly that. The next year's musical was cancelled. No musical involving an onstage kiss was staged at Pellwood for a decade. But even then, stories remained of the legendary onstage fuck fest that was *42nd Street*. By some accounts, it had even involved a fingering.

Which is to say, **THE KISS** had left behind some eggs, small enough to fall through straw blades and catch in planks between warped floorboards. In the years to come, girls trapped in interminable assemblies projected **THE KISS** over their field of vision, imagined an invisible world heaving beneath the starched blazers of their peers, beneath accoutrements, velvet gloves, Bible pages bound with ribbons. To those girls, the story was a lover's kiss, which is to say, a promise.

Tracy barreled through her dressing room, gathering flowers until she realized that they would only incense her father.

Miss Weber opened the door, her lip scar a livid white. "Never in my life . . ."

"We don't call it the Drama Department for nothing," said Tracy.

"You won't be laughing when you hear from the Headmistress on Monday."

Once Miss Weber had left, Tracy rested both hands on the sink. What an idiot. Who was she to think that she could set the world on fire with her matchless talent? Her need for attention was compulsive. But, no. That shifted blame to some monstrous chthonic desire that had, with its dark and seductive glamor, exploited her for its own ends. When she had chosen this.

A screeching shape like a punctured balloon had appeared on Tracy's cheek. It was purpling across the middle, where the mic arm had been. Good, thought Tracy. It might soften her father to see her already punished. She would say she was sorry. Would turn the other cheek.

But the thought of her dad's anger didn't explain the scooped-out feeling in her chest. He'd scream and get over it. And the possible expulsion, given how much the school had invested in her, was an idle threat. No, it was the problem of Julian, who looked at her from the mirror. She'd do anything for a few more minutes of his calm assurance. Julian Marsh, for whom morality was irrelevant. Never again would she grab an audience and compel it to love her. Never again would she strike out and make a mark. She would have to wash off her face soon, but not yet. She waited one minute more.

Later, on her way through the foyer, Tracy passed a dancer. She couldn't muster up the courage to slap her on that perfect ass.

Nominated by Anne Ray

FATHER WEAVER

by JAMAICA BALDWIN

from RHINO

If he wasn't janitor he'd be gravel artist, he'd be glitter farmer, he'd
    groove skate
down beach hill to Isley Brothers. If he wasn't janitor he'd be tennis
    racketeer,
ocean tamer, cicada sequencer, he'd turn his knit cap upside down
    to catch fire

flies, load them into pitching machine, point upwards and shoot
    stars into sky.
If he hadn't been liquor undertaker, booze regulator, drunk-
    gambling-wish denier
he might have been daughter wrangler, fear whisperer, sweet
    lullaby impersonator.

His under-water voice might have sung me to float and swell. If he
    hadn't been vodka
foreman he might have used strands of daughter hair to draw maps
    of blackness
on his body. I might have watched them stretch and curve and
    maze him into father

quest into secret daughter mission. I'd pack a flashlight and three
    meals per day.
I'd stretch and nimble get. I'd compass take, whistle and song and
    song. I'd path
follow and lost get and around turn, around turn till I center reach
    and undead him.

Nominated by Ellen Bass, Rhino

UTTER, EARTH

BY ISAAC YUEN

from AGNI

Weddell seals vocalize nine types of sounds beyond the range of human hearing. Guinea baboons learn to grunt in the accent of their preferred social group. Glass frogs pitch their calls higher near roaring waterfalls while waving hello to potential mates. The croaks of male gulf corvina resemble underwater machine-gun fire in sound and decibel level; spawning aggregations can induce hearing loss in nearby marine mammals. Deaf, earless moths sport wing scales that dampen and deaden predatory sonar. Bats can crash into large sponge walls with weak echoes, not unlike people walking into glass doors. Solitary minke whales seem to abandon efforts to hear and be heard in waters with heavy shipping and military activities. The album *Songs of the Humpback Whale* officially reached interstellar space in August 2012 onboard *Voyager 1*; it is not part of the Golden Record's "Sounds of Earth" track with tame dogs, wild dogs, and hyenas, but mixed amongst the recorded human "Hellos" in fifty-five languages. In 40,000 years, the probe will drift within 1.6 light-years of Gliese 445, a star in the constellation of Camelopardalis. What we think of as a giraffe is in reality four genetically distinct species, some of which have been recorded humming at night. Researchers are unsure if these sounds are passive, like snores, or active messages intended for fellow giraffes, swaying in the black.

Crucian carp can go temporarily blind while swimming through anoxic waters. Naked mole rats can survive eighteen minutes without oxygen using a fructose-fed metabolic pathway normally associated with plants. Hummingbirds fuel their hovering by directly burning just-ingested nectar. The male *Calypte anna* orients his iridescent gorget opposite the sun to ensure females see the optimal hue of pink. Nocturnal dung beetles roll their dung in a straight path by the light of the Milky Way.

Blind cave tetras have left-bending skulls and swim counter-clockwise in their lightless environment. Present-day hagfish have opaque patches over the place where their ancestors' eyes used to be. A squid's optic nerve routes behind its retina without interrupting the photoreceptor layer; thus squid eyes do not contain the blind spot we vertebrates have. Cuttlefish compensate for colourblindness with wide, W-shaped pupils that maximize chromatic aberration, which distorts their vision such that they can access colour information. The California two-spot octopus can sense changes in brightness through its skin without utilizing its central nervous system. Planarian flatworms exhibit negative phototaxis pre- and post-decapitation, suggesting a separate body-based reflex that responds to light. Vladimir Nabokov's 1945 musings that *Polyommatus* blue butterflies migrated to the New World across the Bering Strait were proven correct three decades after his death.

The fins that round goby fish use for perching on rocks are as sensitive as monkey fingertips. Koala fingerprint whorls are so similar to ours that they may contaminate crime scenes. Koalas, manatees, and European hedgehogs have lissencephalic brains; wombats, camels, and collared peccaries have gyrencephalic brains. An elephant's cerebral cortex is twice as folded as a human's but contains one-third the neurons. The elephantnose fish has no cortex at all but is able to switch between sensing and seeing processes, like mammals. The remora adheres to its host with a modified head fin made of soft overlapping ridges called lamellae. The optimal spot for hitchhiking on a cruising whale is either by the blowhole or the dorsal fin, where there is shelter. Flensing is the act of stripping a marine mammal's outer blubber integument from its flesh. No fewer than 42,698 blue whales were processed on the island of South Georgia between 1904 and 1971. A single new sighting was recorded off the island between 1998 and 2018. One survey in 2020 noted fifty-eight new sightings. Migration is a form of culture passed down through generations in both bighorn sheep and moose.

Florida carpenter ants use the formic acid they produce for defence to disinfect their food and their insides. The process by which turkey vultures excrete waste onto their feet to clean and cool them is called urohidrosis. Human stomach pH values are closer to those of carrion feeders than to carnivores or omnivores. Chimps parasitized with toxoplasmosis are drawn to the scent of the urine of leopards, their chief predator. Researchers have formally described the all-purpose cloacal vent of a 100-million-year-old *Psittacosaurus*: the area around the dinosaur's backside, highly pigmented with melanin, was likely used for display and signalling, like the rump of a male baboon. Melanin on the bodies of sixteen species of deep-sea fishes provides "ultra-black" camouflage that absorbs more than 99.5 percent of incoming light. *Fritillaria delavayi*, a bright green flower used in traditional Chinese medicine, evolved brown and grey foliage to make it less visible on mountains with heavy harvesting pressures. The African puff adder employs chemical crypsis to avoid being sniffed out by dogs and meerkats. Lions can spot the outlines of zebras just as well as they can waterbucks, topis, and impalas, but horseflies struggle to land on striped bodies. Bumblebees can sense, discern, and alter the electric fields of flowers they visit. A quarter of wild bee species have gone missing from public records since the 1990s.

Garden-center neonicotinoid pesticides can disrupt the circadian rhythms of insects. White-nose syndrome starves Western North American bats by rousing them from hibernation and wasting calories they can't afford to lose. Providing fruit flies with food choices can shorten their lifespans. When milkweed is scarce, monarch caterpillars are more likely to head-butt each other out of the way. Southern sea otters are at increased risk of heart disease when their diet contains high levels of domoic acid, a neurotoxin produced by warm-water algal blooms. When extreme rain events lower the salinity of their habitats, coastal dolphins can contract "freshwater skin disease," leading to lesions across up to 70 percent of their bodies. White-tailed deer fawns with higher cortisol levels in their saliva have lower survival rates independent of predation levels. Bar-headed geese can hyperventilate at seven times their normoxic resting rate without passing out. Thick-billed murre fledglings can hurl themselves off cliff nests to reach the sea before they are capable of flight.

The diabolical ironclad beetle can survive being run over by a Toyota Camry—twice. Young alligators are able to regenerate their tails up to three-quarters of a foot. The denuded *Geckolepis megalepis* looks like a raw chicken tender, and can regrow its shed scales in a few weeks without scarring. Increased beaver populations in the Cascade Range may raise the reproductive rates of northwestern salamanders. The population of North Chinese leopards in the Loess Plateau is increasing due to the government's five-year reforestation plan. In Fukushima, returning wild boars roam the excluded zones' abandoned streets while Japanese serows stick to human-inhabited areas, possibly to avoid the boars. Macaques prefer the in-between restricted zones. Thick-billed murre fathers can feed fledglings on the open seas twice as often as both parents can feed chicks still nesting on cliffs.

The East Pacific red octopus appears resilient to heightened levels of ocean acidity, given five weeks to acclimate. American pikas cope with rising temperatures by retreating to underground taluses during the day. Coral reefs in the Eastern Tropical Pacific are more heat-resistant than reefs in the Caribbean and the Indo-Pacific, possibly due to ecological memory. "The key to survival for future reefs may not be an immunity to stress, but rather an ability to recover and regrow after stress," writes ecology professor James W. Porter.

It took life on Earth ten million years to recover from the Great Dying a quarter-billion years ago. The first line of *Speak, Memory*: "The cradle rocks above an abyss, and common sense tells us that our existence is but a brief crack of light between two eternities of darkness." Leafcutter ants have been farming fungal cultivars across grasslands and rainforests for sixty million years. Ambrosia beetles, along with ants and humans and certain termites, practice agriculture. The last verse of *On Discovering a Butterfly*: "Dark pictures, thrones, the stones that pilgrims kiss / poems that take a thousand years to die / but ape the immortality of this / red label on a little butterfly." Due in part to its large body-to-wing ratio, the flight of the green dragontail is hypnotic, whirring.

Nominated by David Naimon

COLONIAL CONDITIONS

fiction by BRANDON TAYLOR

from THE YALE REVIEW

The election was on Tuesday, but first, the Halloween bonfire.

When Carson and Roma arrived, Roma discreetly removed her mask and said that she had to find the host, who had spent most of the late summer and fall cycling across the Mountain West. Carson knew this because the host had documented the trip with a string of photos manipulated to look like Polaroids and posted to social media. He was long-haired and from Rhode Island, and he wrote long, flabby essays about having played football in high school and how his father was kind of a mean drunk.

Stranded as he was by Roma, Carson gave some real thought to leaving. Then he dropped down into a battered chair and squinted through the smoke from the petering fire across the yard at the other guests, who stood breathing into each other's faces without masks on. These were not his people. One woman wore a red plastic dress with a high slit and a cutout over a silicon breastplate, as well as a long fur coat constructed out of Christmas tinsel. She looked like a drag queen. There was a man in a skinny suit with a skinny tie and platinum hair who looked like an FBI agent or someone from a mid-2000s music video. And then a man in a loosely deconstructed cowboy outfit. Carson felt insecure because he had come in jeans. He wore a flannel under a navy-blue chore coat. It seemed a little ridiculous to be the only one wearing a mask, so he pulled the mask down under his chin. Besides, he tended to assume a kind of honor system even though he had been told that such an assumption betrayed an overreliance on rugged American individualism.

Just then, a man pulled his own chair over the lawn, digging ruts in the grass. He was a sommelier, he said, and he lived in Des Moines. He'd had plans to open a cocktail bar in Iowa City that ended up getting scuttled after the shutdown, so he moved laterally into wine distro.

"Didn't change my registration though," he said. "Totally slipped my mind."

"I see what you mean." From the way the sommelier sat back on the lawn chair and crossed his legs, Carson sensed that he was a socialist. Carson was not a socialist, but he was interested in having sex, so he nodded along when the sommelier talked about tax code reform and the moral urgency of health care for all.

It wasn't that Carson didn't believe in the need for health care and the redistribution of wealth and all those other things. But something in the socialist fervor among people his age made it seem like their politics were just something they had picked up from their friends at a party, something tantamount to attitudes or styles that would go out of fashion as they got older. They would stop caring quite so much. Or else they'd turn into people who were just rounding into early middle age and still went to protests and composted and had slightly more children than they could afford. There was nothing sadder, Carson thought, than being thirty-eight, married, with a kid, and still complaining about the environment on Twitter or at potlucks. But this Carson kept to himself, and when asked if he'd like to try some of a Pét-Nat that the sommelier had been working on getting into broader distribution, Carson said yes.

The cold wine had a deep but tart flavor. He swished it between his teeth and then gulped it back.

"You can really taste the grapes," he said.

"That's the beauty of it," the sommelier said. "Nothing gets between you and the taste. It's all natural."

"I'm not much of a wine guy. I don't know the *lexicon*. But it's good. Not too sweet."

"Yeah, it's a lighter wine, for sure. Not too acerbic."

The coolness of the wine and the silvery pop of the bubbles made Carson's mouth feel slippery and alive.

"It's great," Carson said.

The brick firepit had gone dark and emitted a stinging scrim of gray smoke. People coughed discreetly or adjusted their shirts up over their noses and mouths. Someone piled a bunch of wood and soaked it down with lighter fluid. The result was a soggy mess, dangerous too, because to light it again would risk an explosion. A girl had been burned on

40 percent of her body just the previous year in North Alabama when one of her friends had gotten a little too zealous with the lighter fluid.

"I don't think they know what they're doing over there," Carson said.

"They didn't have Scouts."

"You were a Scout?"

"Dropped out right before Eagle," the sommelier said. He knocked back the last of what was in his cup and stood. He was tall, but not skinny. He had a solid frame and curly hair. He moved easily, like he could see clearly in the dark. Carson followed him over to the pit and watched him heap more wood onto what was already resting on the gray ashes, then light some newspaper and toss it onto the pile. Carson flinched when the fire flared and hissed. The sommelier grunted and poked at the woodpile with a long stick he'd found.

"That won't work," Carson said.

"Yeah, it will."

The sommelier made a show of handing the stick over to Carson, bowing deeply. Carson busted up the pile. The logs were too wet to light. He reached for some of the dry wood stacked near the pit and made a little tripod over the ashes. Then he shaved some splinters from a log with his pocket knife. The bark came free in loose red fibers. While he was arranging the pit, the conversation quieted down. He could feel, with a cool sweat on the back of his neck, the sharpening focus of the others in the yard. He pushed his knife shut against his thigh and, sitting on the brick foundation of the pit, patted his pockets. Like a damn fool, he hadn't brought his lighter with him. He was trying to slow down on the cigarettes and had, in an act of silly virtue, left his lighter at home.

"Gimme a light," Carson said. The sommelier's lighter was a flash of silver in the night, and Carson plucked it neatly from the air. Striking the lighter one hard time as the sommelier watched him, Carson lit the kindling. The fire was small at first. He willed it to grow. And it did, now that it could breathe. When the fire grew enough to catch hold of the wood, he nodded and stood up from the pit. The yard was full of light then. And he could see their faces. These people he did not know.

The sommelier looked on in awe and with a nervous laugh said, "I did say I dropped out."

"Fair enough," Carson said. It was not the first time that Carson had been at a party with graduate students and people with elite educations who did not know how to start a fire. When he lived in Wisconsin and dated a writer, his starting a fire had been a little bit of a party trick. Every fall, they had dinner parties and potlucks outdoors. And each time, the guests would look at him and say shit like *Oh but you're so good at it* or *I bet you'll have some critique of my technique,* insinuating that he thought he was better than they were because if their roles had been reversed, they certainly would have felt that way. It was the worst kind of fake piety, he thought.

"Man, what did you say you did in town?" the sommelier asked.

"I work at the deli," he said. The sommelier squinted at him.

"You're not in the writing program? I'm used to being the only person at these things with a real job."

"I'm here with a friend."

"Where'd you stash him?'

"She had something she wanted to talk over with the host," Carson said slowly.

"He's such a slut. You know that big trip he took this summer?"

"I have Instagram," Carson said.

"Yeah, well, he did it because he got dumped. And he needed *catharsis.*"

"Getting dumped is rough."

"When you get dumped because your girl catches you on Grindr and you try to make it all go away by saying it's *for the attention,* I have no real sympathy for you."

Carson whistled, both because of what the sommelier had said and how he'd said it, with increasing pettiness and anger.

"She's a friend," the sommelier said. "The one who dumped him."

"And you came to his party? Some show of loyalty."

"Well—she was supposed to come too."

Carson nodded like it made sense.

"Black vintner." The sommelier pointed the bottle at Carson, who shook his head.

"Is that the brand?'

"No. I mean, a black guy. He makes the wine."

"Oh. Good for him."

"It's not very common. Black vintners. I try to point it out when I'm talking to clients about it."

"How does he feel about that?'

"About what?"

"You turning his wine into a *black wine.*"

"There's no such thing as a black wine," the sommelier said.

"No, I mean, like, it's not just wine when you do that. It's suddenly a *black* wine." The sommelier stared at him, and Carson wondered if his

177

meaning was unclear. Or his tone, maybe. He was trying to be funny about the way white people turned race into another one of the things they felt passionately about. Like the way they felt about the tax code or abortion rights or composting. All of it attitudinal, gesture, posture, the right values assembled and deployed at parties in just the right way so that it all hardened and cohered into a liberal argot.

"I don't get your drift," the sommelier said coldly, and Carson could only nod.

"Ah, it's just a joke."

"Black wine. I don't even know what that would look like."

"Well, I imagine it'd be black. Wine."

"Stop saying that," the sommelier said.

"You bet."

His face had gone red, and Carson watched the light lash his eyelids. He was good-looking with a rounded, boyish nose and full cheeks. He had a slightly full but dimpled chin.

"Yeah, fuck you, pal." The sommelier tipped his bottle back and sucked more down. Carson thought about how when he was in middle school, everyone used to grab water bottles at random from the side wall of the gym or fieldhouse, sharing drinks. His mom had utterly melted down in the parking lot when she glimpsed him drinking from a friend's bottle. A few months later, meningitis swept the state, and three kids died. And dozens were laid up for weeks and months. All the fountains in the schools of Alabama were turned off. His mother just said, *See what happens when you drank after folks?*

"I wasn't trying to be racial," the sommelier said. "I was just trying to say something nice."

"I'm happy for the black vintner."

"He works really fucking hard. Grows his grapes right fucking here. Out by Waterloo."

"In the Midwest? Grapes?"

"Hell yeah," the sommelier said. "It's a whole new world, my friend. This guy? He's saving old American varietals. Things we haven't tasted in a century or more. How incredible is that? And he's doing it right. Sustainable. Clean. Organic."

Carson closed his eyes and tried to imagine the grapes and the vines stretching out along a field in rows and rows. He had never been to a vineyard, but he *had* grown up seeing his grandfather planting out greens and beans, peas and okra. He knew how prickly the undersides of leaves could be, how pods came in with a bristly white fur. He knew

178

about the color of the soil, what it meant when it was dark or pale and sandy. Carson had sliced open watermelon in the field with his grandpa and cousins and had sucked the juice from the tender flesh and chewed the rind. When he closed his eyes and tried to imagine the grapes, what he imagined were his grandfather's fields, narrow and dark, stretching out behind and at the side of his house, that creaky blue Jim Walter set up on blocks on what had been an old graveyard.

They sometimes stepped on graves and got their legs or tires caught in holes that appeared right beneath their feet. One time, Carson had seen his grandpa go down with the weed eater, and he'd sprinted across the yard to grab him up by the arms. His grandpa had made the sign of the cross and gripped Carson's hands tight. *Get me out*, he'd said, *Get me out*. Carson pulled and his grandpa came loose, but his foot was bent wrong. He wasn't the same after that. None of them were the same. Because the fields went bad, and the grass grew high, and the cousins did dope, and nobody looked after anything, and then his grandpa died, and the cousins went to jail or else to Texas, North Carolina, or Georgia, and Carson didn't see them anymore, and they were like a different people. Hardly people at all.

"That must be nice," Carson said.

"What?"

"Having your own place. Growing grapes." He was thirsty and wanted some of the wine or beer, but he didn't feel like drinking after the sommelier. So he stood up from the cold ground and heard his knees pop. The sommelier tilted his head back and watched Carson. The firelight was in his eyes. The heat fell on them like cheap wool.

"You heading out?"

"Not yet."

It felt weirdly intimate to say that he was not leaving. Something in his stomach squirmed and beat. The sommelier nodded, and Carson's throat felt drier still. He didn't know what else to say so he walked along the side yard and went up the concrete steps into the house. Music played quietly from the living room. There were people standing around the old-fashioned kitchen. It was all seventies chintz and cupboard doors hanging slightly off their hinges. He did not see Roma anywhere. Nor the host. The sink was filled with ice and beers. On the counter, whiskey and gin and vodka. More ice in a metal basin. He considered his options. He could smell the smoke on his clothes. In his hair. The people in the kitchen were murmuring about books, about movies, about things they would do after the election. Someone was going on a trip back to

Portland to see their family for the first time since they had transitioned. Or come out and begun to transition. One of the poets, tall, thin in a soft wool peacoat. Carson had seen her around downtown. Her eyes tracked to him across the room and she smiled, fleetingly. And then she took the elbow of the person she was talking to and maneuvered them down the hall.

"I know what my brother will say," her voice trailed back into the kitchen. Carson scooped some ice into a clear plastic cup and splashed some vodka over it. He pinched a sad, brown lime from a dish on the counter and dropped it into the cup. Through the window, he could see the sommelier putting more wood onto the fire. Squeezing lighter fluid which made the fire rear back and kick high into the air. People on lawn chairs had taken out their phones to take a picture of it. The sommelier stood with a stick high above his head like he had killed something powerful and mighty. He shook the stick and posed and flexed for the pictures the people took, and Carson liked him a little better.

The kitchen door squeaked open, and the host and Roma came into the house. They were laughing, swaying.

"Oh shit, hey," the host said. He pulled Carson into a hug and clapped him on the back between the shoulders. Carson winced, but then felt his chest swell with warmth and goodness. This, he thought, was what it meant to be a part of mankind. He felt woozy on good feeling, but it was, of course, only the insane rush of touching another person in so casual a way for the first time in months and months. As though they were impervious, invincible. As though the world outside that kitchen weren't on fire or riddled with disease and risk. But perhaps it was the case that the world was always burning and haunted with calamity and disaster. Perhaps it was one of America's greater illusions that those who lived in it had ever been safe.

Roma stood by the archway to the kitchen, her hands clasped behind her back, shifting her weight from side to side. She wouldn't meet Carson's gaze. The host released him and patted Carson's cheek with his cold hands.

"I'm glad you could make it buddy." The host turned to look over his shoulder at Roma, and then patted Carson's cheek again. "Thanks for bringing this one."

"Sure. She brought me," he said.

Roma pushed away from the wall and rolled her eyes.

"Stop talking about me like I'm not here."

The host put his arm around her waist and pulled her up close. They smiled at Carson, though the host's smile came first, and then Roma's.

Carson bit the lip of his plastic cup until it flexed in his teeth.

The music in the living room changed from some classic guitar song that Carson could almost place to sad piano which he could not. But the music, though loud, was so full of human feeling that it was hardly fair to call it the same thing as the banal guitar riffs that had given way to it. The piano sounded real. It sounded alive.

"Oh brother, what's that?" the host asked. He went through the archway. Roma squirmed. She was wearing a man's coat, much too big for her, over the cardigan she'd worn when she and Carson had walked over.

"I did tell you it would be cold," he said.

"Shut up."

The music went back to classic rock, and Carson felt something in him deflate at the shift.

"Well, we better get going," the host said.

"It's your house."

"I meant, upstairs," he said with a smirk, and Roma's face darkened.

"Well, have a great time."

"God," Roma said. "I'm not being given away on my wedding night."

"No, bet," Carson said. He tipped his cup to them. "I wish you great happiness."

"This is killing my boner," Roma said.

The host laughed. But then he took Roma's hand and led her back into the hall and up the stairs. Carson watched them go. He wondered about the poet he knew who had gone down the hall earlier, if she and her friend were still talking about the first trip home.

Sometimes it surprised Carson when people talked about going home for the holidays. He hadn't been home for a holiday since he left five or six years ago. Time added up that way. By the time he had left, there was hardly any holiday left worth celebrating. They had nothing but each other and their cold trailers and cars in need of gas or oil or repair, scrap they burned in barrels in the back yard so they could sell it for booze, for cigarettes, for dope. The last Thanksgiving he'd spent with his family, sleeping on his parents' couch, he was twenty-six and kind of hard up. He was thinking about cutting out for North Carolina to give college another try. His grandmother had said she wouldn't be cooking the big meal. They'd have to fend for themselves. And Carson had woken up to find all the ovens cold and empty. The fridges were humming and so white on the inside it seemed no food had ever touched them. He went across the street to his aunt's house and saw that she wasn't cooking either. No one was cooking.

That was the year of the food bank. Of canned beans and meat that had a purple tint to it. He'd drive his grandma's Blazer out to the small church near the Citgo, and he'd walk down the long gravel driveway to the church kitchen, where he had to stand outside and wait for the old ladies to look up his grandma's name on the clipboard. Then he'd carry the three or four boxes of stale crackers and expired bread and luke-warm lunch meat up to the truck and drive home with it. He lived on the snack cakes and cookies. The instant coffee. Moldy tangerines. He had a job doing little odd things for his great-uncle's widow. She paid him in crumpled twenties and tens with rips down the center. Sometimes the money had been taped back together. The money was always warm when she pressed it to his palm.

He had forgotten what it was like to have a family. To have a place to which he could return. When he lived in Madison and dated the writer who was in the graduate program there, her friends sometimes asked him if he had plans for the break. If he was going home. And he always felt bad for reminding them that he wasn't in school. He had no *break*. How could it be that people in graduate school still presumed that every-one had a place to go back to? How could you go to graduate school with certain illusions still intact? How was it that people could be so smart, so educated, and still so stupid?

Carson sipped his cold vodka and watched the people in the yard. The sommelier. He listened to the sounds of footsteps overhead, the scrape of a door being pulled open. The firelight shivered. The ice in his cup clinked and shifted, opening up channels and grooves through which the vodka flowed. He squeezed the thin plastic, felt the ice gur-gle and slide apart. His palm was tilting from painful to numb. The cold was doing its work.

Back in the yard, Carson sat in his chair. The sommelier was still on the ground near the firepit. One of the nonfiction students pulled a chair up to Carson and asked him for a light. Carson was about to say that he didn't have his lighter on him when he remembered that he still had the sommelier's. He snapped it open and lit the end of her cigarette.

"*Danke*," she said.

"Oh, uh, *bitte*."

Her eyes were dark green, catlike, and she surveyed him for a few moments while she took a few experimental puffs off the cigarette to see if the light would hold.

"Which program you in?"

"None," he said.

"I know you from somewhere though. I've seen you."

"That might be true. I work in the deli."

She narrowed her eyes, inspecting the fact of it on its face but then let it ride.

"At the Bread Garden."

"The very one," Carson said.

"I'm in translation."

"That sounds painful."

She laughed and leaned back in her chair. Crossed her legs at the ankles. Her trim dark jeans were cuffed primly back over brown wool socks. She had on half boots, all scuffed worn leather. Her jean jacket had a shearling fringe, mottled white and green.

"What's your name?" she asked.

"Carson."

"Netty."

"What do you translate?"

She sighed and put her chin on her hand. She flicked some ashes free. "Nothing lately. That's the problem."

"Isn't that what writers always say? That they're blocked?"

"I'm afraid the rumors are true."

"What would you translate if you weren't blocked?"

Netty took another drag off the cigarette. She looked out over the yard, the fire in the pit, the sommelier who was stretched out flat on his back. She looked up into the milky purple sky where shards of firelight rose and broke and vanished. She had curly hair tucked under a knit cap, and there was a dark mole on her right cheek. She seemed to be really thinking about what he had asked, and he regretted it because he hadn't meant to ask something about which he knew nothing and could know nothing. But then she looked back at him and smiled like none of it mattered.

"There's this poet I love, she's Algerian. French, but, like, Algerian. Like Camus, you know? YSL? In the seventies, she wrote this series of poems about Margaret of Anjou and Elizabeth Woodville. Which, like, random. But they're these gorgeous little poems about political intrigue and making horrible choices like giving up your son to his murderous uncle or the great hope of your family dying on a battlefield. And betting what you have against what you might get, I don't know. She compares the wars for Algerian independence, that whole colonial mess, to waiting for the war in England to end. It's a sad series of poems. But that's what I'd want to translate."

"Word? Cool." Carson laughed, but his face was hot. Netty scratched the space above her eyebrow. They had both misjudged something, and instead of drawing them closer, their embarrassment dropped down between them like hard wedge. Carson wanted to say something that would dispel the awkwardness. But he couldn't think of anything to say. He couldn't think of anything that would draw them up next to each other, and so the moment dropped painfully into the next and the next until there was a whole straining mass of moments. When he couldn't stand it anymore, he looked away from her to the sommelier, who had rolled onto his stomach and was looking at his phone. Carson would have given anything to draw him over to them.

"So what makes a normal person come to a party full of writers?" Netty asked.

"I came with a friend," Carson said, hoping that his relief didn't show. Whatever was locking up his chest unclenched. He could breathe again. "She's off somewhere."

"Oh yeah?"

"Yeah, I think she has her sights set on the guy who lives in this house."

"Really?" Netty asked. She leaned forward conspiratorially. "She a glutton for punishment?"

"I think she's just young," Carson said.

"He's got a real talent for dishing it out," Netty said.

Carson looked at her closely then. Something in her face, her voice, pricked at him.

"Wait, were you the one who dumped him?"

Netty took a long pull off the cigarette then dropped it to the ground. She let the smoke issue up over their heads.

"That's kind of a childish formulation."

"You're the *girlfriend*."

"Oh, a million years ago. I haven't dated men in, like, two years."

"My bad. I thought you were the one who found him on Grindr."

"No, that was my friend. Corrine."

"Small world."

"She about hit the roof when she found out I used to mess around with him. But I told her I was basically a different person then. We went to undergrad together."

"Oh," Carson said. It was another of those moments in which he felt that he was among people whose whole churning history was beyond his grasp. They were connected to each other by the weird, deep gravity of stars and planets.

"Wait. Is your friend an undergrad?"

"She graduated this summer," Carson said.

"Fuck, no way."

"Yeah. Why?"

"He was fucking one of his students," Netty said. She had taken out her pack of cigarettes again and was flipping the cardboard tab open and shut. The fire snapped brutally. Carson felt a little queasy, but then it wasn't his business. Roma was an adult. She could do what she wanted and with whom. It was none of his concern, and anyway, he had once slept with a professor during one of his not so successful flirtations with a college education. The professor had taught an introductory math class at NC State, the one Carson had to take because he couldn't afford the AP Exam and had been too late in registering for the placement test. He'd been put into the college algebra class. The professor had a tight, mean mouth and wore her hair in a coppery chignon. She came into the tapas bar where Carson worked that year, and he'd give her free drinks and sometimes he'd ask her about her life. That was how he came to know she'd been a dancer and had grown up in Montana. She didn't sound like a Westerner. She had a clipped New Jersey voice that seemed totally out of place in North Carolina. One night, she said that it got dark out where she was, in the country on the edge of town, and Carson said that he knew what that was like. He was on his break, sweating through his shirt, and tired. His wrists ached from carrying trays of drinks, and his lower back throbbed. He said he'd grown up in the country, in that deep, eternal dark that came when the sun went down and all there was were the lights from the porch and through the trees, the lights of his uncles and aunts' trailers. She said it was primordial. And then she put her hand in his shirt pocket and said that if it was all right with him, she'd like to take him home with her. And then a sad little laugh, so pitiful that he thought it would be worse to say no to her. And he went. And then she pulled his shirt up over his head and they fucked in her narrow bed. The next day, in class, she wouldn't meet his eye. And he didn't meet hers. Instead, he looked down at the handouts she sent around the room. The quadratic equation and the parabolas. He knew about them already. He'd gotten an A in AP Calc.

"Happens," Carson said. "People fuck their profs."

"Yeah, but it is ethically—I mean, it's fucked up," Netty said.

Carson hummed. "It seems like that's a pretty silly idea. People have agency."

"What about coercion. Power dynamics."

Carson struck the lighter and held it out. Netty watched the fire for a moment, and then, as if she had only been waiting for the mere suggestion, took out another cigarette and leaned over for Carson to light it.

"People do what they want to do."

Netty closed her eyes and drew on the cigarette until the fire had a good hold. Then she leaned back and exhaled the wide plume of smoke.

"Men always think it's fair when they feel good."

"I can't say I disagree with that. But I do think if someone doesn't feel taken advantage of, you can't make them feel it."

"It's not *making* someone feel something just to tell the truth and show them. You can't know what you don't know."

Carson sighed. It was all getting too theoretical for him.

"She's my friend," he said. "I don't know what happened when or how or where. I don't know about any of that. All I know is that she seems . . ." he was almost about to say that she seemed happy with her choices. That she seemed to have made her peace with her decision. But then he saw her in the kitchen again, in his mind. That irresolute look on her face. That tenuous, aching strangeness in her eyes. It seemed dishonest to say that she was happy. Or that her choice had been made of her own free will. It seemed ridiculous that the two of them could sit at a bonfire in the most prosperous nation the world had ever seen talking over the immortal soul of another person like it was an argument that could be won. The very act of their talking over her agency seemed unfair. It seemed silly. It was a reductive process, he thought. The machining down of the complicated turns and edges of a person's life into a set of values to be parsed. The extraction and presentation of information as a set of finite values that could be manipulated and computed.

"Seems?" Netty prompted, but Carson shook his head.

"Anyway, tell me about this Margaret you're so invested in."

Netty blinked, then, with a slow dawning smile, she said, "Margaret of Anjou was one of the most powerful women in history."

"I believe that," he said.

"There's this one poem in the cycle I want to translate. It's in the voice of Margaret, at the moment she realizes that all is lost. The battlefield is hazy and there's this cold mist and no one can see anything, but she feels, like, in her heart of hearts that her son has been slain. And she's just looking around the field and her veil is heavy, because she's sweating and bloody, and all she sees is ruin. And it's a really beautiful lamentation. About the moment when you realize that you've bet it all and come out empty-handed."

"That sounds awful," Carson said.

"Yeah, but it's this beautiful, desolate feeling. Like, of total clarity." Netty's eyes glowed as she talked, and Carson could feel the thing behind her words. That spongey soft thing that was meaning and truth. "There's so little clarity in the world."

"That much I do know."

"And then the poem kind of comes back to Algeria—the war for independence. *Whose* independence? The particular, messy intractable colonial condition."

"That's a lot of words," Carson said, laughing. "Whole lot of words."

Netty flicked ashes at him. But then, growing serious, she said, "How about this then. And I'll stop talking your ear off about it. Imagine what it's like to feel owned. And then imagine what it feels like to know that your only recourse is to chew through the hand that's got you held down."

"I can imagine."

"Can you?" Netty asked. "Do you know what it's like to be owned? Held down?"

There was heat behind Carson's eyes then. Sometimes the white people to whom he was speaking forgot that he was not white, forgot that he was not like them, and got so deep down into their abstraction of values and their socialist principles that they overlooked the basic fact of it. How else to account for such a stupid question? Carson thought about the farm. His grandfather's fields. The graves. The empty refrigerators. The moldy tangerines. The watermelon. The empty dark. All the things he knew about but had no way of making legible to these people without it turning into one of their empty, silly ideas like *black* or *working class*. Their idiom, because it was an idiom, was devoid of the real substance of what they were trying to draw into relation. All that existed was the facile charm of making connections between things. They were like children playing board games.

187

"Yeah," he said. "I think I've got some idea of the colonial condition."

"No offense, and really, I say this as someone who likes you, even if I don't know you, but, no offense, that's really naive. And I say that as someone with a little bit of privilege myself, but like, colonialism? There is no greater evil in the history of the world, maybe. And, hey, we live in a First World country? Right? Like, maybe we shouldn't presume to know what it's like to be in a colonial relation to a global superpower."

Carson scanned Netty's face for irony or deceit or some impish humor, but found only refulgent, glowing earnestness. Which made the condescension worse, because it was coming from a good place. That perpetual good place he heard so much about in moments like this. He wished he still had his vodka if only to have something to do with his hands.

"Maybe you're right," he said. "I'm sure you know best."

"Hey, what do I know, right? But I think, hey, you didn't have the leader of the free world flying drones into your uncle's weddings and blowing half your family out of existence."

"I don't think it's really a contest though," Carson said. "It's not, like, whose grief boner is bigger."

"That's so disrespectful, that is way disrespectful, man," Netty said. She sat up straight then leaned toward him like she'd changed her mind. "Look, let's not argue."

"I'm not arguing," Carson said. "I'm not arguing at all. I don't even know how we got into this conversation."

"Look, let's just both admit that as, like, American capitalist drones," here she made a little loop with her hand between the two of them, and did a funny voice like they were on Comedy fucking Central, "that we can't know what it was like for certain people held in subordination in a colonial dialectic."

"I don't speak French," Carson said.

"Okay, funny man. You Dave Chapelle all of the sudden? Don't be defensive. I'm just trying to dialogue with you."

"I almost respect you for that joke," Carson said. Netty didn't answer. Both of them looked out toward the fire. The sommelier had gotten to his feet and was walking, swaying, toward them.

The sommelier was heavier than Carson imagined he would be. They were about the same height, but the sommelier was thicker around the middle. Carson supported him as they walked along the sidewalk. The sommelier had his arm around Carson's neck, and every couple of steps, he would belch and say that he'd had a good time.

"Yeah, I can see that," Carson kept saying.

"You know," the sommelier said. "You're all right. You're an okay dude."

"Thanks. Glad you think so."

When they got to Carson's place, the sommelier tripped on the carpeted outdoor steps and almost cracked his head open on the sidewalk. But Carson caught him just before he fell backward and down. Their first kiss was sour from the wine. The sommelier put his hands down Carson's pants without undoing them. His fingers were cold.

They fucked on Carson's small couch. Which took some doing because they were too big to fit on it at the same time. The sommelier couldn't stay hard because of the drinking and also perhaps because he was unused to men. When he tried to give Carson head, his teeth cut painfully and awkwardly. But he moaned a lot and made his mouth exceedingly slick with saliva. It wasn't the worst blow job that Carson had ever received. But it was not satisfying. Still, Carson slid out of the sommelier's mouth and looked down at his flushed face. He looked happy and silly and had a big grin, and it was the grin that made Carson hard. The happy abandon of someone enjoying themselves. He ground their cocks together and managed to get enough friction to get them both off, and then they kissed again. Long, slow, their semen cooling and sticking to both their stomachs. It was almost like affection. Almost like tenderness.

The sommelier wanted to shower, and Carson showed him how the knobs worked. Then he waited in his room. The apartment was cold, drafty. The heat hadn't been turned on yet. Carson nudged on his space heater and listened to the sound of water striking the tile wall in the bathroom.

The election was on Tuesday. The sommelier came out smelling fresh but cold. He was so pale and white that he seemed to glow in the dim room. He got under Carson's blanket, and wrapped himself around Carson for warmth.

Carson was aware of how raw and how much like sex he still smelled. But the sommelier didn't mind. Carson stroked his hair, and the sommelier sighed and said something quiet and low.

It was the middle of the night when Carson woke with the sommelier still on top of him. Carson's eyes felt dry and stiff. He hadn't had any water before bed, and he could feel the grainy edge of a hangover coming on. He peeled the sommelier off him and got out of the bed into the cold dark of the room, a little sore from the bad blowjob the sommelier had given him earlier. At the window, he peeked down on to the sidewalk, which was empty except for the cars nestled up against the curb. The garage below the large apartment building across the street had a gaping mouth that permitted cars in and out of itself. Carson let the blinds fall shut again, and looked back at the sommelier, who was curled into the blanket now.

In the shower, Carson stood under the warm spray until his skin felt alive again. The numbness receded into the prick of the water's heat. He opened his mouth and let some of the chalky shower water in. He swallowed it down and drank more, all of it hot and fizzing as it slid down his throat. It was like the Pét-Nats before, all those bubbles.

Carson watched the sun come up, and the sommelier grunted himself awake. In the morning, Carson made eggs and toast for him. And offered him water, aspirin, coffee. The sommelier took each of these offerings with groggy gratitude, a flannel blanket wrapped around his naked body. It was Sunday, and Carson didn't have a place to be yet. He thought about calling Roma to see how she was, but decided against it. The sommelier chewed the toast slowly and with great effort. It was endearing. He had ash-blond hair under his arms and around his cock.

It was often the case that Carson didn't know what to say to the people he woke up with. The morning was different from the night. The whole condition and context of your relationship changed when you woke up and were yourself again and not the version of yourself you were the night before. It was embarrassing having to face other people with the vulnerable, anxious self that had to eat and shit and piss and drink coffee and water. He didn't remember what he and the sommelier had talked about the night before, not that they'd done much talking. But he had slept with the sommelier pressed to his chest and he felt a real need to look after him. Was this a part of the colonial condition? Could the colonial condition be expressed as the relation between two hungover people who had fucked the night before? Or did the possibility of such a formulation, as blasphemous as it was, preclude its expression? As in, was it so offensive a thought that the very thought of it had to come undone before it could be thought? Was the colonial condition not only an expression of a relationship of power, of subject and master, but also a series of thoughts that could not be thought? Or thoughts that were not your own but were inherited by you from whatever overcultural

190

imagination had conceived of you in the first place? Was the colonial condition an act of suicide? Could he trust his own impulse to look after the sommelier? Would it have been better to kill him, perhaps? Would it have been better to bash his head open and rob him and throw him out the door? What was the solution to the colonial condition if not violence? If not a rebuke? Was he living in a colonial dialectic as the subjected? As the subordinate? Carson watched the sommelier drink the coffee into which too much milk had been poured. He watched the sommelier breathe and shift the blanket against his shoulders.

Was sex an extension of the colonial argument? Or was the colonial condition just the name you gave the discomfort of the morning after. Or the name you gave your need. Your want. Maybe he was heretical for having the thought. Or maybe it explained his life. Maybe it explained him. Maybe his discomfort with himself was simply the colonial condition. Or maybe that's what white people called it when they felt guilty about something. Maybe every human life was a colony. And everyone you knew was a colonizer. And you took and you took and you took from others and tried to hoard it but were taken from again and again. All of life just one long balance sheet of things taken and things lost.

The sommelier asked if he could play some music. It was almost noon by then, so Carson didn't see a problem. He took the sommelier's phone and connected it to the Bluetooth, and handed it back. The sommelier asked for the WiFi code, and Carson, face going warm with embarrassment told him that it was *littledog*.

"It's the one it came with," he said. But the sommelier just nodded and laughed.

Carson waited to hear what music the sommelier would pick. His eyes squinted, his phone quite close to the end of his nose, the sommelier browsed and nudged and stroked the screen, and then, seeming to light on what he was looking for, he said, "Here we go."

The sommelier flicked ashes into the tray on the kitchen table and then took a long pull. Then waited. They both did, for the music to come on.

Nominated by The Yale Review, Jung Hae Chae, Elizabeth McKenzie, Andrew Porter, Ben Stroud

LOVE & THE MEMORY OF IT

by JAY HOPLER

from THE FLORIDA REVIEW

spook not at the shook world w/ all its viruses & murder hornets
instead that summer evening call to mind when you drove alone
    over iowa
the light in the fields how long it was how in love you were w/ it
& the air & the world & that girl that atomic girl you would one
    day marry
or call to mind a summer evening half a life from then & the park
    by the river the way her laughter
echoed off the rocks
in sparks that sighed
into the water

it was she that lit the world just then
& not that ember of a sun
her light like a struck string fretting its zing against the pic-
nic tables

may that be the music you hear
when they unplug the ventilator

Nominated by Michael Waters, The Florida Review

A BRIEF HISTORY OF THE WAR

by KATHRYN BRATT-PFOTENHAUER

from BELOIT POETRY JOURNAL

The war is a always going badly. Catherynne M. Valente

The war came. Like the other girls, I made myself pretty for the war. I painted snakes and birds on my hands in the style of the war, I cut a black line across my eyes and called that warpaint. I walked the dog on the war's red whip. I pledged allegiance to the war. I proudly parrotted the war's slogans at pep rallies and assemblies. My parents were agents of the war and the war gave them purpose. My brother became one of the war's diplomats, so I learned the mathematics of war and the politics of war and that my politics didn't matter; only the war mattered, the ration cards eaten for fuel when the war took the food. The war had a beating heart, and it played a tambourine, *this, our amazing country, we fight for you.* The war kept time to the footfalls of soldiers. The war took their boots and their toes as trophies, and then took their coats, turned them to tatters. Ours is an old war. It has a beard and calls itself Uncle. It beckons, and we sit on its lap, ready to spill.

Nominated by Beloit Poetry Journal

BACK

fiction by BANZELMAN GURET

from NEW ORLEANS REVIEW

My dad couldn't reach the middle of his back. He waxed every part of his stocky, thick body–and then I hopped in at the end to get the patch between his shoulder blades. It became part of our Sunday afternoon routine.

In the morning, I was trying, yet again, to make some of my own money through the You're In Control app, and when I came home for a break, my dad was waiting for me–puffy and pink.

I spread on the wax as he leaned onto a clean, white towel that I'd draped over the sink. With every rip, his skin reddened, and his shoulders jerked, but his eyes, bloodshot and teary, stared down at the tile, waiting for it to be over, so he could get into bed and bleed onto fresh sheets.

My dad's fear was smelling bad, and he thought that hair trapped bacteria and body odor. He had deodorant rashes under each armpit that made the waxing especially painful.

He said, "They're talking about me up and down this street. They're saying 'He stinks. How can anyone live next to him?'"

I picked up all his scattered deodorant sticks and put them on the counter next to the microwave. He was lying in his tighty-whiteys on bedsheets that he boiled every morning and dried every afternoon.

He got a little weepy, which never would've happened when I was a kid–or even a year ago. Growing up, if he'd had any problems, I never knew about them. He was always steady continuity–never a shout or a loss of composure.

"Not a single person is talking about you," I said. "We're not moving."

"We *have* to move," he said, turning onto his side and shoving his palms together under his cheek. With his knees pulled up, he looked like a shiny toddler. The bed sheets were speckled red where his back had touched them.

At twenty-three, I felt too young for this, and patting his shoulder or rubbing his back was not a possibility. Everything between us had always been formal. As weird as the waxing had been at first, at least it fell under the umbrella of helping with chores.

Eight months before, my dad had been working at ShrenShrenAmerica, a company that specialized in manufacturing indicators for military aircraft.

Apparently, someone complained to HR that he smelled. The person said it was impossible to work near him. His buddies told him it was just made-up, and it was part of the Executives' scheme to get mid-level managers to quit through Passive Humiliation in order to move the company toward full automation.

I never thought of my dad as someone who might break.

He was serious and quiet and solitary and logical.

When I was 11, I wanted to make the basketball team, so he welded a huge metal funnel that caught the ball after it went in and looped it back toward me. I was thrilled and thankful. I never wondered why he didn't just come out and play with me. That wasn't our relationship.

And I imagined that this was how he operated at work too.

At first, he didn't say a word about the complaint. He just started painting himself with deodorant and progressed to waxing his body, and I hoped that whatever this was would resolve itself.

Eventually, one of his old work-buddies called me—which was how I learned about the complaint. This work-buddy was crying, and I kind of had to pull the whole story out of him.

"He won't talk about it," he said about my dad, "but you should know." He sounded relieved. He'd done his part by calling me, and it made me feel like a grown man—being on the receiving end of a very man-to-man phone call.

For the past few months, I'd been doing short, QuickJobs through the You'reInControl app. It was not steady or reliable, but chasing these jobs kept me out of the house.

I liked to park near HobbyGrammies while I waited for a QuickJob to be posted. The location was perfect–surrounded by lots of other businesses in a big strip mall surrounded by other strip malls in concentric circles of strip malls.

Even though my dad was struggling, I felt ready to start worrying exclusively about myself–or at least that was the dream.

The parking area where I was this morning was all taken up, so I had to find a spot in a different lot. And before I could dive into a daydream, I got a notification that FixYup Urgent Care needed someone to combine all the little bits of flu vaccine leftover in the tips of used syringes in order to "Pass Along Thicc-Ass Savings To Customers."

FixYup Urgent Care was almost exactly where I had been parked earlier. It was maybe 300 feet away, and I decided it would be faster for me to run there, than pull out and navigate the traffic. I could actually see the tablet on wheels at the front of the store, waiting for the first phone to ping within 25 feet.

If I hadn't gone home to wax my dad, I would've already secured the QuickJob.

A woman in a business suit was huffing it from the other side of the parking lot. She was farther away, and it seemed like maybe she was coming from either Cheap Ain't Broke or Clean Rick's Dance Academy. Her movements weren't fluid, and her feet seemed to pick up too early with every stride–like when a dog wears shoes. Also, she was carrying a hemorrhoid doughnut.

But she was competition nonetheless, so I pushed hard off of my feet. To my right, I could see a very old man on an ancient Segway, and he was gunning it for FixYup too. The sound of his Segway engine kept whining high and then lowering, like it was struggling to go as fast as he wanted it to. But still, he was zipping along–eleven, maybe twelve, miles per hour. The woman in the business suit just about gave up when she saw me and the older man. But she didn't stop. She was still moving her body forward in the walk-shuffle of someone who's crossing the street while cars waited.

I was ahead of the older man on the Segway who was holding his arms forward like a diver, reducing drag.

The woman sat down on her hemorrhoid doughnut and shouted the c-word loudly at no one.

I was going to get there before him. I could tell. With each leg-kick forward, the best-case scenario started to form in my mind. Ideally, this job at FixYup would become long-term and steady–as unlikely as that was. I'd have to be there day after day for months or years. I'd move out of my dad's house. Get an apartment. Buy groceries. Fall in love. Get married. Have children. Eventually retire to Cape Cod. And also, unrelatedly, my dad would get back to his old self and not need me anymore.

I only had a few dozen more feet to go before this was all possible.

A car screeched to a stop in front of me, and a kid jumped out of the passenger seat.

"I'm here, Sir," he said to the tablet, and he tapped "Accept That You'reIn Control" on his phone.

In the driver's seat of his car, an older woman with rosacea cheeks banged her hands on the steering wheel and said, "Fuck Yeah, Doug!"

She clapped back at me.

"How. You. Like. That. Bitch?"

She started filming herself and Doug–who now had a Quick Job–which, by definition, was no longer than two hours of work–with her phone. She narrated/explained how "Her son Dougie earned himself a new position with a prominent company." Then she pointed the camera at me and the old man and the woman on her hemorrhoid doughnut across the parking lot–and made crying/whimpering sounds to mock us.

The old man on the Segway sucked on an inhaler, and then bit into a beautiful-looking tomato that he'd dug out of his pocket.

I left the HobbyGrammies parking lot. I'd been away a long time, and I needed to check on my dad. I passed by a small gray building that I'd always assumed was abandoned. But today, there was a man in the parking lot.

He was tapping on his phone. And the you'reInControl app buzzed.

I did a quick pullover.

The man said, "Do you QuickJob?"

"Yes," I said. It was so simple. The man tapped on his phone, and the job was canceled. I guessed he didn't want to have to pay the You'reInControl FoundOne Fee–which was kind of a grimy thing to do. But sometimes it's important to look at red flags as just regular flags.

He held out his hand for me. "Stu Deja-Stu," he said, and it took me a second to realize this was his name. "Can you go like this all day?" And he did some of the moves to The Macarena.

"I can," I said–which was true, and also what I would've said if he'd asked me if I could do backflips all day while juggling floppy, mixed-size dildos.

Inside, was just one massive room with machinery everywhere. Conveyor belts, steel and plastic, metal ARMs.

Stu Deja-Stu said, "It's in back. C'mon. I really don't want to be here." He was ducking and jumping and stepping over. There were no walking paths. This place wasn't designed for people.

When we got to the back corner, there were a dozen old-model Industrial Roombas trying to clean around the body of a dead man with a mutilated head.

Stu Deja-Stu explained, almost in one breath when he saw my face, that he was not a murderer. He hadn't set foot in this building in almost eight years. Computers in hospitals placed the orders. The factory fulfilled them. Humans didn't need to think or do anything.

Stu Deja-Stu said, "Listen. I was as surprised as you. I didn't even know I had an employee. I got an alert on my phone that production stopped for a Non-Maintenance Issue." He showed me the suicide note that said, *I think I've had enough.* "Normally, I'd just buy another machine to replace whatever job this guy was doing," he said pointing to the body, "but I'm selling the medical division of my company on the fourteenth. Why would I invest money now?"

The fourteenth wasn't for four whole days. This QuickJob would be my longest one ever.

"What's the job?" I said, still looking at the body.

"I couldn't care less," Stu said. "Actually, the job is—make sure I never get an alert on my phone." He seemed pretty proud of this line. "Just figure it out." And while he was saying all of this, he was back-pedaling out. He gave a big thumbs-up and seemed to hope that I wouldn't say another word. "Figure it out."

And then it was just me standing alone in a factory that was being sterilized without any Roombas big enough to scrub away a dead body.

I called the police and they transferred me to the coroner's office where an automated voice said, "The current wait time for body removal is four hours and thirty-three minutes."

I searched around. In the lofted office above the factory floor, there was a small tablet in the middle of a room that had probably once been filled with dozens of cubicles. Next to the tablet in the empty room, was a Post-It Note that said, *Password is Password$#8.*

I swiped open the tablet and typed it in. I scrolled and clicked, but I couldn't find anything about employees. There were thousands of pages with millions of options.

So, I ran downstairs, and I took the dead man's wallet out of his pocket to look for his name. And it felt terribly, terribly wrong.

His license said, "Jose Dylan Breadmaker."

Back at the tablet, I did a system-wide search of "Breadmaker."

It was under Purchasing. For each unit, thirteen cents were sent to Jose Dylan Breadmaker, SSN 045-05-52JX, Bank routing number and account 109009001-0990889675646. There was nothing listed about him being an employee. He was just another automated purchase built into the price of the product—which I still had no idea about. Just like how 48 cents for each unit were apparently sent to Stenter Medical Plastics and $1.10 to Cardboardz 'n' Thingz.

I deleted Jose's information, and I added my own. Thirteen cents per unit was pretty good money, or not. I had no idea. I didn't know what the factory made or when the machinery would begin. The Roombas seemed to still be going at it pretty hard, but they'd finish at some point. And then what? I looked to the machinery closest to Jose. There was just a conveyor belt positioned next to another conveyer belt.

I couldn't be positive until the production line started, but it seemed like the job was to move whatever came down the conveyor from one belt to the other.

There was a small piece of flat plastic with a handle next to Jose's body—like a square spatula. I practiced doing the Macarena while holding it. It felt really nice to be focused on something new.

And then a little before eight o'clock, the equipment must have been completely sterilized to the satisfaction of the Roombas, because one end of the factory started moving and screaming. Metal spun and turned. ARMs started grabbing. Belts chirped. Drums were opened and poured.

And I got ready. I didn't know how quickly products were going to start spitting out. It was the same feeling as being at the batting cages as a kid. The light was green. The thing was spinning. A ball would come. It was just a matter of exactly when. I always missed the first one.

I concentrated hard and held the tool that a dead man held. It should've meant something, but mostly I just wanted Jose to be gone. In an ideal world, he'd stand up, dust off, pop two aspirin for his mutilated head, and skip out forever.

I stood there for 39 minutes before something eventually came down the conveyor belt. That's how long it took from when the machinery started to when the first thing popped out at me. They were clear, circular blobs–like balloons filled with water–and it seemed like they were breast implants. They shot out at the rate of one every eleven seconds. That was almost 5.5 every minute. 327 per hour. And at thirteen cents each, it was over forty dollars per hour.

It wasn't fun, but it had a rhythmic monotony that allowed me to think about whatever I wanted. I fantasized, and an image kept popping into my brain–me turning on a naked light bulb, late at night, in my own noiseless kitchen and drinking a glass of water underneath the dim bulb.

The noise of the door opening snapped me out of it. I felt my stomach go into my throat–the feeling of having something to lose.

It was, of course, the coroner–who was actually six drones–each attached with a strap to another six drones, making six pairs. The straps were maneuvered under Jose. I had to focus on the breast implants, but I felt like I ought to say something to Jose's body as it left, so I said, "Sorry."

The twelve zipping drones all said in unison, "Our pleasure!" They carried him, pall bearer style, outside, up in the air, higher and higher. And another breast implant came down the line.

The Roombas could finally get under where Jose was. And they sprayed and scrubbed and burned the spot where a body had been–but wasn't anymore.

I took out my phone to let my dad know what was going on. I typed out the message with my left hand which took a while. And it was like texting while driving. Get a few letters down, and then eyes back on the road.

I wrote, "I have a job. Don't know when I'll be home." He texted back, *Okie Dokie. Love, Dad* which was what he always wrote. Under all of that hand sanitizer, he was still my dad.

Around six in the morning, the breast implants stopped coming down the line. I ran over to the end of the production line and read the boxes that they were shipped in. Apparently they were gel pillows to prevent Flat-head in premature babies. I felt pretty embarrassed about all of the squeezing and imagining I'd done before I found out.

I wandered around, knowing that whenever another order was placed, it would start up again, and I'd have 39 minutes to get back to my spot. I was too fired up to sleep. On one of the upstairs doors, there was a little nameplate that said, "Thomas Breadmaker, President," and the reason why Jose had a seemingly unnecessary job all this time made a little bit more sense. The former President of the company must have built a tiny human job into the operation for Jose–who I guessed was his son.

One door was labeled "Lactation Room" and when I opened it, it was a full studio apartment with a kitchenette and a twin bed. There was a small loveseat facing a flatscreen.

It was almost disturbingly modern. It wasn't the hodgepodge mixture of garbage-stuff that should populate the room of a lonesome/suicidal squatter. It was all silver and gray. Clear corners and clean metal. And the sterility of the room made it really easy to take over. This wasn't a man's unique room, loaded with personal touches. It was low-fat, vanilla yogurt.

It was everything I wanted.

I knew that I should go home and check on my dad, but I couldn't leave. What if the machinery started up again?

I'd have to wait until tomorrow to do something to help him. I'd call a doctor tomorrow about his paranoia. I couldn't possibly today. Tomorrow.

But there was also the chance that tomorrow he'd be normal again. Or the day after that.

It was like: hypothetically, if your mom claimed to be a messenger of God who believed she'd be shot dead in two days protecting your cousin's newborn baby–who your mom believed was the second coming of Christ–it would, of course, be crazy. But if it was the twentieth time she'd said it, it would just be Mom being Mom. And it was easier to say, "Yeah/Yeah/Yeah, but what kind of bagel do you want?"

So I felt okay ignoring his problems for another day, and at this factory, I was in love with how easy it was to forget about them.

A baby monitor hooked up to the factory downstairs woke me up with a noise that sounded like an eagle screech.

My dad was in the shower. The water was freezing, and he was shivering. He wasn't sure how long he'd been in there. He looked relieved that someone was there to make a decision about him. When I was younger, if I had ever opened the bathroom and told him to get out, he would have glared at me until I backed out of the room.

I only had 26 minutes to get back to the factory, now that I'd figured out I could leave in 39-minute bursts and make it back in time–even if it started up the second I left. I didn't trust Jose's baby monitor yet. But it was clear that I couldn't just head right back to the factory like I planned. If I hadn't come home, how long would it have been until he slipped/collapsed/froze?

I helped him step out, and I dried him off. I turned on the hair dryer and blow-dried him. His fingers trembled as he worked at the plastic on a new package of underwear.

He started his post-shower routine—putting his new stick of deodorant on, taking a shirt out of the freezer, spreading hand sanitizer up to his elbows. And I finally felt like enough was enough. I hadn't realized I was waiting for this feeling, but it was here.

I went into his dresser and tore into the plastic shrink-wrapped bag that held a new pair of pants. He'd ordered them months ago and had been saving them, clean and ready. He wasn't sure why.

He watched me cut off the tags.

At the hospital, the A.I. screeners/intake computers weren't especially worried about his exposure to the cold water.

"No major effects," the computer said in an artificial staccato voice that was both robotic and somehow British. "What is more concerning is his pattern of abnormal behavior."

It felt good to be talking about it—even if it was with an intake computer. And for the doctor program to not be looking at me like all of this was insane. When I told the program all of his tics and habits, it just showed the face of a handsome doctor nodding, taking notes, and asking me, "What else?" and "For how long?" I knew the answers to all of the questions.

He was transferred to a psychiatric facility called WhyAren'tYouSmiling.

Inside the new facility, a kid walked by with a row of stitches across his throat, and it was clear to me why I needed to bring pajama pants without a drawstring and slippers without laces.

An older man tapped me on the shoulder and said, "Let's see your hot dog, Young Daniel."

The nurses were all soft, dimple-knuckled gals, and the doctor on duty wouldn't look up from her tablet.

"I guess everyone knows now," my dad said. It wasn't visiting hours, which were from six to nine, so all I could do was drop off his stuff.

The next day, I got to WhyAren'tYouSmiling right at six. I had Jose's baby monitor, and I was within its range.

My dad's eyes glistened, and he looked next to him, making sure there was a free chair.

He told me about the exercises he had to do. He talked about the group therapy he didn't feel was useful, but the other people–the ones he said were actually crazy–seemed to enjoy it.

He kept smiling at me with new, unbreaking eye contact. After just the one day, he seemed happier and no longer obsessed with his hygiene.

The staff loved how open and chatty he was. And with the doctor and nurses rewarding his "emotional honesty," I wasn't sure if the version of him I'd grown up with would ever come back.

At one point, he started to get a little weepy. He wasn't blubbering and wailing, but there was a wet shine in his eyes.

He said, "What are you hopeful for?"

"What am I hopeful for?" I repeated back.

"They've been asking me that all day here. The doctor says that even if it's a dessert I want after dinner, it's important to be looking forward to something." His eyes were earnest and pleading.

"I'm hopeful for a lot of things, I guess."

I hated how many times I checked my phone for the time–to see when I *had* to leave, when visiting hours were over. When I'd have no choice but to leave. When it wouldn't be my fault for leaving.

On my way out, one of the nurses needed me to fill out some paper-work.

"Is it okay that I visit like this?" I said.

"Of course," she said. "Everyone loves having visitors."

"No," I said. "I mean is it beneficial to his treatment? Should I not come by as often or stay as long? I just don't want to interfere."

"It's fine," she said. "Stay as long as you'd like."

Stu Deja-Stu had said that the buyer was coming in four days to change ownership, and that was tomorrow. If the new owner knew he had a human employee, he would replace me with an ARM and lock the doors.

At HobbyGrammies, I bought everything I thought I might need–cardboard, spray paint, tape, wires, plastic, glue, tubes, and sheet metal. The bags and boxes barely fit in my dad's car. I kept the baby monitor on me at all times when I was away from the factory, but I still tried to only leave in 39-minute windows.

And I worked on an ARM disguise every spare minute.

When I thought about what my dad might be up to, I told myself that this job mattered more than any immediate problem with his recovery. That securing this job, long-term, would be exactly what my dad wanted–back when he was thinking more logically.

I started to think that maybe leaving the factory for long stretches was wrong. The baby monitor alerted me without fail, but I decided I couldn't trust it.

This was the only reason I wouldn't be able to go to WhyAren'tYouSmiling often or for long. I texted my dad that I wouldn't be able to visit. He texted back, *Okie Dokie. Love, Dad* with a crying emoji. And I could live with that.

I was at my spot on the line. I kept my ARM costume just to the side of my work station, and as soon as I heard the front door open, I slipped into it and hopped back over to my spot. All of the other ARMs were thin and sleek. My costume had to fit me inside, so the base was wider and the whole thing moved with less flexibility. But I did a pretty good impression of the ARM movements, I thought. Sure I looked stupid and obvious–but only if you were looking right at me, and the new owner wouldn't be–if he was anything like Stu Deja-Stu.

The man went almost immediately upstairs-like he already knew where the tablet was. I made sure to lock my apartment door, which was still labeled "Lactation Room."

This had been my home for four days, and my bed smelled like me now and not Jose. I had food in a small refrigerator. I had picked out a place for shoes.

It would have been easier to pull off this ownership transfer if production wasn't running. All I'd have to do was hide. The new owner would never notice that a particular section of this giant floor was missing one single ARM. But right now, my only chance was for him to rush out and not care about what the rest of his factory looked like.

The upstairs door opened and he came down. He gave the floor a tight-lip nod. It was the same look everyone gave the Grand Canyon once they've stood there long enough.

The owner took a first step toward the exit, and then he stopped. He looked up and around. He scanned the floor and then walked over to the very end of the production line. He pressed his fingers into one of the pillows as it zoomed by. Then he did the same to another one. He gave a third one a full-hand squeeze.

"It's like boobs," he said.

I tried to be precise and constant in my movements, but I felt stilted and jerky.

The owner had to walk behind me to get to the exit, and after he finished his poking, it was clear that he was heading that way. He shrugged

204

and even took his sunglasses out of his shirt pocket. He owned the business, and there was no reason for him to be here ever again. But something must have caught his eye, because I could sense him right behind me, way too close.

He said, in a sing-song voice, "Hey guys, It's Tanner. I'm here at my new MoneyMaker I just bought with some of the inheritance my dad left me after my step-mom murdered him. And look what we have here."

I could feel my saliva get thin. I tried to think if it was possible he was talking about someone else.

"Some little cutie," Tanner said, and he was pantomiming something directly behind me. I couldn't know exactly what–but it had to be pinching or pretend-humping. It was just a feeling/instinct. "Yeah, yeah, yeah," Tanner said. "Uhh, uhh, uhh."

And I kept flipping pillows.

"All right Dick-Licks," Tanner said. "Like my Exclamation Post if I should let him do whatever he's doing, and Dislike it if I should call the Cops on him. Results in sixty! Go!"

And then it was quiet except for the constant machinery noises, and I kept flipping the pillows in my ARM costume, one after another, and I waited to find out my results.

Nominated by New Orleans Review

TIKKUN OLAM TED

by NICOLE GRAEV LIPSON

from RIVER TEETH

I'm sitting with my son on the floor of his first-grade Hebrew school classroom, both of us drawing, according to his teacher's instruction, what we'd like to do to repair the world. My four-year-old daughter, tagging along for the morning, is also drawing, and though she's young for this assignment, she gets the basic idea. She scribbles blotches of flowers on her paper while I add a woman—me?—beside a compost bin, depositing food scraps. I'm feeling pretty good about myself for being down here on the rug, in the thick of things, while most parents sit in a semicircle of chairs, watching from afar. *I am a very engaged mother,* I think. *I am modeling enthusiasm for my children!*

It's been a trying weekend, with my husband out of town, just me and the three kids alone—a weekend of back-seat feuds and bedtime brawls, cereal bowls upended and dishes piling up in the sink. I've been vexed by an irritability I don't feel entitled to, that fills me with shame each time I think of the millions of single mothers who do this day in and day out, while three days alone have chafed my patience. But I've made it to Sunday morning. Sun streams through the classroom window and the air smells of cherry-scented markers, and before me stretch three hours that I don't need to plan, in a building—our synagogue—that feels like a second home.

My son's marker scritch-scratches away. He bites the soft flesh of his lower lip and shields his work with his arm, and I keep a respectful distance, knowing how he loves to craft surprises. After a while, he snaps on his marker cap and holds up his work. I see that it's not a picture after all, but a row of words wobbling across the page. My son, who as

206

a toddler had a speech delay, has been struggling at school to write words beyond his name, and I feel a surge of pride in this effort—a surge that lasts just long enough for me to discern what he has written. Could it be? No. But oh my god, yes. *I LUV MI PENES.*

This message, surprising under any circumstance, clashes so profoundly with the spirit of this morning's event that I can hardly register it. We are here for an annual tradition at my children's Hebrew school, Tikkun Olam Day. The phrase *tikkun olam* means "repairing the world" and captures an idea at the heart of Judaism—that the universe is innately good but imperfect, and that our task as human beings is to help restore it to wholeness. *Tikkun olam* is often associated with social activism, but as Rabbi Zecher—who made history at our temple by becoming its first female senior rabbi three years ago—has reminded the students during today's opening assembly, our world teems with small opportunities for repair work. Conserving water is *tikkun olam.* Giving to charity is *tikkun olam.* Opening the door for someone, expressing thanks, welcoming guests into one's home—these, too, are *tikkun olam.* I've long admired Rabbi Zecher, who is not only extraordinarily wise and learned but also beautiful, her face warmly luminous beneath a halo of silver-white hair. And while this introductory talk was meant for the children, it moved me, as her words so often move me, to remember all the ways that I can do better.

Later in the morning, my son's class will be preparing trays of lasagna for Rosie's Place, a local shelter for homeless women. Their teacher Morah Iryna, who has crinkly eyes and a pixie haircut, has just finished reading them *Tikkun Olam Ted,* a picture book about a boy who loves improving the world. "Ted is small, but he spends his days doing very big things," this story begins. On Sundays, Ted scrubs bottles for recycling. On Wednesdays, he walks dogs at the animal shelter. On Thursdays, he waters the garden. Ted has a sweet round face and pink circles on his cheeks. On Shabbat, the Jewish sabbath, he rests and dreams of *tikkun olam.* This book's illustrations are so cheerful, bright and simple, and I'd found myself strangely carried along by them, imagining all the small ways our family could start helping our earth, and our neighbors, right away.

As the children—but not my son—continue drawing, Morah Iryna tiptoes around the room in her leggings and fuzzy sweater, murmuring encouragement. Around me, sheets of construction paper fill with bright yellow suns, smiling stick figures, trees and kittens and doggies—a stark contrast to what my son is holding up before me. He grins at me, his eyes gleaming. Whatever he hopes to see on my face is not there. Who knows what *is* there, what arrangement of features could possibly represent the horrible rainbow of feelings arcing through me: shock, bewilderment, a full-body disappointment that won't stop growing. *Where* did he learn to write this? *What* does he mean by it? And *why* has he chosen this moment to share it, exposing flagrantly and publicly my maternal failings? For these are what this paper seems to announce most spectacularly at this moment, in this room, where I've come expressly as an adult emissary of my family's goodness.

On Monday, Ted makes inappropriate jokes. On Tuesday, he mocks the endeavors of well-meaning people.

Fumbling, I pull my son's paper from his hands and slip it into my bag. Did any of the other parents see? I scan the room. It appears not, but this brings little relief. It turns out it isn't fear of outside judgment that has seized me, but my own self-judgment, more caustic and piercing than another person's eyes could ever be. I know there are child-development experts who believe in the power of nature over nurture, who would tell me my son is his own person, and that I'm no more responsible for his lapses than I am for his triumphs. But I've yet to meet a parent who can untangle their children from themselves this cleanly. In real time, on this real Sunday, my logic works more like this: because I am a mother, I am the moral epicenter of my family's universe; my son's fissures must therefore ripple out from some primal fracture in me.

I glare at my son in a way that's meant to sink deep. My jaw is a hard dam, stanching what threatens to pour out. *We'll talk about this later,* I hiss. Later. In private. Far away from this cramped amphitheater of good men and women and their very good children, ready to do their part to better the earth. A few feet away, a girl in a silver headband sketches herself raking leaves. Beautiful, big-hearted, orange leaves that burst across the page like rising flames.

It's not too late, I think, to put this behind us. My son is only six—probably I'm taking this too seriously. Probably this is something he picked up from a first-grade classmate, one with several sweaty older brothers and no limits, whom he's now imitating. I pass him a fresh piece of paper and a handful of markers. His eyes narrow and his shoulders curl in on themselves like the edges of a Shrinky Dink. But he grabs the paper from my hand, sullenly compliant, and then turns his hunched back to me and gets to work.

On my other side, my daughter has drawn purple dashes above her garden. "What are those?" I ask hopefully, and she tells me they're a bird

208

family. While the birds soar, thoughts descend on me like flies. I think about how we can never fully know our children's minds. I think about Freud and try to remember what I can about the phallic stage. But mostly, I think about how mothering my son so often feels like trying to steer a bike with a wobbly wheel: no matter how determined I am to aim the handlebars, we go crashing together off the curb, again and again.

He is finished with his new drawing. I ask to see it, but he demurs, covering it with the floppy arms of his sweatshirt, and I keep a respectful, and wary, distance. Soon, the activity is wrapping up and the room begins to bustle. One of my son's friends comes over, and they start talking and giggling, and then they've turned their markers into knights' swords. The paper slips free from under my son's elbow.

There's a sea of white and two bobbing words at the center.

FEK MOMMY, they say.

When I recount this incident to friends later, I turn it into a funny story. *"There we were, in the middle of repairing-the-world day, of all things, and he's dropping F-bombs on me!"* I get laughs every time. With three kids and ten years of experience as a mother, I'm practiced at the parental art of turning suffering to comedy. There's the time my younger daughter had the flu and threw up all over me on the prescription pickup line at CVS—ha ha! And the time when, dizzy from lack of sleep, I took my colicky firstborn daughter out in the stroller, and it flipped over when the wheel hit a crack in the sidewalk. *There she was, hanging upside down like a cured ham*—he he! "Humor is just another defense against the universe," the comedian Mel Brooks once said. When it comes to parenting, it's felt like the most powerful defense I have against the orbit of crisis and rapture that is raising children.

Crisis, rapture, and heartache—the unspoken torments beneath parenthood's laugh track. On the floor of my son's Hebrew school classroom, my insides crumple in a way that isn't funny at all. They crumple deep in my center, in the vast, quiet place where my son spun into being, where his heart first quivered to life and his somersaults sent ripples across the flesh of my stomach so that I no longer knew where he ended and I began. I crumple because he's spun out into the world, turning and turning and turning—and because I can't seem to stop him from turning on me.

I love my son as I love all my children—which is to say, staggeringly, with an intensity that sometimes takes my breath away. When he emerged from my body and revealed that he was a boy, I was elated.

We had our daughter, and while I would, of course, have welcomed another healthy baby girl with joy and gratitude, I secretly thanked the universe for giving us this opportunity to parent a boy as well. I felt thankful in a very particular way for my husband, who lost his own father when he was seven, and who now had the chance to honor his dad's memory in perhaps the most cellular way possible—by being for his growing son all that his father had been for him. And I felt thankful that I could now experience what was by all accounts—or at least the accounts of my friends with male children—the uniquely tender bond that develops between a woman and her son. "There's just *something* between a boy and his mama," I remembered my friend Rachel saying. Here was my chance to learn what this something was.

But almost from the get-go, there's been nothing easeful or simple about the interplay between my son and me. I ought not—I know, I know—to compare my children, but the fact is there's an inevitable controlled experiment dynamic to parenting multiple kids, each one moving through the same stages of growth in more or less the same petri dish, announcing their differences whether we want them to or not. As infants, both of my daughters nursed calmly like painted cherubs, their tiny bodies nestled in the crook of my arm. Breastfeeding my son was more like a wrestling match, with him suddenly writhing and wailing at my breast until I lifted him away, and then writhing and wailing more furiously until I pulled him close again. Back and forth we'd go, his face growing redder, each round leaving me sweatier and more despairing than the last. Often, my husband would swoop in to relieve me, gathering up our son and bouncing away with him to another room, shushing and shushing. It wasn't that my husband could always subdue him—but he could, somehow, weather his cries in a way that didn't feel to him intensely personal.

As he's grown from baby to toddler to little boy, my son and I have continued to wrestle. My daughters, of course, have their moments of upset, of supermarket-aisle meltdowns and late-day tantrums and pre-adolescent stomps across the kitchen floor. But with them, I can usually find some way to help restore equilibrium, whether through hugs or soothing words, distraction or minor bribery. Whatever comfort or perspective I offer as a mother, my daughters have received it, absorbed it, unfolded and burgeoned in response to it, whereas my son seems slightly suspicious of it. The tools in my maternal storehouse so often bounce right off him, leaving me powerless to mother him. I'm reminded of the time a Lego helicopter he made fell and broke, and he collapsed on the floor in a seething heap. I knew enough not to downplay this mishap, which would make him feel belittled; or to assure him we could rebuild the helicopter, which would enrage him. So, on a whim, I kneeled down and shared with him something I often do when seized by strong emotions, which is to take three slow, deep breaths. "Do you want to try this with me?" I asked.

He covered his ears with his hands. "Stop talking to me about that yoga stuff!" he yelled.

Later that evening, as my husband and I cleaned up from dinner, I told him about this story. "It's like he's impervious to strategy," I said. My husband listened, scrubbing away at a pan. Then he shrugged a little, a gentle shrug, his forgiving shoulders rising slightly. He shook off the pan and laid it on a towel to dry. "He is who he is," he said, a response that in its understated mercy pretty much sums up why I married him.

It's time for my son's class to make the lasagna. Everyone stands and shuffles with coats and bags toward the social hall, where the meal assembly will take place. My children and I make it as far as the classroom doorway, where I hold them back till we're alone. I thrust my son's paper under his nose with too much feeling. It's the feeling not of a parent, controlled and centered, but of a person—a person who has been wronged and is now proffering proof of her injuries. "Does this say what I think it says?" I demand, my voice strained and tight, and then I say nothing. I don't scold or lecture or make him say "I'm sorry" because all of these require critical distance, which I don't have. At night, I've been reading *Peaceful Parent, Happy Kids*, a parenting manual about the importance of steadiness and calm. I'm supposed to be *mindful*, to make myself a tranquil sea where his pain can dissolve so he doesn't become a damaged and derelict adult. But at this moment, I don't care to feel peaceful, and it's not my son's happiness I'm after. What I'm feeling is wretched. What I want is to make him prove to me his goodness. Something in me will not rest until I've seen it displayed, until he's fulfilled this day's task. Because while there are all sorts of things I'm okay with my kids not being—star athletes or chess whizzes, budding maestros or spelling-bee champions—I cannot abide their not being good. *On Wednesday, Ted ignores his teacher. On Thursday, he curses his mother.*

"You hurt my feelings," I snap. "Look at me—." I grab his chin. I do, I grab his chin. "Look at me. You've hurt my feelings."

My daughter stands perfectly still. She turns to me, then to her brother, then back to me, her face smooth and satisfied in its innocence.

But my son won't look at me. I've never grabbed onto him like this before. He squeezes his eyes tight and claps his hands over his ears and pushes his body hard into the wall. His cheeks twist like wrung-out cloths and he turns his face to the ceiling and silently howls. And then he howls for real: a gush of anger and misery that seems intended to drown out its own noise. Some stragglers in the hallway turn and look, and I see that I've exposed something that doesn't belong here, that I must cover at once. I force my heart into a zone of peace. I open my arms and pull my son close with the strength of my deepest will. He squirms and pushes at me, and I lift him up and pull him to me tighter. The zipper of his sweatshirt pushes against my neck, toothed and cold. Slowly, his muscles ever so slightly ease, but not completely.

"Shhhhhhh," I say, stroking the back of his head. "Shhhhhhh." We end up, somehow, in a chair that's out in the hallway. I've subdued my own agitated self and have become again a mother, soft flesh and bosom, gold-haloed and serene. My daughter trots over and clambers onto the other side of my lap, getting in on the goodness. There is too much weight on me, but this is the choice I've made. I lean my head back and allow myself to be covered.

The concept of *tikkun olam* originates not in the Torah, the Hebrew bible, but in a creation myth envisioned by the sixteenth-century rabbi Isaac Luria, the father of the Jewish mystical tradition known as Kabbalah. I did not know this on Tikkun Olam Day, but learned it a few weeks later in a women's discussion group run by Rabbi Zecher. Six of my closest friends and I sat, as we do once a month, around a coffee table in her book-lined office. On this morning, we read Genesis, and she explained how Judaism actually contains several creation stories, all of them complementing one another. We all knew the version where God created the world in six days, and then rested on the seventh. And the version where God forms Adam out of clay, and Eve from Adam's rib. None of us knew Isaac Luria's version, which Rabbi Zecher described to us.

In everyday life, creating something—a building, a meal, a sculpture— is generally thought of as an act of external production. Here is the architect, the chef, the sculptor, and there, before her, is the thing she's made. In the Judeo-Christian tradition, the world's creation tends to be understood this way, too: on the one side there is God, and on the other there is the world God brings into being and then gazes upon, satisfied. I think of Michelangelo's *Creation of Adam* on the ceiling of the Sistine Chapel. Soaring and diaphanous, God reaches his finger towards Adam's naked, muscled form, as if he has sculpted this figure and is now, with divine power, animating it. Adam is *of* God, but Adam is not God.

But Luria, Rabbi Zecher explained, questioned this model of divine creation. If God is everywhere, he wondered, how can there be any space beyond God for creation to emerge? He envisioned an alternative origin story in which the world arises not through an act of production, but through *tzimtzum*, or an act of contraction. In the beginning, God's presence fills the universe. But then God takes a breath and withdraws deeper into itself, creating a space for earth and life to come into being, making *yesh* (something) from *ayin* (nothing). In this version of the world's beginning, God does not so much impose or demand, but pull back and allow.

I do not yet have Luria to think of as we stand at our lasagna-making station. What I think of is my determination to get the rest of this morning right. The air is sour with tomato sauce and around us spoons clink and bags of shredded cheese rip as the children follow their instructions. My daughter's eyes brighten as I lift her onto the counter and help her pry open a tub of ricotta—she loves messy projects. But my son sits on the floor, rigid and brooding. Once again, he will not do what I want him to do.

The fact that my children's tendencies align perfectly with gender stereotypes—my girls conscientious and people-pleasing, my boy willful and devil-may-care—isn't lost on me. It only magnifies my discomfort, making me strain more aggressively for things to be otherwise. Is this alignment just coincidence? In what unconscious, unspoken ways might my children's community, their teachers, their schools—might *my husband and I*—have steered our children toward these gendered ways of being? At a time when the #MeToo movement continues to reverberate—when "toxic masculinity" has become a household phrase, when more victims of sexual assault and harassment come forward with their stories, when Harvey Weinstein shuffles off our television screens to begin his prison sentence—there's widespread understanding for the first time of the consequences of raising girls to toe the line, and boys to flout it. I've long been a feminist and a champion of gender equality, but as a mother during this time in history, I feel this calling in a new and intimate way. The lessons of our era hover, always, in my mind, reminding me that my girls will become women—my boy, a man—and that what I impart to them in the interim matters. I want all my children, of course, to be empathic and kind, decent and honorable. But what I long for most pressingly—what it feels my work hinges on—is to raise a good son.

On Friday, Ted imposes his will. On Saturday, he acts on his urges.

In our aluminum tray, the lasagna grows. My daughter's lips pucker with concentration as she scoops sauce from a jar and spreads it with the back of her spoon. On and on she goes, scooping and spreading, layering and admiring. Another parent engages me in small talk, and I follow the script as best I can. But everywhere I look, slabs of noodles are being slathered in sauce and sprinkled with fluffy handfuls of mozzarella—offerings of care and nourishment in which my boy will have no part.

Finally, we're released from the room. We pick up my oldest from her fourth-grade classroom, and then I pile the kids into the car and drive the half hour to my sister-in-law Jacqui's house. My niece opens the door in a unicorn headdress, and the four cousins go thumping upstairs together to play.

I have come to Jacqui's because she's my go-to partner in commiseration, my favorite person to turn to in unhappy times. Whatever I tell her, I can count on her to be unshaken, or to outdo me with a worse tale of woe. I lie down on her couch and tell her about my morning while she clears lunch dishes and feeds the dog scraps. I don't sugarcoat or mine my experience for laughs. I don't say, "This might sound funny on the surface, but . . ."

What I say on that dog-hair covered couch, on the sagging end of that tired mothering weekend, is that I have lost myself. I have lost myself in becoming a mother, and I feel I can't project with any truth what I'm, of course, supposed to project, which is that the sacrifices have all been worth it. I've loved and given and toiled and grieved as a mother. I've run marathons that ended in new marathons, and then I've run these new marathons, collapsing exhausted. I've tapped into reserves of energy I never knew existed, and I've siphoned away these reserves, drilling down deeper for more. I know I should rise above the challenges that come my way, for this is what mothers—the world's anointed absorbers of pain—must do. But I cannot rise above my son's *fuck you.*

Jacqui finishes loading the dishwasher and then looks at me, toweling off her hands, her face unchanged.

"So he got angry at you for ruining his penis joke?" she says.

214

"Well, yeah," I say.

"And to deal with that anger, he expressed his feelings on paper, in writing?" she says.

"I guess."

"Even though he has a language delay, and gets Early Intervention, and writing is hard for him?" she says. "He didn't yell or scream?"

I don't say anything.

"That's a fucking awesome parenting success story, if you ask me," she says, and then she sits down on the couch next to me and reaches for the remote control. Outside the window, the barren March afternoon darkens to evening. Inside, the television blooms neon, illuminating Jacqui's face in joyous flashes.

I'm beginning to see how I've gotten this day all wrong.

In Luria's creation myth, something wild and bizarre happens after God contracts, something out of a science-fiction movie. Divine light enters the newly formed darkness, carried there in ten sacred vessels—like a fleet of rockets rising through a cinematic sky. But some of these vessels are too fragile to contain God's light, and they burst and shatter, scattering divine sparks across the world. Luria proposes that if our world is imperfect—if there is evil and injustice and heartache and anguish—it's because of this *shevirah*, this breaking of the vessels, the cosmic accident that thwarted God's plan for us all.

In contemporary Judaism, this idea is at the root of *tikkun olam*. It's through acts of restoration, or *tikkun*, that the world, our *olam*, can be brought closer to the divine wholeness God intended for it. Through *tikkun olam* big and small—from sidestepping an ant in your path to marching twenty miles to protest injustice—humans can become God's co-creators, each of us doing our part to heal the world's fractures.

I love the image of the vessels, so beautiful in their peculiar specificity. And I take comfort in the idea of *tikkun olam* because of its emphasis on action. As a Jew, I am not charged with regular repentance—though often, repenting is what I know I must do. Self-punishment isn't my main task, either, although I silently reproach myself hourly. My main task is to enter each moment looking for the good choice to make, the generous action to take, gathering whatever scattered sparks I see.

My children's sparks are everywhere—on the floor, the stairs, the rug. They accumulate in corners and under tables. They trail their bodies like crumbs. The more I train my eyes to see them, the harder it becomes to lose sight of their light. What more can I do but collect them in my hands, holding them up for my children to see? What more can I say but "Here, here is your goodness. Look how brightly it glows."

It's after dinner, and we're back at home. My husband has returned from his trip, and there's balance again in the house, a lightening in my step at the sight of his bags flung down in the entryway. I want to unburden myself, to tell him everything, but I know this will have to wait until the kids are asleep. For now, it's enough to have him here, his presence alone making my earlier angst feel dreamlike and alien. As we clean up the dinner mess and coax the children upstairs for baths and tooth-brushing, I settle back comfortably into partnership. One of us will put the two girls to bed, and one of us will put our son to bed. I take my son.

His room waits for us—his bed with the checkered comforter, the dresser covered in Legos, the splashes of Pokémon cards on the rug, the overturned beanbag chair. After I read him two picture books, after I pull down his shades and fill his water cup and turn on the white noise of his sound machine, I gather the far-flung pieces of myself and climb into bed with him in the dark.

"This morning, at Hebrew school, you felt upset with Mommy for tak-ing your paper away," I say.

He does not respond.

"I'm *glad* you love all the parts of yourself," I say. "You should! All of you is beautiful and special. And in a way, that note was also kind of funny. I didn't see the funniness earlier because I was too mad. I was mad you weren't doing what you were told to."

The contour of his face tilts in my direction. Light from the street slips through the crack in his shade, making diamond patterns on the wall.

"But I think there are better ways for people to show madness than I did, kinder ways than snatching things away, or using harsh and ugly words. Don't you think?"

His comforter rustles as he turns onto his belly, and I know—because I am his mother—that he hears what I'm saying. I say it out loud any-way.

"I wish I had shown my anger better. I love you so much, baby boy. And I'm sorry."

I feel for my son's hand and squeeze it tight. He wriggles in closer, nudging his head into the space above my shoulder. The white noise whirs. I can feel his hair on my neck, as damp and matted as the day he was born—that April day six years ago, when I took a breath, contracted, and he came to life.

Now, again, I contract, holding back my power and my will, leaving room for him to rise into this moment in his own way, to make of this space his own creation.

Ted holds his mother's cheeks between his hands. Ted kisses one side of her face, and then the other. Ted locks his body around her like a magnet, like a clasp.

"I love you, Mama," he says.

There will be time, maybe tomorrow, to rake the leaves. There will be time for buying a compost bin and walking the dogs at the shelter and watering the plants. But tonight, we lie on the bed looking up at the ceiling. We watch the splinters of light rising up like stars, two fractured beings doing our imperfect best to repair the world, starting right now with each other.

Nominated by River Teeth

DURING THE PANDEMIC I LISTEN TO THE JULY 26, 1965, JUAN-LES PINS RECORDING OF "A LOVE SUPREME"

by ELLEN BASS

from NEW ENGLAND REVIEW

The first familiar, know-them-anywhere notes bless me
this savage morning. Coltrane's horn racing
up and down every alley, in and out of veins and over the faces
of lakes and into the heart of stones.
And when he repeats *A love supreme* again and again,
it's as though, if he says it enough, he can ease
that mercy down into me, into the tiny ossicular chain,
the chemical rush, the spark, and my brain
getting it—if even just
for this thirty-two minutes and forty-eight seconds.
My daughter's been sick seven weeks with the virus.
Yesterday she felt a little bored, she texted. And I grab that
like a shopping cart. I load it up with hope.
Make it prayer. When the day's portion of the Torah is recited,
someone stands by to correct mistakes.
The words must vibrate precisely in the air.
So I open my door
to the breath of his instrument

that refuses nothing, lavishing the grass, gutters, and trees,
concrete, cars, the gopher pulling down the new lettuces.
This generous sound that can mean
anything, nothing, whatever you need.
And isn't that god? Isn't that it?
This shivering? This fall to my knees?
Gods do walk among us.
But humans are, after all, a broken promise.
And yet, these humans seem to be trying
to enter . . . what?
I can almost hear it. This old planet.
Worms passing earth through their tissue.
Orchids, corn, mockingbirds throwing themselves into song
like there's no tomorrow. Which there may not be.
Yet, still a mountain. Still wind.
And Coltrane still offering the same four notes
like a teacher who is infinitely patient.
He's telling me it's worth it
to be in a body. He's telling me
I'm alive in a beach town in California and my daughter
in a high-rise in Vancouver, my girl,
lying feverish on the couch she's been lying on
forty-nine days and forty-nine nights, still alive.

Nominated by Frank X. Gaspar, Robert Wrigley

UNKNOWN

fiction by BENNETT SIMS

from KENYON REVIEW

At the mall a woman asked to use his phone.

Excuse me, he heard from behind. He had just bought A's birthday gift, a new phone from the AT&T store. He was passing through the gauntlet of kiosks on his way to the mall's exit, and he assumed that one of the stalls' sales clerks was calling out to him, inviting him to sample cologne. He ignored the voice and kept walking. But the voice followed after. Excuse me, Sir. Sir. Please, Sir.

When he turned, there was a small, older woman holding up a heavy purse in both hands. She thanked him and made eye contact. Trapped, he waited for her to ask for money. May I borrow your phone, she asked instead. I need to make a call. It's an emergency. He hesitated. If it was an emergency, why was she asking a stranger, rather than a security guard, or the clerk at the AT&T store? He felt certain it was a scam. But when he revolved the scenario in his mind, he couldn't make out what the nature of the scam would be. The worst she could do, it seemed, was take the phone and run, or fling it to the ground.

Please, she said. It's important. I was supposed to call five minutes ago, and I'm already late. It's an emergency, she repeated, and she gestured vaguely in the direction of the AT&T store, where a young boy and girl were peering through the shop window. Neither turned to look back, and it wasn't clear whether they were with her, or whether the emergency concerned them. He considered lying, claiming that his battery had died, but something in her gaze seemed to anticipate the lie, and he felt this path blocked by guilt. It's no trouble, he told her. He took out his phone and tapped the passcode into the lock screen. He swiped open his settings and disabled Bluetooth, then opened his email and logged out. He handed her the phone. Oh, thank you, Sir. She held it in one hand while she dug through her purse with the other. From the bottom of her bag she withdrew a second phone—a newer model, the same model, in fact, that he had just bought for A, not at all an inexpensive phone—and began tapping at it deftly. He felt instant alarm. He still didn't understand the scam, or where the danger might lie, but he did not like the sight of this woman's phone. Wait, he told her. Why don't you make the call on *your* phone? She was glancing from her screen to his, typing something. Without stopping or looking up, she answered: I have no data. I need to find the number. All the politeness and gratitude had drained out of her voice. When she had finished typing, she smiled and stepped aside, holding his phone up to her ear. He told himself to remain calm. There were hundreds of witnesses around them. It wasn't as if she could run away with his phone. And even if she did, what did it matter? It was only a phone. He could go back to the store and buy a new phone.

While waiting for her friend or whomever to answer, she hunched over, hugging her purse to her chest, in the posture of someone cramped into a phone booth. He maintained enough space between them to respect her privacy, but he was still close enough to eavesdrop, and when she finally spoke, he pretended to scan the crowd while straining his ears to listen. He could pick out only snatches. She was whispering angrily. You'll never find me, he thought he heard her say. Never. Her tone—though low—was vehement. She continued in this vein, her voice rarely rising above a murmur. Whoever was on the other end of the line must have been listening in complete silence, for there were no pauses in her monologue. She seemed to be gloating. I escaped, he thought he heard her say, or, It's too late. You'll just have to find someone else, he thought he heard her say. Finally she hung up and handed him his phone. Thank you so much, Sir, she said. You are my savior. Thank you.

She walked off in the direction of the food court. He turned to the shop window, but the children were no longer there. Perhaps they were waiting in the food court to meet her, or maybe they had already left with their real mother. He opened the phone to check the recent calls. There were none. The last number dialed was A's, from earlier that day. Either the woman had deleted her own call from the list—was this possible?—or she had not called anyone at all. Had simply delivered her monologue to a dead phone. When he glanced back at the food court, the woman was gone. He couldn't find her anywhere in the crowd.

Back home, while preparing her birthday dinner, he told A about the woman. He recited what he could remember of her monologue. When he'd finished, she asked who he thought the woman could have been talking to. It sounds like a stalker, A said, a jealous lover. Maybe she didn't want to call from her own phone because she was used to being tracked. Or maybe, he suggested, it was a debt collector. Or a probation officer. In any case, A said, a happy story. With a happy ending. She got away.

After dinner he gave A her presents: the phone and tickets to a play that weekend. They sat on the couch together, and she transferred the SIM card from her old phone to the new one. He helped her link the device to his Find My Phone program, in case she ever lost it, and while she set up her other applications, he took out his own phone. The object seemed compromised in his hand. He couldn't rid himself of the suspicion that the woman had done something to it. It felt changed, charmed. He opened its browser and searched *Lending strangers your phone*. He skimmed an article and read the most alarming passages aloud to A. In one scam, he read, a stranger will ask to use your phone and pretend to dial a number or text their friend. In reality they'll be opening your payment applications and transferring funds to themselves. You don't have any payment applications, do you? she asked. He shook his head. I won't install any either, she said. In another scam, he continued, the stranger will call their own phone to harvest your number for identity theft. Sometimes they'll even call a criminal enterprise—a drug dealer, for instance—so that your number will be on file in their records: later they'll try to use this information to blackmail you. Somehow I don't think that's what she was doing, she said. No, he agreed, it didn't sound like she was talking to a drug dealer. Why not just take her at her word? she asked. He nodded. But when he tried to imagine who the woman could have been talking to, no one came to mind. What had made A so certain it was a lover? He imagined himself on the other end of the line, listening quietly to that monologue. How he would never find her. How he would have to find someone else. How she had escaped.

Later that night, while they were reading in bed, A's new phone kept vibrating on the nightstand. She would reach for it, tap at its screen, set it aside. A minute later it would vibrate again with a new text message.

Now she had placed her book down and was holding the phone in her hand, as if to muffle the buzzing with her flesh. When it vibrated again, she swiped it open and tapped a short reply. Out of the corner of his eye he could see the blue-and-gray bubbles of a message thread, but he couldn't make out the name of the contact or what she was typing. Her expression betrayed nothing. She set her phone back down on the nightstand. What's the news, he asked, without looking up from his book. No news, she said. Birthday wishes. She did not say who from, and he resisted the urge to ask. He was gripped by the image of a strange man, a handsome man, on the other end of the phone: alone at a restaurant table somewhere, sending messages to her. He didn't know where the thought had come from. Whenever she texted in bed—never very often—she usually told him who it was, and it was usually one of the women she worked with. That was probably who it was now. There was no man. The woman in the mall—all this talk of stalkers and lovers— must have put the idea into his head. He was jealous of a phantom. He tried to focus on his book, but her phone vibrated again, buzzing against the hard wood of the nightstand, and the sound of it sawed through his concentration. He willed himself to ignore it, his chest tightening at every noise. She tapped at the screen. He still couldn't see the contact name, could just make out gray bubbles popping into view, surfacing from an unknown source. With each new bubble the phone buzzed in her palm. Can you maybe put it on silent, he asked. She touched his shoulder and kissed his forehead. I'm sorry. She silenced the phone and placed it in her nightstand drawer.

At the same moment, his own phone vibrated on the nightstand beside him. *Unknown*, the screen read. He canceled the call. Who was it, she asked. It's an Unknown, he said. He had learned to ignore unlisted numbers. If it were a real person, they would leave a voice message. It was almost never a real person, just a computer text-to-speech program. The recordings followed a similar script: he was notified that he had committed some oversight or crime—he had defaulted on a debt, there was a warrant out for his arrest—and he was given a number to call back at once. This is an emergency, the thin, urgent, robotic voice would insist. The scam was structured like an anxiety dream. The voice of authority enveloping you, with its spotlight of guilt, to remind you of something you should never have forgotten: the final exam you hadn't studied for, the meeting you were already late to. And then the way you simply accept whatever identity the nightmare assigns you, like an actor possessed by a role. He imagined that some people must respond

223

to these robocalls as he did to his anxiety dreams: the credulity, the panic, the waves of shame. The scam must work part of the time—people must actually call the number and divulge their personal information—or else the calls would stop.

I thought you had blocked unlisted numbers, she reminded him. He regarded the phone with puzzlement. She was right. Now he could remember: about a month ago he had begun receiving several Unknown calls a day, and he had called AT&T for help. They had looked up his account and blocked unlisted numbers for him. He hadn't received any Unknown calls since, not until tonight. That's right, he told her, I did. So how did an unlisted number get through? He thought he heard suspicion in her voice. He opened the phone and checked the recent calls. The Unknown usually had a strange area code, from a state he had never visited. If he searched the number online, he could find message boards full of other people who had also received calls from it, offering each other advice, warning each other not to answer. But when he checked the missed calls log now, there was no number. It just read Unknown. The caller had not left a voice message either. His first thought was of the woman in the mall. Who had she dialed today? If they were determined to find her, they might call him back. They might even be determined enough to mask their number, to circumvent blocking software.

I don't know, he answered finally, they must have some kind of . . . program. Just put it on silent, she suggested. He switched his phone to Do Not Disturb and put it away. She took her phone from the drawer and continued tapping at its screen. He reached for his book, pretending to read.

It wasn't until his lunch break the next day that he remembered to deactivate Do Not Disturb. When he did, his screen cascaded with alerts for missed calls and new voice messages. Most were for work, one from A. But one was another missed call from Unknown, no number listed, and this time they had left a voice message. It was half a minute long. Normally he would delete it without listening, but today he pressed Play and pressed the phone to his ear. He heard A's voice. It sounds like a stalker, he heard her say, a jealous lover. Or maybe, he heard himself say, it was a debt collector. Or a probation officer. In any case, he heard her say, a happy story. With a happy ending. She got away.

He played the message back. Their voices were distant and echoey, and it was clear what had happened: his phone's microphone must have

224

recorded their conversation during dinner last night. His phone had been lying on the kitchen counter, where it would have been able to pick up both their voices. He supposed it was possible that there had been a malfunction: the microphone could have turned on spontaneously, and the resulting recording could have been mistakenly saved to his voicemail. It didn't seem likely. But the other explanations seemed even less likely, and more alarming. Because what if the woman at the mall were responsible? What if, while pretending to talk, she had actually downloaded spyware onto his phone, some kind of eavesdropping program? Maybe she could remotely access his microphone now to listen in on him, and maybe she had sent him this recording as a threat, in advance of future blackmail. Or maybe it was not the woman who was responsible, but whoever she'd been talking to. She had called them from his number, after all, and now this person—whoever they were—might be training their powers of detection and surveillance on his phone, instead of hers. They could have hijacked his phone in their quest to find her and ended up finding him. Wasn't that what she had said to them? You'll just have to find someone else? She could have passed them on to him, the way you pass on a curse, setting into motion a chain of displacements. Now the Unknown would just substitute his phone in her place, calling again and again until he called back from someone else's number.

He pictured a debt collector. He pictured a probation officer. But the more he listened to the recording, the more likely it seemed that A had been right. This was something that a stalker, a jealous lover, might do. When the woman had called them from his phone, and his unfamiliar number had flashed across their screen, he could imagine their reaction. First the confusion, and then—when they heard her voice—the rage. So, they would think, he thought, this must be her new lover's number. Such a person would likely go on calling that number indefinitely. Hacking the microphone. Leaving menacing messages. The moment he handed the woman his phone, he realized, it had become entangled in her story. It was no longer his private property, just a prop in this other drama. So far from stealing his identity from his phone, she had contaminated it with her own.

He played the message back. A happy story, he heard A say. With a happy ending. She got away. If the recording had been made by the woman's stalker, the message it was meant to send would be clear. She may think she has gotten away, but they were still listening.

He opened his phone's browser and searched *Microphone remote listening.* He searched *Microphone malfunction.* He spent the rest of his lunch break reading about security breaches.

That night he played the recording for A. Creepy, she said. He deleted it. He told her about an article he had read at lunch. Apparently there was a bug in their phones' conference call feature: if someone dialed your number, then quickly added their own number to the conference call, your microphone would activate while your phone was still ringing. Then the caller could listen in for as long as it took you to answer or to cancel the call. The article warned readers to check their phones: if they had any mysterious missed calls, someone might have already exploited the bug. That must have been what happened, he told her. That Unknown call. But who would do that, she asked. Anyone could do it, he said. He watched over her as she disabled the conference call feature on her phone.

But later that night, when they were reading in bed, a detail began to trouble him. The recording in his voicemail had been made at dinner. That was when they had discussed the woman in the mall. Yet the Unknown caller had not called until later, when they were already in bed. He picked up his phone. A's phone vibrated on the nightstand, and he ignored it. He checked his calls list and confirmed it: there had been no missed calls during dinner. Her phone vibrated again, and she tapped at its screen. According to the article, the eavesdropper could listen in only while the phone was ringing. So last night, there would have been only a ten-second window in which the Unknown caller could have recorded them. They had been in bed when the call had come. But they had been in the kitchen when the recording was made. A's phone vibrated in her hand while she was still typing her response, and she paused a moment to read. Whoever made the recording, it followed, would not have been exploiting the conference-call bug. They would have had to listen in through some other method, which meant that disabling conference calls would do nothing to prevent them from listening in again. They could be listening in right now. Now he regretted deleting the voice message. He wished he could listen to it one more time, or play it for someone at AT&T.

A tapped at her screen. What's the news, he asked her, and in his ears his voice already sounded disembodied, mechanical, as if he were overhearing a recording of himself. When he looked over at her phone, he could see the blue-and-gray bubbles of a message thread, but she pressed the lock button and the screen went dark. No news, she said. Something at work. She's lying, he thought, and the thought alarmed him. The thought seemed to come from somewhere outside him. She set her phone to silent and put it aside. He opened his own phone's browser and searched *Recovering deleted voice messages*.

At work the next day he installed a file organizer for his phone on his laptop. The program could organize the contents of your phone's hard drive into easily searchable folders. If there was still a copy of the recording anywhere on his phone—even in a deleted folder or in its unallocated space—the program would display it. Then, if he did find it, he could use the program to recover the file.

He plugged his phone into his laptop. All of its folders were visible in the program's sidebar: voicemail, photos, recordings, text messages. He tapped his phone's screen, and it prompted him to enter his passcode. The device was still locked, internally. But the program must have circumvented the lock on his laptop. He clicked on the *Texts* folder. The message threads were arranged in a list, organized by contact, with his most recent contact—A—at the top. He clicked her name. Their entire correspondence was visible: her messages to him, his responses, each time-stamped to the second. He scrolled up several screens, moving back months in their relationship. The silly fights, the accusations, the reconciliations. All of it was open to him. He had not needed to enter his passcode to read them. He had only needed to plug in his phone.

And if his phone didn't need to be unlocked, he realized, then neither did hers. All he had to do was plug it into his laptop and open the program.

He scrolled through the file organizer and clicked on *Voicemails*. He clicked on *Voice memos*. He clicked on *Deleted files*. He could not find the recording anywhere.

When he got home from work, A had laid out dresses on the bed. He asked whether she had dinner plans, careful to keep the suspicion out of his voice. A smirked and reminded him that the play was tonight. He had forgotten all about the birthday tickets. Do you need to shower? she asked, and he shook his head. I won't be long, she told him.

While they were getting ready, he kept an eye on her phone. He had his laptop out on the bed and prepared: the program open, his phone plugged in with a USB cable. It would take only a second to unplug his

227

phone and substitute hers in its place. He didn't even need to read the texts themselves. All he wanted was to see who had been messaging her. He would check the contact's name, verify that it was one of the women she worked with, and unplug her phone. But she didn't leave her phone unattended. Even when she took her shower, she brought it into the bathroom with her. Through the bedroom wall he could hear the muffled voice of a broadcaster echoing off the bathroom tiles. She never listened to the news when she showered. She was only doing it tonight, he found himself thinking, to keep her phone from him.

He looked at the laptop in bed, trailing the white spy siphon of its USB cable, and felt ridiculous. What was he doing? If she caught him reading her texts, he didn't know what she would do. He had never done anything like this. A week ago it would never have occurred to him. It was the kind of thing that the Unknown caller—the woman's stalker— might do. He had allowed this hypothetical jealous lover's jealousy to infect him. He had become possessed by someone else's possessiveness, paranoia, obsession.

The shower cut off and A silenced the radio. When she came back into the bedroom, clad in a towel, she set her phone on the nightstand. From the bed he watched her get dressed. Eventually she went back to the bathroom to put on makeup, and this time she did not bring her phone with her. She left the bathroom door open. He heard water running in the sink. He didn't have much time. He unplugged his phone and connected the USB cable to hers. It buzzed once against the nightstand, and he held his breath at the noise. But the water kept running in the bathroom sink. In the program her phone appeared as a paired device, and he clicked the *Texts* folder in the sidebar. Without bothering to skim the list of message threads, he clicked the topmost conversation, her most recent contact. The contact had no name. She had saved their number under Unknown.

The cunning of this stunned him. This way, he realized, the contact could text or call her even when she was at home: there would be no danger of his glancing over at her phone's screen and seeing their name, since it would just read Unknown. He scrolled up the message thread. There was no mistaking it. The messages were all time-stamped. Unknown was the same person she had been texting in bed the past two nights, the same person who had been sending her so-called birthday wishes and updates from work. He skimmed the most recent messages hurriedly, trying to absorb as much as he could before she returned.

There was a string of gray bubbles in a row, no blue bubbles in response. *You'll never find me*, he read. *You'll just have to find someone else.*

The sink fell silent, and he heard her opening the mirror cabinet. He X-ed out of the program and unplugged her phone, stuffing the USB cable into his nightstand drawer and slamming his laptop closed. When she came into the bedroom, he was lying fully dressed in bed. She paused in the doorway, regarding him. Are you ready? she asked. Yes, he said, I just need to use the bathroom. He thought his voice had been neutral, but she asked, Is everything all right? He kissed her forehead on his way to the bathroom. He locked the door behind him. He ran water in the sink and sat on the toilet.

He went over the messages in his mind. She must have been texting Unknown—whoever they were—about the woman in the mall. She must have been quoting the woman's monologue. But if that were the case, the text bubbles would have been blue. He tried to visualize the thread. *You'll never find me. You'll just have to find someone else.* He felt sure that all the bubbles had been gray. Which meant that Unknown had been the one to text them to her. Which meant that she must have already told this person about the woman beforehand. She had shared this story—his story—and now it must have become something of a running joke between them. *I'll meet you at the mall tomorrow*, she would text them. *You'll never find me*, they would text back, *you'll just have to find someone else.*

He was jumping to conclusions. Maybe Unknown was not a code name at all: maybe it really was an Unknown caller. She could have received these texts from an unlisted number, perhaps even the same unlisted number that had been calling him. The woman in the mall could have easily obtained A's information. While she had been tapping at his phone's screen, pretending to dial, it would have been trivial for her to open his contacts list and copy the numbers. Now she could be texting A the same monologue he had overheard her reciting into his phone at the mall. And if not the woman herself, it could always be her stalker who was sending the messages. If they could hijack his microphone, make remote recordings, they could also hack his contacts and send messages to A.

But if she had been receiving strange texts from an unlisted number, why not tell him?

She knocked on the bathroom door. We're going to be late, she said. I'm coming. I'm finished. He bent over the sink, splashing enough water on his face and hair that she would register the wetness, then turned off the faucet. When he opened the door, she had her phone in hand, as if to check the time.

When they arrived at the theater, they silenced their phones. As they walked down the hallway he saw—alongside the No Smoking signs and Emergency Exit maps on the walls—newer signs forbidding electronic devices. In the illustration, an ambiguous black slab was centered in a red circle, with a barred line running through it. To be safe he took his phone from his pocket and turned it off altogether, holding the power button until it had finished shutting down.

Inside the theater they found their seats in a middle row. They hadn't talked much on the ride over, and they did not talk now. She'd asked once in the car whether something was wrong, and he had said that nothing was wrong—he was just tired. But he wasn't tired. He had never felt more awake. Tomorrow he would get to the bottom of it, he had decided. While she was asleep, he would take her phone and his laptop into the bathroom. He would use the file organizer to download Unknown's text messages, saving them all to his laptop as a PDF, and then he would be able to read them at his leisure. He held her hand as he planned this. She read the playbill. He pretended to scan the crowd.

As people settled into their seats, they opened their phones to mute them. Screens glowed to life in the rows around them, then fell dark. The theater lights stayed on while the crowd accomplished this. It was as if the play were waiting for a perfect seal to form between itself and the outside world before it started: as if the curtains would not part until the last phone had been muted, until there was no portal remaining through which reality could irrupt into the theater, disrupting the play with a foreign logic. When the lights finally dimmed, the audience fell silent. Everyone turned toward the stage. But just as it seemed that the curtains were about to part, a cell phone rang out from the back row, cutting through the quiet.

It was a shrill, insistent marimba—the same ringtone, in fact, as A's—and it reverberated throughout the theater. Something about the acoustics of the space must have amplified the noise, for it sounded impossibly loud, less like a ringing phone than a fire alarm, as if it were being blared through the theater's speakers. He could feel the vibrations in his chest. He shifted in his seat, resisting the urge to crane his head toward the back rows, as the people in front of him were already doing. Their glares, he knew, would magnify the guilt of the phone's owner. At the sight of this sea of turning heads the culprit would dig even more anxiously through their purse, their pants pocket, frantic to find the device and shut it up or off.

But they did not shut it off. It went on ringing, far louder than an average phone and for far longer than it would take the average person to locate their phone, far longer, even, than it would take for the average phone to default to voicemail. Maybe it was buried at the bottom of a heavy purse, impossible to find, or maybe the phone's owner had gone to the bathroom and left it behind as a placeholder on their seat. He pictured a glowing screen, lying face up on the cushion, reading Unknown. He pictured a panicked finger stabbing at the screen, missing the red decline button every time. The crowd began to murmur, and he felt a mob hostility rising against the phone and its owner. Who forgets to silence their phone? How could you ignore all the signs in the hallway? And even if you had, how could you watch everyone in the seats around you silencing their own phones without remembering yours? What call could be so important—what news could you be expecting— that you wouldn't just set the phone to vibrate? At least it was ringing now, he thought, before the curtains had parted, and not midway through a monologue. But still the play would be delayed. It would not start until this final phone had fallen silent.

From the back of the theater, the phone kept ringing. Turn it off, he thought. Turn off your phone. As if she had overheard this thought, A bent to her purse and withdrew her phone, double-checking that it was silenced. On her screen he glimpsed what looked like an alert for a new text message, then she put the phone away. Someone behind him muttered, Turn it *off*, and in the row ahead a man took out his phone to examine it. The crowd was getting restless now. He turned around, searching the back rows, but he couldn't find a likely culprit. No one was standing and patting their pockets. People were turning to each other in their seats and shrugging. The phone kept ringing. Exasperated, he took out his own phone. He knew he had turned it off already, but he was gripped by a compulsion to check.

He pushed the home button. To his surprise, the screen glowed to life. The phone must have been on this entire time. If he hadn't thought to check and the Unknown had called him in the middle of the play, *he* would have been the disruption, the locus of the audience's loathing. But that was impossible. He had a clear memory of turning off his phone when they arrived. Could it have turned back on in his pocket? Maybe he had been sitting on it at an odd angle, putting pressure on the power button with his thigh. Or maybe, he thought, the Unknown had turned it on remotely. Could they do that? In principle, he supposed, it was possible: if they could activate his microphone, they could turn on his phone. He held the power button and watched it shut down a second time. He placed it on the seat cushion, the glassy black screen face up, so that he would see if it turned on again.

The phone in the back row fell silent. Everyone returned their attention to the stage, and the crowd began to murmur good-humoredly. All the tension in the room relaxed. At first he did not understand. Then a prerecorded voice delivered a message through the theater's speaker system: Don't be that person, the voice intoned. Please remember to silence your phone.

Now he understood. The ringtone had been a recording. The rude theatergoer was a fiction, a decoy designed to attract the hatred of the crowd. The theater had played the ringtone in the same way that ornithologists will play back birdcall recordings in the woods: just as a flock will sometimes mob a trilling amplifier, trying to drive away the phantom intruder, the crowd had turned on this nonexistent audience member. Just as there was no bird in the speaker, there was no phone in the back row. It was a virtual point, an empty center toward which real vectors converged. And it had worked: everyone had double-checked their phones. No one wanted to occupy the place of the decoy themselves. No one wanted to be the person who received a call during the play, to have the crowd turn on them. The theater would replay the recording for the next audience, and the next, and with each iteration this decoy—ghostly, acousmatic, a call haunting them from an unknown source—would set off the same chain reaction in the crowd. Everyone's behavior would be bent by this nonexistence.

He reached for A's hand. The curtains parted, and the play began.

During his lunch break the next day, he tested the file organizer with his phone. He opened the *Texts* folder and selected A from his contacts, clicking the *Export as PDF* button. It took longer than he expected—almost five minutes—but in the end their entire correspondence was saved to his desktop. The interface could not have been simpler. It would just be a matter of getting hold of A's phone.

He reached to unplug his phone, but he stopped when he noticed the Voicemail folder in the sidebar. There was one new message there, according to the file organizer. Strange, he thought, that he had somehow missed it on the phone itself. He felt sure there hadn't been an alert. He checked his missed calls now and saw that, indeed, he had one new message: another voicemail from Unknown, a minute long this time. He pressed Play and pressed the phone to his ear. He heard A's voice, or a woman with a remarkably similar voice. I think he's been reading my texts, he thought he heard her say. There was a long silence, as if she were waiting for someone to respond, or as if the response had not been recorded. I'll meet you tomorrow, he thought he heard her say. The same place. She hung up and the recording ended.

He checked the timestamp. He had apparently missed the call and received the voice message last night, when they had still been at the play. So the woman on the recording could not be A. She had been beside him in the theater the entire time. She'd left him only once, during intermission, to use the bathroom. Was he supposed to believe that she had made this call from the stall? That the Unknown had hijacked the microphone on her phone too?

He listened to the recording again, with earphones this time. He maxed out the volume. He tried to distinguish background noises—flushing toilets, sink faucets, hand dryers—but heard nothing other than A's voice, or a voice remarkably similar to her voice. It could not be A's voice. Even if the Unknown had hijacked her microphone—even if they had happened to record her half of a phone call last night—there was no reason for them to send the recording to him.

The likeliest explanation was that this was a wrong number. Some other woman had tried to dial some other lover and had reached his phone instead. It only sounded like A because he was primed to believe it was her. The recording confirmed what he wanted to hear, confirmed his worst fears, so he heard A's voice in it. When, in fact, the message could be from anyone. There were lots of unfaithful partners in the world, lots of jealous lovers.

On the other hand, if A really were meeting someone somewhere today, it would be trivial to check. He opened his Find My Phone application and logged into her account. The map loaded, searching for her phone's GPS location. If he was right, and this voice message were the result of a wrong number, she would be at work as usual. The map zoomed in on the mall, and he saw a blue dot pulsing in the gray wasteland of its parking lot. So. She was at the mall. But that didn't mean she was meeting anyone. She could have brought her phone to the AT&T

store to complain about the strange texts she'd been receiving. He watched the blue dot for a minute, but it didn't move from the parking lot. Maybe she was sitting in her car. Or maybe she had left her phone in the car while she went inside.

He called. It took five rings for her to answer. I'm at work, she said. What's up? He said he'd misdialed and apologized for bothering her: he would see her at home.

He called into work and said that he wouldn't be returning from lunch. He drove toward the mall, leaving the map open on his phone. As he sped down the highway, he kept glancing over to the screen. Her blue dot didn't move. Every time he checked, it was pulsing in the same place in the parking lot. Then, halfway to the mall, the dot disappeared. It evaporated off the map, as if it had never been there. She must have turned off her phone or switched it to airplane mode.

When he arrived in the parking lot, he circled the vicinity where the blue dot had been, but he couldn't find her car. His phone vibrated, and the screen read Unknown. He canceled the call. He switched his phone to Do Not Disturb and entered the mall.

He walked up and down the main hallway, searching the crowd for her face. Excuse me, he heard from behind. A woman's voice. Excuse me, Sir. He turned and saw a sales clerk at one of the kiosks, inviting him to sample cologne. He ignored her and kept walking. At the AT&T store he paused to look in through the shop window. A woman with two children was at the counter, talking to the clerk. She seemed to be returning a phone: she handed a white box with a receipt to the clerk, who scanned its barcode with his laser.

He moved on to the food court. At the tables there were mostly families, groups of teenagers. But at one table he saw a handsome, middle-aged man sitting by himself, with no food. He had placed his phone on the table before him and was tapping at the screen. Discreetly, he moved past the man and sat at a table a few rows behind him. The whole time he watched him, the man never looked up from his phone, not until he pocketed it and rose to leave. Careful to maintain a safe distance, he followed the man. He trailed him across the food court and out the mall's exit. In the parking lot, where A's car was still nowhere to be seen, he watched the man climb into his own car and drive away.

He returned to the mall. He brought his phone to the AT&T store and explained about the Unknown caller. The clerk looked up his account. That's strange, the clerk said. Unlisted numbers weren't blocked anymore. Maybe when he had bought the new phone, the clerk suggested, it had reset his account somehow, restoring the default settings. The clerk called AT&T's customer service, and they reactivated the block.

He returned to the food court and sat by himself at the same table. He deactivated Do Not Disturb, expecting a missed call or text from A. But the only alert was for a new voice message from Unknown. The timestamp was from earlier that day, the call he'd canceled in the parking lot. He pressed Play and pressed the phone to his ear. I know you're lying, he heard himself say. The voice on the recording was strained and angry, and he had no memory of saying the things it was saying. But still, it really did sound like his own voice. Or it sounded unlike his voice in the same disembodied, mechanical way that all recordings sounded unlike him. He recoiled to hear it. *Tell* me, he heard himself say.

The message cut off. He played it back. The more he listened to the recording, the more it sounded like himself. Except he knew he had never said these things. It had to be a recording of Unknown. But whether this message was meant for him, or for A, or for the woman in the mall, he could not tell. In the end, he supposed, it did not matter: it was the last message they would be leaving, now that the block was reactivated. He deleted it.

He opened the Find My Phone map and refreshed it, waiting for A's blue dot to rematerialize. When the time came that he would normally return home from work, he pocketed his phone and left.

Back home, the house was empty. A's car was gone, and—when he checked the closet to confirm—her suitcase.

He sat at the dining room table, waiting for the call. The longer he stared at his phone, the more his confusion turned to rage. He imagined A somewhere with a strange man, a handsome man. He kept picturing the man he had seen in the food court, though he told himself that this was irrational. He tried calling her, but her phone went straight to voicemail. He hung up before the recording started and pushed the phone across the table.

Five minutes later the phone rang, displaying an unfamiliar number. When he answered, he heard A's voice, or a woman with a remarkably similar voice. She was speaking low, and it was hard to hear over the sound of the crowd around her. He could tell from the background noise and the echo that she was in a public place, spacious with high ceilings. He didn't know what number she was calling from—whose phone she had borrowed—but he supposed it might be possible for him to track it. He did not speak, only listened quietly to what she had to tell him. She was whispering angrily. You'll never find me, he thought he heard her say. Never.

I escaped, he thought he heard her say, or maybe, It's too late. You'll just have to find someone else.

Nominated by Ruth Wittman, Lily Henderson

BOCK ROTTOM

by SAM HERSCHEL WEIN

from SHENANDOAH

To use humor to talk about things I don't
like, I often switch the first letters of
words as a ploy, a Medense Fechanism.

Everybody loves jokes, especially therapists.
I'm Deverely Suppressed today, thanks for
asking. I thought about swallowing a Punch

of Bills. I haven't left my Dead in Bays. I'm
soooo funny, I explain to my therapist, though
he's not smiling, giggling, not remotely tickled.

My therapist enjoys my humor though, even
if he keeps bringing it up, what I'm doing,
wants me to know he's figured me out,

tries not to laugh but if I keep with it, often he
chuckles, he can split and heel, he falls directly
out the seat of my mind, he says, you spend

too much of our sessions trying to lighten the
mood, taking care of me, easing the room's
sorrows, the brick room with three chairs,

one couch, a lacy red and green pillow
that I hug, so many boxes of tissues and
he keeps tightening the tension, says no

he would never pressure me he's just trying
to get me to be real but I'm fist closing the
pillow the couch he keeps pressing I keep

yelling you don't get it you Fother Mucking
slender-nosed man you are Bresting my
Puttons and this room is such a thick, pulsing

wet ocean of winded-tight air no matter if
I jab or joke by the time I leave we're rubbing
sadness from our eyes, all the pens snap

Nominated by Shenandoah

FIRE

fiction by THAISA FRANK

from FRACTURED LIT

I'm in Flamineo's trailer when we hear the ringmaster yelling that the fire-eater left to marry his high school sweetheart. We're in bed, pretending I'm a stranger in the audience and Flamineo's guessing my name. The ringmaster must knock three times before we pick our way over Flamineo's sorcerer's hats and the snake costume I wore last night.

He didn't even leave a fucking note, says the ringmaster. He just told the ceiling-walker he was going to Iowa.

He sits at the formica table and pours wine without asking.

Fuck high school sweethearts, he says. You'll be a cobra for five more minutes to make up for his act.

I say I can't manage five more minutes with my legs curled over my head.

Of course you can, he says.

But when Flamineo starts lifting him by the wrists, the ringmaster pulls away, blows his nose and says he'll fill the time himself.

After he leaves, Flamineo says the fire-eater made a good bargain, trading fire for love. I remind him the fire-eater said that swallowing fire is like swallowing a comet and he's sure to trade love for fire again. Flamineo says I'm just saying that to make him feel better because the fire-eater was lucky enough to have a high school sweetheart.

I remind him that all the women in the circus want him, but he kicks me with his heel and says he doesn't want to be with someone who loves him because he can read minds, lift weights twice his size, and recite Hamlet backwards. He wants someone who loved him in high school before all that. But he ran away to be a circus freak and he's nothing but a four-foot pill bug. He wraps himself in the quilt and won't talk.

Flamineo isn't a pill bug. When he introduces his act he's a flaming tumbleweed. All the women in the circus want him and we never know whom he'll sleep with next. Once he read that microbes were 90% of the human body and said he'd drink a bottle of antiseptic and be 100% himself–larger than any of us, who are only 10%. We took turns keeping watch until he said he was joking.

Eventually, Flamineo faces me and once more pretends he's guessing my name. He guesses three times before he gets it right. It's thrilling to be forgotten and remembered.

Nominated by Steve Adams, Jane Ciabattari

MILLION MILLION

by MICHELLE BOISSEAU

from LUMINOUS BLUE VARIABLES AND OTHER MAJOR POEMS (BkMk Press)

=1,000,000,000,000

A trillion seconds ago we danced to bone flutes
The Mountain Marries the Rain. Like petals
on a black bough sentences burst from us
and we hit on handy words right and left.
We scratched the walls deep so the stampede

leapt in firelight, but one of us a million million
seconds ago had sung a song or dug a grave
on this side of the globe. No canyons recorded
the wooly monsters that the Osage-orange tree
still longs for, dangling its softball size fruit

each summer for hungers that never come
while the locust tree bristles with daggers
against eons of empty treats. A billion seconds ago
I ripped through Ohio and half a dozen boyfriends
in two million seconds and you spread a quilt

with your first wife by the Tidal Basin. Mozart,
cherry trees a pink mist. On the high bench
sat nine judicious scholars. Authorities reported
the answer to world hunger was fish
for they were numberless. A thousand million

seconds ago all of our families were still alive,
except our children, yet to be desired. In twenty-five
years we've been apart only a million seconds
and in a million more I'll be driving you home
through an enormous day. Put the thousand count

sheet on the bed, in a million seconds
    I'll be home with you.

Nominated by BkMk Press

IF YOUR DREAMS DONT SCARE YOU

by JONI TEVIS

from THE GEORGIA REVIEW

INITIATION

I don't remember what they called that night. Someone drove us to a house off campus. Someone blindfolded us. Someone lined us up around the perimeter of a pool. They made us practice fundamentals—low mark time (heel up, toes down), high mark time (up to the knee), glide step (dig in the heel, turn up the toe). There was a girl ahead of me in line. I couldn't see her, but I knew she was there.

We were in college marching band together, and there were thirty-five people in our section. Maybe eight of us were new. I tried to think how I would describe this moment, first to myself, then to someone else: that the air pressed in, humid and hot. That the pool's cement edge warmed the soles of my feet. That layers of white tissue bandaged my eyes.

Then the girl ahead of me hit a brick wall. The impact knocked out her front teeth, bloodied her nose, and gave her a concussion. Or maybe it chipped her teeth and cut her mouth so she had to get stitches. I remember she was upset because she'd had braces or other dental work, and her parents would be angry about the damage. Someone drove her to the emergency room, and the night ended. I remember some of the seniors were disappointed they didn't get to do everything they had planned. They were going to tie us hand and foot and throw us blindfolded into the pool.

Was she holding her horn? Was the mouthpiece what damaged her teeth or was it the wall? Was her nose broken or bloodied? Did her parents file a police report? She would have been eighteen, like me. I forget how I got there. I forget how many other initiates there were. Did the university pay for her dental work? I can't remember her name. I can't remember any names.

LEAP

Start with lips on a mouthpiece or fingers loosely gripping sticks of polished hickory. With breath, with heartbeat. What a marching show is especially good at: lines, volume, force. The best shows play to these strengths, bringing scores of musicians together in a tightly bounded art form, the field's white grid pressuring the group's physical motions just as the time limit shapes the arrangement of the music. You need variety: four songs that play well together, even if they vary in tempo and mood. By the end of the season, everyone in the band will know these songs in their blood, will hear them as the soundtrack to their dreams.

Open with an exclamation, an emphatic note: bodies in parallel lines flex and spin, melt into each other, shift into a parallelogram, then flatten into a front. The *whomp* of crescendo hits the audience hard—that's from the turn the players have executed, dynamics at their most primal. Then a ballad, a drum break, and for a change of pace, brass solo. Something new every five to eight seconds. Then a big closer, some surprise or twist: maybe a callback to an earlier phrase, transformed in key or volume. The show's early moments prepared the audience, but if the band does its job, nobody sees this coming.

You have a good ear, my first band director told me. Those high school band directors were the first artists I knew. They arranged music, wrote drill, created the show's every resonant moment. That's why I'd come here, to a school far from home but known for its excellent conservatory. I played piano, French horn, trumpet, a little trombone, a little baritone, and I dreamed of the shows I'd write someday.

Maybe something containing Aaron Copland's music. *Appalachian Spring* was the first piece of serious music I felt was mine. My junior year of high school, we played it in a show, as many bands did; students could play it cleanly, and audiences had loved it since its 1944 premiere. Comprised of eight sections—some joyful, some yearning—it unfolded in the open space of a field, a stage so big you trust only what you see, not what you hear.

Dancers had always prized the spacious quality inherent in Copland's compositions. Said dancer Pearl Lang in 1980: "We thank Aaron for the wide use of time that his music provides, for the energy his music ignites in us, and for the limitless space that we hear in his sound. With Aaron's music, one leaps not across the stage, but across the land."

APRIL

Roll back the clock twenty years. Let me show you my parents, a young couple not long married, digging in a field in Logan County, Ohio. One thousand holes for one thousand seedlings, delivered in brown paper from the soil conservation district. They had not been to college but were determined that any child of theirs would go. Walnut brought a good price. Those trees, they figured, would yield enough lumber to pay tuition when the time came.

They were right in their hunch that two daughters were on their way to them, but wrong about the trees: a dry year killed most of them. Wrong about their assumption that they would stay in Logan County. We moved five hundred miles south, to upstate South Carolina, and different trees furnished my heart: shortleaf pine, white oak, sweetgum. Soon I was seventeen with college on the horizon, but we had nothing saved and no idea how to find the money. Somehow I had to find the money. I applied for scholarship after scholarship, wrote an essay about the biggest problem facing America's youth (apathy), tape-recorded myself playing my piano recital piece. Then a letter arrived. I'd done well on a standardized test, and Florida State University would pay for everything—tuition and fees, room and board, books—if I named them my first choice.

On the campus tour, I wore white flats and my Easter dress. There was a used condom under a live oak that I hoped my folks wouldn't notice. Back home I had a core group of friends—some from band, some not—just as odd as me. We listened to They Might Be Giants and Dwight Yoakam, Buffalo Tom, Dylan, Robert Johnson. FSU was Hootie and the Blowfish, happy clots of people sunbathing on the green, and the Dave Matthews Band. *What's your story?* people asked, but nobody listened to the answer.

Said Martha Graham of *Appalachian Spring*: "There is a house that has not been completed. The bar poles are up. The fence has not been

245

completed. Only a marriage has been celebrated. It is essentially the coming of new life. It has to do with growing things." On the drive home, after the campus tour, we stopped in Panama City, where for homework I read *The Metamorphosis* out loud to my sister. That night, in another room almost three thousand miles northwest, Kurt Cobain killed himself. Said Martha Graham, "Spring is the loveliest and the saddest time of the year."

HUMAN BEHAVIOR

August. I walked across campus on sidewalks inscribed with obscenities that jolted me every time but which I always read became I was always looking down. I carried textbooks, my borrowed horn, sheet music nobody had time to memorize. Every day my route to the practice field took me past an abandoned frat house, its windows boarded up, the site of a gang rape. Over eight hundred people had attended a party there. One of them, a woman, had needed a bathroom.

I pushed open the fire door to my dormitory and climbed the musty stairwell past a torn mural of maidens on their way to a bacchanal. Slick paint, tape stain. My window looked across the street to the Phi Mu house on Sorority Row. As we had lugged in crates of my books, Dad had said he was pretty sure that was where Ted Bundy had murdered those girls. Later I found out it was a different house a block away, but every time I saw that white columned plantation-style mansion I thought of blood.

What are you writing about down there, a friend back home asked, in a penciled letter written on notebook paper that arrived in U-Box 60766, a cubby with a door of glass and brass I unlocked by spinning a dial. I didn't tell him about the night by the pool: I didn't tell anyone about it. He sent me a mix tape that included Bjork's new song, "Human Behaviour," *Be ready, be ready to get confused.*

TOPS FOR FUN

September. Here's a photograph of me in the common room of my dorm, wearing my band uniform, a jacket with long tails trimmed in a diamond pattern in garnet and gold, and trousers creased from waist to ankle. On bye weeks I commandeered the lounge television to watch my favorite show. *Ren & Stimpy*. Animated and strangely paced, it fixated on the gross details of physicality—shiny zits, ingrown toenails, a sentimental fart cloud come to life. Ren was a Chihuahua with a hair-trigger temper. His ears pointed up like a rabbit's or back like a hyena's; his eyes were swollen as blood blisters, his mouth a red kidney. Stimpy the cat stared at the boob tube, rump parked in his litter box.

He unzipped his bulbous blue nose to access a first-aid kit; he drove a truck shaped like a baby bottle, because he was a Rubber Nipple Salesman. He twisted his body into a tight coil or compressed himself into a tuffet or distended his mouth to hwarf a hairball all over Ren. "You filthy swine!" Ren screamed. "I will kill you!"

Back home I went out every Saturday night, but in the crime report of our campus newspaper, the *Florida Flambeau*, I read:

Peeping Tom holes were discovered (again) in the restrooms of an academic building; a suspect was accused of raping a thirteen-year-old; over the weekend, a student was beaten with a baseball bat outside a cemetery so badly he needed reconstructive surgery.

"Sexual assaults can occur in desolate parking lots or at crowded parties. Taking precautions can help to protect yourself from becoming a victim," said the caption beneath a photo (re-creation) of a man forcing a woman into a car.

A cabdriver was killed, a Little Caesar's robbed at gunpoint, and two women from out of town, aged sixty and sixty-one, were robbed at the Days Inn: "The robbers fled the hotel room carrying with them a purse and a suitcase full of clothes."

A squib: "In both incidents, a man broke into apartments at University Towers, forced his way into the apartment and beat the women with a blunt object without taking anything."

And a decomposed body was found behind a power substation. Workers thought it was a pile of clothes. One worker recalled smelling a terrible odor when he had cut the grass in the area a month previous.

And a woman was sexually battered. And another woman was sexually battered. (When it happened, if it happened, you were to blame yourself. I expected it every night.)

"Nothing is funnier than unhappiness, I grant you that," wrote Samuel Beckett in *Endgame*. "Yes, yes, it's the most comical thing in the world." Oh, Ren's rage was the real reason I watched. His body was fragile, but the depth of his anger meant you had to reckon with him. He let himself fly to pieces. He let himself be ugly (curling hair, hammertoe), gibbering (*hee hee, hee hee*), a petty dork, a weirdo.

Last year, Florida State was named the country's Number One Party School. Said the creator of this award, "We only rate the things that

247

make a school fun to attend." Said a student when interviewed about the award: "This year, FSU is tops for fun."

SCREAM

In 1892, in Greenville, Illinois, long before his surname would become synonymous with high-quality marching band apparel, photographer Edmond DeMoulin had an inspiration: build a goat to help draw new members to the Modern Woodmen of America. At the time, the average lifespan for a white American man was forty-seven years. Commercial life insurance wasn't widely available, and fraternal societies like the Woodmen—and the Knights of the Maccabees, the Ancient Order of United Workmen, the Independent Order of Odd Fellows, and dozens more—offered mutual aid. Men joined these societies so that when they died, their brothers would help their widows and children. Member dues sponsored hospitals and orphanages, but if nobody attended meetings, the lodge couldn't collect. More than that, these societies, which traced their lineage back to medieval guilds meant to protect the livelihoods of traveling stonemasons, gave their members a sense of belonging to something larger than themselves. Members were links in a long chain stretching back hundreds of years, and they were responsible for carrying on that tradition. Part of the appeal was the groups' sense of exclusivity; *we're not for everyone*. The initiation process underscored that.

The "riding the goat" initiation ritual, popular among many groups, spoofed the idea that fraternal organizations were secretive cults in league with the devil. How do you build a goat? You kill a goat, skin it, and stretch its hide over an iron frame. How do you make a candidate ride a goat? You blindfold him, buckle him down, and push him around the room.

If ritual places an idea into tangible form, then evil becomes the devil, who becomes a goat. Cloven of hoof, rutty of mind. His scent (rank, cheesy) you will not forget. His unblinking eye (slot, pupil) fixes on what he desires. Put an obstacle in his way: he clambers atop it, or bashes it flat with his skullpan.

Initiation nights drew such crowds that the rituals grew more and more elaborate, becoming the actual point of the meetings. As the years went by, the DeMoulin brothers devised a range of ritual objects. The goat on wheels became the goat on runners became the goat welded to a hoop ("Ferris Wheel Goat"). Trophy trowels and collection plates,

248

Lifting and Spanking Machines, Traitor's Judgment Stand. In 1915, DeMoulin shipped enough catalogs to fill two boxcars. Their list included Baby Dolls, Binding Straps, and the Bleeding Test; Deceptive Burning Brands, human centipede costumes, electrified smoke. "Keep things moving—fast and furious," the catalog advised, alongside a listing of noisemakers from Rickety-Rackety to Rattler to Rooter. "Something doing every minute—that's what the members enjoy."

From the 1915 catalog: "Charleston Girls . . . all dressed up and ready to go." Someone stuffed a life-sized form with sawdust, fitted joints at knee and elbow. Someone sewed the halves of the scalp together and tucked in the knot so it would not show. Someone glued eyes in place, sewed eyelashes, painted a mouth. Someone wired her for electricity. When a candidate took his girl by the hand, a senior brother threw the switch. Said the catalog: "They are the clinging vine type; the fellows that draw them are sure to step high, wide and handsome." The current clenched the candidate's hands and he could not let go. Said the catalog, "They are a scream."

I think now that the elaborate nature of these evening rituals were a way to take the members out of their workaday lives and into a desert, a jungle, a Babylonian pleasure hall. Taking part in these rituals, you are not yourself; as in a dream, you participate in another story. No coincidence that membership in fraternal organizations began to fall after the Great War—and radio—and World War II—and television. Now a man could escape into a fictional world from the comfort of his living room, alone if he chose, and passively. But in the twentieth century's early years, he had to use painted glass and costumes, a metal sheet someone flexed to make the sound of thunder. He had to use his imagination.

DeMoulin stopped production of initiation devices after a factory fire in 1955. Today it is one of the leading manufacturers of band uniforms for high schools, colleges, and drum corps; they do quality work. And if you go to the DeMoulin Museum in Greenville, as I have, you'll see an oaken altar with a skeleton emerging from its tabletop, a false cigar clamped between its teeth. "Wacky fun!" says the museum's website. "You'll walk in wondering why . . . and leave thinking why not?" A trick guillotine with a wooden blade, a Knife-Throwing Machine with straps to hold the candidate in position. All of it showing its age; you can't believe anyone would be fooled. Not here, anyway, under the fluorescent lights. Outside the windows, maples leaf out in the square. But what about in a darkened room, disoriented by a blindfold, noise, exhaustion?

249

What's sinister in and of itself; what isn't? A glass of water. Balled sock. A cord tying your wrists.

PRACTICE

October afternoons, we practiced a stiff prance that popped the knee ninety degrees and needled the toe down into the dirt, bam! Scissor! Bam! Scissor! High mark time went above the knee, which meant we scraped left foot against right calf and then stabbed it into the ground. Because it rained every afternoon, the practice field was muddy, so our legs were muddy, and after a full practice, mine were bloody too, because the grit scraped like sandpaper. Our eyeballs smarted from sweat and somebody was always yelling at us through a bullhorn. *FIIIIIIIIIIVE,* hollered our section leader as we ran through warm-up. None of this was about thinking; it was muscle memory, spots scuffed in the crab-grass, poker chips dropped from darkest color to lightest to help clean the show. My breath turned to water and I pushed it up into a note and a phrase; I poured it onto the ground.

Together we worked to body the green land, sod painted with arrow-straight lines. We had to fill the bowl of the stadium with sound from the field up into the stands and higher, the press box, banks of floodlights, the blimp floating on its cushion of helium a thousand feet up, little planes towing signs advertising pizza and Barnacle Bill's. One person alone couldn't do it. One person's breath was not enough, even pushed through a brass tube stretched at the factory to a total length of fifteen feet, then coiled and turned back on itself so as to be compact to carry.

I can't remember her name. I can't remember whether we ever discussed that night. I don't think we did, although there was plenty of time—during practice, in the stands, in the nice hotel rooms paid for by the booster club. I don't remember any conversations with any of those people, the ones I thought would be my friends for life. For away games we rode charter buses for hours, staring out the greasy windows at fields of saw palmetto. Smell of diesel exhaust. Jacket fitted to the small of my back. Sometimes fans of the opposing teams cursed and screamed and pelted us with trash, but glass bottles had been banned from the stadiums not long before and this was why. Halfway through the season, the section leader ordered shirts for each of us with nicknames across the back. Because I never said anything, he named me "Holly Hobbie."

Across the field from us was the practice ring for the Flying High Circus, the country's only collegiate troupe. I watched the acrobats slap chalk dust from their palms, grab the trapeze bar, and swing into space; watched them release, tuck and tumble, and drop into a giant net that bounced them up again. Somehow I began to pace out a song as I walked from place to place alone, aware of every hedge and shadow; a song of warped plywood, storm, earplugs in a plastic bowl. Legal-sized sheets stapled and rolled: drill charts, each person a numbered X. I had a number of my own, and I split the difference between myself and my neighbors, pacing forward and back, spine straight.

WHO AM I?

In "Space Madness," the best episode of *Ren & Stimpy*, our heroes hurtle through galaxies on a seven-year mission, overcome by claustrophobia and boredom. Stimpy tries to cope, first by preparing a special meal (three tubes of meat paste) and then by drawing Ren a bubble bath. "Yes, sir," he says, "a nice hot bath is just the thing for nerves." Nothing helps, and Ren explodes, accusing Stimpy of trying to steal his bar of soap: "My ice cream bar! Oh, its chocolatey coating, its oh-so-creamy center! People always try to take it from me! I've had it since I was . . . a little child!"

I didn't know it back then, but the notion of space madness had been part of pop culture since before the first astronauts ever entered orbit. To choose the first spacemen—and they were all men—a team of bureaucrats screened applicants with an elaborate battery of tests. The idea was to spot any suicidal thrill-seekers long before liftoff, when they could jeopardize the mission. Candidates wore suits pressurized to mimic 65,000 feet of altitude, sat in rooms heated to 130 degrees for two hours, performed calculations at faster and faster rates. They were left alone in total darkness in a silent room (most fell asleep for at least part of the time). They spent time in the human centrifuge under various g-loads: said a 1959 report I read, "This procedure leads to anxiety, disorientation and blackout in susceptible subjects."

I'm most compelled by the 1950s-era psychological tests: Rorschach, Draw-A-Person, Find the Shape (teapot, handsaw) hidden within the tangle of lines. Guess the right half of the pair in *Shipley's Inventory of Needs*: yes to "I wish I could have more excitement," no to "I wish I weren't bothered by bad dreams." Yes to "I never notice

251

my heart beating," no to "My heart sometimes speeds up for no reason at all." Answer "Who am I?" twenty times over.

In later memos, some of the government agents admitted that the real reason for the tests was to ensure the candidates would do absolutely anything they were asked. The process worked: the astronauts chosen for the Mercury and Apollo missions completed their tasks without fuss, despite incredible stresses. But the notion of space madness endured.

A version of the Minnesota Multiphasic Personality Inventory is still in use today. Its more than five hundred true/false statements include "I have not lived the right kind of life" and "There seems to be a lump in my throat much of the time." I think about that, and about answering the question *Who am I? Who am I? Who am I?* Said *Shipley's Inventory of Needs:* "I have had very peculiar and strange experiences" and "At times I feel like smashing things."

TRIP THROUGH A STORMY DESERT

Start with a man in a darkened room. He wears a blindfold. In each hand he holds a pail heavy with stones still dusty from a nearby field. He tries to believe, as the man beside him whispers, that he is crossing a desert at night as a storm builds. Flash of light. Peal of thunder. He does believe it. "Let us get away from this approaching storm," says his guide, grasping him by the shoulder. "The air and ground seem filled with electricity."

His guide tells him of the trackless waste they wander, where vipers warm their bellies on the sand and bands of marauders lie in wait to torment him until he tell the mystic passwords of this ancient order, whose secret he must never reveal. He must walk the path that burns him. He must heed his guide's every word. Finally, after some hours, his guide unties the blindfold, its velvet facing damp with sweat, and lights the torch. The candidate blinks, dazzled.

You blink, dazzled, trying to discern the hooded figure who holds you by the elbow. Is he a friend? He must be, for he has been kind to you despite your faults. You have done everything he commanded, but you have done it wrong. You have walked too slowly and hindered him from his goal; you have walked too quickly and stumbled. The buckets' wire handles dig into your palms. You hunch your shoulders so as to bear the burden. You strive to become single in mind. "We are now in the center of the desert," says your guide; "yonder remains the only well within fifty miles of us. Shall we not refresh ourselves?" You

252

lean over the lip of the well, but when your lips touch the cup it bites you; a gunshot cracks and you fall.

And when it is over, and the swindle revealed—the lycopodium powder that flashed like lightning, snakes alongside the path (two coiled, three stretched their length) shown to be painted paper, water cup electrified, four brothers come from behind the screen—how will you take it? As you unlatch the electric sandals, will you admire the design of the heavy-duty battery and cord that power them? Will you roll the thunder sheet and tuck it into the Lodge closet? Next time, one of the parts will be yours. (Turn the crank of the wind machine and make the stretched fabric whine.) Or will you remember the room changed, turned shameful for how they hurt you? *Yes* and *I will* the only words they let you say.

SHOCK

In the Odd Fellows' morality play, he's Goliath. He looks out through the eyeholes, touches his fingers to his stiff forehead, his lips of roughened paper. He is alive in another body. He is not himself. From the catalog: "One special advantage of members wearing masks is that they may smile and enjoy the work unknown to the candidate." Here's the Grand Master, silent behind his cowl. From the catalog: "All persons should be careful not to laugh aloud."

In 1916, two initiates in Birmingham, Alabama, died of electrocution during a branding rite and an electrified boxing match. In 1911, in Newark, New Jersey, an initiate had permanent spinal damage after a cartridge casing hit him. In 1907, in the Water Valley Lodge in Mississippi, a blindfolded initiate "was then and there carelessly and roughly assaulted and struck and beaten and wounded with some hard substance of considerable weight and force, upon pelvic bone of hip, so as to cause this plaintiff great bodily pain and suffering, and which has caused him to be permanently injured, and unable to pursue his usual avocation, that of a railroad engineer."

Journalism professor Hank Nuwer has studied hazing since 1978 and maintains a database of hazing deaths on his website, on which he writes: "At least one U.S. school, club or organization hazing death has been reported every year from 1959 to 2019, according to my latest research effective August 2019." I sift through newspaper reports of hazing events. One young man choked to death on a piece of raw liver; another drowned in the Colorado River. A young woman fell seven stories from a balcony; another died in a car crash. Death after death from alcohol poisoning, blunt force trauma. "A terrific blow to the head." "Remained in a coma until he died."

The events I read about range from the military (punctured eardrum; set her clothes on fire) to the workaday (Terre Haute, Indiana: "A federal prison guard fired for hazing a trainee will try to get his job back, saying 'the initiation of a fellow officer was a past practice and it has been condoned for years'"). They take place in colleges ("beaten like an animal") and in high schools (one band in Illinois—with faculty and parents as chaperones—allegedly made students "put bags over their heads [and drove them] on a bus to a wooded area where they were sprayed with bug repellent and led to the ceremony . . . 'similar to a sacrifice scene from an occult movie' and a knighting, 'including tall sword-wielding men in costumes reminiscent of the Ku Klux Klan'").

There's a stance I recognize: the impulse to make it seem like a joke. ("Even the band is in trouble at Florida State," reads a headline about my hazing event.) (The DeMoulin Museum: "You'll walk in wondering why . . . and leave thinking why not?") An article about Major League Baseball in 2002, titled "Dressed Up: Rookie Major Leaguers Endure Pranks, Hazing," describes the outfits the newbies must wear: tutu and leotard, wedding dress, short shorts and crop tops. Says the author of the article, "Everyone seems to be doing it." One of the senior players "flashed a mischievous grin when asked if he's the ringleader. 'Yeah, you could say that,' he said. 'I try to get things together, try to keep that tradition going. We just try to have fun, keep things loose.'" ("We only rate the things that make a school fun to attend.") Hopefully, we can make it even more special this year.'" The audience is necessary here; this is cruelty as spectacle. (Sang Kurt Cobain, *Here we are now / entertain us.*)

Hazing is hard to eradicate, because the ones who do it are the ones who had it done to them. Some experts believe that in order to stop it, you have to suspend the program completely for several years. In a newspaper article about our hazing event, a sophomore from Miami Springs said, "What they call hazing, we call tradition, I guess."

Said a longtime DeMoulin employee: "I don't know how many electric carpets I made. Because of the size, it took another girl that had to stand behind my machine and hold the carpet. It was on leather and we sewed these strips of copper wiring down it . . . I knew what they were and the guys who put the electrical connections to them said they tried it out on somebody and it knocked him to his knees. I knew it was for initiations but at the time I never thought too much about it."

In 2011, members of the Marching 100 at Florida A & M University, also in Tallahassee, beat drum major Robert Champion "more than 100 times as he tried to bulldoze his way from the front of the bus to the back through fellow band members" until he died of "hemorrhagic shock." A spokeswoman said, "There's this culture of secrecy and this conspiracy of silence that has helped to institutionalize hazing." Upon hearing about Champion's death, another band member said, "I was shocked that it happened to him, but not so shocked that it happened."

The very qualities I loved about band—community, hard work, the grand gesture—made it the ideal vehicle for hazing. What was it but walking in a line with others, the measured step, the matching jacket and trousers eliding visual difference? That moment beside the pool felt pointless, but it actually had a very clear aim: to break us down so we would do the next thing the leader demanded, no matter what it was. Press your lips to the silver mouthpiece. *You will have to favor the brothers with a song.* I knew exactly what to do: how to hold my body, where to step and when, what notes to play, how to arrange my face, how to breathe. Pace a careful step, eight per five yards. Adjust where necessary, motion for visual effect. You're always aware of splitting the space between the bodies to your left and right, tuning against each other instead of absolute concert pitch. Listen, breath warm in your throat, then cooling in the horn's bends; after, a red moon on the divot of your lip.

GAME DAY

Start barefoot on wet grass. Tonight the players' cleats will rip the turf, but now it's marked only by our footprints, dark against the sparkling dew.

For me, football is a coincidence of geography: we share a field, time limits, and audience with young men who rise early to punish their bodies, whose discipline decrees what they eat and who their friends are, fractures them, concusses them, stretches and tears their ligaments and muscles. They pad up, tighten their laces, apply grease paint. Faces shielded but their names everybody knows: Dunn, Boulware, Brooks. We love them and fear for their safety. Anyone who would wish them harm must be our enemy too, from some other town; their ways are strange to us.

Hence the rituals: a man in redface and turkey-feather headdress thrusts a flaming spear into the turf. Boys naked from the waist up, coated in glitter, spell words with glyphs painted on their dented chests. Squares of ground cut from enemy fields after important victories are replanted at the Sod Cemetery with granite markers carved with date and opponent. At another school, a famous alum dies and asks that his ashes be scattered at the fifty-yard line. At a third, a famous coach dies and is buried near the stadium, so that on game day he can still hear the roar of the crowd.

Which is considerable, and being dead might not stop your ears to it. On game day, I stand with the rest of the band under the end zone before kickoff, as the fans stomp their feet and the stands above us shake. *I can't do this anymore.* If I stay in, I'll have to haze the new students next year. I'm caught two ways: by this music, which was what I thought I wanted to do with my life, and by the money; if I transfer to another school, I'll lose my academic scholarship. Above my head, a wordless roar from the mob.

I have loved this: sweet smell of valve oil. Orange spray paint, Dixie cups full of Gatorade, pink crepe-de-chine cut in a crescent and un-furled from the silver pole. I have loved taking on a big project with other people. White cotton gloves dotted with rubber grips. I decide to complete the season; you finish what you start. But I'll never play in an ensemble here again. The crowd noise rattles our teeth in our skulls and someone pushes a button and the aluminum garage door clatters open and the blast of the stadium comes shooting in like water through a tail-race and the drum major sounds his whistle, *one, two, one two three four* and we step through the open door onto the springy green turf, the brilliant point of light on which eighty thousand pairs of eyes are fixed, and we all, all of us, we all of us scream.

DRILL CHART

Trace an individual's position through the drill: one mote floating from point to point, a dot pausing two steps right of the thirty-five yard line for seven seconds, then moving backward toward the visitor sideline. A blip in thrall to a larger vision. *Who am I?* Even after I unwrapped the blindfold and walked away, I couldn't shake the feeling of being alone. On New Year's Day we played the Sugar Bowl in New Orleans. The leg-end painted over the gate that led onto the field read ABANDON HOPE,

ALL YE WHO ENTER HERE. When the game ended, I walked off the field for what I knew was the last time.

Some names, not all of them: Richard T. Swanson, Robert Bazile, Theodore R. Ben, Michael Davis, Tucker Hipps, Robert Champion. A thousand holes for a thousand trees. Lined up in tidy rows. A tree is not a person, but—a dry season killed almost all of them. A person is not a tree, but—*struck more than a hundred times until he died. Hit with an open hand more than a hundred times until he lost hearing in his left ear.* Hazing takes practice's good repetition and warps it. I think of crushes never courted, mortgages never signed. Music not adapted for student players. Days and years gone, stolen.

In a 1953 newsletter published by the Masons I read: "The newly rich woman was trying to make an impression. 'I clean my diamonds with ammonia, my rubies with wine, my emeralds with brandy and my sapphires with fresh milk.' A quiet woman sitting next to her looked at her and replied, 'I don't clean mine. When they get dirty, I just throw them away.'"

DADDY UV-UM ALL

The four-lane bridge over the Mississippi River rises toward an unseen vanishing point as tractor trailers pelt along behind and beside me, and under me the river rises, opaque and dark, sliding up the bridge abutments as it carries drowned oak trees along on its current. I came here of my own volition to get something I needed, but now I just want to go home. As my breathing tightens and my vision closes around the edges and the bridge keeps tilting up. Over the pulling river.

Finally I've arrived at the DeMoulin Museum, having taken two planes, a shuttle, and a rental car to get here; having crossed the flooded Mississippi River and driven past fields sheeted with standing water; having brought camera and notebook into this storefront museum kept afloat by the man in front of me. Who unlocks the door and lets me in, on break from his job at the bank across the square. *What brought you here?* he asks, and I end up telling him more than I intend. In five minutes I've told this kind-faced stranger more than I ever told anyone twenty years ago. He leaves to finish his shift and locks me in, says, *Take as long as you need.*

I page through the archives' photo albums. There's a lot of cake: birthday parties and retirements, women modeling band jackets over their street clothes, a hog raffle to benefit a daughter's medical care. Pinned to the wall is a quilt in a tumbling block pattern made of scraps of velvet from robes. Scores of people made and make a good living here. In the factory nearby, I watch a woman embroider loops and lines onto the chest of a white jacket. Meanwhile the river rises. As the people fill sandbags and say they will wait it out, I walk through a place invisibly furnished with a bucket of adulterated blood, men in donkey suits, Yama Yama in good figured cloth, horse head with tongue (five cents extra) that unrolls with a puff of air. Silk pillow shams bear the legend *While we live, let's live in clover / For when we're dead, we're dead all over.*

There's an element of the theatrical in all this: Balloon Ascension or the Parachute Leap, the Rocky Road to Dublin, Raiding the Hornets' Nest (or Trip Thru a Swamp). Here's a photo on the museum wall, a gnome atop a goat atop a wagon. The caption says it's nine feet tall. Surrounding the wagon are four black-robed men in devil masks: horns, wrinkled brows, pointed ears, bulging eyes. Slight differences between the faces show that the masks were made by hand. This one looks like he wants to convert you; this cross-eyed one is more malicious; this one daydreams about something worse; and the last one is proud, chin thrust out, shoulders squared. The sign he holds reads *The Daddy Uv-Um All.* All four demons wear black robes and black neckerchiefs; you can see no skin except for their hands. Hands hanging loose or propped on a hip; hands that turned doorknobs, picked apples, held a fork.

WINDOW

The season ended. Music became for me the mockingbirds imitating car alarms, percussive splat of volleyball connecting with forearm on the sandpit, yet another cover of "Margaritaville" played at the club down the street. The next September, when the football team made a big play, I could hear the roar from my dorm room, carried on the breeze from the stadium two miles away.

I remember the high whine of Highway 319 where it hugged the Gulf's gray sand beach towns: Lanark, Sopchoppy, Carrabelle. In Tallahassee, at the Cow Haus, I swayed along as Will Oldham slurred *Well it's Valentine's Day / And I'm catatonic.* John Darnielle played "Going to Bolivia" on his guitar with such ferocity his fingertips bled. I slept in another dorm by then; painted on the hallway was a Paul Simon line, *Losing love is like a window in your heart.* I used to drive across Georgia in a day, headed home to South Carolina. Cotton scuds on the road shoulder. Billboards: PAPERSHELL PECANS *FRESH CROP.* Rumble strip, big rigs, Gregg Allman singing *I don't own the clothes I'm wearing.* Some other girl sweated through the uniform that used to be mine.

My turn away wasn't dramatic. Not splashy, or even visible to anyone else: the opposite of show. Holly Hobbie, silent. Three years after its inception, Florida State ended the scholarship program that had paid my way; administrators said it cost too much. I got in under the wire. This is a love story, which means it is about heartbreak. I took writing classes in which I worked to understand plot and conflict, but I know now what I really wanted: to get back somehow to that feeling of inexorable beat and melody, the totality of show, which shook anyone that touched it from rib cage to fingertips. *Look at me,* everyone in the press box, everyone in the stands. *I am perfect.* Back straight, carriage commanding, walking a slow measure down the fifty-yard line.

WHERE'S YOUR PROPHET NOW?

I need a song. A song that works like a spell to counteract all these acts of cruelty. And it could be the sorrow and hope that Aaron Copland wove with a Shaker tune in 1944, the sixth year of a long war. It could be a big-eyed girl from Iceland singing *And there's no map / And the compass wouldn't help at all.*

Or it could be a song that takes on evil made flesh, as the fraternal initiations pretended. A song called "The Devil Went Down to Georgia." I'd heard the story my whole life, how Johnny, naïve but talented, takes the devil up on a bet and wins. The shocker is that the devil admits defeat.

I watch a concert clip from 1979, the Charlie Daniels Band barreling through the biggest hit of their career. In the studio, Daniels had played the devil's part seven times over and used overdubbing to create the sound of a demon band. He had custom-strung his fiddle with eight strings instead of the usual four. But even live, the band somehow makes it work, the keyboardist with one arm in a sling, Daniels bored by his own excellence, a cowboy hat pulled low over his face, masking it in shadow. When he tells off the devil at song's end—*Done told you once, you son of a bitch, I'm the best that's ever been*—the packed arena screams.

The song owes a measure of its power to the fact that it carries the DNA of a much older story, like Faust, like the myth of Robert Johnson at the crossroads. Daniels cited his debt to a poem he read in high school,

Stephen Vincent Benet's "The Mountain Whippoorwill," which describes a fiddling contest at the Essex County Fair, a mythic place in Georgia. When our hero, Hill-Billy Jim, shows up, nobody thinks he has much of a shot. But when his turn comes, Jim muses, "They've fiddled the rose, and they've fiddled the thorn / But they haven't fiddled the mountain-corn." He does, and shuts everybody down. Both the song and the poem depend on beating all comers, whether it's Dan Wheeling, little Jimmy Weezer, or Satan himself. Says Hill-Billy Jim, "Where's your prophet now?"

What do you know like nobody else, and how do you carry it in your body? I know feathers wired and twisted into place, stored in tubes to prevent crushing. I know oily kumquat slick in my mouth; cud of tobacco; thigh scraped raw by Florida dirt. My own voice strange from disuse. Sock feet to protect the turf; finish rubbed off the horn; colored fire.

I sing what made me: sawdust and kerosene. Oil ruby red in the pan under the chucker. I sing putting up with John Q. Public at a contract post office at Christmastime. I sing people who loved me who didn't get my chance: who kept chickens, gathered eggs on cold mornings and hot, washed them in the sink, and polished them with Bon Ami to sell. Who worked the laundry in the hospital basement. Speed Queen industrial washers, whine and clang and smell of Clorox. *Land sakes*, she used to say, *for land sakes*.

Statistics are hard to come by, but the year I finished my small-town high school, the graduation rate in South Carolina was 62 percent. This at a time when the textile mills that had employed thousands of local people were closing. Between 1970 and 1996—a generation's time—a million jobs evaporated in South Carolina.

Somewhere in my twenties, I heard that a boy who played baritone with me in high school band had hanged himself. Since 2000, deaths by suicide and overdose have risen among white Americans without a bachelor's degree, write economists Anne Case and Angus Deaton in their 2020 book *Deaths of Despair and the Future of Capitalism*. Part of me recognized that night beside the pool for what it was: another test to secure the middle-class economic stability that men had also wanted from those fraternal organizations. A few Aprils ago, I heard about another friend from band, dead at thirty-nine. At his funeral, his trombone stood next to the preacher's pulpit, where a casket would go. His dad kept saying "my boy, my boy."

And something I had not realized, as many times as I've heard "The Devil Went Down": Charlie Daniels plays both the devil's part and Johnny's. He's both.

So am I.

I sing a song of gust and blood, baseball bat and broken headstones, piles of clothes. Of a narrow bed and lying awake under a plaid blanket. Once I rode out a hurricane in that dorm, windows a blur of black rain. Afterward I walked down the sidewalk in the dark, cracking blowdown pecans against each other and eating them. The sodium streetlights reflected pink on the backs of cockroaches as they streamed out of the storm drain.

Sing sand and granular ash. Pigeon droppings in dark coils on the edge of the poured-concrete balcony. Hidden hallway in the English building, Floor 3 ½, reachable only by a shuddering elevator that smelled of ozone. In the cafeteria, mealworm larvae squirmed in my bowl of granola. One thing I learned was to be inexorable. Sometimes in a clinch and sometimes running full out and always, always, always toward the goal.

Sing the wrecking ball the demolition crew used a few summers back to tear my old dorm down. No implosion: asbestos. Hoses sprayed water to settle the dust, and the crew shoveled rubble into covered dumpsters painted blue. Brushed steel doorknobs, cinderblocks, common-room sofa where I watched *Ren & Stimpy*: everything saturated with unseen poison. This is what it means to become aware of living under threat. As did the fifteen thousand other women who lived there from 1959 until 2015. So knock it down, rebar, cement, light fixture. Break the brittleness I carried curled in my spine. Scrape the ground clean and burn it dry.

WHO I AM

As in a dream, there's something you must do. The particulars might shift but the need insists upon itself. Maybe you have to find your way home, or your way into adulthood. This is a love story: a child grows up. Who am I? *There is no map*, sang Björk, so chart one yourself: I followed the Saluda watershed southwest into the Savannah, then the Chattahoochee basin, then into the Ocmulgee (past the crossroads where Duane Allman died in a motorcycle crash) and the Suwannee, through (remnants of) wiregrass and longleaf and over black water bogs, past vineyards of muscadine and scuppernong, down a road tunneled by live oaks, and there I was.

Musical composition wasn't a language I spoke, but I had the need to shape something that would move people. Something rare and wonderful, possible on field or page, or best, sung aloud. Together we make something that feels freed from normal time, yet built from breath and heartbeat. Something like paradise or play. Brief, blissed. And the listener makes this possible. I see it in the film of the Saratoga Springs crowd in 1979: when Johnny beats the devil (that is, hurt, cruelty, death) we shout for joy because we know: we can beat him too. On good days, we do. But once is not enough. We keep at it.

The company front was always my favorite way to end a show. The whole band stretches in a line from end zone to end zone and moves slowly toward the stands. As an audience member, you don't think about the brass flashing under the big stadium lights, the flags all a flat of color at the same angle, the rounds of bass drums slowly advancing in a rank, the pit percussion hitting the marimba in dancing chords with yarn-wrapped mallets. All of that is present, but it's not what you notice. You feel something past words and you leap to your feet, an uncontrollable physical response, a current passing between you and the people nearby. ("The air and ground seem filled with electricity.") You yell your throat raw to share in the din. You tingle from crown to sole; sparks practically arc from your fingertips.

Look with me over those assembled here. Acrobats, bureaucrats, astronauts, dancers. The girl ahead of me in line. The fifteen thousand women who slept in Dorman Hall. Robert Johnson alongside my high school band directors (Bruce Caldwell, Barry Reese), Charlie Daniels and "Taz" DiGregorio, the keyboardist with his left arm in a sling. A woman with a Gibson Girl updo, addressing a stack of catalogs on a wide worktable, early 1915. A man removing a Goliath mask, wiping his sweaty brow. John Kricfalusi, creator of *Ren & Stimpy*, so obsessed with perfection he spent a year on a single eight-minute cartoon ("Stimpy's Invention"). A woman washing her sapphires with milk. My friends who played baritone and trombone alongside me in the Copland show. Björk Gudmundsdottir, a string of Charleston Girls, and Warrick Dunn (the greatest running back of all time and a tremendous human who forgave the men who murdered his mother). Here, tonight, I'm making supper when *Appalachian Spring* comes on the radio. It does not pretend at a world without sorrow. Copland called it "music for use." We're all gone now, the kids we were.

Sometimes I still dream I'm back at practice with a show to learn and I feel so glad, my foot pressing the springy sod. It has to do with growing things, something doing every minute. One person alone can't do it. Keep things moving—fast and furious. Take as long as you need and finish what you start. Leap from the platform, spindle through the air and catch the trapeze that drops into place at just the right moment and sail into a wordless roar of applause. You're spinning, disoriented, sometimes blacking out and sometimes coming to. *Be ready, be ready to get confused.* A voice on a loudspeaker counts down from ten and the world shifts beneath your weight. For land sakes, while we live, let's live in clover. Where's your prophet now? Who am I? Who am I? Sometimes my heart speeds up for no reason at all. What are you writing about down there? *Yes* and *I will* the only words you need to say.

I know the place where the walnut seedlings grew and died. I know the smell of oil and the burn of sweat, how to work past tired, tune and pitch. He ain't fiddled the walnut tree. He ain't fiddled the sweet-gum gum, or the crabgrass sprouting from the sand. But I have. During a summer storm I hear a thunderclap: C#. I know it's September when acorns drum the neighbor's carport. I walk down the street with my beloved, in step. What we love, we see everywhere. Every choice affects the horn's sound: the particular alloy of copper and zinc, how the artisan shapes the bell with a padded blackjack, this humid air, my lips. Those people whose names I've forgotten: that night by the pool marked them too. I walked away and somehow that decision set my feet on this good path.

We're here now, walking a plain path with patterned steps marked out like dance. Give me green grass, sunlight, a sound big enough to shake the sky on its hinge. Take my hand. No masks, no secrets. Who am I? Tell everyone you know. *Done told you once.* I've had strange experiences in my life, I've crossed the desert on a stormy night, I've danced around the devil struck dumb by defeat. Who am I? *You son of a bitch.* Keep doing it. Once is not enough. Say it. Say it again. Say it so you know. I'm the best that's ever been.

NOTE ON SOURCES:

I'm indebted to many sources for this piece, most crucially John Goldsmith, curator of the DeMoulin Museum, and Donald Adamski, president and CEO of DeMoulin Bros. and Company, who took time out of their busy days to explain the history and manufacture of uniforms and other items to me. Mr. Goldsmith's careful read of the piece saved me from many errors; I'm grateful to him for his help. We have different takes on this material, but I respect the fine history he does. Julia Suits's *The Extraordinary Catalog of Peculiar Inventions* (Perigee, 2011) gives larger historic and cultural context for DeMoulin's initiation devices. For more information on hazing, see Jason M. Silveira and Michael W. Hudson, "Hazing in the College Marching Band," *Journal of Research in Music Education* 2015, vol. 63 (1), 5–27. I also relied on the work of Hank Nuwer, who has spent much of his career writing about hazing. Bill Faucett's *The Marching Chiefs of Florida State University: The Band that Never Lost a Halftime Show* (McFarland, 2017) contained details about the hazing I experienced.

Nominated by The Georgia Review, Edward McPherson, Joan Murray

SCREENSAVER

by ROBERT CORDING

from THE COMMON

Sure, every photograph is an elegy
to what was, but this photograph—
which I've turned into my screensaver—
of my son, dead nearly three years,
has him suspended in mid-air.
He has just jumped from a rocky outcropping
thirty feet above the shimmering water
of Lake George that flashes silver and gold.
The day itself is glittering with light
that has the feeling of being
excessive and there are (I've counted)
seven different shades of green
in the hemlocks and cedars and white pines
growing from the rocky soil of the island.
My son is alive in the thrill of his airborne body,
though it is quiet in the photograph,
no cheers and whoops from his friends
who are waiting at the top to jump,
no sounds of the boats idling below, or the waves
sloshing against their bobbing hulls.
I will not see him cleave the surface of the lake
and vanish with hardly a splash
and then break back into the light,
silvery water cascading from his hair and shoulders.
And I will not see him climb back up the rocks,

eager and intent on his next single-second flight.
But almost daily I give thanks
for this moment in which the past is gone
but never dead, this glimpse
of the terrible sorrow to come, but also
of something like an afterlife
in which his body, relaxed, calm, hovers
as if it's forgotten its heaviness,
the air holding him fast, halfway between
two places at once, the good light of sky
and the ease of bright water that waits.

Nominated by Jeffrey Harrison, Andrea Hollander, William Wenthe

HALF SPENT

fiction by ALICE McDERMOTT

from SEWANEE REVIEW

Four years after Martin's very frugal father passed away, his mother sent him a musical birthday card. It was a huge, garish thing. On the front it said, *Dude, You're Fifty*, and inside: *Rock on!* It played a tinny version of *In-A-Gadda-Da-Vida*—a staple of the garage band of his Jersey youth. It was a six-dollar card. His mother had attached eight Forever stamps for postage.

"As your financial advisor," he said when she called, "May I suggest, next time, words without music—?"

His mother was a silly woman. Martin loved her with all his heart— "She's my *mother*, for God's sake," he would tell his wife—but he knew this to be true. She was an archetype from a time long past: small and blond, wide-eyed, easily distracted, easily given to fits of laughter or bouts of snuffling tears, helpless and inept in a way that must have been appealing to his large and humorless father who made marrying her, in 1960, his life's one concession to whimsy. Throughout Martin's childhood, his mother hit all the sitcom tropes: a fender bender or an uprooted shrub every time she pulled out of the driveway—until his father took her license away. Extravagant credit card bills, her weaknesses being satin blouses and a perfume called Youth Dew—until the credit cards were taken away as well. There were pressure cooker disasters. Misread assembly instructions. The sopping, paper-wrapped neck and gizzards of the Thanksgiving turkey pulled from the bird by his father as he carved.

It would be nice to remember the old man as indulgent of his ditzy wife, fond and forgiving, but that was never the case. Their father didn't tolerate stupidity or silliness in his children, who, all three, grew up to be engineers with MBAs, each scattered now to serious cities—St. Louis, Atlanta, Columbus —so why would he accept nonsense in a wife?

Martin and his two siblings argued in long retrospect that the man was only being consistent: there was no charm for him in foolishness, no matter who in his household had perpetrated it.

They were a cliché from an ancient past, such parents: the cheap, taciturn, undemonstrative husband and the timid woman who had made herself both his prisoner and his ward. Martin knew this and sometimes, when he was younger, when his father's dismissiveness had seemed cruel or his mother's hapless innocence annoying, he wished it to be otherwise. But he and his siblings agreed: you could not call a marriage of forty-seven years a failure simply because it was unoriginal.

When their father died at seventy-five—quickly, efficiently, of a second heart attack the day after he went to the hospital with the first and two hours before an expensive triple bypass was to begin—the three of them, somewhat warily, asked their mother what she would like to do next. The house in Parsippany was mortgage-free. Their father—as he had taken to pointing out in the last years of his life—had never eaten in a five-star restaurant or darkened the door of a Cineplex or bought a car from a dealer, but he had sent three kids to good colleges on an electrician's salary and had invested wisely enough to make sure "your mother" would "never be a burden."

She could age in place, her children assured her. She could choose from a number of local "active adult" senior living high-rises. She could even, as his sister put it, kiss New Jersey goodbye and move to Tahiti.

Their mother smiled and nodded and raised her penciled eyebrows to show she was impressed with each and every one of these suggestions. For a while she spoke enthusiastically about a condo complex in Fort Myers where a number of their neighbors had already gone. There was a lake and a café and a community room with lectures and arts and crafts. She had the brochures. But nothing came of it. None of them imagined that anything would. She was, after all, a woman who had never lived alone, or traveled alone. She had seldom even cashed a check or paid a bill. She had not driven a car in over thirty years. The routine their father had set for them both in the decade of his retirement—newspaper with the *Today* show in the morning, an hour or two tinkering in the garden or the garage, a sandwich, a trip to the store, the evening news, a light dinner and nodding off in front of the TV until bedtime—continued to suit her well enough after he was gone.

Initially, Martin and his siblings were concerned that she would be isolated or lonely in this new, widowed life. Martin also worried (he was his father's son) about how much money she would have to spend on cabs: to get to the doctor or the grocery store, to the shopping mall and the hairdresser's. But the sudden emergence of a coterie of generous neighbors took care of this. These were not the neighbors Martin had known growing up in that narrow cul-de-sac but a new population he'd scarcely been aware of in the years since he'd left home.

There was Rosario who owned the house next door. There were the Brewers, empty nesters across the way, and next to them, a young couple—Bart and Shanthi, his mother called them, as if they were old friends—with school-aged children. There were also the Evanko brothers in the house at the turning, Ukrainian pharmacists. Bill and Luke's yard abutted hers; Sylvie and Maria lived on the corner—"the nice gay people," she called them.

How his mother had befriended them all in what he thought of as the reclusive years after his father's retirement remained unclear to him, but they were there from the moment he and his siblings returned her to the house with their father in an urn.

Soon after, Martin learned in his weekly phone calls home, Rosario had made his mother her "Saturday movie buddy" and "happy hour girl-friend." Bart took her garbage cans to the curb on collection day and mowed her lawn, while Shanthi sent the children over with casseroles or cupcakes. The Brewers bought her groceries, the nice gay couples gave her rides to the mall and to the medical center, and the Evanko brothers knocked on her door every evening as they walked their dogs, to drop off her medications, or her nail polish, or her Youth Dew, or one of those musical greeting cards she loved to send, because, they told her, their own grandmother was so very far away.

When she was diagnosed with leukemia at eighty, Martin and his siblings agreed it was time to find a live-in, someone to take over what cooking and cleaning she still did for herself and also to ensure that these generous friends would not be made to feel overburdened as the demands of her illness increased. Martin called a few agencies, drove to Jersey for the interviews, and hired an Ethiopian woman with an excellent resume and a wide smile.

Her name was Aida. "Like the opera," he told his brother and sister on a conference call.

There was a brief silence. Although all three of them were well-off, educated, upper-middle class, even, Martin recognized in the silence an innate, New Jersey wariness of pretension: *Opera?*

"That tells us absolutely nothing," his sister said.

A full-time live-in was expensive: Aida would be there twenty-four hours a day, six days a week, except for Sundays, when Rosario or the other neighbors filled in. But their father had planned well, the siblings agreed. Their mother could afford it.

Still, there were nights, early on, when Martin woke up suddenly with the comic-book vision of a great hole punched into the fat money bag that was his father's retirement stash. He saw it all trickling away, coin by coin—or, he thought, ticking away, hour by hour, minute by minute, even as Aida merely slept in his boyhood room back in New Jersey.

But his mother quickly came to love her. Now she confessed to Martin and his siblings that she had been terrified all along, sleeping alone in the house. Over these many years, she told them, she had piled the kitchen chairs against the back door every evening, scattered Christmas bells and tin cans across every window sill. She had put their father's old work boots, freshly muddied, on the front step. She had never turned out all the lights.

She clucked her tongue and laughed at herself: "I really did. I never told you kids, but I really did."

But now, with Aida in the next room, she slept as soundly as she had in all the years their father was at her side.

Aida was a Christian woman, she was given to saying. "I will care for your Mommy's soul, even as I take care of her body." His mother never mentioned her soul, although Martin often saw a battered and much underlined Bible on the coffee table during his visits home. But the physical ministrations, the back rubs and scalp massages and pedicures and bubble baths, became a major topic of his mother's conversations in the years of her decline. Aida's hands were large, with broad yellow nails mottled like seashells. And yet, he saw this too on his visits home, his mother closed her eyes in luxurious contentment whenever Aida touched her, if only to put a comb to her thinning hair or to wipe a bit of saliva from her chin. It was childish, yes, the way his mother poked her head into Aida's palm, like a purring kitten, or took the woman's wrist to stay her hand when it brushed her cheek. More childish still, as his mother's health declined, the way she sat so contentedly in the crook of Aida's long arm or leaned into her lap.

"Your Mommy loves me," Aida would tell him when he called. "Your Mommy loves me and I love her. I pray to God for her every day. I am a Christian woman."

"We're Christians, too," he said once, somewhat uneasily. He could not help but feel, at times, that there was something false, even underhanded, in her proclamations of affection—perhaps even in her stubborn repetition of "your Mommy" which, he told his sister, he sort of hated. He tipped her every time he came to visit—every six weeks or so—a couple of fifties left for her on the kitchen table, sometimes even tucked into the battered Bible. His brother and his sister did the same. Of course they were grateful for Aida's presence in the house, her careful ministrations, her affection for their mother, but none of it was the same as the generosity the neighbors offered. She was an employee, after all. And much as he tried to resist it, there was an unshakeable mistrust—probably racist, he admitted to his wife—tied to his experience of those scamming e-mails that purported to be from other earnest African Christians. *I love your Mommy, please send a check.*

"I know you are Christian," Aida had replied, soothingly. "But your Mommy says she don't go to church. She don't pray."

His father had been raised a Lutheran in Pennsylvania but had moved to Jersey as a young man just out of the Army and never bothered to join a church. His mother's family had been Methodist once, but they, too, had long ago fallen away. There had been, in his youth, a boring week at Bible camp one summer, a season playing baseball with a CYO team. Services, when he was young, at Christmas and Easter, but even that ended when he and his siblings hit their teenage years. Martin's wife's family was mildly Presbyterian. They'd been married in her parents' church, where only his mother-in-law seemed to have any prior acquaintance with the minister. His own two children were religion free. He had among his friends and coworkers in Columbus a good number of Catholics and Protestants and Jews, a couple of Hindus, two Muslims, a Mormon, but the majority of his acquaintances were like himself, content enough with the vague claim to be Christian and the good—frugal, perhaps—sense not to make too much of the matter.

"I'm sure she prays," he told her. "Maybe you just don't hear it."

"I pray for her," Aida said. "I pray she will see God."

Another thing that annoyed him (he told his brother) was the way Aida said God with an extra, resonating emphasis on the *d*—as if she herself had learned the word from some TV evangelist, as if she were pointing out some profundity she feared he would never understand.

"I pray she will hear the angels sing."

In the third year of their mother's illness, they hired nurses to come by on alternate days, supplementing Aida's care. Then, four years in, the hospice people arrived. These were mostly middle-aged women who dressed like elementary school teachers and seemed to speak in sentences learned in a training session—professional mourners, his brother called them. His sister, on the phone, did a funny riff on how they had enumerated for her all the Medicare benefits their mother would receive now that the end was near. "The bad news is your mother's dying. The good news is Medicare's now paying for her hospital bed!"

With her health in steady decline, her body shrinking in on itself, growing, literally now, more child-sized every time he saw her, her mind often confused, his mother had asked them for only one favor. She understood that they would want to sell the house when she was gone. The neighborhood was popular with young families, and a house on the cul-de-sac would fetch a good price. But would they please, she said, wait until Aida had found herself a new place to live, a new assignment, or at least an apartment of her own. Would they let her stay in the house, rent-free, for as long as that would take?

"How long?" his brother in St. Louis asked. It was another conference call among the three siblings. "Six months? A year? What if she decides she doesn't want to leave at all? Like a squatter. What if interest rates go up while we're being so generous?"

His sister in Atlanta said some muffled words to a coworker and then turned back to the phone. "It's what Mom wants," she said briskly. "It's the least we can do. Aida has been so great. And Mom loves her."

His brother said, "Mom loves everybody, indiscriminately. She loved Dad, didn't she?"

His sister would not be amused. "I don't know what we would have done without Aida."

"Hired someone else," his brother said. "Fifty thou a year for Christ's sake. Now we're supposed to give her the house?"

"It's what Mom wants," his sister said again, and all three of them knew the depth and complexity of their mother's wishes, their mother's whimsy.

"Let's put a six-month cap on it at least," his brother said.

In early April, Aida called to say, "Come tell your Mommy goodbye."

All three were there by that evening, and on the afternoon of the next day, they were all three in their parents' bedroom when their mother

272

simply turned her head toward the window and stopped breathing. Aida, standing in the doorway of the room, wept large tears, wiping her cheeks with the heel of her palm. The siblings hugged each other without words and then, awkwardly, took Aida in their arms. Martin was surprised to discover how thin she was—hard-boned, yes, but not much flesh. And then they gazed at their mother, so small under the pink quilt. "Now what?" Martin whispered, and his sister picked up the binder the hospice women had left behind. She ran her finger down the index and said, out loud, "Page 8."

That evening, the neighbors in the cul-de-sac began to appear, bringing casseroles and cakes and offering their services—pickups at the airports, runs to the deli—for the days ahead.

They had thought, the three siblings, that as they had done for their father, there would be only a quick cremation, a family dinner, and that would be that, but as the evening wore on and more neighbors dropped by and lingered to talk about their mother—funny things she had said, stories she had told about their childhoods, her appreciation of a good movie, a good laugh, Youth Dew, and those outlandish musical cards—they realized that a service of some sort was in order.

After they ate a subdued dinner gleaned from the neighborhood's offerings, Aida cleaned up the kitchen and then retreated to her room. But she emerged late that first evening to hear them propose it: a memorial service on Saturday afternoon, after the cremation, a way to gather the neighbors and thank them for their kindness, and to celebrate their mother's life. Aida seemed, physically, to have lost something in the hours since their mother's death. She was not as tall as she had seemed when their mother was in her care and her hands, as she touched her own hair and brushed her own wet cheeks, seemed neither efficient nor particularly effective.

"You will have some music?" she asked them. "Some hymns?"

The three exchanged a look. In the hours since their mother's death, Aida had become something of a stranger once again, an employee after all. Six months, Martin thought, was more than generous. No harm to list the house while she lived here.

"Oh gosh," his sister said. "I wouldn't know what kind of hymns to have."

"She liked, 'The Old Rugged Cross,'" Aida said. "She liked me to sing it for her. That's a good one. It could always put her to sleep."

The three siblings glanced at each other across the living room.

"It might be difficult," his sister said kindly, "to find a singer on such short notice. Mom doesn't even have a piano."

"I will sing," Aida said. "I know the songs your Mommy loved." She hummed a bit, deep in her throat, and then moved her lips to shape the humming into a few drawn-out words, "On a hill far away," she began, "stands an old rugged cross . . ."

The three siblings dropped their eyes. Their mother had sung to them when they were young, kiddie songs and popular ballads: "How Much Is That Doggie in the Window" and "Mares Eat Oats," "Getting to Know You." Martin had sung with his garage band in high school—he had a growling baritone that, pressed too hard, always went flat, although he had believed in those years that his voice would bring him fame. Believed it fervently, obsessively. This was mostly his mother's doing, he knew. After a practice, he would come up from the basement or in from the garage, nearly tearful with dissatisfaction and longing—he knew flat when he heard it—and his mother would be there, in the kitchen, behind the basement door. She would touch his wrist. Her girlish face, her bright, flashing blue eyes, even her blond curls would seem to be alight with wonder. Whispering, in case his father or his two non-musical siblings should hear, she would tell him, "You have a great gift," or, "I was transported," or, "Something very wonderful will come of this." Ordinary motherly encouragement, of course, but in those years her silly words had fed his wildest hopes for himself, hopes for some glittering future only he and she had recognized as surely his own. In his fantasies, he told a cheering stadium of adoring fans, "This one is for my mom, who always believed in me."

Now the discomfort he felt as Aida's voice wobbled through the small room—the discomfort he knew his siblings were feeling—evoked as well the embarrassing memory of those deluded teenage years when he had believed his mother's breathless praise was the voice of the oracle.

Aida's voice wavered and grew thin, went flat, on the last drawn-out phrase: ". . . and exchange it someday for a crown."

Martin knew he and his siblings would laugh about this later.

"Very nice," his sister managed to whisper. "Really lovely."

"But I don't think we want to do anything that formal," his brother said gently, dismissing Aida's performance without appearing to. "Just a reception is enough. We'll talk about her a little bit. Thank the neighbors. That's enough."

He turned to the two of them, as if Aida had already left the house. "Remember the three little Easter ducklings she tried to hide from Dad—the ones that pooped in his slippers?"

Aida smiled with them, but said, "'Jerusalem.' She loved 'Jerusalem.'" And pursed her lips for a moment as if she might break into song once again.

It was his sister who found the right tone. "Oh, Aida," she said, warmly, fondly, even as she made it clear that her suggestions had already been dismissed. "Mom's neighbors, they're very diverse." (Martin glanced at his brother, who always smirked at the word.) "Which is wonderful." (His brother raised his eyebrows.) "But we have no idea how they feel, about religion, I mean. We wouldn't want to offend. You know? Make anyone feel uncomfortable. I think a nice afternoon gathering, some tea sandwiches and some cookies, some wine. Saturday afternoon before we all leave. That'll do it."

The families began to arrive in the next few days—the in-laws and the grandchildren and an elderly cousin or two. Martin and his brother took care of the meeting with the funeral director, who steered them away from the plainest of the caskets meant for cremation—the kind they'd bought for their father, who would have been appalled at paying more for something of such limited use—toward a slightly more expensive model that looked a little less like a packing crate.

With Aida still in his bedroom and their parents' room, of course, uninhabitable now, Martin booked a half-dozen suites in a nearby chain, rooms for his own family and his siblings', and the less prosperous relatives. He and his brother agreed to split the costs. His sister, who was staying with her in-laws in Troy Hills, hired the caterer and someone to help serve.

Only the immediate family went to the funeral parlor, where they gazed at their mother for the last time. Aida had selected her clothes: a pink satin blouse with a large bow, a pink barrette for her sparse hair. Aida, too, perhaps, had suggested the turquoise eye shadow, which none of them had seen on their mother in years—since their own childhoods perhaps, when the color matched her eyes. "Maybelline," his sister whispered, a pinky tip to her own eyelid. "Where did Aida even find it?" His brother said, "I've got Mom's perfume stuck in the back of my throat."

Martin said he could smell it too. It was the odor of their childhoods in the small house. It was endless afternoons, endless boredom, the sound of the television somewhere in the background. The sweet, cloying smell of Youth Dew. She always dabbed a fresh supply of the perfume on her wrists and behind her ears in the moments before dinner was served— how many meals had been scorched in those few minutes when she disappeared from the kitchen? In anticipation of what? he wondered now. A weeknight dinner with her husband and her children—a half an hour of the ordinary day, half an hour at most.

He considered how unlike his memories of her, all moist smiles and bright blue eyes and comical mishaps, this pale effigy in the second-tier coffin had become.

When the family returned to the house, a young Black man in a white dress shirt and dark pants was standing on the single concrete step that led to the front door, smoking a cigarette. Martin assumed he was with the caterer, but then Aida appeared behind him as they approached along the limestone path. When they reached him, she opened the door enough to say, "This is my brother, my brother Thomas." The man smiled broadly and held out his hand. Perhaps because he stood in front of the screen door, perhaps because he had been standing there when they arrived, there was a moment's pause after all the introductions were made, after the tangled handshakes were completed, a moment's brief silence into which Thomas said, "Please come in."

The caterers—his sister's high school friend and her college-age daughter—were already in the kitchen. Martin heard his sister exchange a few whispered phrases with her friend: "Who is this guy?" Answered by a shrug. "He was here when we got here."

Martin walked through the kitchen and the dining room. A white cloth had been laid over the table, and three photos of their mother had been set out as a centerpiece: the black and white wedding photo from her bedroom and the colorful Sears family portrait they'd had taken when he was twelve. (The first 8x10 was free, Martin remembered; his father had not purchased the whole package—what was the point, he had asked, "We look the same in every picture." Reasonably enough, Martin and his siblings had agreed.) The third was a candid shot from just a year or two ago—a photo he had never seen before: his mother and Aida, grinning into the camera, holding hands.

The living room, still decorated with the decades-old faux French provincial crap his mother loved, had been tidied for company— magazines put away and the striped beach towel his mother always sat on now gone from the couch, which had grown faded and worn despite his mother's belief that by sitting on the beach towel, she was "saving" it from wear. A florist's arrangement of spring flowers, redolent of lilies, was on the coffee table; another, of supermarket daffodils in a plain vase, was on the mantel. A bar cart had been added to the room, glass and gold trim with spoked wheels. His mother would have loved it, but Martin saw the thing with his father's eyes and thought it both cheap-looking and unnecessary. It held a dozen bottles of wine, one of whiskey, one of gin, some vodka—as if, Martin thought, this was meant to be an Irish wake. Three clear carafes of water, one of them stuffed—a caterer's pretension, he thought—with mint leaves.

He left the room as he heard the rest of the family at the front door, ducking down the narrow corridor toward the bathroom, but then passing it by and going instead to the far end and into his parents' bedroom. In the afternoon light of the fading spring day, the room seemed very still. Now it was and would always be the room his mother had died in. The rented hospital bed was neatly made up with the pink satin quilt his mother had bought only after she was widowed—he recalled a rough wool spread, military green, that had served until then. The ruffled pillow shams were propped neatly against the headboard, and Aida's battered Bible was on the bedside table. He reminded himself to call the hospital supply company in the morning to have the bed returned.

Back in the hallway, he felt an objection rising wordlessly to his throat. He glanced into his old bedroom, his and his brother's, the room where Aida now stayed. There was a large suitcase opened on the floor. Men's clothes, jeans and shirts, and a tossed belt. Thomas's of course. Impulsively, he crossed the hall to the room that had been his sister's. The door was mostly closed but not shut, and he put his fingertips to it, slowly pushing it open. A young woman, perhaps twenty, was sitting at the foot of what had been his sister's bed. She wore a short skirt, her legs stretched out before her. She was barefoot, although there was a tumbled pair of red high heels on the faded shag carpet. She was looking at her phone. She was dark-skinned, thin and wiry. She wore a bright blue head wrap. There was a colorful leather satchel at her feet, clothes erupting from it.

"Hello," he said, or asked.

She glanced up from her phone, unfazed. "Hello," she said.

"And who are you?"

"I'm Bettina," she said. "Aida's niece."

He waited a beat. She had beautiful dark eyes.

"You're visiting." Although he'd meant to make it a question, it sounded to his own ears like a prompt.

She seemed to consider the many ways she might reply, and then said, simply, "That's right." She looked him over, not unfriendly, but with the direct, dismissive sophistication his own children sometimes turned on him. "And you?" she asked coolly.

"I'm Martin," he said. "I used to live here."

As if giving in to a temptation she could no longer resist, the girl glanced at the phone in her palm. "Oh, yeah," she said. She raised her free hand—languid, her bare arm thin and graceful—"Can you tell my Aunt I'll be right out?"

When he returned to the living room, the neighbors had begun to gather. He saw his wife and children among them, as well as his brother's and his sister's kids. At the funeral parlor, he had been surprised to see that his nieces and nephews were all much older than he'd remembered them, all adults now. There had been some joking about who had absconded with the family's little children. But now he recognized them for what they had become in the time—he would have called it a brief time—since they'd all gathered. Was it for his father's funeral?

Thomas was behind the bar cart, serving drinks, and when he handed Martin a whiskey and water, the young man said, sincerely, "I am very sorry for your trouble. It is very difficult to say goodbye to your Mommy." Martin paused—would he too say he was a Christian?—but then relented, accepted the condolence for what it was worth. Turning away, he wondered if this parched anger, this unspoken objection that had risen to his throat, was some race-based resentment of these strangers, or only grief: a knot of unshed tears, his own inability to swallow this loss.

He saw Bettina emerge from the hallway at the other end of the room, wobbling and long-legged in her high heels. He saw her greet another Black couple—who were they?—the woman in a bright green dress, the man in a brown suit, a pale blue shirt, and plaid tie. The small living room was growing crowded. He heard, among the murmuring voices, the lilt of Aida's accent. Three middle-aged women, also in dresses and jewels, one in a felt hat—came in through the kitchen and took Aida in their arms.

"So fond," people, neighbors, mostly strangers, were saying to him. "So fond of your mother." And Martin found himself saying, Yes, yes. But counting all the while, over their heads, beyond their shoulders, these foreigners gathered around Aida, trying to hear, through the music of their voices, just what they were telling her. Was it sympathy they were offering, he wondered, or praise for a job completed?

At one point, his brother was behind him. "What the hell?" he whispered. "Who are these people? Has she got them moving in?" But then he and Martin both had to turn politely to see what Rosario wanted to show them: a dozen musical cards their mother had sent her over the years, splayed out in her hands, proffered like a magic trick.

"Pick one," she said, grinning. She was a short, plump woman with dyed black hair worn straight to her shoulders, red lipstick, and small white teeth. "Full of fun," was how their mother had always described her.

Martin selected one of the cards. It said, "Thanks for being you."

"Open it," Rosario told him.

He did, and the tune that arose out of it was the first few bars of "You Are My Sunshine."

Other nearby guests stopped to listen, everybody grinning.

"Now you," Rosario said to his brother. His brother plucked another card and opened it, "You Say It's Your Birthday."

A tall nephew, his sister's oldest, hair already thinning, said, "She sent me that one too."

Shanthi of Shanthi and Bart reached out for another. "The 1812 Overture." There was a shout of laughter, as if something clever had occurred. "I love that," Bill said, and to his husband, "We should have brought ours. We must have a couple a dozen." And to the rest, "She never forgot our birthdays."

With each opened card, Martin could see the changes in his mother's signature: from the elaborately curling, girlish hand he remembered from his childhood, to a shaking scrawl, to a signature no longer her own—Aida's, he guessed. Only once did he turn the card over to see how much it cost. $7.50. His brother looked at the back of each of them, shaking his head.

Last night, in the too brightly lit bar of their generic hotel, he and his brother and his sister had gone over their mother's last bank statement, which they'd taken from the house. It was her checking account for incidentals—Martin had set up automatic payments for everything else she needed, and his brother kept an eye on her investments. The checks had all been written by Aida, of course, although signed with their mother's name. The three of them laughed about the small donations she had made, right up until the end of her life, TV-induced, they knew. Ten dollars to Save the Children. Ten more to the ASPCA, Wounded Warriors, St. Jude's Hospital. Their mother had always been an easy mark. One of the checks, for two hundred dollars, was to a name they didn't recognize. Elizabeth Clark. A neighbor, they'd guessed. The memo line said, Good luck.

Martin wondered now if Bettina was a nickname for Elizabeth.

Last night, his brother had announced that despite these small indulgences, despite Aida and the nurses and all the good health care she'd had these many years, not to mention the luxury of aging in place, their mother had actually spent very little. Well less than half of what their father had put aside for her. "All credit to Dad," his brother said.

One of the Evanko brothers was explaining how difficult it had become to get these musical cards into his store. "No one wants them anymore," he was saying. "E-cards are just as good and don't cost any postage. I kept telling her, Let me show you how to send an e-card. I can set it up."

Rosario was shaking her head, holding the cards against her breast. "But I cherish these," she cried. She said, "Come on, Milos," a loud, joking, Jersey kind of teasing, "What are you going to cherish after someone's gone—a computer? An e-mail?"

There was much laughter at this. "You are so right," Shanthi added. Martin was aware of a community here, an ongoing mingling of personalities, friends and neighbors, a kind of family—diverse, generous, fond of his mother. So fond.

Inhabitants of that part of his mother's life, the last part, he'd mostly, somehow, missed.

Rosario offered the pack to Martin once more, and he selected a large, glittery card that said "Congratulations" and played "Happy!"

"I got some good news about my health," Rosario explained, her dark brown eyes suddenly tearful. "And the next day, this is in my mailbox." Her tears shivered, glistened, and then, it seemed, overwhelmed their banks. She let out a single, sudden sob, a sound none of them had heard thus far today. Shanthi gently touched her shoulder. Martin wondered if he should do the same. But he hesitated. He was the stranger among them. "I saved them all," Rosario said through her tears.

A spoon against a glass followed by his sister's commanding engineer's voice relieved the awkwardness of all this. Rosario sniffed, put a knuckle to the corner of her eyes. "Hey, everybody," his sister said. "Can I have your attention for a minute. Everybody?"

She was standing before the fireplace, the spoon and the wineglass in her hand. She made all the expected remarks about how grateful she was—to the neighbors, to the family members who had come from so many "far-flung" places, and, of course, to Aida. "What would we have done without you, Aida?"

Martin was aware of his brother beside him, shifting his weight.

His sister said, "Mom had a wonderful life. A great marriage. A great family. If I do say so myself." There was some laughter. "She loved us. She loved her grandkids. She loved her friends. We'll miss her, of course. But really, what more can anyone ask? I mean, of a life?" Her eyes, which had been, public-speaking style, focused somewhere above their heads, now fell on her two brothers. "Am I right?"

Beside him, Martin's brother, who was on his third vodka, called out, "Well done." Meaning, of course, *That's enough.*

There was a smattering of applause and then his sister said, "But please stay and eat up these sandwiches. We've got so much wine. And remember Great Occasions for your next party. Marissa is my old high school buddy. She and her daughter have done such a great job, haven't they? Please keep them in mind. Their business cards are on the table."

And then that change in the air, a vague stirring that portends the beginning of the end of an occasion—great or otherwise, Martin thought. His sister stepped away from the fireplace just as the first departing neighbor stepped forward to say goodbye, and Martin turned to his brother, about to say, "That's that," when a male voice, a strong and steady tenor, cast itself out over their heads. "Lo,"—it sang, sweet and long-drawn, as soft and mellow as a lullaby, and yet sufficient to suddenly silence them all—"Lo, how a rose e'er blooming."

Thomas, who was still behind the wheeled cocktail cart, had one hand on its glass edge; the other was splayed over the breast of his crisp white shirt, just below his throat. His head was thrown back and his eyes closed, his Adam's apple moving as he articulated each word, precise, gentle. "From tender stem hath sprung." Martin could see him take a luxurious breath: "Of Jesse's lineage coming, as men of old have sung."

And then Bettina joined in from the other side of the room. "It came, a floweret bright." Skinny as she was, her voice was astounding, big but modern, an *American Idol* voice, as Martin thought of it, a voice that seized the words, shook them, drew them down into her chest and then sent them toward the ceiling, both plaintive and defiant, somehow. "Amid the cold of winter, when half spent was the night."

Now, from all around the room, Aida's friends raised their voices as well, in perfect, practiced harmony. "Isaiah 'twas foretold it, the Rose I have in mind . . ."

The living room ceiling was low enough, and the singers were distinctive enough in their Sunday suits and jewelry and hats, that for a moment as they sang it seemed to Martin they stood a few steps above everyone else, as if they had indeed mounted a choir stall.

But of course, they had not ascended above the others at all; the others, he saw, the neighbors and friends and family, one by one, were bowing their heads as they listened, or sinking slowly onto the worn couch, into the various chairs.

He saw that his sister was still holding the neighbor's hand, the neighbor who had been about to take her leave, but now she was also leaning against the woman, into her arms. His sister's shoulders were rounded, her spine limp, the very posture of grief. He saw that his brother beside him was stooping, bending, as if preparing to kneel.

The chorus—Aida's unfortunate voice was in there, but it was buoyed and transformed by the better singers among them—slowly faded. And then Bettina soloed again, this time with her head in its bright blue wrap held straight. "This Flower," she sang, her hand raised to mark each word, "Whose fragrance tender"—as if each gliding gesture of her fingers sent the words aloft—"with sweetness fills the air"—directed each phrase into the room like a blown kiss—"Dispels with glorious splendor the darkness everywhere."

And then Thomas, softly, gently, joined her, reintroducing that quiet voice of his, the voice that had silenced them all, halted the end of the party, kept Martin from his own blithe declaration: "That's that." A voice that had changed everything. And, as if to remind them of this, the two repeated the opening verse, letting their voices brush softly against what became the hymn's final words, "When half spent was the night."

The room was paused, stunned, in the brief aftermath of the song. Only Rosario's quiet sobbing disturbed the silence. In Martin's hand, pressed against his heart, the glittery card she had brought. The glitter, gold and silver and turquoise and hot pink, was now all over his fingers and his palm, on his shirt front and his tie; it glistened across the lapels of his blazer.

Impulsively, he opened the card again. His mother's signature here was strong, not her own writing, but Aida's. The sudden, tinny, silly notes—Happy!—jangled through the room. He saw everyone turn toward the sound, simultaneously disapproving and forgiving.

But Bettina heard it and laughed. She clapped her hands. Moved in her tall shoes. And then she sang again.

Nominated by Andrea Hollander

282

WHITE SPACES

by LISA LOW

from ECOTONE

> *This is how to place you in the space in which to see*
> —Layli Long Soldier, "He Sapa"

All day I move from one white space to another.
Today, ranked from whitest to least white: my classroom (as a
    teacher), my classroom (as a student), my apartment,
    Kung Fu Tea.
Yesterday: the library, Target, Kroger, my apartment.
In my duplex, I sleep beside a white person, and two more are
    below me.
The party I attended last weekend was a white space.
I promise myself to say "white" more, even when it discomforts me.
The word almost always trembles no matter who says it.
My commute looks neutral, but I remind myself I live in a city, a
    country that loves whiteness.
I watch a white person say "white" like a hole they must not fall
    into.
I watch the hole in the conversation where "white" was not said.
In white spaces where I am the authority, I question whether I
    really have authority.
Even the spaces around words have already been filled with
    whiteness.
The more distance, the more whiteness, and vice versa.
White reader, see how much space you must leap over to see me?

Nominated by Philip White

THE UNCERTAINTY PRINCIPLE

by DANIELLE CADENA DEULEN

from KENYON REVIEW

It may take federal officials two years to identify what could be thousands of immigrant children who were separated from their families at the southern United States border, the government said in court documents filed on Friday
—Julia Jacobs, New York Times, April 6, 2019

1

Only so much can be known about a part-
icle at any given moment. There is a limit,
Heisenberg stated, to the precision with
which one can measure the exact position
and momentum of a particle. This is not
a statement about a technological dearth,
rather, the uncertainty arises because
the act of measuring affects the object
being measured. The only way to measure
the position of something is by using light
but, on the subatomic scale, the interaction
of light with the object inevitably changes
the object's position and direction of travel.

2

Only so much can be known about a part-
person at any given moment, a refugee
child led into a dim tunnel. There is a limit,
an official stated, to the precision with which

one can measure the exact position of a child
in sleep, how he turns beneath his metallic
blanket, the watchful focus of cameras and
police dogs sniffing the rank neglect of his
body. This is not a statement about a tech-
nological dearth, rather, the uncertainty
arises because the act of measuring affects
the perspective of lawmakers. The only way
to measure the position of lawmakers is by
using light but, on the subatomic scale, the
lawmakers' interaction with light inevitably
changes their position and direction of blame.

3

Only so much can be given to a child
whose parents have tried to save them
from a fragmented life, one of violence
and thirst, and men whose howling greed
for power and blood surpasses all belief
in light. There is a machete swinging wildly
through what is left of the burning forest
but there is a limit to whom we can allow in,
given our scarcity of clean water and cash.
This is not a statement about a financial
dearth, only a way to slide the frame away
from the child in the corner, arms across
her chest because she has forgotten her
mother's face and the face of the armed
guards offer only revulsion. She is three.

4

I know, I know where the lost children go.
Lo sé, sé a dónde van los niños desaparecidos.
I know, I know where the lost children go.
Lo sé, sé a dónde van los niños desaparecidos.
La tierra está tan vacia como el cielo.
Only so much can be known about knowing.
Nuestros niños son tragados por la oscuridad.
They go into the mouths of wolves.

285

5

Some say the lost children are the lucky ones,
their inability to be reached no cause for alarm,
and the focus on these children (who are likely
with family) displaces our focus on the children
detained. On a mundane level, the lulling effect
of safety contaminates our ability to see. See?
No, look here: where the halfway people are
pressed together so close against the chain-link
they can't lie down beneath the Paso del Norte
Bridge, where citizens drive, their eyes narrowed
by an influx of light, the unrelenting sun blurring
their vision. As they pass over they almost hear
the unsettled breathing, the indeterminate notes
of a dying song, but lose the frequency when they
reach the other side. They shrug. They can't be
certain of what they heard, though it haunts them
as they lift cups of coffee to their tender tongues
which they burn, sipping then spilling the dark
drink on their clean clothes, marking themselves
with awkward inattention, which makes them so
resigned they yawn long toward the empty-skied
windshield, their exposed throats revealing a silent
dangle of flesh—the uvula, which grows between
what is uncertain and what has been left unsaid.

Nominated by Genie Chipps

DEAR CORONER, HOW COULD YOU KNOW

by JULIA PAUL

from HERE: A POETRY JOURNAL

that he was articulate, and very, very, funny,
that he once knew all the state capitals in alphabetic order,
won a prize for metalsmithing in high school,
loved reggae, Volkswagens, quesadillas with gorgonzola,
snowboarding, reading Cormac McCarthy
and that he loved how light fell
through stained glass windows,
his brothers, swing sets covered in snow,
blank cavases,
the geometry of a pieced-together bowl,
how sun sparked orange like matchsticks on concrete,
that he loved to dawdle like he had time in his pocket,
believed in ghosts, in not killing spiders,
and forgave, forgave the haters, the suits and shoppers
who brushed past him, muttering under their breath,
but loud enough for him to hear, *Fuck off, junkie.*

Nominated by Here: A Poetry Journal

SLUT DAYS

fiction by SANAM MAHLOUDJI

from THE IDAHO REVIEW

I saw her at the lunch tables after final bell, sitting under a large, shady tree alone. She was actually eating, as in putting food in her mouth and chewing. And not typical girl stuff like frozen yogurt or diet Snapple. She was ripping chicken meat off a bone with her teeth. Chewing and swallowing it. I sat at an empty table, wiped my hand across the dusty surface, and watched.

Her name was Yael, and she was from New York City. Her parents, both brain surgeons, got lured by better pay at Cedars, and bought a mansion in the Valley over the phone. They made a sizeable donation to help build our new science facility so Yael could do her senior year at our school, where the rich brains from as far as the Santa Monica beach clubs to the boonies of the deep Valley came to guarantee entry into the Ivy League, or at least Tufts. The moving truck with their stuff hadn't arrived. I knew all this because everybody was obsessed.

Yael wore the same frayed jean shorts and see-through white T-shirt to school every single day, as if LA were summer camp, and I wasn't the only person who noticed. My little sister, Missy, throwing her volleyball kneepads into the back seat of my car, called her a "ho and a half" and that dumb, but sometimes smart bitch, Heather Gorson, said to me, "Rachel, she reeks of blood. Period blood." Once, when I was standing next to her in the senior locker area, I smelled for it and there it was, pungent and meaty and sour.

Despite all that, or like wild animals because of it, all the boys wanted to have sex with her. I heard she told Ben Warner—who made me crazy with his straight, floppy hair shaved on the sides and sagging basketball shorts—

288

that she'd sit in his car all day, and between classes he could come and fuck her, and she'd stay in the car no matter what. So apparently he did. After every period. He missed every bell today because he was in his rusty green Jeep Cherokee fucking the new girl. Right next to his dirty, buttered-popcorn-smelling tube socks. I imagined it. The sun way up high, then lower, then crawling slyly, Peeping Tom-style through his back windows. All day. It was so outrageous I was not just jealous. I was impressed.

I slung my backpack over one shoulder and strode over to sit right across from her at the lunch table, pretending to listen to the *Hair* soundtrack on my big black headphones. Our school was putting on a G-rated production of it, and although it wasn't my thing—the beauty pageant girls turned snobby theatre people belting it out as if they didn't still just want to get on *Star Search*—we were all swept up in their nasal vibratos, wearing mud-colored corduroys and paisley whatevers.

A cool breeze, highly unusual for September in the Val, ran through my chest. I resisted hugging my arms and let myself experience the bubbly soda feeling of cold. I played C-major scales along the goosebumps on the underside of my arms. I always loved that side because it was hairless and soft and tingled when I touched it as if my fingers weren't my own.

Yael was so uninterested in me, the only thing she did when I sat down was open her copy of *Frankenstein* and turn pages. I didn't know how to start a conversation. Nobody had taught me. Eventually I said something stupid. "So I heard you're into Ben," I said. "I love his hair."

"Yeah, it's so shiny I can see myself in it," she said and smiled with a closed mouth. "What did you *really* hear?"

"Oh nothing," I said. "Just, like. Maybe you're on his jock. Or, he's on yours? That's all. Swear to God." I didn't know how I was talking like this, I just was.

"Bite me," Yael said. She rolled her eyes and went back to eating—now watermelon slices from a square of Tupperware, the pink juice swarming over her hands.

I fiddled with my Discman. I pressed the button in the front and the lid lifted slowly like stage curtains. I shut it with my fingers, opened it against my palm, and shut it again. I wanted to pull her over to me by her loose white T-shirt and make her tell me all the secrets of how to be a self-assured person. I looked at her while I pretended to be interested in the clock on the classroom building behind her, and also as I turned the volume wheel left then right, quiet then loud, digging the tiny ridges of the wheel into my fingertips, and it sounded like a train coming at me, a million voices rising.

Her eyebrows were amazing. I couldn't stop looking at them. They were plucked so thin they looked drawn in with the single line of a blunt pencil. Curved like rainbows, the sexiest thing about her. With them, she seemed older and damaged. Like she pulled out her eyebrow hairs involuntarily. Obviously I knew boys didn't make that connection. I didn't care. I looked at her shirt and pictured her perfect tiny erect nipples in the center of her large breasts as eyes smiling at me under a bra of lace—at me and at all of the boys. She picked up a rectangle of yellow cheese from a nest of foil. Her nails also were shaped like rainbows and painted purple. The neckline on her T-shirt was curved like a rainbow too, dipping down towards her boobs.

"Look. Whatever your name is," she said.

"Rachel," I said and lifted my head and stared, glad to finally do it freely. She sucked whatever chicken and watermelon and cheese was left on her fingers. I stopped the machine and the CD spun to a stop, sounding like our salad spinner. I hated that. I hated salad, those dumb wet and slimy leaves.

"At my old school everyone was having sex and it was no big deal. It's what you did if you were remotely cool. Here, it's like I've come to a Catholic nunnery or some shit."

"Really? Everyone?"

"Of course not. But more." She widened her eyes as if by doing that she was proving her point, like she was inviting people to have sex inside her eyes or something. Whatever it was, I believed her and more. That she came from a magical place where the kids were fucking each other in front of the teacher in class, for their group science projects, to pass PE.

I watched her stuff foil and plastic baggies into a brown bag and crush it into a ball. I pressed the open button on the CD player and the lid lifted. I pressed it down. The click and the way it felt in my body. It was satisfying, like knuckles cracking. I almost burst with pleasure.

She ran her chicken, cheese, watermelon, saliva fingers through her thick brown hair and shook it out. "What's your name again?"

"Rachel," I said and smiled.

I sat at my desk and looked at myself in the special pink light-up mirror I used to put in my contact lenses, which I'd worn since I was twelve without an infection because, like the doctor with greasy black hairs clogging his ears said, my eyes were especially clean, with very little mucus. The rest of my face really wasn't so bad. My eyes, dirt brown, spaced too close together, my nose too big so when I turned to look at my profile I would twist it to the other side and pretend I had a smaller nose. I wasn't objectively ugly, just nothing special.

I flipped the regular mirror around to the one that magnified "blemishes," as the booklet in my desk drawer said, and thought of Missy. When I was twelve and my sister was eleven, acne spread across her forehead like a layer of red pus-filled Rice Krispies treat. Even so, she was the first person I knew to seriously hook up with anyone. Now she and her boyfriend, Damon, had already been together three months. Her acne signaled she was ready. Like Yael's boobs or her smelly period blood. I did not signal I was ready. Even at seventeen. My face, humungous in the mirror, looked like dirty sand, bits of trash revealing themselves when I looked closely, black specks and hairs and crumbs of greasy crust. I turned it back to the regular side.

I watched Yael in the morning from my car, my palms warm on the steering wheel. I rolled down the window for air and because it was September, and hot as shit, and I'd fry like a steak otherwise. She wore a different outfit, and I knew her New York stuff had arrived. Ripped up Levis, Keds, and a black halter top whose bottom edge floated un-encumbered an inch above her bellybutton. Her brown hair long and tangled. She'd put grandma glasses over her big brown eyes. Her shoulders were always slumped. I liked that, as much as purple bruises on legs. They gave an impression of not caring, of being focused on something more important and internal, of being bad. Also, they reminded me of runway models. The irony was not lost on me. She ran her hand through her hair. I'd always dreamed of running my hands through my hair and looking like that.

Matt and Corey, the two nice, funny guys who played in a band and pretended they were just goofy eunuchs until you had a couple diet kiwi-strawberry vodkas and their hands were unhooking your bra after one of their pay-to-play concerts at the Whisky a Go Go, were talking next to my car, but really they were watching her. They kept forgetting they were talking to each other and then would say, "Wait, where were we again?" and laugh like hyenas.

Did she know people watched her? Matt told me once he liked girl singers like Suzanne Vega. I asked why and he said he liked her soft voice and when she whispered "duh duh duuh da, duh duh-duuh da" that she looked like a hot librarian. That was so different from why I liked girls in bands.

I liked seeing girls do what girls weren't supposed to do.

Eventually Yael looked in my direction and put one hand perpendicular over her sunglasses and waved with the other. A big, fast wax-on wax-off. I was still sitting in my car and my windshield was dirty. I wondered if she could be thinking that I was someone else, the sun as it sifted through the black dirt altering my face. She walked up to the window. I poked out my head.

"Hey, you," she said.

I smiled. I didn't expect to be called "you" so soon. Electric sparks lit up my brain and my body buzzed.

"Gold cars are for old people," she said, sliding her fingers, the fingers that were just in her hair, sideways on the gold paint. "Ewww," she said, looking at her blackened flesh. She wiped them on the back of her jeans.

I made myself be bold. "Shut the hells up."

"Meow," she said and pawed at the air.

I smiled again. I was so ready to ditch my friends—Terry, Sapna, and Marisa with the legs that looked like logs. They were still spending free periods in the library circulating a group diary and pretending the library boys—who they gave secret code names to—had devastating crushes on them.

I said, "Fine, okay, you got me. This used to be my mom's. Can I just be old and wear a visor and have a tiny white dog on my lap already?"

"How old's your mom?" she said.

"Well, it was my mom's mom's. She's like a million, I don't know."

A smile formed on her mouth. It was sparkly and white and perfect.

I started to have conversations with Yael in my head. It was really weird and I didn't realize I was doing it at first. I'd be taking a shower before bed, or assisting Dad, the dishwasher Nazi, load the dirty dishes, and find myself telling her about how Ms. Martelle said I had a 50 percent chance of getting into Yale, and it made me think that college counselors are like weathermen and doctors the way they make these predictions. I'd tell her she had to go to Yale too because they were anagrams of each other. Silly things like that. Usually what I'd say I found funny, and in my imagination Yael would laugh and tell me I was funny, that smile slowly forming on her mouth.

My whole life, Missy had all the friends. Mom knew all Missy's friends' names, their last names and sports and boyfriends. Mostly they played volleyball like her, long tan legs in tiny bike shorts. Apart from Missy, they all met in some sandbox at Presbyterian elementary school in the Pacific Palisades. With me, on the rare occasion I was invited to a birthday party, Mom and Missy would laugh at the kid's name or yearbook photo because the kid would have a name like Aditya, or Hyuan, or a face with asymmetrical nostrils or weird facial hair.

Yael had a funny name, but she did not have a funny face. Her face was beautiful to me—like my favorite childhood doll. Her eyebrows, her brown brown eyes, and her purse-shaped lips. She was perfect. I wanted to talk to her about everything—like why I was so obsessed with the way she looked and yet I felt judging people based on looks was pathetic. Everywhere I turned, people paired off with those who looked like them, and so I'd think the morally superior people hung out with those who didn't look like them, or were ugly. Yael was neutral for my moral superiority because although she looked nothing like me, she was breathtaking.

I was putting the glass cups and coffee mugs in the dishwasher the way Dad liked—big mugs on the bottom back, glass cups on the top sides— while he oversaw me and shook his mostly bald head and corrected the ordering within the ordering. While I did this, I was having a chat with Yael. I was telling her how a girl I went to camp with from Chicago thought "wind chill factor" was "windshield factor" and yet she got an 800 on her verbal SATs. My sister was arguing in the living room with Mom about a new dress she needed.

"Why can't you wear the same dress as last month?" Mom said, her voice quiet behind the wall, but I could tell she was speaking loudly because of how her words were slow and overly enunciated.

"I just can't. No one does that," Missy said.

I felt immensely sad. What a world. I was always using college as my way out, but now suddenly I was happy at school and all because I had one possible friend, and I considered that maybe my sister had never been happy. Then I realized that was just one possibility and maybe she was so happy she had to pick fights with Mom to challenge it, and so my sadness faded.

Missy darted in through the swinging white doors. "Da-ad," she sang. "Mom said give me a hundred bucks for my dress."

"She said that?" He was checking my placement of mugs and looked up at Missy.

"Swear to God." She smiled at me. But it wasn't a smile like Yael's. It was mean, which I saw in her eyes and her eyebrow that lifted.

I squinted. Yet being happy was making me generous. "Yeah, Dad." I smiled at Missy. "What's the big whoop?"

Dad mumbled something and left without pulling out his wallet.

"Just ask her," Missy yelled at the door. "Nice try, beotch." She turned to me, put her hands on her hips, tapped her muscular foot. "So. You got a date?"

"No."

"What about Yael?"

"Hardy har har," I said. That was Missy's way of talking. Like "bros before hos" which Missy used in an ironic way with her volleyball friends to talk about the "ballers," the boy athletes.

"She's a huge slut. Is that what you want?" she said.

"Want what?" I said.

"To be a slut."

"You're way worse," I said, and smiled.

"Oh, sure. Because I have an actual real-life boyfriend," she said. I could tell Missy was getting excited because she made her voice higher and louder and her ponytail was getting a little excited, too, and shaking like a pom-pom.

"I mean, you do whatever those 'ballers' tell you," I said. "You listen to what they listen to. You watch what they tell you to watch. Do you even like rap? EPMD? Honestly. At least Yael has her own opinions."

Missy rolled her eyes. She scrunched her face and looked up at the ceiling. "At least Yael waa waa waa. She's just getting away with it because she's new. We're only getting used to her. You'll see," she said, shaking her head. She raised her arm to, I'm guessing, give me the finger, but then she stopped, lowered her arm and gave me this weird half-smile. She pushed the door open and left.

I bent over the dishwasher and dropped the forks, tine sides up, into the fork utensil basket. One at a time, plunk, plunk, plunk. I considered whether Missy was looking out for me, that deep down she cared. I wasn't surprised people called Yael a slut—that was the first word I thought when I heard the story about Ben. And that was what I thought when I talked to her at the lunch tables, and it was what I thought when I saw her in the parking lot. I still thought it. Maybe it was because I wanted to be one too.

I met Yael at the back of the school by the dumpsters. She was smoking a cigarette, leaning against a wall. She wore her white low-cut T-shirt, a plaid schoolgirl skirt, thigh highs and Docs. Her skirt was as narrow as a Girl Scout sash and she was not wearing boxer shorts underneath like the Catholic schoolgirls did when I saw them ordering sundaes at the ice cream store Friday afternoons. I, on the other hand, looked weird if I wore patterns or all black or something bright or too tight. Nothing fit me right. My body was lumpy, my head big, my feet narrow, my hair frizzy—so as usual I wore one of Dad's old work shirts, used Levi's and Adidas lace-ups, mainly to disappear. I did consider the possibility that my perceptions weren't fact but opinion, except it's hard to argue with yourself and win.

Yael blew the smoke straight up and then lowered her head to look at me. "None of the guys want me anymore," she said. "But I don't like those losers anyways. They say I've got AIDS. That I sucked thousands of dicks."

"No way. How lame," I said.

"I know, right," she said. "In New York I slept with my English teacher, Mr. Haskell. Twice and we used a rubber. He's the only one I ever slept with before Ben. But it was enough to majorly fuck with him and he quit. It's not like they found out, but Mr. Haskell felt really bad. Like he raped a little girl or something. I told him I was fine, but he wouldn't listen."

"Did you like him?"

"Everyone thought he was cute. He was, you know, the young, hot teacher. I heard his voice while I did my homework and then I dreamed about him and creamed my pants. He was always riding a horse like one of King Arthur's knights, and then he'd swoop me up into the sunset." She examined the cigarette between her two fingers.

I wondered if the skin between her fingers was indented even minutely or smelled like cigarettes even after she washed her hands.

"Can I borrow a cigarette?" I said.

"Yeah, but give it back when you're done."

We laughed. I coughed a few times before I got the hang of it. And even then I wasn't sure if I was supposed to keep the smoke in my mouth for a few seconds, or just let it out right away. It hurt. A good hurt.

One day in October, I brought her home. I was still trying at school because I hadn't gotten into college yet. We were supposed to study for AP Calc together. I was taking more APs than any other senior—at least that's what my parents thought.

My sister sat in the kitchen peeling a banana, her tan muscled legs up on the table, dirty shoelaces and all. I put my binder down in front of her.

"Hey, ho-bags. I didn't know you were a math geek, too," she said and smiled at Yael.

"What does that mean?" I said.

Missy laughed. "I heard she's like a mad genius at science—like Marie Curie level. But how come you failed out of the easiest subject? With boobs like that. Good going, dude. How are you for real?" She swung down her legs, threw the half-eaten banana onto my binder and stood facing Yael.

Yael's eyebrows crinkled and her beautiful porcelain skin turned red, the heart shape of her lips flattened. "Are you jealous of me? Is that what's going on?"

Missy laughed and said, "Whatever. I don't get what you think you're accomplishing. What's the point?" and pushed the kitchen door hard enough on her way out to create a small breeze as the door swung back and forth.

I wanted to say sorry for Missy, but when I looked over at Yael she was sitting and writing something in her textbook. I felt bad for Yael. But I was meant to be like Yael and wasn't, and that made me feel less bad for her and more bad for me.

We stepped into my room and Yael dropped her backpack and took some magazines off the floor to my bed. *Rolling Stone* and *Seventeen* and sometimes a smart magazine Dad threw in. She flipped through them just like Mom, from back to front, licking her finger to help separate pages.

I watched. Then when she kept reading, I tried to do my lab homework, but soon I was just pretending to do it while I watched her. She laughed at some stuff in an *Economist*. "Did I ever tell you I want to be an economist?" she said.

"Really?" I said. I'd never known a kid, a non-adult, who thought economics was interesting.

"Doesn't it explain so much?" she said. "The whole world is economics. We want what's rare, what's in demand." Yael smiled, but I thought I saw a tiny bit of sadness in her brown eyes. Something unlike her. Then she said, "Come here."

"What's up?" I took a big breath. I got up from the rug and sat down on the bed next to her feet.

"So. Who're you into? Ben?"

"Ben's not my type," I said. I knew the rules—I wasn't dumb.

Yael laughed.

"Well, I guess I don't know. No one lately." I looked at her purple toenails—wiggling, polish peeling. She wore her white tank top tucked into a giant red peasant skirt that made her look hippyish. It lay across my bed like a spill.

"Don't be scared of going after what you want. Choose and ye shall succeed."

I laughed.

"Rachel," she said, and tilted her head.

I grabbed her big toe. It was warm and movable. "What?"

She giggled. Yael loosened her foot and dug it into my butt. I sat up straight and twisted to see if she was trying to shove me off the bed. She smiled. "Come here a sec," she said.

I didn't move.

"You're so dense," she said. She sat up and pushed me down onto the bed. She sat over me. Straightened out her flowy red skirt and covered my torso with it. She looked like the stamen of a flower, her skirt the petals. She leaned closer and kissed me. I kissed her back. It felt wet and mushy. My body tingled. We kept pecking our heads up and down at each other. Every time, I got more dizzy. Her fingers slid under my shirt, and she touched me all over my stomach and under my bra. Goose bumps rose up. I thought about her and Ben and felt warmer. I moaned, opened my eyes and closed them. Was this Yael going after what she wanted?

Then suddenly she sat up and wiped her mouth on the shoulder of her T-shirt. "I'm not gay, just so you know," she said.

"I know," I said. "Me neither."

She got her tasseled vest off the floor and walked out.

I didn't see her again for a few days. I thought she was sick. Then I heard she was in Ben's car, and they'd fucked 108 times in two days. I didn't believe it, at least not the number of times, but I was mad as hell because I thought whatever she'd done was in reaction to kissing me. That it had been a big mistake. And then when I considered it had nothing to do with me, that maybe I wasn't a factor, I was even madder. She also fucked Matt and Corey—they weren't buying the AIDS rumors either, I guess. Maybe she was a liar about all of it—that Mr. Haskell was her only fuck pre-Ben, that the boys didn't want her anymore, that she really thought a guy would go for me. But then part of me didn't want to believe that. She was my friend, and she chose me. Just like I chose her.

I wandered around the school hallway during AP Government because I couldn't handle sitting any longer. Grey lockers galore. Whenever I saw an open one—the empty and unclaimed—I slammed its door, but it would bounce back because the lock was engaged, and hit the door of the locker behind it. The loud metal banging echoed, and I was happy to hurt something. I saw a locker decorated with wrapping paper, ribbon, birthday candles, candy stuck with tape. I ripped off the paper and threw the Sour Tarts packet across the hall. It slid to a stop. A teacher I didn't know poked his head out of a class, and I hid behind a corner.

When I got home I called Ben. I wanted to tell him that the girl he was fucking also liked me, needed me, but I asked if he could tell me what our English homework was. He told me we had to read *The Overcoat*, and I said thanks and hung up.

Then I called Yael. I'd never talked to her on the phone. Was never one of those girls. She picked up on the first ring. Her voice sounded distant, like I was looking in at the wrong end of binoculars.

"Where've you been?" I said.

"Around," she said.

I had figured out what to say to her. "I think Missy's breaking up with Damon. She said how he's just a baby at dinner. That she's too mature for him. Whatever, she has guys lined up waiting."

"So?"

"Well, he's always been nice to me. I think he just needs someone like us. Like me. To bring out his wild side. He's a hottie, don't you think?"

"In-ter-esting," she said. I could feel her smile. "If that's what you want, go get it. He's all yours."

I laughed. Nobody else had ever talked to me in this way. "Okay," I said. My old friend was back.

The next morning, I woke up early. I took my time getting dressed. Put in some of Missy's hair stuff for shininess, used her raspberry lip gloss. I always enjoyed how gloss stuck to my lips and the slippery feeling of rubbing them together, the waxy sweetness. I wore a dress—one Mom bought me but I'd never worn—a baby doll one with subtle green and purple flowers and a ribbon tie at the back.

Kids looked at me all morning. Or I suspected they did, that some were smiling and some were spying from the corners of their eyes. When Missy and her volleyball crew—Carter, Brooke, and McKenzie—walked past me in the hallway in their short shorts and high ponytails, Damon followed them, strutting slowly, not holding hands with Missy. He seemed sad, and as I looked back at them, I waited to see if maybe, magically, he'd turn, too. He didn't.

At lunch, Yael sat down with me. She didn't say a word about anything. She didn't even say hi. She took a bag of chips and smashed it with both hands. The pop sound was deafening. She crunched her chips loud, her mouth open. Then she pulled a small plastic bag from her backpack and threw it at me. "Wear these," she said. "I felt your tits. You can show them." I knew it: she believed in me. She cared.

I sat under the bleachers and waited for Damon to start walking back to the locker room. Yael told me this was the best time to approach a guy—after he'd worked for his sweat. It wasn't yet dark and when I looked up the underside of the bleachers were covered in thousands of pieces of gum, pink and mint-green and light blue. I was amazed at how dirty they were.

Someone blew a whistle, and I heard the pattering of feet and looked out and saw the whole team running towards me. The locker room was just behind the bleachers. I looked for Damon and didn't see him.

When I did, after it got quiet again and dark and then someone snapped on the athletic building's outside lights, he was alone. I stood up, careful not to bump my head, and walked to the left of the bleachers. He saw me.

"Hey," I said.

"Hey, Rachel," he said. "Where's Missy?"

"I don't know. I wanted to show you something," I said, and pulled his hand which was hot and sweaty. He ducked under the bleachers with me. I walked us to the top where we could stand upright. At our feet, the packed dirt was lit up in a crisscross pattern of light marking the spaces between beams.

I stared at him. He looked at me blankly. "Did you find those weird worms or something?" he said.

"No, stupid." I unzipped my canvas jacket and let it drop so he could see me. All I had on were gold pasties, thong underwear, and boots. I think I knew deep down that I looked ridiculous, but I stood there, in the cold, and all I could think was I was wearing Yael's pasties and hot pink underwear and I was a goddess, too.

He raised his eyebrows. Oh, he was beautiful in that unattainable but easy way—skin smooth like a brown egg, every muscle flipped on, his eyes twinkling against the artificial light. Tufts of thick bronze hair curled out the sides of his cap. I looked down at his white baseball pants. They were tight and I could see the silhouette of his bunched up boxer shorts.

Damon laughed. "What the hell? Did Missy put you up to this?" he said. His feet kicked the dirt.

I looked at him and his perfect skin, then down at myself. Lumps of stomach, short torso. The thong and pasties like chocolate frosting over salad. But it was more. It mattered also who was receiving this and what traveled between. That's what made it not fit.

"Figures," I said.

"Huh?" he said and stared. "This is weird."

"What's sexy about this?" I said. "It's not the animal in me. Not this way. Not with you." I thought of Yael, in all her dirty clothed, sliced eye-browed, messy eating, period-smell glory. But also how she pulled me in, the electricity of it, and us.

I peeled off the gold medallions, let them drop into the earth. They glistened like lost treasures. I didn't even care that my boobs were now entirely exposed. I wasn't trying to impress Damon. Instead, I thought, what would I tell Yael, and what would she think? Would she even be sad for me? I tried to push that thought away.

Damon frowned and shook his head. Bending low, he left me under the seats.

Her house looked like buildings we saw in AP Art History slides, only brand-new. A million arches and columns. Three fountains. The housekeeper, the one who made her lunches of chicken and cheese and casserole, shooed me in. I pretended we had a study date even though I came with no books. She pointed to the back of the house and vanished. I was going to get everything out in the open—demand it.

It took five minutes to find her room. I felt like an intruder in an exhilarating way. My pulse was fast down the long hallways. We hadn't spoken since lunch period yesterday. After I got home, after Damon, I'd cried. I wasn't exactly sure why.

Yael was at her desk, studying, a thick braid curving down her back like a second spine. She wore a tank top and those seventies gym shorts with white piping at the ends.

All day, I'd pictured a hazy room of dripping candles, Sharpie graffiti, slashed bras drying on a lamp, a needle repeating the blank crackly end of a record. But at the threshold to her room, I saw debate team trophies and a bulletin board, a poster of Eddie Vedder, hunched, crooning in a corduroy jacket, and I stood and stared. It was all so normal. I was confused, and it made me like her less. And also more.

I shifted in my Shelltoes. Get it over with, I told myself. She still didn't see me. I walked up to her bookshelf. I didn't know exactly how to start so I picked up the first trophy, a golden girl gesticulating next to a lectern, and while I imagined pitching it at her window, hearing the sound ring in my ears, shards fall to the floor, I just lobbed it at her pillows and it tumbled against her headboard.

She turned anyways. Jumped out of her chair. "What the fuck? Rachel?" She stroked her hair. "You freaked me out."

I put my finger on the edge of the poster and ripped out Eddie Vedder from the thighs up, guitar included, as if from a book. The tearing sound was satisfying. I dropped the big curling piece onto the ground. "Whatever. You're just a fake. You know shit about shit." Already I was holding myself back.

"What else do you want to ruin?"

"You," I said, almost a whisper.

She tilted her head to show me compassion. "Did Damon not go for you?"

I laughed the way someone laughs when something isn't funny.

"How is that my fault?" she said, hand on hip.

I crossed my arms. "You should have known. And saying I should wear that bullshit? For him? Or—maybe you did know. What do you even want from me?"

"So, you can't tell if someone likes you? You can't wear what you want? No one forced you to wear my pasties."

"I did it to show you," I said. "I did it for you."

She stared at me without blinking. "It's in their eyes. It should be obvious if they like you," she said.

I felt the warm-wet on my cheeks.

She reached out her arm. "Show me what?"

I didn't give her my hand. I looked at my feet and toed Eddie Vedder around on the carpet. Wiped my face with the back of my hand.

"What is it?"

"Whatever, it doesn't matter," I said, staring at Eddie Vedder. Hair sweat soaked. Vein bulging on the side of his head, exasperated with his art, legless, freed. His eyes looked like they wanted me, and also everyone. It was his job.

"No. Say it," she said.

"No," I said. "Fine." I looked up. "Then why the fuck did you kiss me?"

She twisted her mouth, and I could tell she was thinking how to put her words. "I didn't think it would be a big deal."

I nodded. Ablaze. Of course not, whatever, my face said. No big deal.

But standing there in silence, I was drawn, sucked into another time and place, watching us. No biggie, no big whoop. A future me would know better: none of this was not a big deal. Every time I'd kiss a new person, girl or boy, I'd compare it to that pure experience, of not knowing what I felt—whether love, lust, admiration or something else, like discovery. Or all of it. And the enormity of that feeling. From our slut days. I would long for it, everything new, unassigned. Maybe. Standing there in front of Yael, my breasts secretly cupped in her pasties—for her.

I knew then this longing would come—yet how could I?

Nominated by The Idaho Review

PEARL GHAZAL

by LEILA CHATTI

from BLACKBIRD

My mother's mother was named for a bright shining; my mother,
    a pearl.
Myself: dark floor of heaven, across which the moon rolls like a
    pearl.

As a child, I tried to die. The school called my mother and my
    mother called me
to say *Sometimes I wish you had never been born.* Before I was
    born, I was a pearl

in my mother's pocket. I try to imagine what it was like to be inside
my mother inside her mother, try to see myself in the girl flashing
    pearly

-whites in a sepia photograph in the last year of her twenties,
    imagine myself part of some light
shining through her—the layer beneath the layer of the pearl

which makes it glow. My grandmother was born in June, like me,
    twin
Geminis fifty-five years apart. Our birthstone: pearl,

which is not a stone but a gem, queen of them, once valued beyond
    measure.
In the Parable of the Pearl of Great Price, heaven is the pearl

303

for which the merchant trades all else to attain. *Momme*
is a Japanese unit of weight—3.75 grams—used to value loose or
    stringed pearls,

pronounced *mommy.* Perhaps foolishly, I've assumed, because I was
    born
first, my mother wanted me. Wise enough, never asked. A pearl

is made in defense against an irritant, a parasite
or fragment invading the mollusk's soft center. Mother of pearl

is named such for a root of mother—*modder*—means sediment,
    dregs,
filth. Briefly, I mothered; what I made dropped from me like pearls

from a strand cut. Before my mother was
my mother, her hair was black as Cleopatra's, clever woman who
    dropped her pearl

earring into vinegar and swallowed its sediment, for a bet. I am the
    mother of no one
ever born. My no one was due in June. Eve, the first mother, wept
    pearls

when she was cast from heaven. My mother never wept
in front of me, was never soft, hardened early. She lost her mother
    like a pearl

earring as a teen. Hardly had one before that. Despair for weeks,
    years, then—Snow glittered in the yard like crushed pearls.

As a girl, I asked my mother where her mother was. My mother
    turned to look
at me, her look blank as the face of a pearl,

which never ends. Hard as my mother is, I've always wanted
    her
life to be easier, so mine might be. Grief is an heirloom, a rope of
    pearls

304

handed down. Oh girls, where were your mothers. I am a woman
  now trying
to live. For weeks, years. I daughter my mother. I treasure my little
  pearl

of foolishness, the belief I may be different. May survive the dark
  dark
as my mother's hair. May string a life of days like pearls,

hoard them preciously. *Margaret, are you grieving?* Hurt shines on
  both sides,
like heaven. I call my mother. All day the sky comes down. Leaves,
  on the window, pearls.

Nominated by Blackbird, John Drury

FIREFLIES

by KAMILAH AISHA MOON

from WORLD LITERATURE TODAY

The air in this house
is so warm, closer
than close.
In different rooms
they flutter,
eyes closed within
their own worlds.

Faces bathed in twilight,
headphones mainline
Jackie, Sam, Aretha
Dionne, James or Smokey
into their pulsing bodies—
who they were then
lives inside every adlib
& holler, shooting
from fingertips spread
above their heads.

Inside the brightest nook
of themselves, they are
everything they did
right, everything that
made sense at the time
still bringing

residual joy. Ambient,
my parents winged
& lit from every angle
hover, untaxed delight!

I don't blink, don't dare
try to capture them
in the mason jar
of my hungers
nor halt them
shimmering, spellbound.

Nominated by World Literature Today

I SEE A SILENCE

by ILYA KAMINSKY

from ARTANGEL

This, officers, is common chickweed,
cousin of a prickly sow thistle.

If you lean your ear
to her stem

you can hear
yourself leaving.

Nominated by Jane Hirshfield

REMEMBRANCE POPPY

by KATRINA VANDENBERG

from ORION

1.

About the time a pregnancy test registers as positive, a fertilized human ovum is the same size as a poppy seed.

2.

I sing and celebrate the poppy.

Our daughter was born by an emergency C-section. She was already more than two weeks late, and even then she did not want to come. Her heart rate had dropped dangerously low. Before the surgery, the anesthesiologist came to deliver the spinal block, a numbing anesthetic combined with a powerful form of synthetic morphine. He was blunt and smart, highly skilled and not kind.

I have a needle next to your spinal cord right now, he hissed. *I don't care how bad your next contraction is. Don't. Move.*

I hated him and adored the bite of his needle all at once.

The surgeon I trusted. His hospital had one of the lowest C-section rates in the nation. The surgery was not a frivolous one. After my abdomen was opened, he found that there was almost no opening into the birth canal, that the contractions had been crushing the baby's head into my pelvic bone. *Completely unengaged,* he said, and I pictured a bored baby, thumbing through a magazine. Then, likely noticing my downcast face, he added, *In the old days, she never would have gotten out. You both would have died.*

And I remain privately surprised by my memory of that day, when I felt as if she were a seed and I the husk. In that moment, my body accepted that her coming might require me to be shed, from her life and everything I knew. It did not feel as morbid as I am sure it sounds now. Giving birth, I felt that I had entered a sacred place where life and death touched.

Our daughter is nearly ten years old now. Every morning when she stumbles out of bed, her tangled long hair making her look like a wild sprite who found her way into our house by mistake, I feel grateful and victorious: We're here! Together! All hail the poppy, to which we owe our lives.

3.

My mother's father died on Christmas Eve. I was seventeen. After our family left the hospital, we had just enough time to pick up our dinner rolls before the bakery closed for the holiday. *In Yugoslavia, we say that only saints die on Christmas*, said the baker, Gino, offering his condolences. *To have such a father, you have been very blessed.* Along with the rolls, he boxed up a ring-shaped poppy-seed kalach, on the house.

I thought Gino had given our family a free coffee cake to be nice. My mother, who had grown up in a neighborhood full of eastern European immigrants, knew that his gesture meant more: Kalach is sweetened holiday bread, a ritual bread. The seeds had been ground to a fine powder, simmered in milk and honey, and thickened with tempered egg until the mixture became a black, nutty, jam-like filling. The bread's round shape has no beginning and no end, like a life that goes on forever. Eating the poppy seeds would bode well for the coming year, she said.

4.

Poppy seeds can represent fertility or abundance, luck or money. Because poppies contain so many seeds, the seeds are often used in baked goods as a cultural stand-in for *a lot-ness*. It's no surprise that they make their showiest appearance in breads and cakes during winter holidays, when our cups are meant to overflow.

It takes close to a million poppy seeds to weigh a pound. Six thousand to top your average morning bagel.

310

The poppy seeds that we scatter over bagel tops, that punctuate the flesh of muffins—they are not black. They are pewter-colored, nearly blue, like shadows on the snow near dusk, which on Christmas Eve in Michigan comes around four in the afternoon, just a few hours before my extended family would gather for dinner. The smallest among us would each get to open one present, and we would go together to fill an entire long pew at the candlelight service at our church. The seating arrangement was dictated by the mothers, an elaborate and mostly un-successful effort to separate the jokers.

We lived on an island and the church was on its eastern shore. From the windows, you could look out at the frozen river. You could see the shoreline of Canada and long skeins of migratory geese. Sometimes people—teenagers, and, further back in time, bootleggers, enslaved people traveling the underground railroad—crossed the river on the ice.

Even then I did not believe in some faraway heaven. Even then I believed that many of the stories read to me from the pulpit were meta-phors or parables. I didn't find them less real or urgent for being that. Mostly I believed what I still believe: that the vast majority of our acts of love are humble and seldom witnessed. Yet act by act by act, we shape our culture and even have the power to change life itself, and our par-ticipation in that collective life force does not end with our deaths. What I mean is, heaven is here.

5.

In the last few years of my grandfather's life, he grew intimate with mor-phine. He swallowed over a hundred pain pills every week. A large cancerous tumor pressed against the base of his spinal cord.

My grandfather wore a cowboy hat and a bolo tie, decades after the Dust Bowl forced his family from their homestead back east into the factories and rail yards of Detroit. He came up in a more rough-and-tumble world than did we, his grandchildren. We all had learned the hard way not to trust him when he said, *You got a loose tooth? I just want to wiggle it.*

My grandfather had grown up in a two-room homestead in North Da-kota with no electricity or running water, and quit school at the age of eight to work, guarding another family's cattle all night from wolves. He was the upbeat, cheerful type, not one to complain. Yet his doctor told us that his pain must have been excruciating, and thus the mor-phine.

What would night on the prairie be like for a child? Long grass, a rifle, the sound of wind, bright spackle of Milky Way above. He told me that he had been lonely, and often cried. He reminded me of the *sore afraid* shepherds guarding their flocks, in the part of the Christmas story where the angel comes to them. I imagine that he had to teach himself how to hear *Fear not*—not from any sort of outside visitation, but from within.

6.

Morphine remains the most significant painkilling drug in contemporary medicine. Thousands upon thousands of plants make flowers in our world, yet only the species *Papaver somniferum*, the opium or "sleep-bringing" poppy, can make morphine in any significant quantity. (*Papaver*, Latin for "poppy," is said to be derived from the sound made when chewing poppy seeds, or from the Celtic *pap*, because the poppy's juice was given to fussy children to help them sleep.) The molecule has no equal in nature. Somehow it evolved to fit key-in-lock into the receptors that we have in our brains and spines, which are designed to receive our bodies' own endorphins and provoke a relief of pain and a feeling of pleasure. These same receptors dutifully provoke the same experience at the touch of morphine, seemingly oblivious to the interloper.

A brief detour for an explanation of how these terms all fit together: Opium is the milky latex that oozes from an unripe poppy seed capsule, dries to a gum, and is scraped from the plant to be rolled into balls and sold. Opium contains dozens of complex chemicals, three of which scientists in the nineteenth century figured out how to separate—morphine, thebaine, and codeine. From these three narcotics, we have since derived over two hundred additional drugs, which include laudanum, heroin, hydrocodone, oxycodone, oxymorphone, methadone, and fentanyl. These drugs are referred to as *opioids*.

My sister and I were among the final group of American kids given over-the-counter children's cough syrup laced with codeine before the FDA outlawed the practice. The nighttime variety was thick and grape-flavored, with the dull sheen of an eggplant. Probably it soothed our coughs and helped us sleep, but what I remember most about it was the feeling of well-being it created, as if I'd been swaddled in purple blankets and allowed to sleep all night in my mother's arms.

In the years since, I've gulped down glasses of water fizzling with effervescent cold tablets, other syrups, countless gel caps. But nothing, *nothing*, has ever replaced the feeling of being a child floating off into poppy-induced sleep. When my sister and I reminisce about growing up, it's the banned cough syrup that gets our most dreamy praise. This must be one of the more sinister aspects of narcotics: no other drug has made me feel beloved.

7.

For thousands of years, humans have tried to understand the nature of the poppy. No plant has been studied more for its medical properties. We have steeped its seeds in hot water to brew tea; we have chewed them. We have scored the capsule of its flower with a blade and collected the milky latex inside. We have invented the hollow needle and the syringe to marry the poppy to our blood. We have mixed it with nettle seeds, mixed it with the excrement of flies, mixed it with citrus juice and fashioned it into a circle we then christened the "stone of immortality." We have mixed it in alcohol for Victorian housewives to sip. We have soaked sponges in the poppy's milk to give to patients to suck during surgery. We have smoked it in elaborate pipes.

The story of our relationship with opium is sometimes one of the deepest of human depravity; think, for example, of the Opium Wars of the nineteenth century, in which Western trade powers fought China for commercial access to their own country, including the "right" to sell the Chinese opium, even as China was struggling with a massive addiction problem.

Our relationship with opium is also one of good intentions gone awry. One of the many hopes of Friedrich Wilhelm Adam Sertürner, who in the early nineteenth century figured out how to isolate morphine from opium sap, was that morphine would be more predictable and less addictive. When morphine too proved addictive, heroin was introduced as a way to wean people from morphine.

A lot of us know only too well what the poppy can do. In addition to allowing countless lifesaving surgeries and control of chronic pain, morphine has the power to enslave. The morphine molecule doesn't so much trigger our receptors as it crashes them, creating the most intense feeling of euphoria our bodies have ever felt. Opioids are ruthlessly addictive, nearly cruel. Fifty thousand Americans died from opioid-related overdoses in 2019, almost the same number of Americans who died in the Vietnam War.

I first took the opioid Percocet one winter, after minor outpatient surgery. From our living room couch, I watched the snow fall for hours in big Charlie Brown chunks. Time thickened and turned into syrup; all sound grew cotton-muffled. It snowed and it snowed. Later, I returned the bottle, still with fifty-nine more of the full-moon tablets inside, to the pharmacy. I had a feeling that if I didn't, I would want to stay inside the snow globe forever.

8.

Poppy seeds look as if someone took all the periods from a typesetter's case and scattered them. Somewhere there exists a marvelous three-hundred-page book with all of its hesitations cast away.

9.

The opium poppy has been cultivated since the times of our earliest civilizations, for oil and food, for sleep and easing pain. Poppy residue has been found on clay pottery in Neolithic settlements all through Europe. Fossilized poppy capsules have been found around human skeletons carbon-dated to 4000 BCE, in a cave in Spain—the oldest evidence we have of people laying poppies on others' graves. Images of poppies have been found as woven crowns on the head, or cradled in the arms of fertility goddesses in Egypt, Assyria, Greece.

The poppy family has two hundred fifty species, most of which are found in the Northern Hemisphere and have large, bright, showy flowers. Here is the golden blaze of California poppies, and the scarlet red corn poppies that grew in Belgium. Here are snow poppies from China, desert bearpaw poppies, and fire poppies that grow on land recently burned. Prickly poppies, pygmy poppies, flaming poppies, dwarf poppies, tulip poppies, and the rare Himalayan blue. Here are poppies named for places, Oriental and Welsh and Iceland and California poppies, which actually come from India. Here is the Matilija poppy: with its white petals and yellow center, it looks like a fried egg. The petals are silky and paper-thin, magenta and orange, cream and pink.

10.

In whose doorways does the poppy grow? At the mouth of the cave belonging to Hypnos, the Greek god of sleep. The medieval apothecaries. The ancient Slavs, who believed it gave people the power to move between the lands of the living and the dead. My mother, who's now eighty years old, the same age my grandfather was when he died, and who's had multiple strokes and a hip replaced and no longer remembers much of anything. She needs a walker to leave the house, so she isn't out in her garden much these days, but her poppies still bloom in her absence. The poppy lives at the threshold.

Writes a poet, in the voice of a flower, "At the end of my suffering there was a door."

Perhaps the poppy itself is a type of door. It swings *open-closed, life-death, pleasure-pain, freedom-slavery, remember-forget, suffer-release,* and when not swinging, it lives on its threshold, ready. It knows how to be more than one thing at a time, even when those things contradict one another. It knows everything about living and dying that we struggle to understand.

The poppy mind would call my theory an oversimplification, of course, but the poppy mind is a fecund one, multifaceted as the mind of God.

11.

You would think I'd be a prime candidate for opioid abuse.

A few years ago, I was diagnosed with post-traumatic stress. The diagnosis was not especially remarkable. I had an early and brief first marriage, to a boy I had met at college who was HIV positive. It was the early nineties, the height of the ACT UP movement, and we lived near the center of a vigorous national activist community. Nearly all of the HIV-positive men I knew then are now dead. Most of their surviving loved ones struggle with insomnia and startling easily, guardedness and numbness. I've learned how to manage my symptoms; I know what to say to myself when I wake up, panicked and unable to breathe, after a particularly carefree evening. Most of the time I forget that I have PTSD.

I would like some sleep, though. I got by on five hours a night for decades, and most of that time, I did not nap. I fetishize pajamas and collect Japanese bath salts and go to bed earlier than my daughter, who is agog that I forgo the adult privilege of late nights. I don't take any sedatives, even melatonin. I do think about them a lot.

But I'm not sorry for it. I was given a gift, to be able to live while knowing that death is close. Lots of people have a core experience around which their lives wrap, and we know, through our pain, more intimately the luminous center of the world.

12.

In the last century, we in the West have made the poppy an artifact for remembering.

In the United States, 14 million artificial remembrance poppies, or "Buddy Poppies," are distributed every year. Many more are distributed in other countries. Where I grew up, older veterans in their dress uniforms usually handed them out at traffic intersections around Veterans Day, in exchange for money. The remembrance poppy was originally inspired by John McCrae's poem "In Flanders Fields," and first worn in 1922, to "honor the dead by helping the living," and to remember those who fought or assisted in the First World War. Designed to be assembled with only one hand (to give disabled veterans work), they are inexpensive lapel flowers with a fortune cookie-like tag attached that reads WEAR IT PROUDLY.

I used to see veterans passing out Buddy Poppies all the time, but I seldom see them anymore. I still have one in my jewelry box, given to me maybe seven years back. Where did that come from?

A tiny poppy memory: It's a November weekday morning more than forty years ago, in the mid-1970s, outside Detroit. My handsome uncle stands between lanes of traffic at the island's only stoplight, wearing his World War II Navy dress uniform and collecting money. The last troops have been airlifted from Vietnam, and every adult assures us that all war, forever, is done: surely no one will ever again be so stupid. My sister and I are maybe five and three years old, sailing along in the back of our made-in-Detroit sedan. My mother stuffs a dollar in my uncle's plastic jug, and my uncle hands her a poppy made of red paper and a twist of green wire. My mother fixes the poppy onto the rearview mirror, and the light turns green.

13.

Mostly, poppies don't grow right away. They lie dormant in the earth until they are disturbed, often by a plow.

In spring of 1915, in Flanders, the cornfields had been turned to battlegrounds, and whole nations full of young men waited in the dirt, in trenches they dug for themselves. The battlegrounds had been so disturbed by mines and trench digging that nothing was left, not a single tree or blade of grass, not one building. But all the dormant poppy seeds were awakened. Blood-colored poppies began to grow. For the next four summers, until the fighting ended, poppies were everywhere.

A century after the trench-warfare battles in Ypres, Flanders, I stayed for two weeks on the same land, in the house of a poet. Flax fields, high and golden, as far as I could see. Two fat ponies, one brown and one white, were tethered in the yard outside my window. Early in the morning, I could hear them chuffing. There were four sheep and a smattering of chickens and cats.

It was impossible for an outsider like me to know what had happened the century before, just by looking. But the locals knew. Éireann and Jonathan told me during dinner that the area farmers were forever unearthing skulls, eyeglasses, and razors in their fields; and in a nearby village, a dumpster was specially designated for any unexploded land mines they found. Along the sides of roads were blue cornflowers, and still the occasional shock of a cluster of poppies, bright and ragged.

It was also the summer after the Americans had elected the demagogue. A heat wave was on. The Belgians I met in a café off the *jaagpad*, the path that ran past the poet's house, found the predicament hysterically funny. When I ordered my drink—in Flemish, with a clearly American accent—the bartender-owner smiled gleefully, leaned toward my face, and crowed the demagogue's name. He and his friends at the bar all laughed. The big powerful country had been played!

Their country, meanwhile, had been neutral during the war, yet their grandparents' and great-grandparents' farms had been destroyed. Some of the farmers had committed suicide when they saw what had become of their land. Unlike the French, who declared a portion of their country an uninhabitable zone after the First World War, the Belgians needed the land of their tiny country too much to abandon it. One century later, not much seemed to faze their grandchildren and great-grandchildren. The deep losses in their families' pasts had set them free, in certain ways, from fear.

14.

A corn poppy seed can remain dormant for up to a hundred years.

15.

Unpredictable as the wind, the poppy comes no closer to domesticity than the garden, and defies our desire to contain it. Because its blooms die within three or four days, they make poor cut flowers and seldom find their way into bouquets. They are almost never displayed in con-

317

servatories. They are at once too common and too rare, too vigorous and too fickle.

The poet writes, "The poppies are wild, they are only beautiful and tall / so long as you do not cut them, / they are like the feral cat who purrs and rubs against your leg / but will scratch you if you touch back. / Love is letting the world be half-tamed."

Michael Pollan was the first writer I read who posited that plants and people have reciprocal relationships—that plants domesticate us at the same time that we domesticate them, and that they evolve to respond to basic human yearnings. In *The Botany of Desire*, he writes about four human desires—beauty, sweetness, intoxication, and control—and our social history with the tulip, the apple, marijuana, and the potato. I enjoyed reading the book when it first came out, but it also struck me at the time as romantic, even cloying. Twenty years later, after hearing Suzanne Simard describe a community of trees that speaks the languages of carbon and nitrogen, I reread Pollan's book and realized he isn't talking about anthropomorphized plants—no stems with googly eyes or brains. He is talking about a deeper intelligence within nature, one we may never fully understand.

For now, the poppy remains a mystery. We have never found the opium poppy's wild ancestor. Morphine remains the only drug in nature that resists being expelled from the body. We will never know why, of all the species of plants in the world, one and only one developed the ability to flawlessly impersonate our body's own chemical messengers, a flower whose painkilling properties we have never found anywhere else. Somehow, early on, the opium poppy learned—however it is that plants learn—what we most desire to feel, and discovered that birth and death are often painful and always mysterious. And then it evolved to become our companion in the Mysteries.

16.

What did the poppy know of my grandfather's death that Christmas Eve? Its essence had been inside his body through his illness. It had been part of him when he died. What did the poppy know of our daughter's birth?

We want the world to cleave neatly into halves, no and yes, evil and goodness, fantastic and real. We want it to be clear what to choose and who to hate. We want life and death to be opposite endpoints on a single line. The poppy reveals this kind of thinking to be hopelessly naive.

Poppy seeds are not circular. They are pitted and kidney-shaped.

The poet says in the voice of one of the Magi, three astrologers schooled in prophecy who were guided by a star to witness the birth of Jesus, "I had seen birth and death, but had thought they were different."

Mysteries are places where opposites touch.

On the first day of our daughter's life, the nurse took her father and I to the clear plastic bassinet and showed us how to change her first diapers, teaching us the name for the thick tarry substance that makes a child's first bowel movements: *Meconium,* from the Greek word for "poppy," *mekon,* named for the way that opium is also sticky and black.

Did our daughter leave her dream world, or did she enter ours? Writes John Keats, poet, consumptive, opium addict: "Fled is that music:—Do I wake or sleep?"

Nominated by Orion

TO CIGARETTES

by NANCY CONNORS

from STONECOAST REVIEW

I don't smoke, but not for lack of trying.
In high school I filched Tareytons from the kitchen table,
bummed Luckies from a friend's brother
till he went to Vietnam, palmed Trues at the bus stop,
my younger sister hissing, *I'm gonna tell.*

I sucked Marlboros in the college dive,
sipped tequila sunrises and sent
thick smoke signals to the lead guitarist,
who missed the message,
struggling as he was through *Purple Haze.*

And in France, it was yellow Gitanes,
red wine and sex—sometimes all at once.
Ah, France! Europe's three-hundred-year
experiment in corporal sin. France, where
je ne fume pas means I'm not smoking
right this minute, but I certainly will soon.

Smokes, butts, ciggies, coffin nails—
I tried every brand. Held them languidly between
my fingers while I spoke with wisdom on all manner
of vital subjects, balanced them between my lips
while I typed important works on my
Olympia with the missing m key,

used them as pointers, props, smokescreens,
reasons to have a drink, ways to introduce myself,
and justification for leaning seductively over a candle flame.

They made my chest feel tight and my head whirl,
and try as I might, I couldn't hook myself to them.
They would not have me.
I know now that I didn't have the look they wanted:
neither suicide blonde nor black widow brunette.
I was stuck with the sunny look of Doris Day,
whose lips never met a cigarette and who
was in her chaste bed by 10 at the latest,
dreaming of puppies.

Now I drive by the high school and see the girls outside,
dressed in black, elaborate black hair, black-rimmed eyes,
cigarettes in their blood-painted fingers,
and the boys swirling around them, mystified by smoke.

Nominated by Philip Schultz, Stonecoast

SKINFOLK

fiction by ELAINE HSIEH CHOU

from PLOUGHSHARES

She perfects her look on Myspace. The brightness and contrast in her photos are turned up to 70 percent so she looks like an animation most of the time. It's the mid '00s and she wears metallic cream eyeshadow, has red highlights in her layered hair, acrylics on her nails. Her belly button is pierced (her favorite piece of jewelry, a dangling rhinestone heart). On her lower back, between those two infamous dimples, rests a black butterfly tattoo inked at a parlor that doesn't card. Her AIM screenname is AzNbByGrL88.

His Calvin Klein boxers are positioned two inches above his hip-bones. He tightens his belt just where his dick begins, so his pants are in a constant state of falling down. His sneakers are FUBU and his car is a lowered Honda Accord, celestial white, windows tinted black, with a custom rear wing on the trunk. It's a car you hear, both when it arrives and when it leaves. His hair is bleached at the tips and spiked into symmetrical points, like an underwater anemone. He leaves two long, thin strands at the front, crinkly with L.A. Looks gel; he likes to think they frame his face. When you click on his Myspace page, a familiar melody plays, though the lyrics have been changed: "Got rice, bitch? Got rice?"

They apply to college because their parents are immigrant parents after all. She attends community for two years, transfers to a four-year, majors in nursing, then sociology. He goes to State not too far from home. He manages to graduate with a degree in business, his GPA hovering just above a 2.8. She drops out with twelve credits left.

She's moved on from Myspace to ModelMayhem. Instead of capturing her own pout with her digital Canon PowerShot, someone does it for her and it feels legitimate, though she doesn't get paid. Men message her saying they can trade portfolio for portfolio: she gets free modeling pics, they get to claim they're real photographers. She drives to apartments in Long Beach and El Segundo and lies on strange sofas in a lace pushup bra and panties shoplifted from Forever 21. She curates all kinds of looks: suntanned *Laguna Beach*-esque bikini babe, emo kid adorned with checkered wristbands and plastic barrettes, hip-hop b-girl with her hair in a tight ponytail, Reeboks, baby hairs curled and gelled down. She wants people to know she's versatile.

He joins an Asian frat at his college. They take ecstasy, pink and blue and green pills printed with smiley faces and peace signs, pack into clubs on Wilshire Boulevard in Hollywood and ask each other, Yo, are you rolling yet? until their pupils swirl black. They wear chinos and pressed dress shirts, leather shoes, 14K gold bracelets, watches that look more expensive than they are. When they walk into a room, an intoxicating cloud of Acqua Di Gio drifts behind them—intoxicating because it makes everyone, even them, a little drowsy. They pay for girls' vodka tonics and in the pit of the club's dark, beating heart, they close their eyes and grind against their asses.

At EDC that summer, a blond Asian girl whose boyfriend she fucked yanks her hair down to the sun-soaked pavement and threatens to kill her. She punches the girl in the mouth. Blood dribbles out; it reminds her of red icing. She decides she likes her *Ruff Ryders* inspired look best, maybe because she doesn't see a lot of other Asian girls doing it, who are all too busy trying to look like Paris Hilton. She dyes her hair Revlon 5.1 Medium Ash Brown, arches her eyebrows high and thin, lines her lips in a color darker than her mauve lipstick, dons four-inch hoop earrings that graze her shoulders. She strips her MP3 player clean, downloads Missy Elliott, DMX, Bone Thugs & Harmony, Dr. Dre, Lauryn Hill.

On Craigslist, he buys a scratched-up sound mixer, but it works just fine. He fabricates a stage name, deletes "Got rice?" from his Myspace page and uploads a demo he recorded in his room. That was some pretend shit, he says. Two Asian F.O.B.s playing at rapping. He can do it better, he can do it for real. He asks a friend from college if he can offload a few baggies of X, he needs money to produce a real music video. Six weeks later, he drives to Las Vegas and pays too much to film it in XS's pool. It's a night shoot: gyrating half-naked girls clutch cocktails and neon lights refract against their high-sheen skin, against the aquamarine, chlorinated water. His sister demands to be in it; he relents.

Their diction and syntax are morphing and it's happening so effortlessly it doesn't even feel like a twenty-four-hour performance. They don't have to study much. They've always been keen observers and adapters, the kind of kids who watched their parents fight and repeated it like a rehearsal; they the actors, the argument the script. They end up with a new shiny box of vocabulary at their disposal. Inflection and stress—that's important too. Much later, when people ask *Where are you from?*, they nudge their places of birth a little south. Less Inland Empire, more on the edge of Inglewood. In his songs, he references "the hood" but is careful to never get too specific. In an interview years later, she says that growing up, all her best friends were black.

When they visit their parents, they know to select words from a different box of vocabulary. Their teeth, lips, tongues, and palatine uvula shift. The tone and pitch of their voices too: less boisterous, more restrained; a soda that's lost its carbonation. They look around their parents' house: an altar in the front room, good-luck cloth charms from Hsi Lai Temple, steamed ground pork with salted duck egg on the vinyl-wrapped table. When their grandparents come over, they stare at the ground and mumble a few Cantonese phrases. Under their watchful eyes, they kneel on the floor, grasp joss sticks between their palms, bend their foreheads low to the floor, glance up at their ancestors' photos. Repeat two more times. Their grandparents look them up and down and sigh.

He records an EP. When he meets other rappers, he mentions 2Pac and Warren G, talks about respect and admiration, tradition and changing the game. Most of the time, he's ignored. People raise their eyebrows, occasionally laugh behind closed doors. *Who is this guy? Where did he come from?* He feels self-conscious for the first time, the way he never did with his old crew, ponders the new tattoo under his right eye and on all ten knuckles, if he's dropping his pants just a little too low, if he should have shaved his head instead of getting corn rows. But all it takes is one guy—RJ, rambunctious and unpredictable RJ who's got a heart of gold, doesn't know what judgment is—to change things. Not everything. But when RJ says *Hey, he's with me*, the others welcome him, cautiously. The first time he walks into a room where everyone is black but him, where he's fist-bumped and shoulder-smacked, he feels like he's in first grade again, friendless and lonely, and someone just asked if he wants to play on the swings. He makes sure to take pictures of them all together, flashing his grillz, gripping a paper-bagged forty by the throat, and posts them on his Myspace.

She wants fame to be her career, can see herself looking at herself so clearly, as if she's her own fan. So she comes up with a stage name. Her brother's following is growing, he's performing at small venues, he's even getting collabs, but being in his music videos isn't getting her anywhere. There's a new thing called YouTube and she records a couple videos flipping her hair, shaking her ass. It doesn't really help. She begs her parents for three grand and gets implants at a clinic in Corona: 34DD. It helps. Once the scars heal, she starts go-go dancing at clubs, in a neon bra and panties set, wearing fuzzy boots that tickle her knees. On weekends, she goes to car racing events and splays against the lacquered cherry reds and electric blues. She sits on the hood with her breasts thrust toward the camera's eye, or bends over in six-inch clear stilettos, calves taut. Her name appears in airbrushed font on event flyers: watch her dance, get your picture taken with her, get her autograph. Sometimes hair and makeup try to change her look: maybe a frosted pink lip, silver eye shadow, hair curled into loose waves? Something a little less . . . urban? She tells them no. This isn't a look; it's who she is.

Fame finally arrives in the form of a reality TV show on MTV. She tries to get on the show by herself, but they want them both, a two-for-one package deal. They'll be marketed as the controversial, in-your-face brother and sister duo. MTV approves their urban look, even suggests they throw some bandanas into their wardrobe (not red or blue, are you crazy?) and is a do-rag asking too much? They live with ten other C-to D-list celebrities in a Silver Lake villa. Everyone competes in teams: there are couples, friends, siblings. Each day, they're given a stupidly difficult challenge: Sell as many of these 10,000 T-shirts as you can on the Venice boardwalk. Persuade a stranger over the telephone to give you a hundred dollars. Eat a four-foot-long burrito; keep going if you throw up. The winners get $50,000 to split. They cultivate and harvest their personalities, make them better than the producers could have ever dreamed of. When they're not doing challenges, they're screaming, punching fists into walls, crying streaky mascara, hooking up with the other celebrities under the greenish glow of a night-vision camera. There's one moment on day seven of filming when he says a slur, ending in—*a* but nonetheless it's the refashioned son of a slur, *the* slur, and a black contestant overhears him and an argument ensues. It didn't air. They came in second place.

After the show ends, they feel strange when they're not being filmed. They can't decide why they're doing what they're doing or saying what they're saying when no one's watching. They want the camera's lens back on them; it makes them feel real. Paparazzi, TMZ, Perez Hilton, they don't care if it's good or bad press. There is a stint in rehab and one disorderly conduct arrest. In these photos, they look stumbling and glazed over or else hesitantly doelike, caught in the camera's flash. He makes a second album that takes too long to record because he's always on something when he comes to the studio. He throws up at a performance in Union City in the middle of his set. Some people leave early. She gets more plastic surgery (lip injections and liposuction on her upper arms and lower stomach). She dates an NFL football player for a few months and dreams of being a Real Housewife of Atlanta but the NFL player tells her he's not ready to commit, baby, not yet.

For the first time, they have money. Instead of going home, they send their parents a six-piece Gucci luggage set, though their parents have never taken a vacation. It's displayed in the living room like installation art.

High on Special K one night, they drive to the Hollywood sign. They clamber over itchy brush and maneuver around snake holes and look over the throbbing lit-up city and hold their breaths. Most of the time, when they're alone with each other, they keep it up. But for a moment they forget, or maybe they're just tired, and they say in their old voices *Hey, we made it.*

They're at a Malibu mansion when the news breaks. It's a party for one of his friends, acquaintances actually, a producer at Aftermath. They are drunk and have done two or three lines of coke each. Someone turns off the music. There was a shooting on North Santa Fe and Cypress. A cop pulled over Terrence Jones, also known as Ha-Voc, a newcomer in the industry, just nineteen years old and about to drop his first single. He was reaching for his license and registration when the cop fired three rounds into his back.

She shakes her head and looks down at the floor in silence, the coke beginning to leach out of her. He pulls RJ into a side hug and quotes NWA, *redneck, white bread, chickenshit motherfucker.* Someone watching the news corrects him, says a first name and a last name. The last name is a lot like theirs, though they don't use it anymore, only when filling out legal paperwork.

Everyone is looking at them, as though waiting for them to say something. But what do you say in a moment like that? And in what voice do you say it?

When they leave the party, it feels as if people are looking at them differently. Or maybe they're looking at them the way they've always felt about them.

In the car, he thinks about his second album that's releasing soon. Track nine is called "Azn brothas bleed too," and somehow the sentiment goes from feeling powerfully legit to feeling foolish, really foolish, in a matter of seconds.

The cop is indicted. A rarity. Some people in their hometown stage a protest in front of the First Chinese Baptist Church. There are two, maybe three dozen protestors—as young as sixteen and as old as sixty, holding up posters in both English and Chinese: "We Love LAPD," "Protect Cops." She drives by in her car, Sean John sunglasses shielding half her face, and reads on one of them, "Free Officer Tsai."

It's an unusually cold winter in Southern California. The palm trees droop against the gray sky, buckled by the wind, and the grass seizes up with frost, turns a surreal purplish-green. The beaches are empty. There's only the occasional tourist wandering around, disappointed.

Twenty people come to his drop party. His second album is a flop. His Myspace posts grow frequent and erratic. When he shows up at RJ's house one night at four a.m., unintelligible and belligerent, RJ looks at him, his carefree expression somber for once, and tells him to get help.

He is found passed-out on the sidewalk, his mouth patchy with white. The doctors identify meth in his system.

The modeling and dancing feel stagnant, like they're not taking her anywhere, but all of that changes when her sex tape leaks, the one with her NFL player ex. Watching it, she can't help thinking that she looks good, as though all the while she is moaning and twisting, she somehow realized that someone, somewhere, was going to watch it on the big screen one day. She wonders if sex has always been that way for her—a spectator witnessing her own pleasure. There's a moment toward the end where she looks directly into the camera and, after a moment, remembers to smile.

He is sent to rehab.

She is offered a three-video deal by Sapphire Pictures.

The next time they go to their parents' house, it's their grandmother's eightieth birthday. Their voices shift gears as their voices always do, some long-ago-inherited Cantonese phrases resurface as they always do, their diamond chains and grillz removed for the occasion, plain T-shirts and jeans slipped on, and they sit on the plastic-covered sofa, egg-roll cookies in a glass dish on the coffee table, Danny Chan crooning on the CD player, and they look around at the people gathered and think *does the killer cop's family listen to Danny Chan, do they eat egg-roll cookies, do they rub Mentholatum on everything even when it doesn't make sense?*

After dinner, they're watching the evening news and ABC is doing that thing where they bust into a house with a handheld camera and line up all the people facedown on the sidewalk. They're all men, boys really, and black. Their father makes a comment in Cantonese. Something about the neighborhood, how if it keeps going where it's going, he'll buy a gun.

They pretend not to understand him.

It's the mid '10s and they are older and maybe a little wiser.

Instagram is her new domain. She takes pictures of herself in Nike everything: sneakers, track pants, sports bra, baseball cap, and tags @ Nike on each item. She's always leaning against a railing or a bench or a brick wall, her gaze angled toward something in the far-off distance. Or she wears bandage dresses without a bra or underwear (it shows through) and takes pictures of herself on hotel balconies, eyes (with lash extensions) looking shyly downward. She sucks her waist in and pushes her lips out (just a little) and balances on the balls of her feet because she swears it makes her ass look tighter. There are apps to make her waist smaller, her lips plumper, her skin poreless, her chin tapered, her eyes larger, her nose thinner, her cheekbones higher, her forehead wider. Out of pride, she refuses to post edited pics, uses #no-filter instead, but hey, she's older and these other little twats she has to compete with are barely seventeen, so after a few months, she decides it's only fair. Her photos look airbrushed, take on a slightly alien quality. She gets more followers.

He's always on some kind of hustle. He tried to slide into the producing side of things, failed, was a club promoter for a while. Whenever he was running low on cash, he could always drive to Chapman or Pepperdine and offload a few baggies of Molly (the kids had changed the name and the look, tried to make it wholesome, like vitamins). He finds himself briefly back in the public eye when he's invited to be a contestant on a VH1 dating show. Instead of wild and unstable, he cultivates a new image: silent, cool, doesn't-take-shit. Two girls on the show fight each other over him; one of them is pushed out of a car onto the highway. The cops are called and there's a bump in the show's ratings. The other guys start asking him for advice, listening to him with faces that are meant to look blasé but underneath, too hopeful, too eager. When the show ends, he dips into the Pick-Up Artist world, makes a website, pays for ads. He hosts seminars at hotel conference rooms, where men come to see him talk, but after just a few sessions, he starts showing up late, then missing dates altogether. He doesn't want to hang out with these losers for hours and hours, he's not some tenderhearted social worker, and even though he gets paid, it all starts to feel like charity. Sitting on a fold-out plastic chair, telling braces-wearing Christopher from Bakersville how to get a girl's number in ten minutes or less is not who he is, he decides, looking down at his tattooed knuckles, no, it's not the image he's going for.

She is learning that in this new decade, she is the product and she has to sell. That's what people are buying when they pay for the junk she sponsors: tea that makes you shit water, gummies that claim to turn your split-ends into a lush mane, UV lights to jam over your crooked off-white teeth. What they really want is to look like her, be like her. Whatever alterations they do to themselves, she knows, they'll still just be themselves. She stays up until five a.m., deleting comments that resurface her past, the arrest, the sex tape, comments asking why she never posts pics of her parents or childhood photos on #throwbackthursdays, comments asking *why do you talk like that?*, comments asking if she's half black, and if so, does she have proof, comments asking about her skin tone, why her old Myspace pics are clearly a no. 2 fair ivory and now she's inching toward no. 7 dark caramel. She deletes and scrolls, deletes and scrolls. Scrolls some more. There are so many other women to both envy and hate. She has to perform and edit and curate to get likes, though she tries to make it look painless. But for some of these women, she suspects, it *is* painless. What is it that she's missing? She's paid for an algorithm that got her past the 10,000 mark, then she bought 10,000 more followers, but she's still well below the 100,000 mark, not even close to the seven-figure Insta stars. What is it that she's missing? Her entire life, she has been grooming herself for this technologically ripe moment. Model, music video dancer, go-go girl—all of that has led her here, to the ultimate platform to sell her image. She has always looked at herself from outside herself, evaluating the girl on the screen as its own autonomous commodity, how to package her, how to maximize her, how to optimize her. What is she missing?

On the rare occasion they go home, their parents have stopped asking *When are you finding a real job? When are you getting married? When are you going to have kids? When will you give us all the things we deserve because we came to this country for you? Why are you like this? What made you like this? Why do you like black people so much, why are you always listening to their music, why are you always hanging out with them*, why and why and why?

They watch TV in silence, comment on the weather, leave some money on the coffee table, don't stay for dinner.

He decides to use his business degree for something after all. He gets RJ involved, good old RJ, they've been friends for almost a decade now, he'll always come through for him, right? Business partners 2.0, together the sky's the limit, me and you—RJ loves that inspirational kind of stuff, talks tough, but inside, he's a sweetheart, a total teddy bear. OK, so. The idea is a start-up. It's called The Exchange, accessible for a monthly fee. Hip-hop singers, rappers, professional athletes— they all want to meet beautiful single women, don't they? And beautiful single women want to meet hip-hop singers, rappers, and professional athletes, don't they? No, it's not a dating app, not officially anyway. Attractive people want to party together, enhance each other's images, there'll be a professional photographer on site, a win-win situation for all. It's sort of like networking. Yeah, there'll be alcohol (and other chemical goodies). They'll rent out penthouses and mansions in LA, SF, NYC, Atlanta, Miami. If all goes well, the girls will be transported via private jets. No one can get in without an individualized, temporary QR code, because he understands exclusivity is key to desirability. The girls will be carefully selected and screened, only the cream of the crop, naturally. It's discreet too, if any married men want to partake. On top of that, they'll be sponsored by Bacardi, Red Bull, Evian, etc. In the bathrooms it will be the same, only La Mer lotion or whatever girls are paying too much for in the name of immortality. He's got it all worked out, don't worry RJ, he's got it. He's got it.

Hanging around clubs, fucking around on reality TV, peddling pills, he understands now that all of that was child's play, no wonder his parents were never proud of him. The Exchange is different. Legitimate. He's backed by white investors dressed in suits he could never afford.

He attends meetings, gives presentations. He wonders if he should adjust his voice, try to sound like them, nasally and strident and *how about those Lakers!* but they don't seem to mind—they want to invest in him, in the authenticity of him.

His sister comes on board. Most of her followers are girls who dress and talk just like her. She knows thousands of them, can supply him with pretty face after pretty face. She updates her bio to The Exchange VP, which sounds official, adds a pink lip emoji plus flying stack of bills emoji. She takes over for The Exchange's account and posts enigmatic photos of infinity pools, slippery sleek hotel bars with champagne lounging in a tub of ice, anonymous rappers posing with women from the waist down, diamond-wrapped fingers clutching hips, adds #inviteonly #comingsoon.

When she takes off all her makeup and looks in the mirror, she realizes this role relegates her to the background, to behind-the-scenes, no longer the leg dangling out the car door like bait, the one men are paying to be near, as though her presence alone makes them into someone better, someone with more capital. And she isn't too bothered by it. She's getting tired. She wants Jordan to propose; they've been together for fourteen months, which is long in her book, maybe the longest she's ever had. She likes thinking about having his baby, a little girl, what she'd look like, *blasian*, that most coveted mix, what clothes she'd put her in, what her skin would look like, what her hair would look like, if she could do her hair, do it right.

The penthouse is in Malibu, coincidentally the same one where the Aftermath producer had his party, where they learned about the killer cop with a last name too close to theirs. All of that seems a long time ago. They can hardly remember that night, what was said, what wasn't said.

The penthouse features a rotating circular bed in the master bedroom, two floors, an infinity pool, a balcony, a fully stocked bar, a Jacuzzi, a view out of a magazine. They had to rent it because tonight is the launch of the Exchange and everything has to be perfect.

They plan to get things ready at nine before people show up at ten. She arrives on time, he and RJ arrive twenty minutes late.

She's wearing a silk camo jumpsuit with gold accents, paired with lace-up high-heeled boots, her nails are a reasonable two inches instead of three, and her hair doubles the size of her head. He's in head-to-toe

331

Supreme, from his bucket hat to his sneakers, his entire outfit costing a monthly mortgage payment.

She runs around, frantic, like someone's holding a gun to her head, taking videos and selfies and uploading them to the Exchange's account, remembers to add #thisisit #launchparty.

He's on the phone, pacing in front of the floor-to-ceiling windows; some idiot double-booked two photographers and where is the ice, did no one remember to get fucking ice? and why is this idiot fucker calling him about airport pickup for the girls, does he not have Google Maps, does he have to do everything around here for everyone?

RJ says he's going to check out the Jacuzzi, ends up taking a nap in one of the bedrooms.

She runs out of things to do, starts fluffing cushions, straightening wine glasses, keeps checking her face in the mirror.

A batch of girls arrives first, they stand in the hallway, laughing and gasping *it's so beautiful and big, even better than the pictures, can you believe we're here? I heard he's coming, he's so hot, I call dibs, oh my god OK fine.*

They look a little awkward and shy, crowded together in their platform heels and cheap polyester dresses, with twiggy legs and uneven eyeliner and hair that was flat-ironed a little too long, not exactly what she had hoped for—glamorous, sophisticated, icy. She calls them into the master bedroom, splays open her enormous makeup kit, someone turns Spotify on, and here's some sparkling rosé (they have to save the expensive stuff for later), they start laughing and taking selfies and asking what's your handle, I'll tag you, so it's cool, alcohol and a pounding subwoofer make everything better.

Another batch of girls arrives and the first batch is there to welcome them in. They're fluffed up with giddy excitement, self-conscious of where the photographer is in the room, tucking their hair behind their ears, working their best angles, smiling without showing their teeth.

He has relaxed enough to allow himself a single line and he and RJ freestyle a bit, the girls begin to dance, heads bobbing and hips swiveling, though they never seem to move their feet.

It's getting late and the main events are finally arriving, the hip-hop singers, rappers, and professional athletes. The atmosphere changes immediately, becomes taut, like this is serious business, we're starring in our own movie and watching it happen as it happens.

She opens bottles of champagne and everyone gets a glass—all these perfect young people, like 3D cutouts from Instagram—raising them into the air and he says a few words, something about starting a move-ment, thank you for being here, enjoy, and everyone feels that this will be the best night of their lives, or at least, one of the best nights of their lives and this feeling is heightened, no, predicated on, the fact that it must be recorded, saved, and shared because if it's not, it's not real, you can't prove it happened. She reminds them that it's a discreet and invitation-only event, they can only post anonymous pics of the mar-ried hip-hop singers, rappers, and professional athletes—no faces, no identifying tattoos or marks—but feel free otherwise, it's the tease of information that will make consumers inconsolable with not knowing and wanting to know, enough to sign up for a pricey membership.

He cannot believe this is all happening and look, he didn't even fuck it up, everyone thinks he fucks everything up, but it's happening just like he planned and hey, two photographers are better than one, and people keep telling him this is dope, the women are fine, and in spite of himself he breaks into an unplanned, goofy grin.

The bartenders are working hard serving drinks, the sweet, damp stink of weed floats from the first to the second floor, a few pastel pills are passed around inconspicuously and swallowed. People are gyrating to the music in dark corners with their eyes closed, they're sitting en-twined on the velvet sofas and whispering in each other's ears, one guy's got two girls balanced on both knees, people are stripping off their clothes and cannonballing into the pool, girls are making out with each other and guys are clapping and hollering, a few couples and threes and fours slip into rooms, close the doors.

She finds him outside by the pool, staring down into the houses and lights below, and it reminds her of the time they climbed to the Holly-wood sign.

Remember when—she begins, but he already knows. They look at each other and laugh. It's been a crazy decade, they've made some mistakes along the way, but they wouldn't trade it for anything. Look how far we've come, they say to each other without having to say any-thing. *Hey, we made it.*

He glances around, sees the party is still popping (remember when they used to say "the party is popping") and decides he can relax now, really relax, it's his party after all. He came into some new stuff, it's strong but clean and good, does she want to try it? She decides she wants to stop checking her phone (Jordan hasn't replied to her texts, what the hell is he doing? Where is he? Why did he like that bitch's post on Ins-tagram five minutes ago?) and says, fuck it. They rub a pinkie's worth on their gums, and minutes later, they don't even know their own names, their pupils feel like the size of jaw breakers, everything is a halogen carousel of kaleidoscopic lights, their bodies are paper thin, every sound and vibration melts through them until their bodies give way entirely, and they're unanchored, floating.

They lie on their backs facing the house, eyeballs roving and jerking toward the glimmer of light coming from inside, everyone's bodies moving on land like they're swimming. The music vibrates the palm trees, they can see the minutest tremble before it liquefies into a swirling puddle again. They have vague impressions of people asking, "You good?" and they laugh, touch their fingers to their mouths.

It's nearing four a.m. when they hear yelling and crying and they wobble inside, try to focus enough to visualize what's happening, connect the sounds to people's mouths. His mouth feels like a cotton ball. Her head is a helium balloon.

The bedroom is glass-paned with a chandelier dangling from the ceiling. He looks in the mirror, sees himself refracted into pieces, blinks, tugs his vision away toward the commotion.

She moves closer and registers that the figure standing at the edge of the bed is a man, a black man, an NFL player for the Raiders. His mouth is popping open and shut, open and shut. It sounds like *How old are you? How old are you?*

There's a girl on the bed with the sheets pulled up to her neck. Her hair is in twist braids, her highlighted and contoured face exquisite.

There's a small crowd around him telling him to calm down, man, what the fuck happened?

He says, We start hooking up and she's into it, then she starts crying and telling me she's a virgin and some shit about high school and she wants to call her mom to come get her.

Someone cracks a joke and the NFL player says that's not fucking funny, he's got a sister, same age, this shit is fucked up.

She starts laughing because it is fucked up, it's royally fucked up, her being the same age as his sister, the universe is a sick joke, and it's always been, it doesn't lead to transcendence, it only leads downward and why did she ever believe otherwise and why did she ever think she could rise above the muck.

Everyone turns to stare at her.

There's more yelling coming from outside the door, someone saying let me through, let me through, I'm her mother.

A woman—probably just a few years older than her—pushes into the bedroom and looks around, eyes snapping, furious, orders people to get the fuck out, tells her daughter to get dressed, now.

I didn't know, the NFL player keeps repeating, I didn't fucking know. He looks at her and asks, Did you know?

She's still laughing, her brother is gripping her wrist, hard, hoping to jolt her from that other place she's still trapped in, but she can't walk because her legs have jellied and she collapses onto the floor.

The mother points at the girls with skittish eyes crowded outside the bedroom door, and asks again, Did you know?

She doesn't really understand what those words mean, English is just a collection of meaningless vowels and consonants at this point.

My daughter is fifteen, the mother says, what kind of shit are you running—I will have you arrested—did you target—just a child—tell me, did you—exploitation—black bodies—

She closes her eyes, covers her ears, and screams. The mother shakes her head, holds her daughter's hand, says, we are getting the fuck out of here.

He trails behind her, telling her it was just a misunderstanding, don't press charges lady, please, yo, lady—He stops and wills his voice to rewind to its normal state, tries again—yo, lady—Where did his old voice go? His lips strain toward it, but it's already years behind him, ditched and buried.

The mother steps into the elevator with her daughter, looks at him with bottomless pity. It's a look that slaps him backwards. It's how everyone looked at him the night Ha-Voc was shot by the killer cop.

He stares back at her, dumbfounded, gropes at his throat. When the elevator doors close, he stumbles toward the bathroom and vomits, tucks himself into the fetal position on the tiled floor.

She looks up to see shifting faces and crossed arms, the NFL player is saying if he gets charged with anything, he's going to sue, what the fuck was she thinking, should have never signed up, some sort of sick scam, what a fucking bullshit party. Everyone's asking the girls to show their IDs, right fucking now or leave—

Did you know? someone asks again, shaking her by the shoulders.

She just wants everyone to shut up, she screams for them to shut the fuck up, but the sound isn't exiting her mouth. Her throat is clamped, her head is a black hole, her eyeballs are going to splinter from their sockets and she just wants to feel unanchored again, to disentangle herself from this body, this poor sack of flesh that she has denied and that has denied her, again and again.

When she runs out of the room toward the balcony, it happens so fast no one knows where she's gone.

It's only a handful of people on the first floor who see her, a splash into the pool, a white crash of foam, then silence, ripples. A diluted, pale pink rises to the surface.

Above her floating body, the city's lights and palm trees keep swaying.

He wears all black to her funeral, no name brands. His cornrows have been shaved off. Their father has shaved his head too. Their mother wears a black YSL dress her daughter bought her, never worn before.

Afterward, people cry outside the temple where a burning metal trash can has been placed. The fire fuses into the summer heat wave, makes the air shimmer. On their knees, relatives toss in paper wads of money, paper McDonalds, paper Chanel purses, paper iPhones and iPads, paper Louis Vuitton luggage, so she'll have them in the afterlife, so the ghostly ashes of these objects will rise up into her possession.

Only three of her friends from her go-go dancing days show up, clustered at the edge of the crowd.

He kneels too close to the fire, stares into the heart of the flames, his skin hot to the touch, sweat soaking him, until his mother pulls him away, shouting in Cantonese.

Her photo is on the altar now at his parents' house, beside his ancestors'.

There are so many photos of her to choose from—on mobile apps, on the internet, on her phone, stored in backup disks. But the only good one they could find of her, just her, is from her high-school yearbook, tenth grade. She's wearing a long-sleeved baby-blue shirt with buttons down the front and a necklace of sterling silver stars. Her undyed hair is in a ponytail, her smile toothy and wide. She isn't wearing any makeup.

When he bows three times, the joss sticks grasped in both his palms, he places his forehead against the floor, lets his tears stain the carpet and says her name: Nina.

Nina Tsiang.

Nominated by Anne Ray

AS A CHILD OF NORTH AMERICA

by ROGER REEVES

from FIVE POINTS

And Abraham lifted up his eyes, and looked, and behold behind him a ram caught in a thicket by his horns: and Abraham went and took the ram, and offered him up for a burnt offering in the stead of his son. Genesis 22:13

I wept for the ram and was told not to—
His life—in the thicket, horn-held and groped
By thorn and God, stone table and knife—his
Life—crazed for sure, a free animal
Until master, mastery, and the Lord
Grants his vision—capture—the ram's flesh
Chattering, smoke covering the face of God.
I was told to celebrate this vision—
The tambourine knocked and fluttering
Against the heel of my mother's hand
Drove the smoke higher—and higher the church
Climbed to witness the smoke, the ram,
A burning angel burning in the eye of God,
And God wild as the eye of goat
Watching its body walk out from beneath it
In prophecy, in flame. How does it feel
To be a problem, my mother once asked
From behind a knife and the first ten years of a century
Whose last ten years will resemble a goat
Hemmed in thorns, awaiting a knife, a new century to die
In. How does it feel to be a problem?

I answer upon a stone table, conscripted
By tambourine and its talons drawing me higher,
Higher until I am what vision forgets—
Something thrashing, a second sun of blood
Coming out of the day's slow thighs,
Mismanaged mercy so silent. I would remind you
I did not coo into the knife, I did not coo
Though I wept like a goat and was glad.

Nominated by Maxine Scates, Five Points

AUTOBIOGRAPHY VIA FORGETTING

by MARIANNE CHAN

from KENYON REVIEW

1

I once heard someone call themselves "a string of memories." The opposite is true for me. I'm a cement block of forgetfulness. For every new memory, something else gets lost or disfigured: a recipe for lentils, dance moves, someone's birthday, names of directors and actors. I manage to get them all wrong. Some people claim that they've retained memories from past lives. I can't remember what happened in this one.

2

Most of my childhood on the military base or in Biddle City is gone from my brain. I ask my brother questions, and we sort out what we know. I say, *But didn't we?* And he says, *I think that was someone else.* The thing I remember most is the blue feeling in my chest as a child, that sudden gloom. My dad told me that he spoke to a colonel he worked for in the nineties. The colonel remembered me as "the child who used to cry all the time." I don't remember crying all the time, but it's possible I did because I forgot that I was safe and happy.

3.

I read somewhere that memory is not stored as it is on a hard drive. Instead, it is something you recreate in each version of remembering. It is a process of sculpting. Perhaps, the difference between memory and imagination is simply the clay you use.

4.

When I was about eight or nine (or six or seven?) I asked my mother to please give me another sibling. It was not that my brother wasn't enough, but I wanted to be the middle child, to sit between two bodies where I could be securely tucked away. This child would be another brain for our family, another memory maker. My parents said no, didn't even try! Therefore, I remained the youngest in my family, a flea clinging to the tip of our animal tail. We don't know and will never know what that third child could've remembered that we've all now forgotten.

5.

In my early twenties, I had a boyfriend who asked me if I ever forgot I was a racial minority. I said, *Yes, I forget everything*. But of course, it was a stupid answer to a stupid question. I mean, who walks around thinking all the time: *I'm a minority, I'm a minority*.

6.

There are places in the U.S. like Daly City in northern California where more than half the people are Asian, where cultures and languages from nations of origin are remembered, maintained. This is all to say: People of color in America experience moments of majority. In the Midwest, at a Filipino gathering for example, I am awash in majorityness. In this room where I am alone, I am majority. And in my body, my spirit takes up more space than any other spirit. The majority of me is me, while the minority of me is me as a minority.

7.

What does it mean to forget something really? When I am asked to speak Bisaya, my parents' language, I struggle to put two words together. Certain words don't flake off the tongue like stewed meat from bone. But when I hear Bisaya spoken, I understand its meanings. The language is there in the mind behind a closed door, key dangling from the knob. I only have access to the meanings when someone else turns the key. It is the same as me remembering that I am a racial minority. When some external thing reminds me is when I know it most fully.

8.

Now, in my thirties, despite the state of the world, I want a baby. I want to hold a new memory-maker against my chest like fragile glass. It amazes me how strong the desire is. S. tells me to forget about it. *Don't think, don't write, don't talk about it,* she says, *and it'll happen.* And yet, I cannot resist writing about it. And yet, sometimes I say *baby* to myself as I fall asleep with my ear against my cat's ribs, her purrs buzzing against my head. *My baby.*

9.

One cannot try to forget something without remembering it. Emily Dickinson writes, *Heart, we will forget him! / You and I, to-night!* and yet, *he* is in the poem, immortalized like the beloved in Shakespeare's "Sonnet 18." And in this poem that I am writing, my beloved is forgetfulness. Forgetting is remembered, immortalized *so long as men can breathe or eyes can see.* To get me to fall asleep, my father used to tell me to think of nothing. Tell someone not to think, and the brain will run wild. The mind is fiddly that way. The mind is only manipulated by trickery: sheep counting, body scans, a catalogue of the things you don't remember.

Nominated by John Drury

WHEN THE BODY SAYS NO BUT YOU CAN'T STOP SWALLOWING

by STEVEN ESPADA DAWSON

from GULF COAST

after "On Being Suicidal" by b: william bearhart

From twenty yards away the adult megaplexxx sign
looks like a crescent moon stuck on its beetle back.

On the bus I use my fingernail to etch figure eights
into a styrofoam cup. The mean idea of vanishing

myself is a seed I can't unplant. A stranger tells me
her kidney stones ache. Every flaw in the road

rattles her like a handful of glass. I pine for
that gorgeous myth of childhood. How I lost

good sleep worrying over watermelon seeds.
Thought they'd gut sprout, impale upwards, straight

through god's windshield. The thought of being
dead returns unwelcome like a landlord.

In Colorado I pushed two motel beds together,
left the door wide open. Anything to be held

while unrecognizable. Regarding wellness
checks: I cut into a forearm length of bread,

finessed the knife like a violin bow. I tried
to convince that angry cop I never swallowed,

then threw up in his back seat. Had instead
he been my father opening, for me, a door—

not out but towards somewhere tender. Had he
held me there, so I might practice delight.

Nominated by Peter LaBerge, Gulf Coast

TOO ATTACHED

by WHITNEY LEE

from THE THREEPENNY REVIEW

Mila lay on my ultrasound table, her tan skin stretched over a twenty-two-week pregnant belly. Across the room, Joaquín, Mila's husband, rested his elbows on his knees. I had graduated from a High-Risk Obstetrics fellowship seven months earlier and was serving as a military physician, and Joaquín was a Marine. His thick, defined arms, broad shoulders, and narrow waist offset a short stature—his presence was conspicuous. Yet when he smiled, his eyes disappeared behind full cheeks, giving him an air of youth and kindness.

Their five-year-old son, James, slouched on the chair next to Joaquín, watching *Dora the Explorer* on an iPad.

"Hi, buddy," I said.

When he did not answer, Joaquín tickled his side. The little boy laughed but kept his eyes on Dora.

I squeezed a tube of blue ultrasound gel onto Mila's abdomen, then swept the probe over her skin, careful to avoid her plain blue T-shirt and jeans. The three of us engaged in banal chitchat. "Do you know the sex of your baby?" "Have you picked a name?" "The weather is nice for January."

Though I had not met the couple before, I knew from Mila's chart that their baby had a lung tumor. But I also knew it had been stable for a few weeks. The purpose of this visit was to make sure the fetus was not getting sick, that everything was status quo. But it wasn't.

Images of the little girl they had already named Williamina appeared on the monitor. I pointed out their daughter's head, arms, legs, feet, hands, fingers, toes, nose, lips, and spine as she wiggled, stretched, and turned inside Mila's body. Though the couple marveled at the images, they could sense I was worried and they could see why. The baby's lungs, intestines, stomach, heart, and liver floated in a sea of black. Over the last week, fluid had accumulated in her thorax and abdomen while a white mass—a tumor—filled the left half of her chest. Their daughter's body was failing.

The tumor Williamina had is called a congenital pulmonary airway malformation (CPAM). Often, these masses are small and of little consequence to a fetus. But when one grows as large as Williamina's, it compresses the heart as well as the tributaries of arteries and veins that course through the chest. Consequently, her blood failed to circulate and the pressure of stagnant fluid inside her vessels forced water to leak into all of her tissues. The medical term for this condition is fetal hydrops, and it is an ominous sign.

Mila and Joaquín already knew about the CPAM. They already knew their daughter could get sick before she was born. They already knew the mass was potentially large enough to crowd her lung tissue and impede its normal growth, so that even if she survived in utero, the little girl could die of respiratory failure at birth.

What they didn't know was that I had three children, and their family reminded me of my own.

I had just returned from maternity leave. Like Mila, I'd recently lain on an exam table watching my baby on an ultrasound screen. It was easy to see myself in Mila and my baby in Williamina. But I also saw my four-year-old in James. They both had dark hair, tan skin, and a shy demeanor. Though new, our connection—their reflection of me—meant I did not want to tell them how hydrops portended a bad prognosis, how their baby's body was starting to fail, and how I had little to offer.

Mila swung her legs to the side of the bed, sat up, and pulled the bottom of her T-shirt over her belly. Joaquín walked to her side and rested his hand on her knee, then asked, "What's the plan, doc?"

When I was in training, I had seen babies like Williamina. I'd counseled families about the gravity of this situation. I was certain that Williamina was sick and gravely so. But I did not know what would happen to her: if she would die before birth, if she would die after birth, or if she would survive and have surgery. I did not want to be responsible for all the uncertainty such a tumor introduces to a family. And yet, like most families, Joaquín and Mila wanted me to make predictions about their daughter so they could make decisions. Should they terminate the pregnancy? Should they buy a crib? What about a baby shower? Should they plan for a funeral?

The simple truth was, I didn't know.

I quoted studies, recited odds, shared my experiences with other babies like Williamina. But they wanted black-and-white. Hell, *I* wanted black-and-white. However, my expertise did not afford me the ability to make predictions. Rather, my training helped me set expectations, temper Mila and Joaquín's hope. But first I had to temper my own, and I did not want to; I wanted to believe it would be okay.

So I told the couple I'd read studies where doctors gave a mother two steroid injections over the course of two days and masses like Williamina's shrunk. Then their babies got better. At that time, the treatment was new and not standard of care.

"I want to do it," Mila said.

But Joaquín did not share her enthusiasm. "Are steroids dangerous for my wife?" He was not willing to sacrifice his wife's health, even to save his unborn daughter.

I knew that the medication was safe, with few side effects: it's something we administer frequently in pregnancies, for other indications. I did not know if it would help Williamina.

While the data were not in Williamina's favor, the couple would have trusted anything I told them, followed any advice I offered. Joaquín picked up James and the little boy wrapped his arms around Joaquín's neck. I thought about my family and how I would feel if my doctor had said my baby was critically ill and the only treatment available offered little hope. For me, that would be an unbearable reality.

So I said, "I think this will work."

I lied. I did not think it would work. Yet hope was what I knew they wanted to hear, and so it was what I wanted to provide. Maybe I thought I could will what the couple wished for Williamina—what I wished for Williamina—with optimism. Or maybe I just kicked the proverbial can.

Over the next two days, Mila came to the clinic and our nurse gave her the two steroid injections. A week later, she and Joaquín returned for another ultrasound, one that would show whether the medications I'd prescribed had shrunken the CPAM.

When the nurse told me that Mila was in the ultrasound room, I stayed in my office returning emails. I did not want to see the family. I wanted someone else to do the ultrasound. Pushed off the sad news until this. But now I knew I had to confront Mila and Joaquín's pain. If

Williamina's condition had not changed—and it likely had not—I desperately wanted someone else to tell them.

I walked down the hall, knocked on the exam room door, opened it, smiled, and greeted the couple. This time, James raised his right hand and waved.

"You are back," I said to James. "I am glad to see you."

I patted the ultrasound table and said to Mila, "Hop on up." I was overcompensating for my anxiety with a cheerful and light tone.

As Mila lay down and lifted her T-shirt, James climbed into his father's lap.

Images of Williamina appeared on the screen, and it was obvious the mass was unchanged and the fluid remained. In fact, there was more fluid—the hydrops was worse. I put the probe down and turned toward Mila. She saw the images. She knew.

"Sometimes CPAMs can get smaller on their own," I said.

"So, we just wait?" Joaquín asked. "There is nothing left to do?"

A week later, fluid had not only accumulated inside Williamina's body but also around her. When a baby develops hydrops, water does not just accumulate inside the baby but outside of her too. Furthermore, the mass pushed on Williamina's esophagus so that she could not swallow. When a fetus is healthy, amniotic fluid is made by the baby and cleared from the uterus when the baby swallows. But Mila's baby girl could not clear the fluid, so it collected inside Mila's uterus, forcing the muscle to stretch. Once the organ grew to the size of a full-term pregnancy, she went into labor.

But Williamina needed more time to gestate. Her lungs needed more time to develop. Her body was already stressed. If she delivered at twenty-four weeks, she would die.

Mila's contractions would not stop unless her uterus was smaller, and even then she might continue to labor. I explained I could insert a needle into her skin, through her uterus, and drain some of the fluid so the muscle would relax, a procedure called an amnioreduction.

Even after I listed all the risks, including infection, bleeding, progression of her labor, injury to the baby, and breaking her bag of water, Mila told me to do it.

"It sounds dangerous," Joaquín said.

"I would not suggest the procedure if it were dangerous," I said. "It will work."

Again, I sounded more confident than I felt, more confident than I knew I should be in that moment.

I prepped the exam room and gathered all of the supplies. Mila's cervix was already dilated. The bag of water surrounding Williamina was tense and tenuous, like a balloon stretched beyond capacity. Mila's body was small and her large uterus filled her abdomen, pushing on her diaphragm so that her lungs could not expand. Lying back, she had trouble breathing.

I used a sponge to spread Betadine, a brown disinfectant, over her abdomen, making concentric rings. Using an ultrasound, I found a pocket of fluid free from Williamina's head, face, limbs, and umbilical cord, then pushed a three-inch needle through Mila's skin and watched it on the ultrasound as it entered her uterus. Then I connected tubing that led to a large container, and the straw-colored amniotic fluid flowed out of her abdomen. When I was done, I'd removed two liters. At that point she stopped contracting.

The couple went home, only to return a week later with the same problem. Again I drained two liters of fluid from Mila's uterus. But now she was twenty-five weeks pregnant, a gestational age some babies can survive if they deliver. Though it was unlikely Williamina could live outside Mila's body, Mila and Joaquín said if Williamina delivered, they wanted the pediatricians to try to keep her alive.

Even though I had drained liters of fluid from Mila's uterus, an excessive amount remained. Consequently, the baby floated and flipped, putting her umbilical cord at risk. If Mila's water broke, the cord could slip through her dilated cervix in front of Williamina, and her body would compress the blood vessels that kept her alive, requiring an emergency Cesarean delivery.

I admitted Mila to the hospital so that I could quickly get her to the operating room if her water were to break and the umbilical cord prolapse. Every few days, I put a needle into Mila's abdomen to drain amniotic fluid. Joaquín wanted to be there for every procedure. So on the days I preformed the amnioreduction, I waited for him to retrieve James from daycare and then come to the hospital. Often he'd still be in uniform, his khaki shirt neatly tucked into blue pants with a vertical red stripe. Rows of military ribbons were meticulously pinned above his left breast pocket. He had perfect military bearing.

The procedure took at least thirty minutes. During that time, I talked with James about his cartoons and toys. My son loved the same characters, shows, and animals: Lightning McQueen, *Little Einsteins*, and *Blues Clues*. Joaquín, Mila, and I laughed about the perils of parenting and the funny things James would say. When the procedure was done, I would linger in their room to continue our conversations. Soon, they started to inquire about my children. The roles of doctor and patient were blurring into friendship, further complicating the balance between the reality of Williamina's condition and my hope.

I never told them that everything we were doing was a desperate measure to keep their baby girl alive. I never said I did not know if it would work. They understood their daughter was sick, but I don't know if they understood how sick.

Sometimes, in extreme cases, with the right patient and the right type of CPAM, surgery can be done on the fetus while it remains inside the mother's uterus. Mila had read about this option. I knew Mila was not a candidate for fetal surgery, but I did not want to be the one to say no to her. So I called a surgeon in San Francisco. He confirmed what I already knew, but I wanted him—anyone else but me—to be the one to say there was nothing to be done. And he did.

Three weeks after I admitted Mila to the hospital, twenty-eight weeks into her pregnancy, my pager woke me at five A.M. Her water had broken. On the phone, one of the obstetrics residents explained that a loop of Williamina's umbilical cord had slipped into Mila's vagina, cutting off the little girl's circulation, so the on-call obstetrics team had performed an emergency Cesarean delivery. A pediatric surgeon was already operating on the baby.

"I'm on my way," I said.

I put on clothes, kissed my three sleeping children goodbye, got into my car, and sped down the highway in the dark. I shared the roads with only a few morning commuters. Though the hospital was not far from my house, the drive felt long. Looking back, I don't know why I rushed. I was not the one who would operate on Williamina. Mila was stable after the delivery. At that point, I had no role. My presence was superfluous. But my connection to this family, my deep reverence for their story, compelled me to be present.

I parked, ran though the hospital's double doors, and did not bother to change into scrubs or a uniform. I climbed the stairs two at a time, ran through a windowed hallway and onto Labor and Delivery. A resident sat at her work station in the middle of the unit. When she saw me, the first thing she said was "I'm sorry, Dr. Lee, the baby died."

The mass had taken up too much space in Williamina's chest. There was not enough lung tissue left for her to breathe. I sat down at the nurses' station, rested my head on the back of the chair, gazed at the ceiling, and said, "Fuck."

After I changed into my scrubs, I told the resident team on the ward I'd round with them later in the day, and went to Mila's room. I sat on the bed and said I was sorry; then I cried. I told them I was glad we tried but I was so sorry. Joaquin said his daughter fought to stay alive. He said she had her fists in the air when he got to hold her and she was strong. Mila told me she was beautiful. Their peace was staggering. They told me it was okay. They were okay.

But I was not okay.

I don't know how long I stayed in their room. An hour? Three minutes? Time disappeared. When I finally left them, I went to the NICU and asked if I could see Williamina. A nurse led me into an alcove where the baby lay on a small bed. Mila and Joaquín had dressed her in a white gown embroidered with flowers. She had dark thick hair like James. Her fingers were long and her eyes closed. She was gorgeous.

Mary, a social worker I had known since I'd started my job at the military command, was taking pictures of Williamina for Mila and Joaquín—a standard practice at our hospital when a baby dies at birth. She had dealt with the death of babies for decades, much longer than I had practiced medicine. She hugged me while I cried until my chest hurt.

"You will never survive like this, Whitney," she said. "You are too attached."

She was right, and I have thought a lot about her words over the years. But when I took care of Mila, I did not like the doctor I would become if I were less attached. I still don't. I have not learned to find both deep compassion and emotional distance in the same space. A decade later, I've not reconciled what that reality means for my heart or my job, but I suspect this tug-of-war will eventually end my career as a physician.

I chose to attend Williamina's funeral. I drove two hours north of where I lived, through mountains, creosote bush, cholla, and windmill farms to a small church in the Mojave Desert. The service had already started when I crept into the back and sat alone in a pew away from the rest of the congregation. The dry air smelled like wood and stone. Joaquín was telling his friends and family about the strength his daughter displayed in the few hours she lived. He expressed the pride he possessed as a father. Then he saw me in the back of the church. He pointed at me, put his other hand on his heart, and began to cry.

When the service ended, I stood at the end of the line to pay respects to Williamina and to hug Joaquín and Mila. I don't remember if Joaquín was in uniform or what Mila wore. But I remember I did not want to see the baby's body. I don't like seeing dead babies. I was present with her when she was vibrant and alive inside Mila's body. I was present immediately after she died. I did not need to see her dead in a tiny casket. I embraced the couple, who thanked me for coming. "We started this together and we will move on together," I said.

At the time, I did not know what I meant by this comment. It felt like a good placeholder, a door open to hope. I was not willing to say goodbye or acknowledge I might never see them again.

The next week, Joaquín deployed to Afghanistan.

Two years later, still in San Diego, I knock on a door behind which Joaquín and Mila are waiting. I noticed Mila's name on my clinic schedule early in the day, and the hours leading up to her appointment felt long and arduous.

When I enter the exam room, both Mila and Joaquín stand to hug me. An ultrasound taken earlier in the day confirmed she is eight weeks pregnant. I congratulate them and we laugh as we embrace. Mila smells like laundry. Joaquín still has impeccable military bearing. Like old friends, we catch up on life events and share stories about our children.

Then Joaquín sits and says he has something for me. He reaches into a bag and pulls out a folded flag with a certificate stating that it was flown on October 16th in my honor by the Marine Light Attach Helicopter Squadron 267. He explains that after a rough day in Afghanistan, he asked that they fly the flag in my name. It is humbling to accept such a gift, one I am not certain I deserve.

"I would really love it if you would be my doctor this pregnancy," Mila says.

My favorite patients are the ones who allow me to walk with them through a pregnancy that follows the loss of a child. Those pregnancies are long. Each office visit, ultrasound, and test carries the weight of the loss they have already suffered. That heaviness is part of Mila's pregnancy, too. I want to absorb her fear and worry, but it is not mine to own or fully understand. Yet Mila, Joaquin, and I walk together—each milestone normal and reassuring. First, she has normal genetic testing. Eight weeks later, a normal ultrasound. Then there is normal fetal growth and normal amniotic fluid. Every piece of information we have tells us Mila and her baby are well and healthy. But there is always something that could go wrong; every day of every pregnancy is an opportunity for devastation. Though I do not think about such morbidity during most pregnancies, I harbor an irrational fear about Mila's that I keep secret.

After eight months of anxiety and anticipation pass, I stand in an operating room wearing a surgical gown, mask, goggles, and gloves. Mila is on the OR table and Joaquin is sitting on a stool by her side. A resident and I have already covered her body with a sterile blue drape, positioned suction, and tested our surgical cautery. A gold locket that contains a clipping of Williamina's hair hangs around Mila's neck.

As in most Cesarean sections, Mila is on the table awake. But when Williamina was born, she was asleep—there was not time for spinal anesthesia or an epidural. So this experience is new, and she is nervous. Admittedly, so am I. We still have not crossed the finish line. My brain knows everything is fine. But my heart is terrified of the devastation that would ensue if anything went wrong during the surgery, if this baby had an anomaly I missed, or if for some reason I cannot anticipate she were to die.

I pull a scalpel over Mila's skin, slicing through the scar left from Williamina's birth. Though I am anxious to deliver this baby, the resident and I take our time to get into Mila's abdomen. Careful and meticulous, we cauterize bleeding blood vessels, and we are cautious of scarring that may have formed inside her abdomen as a result of the last C-section. We take nothing for granted.

Just before I incise Mila's uterus, I announce, "She is almost here."

When I cut into the uterine muscle, clear amniotic fluid gushes from the incision spilling over Mila's flanks. I reach into her pelvis and wrap my hand around her daughter's head. I am anxious to hear the baby cry. We are so close to the end and I just want to hear her cry. I deliver the little girl's head, then her shoulders, belly, and legs. For a moment, lying in front of me, she is quiet and still and it is awful. A thousand "what ifs" run through my mind. What if I took too long to deliver her? What if I hurt her during the delivery? What if she cannot transition into the outside world? But after the pause—seconds that feel like centuries—the baby girl wakes to the world and wails. I gather her in my arms and the anesthesiologist pulls down the drape that separates me from Mila and Joaquin so that I can hold up their daughter for them to see.

Though the baby is screaming and squirming, Mila looks terrified.

"Is she okay?" Mila asks, gripping Joaquín's arm.

"Mila," I say. "She is perfect."

Nominated by Threepenny Review

IF YOU WOULD LET ME

by MAGGIE DIETZ

from SALMAGUNDI

If you would let me hold you I could breathe
Your purple hair, the flakes of makeup breaking
From your boiling eyes. You'd see how much you need

Cool words. Outside the door I've heard you seethe
Through years of trouble. I'd press away the shaking
If you would let me hold you. I could breathe

The atoms of your dreams, my face so close I'd eat
Your anguish, taste the tang of black tears leaking
From your locked-down eyes. You'd see how much you need

To forgive, to be forgiven, to reach and cleave
To something incorruptible and unforsaken.
If you would let me hold you I could breathe

Away your brinks, lay cushions underneath
Your cliffs. I'd let no shiv of light be taken
From your arctic eyes, you'd see. How much you need!

Is there no salve, no balm in Gilead
To breach the brick and thistle of your hatred?
If you would let me hold you I could breathe.
Your broken eyes would see how much you need me.

Nominated by Maureen Seaton

WISHBONE

by JOSEPH SIGURDSON

from REED

You start in Anchorage: you get your gun, a new cell phone plan, winter gear to withstand −40° temperatures, your final dose of civilization for quite some time. The planes that take you to these Alaskan villages feel like minivans that are somehow flying. The pilot's gym clothes were in the seat beside me. He was eating a sandwich as he flew. We were low enough and moose are big enough where you could see them from up there, meditating in the tundra pools formed from yesterwinter's melted snow. The pilot leaned over to point to one and brought the whole plane with him. "YOU SEE THAT MOOSE DOWN THERE?"

"YES," I said.

"HUH?"

"YES."

We were still descending. "BEAUTIFUL CREATURES AREN'T THEY?" he asked.

The village where I teach is called Kalskag. A Yup'ik fishing village on the Kuskokwim River. For thousands of years these people have harvested the masses of salmon who come upriver to lay eggs and die. A Paleolithic lifestyle is still alive here, although the kids love basketball and Machine Gun Kelly just as much as any other. It's a mix of two worlds. People harvest moose then go to bingo.

The stuff I shipped was at the school, so I went there first and explored my new workplace. My classroom was modern. Rows of desks, big whiteboard, big TV, thin carpet. The gym was large and clean. Its walls were decorated with the tapestries of past victories in basketball and volleyball and wrestling. I explored the teachers' lounge to find the sink piled with blood-soaked cutting boards. Knives caked in moose hair and blood and tendons lay in the mix. I opened the fridge and there was nothing but a forsaken jar of mayonnaise. I opened the freezer and there was a beaver. I flinched so hard I nearly burst my appendix. The huge frozen rodent was still fully intact. Its face was in a screaming posture, its paws were upright, ready to scratch.

My house was red and small and ice-worn and tattered but cozy nonetheless. On the first day children were knocking on my door, asking to come in. Some wanted to use the shower or the toilet, because there was no running water at their house. They would say, "You live in there all by yourself? Are you rich?" They were infatuated by my cigars. The fifth-grade boys stole the butts from my porch ashtray.

Permanently chained dogs were everywhere. Loose dogs were everywhere. I played with them on my morning smokes. These bedraggled mutts were just as loving as a suburban golden retriever. Some of them limped though, from injuries uncertain to me. Some were rib-skinny. One was covered in spray paint.

My neighbor said, "I won't look at them, because then I'll get sad."

"Uh-huh," I said, puffing some Honduran cigar.

"They won't last. The dog-catcher will get them eventually."

Here, there are no spay and neuter clinics. No veterinarians. The town hires a man with a .22 to shoot the strays. $20 a tail.

The sun wouldn't go down until midnight. I'd come home from fishing and sit in my sunlit living room well into the night. Internet was scarce. I read until I needed eyedrops.

One day, I opened the door for another smoke, and a little black dog ran right in. Though he was collarless, his fur was smooth and his belly was chunky. A well-kempt, well-fed little boy. Full of energy. Full of love. He became my favorite.

He loved trash. He'd explore the village for rotten trinkets such as pop cans and halves of scissors and fish guts. He followed me to the post office one time and found some ribcage that he quickly fell in love with. He gnawed at it real good. Dragged it this way. That way.

"Is that your dog?" said a man. He was sitting on a railing, a rifle yoked across his lap. He was young and had a thin goatee. Slender, but strong. A calm yet somehow violent glower.

"Sort of," I said.

"What?"

"Sort of. Yeah. I don't know whose he is."

"Well, I'm hunting dogs."

Now I could see that the ribcage was bait and the dog catcher was waiting. He was good at what he did. Even I didn't notice this hunter until he spoke. I picked up the little black dog. He loved his new rib-cage so he began to scream and bite at my arms. He tried to squirm free but I held on.

"I'm saving your life," I said.

Another neighbor approached me and asked, "You been letting that dog in your house?"

"Sometimes."

"You want it?"

I smiled. He smiled.

"I'm being completely serious," he said.

"Well," I said.

"You look like you could use the companionship."

Behind me lay my house of no furniture save a couch and a lampless end stand. No bed. No TV. No pictures. No LIVE LAUGH LOVE.

"Well," I said. "All right."

He went back to his house and returned with treats. "We've just been feeding him scraps and these. He likes fish."

"Is he fixed?"

"Oh, no. None of them are." The little dog came to him and jumped up on his leg. "This is your new master now."

When the treats were transferred to me the dog's love was transferred too. He scarfed down the moist and meaty treat and stood anxiously, wanting another. The man took this time to leave.

Just before he entered his home I said, "Wait."

"What?"

"What's his name?"

"The kids named him Wishbone."

I was told the dog catcher wasn't supposed to kill them if they had a collar. I got him a camouflage collar, because I wanted to take him hunting. I'd never been hunting before, but I figured I'd start if I lived out in the Alaskan bush. And all the hunting dogs I'd see online had camouflage collars. Wishbone had the face of a lab, but was smaller. I figured it'd be enough to make him a bird dog. He was all black, save a diamond of white on his heart.

We walked the dirt roads of the village. My shotgun was over my shoulders. Wielding a firearm was not strange here, though I felt strange doing so. Children came to me asking if I was going hunting, asking if they could come with me. Cabins older than the elders lay every which way, with lawns of decaying vehicles and howling dogs on chains. Wishbone wanted to approach them, but was nervous.

"Come on little boy," I said.

A big woman was up a ways and Wishbone sneaked behind her and stuck his nose into her butt crack. She yelped then turned around and kicked him. I couldn't blame her.

"Sorry. Sorry. Come on. Come on you damn dog. Git over here."

He was confused as to why she was so angered by his curiosity. He meant nothing by it.

Behind Kalskag there are trails. Long stone trails where the grouse come from their secret places to feed on the gravel for their gizzards. I got cold feet the first time and delayed pulling the trigger until the bird flapped to the spruce trees and was gone.

Further down we found the foreleg of a moose. People hunted them then dumped the scraps wherever. Bald eagles and foxes and dogs would pick them up and take them. Soon you had hides and heads and legs and antlers scattered in random places, like some forgotten God of the hunt went whacky and poofed strange things into existence. Wishbone gnawed on the leg.

"Stop."

He gnawed.

"Stop, you'll get sick."

My demands were useless. He only listened when he wanted to.

"Fine." I carried on until I saw three grouse ahead, sauntering in and out of the path. I got close enough where they froze, but not close enough where they fled. The safety was clicked off and the aim was true. When the shell expelled, the bang made my ears ring and the wounded grouse flapped awkwardly in its cloud of feathers. Wishbone came darting from behind me and soon had the grouse by the neck, dead, out of suffering.

He was a natural.

One of my students taught me how to gut and clean a grouse. You place both your feet on its wings, then grab hold of its talons, and pull until it's disemboweled. It works well. No plucking.

Wishbone and I shared the grouse. It tasted like the dark meat of turkey, but a bit greasier.

School began, but because of the virus, we had various blocks. The high school's block was last, going from 1:15 to 7:30. I'd let Wishbone out to play with the elementary school kids on their recess. He was loved by them all. They weren't allowed to touch any balls with their hands, so they resorted to soccer, running and kicking on the dirt roads, running and kicking with Wishbone and the other loose dogs, laughing, screaming.

He came to learn that 12:50 meant he was getting locked in the house. The first few days he destroyed everything he could. Whole stacks of books were in shreds. The dish towels too. The handles of my knives had bite marks. He clawed so hard at the door there was a pile of wood shavings beneath it, and his paws were bloody.

They made us sanitize all the desks before we left. Wishbone was often locked in the house for ten hours. He'd get so upset with joy when I returned, he'd pee everywhere, cry in screams.

"You thought I'd leave you little boy?"

Yes. Yes he did. So now when 12:50 came, he would hide in the brush.

Though he now had a bed, a food dish, two different collars, he was still very much a village dog and it seemed there was no way of changing that. He played with the other village dogs. He fought with the other village dogs. He scavenged the beach, the trails, for carcasses and trash. He was happy outside.

Autumn came and killed off all the swarms of mosquitoes and gnats. Wishbone and I ventured off the trail in search of geese and tundra swans. We came to a meadow that must have once been a quagmire, for the grass had the feel of a dried sponge. Goose droppings everywhere. They were once here, or maybe further down.

We walked so far that the way home was uncertain. Wishbone had his snout in the grass, a ways ahead of me. The sun shone through the tree line, blinding me, but not enough to mask the movement of some large animal. I moved a few paces to block the sun with a tree, revealing that this animal was a bear on two legs, staring at me.

This was right before their long sleep when they're desperate for their final pounds of protein. I had my gun, but it was only a 20-gauge loaded with birdshot. That would tickle a bear at best. I knew not to panic though. I knew not to run.

I stepped back into the blinding sun and could no longer see the bear watching me. Wishbone couldn't either, but now he sensed it. That air of no longer being the hunter, but the hunted.

We made our way slowly to the tree line. I paused and found the bear's silhouette. It was still standing. I grew bold and said loudly, "I see you bear! Get out of here!"

It responded with a deep and guttural bark that echoed across the meadow. My knees lost their lock. Wishbone whimpered.

"Come on little boy. Follow me."

Trembling, we ventured deep into the brush, scraping our limbs and faces on thorns and protruding branches. Their sharp edges, like the tickling fingers of witches. I prayed we wouldn't hear the rustle of foliage, the stomp of a running bear, from behind.

We never did.

It was dark by the time we found the trail again. We went home and I took a shower. As the hot water pulled the dirt and blood from my skin, I could hear Wishbone crying from behind the bathroom door.

"I'm right here Wishbone."

When I got out, I found him on the couch with pants and socks from my dirty laundry. He wanted my scent.

"You thought I'd leave you little boy?"

I couldn't afford a four-wheeler so I had to take the bus home with the kids. When I'd get off, I'd tear off my mask and Wishbone would run to me. He'd jump up on me, bite at my arms playfully. He'd want me to come play with him and his dog friends, but I was always too tired to do anything but sit on the couch and smoke cigarettes.

I'd peek out the window often to check on him. One time I spotted him mounted atop a female, thrusting.

"God dammit Wishbone!"

I ran out there and tried to put an end to their natural instincts. Now the strange thing about a dog's anatomy, is that when the two of them connect, they truly connect until the job is done. It can't just slip out. Some mechanism stiffens in a certain way to lock in place. That's why you may have encountered two dogs stuck butt to butt.

Now the female dog was truly stray. She was afraid of humans. So when I approached them her natural reaction was to run—didn't matter if they were in the middle of this intimate experience. She booked it, and because of the strange sexual anatomy of dogs, dragged Wishbone with her. He was dragged by his little red rocket for a good twenty-five yards. I'd never heard such agonizing screams. What a way to lose your virginity.

But he was resilient. When the job was done he came back in, licked himself down there, and was back to normal. I actually sensed a hint of pride in how he carried himself. He was no longer a puppy.

He spent the day outside with the other dogs while I worked. Still, each morning, I was nervous. There are no fences in Kalskag. I'd try to coerce him into the house but he was too smart. He knew what that meant.

One morning I was off to make my walk to school. My student and his mother were on a four-wheeler and they offered me a ride. I hopped on, held my bag tight.

When we took off, I caught a glimpse of black running through the foliage. It was Wishbone. He kept up with us for a while, but the four-wheeler was too fast.

The last time I ever saw him alive he was running for me, not wanting me to leave him.

I knew what happened but I refused to believe it. When I got off the bus that evening, all his friends greeted me, but he was nowhere to be seen. I walked the dirt roads through the frigid dark, calling his name. I walked our hunting trails, fearless of moose or bear, praying I'd find him.

That night I slept on the couch. I got up each hour to go outside and call his name, but there was nothing.

I posted his picture on Kalskag's Facebook page. Somebody responded that the dog catcher threatened her dogs. He said he'd kill any dog he sees. Collar or no collar.

I called the town office and the lady said she didn't know where the dog catcher was.

"Did he kill any dogs yesterday?"

"I don't know."

"Is there a way I can find out?"

"I don't know."

I hung up, then called again. "If he were to shoot a dog, where would he dispose of the body?"

"I don't know. The dump I guess."

It had been two days. I knew to bring a garbage bag, but I did not articulate why. The dump is at the far end of Kalskag. I woke before anyone else and walked the roads, past the houses now leaking smoke from the chimneys, expelling the smell of scorched wilderness throughout the village.

At the dump there were over fifty ravens. Big as eagles. Black as nothingness. They picked through the trash and made their toadish croaks. I walked the whole dump but could not find him, or any dead dog.

I went around one more time just to be sure.

In the tall grass there was an area that was flattened that I had not noticed the first time. I peeked around it and saw the snarling skull of a dog. Only half of its face had decayed. I stepped closer and the smell hit me. I stepped closer to find a whole pile of dead dogs, many of which were puppies.

I saw his white diamond chest.

"Oh Wishbone."

I plugged my nose and stepped closer. He lay there dead—a bullet wound in his head, dried blood in his ears. His tongue was crushed between his teeth. "I'm here. It's okay."

I grabbed hold of him and lifted him from that pile of horror. I placed him down on the path. I could hardly breathe through my cries.

"You thought I'd leave you little boy?"

His body froze over the cold nights, making him awkward to carry. I put him in the garbage bag, reminding him that it was okay, I was here, and carried him on my shoulder. I carried him nearly two miles across the village and far down the beach where no one would see us. This was one of his favorite spots to explore.

My back was raw when I placed him down. The earth was too frozen to dig a grave, so I laid a bed of logs on the hardened mud. I took his tongue from his teeth and put it pack in his mouth. I smiled over the cries. "You don't want to look vicious when you get to heaven." I closed his eyes, stroked his silky fur. "I'm so sorry."

It took a while to gather all the wood to make a fire strong enough. Log after log—eventually I could no longer see him. "I'm still here. It's okay."

I waited until there was nothing but ash. I sat there staring at the Kuskokwim. His remains would blow into this ancient river and get carried away into the nooks of the world no man or dog had ever set foot in.

They asked me if I was leaving after that, and I said no.

Nominated by Reed

361

THE DESPERATE PLACE

by GAIL GODWIN

from NARRATIVE

[de- +sperare; de = reverse the action of + sperare = to hope]
I can't see a way out of this.
Things will not necessarily get better.
This is my life, but I may not get to do what I want in it.

This is the language that speaks to you in the desperate place.

A place from which you lack the means or power to escape.

A place in which you realize that someone you love does not, and will not ever, love you back.

A place in which you acknowledge your steep falling off in health, or strength, or status. A place in which you must accept that you are losing ground, losing face.

I have been close to people who one day found themselves in the desperate place and didn't make it out. I remember struggling to write a letter to a young man whose father had just hanged himself. The father had been the builder of our house. He was charming and talented and proud of his son. I wrote these things to the son, and then came the point in the letter where I was supposed to write something hopeful for the future. All I could think of to convey was, *No, you'll never get over it, but the time will come when you will be glad you can't get over it because the loved one remains alive in your heart as you continue to engage with the who and the why of him.*

Two people in my family didn't make it out of the desperate place. My father and my brother.

Though I had seen him only twice when I was a child, I sent my father an invitation to my high school graduation. Mother said not to expect him to show up, but he did. He and his new wife and his brother drove from Smithfield, North Carolina, to Portsmouth, Virginia, for the ceremony. In the early summer weeks to follow, we wrote letters to each other. He had elegant handwriting, and prose to match. He wrote that he would like more than anything to get to know me better. Could I, would it be possible for me to spend a few weeks with them this summer at the beach? I was in my first desperate place at that time and decided to tell him about it—though not all of it. I ended up going to the beach and returning with them to Smithfield and entering Peace Junior College in the fall, paid for by my father.

My father had been doing some personal bookkeeping of his own. At the age of fifty, he had at last achieved a measure of stability. Finally, after thirty years of intemperate living he had managed to stop drinking, had married a widow in town with a prosperous brother-in-law, and was the manager of sales at the brother-in-law's car dealership. For years he had envied his older brother the judge, whose profession gave him status and power and backslapping lunches with lawyers and businessmen, not to mention the stage-like gratification of being the calm character of authority who held sway over messier lives. My father confided to me during the weeks we spent at his brother-in-law's beach cottage that he regretted not having made more of himself. "You mustn't let it happen to you," he said. "Nobody is prepared for how quickly time passes," he said, "and you don't want to be one of those people who wakes up in the late afternoon with nothing to show for it." But later, in a radiant moment while we were lying on the beach working on our tans, he told me that I had come along at just the right time, and if he continued to win his battle against depression and alcohol, and if automobile sales continued like this, well, the future didn't look so hopeless after all.

As we lay side by side, congratulating ourselves for finding each other, I had no idea that old disappointments were biding their time, stealthily building like waves, which in less than three years would drown him. One winter afternoon when I was a junior at Chapel Hill, he phoned his brother at his office. "Just felt like saying hello, old son," he said. "Son" was what the brothers called each other. After he hung up, he lay down on the floor of his bedroom in Smithfield and shot himself in the head.

Losing ground. Was that the thing that ultimately killed him? In his twenties he began losing jobs, losing status, but always got back on his feet. A charming, handsome man, he did not need to keep a steady job as long as his mother was alive. And after her death there would be other admirers waiting in line for whom his looks and charm were enough. By the time he met my mother he was an alcoholic. After that came the mental disorders, given different psychiatric names as the years went by. Once after he had been under treatment, he stopped by to see me at Chapel Hill. He was in a good mood. He had risen again. Smiling, he rummaged in his jacket pocket and pulled out a piece of paper he had torn off a pack of cigarettes. "Here," he said with a laugh. "This is what they said I am this time. I wrote it down." He handed it over and I read in his elegant handwriting, "Psychoneurotic, with compulsion to drink."

When they were driving back to Smithfield after my high school graduation, he had come down with a raging toothache. They found a dentist along the road who pulled the tooth. But the pain continued and when they got home his dentist told him it had been the wrong tooth. "I should have known," he would finish this story, laughing. "I should have known when we drove into the parking lot and his shingle read: Dr. Payne."

He still had the charm but the looks were going.

This is from a June 16, 2018, *New York Times* opinion piece, "What Kept Me from Killing Myself," by Iraq War veteran Kevin Powers.

"Throughout that summer and into the fall . . . just below the surface of my semi-consciousness, was the constant thought: Maybe I won't wake up this time."

Powers continues, "I doubt much needs to be said about the kind of despair that would make such an idea a source of comfort, despair that came not from accepting that things were as bad as they were going to get, but, worse, that they might go on like that forever. The next step felt both logical and inevitable."

Which sounds along the lines of what my twenty-eight-year-old brother might have been thinking in the hours that led up to his death.

In the last week of his life, Tommy was working on a long poem. He left behind two drafts. He titled one "Why Not Just Leave It Alone?" He titled the other "Why Change the World?" One line is the same in both drafts: "My pride is broken since my lover's gone." Both drafts end with the same image of the poet being laid to rest in his wooden home, "With my trooper hat on my chest bone."

He was my half-brother, but why quibble about the half when he and I kicked and floated, eighteen years apart, in the same watery womb and grew to the rhythms of the same mother's heart?

It was October 2, 1983. October 1 was our mother's birthday, which is why I was in North Carolina: she liked all her children to be there for her birthday. I flew down from New York; my half-sister, Franchelle, drove up from Columbia with her family; my half-brother Rebel drove across the state from Chapel Hill. I wrote about this in my novel *A Southern Family*. Tommy became Theo, a name that would have suited him. Rebel became Rafe. I chose the name Clare for myself because I hoped for clarity. There is no younger sister in *A Southern Family* because—once again, why quibble about the half?—my sister, who is an attorney, told me after the publication of *The Odd Woman* that she would rather be excused from serving for any characters in my future novels.

What happened, what we *know* happened, as opposed to all that we can never know, was that on the Sunday afternoon after Mother's Saturday birthday, Tommy, who had just turned twenty-eight, ironed a shirt at his parents' house, where he had been living with his three-year-old son. He told Mother he was going over to see J., the woman he loved, a nurse, who also had a three-year-old son. They had planned to marry, they had even made out a budget. Then J. suddenly broke it off. Tommy told Mother he was going over to ask J. to reconsider. "I'm going to settle it one way or another before the afternoon is out," he said, and drove off alone.

"Couple Found Shot" was the headline in the newspaper next morning. Afterward, we would go over and over it. My stepfather would hire a detective. The police report would be taken out of the files again and again and scrutinized: maybe we would see something that we had missed before. "The real truth" would suddenly reveal itself on some overlooked line in the official text. "The real truth" being something everybody could bear.

This much we knew. Tommy, J., and J.'s three-year-old son were in J.'s car. The child was in the back seat. The car pulled over on a shady residential street. A boy riding his bicycle saw two people arguing inside the car. Shots were fired. A neighbor called the police. When they arrived, the woman lay on the street on the passenger's side of the car. She was already dead. The man was unconscious and writhing on the ground on the driver's side. A .25-caliber Belgian semiautomatic lay on the front seat of the car. J.'s son was found uninjured in the back seat.

Tommy had his own pistols. He belonged to the National Rifle Association. He won prizes for marksmanship. But this particular pistol belonged to his father, Frank. He and Frank had lent it to J. several weeks before to keep in her glove compartment because she said a man had been stalking her. J. had been in the army and knew how to shoot too.

The day before, on Mother's birthday, I knew Tommy was unhappy. But Tommy was always unhappy. He "felt things more than most," was the family euphemism for his troubled nature. He took most to heart the family's fractures as well as the world's. Drawing you in with his shy, closemouthed smile, he would offer his latest tale of woe. But always, always before in his stories, there had been a quality of suspense, of entertainment. He starred in them as the knight errant, complete with pratfalls and setbacks, but a knight errant who picked himself up, dusted himself off, and set out on his next mission. Tommy was a modern Samaritan who carried a first aid kit and a blue flasher in his car in case he came across an accident. He had wanted to become a state trooper, but even the state troopers he hung around with urged him to get a college education first and "then see." So he went to college and became an accountant. Weeks before his death, he had applied for a job with the IRS. He was sick and tired of helping boring businesspeople keep more of their money, he said; he wanted the high drama of catching the cheaters.

The afternoon before his death, on my mother's birthday, we were in the kitchen and he told me the story of his girlfriend suddenly breaking off with him. But this time something was different. I was not deriving the usual listener's satisfaction from his story. Many years later when remembering that kitchen scene, I realized what had spooked me about it: Not only was there not a trace of the shy, closemouthed smile, but there was no knight errant starring in my brother's story. The tone was new: one of bafflement and resignation. There was no sense of any future missions. There was no tug of suspense. It was like a story that had already happened.

Tommy would be sixty-three now. He was born the same summer that my father drove from Smithfield to Glen Burnie, Maryland, and rescued me from my desperate place. If on that October 2nd afternoon twenty-six years later there had not been a pistol handy in the glove compartment of J.'s car, would Tommy have married somebody else and raised his son and reconciled himself to a fallen world, as long as he had a first aid kit and a job that gave him the satisfaction that he was rescuing people from injustices?

But now I do hear his voice, the old Tommy voice, just as it was in life, chiding me as he defends the position of his beloved NRA with its singsong refrain: "Gail, *guns* don't kill people, people do."

During the winter following Tommy's death, I had an awful dream. I awakened with my heart thudding, and it took a minute to remember who I was and a few more minutes for the rage and hopelessness to drain out of me. It was unlike any dream I'd ever had. There was no action in it. There were no visuals. I didn't see anything or hear anything. I was in the black box of myself and felt only pure, stark emotion. I wanted to die, or kill somebody, *or both*, because this person didn't love me. The person was genderless. I was genderless. It was just the unbearable agony of knowing myself *not loved* and wanting to kill/die to avenge myself and put an end to the pain. After I had calmed down, I lay in bed and thought: that would be just like Tommy to find a posthumous way to hand over this dream like a neat, well-wrapped package: "Here you go, Gail. Feel my pain."

When we left the twenty-five-year-old Iraq War veteran Kevin Powers, he had plunked down the last of his army pay on a year's rent for a small apartment, kept the shades down and the door locked except for his daily trip to the 7-Eleven store for a case of beer, two packs of cigarettes, and two big-bite hot dogs. He spent six months of 2005 drunk. "And yet," he tells us, "I'm here writing this almost thirteen years later, despite the fact that in the perpetual semidarkness of that Richmond apartment, I wanted to not be, wanted to not be with an intensity that very few desires in my subsequent life have ever equaled."

He got so he couldn't read. His hand trembled and he kept one eye closed. Then, for some reason, he picked up *The Collected Poems of Dylan Thomas*, and opened to the first page in which the poet offers the reader his poems "with all their crudities, doubts, and confusions." For the first time, Power recognized himself in another person. ("Nothing came as close to characterizing what my life had become as those three words ['crudities, doubts, and confusions'] . . . and somehow that simple tether allowed me to slowly pull myself away from one of the most terrifying beliefs common to the kind of ailment I'm describing: that one is utterly alone, uniquely so, and that this condition is permanent."

Over a significant period of time Powers read more books, went to college courtesy of the army, and began to write poetry and fiction. In 2012 his novel *The Yellow Birds* became a celebrated war novel. Next he took on the horrors of the Civil War: *A Shout in the Ruins* was published in 2018. He also wrote a book of poems, *Letter Composed During a Lull in Fighting.*

Just as I continue to engage with the who and the why of my father and my brother, I also ask myself what small detail might have made the difference in Kevin Powers's case? It works both ways. What if he hadn't happened to pick up that Dylan Thomas collection, or opened to those words: "crudities, doubts, and confusions"?

During my life, I found myself in the desperate place four times. But that first time, at age eighteen, was by far the worst.

Summer 1955. We were living in a tract house in Glen Burnie, Maryland. There were a hundred or so identical houses in the development, which ran alongside a busy highway. Inside our house was my pregnant mother, my two-and-a-half-year-old half-sister, my stepfather, who had been transferred from chain stores six times in four years. And myself, who had just graduated as salutatorian from Woodrow Wilson High School in Portsmouth, Virginia. Because of my stepfather's many transfers, I had gone to six high schools in four years. Ninth grade at St. Genevieve's, in Asheville, North Carolina, on a full scholarship to high school, which I had to abandon when we left town at the end of ninth grade. Tenth grade in Anderson, South Carolina, where my little sister was born. Eleventh grade split between Norview High in Norfolk, Virginia, and Woodrow Wilson, across the river in Portsmouth. Twelfth grade divided between a first semester at Woodrow Wilson, three weeks in a high school in Louisville, Kentucky, then the last two months at Glen Burnie High School, and back to Woodrow Wilson for graduation.

Now summer was beginning and everybody seemed to have a future but me. My mother was expecting her second child with my stepfather in August. My stepfather was starting over at a new W. T. Grant store, in Baltimore, where he had not yet alienated the boss. That morning I had received a letter from Mother Winters at St. Genevieve's, a wise figure in my past. She congratulated me on being salutatorian, asked about my plans for college, and brought me news of some of my class-mates. "Pat has won the four-year Angier B. Duke Scholarship to Duke, Carolyn will be going to Radcliffe, Stuart and Lee to St. Mary's in Raleigh . . ."

Here I stopped reading and felt . . . what? A dry mouth, a pang in the chest, a sense of going down, of losing myself. All I knew to do was mark my position.

My position. At that time I couldn't hold all of it in my mind. If I had tried, I might have despaired, or lashed out and hurt myself or somebody else. I had so little experience to draw from, and there was no escape.

A distinct sense of loss, a flavour in the mouth of the real, abiding danger that lurks in all forms of human existence.

That is Joseph Conrad describing the sensation of the commander of a stranded ship in *The Mirror of the Sea*. But I had not read Conrad yet, or any of the richly chronicled descriptions in the literature and religions of the world of what it feels like to be in the desperate place.

It would be years before I came across passages in books or met people who described the place in which I was embedded. It would be years more before I began writing books in which people found themselves in the desperate place.

Since my early teens, I had been building my life on false premises, creating a persona to meet the requirements of my family's frequent moves. This persona was more extroverted than I. She pretended to more confidence and security than I felt. I became a pro at embellishing and editing my history. When I entered a new school, I "went out" for things I was good at that would bring me attention. The school paper, the drama club, painting posters and scenery, entering speech competitions—and of course getting high grades. I dated lots of boys, made it a point to be cagey and hard-to-get until each got fed up and moved on, usually just as I had begun to appreciate him.

That was the outside of things. Inside our various rented domiciles other dramas were playing out. We were not free people. Our embattled breadwinner, who was angry much of the time, sometimes knocked one of us to the floor for challenging him. There was no money for us except what he doled out and no going anywhere he didn't drive us. As I entered my teens, the breadwinner, who was only twelve years older than me, often spoke of how he "loved" me. At night I would wake to find him kneeling beside my bed, his hand taking liberties.

My mother had shed her former confident self. As a child, I knew a mother who arrived home on the 10:00 p.m. bus after her wartime job on the newspaper, a woman who taught college and on weekends typed up love stories that earned $100 apiece. This powerless woman seemed more like someone I was visiting in prison. Only I was in prison with her. She suffered because there was no money to send me to college. She made phone calls to a private college in Baltimore to see if I could go as a day student. The registrar said a partial scholarship might be arranged, given my academic record, but where was the rest of the money to come from? There was no "rest of the money," my stepfather reminded us, as though we were dim-witted. He suggested I take a year off and find a job, "maybe in sales work," and save up for that college next year. He added magnanimously that I could continue to live under his roof for the time being without paying rent.

That's the way the ground lay, that 1955 June morning in Glen Burnie, when the girl sat cross-legged on her bed, the letter from her old teacher clutched in her fist. "Pat to Duke, Carolyn to Radcliffe, Stuart and Lee to St. Mary's . . ."

This is my life, but I may not get to do what I want in it.

I can't see a way out of this.

Things will not necessarily get better.

In my novel *Unfinished Desires*, about life at a girls' school, two old nuns are being driven back to their retirement house from doctors' visits, and one says to the other, "There was a sentence this morning in that Prayer for Holy Women: 'In our weakness your power reaches our perfection.' What do you think it means, Sister Paula?" Sister Paula thinks for a minute and replies, "I think it means you have to fully admit you can't save yourself before you're fully available to God."

That morning in Glen Burnie, God was undergoing some very slippery changes in my psyche. He had ceased being the attentive heavenly father who was always aware of me, and he had not yet expanded into the mystery beyond my understanding that I am still pursuing today.

All I could be certain of, that long-ago summer morning, was that I could not save myself.

But something else did, something already embedded in the tissue of my particular circumstances: the earthly father who had been the absent father. In a mood of defiant resignation, I decided to send him an invitation to the graduation anyway. Of course he wouldn't come.

But he did come. And when we were lying beside each other on the beach, he said, "When I opened your invitation, after I got over being pleasantly surprised, I thought to myself, 'Well, this is one thing I did that came to fruition.' And then, after we began to write letters to each other, it struck me that I might be the rescuer you needed."

Nominated by Narrative

THE UNION WALTZ

by DOUG CRANDELL

from THE SUN

Another labor strike had ended. The Local 563 Paper-Workers' Union had rolled the dice and come up a winner. To celebrate, my folks threw a potluck: piping-hot casseroles, homemade bread, and crock-pots of beef and cheese with tortilla chips for dipping. There was ham, roast beef, and chicken. There was sweet tea, Pepsi, Sprite, hot chocolate, coffee—and beer. Dad's union brother George pulled a cooler to the edge of the bonfire, slung it open, and thrust his forearm into the cold water as if to save someone from drowning. He tossed cold beers to people while he shimmied to the music. From where I sat on a bale of straw, I could smell oak and hops and the tang of sweat. I was ten.

My parents were fine with beer in moderation; both caught the cans George fired at them. They took small sips, smiles appearing on their ruddy faces, as if the beer were an elixir. I was struggling to stay awake, my eyelids heavy. I didn't want to miss anything, especially the dancing.

The air was brisk, and the nubs of the harvested cornstalks were covered with hoarfrost. A cassette player blared a Waylon Jennings song someone had recorded from the radio. George hooted at the dark autumn sky as if trying to summon some animal spirit. In the shadowy light I caught the disapproving glances my parents gave each other. It wasn't that all dancing was bad in their eyes, but it was shameful if you did it like George: with a passion, legs jigging, steps straight out of the Appalachians. Our father wanted my siblings and me to be more than foolish hicks like our great-great-grandfather, who had been run out of Kentucky for unspecified crimes and ended up here in Indiana. But George's dance fascinated me like nothing else, the taboo sway of his knees and hips. I had seen men dance like this before: at high-school graduation parties or weddings, the graduate or bride and groom children of other union members. I longed to watch and learn.

My two brothers were playing cards, and my two sisters were engaged in a game of hide-and-go-seek in our landlord's haymow. The bonfire dwindled, and someone tossed on some desiccated tree limbs, planks from old livestock trucks, and the quartered hunks of a downed tulip poplar my father had split nearly a year before. The fresh wood crackled like popping corn, and the flames shot upward. George stood on a bale of straw to declare his love of the union and his undying gratitude to my parents, the Crandells. They looked nervous, probably afraid our landlord might get a call about the noise. My father took a few steps toward George, who by now was drunkenly singing along with the music, but George skittered away around the fire, his elbows lifted from his side like a rooster in midcrow.

There were several families left, and I sensed they were getting ready to go but also wanted to stay and see what would happen. George cantered to the music, blowing kisses to the people around the fire. His wife, Sandra, had gone to sleep in their Camaro hours earlier, her short skirt so tight it constricted her thighs. I thought she was beautiful. I thought George was wonderful, and his dancing was extraordinary, but I could not say so out loud where my parents might hear. I'd never seen my father even tap his toe to music.

Dad finally took ahold of George's arm and looked at him with pity. George escaped the grasp, waved my father off, and started a slow, rhythmic side step, as if edging around a deep hole no bigger than a dinner plate. An owl hooted in the copse of leafless trees behind us. Cars revved to life, and their headlights passed over the bonfire area, leaving it seeming darker than before. The smell of burnt marshmallows and oily meat filled my nose.

My dad told George he'd had enough to drink. My mother said, "Why don't you put that beer down, Georgie, and let me take you inside and cook up some scrambled eggs?" But George only danced harder, even after Dad had shut off the tape player. I stretched out on the hay bale and pretended to be asleep, keeping one eye open a bit.

George looked over his shoulder at my father, face full of glee, cheeks afire. I'd never seen a person so drunk, and it was both scary and funny. George's arms and legs seemed hinged like a stringed puppet's.

As the few remaining couples dispersed, Dad gave my mother a nod and then cut his eyes toward me. She stood up and tugged on my jacket sleeve to tell me it was time to go to bed. When we reached the steps of our rented farmhouse, I glanced back at the fire and saw George silhouetted like a cutout against the flames. Then Mom tugged me inside, and my siblings and I all washed up and went to our rooms.

Later I crept to the stairs to eavesdrop on Dad telling Mom that George had passed out. "Makes a fool of himself with that hillbilly dancing," my father said. He slurped some coffee; I could smell his Salem Light. I knew we were sort of hillbillies, too. My mother's father was a coal miner who had died of black lung at sixty-seven. Dad would tease my mother that they had barely made it out of Vigo County themselves before the mine sucked them down. It was a joke but also a warning. He was fastidious and shaved twice a day, kept Scope mouthwash and Mitchum deodorant in his truck. He insisted my siblings and I keep ourselves and our clothes clean. Dad told Mom he wouldn't invite George again if he was going to act "that way."

I slowly made my way back to bed, already missing George. He'd seemed happy while he was dancing, as if he'd been drunk not on beer but on the music. I would even have said I loved George, but I'd been told a few months earlier that it was wrong to say that about a man: Another of Dad's union brothers, Monty, had stopped by our house to talk union business. I liked the way Monty's bad teeth made him look like he was pouting. He made excellent paper airplanes and could gargle water and talk at the same time. After he left, as we ate our chipped beef and gravy over white toast for dinner, I told my family that I loved Monty. Dad perched his cigarette carefully in the ashtray and said, "You don't love him, Son. You admire him. You respect him." As he picked his cigarette back up, shame warmed my cheeks.

When I was fourteen, I took a job on another farm, scooping manure and bedding hogs with straw, often on nights when the temperature fell near zero. George worked there, too—a second job for him—and he became my ride to work. On the twenty-minute drive George would smile that gap-toothed grin and crank up Hank Williams on his Kenwood cassette deck. He'd splurged on an amp and big subwoofers behind the seat that gave my back a massage. George provided me with cigarettes and cans of Mountain Dew, and by the time we reached the farm, I believed I could do any job there was, as long as he was my partner.

While we spread straw in the hog pens, George showed me the "flatfoot two-count," a seemingly simple move called "step dancing," and something named the "kickin' Alice." For the first time I was aware of a brighter side to my hillbilly ancestry. I hadn't come from a culture that was just endless toil. I was part of something joyous, too.

We were doing the flatfoot to a song on George's boom box when my dad showed up unannounced. A circuit breaker had been tripped at the factory, and everyone had been sent home early. Dad stood silently under one of the hewn-timber beams, smoking. George saw him first.

"Just about done, Dan," George announced to my father, and he poked me in the ribs and flashed that smile. I stopped dancing, too.

Dad walked over to George's boom box and turned it down, then waited for us to finish the job. On the ride home, Dad instructed me to avoid distractions and focus on my work. At a four-way stop he asked if I understood. I nodded. The eyes of deer in a dark field reflected the truck's headlights back at us, and the music from George's boom box echoed in my head. We rode the rest of the way home in silence, the radio off, as usual.

Seven years later, to pay for college tuition, I got a job at the ceiling-tile factory, working alongside George, who taught me more dance moves. George was fond of calling me "Baby," and though it was slightly embarrassing, I liked it. I tried to keep this fact and the dancing from my father, who also worked there, driving a forklift. I was the first in my family to go to college, which meant anything I did to reflect an aptitude or desire for manual labor would be seen as a threat to my future. But during those summer months at the ceiling-tile factory, I found myself drawn to the easy ways of George and his pals, men who worked sixty-hour weeks and on the weekends still had the energy to shuffle their feet across a cracked linoleum dance floor sticky from spilled dollar beers.

My father made it clear to me on our rides to work: "Not my business if you're foolish enough to spend your hard-earned money on tavern beer, but you'd be well advised to steer clear of George. He and his kind throw away their money and act the fool."

I'd stare out the car window and secretly wish my dad could find room for some frivolity.

At work, asbestos fibers drifted down from the catwalks like sharp snowflakes. The stuff burrowed into your skin and left red bumps, but it was a crucial ingredient in ceiling tile. Workers in hazmat suits used industrial vacuums on the beams fifty yards above George and me.

The area where we worked was isolated from the rest of the factory. I rarely saw my father, except when he zipped in on the forklift to remove our cartons of ceiling tiles from the scales, then sped off again. George kept a sheet of plywood behind some wall slats and pulled it out once in a while to show me new footwork, the sound of his feet striking the surface audible even over the roar of the factory's furnaces.

At the end of one shift, as the whistle blew at midnight, I told George, "I get this. I can feel it in my bones."

He grinned. "Baby, don't ever say that to your daddy." He patted me on the back and turned up a radio strapped to a steel beam.

With George's help I did learn how to dance like my distant kin. We kicked up factory dust to Glen Campbell and Roger Miller and the old Possum, George Jones himself. As the hot summer days crawled by, George prepared me for my big debut: a night at the local tavern, where I'd showcase on the dance floor all that my body had learned but my mind still feared was improper.

Even as George brought me closer to my ancestry, I was aware that I would soon be getting my degree and moving away from that job, that place. George was curious about college life. He thought my being an undergrad psychology major meant that, after I graduated, I could prescribe him drugs: "Don't you go forgetting that ol' George taught you how to cook this cancer tile and showed you how to do the two-count." My heart sank, because I realized I wouldn't be staying on at the factory after college, which meant I might not know George much longer. I felt caught in a tug of war between the old life my parents somberly led and something new I could not wholly grasp. And the old life was slipping away.

George's brown eyes widened. "If you're ashamed to dance," he said, "well, that's just a shame." Then he elbowed me and pulled me in for a hug.

It was late summer, only a week or so before I'd head back to college in Muncie. The air outside the dock doors was sticky with humidity, and the waste lagoons gave off a rusted-iron smell as strong as a bloody nose. George and I were working the noon-to-midnight shift. He danced past me, arms out at his sides, then circled back and performed a tangled shuffle, intentionally goofy, self-mocking. After work we would be headed to Smitty's Bar, where the twangy music would kick up, and I'd try to find the courage to dance in public.

George used to tell me, "Son, there ain't no way you can outrun your kin." He meant the dance and the music were in my bones, though my father thought letting your feet follow the beat was disgraceful, undignified. He rarely went to the bar, but occasionally he'd make a showing, to drink the free black coffee and snack on peanuts. Part of me hoped he would be there that night—or, at least, that he'd hear about it. My plan was to drink and drink some more, then dance and dance some more.

When the lunch whistle blew at 8 PM, I did not go and get my lunch box. I remained with George, who proceeded to give me some last-minute pointers. He turned up a country station on the radio, put his fingertips on my temples to position my head, and told me to stare straight ahead, never let my eyes stray. George gave my foot a soft kick, to get my leg stance correct. We did a few steps together, the whiskey on his breath strong, and he laughed and told me I might end up a dancer after all.

Four hours later, at Smitty's Bar, I cashed my check and bought George and me a round. The dance floor was still empty, but a man and his uncle—both former factory employees, disabled in a car wreck—hobbled through the back door and began setting up their gear on the meager stage: a snare drum, a fiddle, and an acoustic guitar connected to a worn amp. The mirror above the bar was adorned in white Christmas lights, and the bottles of booze gleamed. Jars of hard-boiled eggs, sugary cherries, and green olives sat open, silver tongs hanging at their edges. The red vinyl stools, small tufts of white sprouting from their cracked seams, were reserved for the union leadership. I could hear the snap and pop of chicken tenders descending into fry oil, giving the space the warm smell of batter and onions.

We moved toward the smooth dance floor. The dancing always started out slow, with the tap of a work boot. Then the arms would loosen, the neck and head held squarely in place. When a grunt or single clap egged the dancer on, the shuffling turned into feet flashing in a blur, the taps of soles sharp and rapid, the eyes always straight ahead, as if in a trance, trying to make their visions real.

After three beers and several cigarettes, something eased inside of me. My worries lifted. George and I stood at the edge of the dance floor, warming up. The music made my entire body feel electric.

The fiddler began to play. The clapping got louder. Outside the humidity was stifling, but inside I had goose bumps. I supposed what I felt was wrong, but I didn't care. George nudged me, then did a crawdad onto the floor before transitioning to a box-step. Under the red lights he claimed an invisible square around him and let loose in ecstasy, allowing the whining fiddle and the guttural croaks of the singer to enter his body. I watched from the perimeter, in awe of how a man my father's age could still find joy in the sadness of a fiddle riff. George beckoned me with his eyes, then went back into his trance. I gave in and joined him.

Like dance partners, we anticipated each other's movements. I wanted to dance this way forever, but also never again. I longed to leave this life behind, yet hesitated when I thought about abandoning this place and these people, who worked with their bodies to keep their families fed. The lonesome fiddle wailed, the floor tilted, and I reached for George, who righted me and steadied me for the finale to our dance. When the music stopped, we bowed to the tipsy crowd and exited the dance floor to merge into the mass of sweaty bodies. We sat down at a table, ordered two more beers, and lit one Salem after another. The menthol seemed to relieve the hurt in my heart.

For the next hour or so we chugged our feet to improvised bluegrass. (Only occasionally did I hear a recognizable song.) My father never made an appearance, but I knew he'd likely hear about my hoedown the next day.

Near 2 AM George and I stumbled into the gravel parking lot with our arms around one another, his dyed-black hair damp at the nape of his neck. Our vehicles sat under a sickly yellow security light. The briny funk of the Wabash River wafted over us, and inside the cab of George's F-150 we took shots from a bottle of Jack Daniel's. George rolled down his window and lit us both cigarettes. We would sleep in his truck until the morning. Exhausted from work and dancing, we stared out the windshield toward the tiny town of Lagro, Indiana. George sighed and, without looking at me, said, "Baby, I can't for the life of me tell you why I'm still doing this."

His labored breathing seemed to fill the truck's cab.

I took a long drag from the bottle. The vehicles around us spit gravel as they left the parking lot.

George said, "My own daddy was a drunk, sure enough." He pulled a piece of tobacco from his lip. He and Sandra had gotten divorced years before. I knew he had two daughters he loved and was proud of, but they'd moved out of state. George lived alone in a duplex rental. On the small front porch he kept a boom box and a piece of plywood to dance on. Music was all he had now. My head was bogged down by the humidity and alcohol. I thought of that night eleven years earlier, after the strike was over, his pure exhilaration in the dance. My chest felt tight.

I asked, "How do you do the part where your feet don't seem to touch the ground?"

George grinned and dabbed out his cigarette in the ashtray. "Baby, all you got to do is pretend you're already dead, and the steps will follow."

I snuck a look at him, his sideburns turning silver, his face as familiar as my father's, or my own.

When I woke in his truck early the next morning, George was smiling and lighting two cigarettes. We smoked as the sun edged up over the river. We did not talk. Sparrows cheeped in chorus. The power lines came into focus, the morning light growing brighter. I wanted to tell George that he meant more to me than he could know, but before I could form the words, he found a staticky station on the radio, and we listened to songs from somewhere else. My throat ached, and I felt like anything I might try to say would ruin the moment.

My father heard about my debut at Smitty's, and, though he didn't say much, I was embarrassed. I saw George a few more times at work before I went back to college, and one last time at Smitty's, where I couldn't make myself get up and dance. He waved for me to join him, but I just watched and nursed a Bud Light in the darkness. He pranced around the linoleum and then bore down into a slide so fierce his feet seemed to hover. His work boots were a blur, his gaze fixed as his steps picked up speed. People hollered, and George took a long swig of beer from someone, then looked right at me and performed a slow, silly side step, his eyes bulging in pantomime.

Occasionally I dream of him stepping from the factory doors. He's not dancing, just walking straight toward me. "There you are, Baby," he says. "I've been looking for you." I hug him tight, then wake up. Throughout the day I can hear music.

Nominated by Nancy Geyer, Jennifer Lunden

THE LAND OF UZ

fiction by ALEYNA RENTZ

from THE CINCINNATI REVIEW

It's the first night I've slept over at Gerald's. Yes, I am dating someone named Gerald. I asked if I could come up with a cooler name for him, something modern, geometric, all sharp angles and dangerous overtones—Axel, Gunner, Blaze—but he declined. Gerald's cute in an awkward way, wears rectangular glasses and ties patterned with the kinds of animals people shoo from their garages: hedgehogs and raccoons, neon-colored lizards if he's feeling a little feisty. He works in strategic data solutions. I have no idea what this means. I'm just a high-school English teacher, a recent college graduate with poems languishing in obscure literary journals. For whatever reason, Gerald loves this about me. He was impressed when my short poem about pain relievers (*My heart has been broken / by so many men, / each night I fall asleep with / acetaminophen*) appeared in *Paper Fan Quarterly*. He swoons whenever I tell him things like "we're all islands unto ourselves" or "metaphor is just a writer's way of imposing meaning on a chaotic universe." Instead of dirty words, I whisper literary terms in his ear. *Climax. Euphemism.* He thinks this is clever. His name is fucking Gerald. We had our third date tonight. He took me to Olive Garden, ordered both appetizers and dessert. Certain amorous activities transpired afterward. I guess you could say things are getting serious.

We settle into his bed, holding each other. This should be a tender moment, but all I can think about is the spaghetti I ate earlier, all that tomato sauce that just got jostled around my stomach. I'd specifically asked for no sauce, but they put it on anyway, and I didn't want to make a scene. Even though Gerald wears goofy ties and is named Gerald, I still can't bring myself to tell him I've got severe acid-reflux disease, and unless he's got an extra pillow somewhere to keep my head elevated, there's no way I can spend the night.

"Hey, Ava," he breathes into my ear. "Say something sexy. Just one more word before we go to sleep."

I shrug. I'm trying not to burp, or anything worse. "Zeugma."

"Zeugma," he repeats slowly, relishing each syllable. "What's zeugma?

"It's like . . . well, an example would be . . . 'she stole his heart and his wallet.'"

"Ha ha," he says. Poor Gerald. He's genuinely amused.

"So, basically only one of the objects of the sentence is semantically suited for the verb. See? One's figurative, the other literal."

"Do another."

"Um . . . let's see . . . he swallowed an aspirin . . . and his pride." A certain enchanted look in his eyes prompts me to keep going. I can't remember the last time a man looked at me like this. "He buried his hopes and his father. She regurgitated useless facts and last night's dinner."

"Genius."

I disentangle myself from him and raise myself up against my single pillow. "I'm not a genius," I tell him, and this is true. Not a genius, but smart. Smart enough, at least, to have won a Fulbright to study literature at Trinity College in Dublin. If I were a genius, I would've admitted to myself I was too sick to apply. My senior year at Duke was a blur of mock interviews and missed classes, résumé workshops and doctor visits, the sickest I'd been since my diagnosis at seventeen. A month after winning my Fulbright, I was informed I didn't pass the medical clearance. Even though I was accepted into a handful of master's programs, my gastroenterologist said I needed to come home, stay in a low-stress environment for a while. I asked him how long a while was, but he didn't say.

Physically, I'm in Georgia, but my brain's stuck overseas. I should be there now, hiking verdant cliffs, sending home tacky leprechaun postcards, stumbling home from pubs with dark-haired boys named Cillian and Fergus. I could've been that mysterious, bookish girl sitting in the corner of a small café, enjoying a glass of milk (never tea or coffee) and a volume of Beckett.

Really, I'm not in Georgia or Ireland but holed up inside my belly, nestled there like some hibernating animal. Sickness is its own terrain, its own country.

"Okay," he says, "I'm gonna try one."

"Try one what?"

381

"A zeugma." Scrunching up his face, he stares across the room, his eyes landing on a nondescript painting of a fisherman—yellow raincoat, white beard: a misplaced Captain Ahab—standing on a dock at sunset. This is the kind of art Gerald hangs in his apartment. "He sunk his boat and his, his . . ."

"His credit score."

He smiles at me as if I've just told him I love him. "Brilliant. Do another."

Something that tastes like tiramisu coated in parmesan cheese creeps up my throat. "I'm afraid I'm zeugma'd out for the evening."

"Something wrong?" he asks.

"Do you have an extra pillow?"

"I've got that one throw pillow in the living room, but . . ." My face must cause him to trail off. "No, no pillows for, like, actual sleeping."

"Oh."

"Is that a problem?"

"Well, uh—um, sorry, this is a bit gross—I get bad acid reflux if I don't have two pillows. I need my head elevated or else it just kind of . . ."

"Oh, well, these are all I've got, but maybe—"

I'm already up, getting dressed. This is how it always goes. My therapist told me it might be best not to date until I had my symptoms more under control, but I met Gerald in line at Walmart (he was buying a large book of sudoku puzzles) and thought it'd feel good to contradict her. Empowering, maybe.

"You don't have to leave," he says as I sling my purse over my shoulder. "You can have my pillow, if you want. I can just use the throw pillow."

Earlier this evening, he showed it to me. Cross-stitched by his grandmother, the pillow depicts two nuzzling bunnies, a heart floating above their heads. He told me he put it out only due to a sense of familial duty. I have my doubts, though. Picturing him tossing and turning all night on that throw pillow, a tortured, sleepless martyr, makes me feel even worse. Dizzy. Nauseous.

I can't hold it in anymore. I throw up all over his bedroom floor.

"Oh, goodness," he exclaims softly. This is really what he says: *goodness*.

My favorite kind of poetry is nonsense verse. Gibberish words, ridiculous rhymes, no logical progression—nothing captures the human experience better than this. After my date with Gerald, I decided to memorialize the evening in a double dactyl:

382

Higgledy-piggledy
Poor Ava Slate
Once again brought down by
Something she ate.
It's catastrophical
Gastroesophageal
Reflux that caused her this
Miserable state.

Yes, that's my full name, Ava Slate. The kids in my class just call me Ms. Slate. Sometimes their parents write "Mrs." when addressing me in emails, presumably to taunt me, to rub it in my face that I'm making poor romantic progress with someone named Gerald. I hate being called Ms. Slate. It makes me feel like a widow, a lonely spinster who takes in stray cats. Honestly, I'm not too fond of Ava Slate in general. My first name's a palindrome, my last is a writing utensil—it sounds like a pseudonym you'd find on the back of some self-published poetry chapbook. I guess you could do a lot worse.

Gerald, for instance.

He left a message on my phone this morning. I'm not sure why he tried to call when I didn't even stay to help clean up his bedroom floor last night.

While most of the teachers at Altamaha County Magnet School teach three classes, I'm teaching only one. The principal wouldn't have pulled these kind of strings for just anybody. I have a certain reputation here. Valedictorian 2012, student-body secretary, founding editor of *Lemonbiscuit Literary*. My parents were the ones who talked the administration into giving me a lighter teaching load. Because I was deemed incapable of handling a year of heavy research, my parents think I'm incapable of handling anything. They want me lying on the couch, sipping ginger ale and watching *The Price Is Right*. They keep trying to bring me soup in bed. Campbell's, but the thought still counts. They cut my poems out of magazines (*Sad Dog Review*, *All-Purpose Flour*) and hang them on the refrigerator with alphabet magnets.

The class I'm teaching is tenth-grade Honors English, a course I sat in years ago, scribbling subversive limericks in the margins of Nathaniel Hawthorne stories. Back then, I endured a one-and-a-half-hour bus ride each morning for the opportunity to attend a slightly better high school ("a *magnet* school," I reminded my friends at home every chance

I had) than the one five minutes from my parents' house. I felt certain I was destined for someplace greater than South Georgia, and so do these kids. They've been deemed special, anointed, because of their excellent standardized test scores; they come from as far as three counties over. They're the ones who will win scholarships to faraway schools, become pro-choice in college, and not come back once they leave. When I told them on the first day of school that I'd just graduated from Duke, they looked at me sideways, the way you look at prune-shriveled grandparents in nursing homes.

"But why did you come back *here*?" they asked. "There's nothing to do."

These kids never want to shut up, are always asking me questions, so I made up a new rule to slow them down: they're allowed to speak only in iambic meter, which they usually fail to do; instead, they just avoid modern English.

"Miss Slate," Polly Wilkinson says, using a spondee instead. She's the only student I have from my hometown. I've known her since she was a little girl, a pudgy soprano in the Methodist church's children's choir. She's slightly overweight, her skin red and splotchy, the best writer in my class. Sometimes when we read poems aloud, she actually starts to cry a little bit.

"Yes?"

"Art thou feeling well today?"

A valid question. I'd just left mid–*Macbeth* lecture to throw up my lunch. Before class, my lifelong best friend, Gisberta, had taken me to a sandwich place. When she noticed the new rasp in my voice, she asked if I was all right, and in an aggressive show that said yes, I was indeed all right, I'd left the tomato on my turkey club, ordered extra mayo just for emphasis.

I say to Polly, "Oh, I'm fine, thanks."

"Art thou *cer*tain thou art well?"

"I mean, I'm here." I give a weak smile that melts Polly's little heart. "Can't complain."

Another hand shoots into the air. From the back of the classroom, Henry asks, "How dost thou chemo treatments go?"

Oh, yeah. I kind of told them I have cancer.

The only person my age with cancer I've known was a girl in my junior-year British Romanticism class. A pain she occasionally felt at tennis practice turned out to be something much worse. Osteosarcoma, a growth in the knee. She limped around campus in a pink brace, clutching her boyfriend's arm for support. People held doors open for her, were moved to tears whenever she scaled small staircases. Such a brave girl, they said. Whatever secret fear or pain she felt she channeled into an essay with some melodramatic wordplay in the title—"Bracing Myself," "A Leg to Stand On"—that won a contest and was featured in *Seventeen* magazine. I have no idea what she's doing now. Coming up with clever names for nail-polish colors, hobbling through weeping crowds at half marathons. *Osteosarcoma* is hexasyllabic but conforms to no meter, too beautiful and dignified for double-dactylic nonsense verse. Compare that to *gastroesophageal reflux disease.*

Today isn't the first time I've left class to throw up, and my students have noticed. Rumors started spreading: that I have mesothelioma and never called the 1-800 number, that I've contracted a rare but deadly STD, that I have terminal cancer. Naturally, I went with the most attractive option. What was I supposed to tell them? That drinking a glass of orange juice feels like a knife to the gut? That an illness most people overcome with a can of ginger ale has me shackled to prescription pills, imprisoned in South Georgia? Maybe I ought to have related my disease back to our coursework. I could've told them my stomach, that leaky cauldron bubbling with acid, would make an ideal set piece for a production of *Macbeth.* Mount a play inside my body, I would've said. Make this wreckage into art. They wouldn't have understood. I got the same reaction in college, boys willing to kiss me until my lips began to taste like whatever we'd just had for dinner.

You can see, I hope, why I lied about the cancer.

Having spent the past four years studying literature, I know how to tell a lie. If you're going to tell someone you have cancer, don't choose something obvious. No leukemia, no lung cancer. You have to pick something nonspecific that really captures the *essence* of the disease. No organs in the title, nothing too common. Non-Hodgkin's lymphoma, for instance. I have no idea what non-Hodgkin's lymphoma is, but my students are under the impression it causes a lot of indigestion.

"Chemo's tough, but it's going pretty well," I tell Henry. Even though he scored perfectly on his verbal PSAT, he pays attention only when I'm talking about my cancer. Shakespeare doesn't engage him. This is the kind of drama he wants, immediate and dangerous, playing out in real time. "Good news, though: the doctors said I might have ten years left instead of five."

Relieved applause.

385

"How're you gonna spend your last five years?" someone wants to know.

"I don't know. Maybe I'll travel."

"Where?"

"Hmmm. Portugal, maybe. Greece. Ireland. If I'm well enough to travel, of course."

"Your husband must be happy you've got more time," a girl in the corner remarks.

"If I had a husband, I'm sure he'd be thrilled."

"Oh." Remembering that she's supposed to be using iambs, the girl asks, "Dost thou have a man thou date?"

I narrow my eyes in a sinister way to establish credibility. "Men are scared of me."

The room falls silent, perhaps in fear, until Polly speaks up. "Thou must really suffer," she says in a quiet voice. I think there might be tears in her eyes.

Her meter's all over the place, but I don't tell her this, just nod. "Yes," I tell her. "Yes, I do."

I tug at my hair as though I'm adjusting a wig, eliciting sighs of pity. What kind of sicko does this?

If you type up a prayer request and send it to Miss Sheila Carmichael, secretary at the First United Methodist Church, she'll print it in the Sunday bulletin. Please keep Reggie Sykes in your prayers as he undergoes hip-replacement surgery this week. Lift up Kathleen Anderson, who starts dialysis this Friday. Pray for Gerald, who's still dating someone who threw up on his bedroom floor. Yeah, I called him back. Earlier this week, he took me to see some cheesy rom-com at the Regal Cinemas. He didn't flinch when I asked for no butter on our popcorn. In fact, he said butter messes with the integrity of popcorn's flavor, whatever that means. He actually wore a tie to the movie theater, this one dotted with bright green parakeets.

The movie chronicled the trials and tribulations of a young American couple backpacking across Europe. I paced myself with the popcorn, one piece at a time, and tried to immerse myself in the film. Aside from a slight stabbing pain in my stomach, I felt pretty okay. Gerald kept trying to maneuver his arm around me and chickening out, the poor guy. We'd already had sex, yet he couldn't bring himself to touch my shoulder. The couple on-screen was astonishingly adept in foreign languages: they fought in hissing Italian, made up in doe-eyed French, gave directions to weary peasants in rapid-fire Russian.

Gerald whispered in my ear a line lifted from the movie: "*Je t'adore, ma cherie.*"

Then his hand became more adventurous, or perhaps resigned itself to a more accessible region of my body. He placed it on my knee, let it slowly travel up my thigh before stopping, rigid, mortified. I was fine with this. I liked the way it felt there. The couple boarded a plane, never once reached for their sick bags. How nice for them, I thought. Gerald passed me the popcorn, but, feeling that the invisible knife in my stomach had sharpened, I declined. I tried not to think about the parakeets on his tie and focused instead on his hand, its dull bravery. I watched the screen: rolling green fields, cows in sun-drenched pastures, our beloved couple running through the rain to take cover in a pub.

Ireland. They'd gone to Ireland.

I felt Gerald's breath in my ear again. This time, he spoke in English. "Ava, are you okay?" His hand left my leg and wiped a tear from beneath my eye.

"I want to go home," I told him.

So he took me home, walked me to the door, kissed me good-night, all that. My parents weren't even up. It was hardly ten thirty. Living at home at twenty-three isn't as bad as you'd think. Free rent, all my medicine paid for. Granted, it's not great, either. At the behest of my therapist, who thinks I need to get out of the house more often, my parents keep dragging me to different social events. Dinners at the McPhersons' house next door, brunches with my mom's Bible-study group. I've become an expert at rearranging food on a plate so it looks eaten. Sunday mornings, I go with my parents to church. I don't have the heart to tell them my mouth hasn't opened during the Apostles' Creed since I was seventeen.

Mom, Dad, and I have been regulars at the FUMC as long as I can remember. When I won the annual middle-school poetry contest in sixth grade, Miss Sheila asked me to start contributing Bible poems to the bulletin. My first one was called "Bible People" and went like this:

Shadrach, Meshach, and Abednego,
Moses shouting "Let my people go!"
Jesus made water turn into red wine,
Methuselah turned 969.

The Bible is full of people great and small,
But the best one is God, the greatest of them all!

When I first came back home after graduation, she asked me to send her a new poem, so I wrote one about Job:

There once was a man from the land of Uz,
Whom the Good Lord tortured simply because.
He killed the man's wife
And fucked up his life
Then dismissed the whole thing with a shrug.

"I'm not so sure we can run this," she told me with a nervous laugh.

Believe me when I say I know how to take rejection. Four years of bad dates in college have prepared me for this. I've recently published a few better poems in independent journals—*Flat Soda*, the *Hopscotch Review*, *Lobster Ferry Press*. Maybe one day I'll work up the nerve to submit to more prestigious places. I decided to send the Job poem to a place called *The Newer Testament* just for the hell of it. Their masthead says they're devoted to promoting subversive religious humor. Publish this entire planet, this whole cursed realm, I wanted to tell them.

After Miss Sheila read my poem, my mom explained to her that I'm sick and "just trying to process things." Miss Sheila hasn't listed my name in the bulletin, though. I mean, what would she even say? Please pray for Ava Slate, who's having trouble digesting tomato sauce. Lift up this poor girl whose lipstick print ought to be smeared on the Blarney Stone. Send a guardian angel down to keep her from going on another date with Gerald, who wears exotic birds on his ties and uses words like *integrity* to describe popcorn. Really, just pray for Gerald. He keeps insisting he wants to see me again. Clearly he needs God's help more than I do.

My gastroenterologist is named Ted. I like to use this against him. I never call him Dr. Mackler, or even Dr. Ted. Just Ted. Teddy, if I'm feeling particularly audacious. You can insult somebody with their own first name if you use the right inflection.

Ted and I have been seeing each other regularly since I was seventeen. It's the most stable relationship I've ever had with a man, and easily the most intimate. He's seen the scarred lining of my stomach, the charred walls of my esophagus. He knows more about my bowel movements than anyone else ever will. We talk about literature, too. Not my writing—his. Yes, Ted the gastroenterologist, the man who probes intestines for a living, is a writer.

"I'm really quite good," he told me during our first appointment. I'd made the mistake of telling him I founded our high school's literary journal. "Whenever I have to write letters to other doctors, everyone in the office will crowd around to see what I've written. They say I have a distinct voice."

Today he's doing the usual abdominal exam. I lie on a table while he pokes and prods and asks me what hurts.

"I was sorry to hear the Fulbright didn't work out. That hurt?"

"Oh, well, it's whatever. And no, it didn't."

"What about this? Your mom says you wanted to study nonsense."

"That's partially true. I wanted to study the influence of nonsense poetry on Joyce and Beckett. Or maybe Joyce and Beckett's influence on nonsense poetry." Whenever people ask about my research, I keep doing this, pretending I can't remember my own idea. Usually I say James Joyce and Samuel Beckett, but this is Ted I'm talking to. I use last names to intimidate him. If he's a real writer, he ought to know the people, the jargon.

"Well?"

"Well what?"

He gives what I imagine is my appendix a quick jab. "Did it hurt?"

"Oh, sorry. No."

"Sounds like you don't quite have things figured out."

"I said no, it didn't hurt."

"I mean about the nonsense."

"What?"

"Does this hurt? What I'm saying is, do you actually know what you want to study?"

"Yes."

"That's not good."

"Hold on a second, Ted." I sit up. "How is that not good?"

"You felt pain when I pressed on your upper abdomen. We're looking at potential esophageal ulcers here. You having esophageal ulcers would be a very bad sign."

"No, I meant I know what I want to study. Wanted to, anyway. I mean, why else would I have applied for a Fulbright?"

"So, it didn't hurt?"

"Wait, actually, yes, it did."

"Are you sure?"

This is usually how it goes. Confusion, nonsense, the whole Vladimir and Estragon routine. Ted tells me how he once received some less prestigious grant to research gut flora in Sweden, then moves on to the novel he's been working on for the past decade. As it turns out, gut flora figure quite prominently into the plot, a multigenerational saga told through the plucky voice of the family's youngest boy, Quentin, who longs to escape the chain of Catholic priests his family has been producing since 1798, so he can become none other than a gastroenterologist. I'd like to ask him why all the priests in his novel are having sex, but I don't want to hurt his feelings too much. He's an old man who's spent his life talking with strangers about poop.

After the abdominal exam, he has me do a barium swallow, a procedure that allows him to X-ray my digestive system, and finds a cluster of ulcers, tiny craters in the junction between my esophagus and stomach.

"Well," he says, studying the X-ray.

"Well," I say, and the word takes on an incantatory quality, as if we are both trying to will me into wellness through some ancient pagan spell.

Once our appointment is over, I stand outside my car in the parking lot, letting the September sun cook my skin. I'm pale, burn easily. My phone buzzes with another text from Gerald: *I want to see you.* To be honest, I've been avoiding his texts since our date last week. He keeps sending me zeugmas:

The food came and so did the check
Wait no
He made up his bed and his mind
The stars twinkled and so did her smile
I am the champion of zeugmas
haha just kidding, that title belongs to you:)
heeeey Ava
you okay???

I read his last text again, study it like a poem. He wants to see me again. What for? So I can excuse myself from our table at Chili's to vomit in the ladies' room? So he can scrub more of my half-digested food out of

390

his carpet? What the fuck is in it for him? I don't know what causes me to do it, but I compose a response: *I want to see you too.*

My thumb hovers over the send button, but I don't press it.

"My oncologist says the cancer's getting worse, that maybe he was wrong about the ten years. There was a tumor that didn't show up in the initial X-ray. He says I only have three left."

"Art thou sure about this thing?" Polly asks.

"Yes, I'm sure."

We all put down our copies of *Macbeth* and cry together. I love being a teacher.

I'm at the Applebee's bar with Gisberta. Since her wedding last summer, our friendship has become a thing that exists entirely in restaurants. This is the only decent bar for miles. We take what we can get. Gisberta is drinking something that looks radioactive, bright blue liquid contained in a mason jar. I ask the bartender to put a little plastic umbrella in my glass of water. I want people to think I'm drinking straight vodka.

Gisberta is half-German and beautiful, high cheekbones and blond hair. Pretty enough to get away with having the name Gisberta. Practically the whole restaurant is in love with her. She's been having a lot of fun turning her wedding ring around her finger while men attempt to flirt with her.

"That poem was hilarious," she keeps telling me. I can tell she's just trying to be nice. "Everything you write is hilarious."

She's talking about the Job poem, which was picked up by *The Newer Testament* after all. They've got incredibly quick turnaround. Too quick, really. Maybe it was a mistake to submit to a website that still has a brown background and yellow text. There's actually a hit counter at the bottom of the page: 8,090 total website views. My parents, long-standing suppliers of potato casserole at church luncheons, opted not to hang this particular poem on the refrigerator.

"It was shitty doggerel," I say. "Everything I've written lately is shitty doggerel."

"Dog-a-what? Don't be modest. Guys are super into poets. Like what's his name—Gary?"

"Ger-ald," I hiss, feeling defensive. My tone is nasty, mean. Her name is Gisberta, which is way worse.

"Are you still dating him? Do you write him romantic sonnets?"

"Shut up."

"Are you dating him or not?"

"I don't know."

"You don't know?"

I haven't texted him back, don't plan to. He's better off this way. Let him have some alone time with his hedgehogs, his parakeets, creatures who won't throw up on his bedroom floor.

"I should just go home." I look at my menu and spot something called cheeseburger egg rolls. I want to burn this place to the ground. "Fucking Applebee's."

"No! You, Ava Slate, are not leaving here alone tonight."

"Ha, right."

"Come on, forget Gerald. You're smart. You're a poet, for fuck's sake. You won a Fulbright. Look at you! That dress is amazing."

As a former English major, I've been trained to notice this kind of phrasing as a means of sly insult. The dress is amazing, not the girl who's wearing it.

"It looks like a bag on me."

"No, you're waifish. Supermodel skinny."

"Whatever."

"You've got that sexy raspy voice. Guys are into that."

"The guys here are only interested in you."

"They're just intimidated by you, that's all." She looks at my glass and smirks. "Men are scared of girls who can hold their liquor."

Except I haven't drunk alcohol since my freshman year of college. It was my first and last time. The girls in my hall were gathered in somebody's room, sitting in a circle on a blue shag rug, passing around a bottle of something redolent of nail-polish remover. Everclear, I think. We were all in our pajamas, hair in disarray: one of those hazy midnights with nothing to do but get ourselves in trouble. Everyone was giggling at nothing, running into furniture on the way to the bathroom.

"Come on, Ava," they all kept saying, "aren't you going to drink anything?"

I hadn't said much all night. Aside from my senior year of college, I was sickest during that first semester, nursing my first ulcer while trying to navigate the foreign land in which I'd been abandoned. On that blue rug, I thought we all looked like islands, a little archipelago. Everyone was blurting out secrets: I'm cheating on my boyfriend! Jason from down the hall has a crush on me! Katie is fucking her chemistry professor!

Even though we were crowded into a tiny room, I felt far away from everyone, shipwrecked on some remote, faraway shore. I wanted to join them. I wanted to share my secrets, to take part in this unorthodox communion. Inhaling deeply, I announced, "I can't drink alcohol because I've got acid-reflux disease."

Silence. Everyone stared, then burst into hysterical laughter. They must've thought I was joking, or maybe they were too drunk to understand. I wanted to sink into the ocean, let it erode me completely. What I did instead was drown myself in Everclear. I took that bottle and chugged it until I couldn't anymore, everyone cheering me on. When I spent the next day in the hospital, too dehydrated from all the puking to keep anything down, they were all too hungover to visit me. Whenever I closed my eyes, though, I could see their smudged inebriated figures applauding me. I could hear them chanting my name.

Right now, in this goddamned Applebee's, I'm thinking about doing it again. I want to feel bombs bursting inside me, fireworks, bottle rockets. I want people to watch in awe as I explode. Swiveling on my barstool, I turn to ask Gisberta for a sip of her drink, but she's all the way across the room talking with another man, twisting her wedding ring around her finger.

She left behind that blue stuff, though.

I hate to admit it, but I texted Gerald: *Hey, this is kinda out of the blue, but I'm in the hospital. You definitely don't have to come but I thought you should know.* An hour later, he showed up with a sudoku book, several back issues of the *New Yorker*, a package of fuzzy socks, and a Mylar balloon shaped like a bumblebee. He also brought a pillow, one of those goose-feather things. In case the nurses didn't bring me enough, he said.

They've got me hooked up to an IV, pumping in fluids or something. Things are kind of messy. Lots of puking, a bleeding ulcer. I'd rather not go into details. Aside from my parents, I haven't had too many visitors. Gisberta stopped in for a minute on her way to work, said she was in a rush. There's a Hallmark card from her on the nightstand. Ted, that unsentimental fucker, hadn't thought to bring me anything, just came by and talked about his novel for half an hour. I kept zoning out, wondering where I'd fit into a book or play, what Shakespeare or Aeschylus could possibly do with a girl like me. The tragic heroine generally stumbles into weeping brooks, cleaves her heart in two with a dagger. Imagine a greasy-haired Cordelia sweating in a hospital gown, Helen of Troy coughing blood into a tissue. Tell me, who should weep for Hecuba when she carries her tragedy around in her stomach, when she wants for nothing but a warm, familiar hand on her knee?

"I brought my mom's homemade carrot-soup recipe, for whenever you get out," Gerald says. He's not wearing a tie, thank God. The strategic data analysts of Southwest Georgia are enjoying their weekly Casual Monday. "One of my favorites. I tucked it in the pages of the sudoku book."

"Thanks," I croak, my voice staticky and hoarse.

"Geez," he says, sinking into the chair next to me. "I didn't know how bad off you were. You're in the *hos*pital. I was talking to your mom out in the hallway, and—"

"My mom?"

"Yeah. She was saying you were supposed to go to Ireland. I had no idea you were so sick. Why didn't you tell me?"

I shrug, sparing my voice.

"You know what else your mom said? She said she thinks you're secretly drinking up all the orange juice in the house. She's really worried about you." He pauses for dramatic effect. "And I am too."

Now I'm thinking of Achilles, King Henry, the mighty Beowulf. Armor clanking through the aisles of Walmart as they scan the selection of puzzle books. Swords traded in for balloons and socks. I see demigods and warriors with cell phones pressed against their ears, their mothers rattling off carrot-soup ingredients. Broth, celery, the scratching of pens. There's heroism in all of this, I realize, an absurd brand of valor. Wasted sacrifice.

"It's gonna be okay, though," he says, "because one day you're gonna be better, and you know where you're gonna be? Right here." He points to one of his *New Yorker* back issues. "Right between these pages, that's where. Or in Ireland. Doing your research. Teaching at Harvard, Yale, wherever. The world is your oyster."

"No, it isn't," I say, my voice a jagged whisper.

"Sure it is. I promise." He tries to grab my hand, but I pull away.

"You don't know where I'm going to be. You don't have a fucking clue." I flinch at my own cruelty, and so does he. "I'm sorry." I pause to clear my throat. "Please, just leave."

"But why?"

I try to tell him, but the words get lost in a coughing fit. Even when I compose myself, the words won't come loose, are still stuck in my ravaged windpipe. Finally, resignedly, I mouth for him to please go.

"But—"

I just shake my head. It's all I can do.

Gathering his magazines, he gets up and gives me one last sad look. "Goodbye, Ava," he says, and I wince at the sound of my own name. Unpoetic and blunt, like the end unit of some lost Shakespearean insult. You pigeon-livered, plague-sored, poison-bellied Ava. You are as a candle, the better burnt out. I am sick when I do look on thee. I am so, so sick.

Once a week I go to therapy. These meetings, of course, are confidential.

The quality of poetry in the church bulletin has fallen substantially. Not that my Job poem would've helped any, I guess. Last night, I looked it up in *The Newer Testament* with intentions of maybe texting the link to Gerald, patching things up—he was nuts about that painkiller poem, after all—but discovered their website had been replaced with a bright flashing banner: DOMAIN NAME EXPIRED. Beneath this message were links to virtual churches and chat rooms where one could converse with sexy Latinas. I closed the browser and went to bed.

My parents are fond of coercing me into going to church, think it's good for my spirit or whatever, so that's where I am, looking over the bulletin instead of listening to the preacher. This Sunday's poem, written by nine-year-old Yasmine Pope, is simply titled "Jesus."

His hand can heal
The sick and the lame,
The blind and the deaf
Praise His name!

"Amateur," I mutter under my breath.

"You say something?" my dad whispers to me.

"Oh, no."

I'm sitting between my parents in our regular pew, and we turn our attention back to the preacher. He's still on the prayer requests, all these poor people bearing the consequences of some secret wager between Heaven and Hell: Reggie Sykes is suffering complications from his hip-replacement surgery. Kathleen Anderson isn't adjusting well to dialysis. Someone's grandfather is dying in Atlanta. A mother gave birth to a stillborn child. Everybody's got fucking cancer.

"Any other prayer requests?" the preacher asks.

Toward the front of the church, a familiar figure stands up. Short, blond, arms splotched with eczema: Polly Wilkinson. All I ate for breakfast was toast, but I can feel it creeping back up my throat.

"I want to put in a prayer request for my English teacher, Miss Slate," she says, her voice quavering. She actually turns around and smiles at me. "She's been in the hospital with non-Hodgkin's lymphoma. She's out now, but she could still use our prayers."

"Wait, you mean Ava Slate?"

She nods vigorously. "Yes, sir."

Everyone stares at me, and for a brief moment, I relish their stunned pity. How tragic I must seem, how noble, a cancer patient who suffers in silence. But then Mom squeezes my arm, not in a comforting way. "I'm afraid there must be some kind of mistake," she says. "Our Ava doesn't have cancer."

The preacher breathes a relieved sigh. "Okay, phew. That's what I thought. Glad to see you're doing well, Ava."

Everyone laughs in a claustrophobic way. I wonder if it's possible to will myself into spontaneous combustion. The preacher moves onto the next tragedy, car crash off State Road 6, but I'm still stuck in the last one. Polly turns around and stares at me, asking all the questions iambic meter won't allow, but I don't return her gaze. I'm not even here.

Where I am, there is no State Road 6. There's just me, nothing else for miles.

Polly's parents filed a complaint with the school about me. The principal was unduly sympathetic; she said what I did was wrong but forgivable, if I wanted to stick around. I didn't. It was unhealthy, working in a place with so many Rand McNally maps.

A substitute is teaching my class while they look for a permanent replacement, meaning today I'm free to go to Walmart with my mom. Spending time with her is the least I can do, I suppose, after last week's scene at church. I keep trying to come up with apologies—*Sorry, I didn't mean for you to find out about my fake cancer!*—but none of them feels quite right.

"Did we miss anything?" she asks, pushing the buggy down the cookie aisle.

"Give me a sec to decipher Dad's handwriting." I scan the list. "Looks like yogurt . . . Dr Pepper . . . unintelligible scribbles . . . DJ?" I squint, read it again. "Oh, OJ. Orange juice."

Mom stiffens. "He can pick those things up later." She lets out an awkward laugh. "Punishment for poor penmanship."

"Okay," I say. We roll on in silence, past rows of Zebra Cakes and Moon Pies, snacks I haven't touched in years, relics of ancient history. "I didn't drink any of it, you know," I tell her. "Just wanted to clear that up."

She breathes in deeply, like she's about to say something, then thinks the better of it.

"I wouldn't do something like that," I insist. "I've never even liked orange juice in my whole life."

Mom is quiet for a moment, but then she says, "That's not true. You used to love it. I used to buy the ones with Donald Duck on the side."

"I don't remember that."

"You used to love Donald Duck. We had all those Mickey cartoons on VHS tape, and you'd watch them over and over. I remember you'd be in hysterics whenever Donald Duck came on."

Her face is wistful, teary eyed, provoking multiple reactions in me. I want to slap her, hug her, grovel at her feet. Instead, I silently follow her into the checkout line, one register over from where I first met Gerald. While we wait, I pull out my phone. For what feels like the one thousandth time, I reread an unanswered text I sent last night:

> Hey, I know things ended badly in the hospital but I was gonna send you this poem I wrote that was published online but I guess the editors or whoever didn't pay their bills because the domain name expired . . . their domain name expired, and so did my poem. Ha ha but anyway if you wanna read it text me and I'll send it (again REALLY sorry, please lets talk)

I guess I thought Gerald would answer, you know? He'd really offered me his pillow.

After shopping, I go by the school to collect my stuff. Had I been teaching today, we would've gone over figurative language, all those complicated evasive maneuvers poets are so fond of: litotes, hypallages, zeugmas. How to say a thing in the most inscrutable way possible.

Emptying out my desk, I'm confronted with the flotsam of an abridged career in teaching high-school literature. Confiscated fidget spinners, broken pens, indecipherable notes passed between giggling friends. I unfold them, try to interpret their gel-pen hieroglyphics, all curly tails and heart-dotted *I's*. I used to write in this language once. Boys would pass me notes: *Do you like me circle yes or no.* I had one of those pens that let you write in any color. Blue, green, purple. There's a card for me, signed by the whole class. A rabbit holding an ice pack to his head, the words "Get well soon" floating next to him. Here's a roll of Tums, a mutilated paper clip, a stick of peppermint gum to cover my breath in case I get sick. I remember the giddy thrill of circling *yes*, the smugness of circling *no*. Every day a fist uncurling, revealing a delicious surprise.

My mom's not just imagining things. I really have been drinking the orange juice, a few sips here and there. I've been drinking it for the same reason other girls slit their wrists.

"Miss Slate," a voice says. "Why dost thou have your head put down?"

I lift my head from the desk and find Polly Wilkinson standing before me, rocking back and forth on the heels of her tennis shoes. Her cheeks are pink, her forehead shiny with sweat; judging by her gym shorts and the flute case in her hand, I assume she's just come in from marching-band practice. I guess I've been sitting here for a while.

"Hi," I say.

"How dost thou do this afternoon?" she asks in a barely audible voice.

Then the room goes mute. This silence persists for several seconds, me staring down at the ephemera covering my desk, Polly swaying uneasily like a ship at sea until finally she bursts out in a bruised voice, "Thou hurtest me."

"I'm sorry."

"Dost thou really not have cancer?"

"No, but—"

"Art thou even sick at all?"

"Well . . ."

"Canst thou answer what I ask?"

"For God's sake, cut it out with the fucking Shakespeare shit."

She puts a hand over her mouth. Tears well in her eyes. John Donne and Walt Whitman make her cry in class, and now I guess I do too.

"Hey, hey," I say, rising from my chair. "I didn't mean it. I'm sorry. I'm really sorry."

She refuses to look at me.

"Hey, Polly. Come on. I swear I didn't mean it."

Sniffling, she asks, "Are you sick, though? Or was that all fake too?"

"No, it was real." I think about placing a comforting hand on her shoulder, but instead I just stand in front of my desk, leaning the back of my legs against it.

"Then what is it?" Polly asks with a little hiccup. "What's wrong with you?"

I hesitate. "It's hard to explain."

"I knew it. You're lying."

"I'm not, though!"

"Then tell me what's wrong."

"It's just this stomach problem," I say, feeling absurd. "Acid reflux."

She makes a face. "It's that bad?"

"For some people it gets really serious. I get ulcers and stuff. Makes me sick a lot."

"Oh," she says. Something in her hardened expression relaxes. "So, you're not going to die in three years?"

"No."

"Not even in five years?"

I shake my head. "It's not like that. It's not terminal."

"That means you're going to live?"

"I'm gonna live a long time," I say. The words feel like a prison sentence.

The corners of her mouth turn up. She's smiling. She even lets out a little laugh. "Oh. Good." She laughs again. "I'm so glad." And suddenly her arms are wrapped around my middle, her flute case banging against my hip. This embrace lasts only a split second, and then we're apart again, her face shy, eyes roaming the tiled floor. "Bye, Miss Slate," she mumbles, then disappears.

There's nothing left for me to do but finish packing, take down my decorations. The lace curtains, the string lights, the plastic bust of Shakespeare in the corner. I've tacked glossy poetry broadsides all over the room. We've got the entire Western canon here, its coy mistresses and dreary ravens and lonely clouds. There's enigmatic punctuation from Emily Dickinson, delightful gibberish from Edward Lear. I strip them from the cinder-block walls and hold them close to my chest. Reluctantly, I stow them away in cardboard boxes, wondering when I'll see them again, when they'll have another chance to speak. If I could live anywhere, I'd choose the white space between stanzas, that sweet breath between words.

With the broadsides packed away, I return to my desk, rake the clutter into the wastebasket and cram what's worth keeping into my purse. I pick up the metallic nameplate on my desk, watch it glint in the sun. Ava Slate, it reads, one last poem to carry home.

Nominated by The Cincinnati Review

CONFESSION

by ELIZABETH ROBINSON

from SAGINAW

For the homeless woman who hanged herself in the Denver County Jail

I write to you today when "today" hesitates
to arrive, stumbling in the darkness that precedes
sunrise. This is confession
and I am wondering if all

efforts at telling stories are
our struggles to confess. A confession might not

be an admission of sin, just an admission—
the way I overheard a man yesterday say,

"I'm an alcoholic, but not a drunk." Confession
easing the burden of narrative-as-it-is-supposed-
to-be in favor of

a positing, a position,
a vision of the possible,
a retraction of what has been.

❊

I confess,

and that means only
that I am witnessing
what surrounds me.

Now I also confess that when I first began
working at the shelter,
I resented the insistence of stories.

Yesterday: 121 messages on voicemail

and, listening, one woman talked urgently,
for eight minutes until the phone cut her off.
I resented my own obsessiveness in
the face of all I was forced to see: the skirmishes

that occur when a person has been shoved
out of their home, then out of their narrative
and fights to get both back.

So much worse than losing the apartment
or car you have lived in, worse even than having
someone steal your tent or sleeping bag—

it seems that to have your account of
yourself disrupted
is the greater loss.

Shoved so rudely
out of your own biography,

you or you or you cut in line to tell me, tell me
and tell me, what your story is, or you

relinquish what, in practical terms, was
a fruitless effort to get your food stamps reinstated

with a sigh of satisfaction
because at least you got to tell the story

of why they were so whimsically
taken away.

*

It's still dim outside and I am
aware that people I care about are

as awake as I am, but for different reasons.
We are each trying to stay alive, until we aren't.

So much for the unity and fulfillment of narrative.

*

A man bursts into the office shouting that we must
find a place for him to stay, "I can't be homeless, I can't

live outside!"

That day, you took his hand,
understand with such grace that the narrative

that imposes itself on him *right now*
is intolerable, and that's
another kind of homelessness.

"You think you can't bear this," you tell him,
"but you can. There are places you can go
—to eat, to get a shower. We can show

you a park where the police won't bother you
too much, how to sleep with the blankets
around you, instead of *on* you—

so you are warm but not covered up
and they can't say that you are camping
and ticket you." The man looks at you mutely.

"You think that you can't do this," you go on,
"but you can. Just don't look

too far ahead." Don't try, in

other words, to understand yourself

moving over the earth as if
toward a destination.

Confessing
to the moment as bearable when it's not.

＊

As though life were something other

than a problem to be resolved.

Instead: life as an effort to find

a human—you—
who is gone. You have disappeared
into the absence
of evidence that you
were ever present.

Now, the beautiful parallels, the circuits,
the snowflake-like symmetries that I have

inhabited all my life, I confess,

really inhabit *me*. A homeless

man pausing at a park as I gave
a poetry reading approached me afterwards

to say, "I enjoyed what you read because
it sounded like the way I thought when I was psychotic."

All my patterns broken into weightless
fragments, disturbed on the breath
I exhale within my mind.

＊

I did resent the stories for
overwhelming me, for failing in some way to merge

into a whole.
All that I have is a raucous list of accounts
each vying for place, for acknowledgement. But together,

they lack a reliable surface I could polish
into meaning.

People, like stories, disappear and then reappear,
sometimes with familiar faces that
expect me to recognize them.

Is it a story if I can remember no name,
no date, no contiguous facts, but feel.

a rush of affection and recognition?

✳

Your hand on the hand of the man
as he drew back, furious that, no,

we couldn't get him a hotel room. Whereas

you, interrupted, had just told me
why you were in pain, what the medication
was for, as we tried to figure out how to get
and pay for it

We never saw him again.

✳

I never saw you again.

✳

After you hanged yourself in the county jail,
I walked to the post office with your husband,

to pick up a package that had been mailed to you.
I asked him for a story that I could keep, not a story
that was your "life story" but

a kind of a keepsake anecdote. He showed the postal clerk
the package slip, and a letter that we had produced

vowing that he was a resident of the city and so
entitled to pick up your mail.

The clerk went to the back,
brought the box up and paused: "I'm sorry for your loss."

❀

I asked your husband when the two of you had met, where you had
    traveled,
and he opened the package, pulling out a picture of your son
who looks like him, not like you.

Still, it was a resemblance, and a resemblance is a kind of
continuity that makes its own story.

Your husband said,

"I knew she was dead
because she came to me in a vision one night. She came with
    others,
and I knew them, but I didn't. And then they were all gone."

I had seen him walking down the sidewalk
and thought he too was probably
waiting for your return.

❀

You don't come back, I do.
I argue with myself: Isn't recognition a form of return?
A return of—
we shorten its syntax to say that

recognition is a form of presence, *is*
presence.

✳

I confess that you, your *self* came to me
as relief. I liked you.

This sort of recognition is neither return nor arrival.

I thought you would come back.
I thought you would not disappear.

Helplessness is another form of recognition.

✳

When I anticipated your return, what
I confess I wanted was the simple comfort

of conversation, a moment when
the dilemma of how

to understand a narrative or any pattern

didn't, finally, matter.

Maybe grace

is the bereft comforting the bereft with nothing.

Your hand never touched my hand,
but I saw it touch another's, a real

contact that now refuses to be gone.

Nominated by Annie Sheppard, Saginaw

SHAKESPEARE DOESN'T CARE

by RITA DOVE

from CHICAGO QUARTERLY REVIEW

where Sylvia put her head. His Ophelia
suffered far worse, shamed by slurs, drenched
merely to advance the plot. "Buck up Sylvia"
he'd say. "Who needs a gloomy prince
spouting iambs while minions drag the river?
Sharpen your lead and carve us
a fresh pound of Daddy's flesh
before the rabble in the pit

starts launching tomatoes!"
Shakespeare's taking no prisoners,
he's purloined the latest gossip
to plump up his next comedy,
pens a sonnet while building
a playlist for the apocalypse.
When you gripe at reviews.
he snickers: How would you like

to be called an "upstart crow"
just because you dared to write a play
instead of more "sugared sonnets"?
How's them apples next to your shriveled
sour grapes? As for the world
going to hell alas! alack! whatever.

ditch the dramatics. He's already done
a number on that hand basket
what with pox and the plague
bubbling up here and there,
now and then afflictions
one could not cough away nor soothe
with piecemeal science. So chew it up
or spit it out, he might say.

although more likely he'd just shrug.
What does he care
If we all die tomorrow?
He lives in his words. You wrestle
Enraptured with yours.
What time does with them
next, or ever after,
Is someone else's rodeo.

Nominated by Elizabeth McKenzie, Chicago Quarterly Review

SATYR'S FLUTE

by SHANGYANG FANG

from THE YALE REVIEW

I was skinning a goat's penis to prepare
   the dish my mother had taught me.
This was not in a dream, though, with a dream's
   deliciousness, the knife—a stroke of blueness
—tapered the bleeding thing into a sheer bruise.
   One must always be careful with a penis.
One must marinate it in a pool of oyster sauce
   with starch, sprinkle ginger juice to cleanse
its urinous smell—smell of fish—ithyphallic,
   as Rimbaud may have said—let the residue
of semen ferment with blood and the blueness
   into an evening sky like this: when the penis
starts weeping ceaselessly, softly at first,
   like a newborn, then louder, until the kitchen
turns into a train station, from which the goat
   was brought to the nearest butchery.
The penis cries like a baby, like a baby it cries
   for its wanting—without the mind
the penis is innocent. The penis wants
   its goat back. The way a child wants
his mother's milk. And the goat,
   without its penis, is it anyway
a goat? Half-male? Will it go crazy looking
   at the moon? Will it serve the Goat King

like a eunuch in a primeval dynasty?
   Or it will follow the rancid smell of dead
fish, past the meadow, past the bullying woods,
   to reach the lampblack river and watch
the water flow. Watch the needles
   of fish sewing the stream and wish
one of them was his genital. The penis in my hand
   is thick and emblematic, something I cannot
fully fathom. A device without the service
   of its mind, how does that work?
How, in heaven's name, can a mind bear to lose a part
   of its form and stomach the loss as a thought?
The thought of a penis, being nothing otherwise,
   is not a penis. How my mother once saw
me with a boy. How she said, no. The n preceding
   the choir of the o is like a castration
that severed me from her. O, am I anyway the penis
   my mother had once lost? I rushed
back to my room, stayed a whole afternoon
   in front of the mirror and thought I am not
beautiful, thought she was right, no, I cannot
   love this boy in front of me. And wished
he had not been born. Now I can see how the goat,
   disturbed by his forbidden thought, staggers
toward that river, mates with deliquescent
   nymphs—Hermes into Hermaphroditus,
whose lilac-encased body, androgynous
   and gorgeous, once drowned and rose
from the rootless water. And I see
   the meadow outside the kitchen
is purple, an infecting pool of neutering
   tincture. The penis, enveloped inside
my hands, is old and tired, like a fetus curling
   back toward an anonymous uterus.

Nominated by The Yale Review, Rodney Jones, Peter LaBerge

THERE I ALMOST AM: ON ENVY AND TWINSHIP

by JEAN GARNETT

from THE YALE REVIEW

Recently, I walked into a small grocery store near my house and the owner, a shy but sociable man, looked up at me and said, "Are you *you*, or the other one?"

"I always wanted a twin," some singletons say, and I believe them. To be a twin is glorious. We get lots of attention. Sometimes it's an insulting kind—a man on a boat once said, "Don't even bother telling me which is which; I won't remember"—but attention is attention, and it feels good. Plus, we have each other, which is no small thing to have.

Not long ago, stepping out of the rain into a crowded vestibule, there she was, my own face among strangers. Relief. We pressed our dripping cheeks together and instantly became, if not one body, then a kind of puppet that takes two operators, me fishing chapstick out of her bag, her biting into the energy bar I had in my pocket.

Up the stairs, surrounded by intimidating young people, we held our ground as though by forcefield, whispering and laughing, not needing anyone else. I thought, *I have brought my second to this duel.* You may know the feeling of taking proud shelter in a sibling, someone who knows how to assemble and disassemble you, someone with whom you share blood, history, memory. Imagine sharing not only all of that but also hair, skin, iris, nipple, the same winces of pain caused by the same herniation in the same cervical disks, the same laugh sounds and laugh lines, the very same early marks of age; the same face—your *face*, the signature that proves the youness of you—so that you can look at another person and think, There I am. There I *almost* am.

This was a work event: My sister and I are in the same business; in fact we have the exact same editorial position at different publishing companies and are in direct competition with each other, sometimes even bidding against each other in auctions. I started out in publishing a few years before she did, and at first I enjoyed playing mentor, offering advice on agents and office politics and author care; sometimes she would even ask me to read something to verify her opinion. I can be a very generous sister—maternal, even—as long as I am winning. Now, just as I feels my own career stalling, overtaken by domestic sprawl and motherhood, my sister's seems to be taking off, her ambition suddenly asserting itself though filling the vacuum left by mine. I have stopped going to work events—I never liked them, and with a small child I have an excellent excuse not to attend them—while she makes a point of showing up to everything. When I skip a big literary benefit or agent mixer, I am almost certain to hear from a colleague the next day, "I waved to you across the room last night, but you didn't see me," or, "Wait, yesterday you had a different haircut."

It causes me a strange mix of pride and panic to hear about my sister from people in my own sphere. For us, meeting people has always involved a sort of flag planting. The system goes like this: If you meet me first, I have planted my flag in you; even if we are not friends and never will be, I expect a certain loyalty from you—meaning, I guess, that I expect you to see me as being more real than my sister. If she meets you first, ok, she has planted her flag, and I am resigned to being "the other one." These days, I find myself feeling more and more like the other one—not the right one, not the looked-for one, not "the *one*." This feeling is nothing new (though to some extent it is in keeping with the sense of ceding ground that, I am discovering, comes with parenthood). It is, and always has been, a part of the natural twin cycle. She is having her turn.

My sister has had a good year. At the event, people kept coming up to her. "You've had a good year!" they'd say, and I would smile and nod and say, "She really has." After one congratulator walked away my sister leaned close to me and whispered, "What am I supposed to say to them? 'Thanks, errrr, you haven't!'" I laughed. The room went quiet as a reader took the stage and we stood together, shoulder to shoulder, arms slung around waists, self-conjoining. As usual, her nearness flooded me with,

413

first, a profound sense of peace and well-being and, second, anxiety about my comparative worth. I was, for example, aware of being the shorter twin. No one can say when this one-inch difference pried its way between us; we didn't start to notice it until we were almost thirty. Maybe she did more yoga, elongating herself. Maybe certain chapters stunted my growth. Maybe I've been shrinking.

A few minutes into the reading, suddenly, without warning, her body shifted away from mine, leaving me physically lonely and cold, as though she had been sheltering me from a breeze or had removed my clothes by un-touching me. She pulled ahead, stepping softly through the quiet room of listeners, over to a cluster of people sitting on the floor near the stage. I watched her lean down toward them, exchange warm smiles and whispers of greeting, and then, turning her back to me, fold her long legs and sink down until all but the part in her brand-new haircut disappeared.

Not long after that, standing in line for the bathroom at a poetry reading, I strike up a conversation with an acquaintance of my sister's, a young man named Daniel. He expresses surprise that she and I are both book editors, and I tell him that it's actually pretty common for identical twins to have the same job, something I learned from a *National Geographic* documentary. "I guess that makes sense," says Daniel, and then he tells me about a pair of identical twins he knows who are both poets. "Which one is better?" I ask him, as a joke. Without missing a beat he nods and says, "That comes up a lot." And then he gives me an unequivocal answer.

"Twins are the same because they are twins," the psychologist (and twin) Barbara Klein writes in *Alone in the Mirror: Twins in Therapy,* her 2012 book on the struggles of twins in a singleton world. In many ways my compound identity with my sister is home. I would like to stay home, in Klein's cozy tautology, but she immediately about-faces and spoils it: "At the same time, twins have the right to be different and to create their own sense of themselves." As an adolescent I was eager to exercise this right. Now I worry that, no matter what happens, I am unfinished, synecdoche, half the apple.

What do you do with two people who share a face? The old way was to lean into the curiosity of doppelgangerdom, have some fun with it. Parents might dress their twins in matching outfits, maybe even christen them alliteratively. By the 1980s, this model had become suspect (a symptom of Cold War distrust of sameness, maybe?); now each twin was required to be an individual. In America, "How are you different?" and "How are you special?" are the same question. We must all be equal, but also different and special, and so with twins, who are the same but different, a dizzying, ever-vigilant accounting is necessary. Red overalls and a blue shirt for one; blue overalls and a red shirt for the other. The exact same *number* of presents on birthdays and Christmas, but not the same presents. A box of colored pencils for one and a beading kit for the other, wrapped identically as a kind of coding for us (apparent duplicates reveal distinct interiors!).

Adults don't compare and contrast my sister and me aloud like some kids and family members used to, but they do stare. Sometimes a new acquaintance (usually a man) will stand there looking back and forth between us, and then say, "Yes, I see the difference." And because I'm vain and frightened I always want to ask, "What is it? What *is* the difference?"

To the twin, motherhood holds out the promise of a final, elevating inequality. For this one person, my child, I am singular, irreplaceable. I have no equal.

I have never felt like more of a singleton than during the first few months after my child was born. She wailed when my sister took her, missing my smell. Now that she is older, it's my sister's neck she clings to while I try to pull her away, and I can hear the false cheer in my voice as I coax her.

Even as I go through the motions of building my own life, in many ways my sister still holds the key to its meaning. For example, I believe I am happily married. My husband and I have been together for many years, and if some of the passion and desire we once felt for each other has been muffled by routine, familiarity, and the stress of parenthood, that is no tragedy; it happens to lots of marriages. But if my sister, whose current relationship is similar to mine in being well-worn, were tomorrow to go out and fall madly in love with some new man, embarking on a thrilling, terrifying romantic adventure, the character of my marriage would be transformed. Outwardly, nothing in my life would have changed, but the story of my happiness would be undone.

One twin is always better looking than the other. One is always "doing better." Happier. Healthier. Thinner. Time acts upon us. Food and drink. Cigarettes. Anxiety. Childbirth. I used to privately note that my tits were perkier; now that I have nursed this is no longer true. I think her teeth might be slightly whiter. My nose is pointier. Her lips are fuller. I could go on.

Envy. Francis Bacon called it "the vilest affection, and the most depraved." To Socrates it was "the ulcer of the soul." It is, the critic Sianne Ngai tells us, an ugly feeling, meaning that it is noncathartic, arising from a "situation of obstructed agency." You can do nothing to stop it, nothing to control it, nothing to bring it to any conclusion. It will have its interminable way with you. Unlike the grander passions—rage, despair—it endures while offering "no satisfactions of virtue . . . nor any therapeutic or purifying release."

Not surprisingly, both Nietzsche and Ayn Rand dismissed it as the province of petulant losers: "the vengefulness of the impotent" (Nietzsche), "the hallmark of a second rater" (Rand). According to Melanie Klein, it is "operative from the beginning of life" and "affects the earliest relation of all." It occurs, says the Austrian sociologist Helmut Schoeck, "as soon as two individuals become capable of mutual comparison."

I remember how, in our early twenties when my sister was at her thinnest, I was always angling for a view of her, using barback mirrors and public bathrooms and shop windows to catch secret glimpses. I remember how perverted I felt whenever our eyes met in the reflection and she caught me in the act of envy. I am never more disgusted with myself than when I am engaged in this covert looking and assessing, treating her body as a human mirror. But I still do it. I spy on her. She'll be walking or crying or dancing or getting dressed or trying to tell me something important, and I'll become aware that my eyes are scanning her as though she were a bar code. You want your identical twin to be beautiful, to confirm that you are beautiful, but you also want her to be ugly, to confirm that she is uglier than you.

Aristotle put it like this: "We envy those who are near us in time, place, age, or reputation . . . those whose possession of or success in a thing is a reproach to us: these are our neighbors and equals; for it is clear that it is our own fault we have missed the good thing in question." *Missed* is the knife-twisting word here, so much of envy having to do with the feeling of a near miss, an *almost*.

When does Envy begin? In her essay "Envy and Gratitude," Melanie Klein traces it to the body of the mother. I find her writing difficult to understand, and so, recently, when I found myself sitting next to a psychoanalyst at a dinner party, I asked if he could break it down for me.

He said, "Think of the breast from the infant's point of view: I am suffering, I am wanting, I am alone. And then, as if by magic, a nurturing object appears and quenches every thirst, removes every anxiety, wraps me in a cocoon of safety and love."

While he was talking the server came up behind us and poured red wine into the heavy bowl of his glass (perched on its slender, feminine stem, very breast-like), and I was thinking how I wanted some and how easily I could ask for it and take a warm, acid sip and break four years of sobriety that came about not because I hit any rock bottom but simply because I am bottomlessly thirsty.

"So," continued the analyst, "Mother has the thing that will end all discomfort. But she doesn't always give it up, at least not fast enough, which must mean she's keeping some for herself. That produces envy."

"Wanting what someone else has," I said.

"Wanting to *destroy* what you want that someone else has."

"Fling poop at the breast," I said.

His owlish face broke into a smile. "Exactly."

A desire that seeks to destroy: that is one definition of envy. "The professional thief is less tormented, less motivated by envy, than is the arsonist," writes Schoeck.

Klein talks about breastfeeding as restoring, to some extent, the "lost prenatal unity with the mother." My sister and I were never breastfed; we were too small and weak to suck strongly enough. But with twins it is never just fetus and mother; there is always triangulation. We are not only dependent on our mother to nourish, but on each other to share rather than steal. Each of us withholds from the other—each of us constitutes, for the other—the thing that would end all discomfort by conferring wholeness.

I first recognized it in the cartoon villains of our youth. Wicked stepmothers, illegitimate kings, lonely sorceresses. Of these, I particularly identified with Ursula, the sea witch in *The Little Mermaid*. With her crystal ball spying, her glowing eyes (envy *looks*), and her yearning for Triton's three-pronged golden schlong, she was dripping with envy's signifiers. At one point, a pair of enormous, pea-green hands come steaming out of her and hover winglike for a second before caressing their way toward Ariel's face, like a bad smell that makes you horny. Ariel throws her head back as the hands penetrate her, deep throat, no gag reflex, her eyes closed, her neck engorged.

417

Even as a young child I knew what those hands meant, and that if I was not careful my own would be visible.

A book my sister edited is on the *New York Times* list of the ten best books of the year, a career milestone I've never achieved. I text her: "OMGGGGG! CONGRATULATIONS!!!" I am screaming in her face. I use my baby name for her, at the very moment of her adult and individual success. I am aware that I am asking her for something. An apology? A disavowal? Reassurance? Or maybe I am warning her, emitting a shrill alarm. Mind the gap between us. One victory is permissible, but take care.

I call my mother and break the news of my sister's triumph, making it mine this way. Isn't it exciting? Aren't we so proud? I don't have to pretend to be excited and proud; I *am* excited and proud, just also miserable and empty. My mother is overjoyed. "Wow," she says, "that's—" and she pauses for a split second before concluding, "you two are really something."

I remember us, face-to-face across the kitchen table after school eating identical snacks—two fruit roll-ups, a bowl of cheese puffs apiece— watching each other chew with excruciating slowness. The goal was to finish last, to be left with something when the other had nothing. Sometimes I would seem to finish first, and she would gloat briefly over her remaining treasure, and then, once she had swallowed every last crumb, I would bring out the morsel I had hidden in my lap and make a show of savoring it.

Years later, the goal was to push the still full plate away, another kind of not finishing. When, at eighteen, she came back from several months abroad, our first sustained physical separation, she had lost a lot of weight. I tried restricting, and managed to starve myself down about twenty pounds, but sooner or later deprivation always gave way to a gorge. I ended up in an in-patient facility where the rooms and halls and lawns were bursting with barely suppressed envy.

The bulimics coveted the willpower of the anorexics; the anorexics wished they could let loose like us. (It's hard to think of a more destructive "cure" than bringing a bunch of eating disordered girls and women together under one roof so that they can go on a manic comparison spree, but that's what this facility did, and our parents paid them for it.) It strikes me now that restriction, bingeing, and purging are, among other things, attempts to get the ugliness of envy, the ugliness of de-

418

sire under control, by starving it, or sating it, or releasing it once and for all.

My roommate was a fifty-year-old suburban housewife so tentative in her existence that her eyeballs seemed to tremble in their sockets. At home she consumed exactly one cup of grapes per day; at the facility she had to chew and swallow her meals under surveillance like the rest of us.

One walleyed dirty blonde had been driven deranged by her basement treadmill. I never heard her complete a sentence that did not reference this treadmill: how many miles she had got up to, how many hours and calories burned, which man said he was impressed by her endurance, which bad family member had tried to keep her from her machine. She had spent a quarter of her life sprinting in place and she was going to run out the rest the same way.

I think about these women now, and how obvious it was that at every session we were all (patients and counselors) mentally comparing the bodies in the room and the stories attached to them. I wonder why we talked so much about food, weight, family, sex, but never about the one feeling that united us.

Envy is silent. It leaves us ashamed, inarticulate. As Schoeck observes, "It is remarkable how seldom the vernacular forms of different languages permit one to say directly to another person: 'Don't do that. It will make me envious!'"

A stunningly beautiful famous woman posts a picture of herself, always with a caption that is either jokey or empowering, as though the proud display of her beauty represents oppression overcome. Every so often one of her millions of followers will reply with an "ugh, so gorgeous" or an "I can't even" or occasionally a friendly "OMG I hate you." This is the closest we come to discharging the barely contained fury coursing through the comment feed. "ANGEL!" people shout. "PURE WARRIOR GODDESS!" "YASS!" "YOU'RE SO PERFECT!" It's like we are stoning her with compliments.

My sister has been staying with me during the outbreak, helping with childcare. Tonight in the kitchen my husband and I start fighting again about something stupid—whether it's safe to refrigerate tomato paste in the can. When our voices get sharp my sister quietly leads my daughter upstairs and starts running the bath. I hear her sweet, clear voice singing an improvised song about scrubbing, punctuated by gleeful shrieks and demands for more. She is the kind of aunt who throws her whole soul into every goof. I am grateful; during her stay here I have come to rely on her as a coparent. Yet there are times when the love between the two people I need most in the world threatens me. "You can't need anything from your child," says my mother when I call her in tears.

After my daughter falls asleep I knock softly on my sister's door. She is sitting in bed with her laptop on her lap. "Whatcha reading?" is never an innocent question with us now; we are often racing to finish the same batch of submissions. Sitting alone at my desk, skimming pages, I wonder, What does she think of this manuscript? If she values it, then I will value it. If she dismisses it, then I am bored.

The great dream of my life is to succeed in collaboration with my sister, harmonize with her, shine with her, but the reality is that we almost never manage this. Instead I am often stupefied by her eloquence, disturbed by her peace, extinguished by her light. She seems to cancel me. When she gains weight or gets a pimple on her face or fails at something, I rejoice inwardly for a millisecond before I recover myself and quash this hideous joy with shame.

In Miloš Forman's *amadeus*, the composer Salieri, who calls himself the "patron saint" of mediocrities, is tormented by envy of Mozart. In middle school I became fixated on Salieri, recording his monologues from the movie, which are accompanied by musical movements, and listening to them on my Walkman while at school. I felt, though I couldn't have expressed it at the time, that Mozart's music became more beautiful—inexpressibly, unbearably beautiful—when heard through the scrim of impotence and longing that was the Salieri filter. He suggested to me that a note of envy might be inextricable from the experience of beauty, and maybe the experience of love, too. Schopenhauer writes that envy "builds the wall between *Thee* and *Me* thicker and stronger"; sympathy, in his formulation, tears the wall down. But maybe they're both adaptations to each other—sympathy a penance for primal aggression, envy a defense against annihilating love.

❋   ❋   ❋

At ten, my sister and I had been sent to separate schools so that we could develop our own identities. I never questioned the logic of this separation, and I don't think my parents did either; it was simply the done thing. At my new school I set to work. The quickest and easiest way to differentiate was to become "the bad one." I dyed my hair a dark color and took up smoking. I got my period first. Smoked a joint first. Kissed a boy first. Dropped acid first. Got to first, second, and third base first. Got home first. Got home with my sister in the room, lying perfectly still under the covers of her twin bed while I inhaled sharply.

I got home with a boy we'll call A. He was on the basketball team, and after school I would sit and watch his lanky body move under the yellow lights of the gym. I was so in love with him that my hands shook whenever he was in the same room with me. This continued well into my twenties.

A therapist would say I was looking to re-create the closeness of the twin bond and was doomed to disappointment, and yes, I behaved with A as though we shared one body. I found separating from him even for just a matter of hours physically painful. Once I got down on my knees on the sidewalk outside of school and grabbed him around the legs to keep him from walking away, but he walked away anyway, his black Air Jordans dragging me down the street until I came undone. And yes, of course he befriended my sister and they remained friends after he told me he didn't love me anymore.

When, at twenty-six, my sister told me that my worst fear about A had been justified—that he had pursued her, declared his feelings for her—I drew a blank and laughed. Why hadn't she told me sooner? "I thought it would be better if you didn't know," she said. I was never angry with her, or I never expressed my anger. How could I? It wasn't her fault she was so lovable, so calm and unassuming and perfectly opposite to me, who had screamed and begged and sent A email upon email filled with below-the-belt insults and declarations of everlasting devotion, who had been so needy, so totally bulimic in every way. For months I wrote to him and heard nothing. Until suddenly there was a reply and I was sick with excitement. I clicked the bold text. He had written me one line: "Stop. You have earned enough credits to graduate."

In retrospect I think I gave up on the idea of trying to be a writer at that moment. What is the point of stringing words together if you can't argue someone into loving you? How good can you possibly be if you fail to persuade?

Of all the definitions of envy I have read, the simplest and most terrifying comes from the psychoanalyst Harry Stack Sullivan, who wrote, "Envy may be an active realization that one is not good enough."

For years the thought of A, always intrusive, was accompanied by an image: I pictured a tall glass filled to the lip with the foulest black liquid, and I knew that I would have to drink it all. I repeated a merciless mantra to myself, hoping that it would toughen me up, though it turned out the tall glass was bottomless—the breast that never stops lactating, because you never stop sucking it. "For a fact, A does not love you. For a fact, he loves your sister."

Here is where the metamorphosis begins. You take to your bed and daydream a different outcome for days, pausing only to sleep, and when daylight attacks, you roll over and daydream some more. You make a comfortable home in what Dickens called "the vanity of unworthiness." Here, you cannot go any farther down. You are at the bottom of the ocean, the bottom of the family. You stay down there, streaming entire seasons of whatever on your iPad, going back and forth from bed to kitchen, chewing and swallowing until your jaw aches, salty chips from the bag, whole packages of stale rye crackers smeared with cold butter, ice cream that comes back up into the toilet in cold sweet glugs. Here at the bottom, in your state of obstructed agency, you are free to hoard all the ugliness—and by extension, all the humanity—for yourself.

This can't last. You may not be good enough, but you are still going to get up and leave the house and work and get married and have a child and love your sister and try to be there for her when she feels like the other one. I remember the night a few years ago, when I came home to find her sitting hunched on my front steps, her long hair curtained in front of her splotchy wet face. I was doing well then, seeing an excellent therapist twice a week, exercising regularly, sticking to a healthy diet, getting promoted, working on a new style of self-talk that I planned to use on my sister when she calmed down a little.

It took us forever to climb the four flights to my apartment because she kept stopping to clutch the bannister and sob, as though something were trying violently to escape her body and she had to stand still to help it. I remember being in a light, strong, masterful mood. Upstairs, as soon as I got my apartment door open she collapsed on the rug, unable to make it the extra few steps that would have landed her on the couch. I put the kettle on, then went and sat cross-legged on the floor and lifted her head into my lap and rubbed it gently, noticing the slight stiffness at the roots of her hair. (I remember sitting like this, but reversed, my head in her lap, on the steps of a church in Paris while she carefully cleaned my ears. We were teenagers and hadn't seen each other in months and we had gone straight from the airport to a pharmacy to buy Q-tips because we knew that *this* would be the way back, to sit quietly and groom each other like monkeys.) After a while her breathing slowed and I thought she might be asleep, or in the trance-like state that sometimes steals over a person in the middle of a breakdown and that can, in my experience, be quite pleasant. But then she turned and looked up at me and said, her lips twisting, "I feel like you're leaving me behind."

Nominated by The Yale Review

POETS

fiction by ELIZABETH TALLENT

from THE THREEPENNY REVIEW

To begin with I held them in awe. Tell me one time awe turned out well.

The poet with the frank gap between her front teeth was once the seraph *Suburban Housewife*. Babies, martinis. Her gestures run from folding to stacking to tucking in to combing out snarls to stirring to cutting into little pieces to buttering to dishing out to drying off to fucking to smoothing down his tie before the husband goes out the door until one evening Vietnamese kids running from the cloud gaining on them cower behind her ribs. Cambridge, crowns of sonnets, Lowell smoking and holding forth, pacing miles around the seminar table, ranting them into transcendence, pausing to lay a hand on her head, blessing that became the first poem in *Napalm*. Yale Series of Younger, ylang-ylang on her pulse points, abortions, Rinpoche, vision quest in Joshua Tree, second book, third, tenure. Fourth, fifth, fame. Her name became shorthand for seducing a straight girl, her Pulitzer'd essays hitchhiked in ten thousand backpacks, on a talk show she unbuttoned to display the rose thorned by double mastectomy stitchery. *Cinderblock*, she nicknamed *Collected Poems of*. Through all of this the gap between the poet's teeth stood by her.

I know a poet who's ridden for thousands of miles in boxcars and a poet who's driven everywhere in a black limousine so long it has trouble turning a corner. The boxcars clatter through poem after poem. The limousine idles at the curb just outside.

The poet and I, introduced five minutes before, were naming names, seeking affinities, curating minor coincidences. She mentioned another poet, a generation older, who'd been something of a mentor to her without ever having seemed to particularly like her, and I'd said that was funny, I taught there for a while, she never liked me, either, after which the newly met poet and I traded details of the older poet's unraveling. How nobody knew *what* was going on. The older poet's tone, in conversation and in poems, had always been fey, trance-like, her perfume had cost a fortune and her eyes were very green—they still were, but it wasn't fun, what was going on in them. The word in her jacket blurbs had been *otherworldly*, but people understood something had gone really wrong and had stopped saying it. Her original lyric hallucinations seemed like warnings, now.

I remember when I found *Siren*, I said. I stole it from the bookstore where I was working.

There weren't that many of them, the poet said. Women whose books were worth stealing.

Schadenfreude had vanished from our attitudes, mine and the poet's.

She was who I wanted to be, the poet said.

I heard she showed up barefoot for a reading.

We had stripped down to heartsickness.

The poet said:

Once I was at her house for dinner, and she goes, You've got to see my little girl. Who was barely one. We'd been drinking and it was really late and I said But she's asleep right? but she's insisting, insists I follow her up the stairs and then she opens the door to the baby's room and hits the light switch and the baby wakes up blinking. Because the light smashed down. We're in the doorway looking in. And she, she turns to me like okay? And clicks the light off and closes the door and we go back downstairs and she tips more wine into our glasses as if nothing's wrong. As if there's no howling.

The poet and I crouched close. We might have been stranded in the taiga, blowing together on a little heap of tinder.

Poets suspect that fiction writers say things about their books like *Excellent use of white space*, and they're not wrong.

Academia, it turns out, isn't a party you can lurk in a corner of, unnoticed. That had been my plan, to receive a paycheck and so-called

425

health benefits while being left alone. I was unaware of academia's worst sin, *lack of collegiality*, but I soon found out. Creative Writing Programs operated like remote mountain villages, by ancestor worship, ritual scarification, covert infatuations across clan boundaries. You would have thought my personality would have fended off attraction, incandescently fucked-up as I was, but fucked-uped-ness proved no impediment to sleeping with poets, those first responders of the soul. Still, I was sorry to be the burning building, story after story needing to be searched. Or, first I was sorry, then I was jealous: hideous awkwardness that struck me as needing three hundred pages' explanation became, in a poem, the kinked hair stuck to a lover's tongue. I would have liked to have gone into the night as myself and to have come out of it smelling of smoke, cat cradled in my arms, or something, just something alive.

There are poets who want the whole thunderstorm and poets for whom the shine left in an antelope's hoofprint is enough.

There was one poem of his that killed me. In the poem a woman was cheating on her husband with the poet. She and the poet slept together in her bed, in her house; in the poem, it couldn't be helped, what they felt for each other. Other obsessions of mine at the time were Cat Stevens singing "Wild World" and JFK-assassination conspiracy theories, and while I didn't give those up, I understood the poem had induced a more worthwhile greed. *Throw your shoe, hit a writer*, my students said about the little Iowa town. The poet had a new book and it wasn't long before he came for a reading. Winter, the windshield snowing over in the time I spent twisting the key, reciting my dad's old incantation when yanking the cords of lawnmowers or fishing-boat outboards, Comeon comeon comeon, invoking the tender futility that had been my dad's apology to recalcitrant machinery for his baffled, conciliatory manner of dealing with it, an apology my gender should have rendered extraneous, but I was his daughter and his *Comeons* issued from my mouth in the frigid space capsule of the partially buried Bug and his emotions rose in my heart and milled around uncertainly, and I was ashamed that he, my father, was in some sense *here* for this freezing inkling, these minutes of trying to start the freezing car that would carry me to—right there, it felt shameful to recognize what I had of course known all along, that what I wanted was to fuck the poet, to become aware of that before my father with the weird sincerity he had directed at inanimate objects had completely vacated my heart, but then, luckily, or I thought "luckily," my father, the particular adorable shade of my father conjured by a good dose of futility in relation to a dead-seeming machine, *trailed off* in the dodgy transit through streets vacated by the power outtage to Prairie Lights. I eked the VW into the last available niche and climbed out to find the world had come much closer than ever before, and was, in a sense, meeting my gaze with its own gaze, crowding in toward me, rushing, urgent, but soft, too, coming in the softest touches I was capable of perceiving, and I was rising through them to the black from which they issued, it seemed to me I could easily have vanished then and there, that with another breath I could, if I gave the purest, most absolute consent, align myself with the force willing me to disappear into it. In its rawness it was the coldest, quietest wildness I have ever come close to, but what is the *it* of *its rawness*? I'm not, now, in a position to lecture that girl with the snow falling toward her. Something writers envy poets for is the way, pausing at the mike between poems, they get to do a little soft-shoe, explain allusions, flash their charming real selves. In the poem I wanted to hear, the woman he's just slept with is standing in the doorway watching the poet go, and you know he has to go, and you know it's killing them. Suddenly she kisses the doorframe. I walked in just in time. That poem, he prefaced by saying *Everybody who's had an affair raise your hand*. In his loft in Salt Lake City he had a brass bed and the Indian motorcycle he rode into the desert, moonlit nights. He was easy-going, elusive, suicidal. I didn't get the chance to know him well. There was only what he was willing to let me see, which—I understand now—was wisely calibrated to what I was willing to see. *It wasn't serious* is the sentence that offers itself when I wonder about what happened between me and him, and it's true, it was only serious beforehand, it was only, for two minutes in an empty parking lot, a matter of life or death.

A red-haired *Truth is beauty, beauty truth* acolyte so prone to quoting the letters that an hour of talking to the poet held the exasperation you'd experience talking to the actual Keats—resurrected, hauled through time, affronted by the speed of everything's unfolding, by the dominion of brutality. The poet even went in for a pale, vested, high-collared look. On the page this anachronistic courtliness continued, lines ruled by meter and wistfulness. One day a young woman showed me a note he had written. *You fucking cunt*, it began.

The first time we met, the poet threw her arms wide and waited. Almost nobody persists in such a gesture if the summonee stays put, but the poet was known for her unwillingness ever to back down, and even if that unwillingness struck me as wrongly deployed against my hanging-back, which I would have imagined, from her work, she'd be sensitive to, alert as her poems are to multiple shadings of transgression and coercion, still her flung-wide welcome, sustained, cast my immobility, more and more, as gracelessness, and if there's one thing I can't bear facing it's that glaring deficit, my gracelessness, next thing I knew she was stream-of-consciousnessing hotly into my ear: *You won't break will you?—the solstice, fortuitous!—it's been men men men men men here, I mean I love men—feel your teensy shoulderblades!—I told everyone oh, no I've never even met her—teensy—really I stayed out of it, I was away while she was hired, said not a word, the men did something good for once!*—the disillusionment of finding out zero sisterhood had been involved, she hadn't fought for me after all, should have hit me like a ton of bricks, but didn't. Somehow, I could never figure out how, she had a way of making her obliviousness entrancing. Charismatic, as if what you'd secretly always longed for in your dealings with others was not, as you'd believed, clear-eyed comprehension of who you really were, but just this anxious, self-serving puzzling-out of what use you could be, to her. An editor at the magazine, having red-pencilled the word, explained *The magazine frowns on the use of "oblivious."* Frowns. This was on the phone. In phone conversations I was always ending up with my hands full, emotionally. The littlest things were always causing me to have to stop to try to damp down emotion, and because I was busy minding that billboard-sized magazine frown, what I said back had the note I most loathed in my own repertoire, a chastened feminine obligingness ineptly masking acid dissent: *Oh.* Pause. *Why?* The editor: *It can mean "unaware of," or it can mean "indifferent to," either of which is more exact than "oblivious," and they're different, and the writer ought to know which it is,* and without knowing what I was going to say I said *But what if the writer doesn't know, if the not-knowing, not being sure, is more interesting than exactness, then isn't "oblivious" the word?* but *oblivious* didn't get back into that story, though it can stay here, in this scene where I probably should have been able to tell whether what the poet was was *unaware of* or *indifferent to,* because I was right there. I mean, I was in her arms.

Keats was in the wrong century, otherwise we would have *Fanny. You fucking cunt.*

In Washington DC for a conference I sat in the hotel's rooftop bar with other writers. I was wearing a sleeveless little black dress and had kicked my heels off and was rubbing my stockinged feet against each other, *sssst sssssst ssssst*, till I told myself in my mother's voice *Cut it out, that's annoying.* The bar overlooked the White House, whose pillars were theatrically uplit. The white-neon lonesomeness of those pillars was opposed by the misted-over modesty of the surrounding low-lying cityscape. Diffused light glowed brighter and blurred out as the fog came in and it took me a while to comprehend that while its crawl seemed uniform in depth the fog was gaining and buildings were disappearing. Boas of gray furred the uplights below the pillars, diffusing their blaze to a weak pallor. Only upper stories were left and even the high air we were breathing began to smell of river. I told the poet sitting near me that it seemed like our view ought to have been outlawed on the grounds that it would be excellent for snipers. The poet had been musing and should have been left alone, but that was the sort of mistake I could get away with then. He was among the last of the Beats, old, cowboy-lean, glamorous, with a black eye-patch half-hidden by a boyish hank of hair. The eye-patch took me in. He turned from me back to the stray lights filtering through the crawl of fog and said *If that was the world, I would walk out into it.*

And, see, he knew I was never going to know what he meant. He black-eyepatched me for good.

The poet was troubled, she told me, by my disputatious attitude toward male colleagues. In particular, she told me, I needed to learn to like F. Her tone startled me—a little grenade of savagery. The poet lived in the same faculty-housing complex I did, and, without intending to, we often ended up walking home together after events, and at the sidewalk leading to her door, we would pause, and the pause nearly always occasioned a reprimand along these lines. The first time this happened, I laughed—the quick, disbelieving hiccup of being jarred from one's presumed immunity to attack. Time after time, despite the suffering asperity of her manner as she broached the question of my disliking F, I made things worse with that laugh. Often, defensively—and defensiveness was a mistake—I objected that I worked hard at collegiality with F. Things I failed to say: *You're a famous feminist!*, *What are you doing!*, *You know why I don't like F!* and if I had told her how compulsive and intrusive this conversation seemed to me, what might have changed, would anything have changed?, but as it was I grew, in a minor way, harder of heart, achieving the ultimate rudeness, through bearing with her as-I-saw-it craziness, of dismissing the person we are with as inconsequential, figuring these attempts at correction were her way of saying goodnight. This night, though, well before the usual moment at her door, she lost her temper, and I did, too, all my stored-up incredulity emptied into the shout *You've got to be fucking kidding me*, and the longer we stood there, sliced at by mercurial March rain, the worse this was going to get, her vitality made it impossible to think of her as frail but she was asthmatic and we still had three-quarters of a cold dark mile to go. Without waiting for a lull in her rant I walked away. Only after five or six steps did I grasp what I had been seeing: she was shaking. The terribleness of that flickered at me but failed to claim my attention. I was thinking in slashes, in obliterations, *Crazy* and *I should neverof stood still for this* and *Why, why, why are we even talking about asshole F*, the rain really coming down, my glasses fogging. I took them off and walked blind. She was seventy-five, she was shouting, farther and farther behind, *Elizabeth!* April was the month of her death. When I read them now her poems are—but my relation to her poems can't be called *reading*, it's just me trying to scrabble back to that night and re-write it, by which I mean re-live, willing myself to turn around and go back and try, to at least try, and while you're at it, fool, take an umbrella to hold over her head.

When I was twenty-four, in Santa Fe, I was a little in love with my best friend, a fragile-seeming poet of Chinese descent who lived alone on a mesa three hours' drive north and who, liking solitude and having almost no money, had little reason ever to come to the city. For the dangerous slump of its adobe walls, the sheets of corrugated tin threatening to sail from its roof, and antique electrical wiring, the house she lived in should have been condemned; her rent was fifty dollars a month. Its narrow windows had the original glass, showing oval bubbles of the glassblower's breath—exhaled in 1874, the poet liked to say, touching the tip of her tongue to the pane. When I spent the night, we slept chastely in her bed. Apart from the bed, her possessions made a Rilkean inventory, as in *Maybe we're here only to say* typewriter, table, chair, cup, bowl, fork, spoon, knife, *things that in themselves never dreamed of existing so intently.* I used to tease that if I ever pulled open a kitchen drawer to find two forks, I would know she was in love. Once we were under the quilt she would tell me to look up and I would say What? and she would say Keep looking and I would say It's not a spider is it? because it wasn't impossible that she would have come to love a spider if one lived there, and she would take my hand and straighten my pointer finger and point it, saying softly: Bang. There it was there for the seeing, the bullet hole in the rough smoke-dimmed plaster. She was not a holder or toucher, and I was enchanted by her seizing my finger, willing to pretend I had no idea what was up there, though on each of the half dozen nights I spent under her raggedy quilt, which smelled inexplicably of dry grass, she pointed it out, and it seemed unlikely that she'd have forgotten, but maybe it was a playlet about what sex would have been like between us, first the having-no-idea-what-comes-next, then the Oh, then the pretense of complete forgetting. In that comfortless three-room warren her migraines disappeared, and the insomnia that had been her life's torment. Mice ate the corners of her books, she went without wood for the woodstove in order to pay for typewriter ribbons, she wrote page after page and her lines were getting so long, she said, she had to turn the paper sideways before feeding it into the platen. I got it into my head that she ought to meet another poet, older, more famous, a big, rangy, feral, several-affairs-at-once spellbinder who was also precarious beyond belief, though because he was six foot three and a world-class dissembler, he struck me as being vulnerable when, and only when, it suited him—manipulatively vulnerable. In short: anyone could have seen that for the two of them to meet could only bring disaster. In the restaurant, while the older, more famous poet and I waited for her, and though I tried to talk him out of ordering wine, he began drinking, and he drank through the first and into the second hour of her failing to show up, and then he was done. He was like that, he could be suddenly, absolutely done. Standing up, he said *Why are you doing this?* I said *There she is* and she was coming through the crowd toward us and every head turned to watch her. She had not tried, she was above trying, she wanted nothing from anyone. When she sat down at our table, I told them each other's names, and they said their first sentences to each other—shy, fraught. The older poet poured wine into the glass that had been waiting for her, and she drank, and they talked, and when they left off talking, she bent her head so that her hair fell forward, not slippingly, like mine might have done, but all at once, black claps of hair, and then she was quiet. They both were. She appeared to be exerting prodigious effort to stay in her chair. To hold supremely still. And my sense was that she was honoring the advent of life-altering emotion. And that I was at least there to see it happen. To see her fall. But I minded it, too—minded the inevitability of their devouring each other's attention. Each other's lives, maybe. She was wearing a long-gone boyfriend's pajama bottoms and the huge, smoke-scented, crudely knitted, black sweater she said she needed to wear while writing, a talismanic garment I'd never seen her wear out of the house before, whose unravelling cuffs could be pulled down over her hands when she could no longer feel her hands, but they were out now, her hands, white-knuckled around the stem of a wineglass. Apart from the wineglass stem there was no other touching, and as it became clearer and clearer that the two of them were not into each other, my relief grew, and gratitude to the poet for having deflected his interest by her strange, stalwart immobility. Only later did she explain. Overnight, fleas had infested her house, and they'd come along—as soon as she sat down at the table, inside the black sweater, fleas started jumping. It was very distracting, she said, being bitten while you are trying to talk. Bitten all over, and all I wanted to do was scratch, and I knew if I scratched just once, I wouldn't be able to stop.

The wintry, quaintly goatee'd countenance of the poet who'd gone to Japan before anyone, five lean and barefoot Zen-monastery years had left him knowing the ropes, and they were in his poems, the ropes, things-as-they-are poems of falling snow and the breasts of women and highways and hawks riding thermals, *catnip to women* was what my colleague said he'd been, irresistible, haven't you read *Dharma Bums*, that's him, you know, who does that sex thing, said my punk Woolf-scholar colleague, that thing where a woman takes him inside her while he sits cross-legged without moving and he's rock hard and it lasts for hours, I've always wanted to try it, she said, and I said, Now? She had one of those quicksilver temperaments, herself—good for Woolf scholarship, inclined to impatience in civilian conversations. I said He's old. She said In years maybe. I was sort of into her and willing to play along. As opposed to soul, you mean? Because haggard. Old. Old. Old! Is how he seems soul-wise. She said she was talking about dick age. For proof she pointed out the *Chronicle*'s reporting some wisecrack of his mother's about his having left his fifth wife and taken up with what the paper called a younger woman who was now installed in the cabin he'd hand-hewn from ponderosa pines he'd felled himself on his land in the Sierras, property whose hot spring featured in the poem he liked to open his readings with, a poem in which he and his then wife and their little boy waded in naked and the son's penis perks up and the poet ruefully celebrates the little erection for embodying the beauty of the world as he has known it, the world his son will walk out into, and the Woolf scholar wondered if that had been her who'd gotten into the paper as the woman he'd left his fifth wife for if she'd have been called a younger woman and then she said the way things were going she was never going to get to sit on the poet's dick for hours. He had asthma and after everything he'd been through his Roshi was refusing to deem him a Zen master. I had grown up with a father who went around smoldering and I recognized the force field radiating from the poet so the refusal to deem him a Master seemed fair enough to me but I kept my mouth shut because I had to work with the guy, and who did I have to talk to, anyway, except a punk Woolf scholar who all that year mourned missing the chance to sit on his dick, maybe meaning it, maybe not? In faculty meetings, she and I, the only women, would sit at a corner of the table, and with her hand hidden from view, she would gaze meaningfully across the room at the otherwise-absorbed poet while the hand in her lap made an eloquent jacking-off motion whose prowess and mockery were witnessed only by me. And I wish I could write that that was fun, or that it was subversive, or that the mischief of it bonded us, but all it did, really, was worry me, because she was sort of compulsive about it and because it began to seem like a worse and worse thing to be secretly doing, and it was strange to find this brilliant exquisitely sensitive person obsessively enacting a sexual taunt directed at a poet she claimed, in every other context, to revere, and didn't it diminish him somehow, in his unawareness, to be mocked with furtive prowess, under the table we all sat around, and why, really, why was I sitting there with my craven mouth shut, thinking Stop. I would contract my peripheral vision until my focus was narrowly directed at the place where he sat. The poise of his motionlessness was perfect. Strange, too. I tried to describe it to myself by thinking of him as being distinctly outlined. If you looked away from him, the next person you focused on appeared to be leaking from themselves. Sitters oozing out not-really-here-ness, just as I was always doing. Not-really-meaning-it-ness showed in face after face after face till you got to his. Old words wanted to be used in his case. The jawbone below the glaze of stubble was as suddenly beautiful as if I'd been hit over the head with it. The set of the shoulders in the artful Japanese denim shirt told of authority with an ax, and it was reassuring to think that if you got stranded out in the wilderness with him the blade would ring through kindling and the spark nestled in tinder would answer to his breath and you could warm yourself at the blaze he had made—some *despair* arose due to this, my quasi-confrontation with him, whoever he was, and I balked, I wanted to get a hold on things, the hold I usually had, I was acquainted with my despairs and thought I knew them all, but this one, anarchic and indifferent but feeling mostly old, old, old, old, *old*, insanely old and wily and inarticulate, insouciantly potent, prodigal, unasked-for, *fleet* was my thought, as fleet as if it came from way far back, was nothing I'd ever felt before, and by this onslaught I was dragged from my known self, that fortress, dragged out a ragdoll fool—and right then, with a fractional turn of his head, he caught me staring, and by some quirk of timing we gave each other these real little smiles, his lacking his trademark fearful symmetry, deeper in one corner than the other, droll, intimate, yes that was it, it was intimate!, and mine, mine was steady and freakishly tender, a smile that gave away the whole shebang, ending when I tuned into the voice of the Woolf scholar. She had leaned close to my shoulder and was saying something truculent and funny, which I heard and immediately forgot, because who wants ironic knowingness when life can do this, write something beautiful in a heartbeat?

The canaries have been singing like mad for a hundred years now, and we're all still down in the mines.

The poet with beautiful dreads talked gorgeously, offensively, with jouissance, with nerve, fantastically, somberly, ironically, self-deconstructingly, jumbledly, first lines of neverwrittendown poems flying by, images gleaming and sucked under, neverwrittendown last lines like wasp stings, like dying falls, talked headlong, righteously, bruisingly, talked as if she had been told she was to have her throat cut in the morning and had one night to get all the words out, with despairing ferocity, improvisationally but with guileful set pieces inserted here and there, rants whose theatricality would have worked before an audience of four hundred, meaning that, because it was only the poet and me, three hundred and ninety-nine people were missing.

If poets and fiction writers attend a party, they'll segregate themselves, each cluster as comradely and comfortable as Victorian men settling down for cigars and serious talk, now that the pernicious listeners have been banished.

Beginning about a year ago, the Irish poet began interrupting conversations about quite other things in order to narrate some incident or other from her childhood, except *interrupting* is wrong, she was such a beguiling and authoritative talker that when she began it was not as if others' interests had been forsaken but as if the entire table's submerged obsession had at last asserted itself and we were all finally on the right track. At program dinners she told of the illiterate cook who had fed and cosseted her in the kitchen of the residence allotted to her ambassador father; her mother's having been talked out of an abortion by a charming doctor while pregnant with her, the poet; her father's admiration for the American delegates who in post-Versailles negotiations advocated for giving tractors to desperate German farmers. What is a *childhood*, and why was she parceling it out now to tablesful of listeners, when she had always held forth about everyone except herself? She was a sluice-style talker, mischievous, formidable, a compulsive pourer-out of others' secrets, but these were the only self-disclosing stories I had known the poet to tell, though I'm not sure how much exactly one discloses about oneself if that self is, in the stories, a child. Her mother telling her "My dear, I've had more affairs than you've had hot suppers." The stories were anti-mysterious, barely a sentence or two. Seldom more. Her glee was lovely, and her imitation of voices long gone. And you might have been charmed, but you probably wouldn't have thought the stories themselves remarkable. Nothing was unfolded, no truth driven home. Things-as-they-once-were glinted from the dark, that was all. After this year of changed stories, the poet suddenly died.

A poet who never uses italics said of her: Of everyone I know, she was the *least* likely to die.

Sometimes I think we are all in the dark, we keep ourselves in the dark and other forces keep us in the dark, and the poets, at least, are digging.

Tell me what you'd give for a little light.

Nominated by The Threepress Review

MOTHERFUCKERS TALKING SHIT ABOUT AMERICAN SONNETS

by SAM CHA

from CLARION MAGAZINE

I know what you want: to waggle your tongue
in the old ferment, the pure Elizabethan
product, hundred proof, guaran fucking teed
to make you go buckwild, flushed, knock kneed,
toe-curled, blank-eyed, blank-versed, brain all snow-white
till you spill your thin blancmange down your tidy-
whiteys and come—back to yourself. I get
it. Sometimes I'd also like to forget
that I'm no longer young. But the sonnet doesn't
belong to you. There's nothing to own. Not a spit
of land nor spitcurl of rivulet for your chickenwire,
   your snares,
your chickenshit sneers—where's the rhyme scheme?
   Who cares.
Not Shakespeare. Not Keats, not Drayton, not Donner.
It's not your lawn. (Yawn.) Stop yelling. Be done.

Nominated by Lloyd Schwartz

MALY, MALY, MALY

fiction by ANTHONY VEASNA SO

from THE PARIS REVIEW

Always they find us inappropriate, but today especially so. Here we are with nowhere to go and nothing to do, sitting in a rusty pickup truck, the one leaking oil, the one with the busted transmission that sounds like the Texas Chainsaw Massacre. Here we are with the engine running for the AC, the doors wide open for our bare legs to spill out. Because this, right here, to survive the heat, this is all we have.

An hour ago we became outcasts. One of us—not me—would not shut the fuck up. And since the grandmas are prepping for the monks and need to focus, we've been banished outside to choke on traces of manure blown in from the asparagus farms surrounding us, our hometown, this shitty place of boring dudes always pissing green stink.

And according to the Mas, everything about us appears at once too masculine and too feminine: our posture—backs arching like the models in the magazines we steal; our clothes—the rips, studs, and jagged edges—none of it makes sense to them. The two of us are wrong in every direction. Though Maly, the girl cousin, strikes them as less wrong than the boy cousin, me.

"Ma Eng can suck my dick," Maly says, still not shutting the fuck up, her long hair rippling in the gas-tainted breeze of the vents, her blond-orange highlights dancing, or trying to, anyway. "What is up her ass? Seriously, I should have a say in this party's fucking agenda. It's my birthright!"

"At least Ma Eng gives a fuck about you," I say, my chin resting on the steering wheel. Under the truck, the cracked concrete of Ma Eng's driveway seems to be steaming, and I swear the very dust in the air is

437

burning, it's so hard to breathe. We can't even listen to the radio, you know? Can't focus on anything but our own sweaty boredom. I look up at the harsh blue sky, how it crushes the squat duplexes of G Block. I am trying to deprive Maly of my full attention, but her vivid presence, that vortex of cheap highlights, it exhausts my energy. Plus, she's slapping the side of my head.

"Ves, Ves, Ves!" Maly says. "Look at me!"

"Jesus," I whine, batting her hand away. "I thought you 'gave zero fucks' about this party. Why do you care if they're making amok or not?"

"It's what *I* want to eat, okay, and it's *my* dead mom." She violently throws her head sideways, cracking her neck. "I mean, apparently she's not *dead* dead, anymore, but still . . ."

Unsure of what to say, I clench my teeth into a lopsided smile. I can't help but admire her looks, as I always do. Almost with pride. Maly's got it going on, no matter how disheveled. Even today, on this random August Sunday, as we wait to celebrate the rebirth of her dead mother's spirit in the body of our second cousin's baby, she looks good. Her left leg's thrown up onto the dashboard, and I wouldn't be surprised if she started clipping her toenails. She's in a pair of jean shorts she stole from our other cousin, who was too chunky for them anyway, and a white T-shirt cut into a tank—also stolen—which she's stuffed down her panties so you can notice her thin waist. Hard to say if it's intentional, the way her clothes fit, all these hand-me-downs, which is the effect she uses, I guess, to chew up guys too dumb to realize she will spit them right out.

Through her cheap sunglasses, I see her bug eyes looking at me and past me at the same time, an expression affirming how I feel sometimes, like she's *my* responsibility, like I'm a dead broom reincarnated into a human, my sole purpose to sweep away her messes—whatever Maly happens to shatter next.

"Stop being dramatic," I tell her, my hands tapping the steering wheel. "You know it's all bullshit—the celebration, the monks, our third cousin or whoever the hell she is." I'm not sure I believe what I'm saying or if I'm just trying to make Maly feel better. "It makes zero sense, right?" I add. "Like, I'm no expert, but why would your mom reappear over a decade later?"

Maly shrugs her shoulders, indifferent now, too full of herself to entertain my attempts to console her. It reminds me of our sleepovers. Whenever my dad got stupid drunk, my mom would send me to Ma

Eng's. He was never violent in front of me, but who knows what happened between my parents when I was sleeping on Maly's bedroom floor, especially in those years when my dad was jobless—after his restaurant failed and before he started cooking lunch for a rich-kid school—and when it became obvious I wasn't, you know, a normal boy, that I was a girly wimp who despised sports and watched weird movies. I was a precocious freak who came out before puberty, and I was clearly doomed. It's hard enough for people like us, my mom would say. All very cliché, in that gay sob story kind of way, but I can't explain it any better than that. They are my immigrant parents.

Anyway, every night of what my mom called "bonding time with grandma," even though technically Ma Eng's my great-aunt, Maly would nudge me awake with some fake urgent question, like was she actually pretty, or even that funny? For weeks, she obsessed over our eighth grade English teacher, how he claimed she wasn't ready for the high school honors track and then refused to write her a letter of recommendation. Why do teachers always hate me? What if that stupid dirtbag is right? Every night I told her, You're awesome, everyone's a dick, and so on, only to discover that she'd fallen asleep before I even stopped talking.

I was always there for Maly, right where she wanted me, on the floor beside her bed, doling out reassurances until she sank into her dreams. Though maybe she's getting worse these days, needier than usual. Because in less than a week, I'm heading to a four-year university in LA, while Maly's stranded, stuck with Ma Eng for another two years, at least, as she makes do with community college.

Maly has closed the passenger door and is now sticking her head out of the window. She leans her right hip against the door, presses her left foot onto the center console, holding herself in place for a moment, grabbing on to the truck's roof, until she steadies herself into a stillness, like she's posing for a famous photographer. I watch her, skeptically, as she dares to go handless, crams her fingers into her mouth, and whistles a deafening sound.

"Get over here, bitch!" she shouts, and my limbs tense up.

Jogging toward us now is Rithy, his arms bulging around a basketball, baggy gym shorts flopping. He looks like he always does, all brown-kid swagger. He's the kind of guy who recites 50 Cent lyrics and loves *Boyz n the Hood* and *8 Mile* even though he doesn't—I suspect—get their political themes. This summer Rithy and Maly started fucking,

439

which makes sense, as both of them have dead moms and shitty dads, but now I have to remind myself that I've *also* known Rithy forever. That he's not just Maly's personal plaything. Her boy toy, as she calls him.

Maly returns to her seat and tilts her sunglasses down while licking her teeth. Rithy's not even at the truck yet, but there it is: *Lolita*. Neither of us has read the book, and only I've seen the movie, but working at the video store, we both stare at that fading *Lolita* poster. Usually stoned. Stoned enough we get sucked into those heart-shaped glasses, that chick's wild, don't-give-a-fuck look, the crazy bravado of that tagline— "How Did They Ever Make a Movie of *Lolita*?"—as we burn illegal DVDs for our dipshit uncle to rent out.

"Aren't you supposed to be, like, setting up a *party*?" Rithy teases as he leans against the truck's door and stretches out his legs. He's sweating all over, probably from shooting hoops at his cousin's house, and I can almost smell him. Everything Maly says about his body swirls in my head.

"We've been exiled," she tells him flatly. "'Cause every Ma has been a psycho since the genocide. It's like, as long as they don't overthrow a government and, you know, install a communist regime, they aren't being total dicks." Pleased with herself, Maly laughs.

"Your Ma's hella rad, you know it," Rithy responds. "Old lady comes through with the beef sticks." He raises the bottom of his shirt to wipe the sweat off his forehead, flashing that flat stomach of his. I don't even care if it's intentional. "What time's the party again?"

Maly flings both her hands toward the duplex, as though pushing it all away. "Go ask Ma Eng yourself. I'm fucking tired of her bullshit."

"Girl, just tell me," Rithy says, biting his lip.

"Look, we can be late for my dead mom's birthday bash, okay, it's *fine*." She closes the distance between her face and Rithy's. "We're young and beautiful and the concept of time is a fucking buzzkill."

"Six is fine," I chime in.

"Oh, hey, Ves," Rithy says, oblivious to my focus on the veins of his forearms. "Excited for college?"

"You got any weed, Rithy?" Maly interjects, slamming back into her seat.

Rithy twists his face into an even bigger smile. "You know I do."

With barely a nod, Maly tells me she'll be right back, that if I leave she'll be pissed. She gets out of the truck and walks Rithy to his uncle's duplex, just down the block, as if leading a disoriented puppy home. His hand slides down her back to hover over her ass, which sways just enough with every step. He cocks his head slightly, to witness Maly by his side, before looking forward again. Even from here, I can tell how enraptured he is by her, how much his own dumb luck astounds him, that he should be so blessed this early in his life, all of us only three months into adulthood.

And here's the part where shit gets common, right? Or rather, here's the part that makes outgrown Power Rangers twin sheets feel pretty awesome, allowing the srey to understand how men see her thick eyeliner and her fake nails, letting the proh assert power, for just a moment, over his own dark skin and his addict father with the bad, broken English. Here's the part that seems like a revelation until it's forgotten as life is lived, because nothing's special about an adulthood spent in the asshole of California, which some government official deemed worthy of a bunch of PTSD'd-out refugees, farting out dreams like it's success intolerant.

This is the part just like the thai lakorns, those soap operas from Bangkok dubbed into Khmer and burned onto wholesale discs from Costco. The srey—raggedy and poor, flush with the blood of forgotten royalty, angry from the backstabbing of wills and inheritances—cons her way into the arms of the prince whose family is the very cause of her misfortune. She allows the scheme to redeem her family's name to blind her to the feelings of real love developing beneath the high jinks, the pratfalls, her awkward but whimsical personality. Little does she know, everything will soon feel like a missed opportunity, as the prince enlists in the army to prove his manhood, because every Thai prince in every Thai soap, like every shitty proh in every shitty neighborhood, always craves some higher purpose.

For now, though, the srey basks in the prince's hot breath, the shock of secret touches, the rush of manipulation. And, hey, at least she isn't the sidekick, the faggy best friend. Because there he is, in every episode of every different version of the same dumb story: the kteuy, sidelined to the bleachers, baking in the sun, expected to get off not by his own proh but simply by the idea of the srey he supports getting hers.

Of course, all these depressing thoughts aside, I am relieved, regardless of how demeaning it feels, to have some peace as I wait for Maly and Rithy to finish fucking. I'm even happy for her, that on this nightmare of a day, she can find solace in her boy toy's tight body. Though

I'm assuming that's how Maly feels about it. She hardly ever talks about her mom in a serious way.

I look into the windows of the duplex where Ma Eng has lived since the eighties, since before Maly's mom, her niece, committed suicide, and long before she took in Maly when Maly's dad proved just another fuck-off Cambodian man. Ma Eng's pointing antagonistically at the other Mas in her kitchen, instructing them on how to cook certain dishes—not amok—for the party tonight. She's probably still pissed that Maly's shown so little respect for the ceremony's preparations. I wonder how Ma Eng must feel right now, clinging to the desperate wish that her dead sister's dead daughter has another chance at life, that the forces of rein-carnation are working their voo-doo spells to rebirth lost souls. Espe-cially those who died as pointlessly as Maly's mom, an immigrant woman who just couldn't beat her memories of the genocide, a single mom who looked to the next day, and the day after that, only to see more suffering.

Honestly, if I think about it too hard, I get really mad. I know it's ter-rible to ask, but why did Maly's mom even *have* a kid? And why does only she get to tap out of living? Well, joke's on her, I guess, because now she has to deal with yet another life, and in G Block, too.

Ma Eng's garage door opens, an uproar of Khmer thundering out of the house. Two Mas I recognize from the video store begin sweeping the concrete floor, where we will pray and eat during the party, on sedge mats that imprint our legs with red, throbbing stripes. Again I turn to face the kitchen windows, but Ma Eng has walked out of my sight. Wrap-ping my hands around the steering wheel, I think about driving off to college right now, leaving behind my worthless possessions, my second-hand clothes—all of it. I could finally start my life, with a blank slate. Only I can't, not yet anyway, as the Mas helping Ma Eng have parked their cars behind mine, blocking the driveway indefinitely.

I am about to fall asleep, the cold air from the vent and the oppressive dry heat of the afternoon competing for my skin, when Maly jumps up from under the car window and screams, "Boo!"

"What the fuck is wrong with you?" I say through the coughing fit I've been shocked into, as Maly recovers from laughing hysterically at her own antics.

She throws a joint into my lap. "Say thank you," she tells me, and waves at the Mas in the garage with a fake smile. They only stare at her, clutching their brooms like they're prepared to whack us. "Least now we won't be sober for this shit."

Yet again, like all the times she hid alcohol or lube in my bedroom, offering me a share, Maly looks out for me while remaining, to the very core, self-absorbed. "Well, we can't smoke it here," I say. "Not in front of Ma Eng's henchmen."

We agree to toke up in the closed video store, because we enjoy messing with our uncle's stuff when we're high, so we start walking the quarter mile to get out of G Block, passing duplex after duplex, all of them packed with Cambodian families and guarded by chain-link fences and patches of dirt where grass should be. Halfway to the store, I see the pink duplex my parents rented before we moved, and I remember that G Block used to be called Ghetto Way. I think of how lame and uninspired everything is, these nicknames, this neighborhood.

By the time we reach the video store's strip mall, we're drenched in sweat. The Iranian man who owns the liquor market is smoking a cigarette on the sidewalk. He ignores us, too busy leering at the Vietnamese boys outside the Adalberto's. They are throwing cherry poppers at each other's feet and passing around a Styrofoam cup—probably horchata, that's the big hit at Adalberto's—and I imagine these boys growing up into Rithys and pairing off with their own Malys. The boys now explode into laughter as one of them freaks out over the sparks of those mini firecrackers. The poor kid bolts away and Maly shouts, "Run, Forrest, run!"

Inside the empty store, we light the joint, both take hits, and then I watch Maly shuffle through the art house films our uncle inherited from the previous owner. Usually she goes straight to the back room and sprawls onto the couch, but not today. She's pretending to be a customer, for shits and giggles, and I guess I'm also pretending, by being around her. We usually split an extra-large horchata, too, and if we have enough cash a carne asada burrito—the California kind, stuffed with french fries—but only Maly manages to never gain weight, that asshole. Really, I shouldn't be complaining, even if the weed's making me bloated. I'm okay, body-wise, and the handful of times I cruised in Victory Park I learned that guys aren't picky as long as my mouth is wet and I keep my teeth in check. It was Maly, of course, who taught me how to give a proper blowjob.

I suck in another drag and take in the front room. The tacky sales rack of ten-dollar Angkor Wat shirts. The clueless stupidity of our uncle placing the candy dispensers—which are for kids, obviously—right next to the dirt-red curtain of the porn section. The store's supposed to look like a Blockbuster, but the shelves and bins are spaced out unevenly, with some aisles fitting only one person and others wide enough for jumping jacks. Right now, Maly's in a small aisle and I'm in a big one, the "horror" DVD island separating us.

Our uncle, who's actually the cousin of both my mom and Maly's mom, peaced out to the homeland for the month—probably to play house with his second family—leaving his younger brother in charge and us with the spare keys. With our older uncle gone, our other uncle disappears from lunch till closing on most days. He also refuses to work on the weekends, so the store's not open right now. A week ago, we were told to burn copies of the latest shipment of thai lakorns, to make ourselves *useful* at work, but instead we take turns smoking weed in the alley, and then pig out on candy bananas from the dispensers. We get up from the couch to man the cash register only when the front door jingles. I'm not about to spend my last week at home ripping bootleg soap operas on DVD Shrink with a second-rate laptop. Maybe that's why all the G Block grandmas are so cranky, so filled with contempt, like they're on some karmic warpath of eye rolls. We haven't burned the new thai lakorns, and thus we have cheated them of their one pleasure here in America, thousands of miles away from anything they can actually stand. At least that's what I think to myself, now, stoned as fuck.

"Swear to God," Maly says, still wearing her oversize sunglasses, even here, in this illegitimate video rental business. "These movies are fucking *weird*." In the dark reflection of her lenses, I see Maly draping me in her mom's old dresses as I wobbled on high heels, our lips painted red, eyelids smeared with shadows, before we screened another movie— like *Candyman*, we viewed that one so many times—on the PlayStation 2 my dad bought me, even though he couldn't afford it, hoping I'd be like the normal boys. "Earth to Ves!" she shouts. "The fuck's a Videodrome?"

I snap out of my daze to squint at the DVD she's now holding, by the corner like it's a dirty diaper. "Oh, yeah, I've seen that one," I say, recalling the last time I watched an actual good movie with Maly— *Suspiria*—and how she couldn't stop cracking up. Fucking idiot, Maly said when a character fell into a pit of wire and got her throat slit. "It's about this lame white guy," I explain, "who's obsessed with a TV station called Videodrome." I hit the joint and blow rings of smoke into the air, which Maly studies closely, scrunching up her face. "The station plays, like, snuff porn. You know, people being sex-tortured."

"Why not jack off to actual snuff porn?" Maly asks. "Why even bother with a dull artsy film?"

444

"It's a metaphor," I answer.

"And the metaphor means . . . what?"

"It's about how we are constantly violated by the media and . . . like . . . TV commercials . . ." I pause to flip through the thai lakorns Ma Eng forced us to watch as kids, which makes me, stupidly, think of my college essay topic: how our Khmer lessons were dubbed Thai shows with confusing plots, shitty camerawork, and female characters who all spoke with the voice of the same voiceover actress. I wrote about that, Maly, my gay sob story. "There's this part of the movie," I continue, "where the white guy's stomach turns into a vagina, you know, and then some other white guy forces a videotape into his vagina-tummy . . . The rape of our minds, or some shit."

I don't admit that when I first saw this scene, I found it tempting, and hated myself for that. Instead I pass the joint.

"That's fucking idiotic." Maly breathes the smoke into and out of her lungs, leaving the joint hanging from her mouth like a French girl in a Godard film, only brown and poor. "Raped by the media," she says, and kills the rest of the joint. "Would we even *know* English without Judge Judy?"

"Guess it's the only way we survived," I say, still searching, absentmindedly, for a thai lakorn I might recognize, for something that really pulls, or strikes, me. "Like, we had to let ourselves be violated by all those shows we loved as kids . . . *Full House, Step by Step, Family Matters*—Steve Urkel fucked us in the brains every day after school on ABC Family. 'Did *I* do that?'"

"Yes . . . that's, like, really messed up," Maly replies, and we stare at each other in silence, for a split second, before sliding into laughter.

We stay giggling until a thai lakorn finally catches my eye. "Oh, shit, remember Nang Nak?" I pick up the DVD and hold it over my face, covering my bloodshot eyes with the image of a demented woman, all black hair, pasty skin, and ghostly presence, like the Thai, low-budget version of *The Grudge*. When I lower the DVD, Maly's face looks frozen.

"Holy fuck," she says, removing her sunglasses. Without much body awareness, it seems, she tries to climb over the movie bin, almost in slow motion, as though the air has turned into a thick mud. Somehow she makes it to my aisle, struggling, tumbling onto the floor, kicking the entire Kubrick section, and right after she recovers from that unnecessary stunt, she snatches the DVD from my hands. "I haven't thought about this in years. Is this the whole thing?" She peers over the Khmer words she can't even read. "Wasn't it, like, ten thousand hours long?"

445

"I mostly remember that crazy shrieking," I say, and start impersonating Nang Nak as a vengeful mother spirit, but Maly doesn't react, so I shut up, mid-haunting screech. Then I examine her expression as she contemplates the faded DVD cover, her puffy eyes locked in a staring contest with Nang Nak's.

An eternity passes before Maly suddenly says, with a strange sincerity, "I've always thought Nang Nak was a badass." She lifts her head, and her eyes, dark orbs in the dim light, cut straight through me. "I'm serious," she says, "like . . . *fuck*, man. She haunted those assholes for years."

Just then I wish Maly could move to LA with me, that we'd keep hanging out until one of us—Maly, obviously—got discovered by some Hollywood hotshot, and then maybe I'd make movies of her, because she'd probably be a great actor, actually, the perfect muse, and what else was she going to do? Though that's also the last thing I want, and besides, I'm not attending film school. I applied and was accepted, but it was too expensive.

"I know it's stupid," Maly adds, almost shaking, "but I want my mom, like, out there, you know? Like . . . shouldn't *she* get to torment everyone, too . . . everyone who wronged her . . ."

"Right," I begin to say, unable to finish my thought. I'm not even sure I understand what she means. I place my hand on her shoulder—a useless move, I know, but it's the only thing I can offer. We hold this position, not talking or making eye contact, until Maly stops trembling. Then she nudges me off and throws the DVD down the other aisle.

She shouts in my face: "You know what we should do right now? We should play a fucking movie! One last time before you, like, leave me *forever*, you dick asshole. And let's make it big this time—epic. Okay? Let's fucking watch a porno! Seriously, stop talking about vagina-tummies and just watch some *porn* with me. See how long it takes for our minds to feel violated by the media, you know?"

I'm not sure how to gauge her enthusiasm, but then Maly dashes for the porn section. "It won't be weird," she says, her voice moving farther and farther from me. "'Cause you're gay and I'm a girl!"

The porno Maly chooses to screen on our uncle's digital projector comes across as standard shit—bright lights flattering to nothing but bouncing breasts and engorged clits and veiny dicks, all stilted dialogue and stilted facial expressions and stilted moans, the porn actors as enviable as they are gross. The whole shebang. Too many POV shots, too many close-ups meant to put the viewer right there. Seeing a sloppy wet penis enter a sloppy wet vagina, from above, going in and out with the practiced tempo of professionals, strikes me as yet another drama for the ages I am meant only to witness, rather than learn from, like the Olympics or presidential debates. My own penis feels faint, nonexistent, and not just because Maly's presence has scared it into hiding but also because I can barely project myself onto the digital projection; what am I, really, but a knockoff version of the woman getting pounded, my dick vestigial and just . . . in the way?

It's beside the point, though, whether I see myself in this porno world—where a mustachioed plumber can unclothe a big-tittied MILF with a devious smirk, an arch of the eyebrow—because, as always, Maly is forcing herself into the center of my perspective, obstructing my view of the giant, high-def vagina.

"Look . . . he's literally fucking my brains out," Maly says, standing in front of the wall we are using as a screen. From where I'm sitting on the couch, the colossal dick appears to thrust in and out of her left ear, across and through her face.

"That's cool," I say, with a half-heartedness I don't try to hide.

"The hell is your problem?" Maly snaps. "That was hilarious," she says, pacing back and forth, as she always does when her high peaks, her attempts to be fun crossing into belligerence. The image of straight sex contorts around her body, wrapping her in fleshy colors.

"Calm down, okay?" I say. "It's *your* porno."

Maly places her hand on her hips and strikes a pose, shooting me an exasperated look, and then sits down.

The porn actors are now fucking more aggressively, and I expect Maly to start heckling them, to crack a joke about the guy's grunting or the woman's moaning. I want her to make a comment that confirms the insanity of this situation. Anything that would align us together as observers of the world, of everyone else but us, outsiders who can see through the bullshit; but instead, she just goes sullen. Lost in thought, she studies the porno. So we sit in silence as the scene nears its climax, as the male actor pulls out of the female actor, as he masturbates vigorously and she writhes in ecstasy, her vagina almost calling out to his penis to unload itself. And unload it sure does, all over her inner thighs, so much so that Maly, jumping from her seat, seems to be exploding herself with some newfound motivation.

"I need to see this baby," Maly says, darting to the door.

Cleaning up so I can run after her, I stop the film and struggle to find the DVD case. Then, before I hit the eject button, the frozen image compels me to pause, and sit there, dumbfounded, stoned. I am entranced by the cum covering the woman's bottom half, though not the vagina itself, and, despite my own preferences, this reminds me of failure, somehow. Failure in its most legit form.

By the time I catch up with her, Maly's jumping the fence of our second cousin's duplex. Maybe our second cousin wouldn't mind that we're sneaking into her house, but I'm too high and paranoid to deal, and apparently Maly doesn't care about anyone's privacy or taking the extra steps to ask for permission. Anyway, it's too late to calm her down, convince her this may be unwise—breaking into the nursery of a baby who happens to be her dead mother—so I follow her nervously through the back door.

Our second cousin's napping on the couch, and I fight the urge to yell for Maly to abort her mission, to grab her by the shoulders and remind her that none of this matters, that we shouldn't partake in the stupid delusions of old people wishing their lives had gone another way, that we have each other, just as we always have, even if we're about to be separated by three hundred miles, a whole mountain range. Fuck everyone else, I want to say, for burdening the two of us with all their baggage. Let's go back to minding our own business, anything but this. Who cares about our family? What have they ever done but keep us alive only to make us feel like shit?

We find the baby's room without any mishaps, other than my growing sense of unease about following Maly down this fucked-up rabbit hole of hers. Once inside the bedroom, Maly cautiously approaches the sleeping baby. She shakes her head and clutches the rails of the crib. She looms over this tiny and new body of the mother she grew up without.

"It's uglier than I thought it would be," Maly says.

"What did you expect?" I ask from behind her, wondering what she is seeing in the baby's face, whether she recognizes a flicker of her mother's soul, or nothing at all.

"I . . ." She shakes her head again, but quickly this time. "Who do you think my kid will be?"

"You actually believe this?"

"I mean, hypothetically. What if it's Ma Eng? You know, after she dies."

"Now *that* would be serious karma."

"Shit, that'd fucking suck," Maly says. "I have zero interest in facilitating the rebirth of Ma Eng. She'll pop from my vagina reeking of Tiger Balm, pinching my ears 'cause she's, like . . . already disappointed in me. No way I'm unleashing Ma Eng onto the world all over again."

We laugh until we don't, and endure a silence together, with her back still turned to me.

Finally: "I'd totally have an abortion if I knew—like *really* knew—that Ma Eng was gestating inside of me."

"Even as a dead embryo, reincarnated, she'd haunt the fuck out of you."

"Probs," Maly responds, glancing at me from a slant. It's almost like she can't move away from the baby, like something's forcing her to confront it. "Ves . . . is it weird I want my mom reborn as . . . *my* child?"

"I don't think so," I answer. Because what else can I say?

Watching as she redirects her gaze, as she lowers her hand into the crib, I can't help but imagine Maly hurting the baby. I know that doesn't make any sense, but I worry she's about to do something terrible, even as she caresses its head, delicately, with the gentlest touch of her fingers.

"I've changed my mind," Maly says. "She's actually pretty cute."

And this, out of everything, is what chokes me up. The air suddenly stuffy, I feel the cramped dimensions of the room, the dry roof of my mouth, all the words trying to claw their way out of my throat. *Fuck*, I now think, teary-eyed, trespassing not in our second cousin's house but in Maly's world, her one opportunity of peace with this baby. Of course Maly would want to be with her mom, no matter how. Of course she never needed me, not really. Maybe I was the one who was angry, with Maly's mom, with everyone, this entire time. Just me.

Right then, Ma Eng opens the door, presumably to collect our second cousin's baby for the party. Her eyebrows collide. She's surprised to see us, but she only tells us to hurry up, that the food is ready, the monks are at her house, and then orders us to bring the baby. So Maly swoops it up and turns around. Standing before me, her reincarnated mom pressed against her body like armor, Maly looks natural, as if she's been preparing to hold this baby her whole life, her cocky anarchy so easily swept away.

"Let's go," she whispers, following Ma Eng.

It takes me a second to realize Maly is talking to the baby, and I find myself overwhelmed by the quiet of the nursery. For a moment, I am the only person in the neighborhood separate from the celebration, from the grandparents and the parents, including my own, and the babies. From all the generations, old and new, dead and alive, or even reborn. Staying here, in Maly's wake, I understand how truly alone I am.

This night—after the monks bless Maly's reincarnated mom, after our drunken uncles sing too many karaoke songs, and after Rithy whisks Maly away, for only an hour, to bring her back with nothing but hickeys—I dream I'm in the Videodrome. Around me towers of TVs broadcast the programs meant to brainwash our minds, the conspiracies of our time on every channel, including Maly's lives playing in tandem on hundreds of screens. In every single one, she's a different girl, with different caretakers who express their affection in odd ways, who sacrifice too much to raise her, who abandon her for various reasons. Self-loathing scumbags and narcissitic good guys and corrupt role models of all genders float in and out of her lives, hurting her most of the time, but others, when she's lucky, they push her into something like happiness. Regardless, she eventually has kids, sometimes many, sometimes only one, all of them growing up with forms of entitlement she never understands, all of them loved by her, fiercely, no matter what. And still, every iteration of Maly's life, despite any trace of rebellion, any nitty-gritty details, they all map out to a similar pattern, follow the same arc into the very same ending.

Surrounded by visions of Maly, I regret that I won't remember each of her lives, but I will keep this: standing here in the Videodrome, watching my cousin grow into the same mother across all her reincarnated selves, as I wonder about my kteuy-ness, how it fits into the equation before me, and doesn't.

Then I wake up. I rise out of my twin bed, look around my room, the sunlight from the window exposing the floating dust, like the phantom beam of a projector. And finally, I start packing.

Nominated by Peter LaBerge, Ethan Chatagnier, Dominica Phetteplace, Shelley Wong

AN ESSAY ON WAR

by JENNIFER CHANG

from THE GEORGIA REVIEW

As I do nearly every night,
I will sweep the floor
when my mother dies.
I will miss her and
not call her

and little will change,
like the not calling. Every night
I think of her and don't call
because the thinking is soothing

and the calling is not. I sweep the floor
and think about what I've been asked
to write, an essay on war.

———

"Most of us have not been to war," I begin,
"yet certain photographs
make us remember
what never happened to us.
Either our imaginations are marked
or no longer our own."

Dust dwelling in corners deforms
what I think of as an edge. There is the wall,

and there, alongside it, trails the dust,
stubborn, unrelenting. There—

a boy asleep on the beach,
a girl turned into flame.
In my mind I am at war
with images, my mother brazenly
unsmiling in a photograph

until the end of time. Her mouth's dark
red, a terrible ellipsis. Now, awed
by the body in time, she dons a smile
rinsed out like an absence.
I hate poetry. I hate art. One broad sweep,
and still the house will not be cleaned. My floors.
My nighttime habits. I write
without experience: "Dying is a fact
few of us can bear."

———

My mother is dying and we pretend
nothing will happen. There
is the onslaught. Tiny particles
of my children proliferate . . .
our breakfast crumbs, my grief,
the nothing that scatters across the room,
that won't be swept away. I try
to not burn the toast. I try to not bend
to abstraction, this page
torn out of nothing.
What did you pluck out of the tree?
What did you put in your mouth?

My mother, who is dying,
tells me to lock the doors and windows.
Winter is coming. Every house
is a target. I live
in a house with a writing desk.
As a child, H's mother,

barely escaping the war,
left everything behind—a well-stocked
kitchen, the first books she read in English.
She held onto her
small self, her only baggage,
covetously, terrified
in the backseat of a stranger's car
barreling toward a border.

Now in America
my mother is dying. She is scared of deer,
snakes, caterpillars, rats, and some
men. And windows and doors.
I no longer know where she puts the broom,
if she sweeps the house or
answers the phone.

———

Who made this mess?

I write,

"The mother of all wars
is inside ourselves: I cannot decide
whether to speak or stay silent, or
I speak only ineffectual words,
the crackling sounds that trees make
on a windy night." The season changes; again
nothing is coming out of my mouth.

I read a poem about a family
photograph, the son long gone,
the mother years into a second
language, second life. Her hair is a black wave
in a black ocean. I write,
"Why do we not think of this
as an image of war?" The daughters
look nothing alike.

I am leaving the door open,
the windows unlatched.
I sweep the floor as my children sleep,
I sweep out the leaves
they've carried into the house, every corner
the dust, the dust, the dust.

My mother was born in a war,
outlasted wars I studied
and wars I never heard of.
Never saw. My whole life.

Nominated by Shelley Wong, The Georgia Review

TO SHARKS

fiction by STEPHEN FISHBACH

from ONE STORY

When the phone rings, Kent Duvall is in the Memorabilia Room watching himself on the reality show *Endure*. On days when he is feeling his age and the slab of gut hangs like an anchor at his waist, he often finds himself popping the disc into his DVD player, which clicks and snaps like an arthritic joint. He doesn't need much. The show's intro features a three-second, slow-motion shot of him pounding his chest in the tropical light, hair billowing around his face. God, he had epic hair, long blond locks that in the island's unreasonable humidity looked like they belonged to the lead singer of an eighties glam band. Last year, Margaret insisted he shave his head. "You're starting to look like you have a comb over," she said, walking her conversational tightrope between loving joke and withering insult. He'll watch that three-second clip again and again, rewinding and replaying, rewinding and replaying, and think to himself, *That is me.*

They still call it his Memorabilia Room, though almost all of the memorabilia has been auctioned off on eBay. He argued that they were selling his treasures for much less than the items were worth. Margaret said they were only "worth" what someone was willing to pay. All that's left are the discolorations on the wallpaper to mark where he mounted the dull machete ($50), the necklace that he carved out of driftwood and strung along a circlet of woven grass ($75), and the single set of clothes that he wore throughout the show's forty-five days, which reeked of sweat and wood smoke even through the pane of protective glass ($30). The last piece of memorabilia left is a photograph of him holding his $100,000 check and smiling into the universe.

Kent reluctantly pauses the DVD to answer the phone. A woman with the improbable name of Gita Seuss is on the line. She's organizing a charity event, she says in a voice like a cowbell, where former reality television contestants will sign autographs and mingle with paying fans. The signing will benefit . . . He misses who exactly it is supposed to benefit.

"I asked the fans who they wanted to see," Gita Seuss is saying, "and your name came up again and again. I said, Kent Duvall? He was on over twelve years ago. But your fans *love* you, with a love that transcends time."

"I'll need some kind of appearance fee."

"We can pay for your travel and lodging, just like we will for all our guests."

"My appearance fee is $1,500."

"This is for *charity*," she says.

"You have to understand, I get a lot of invitations—"

Gita rattles off a list of other reality TV contestants who will be attending. Mostly they are names he doesn't recognize or wishes he didn't recognize. A survivalist from *Naked and Afraid*, a finalist from *The Bachelor*, two *Amazing Race* winners, a longtime participant on MTV's *The Challenge*. Some of the people are from television shows he's never heard of, shows he isn't even sure exist. *Beauty and the Geek. Extreme Pregnancy.* But Kent refuses to give in, and eventually Gita relents.

"The fans really want to see you," she says, the cowbell clanking mournfully.

Fifteen hundred dollars off the top—what will it even matter to the diabetic orphans or homeless pets? Kent was once a mainstay on the reality charity event circuit, and he was always mystified by the economics of these affairs. A few hundred reality TV fans paid what—$30? $50?—for the privilege of getting drunk with contestants from their favorite shows. Out of that, the event organizer paid airfare and lodging for fifty-some reality contestants. What could possibly be left for charity? He imagines Gita Seuss proudly handing an oversized novelty check for $23.57 to a group of confused kids from the children's hospital. But then, he thinks, the economics aren't the point. He and fifty other has-beens can recapture for a few fleeting hours the feeling of being famous; the fans get to fill the void in their lives that can be addressed only by the autographs of former reality TV stars; and Gita Seuss can ascend to heaven for arranging it all.

"It's for *charity*," Kent says to Margaret over dinner that night.

"You're not digging water wells in Africa. You're getting drunk at a bar."

"Why don't you come? It's fun. I'm sure I can get them to pay for—"

"No way, buster. I end up holding the camera and taking pictures while you play celebrity." Margaret has just come home from her shift at the hospital, and her face looks like a bruised orange.

"That's not true," Kent says.

"You *hate* these things. You come back miserable and talk about how annoying everybody is. Everyone spends the entire time either explaining why they really deserved to win their show, or making alliances for a future season, so you drink too much and get a massive hangover. Then I have to spend the next day nursing you like a wounded bird."

"It's $1,500," he says, holding out his hands. The truth is, even more than they need the money, *he* needs the money. He's tired of being a freeloader, tired of watching his wife drink day-old coffee that she saves in the refrigerator. Kent Duvall's wife deserves $5 lattes! Most of all, Kent is tired of the way Margaret looks at him. Like she doesn't expect anything more. Like she's resigned herself to living with a lump.

When he won the show, he quit his job to travel the country speaking to enthralled students. His last paid speech was over six months ago. They gave him travel expenses and a $500 honorarium, and for that he rode a bus twelve hours to Shamrock Lakes, Indiana, on a frigid December afternoon. Seven bored kids swiped on their phones while he clicked through his PowerPoint and told them that if they believed in themselves, they could accomplish anything. Afterward, the tweedy professor who had organized the event drove him back to the bus depot.

"It's *very* cold," the professor said. "I can think of quite a few people who said they would come, but it's very cold."

Kent nodded.

"And the students have finals next week."

"Bad timing," Kent agreed.

"Well, *I'm* a huge fan," the tweedy professor said, bristling as if Kent were blaming him. "But I have to get back to campus. Do you mind if . . . ? The bus should be here any minute." And Kent waited for an hour in the bus depot, which was nothing more than a ticket kiosk and an out-of-order toilet that stank of piss, watching two meth heads bicker over which of them was at fault for ruining the other's life.

Margaret used to come with him to these speeches, back when he still filled auditoriums. While he spoke, he would find her in the first row of the audience, and they would lock eyes and share a little smile that said, *isn't this all so silly?* She'd drive him home, his right leg still jack-rabbiting from the adrenaline, and she would mock the tweedy professors and the pompous administrators who'd said they were so honored to introduce him—"Honored? Really? No offense, babe, but you're not the president"—and he loved it because he could see her pride. He knew that buried under all her layers of Boston sarcasm—reaching back past the three caustic older brothers who picked apart each other's flaws for sport, past the father whose dry wall business had left him with two herniated disks, who had faithfully rooted for the Red Sox all her childhood until they actually won the World Series in 2004, at which point he turned off the TV in disgust as though he'd been personally betrayed—something about the reality carnival touched a dormant childhood fantasy. Maybe life wasn't just a ceaseless grind. He would see it in the twist of her mouth when people stopped him on the street, or that time he was on the cover of a magazine. Sure, it was his high school alumni publication, but still, a glossy object you could hold in your hand. Hers was the look of a skeptic just waiting for the two-bit magician to reveal the wrong card, when suddenly he pulls a dove from the air. She *liked* dating a reality star. And it seemed in those days that maybe the audiences for the speeches would grow. That maybe a meeting with a producer could turn into a TV hosting gig.

But for Margaret that dream died long ago, and in dying embarrassed her, like he had tricked her into exposing some secret part of herself. And he was still giving these speeches.

"This could be an opportunity," he says to her now. "Billy Phillips will be there—"

"Billy Phillips the tech entrepreneur?"

"He was on this past season."

"Why would Billy Phillips do reality television?" she asks, with the disdain she now has for the one significant thing in his life.

"I don't know. Because he can? I was thinking—I could ask him for a job."

"A job?" She looks suspicious. "What kind of job?"

"Any job," Kent says. He hadn't even thought of it before this moment, but it's true; he really could ask Billy Phillips for a job. The man employs hundreds, maybe thousands, and Kent always had a way with people. "You know how these things work. Some mid-level HR employee gets a résumé forwarded by the CEO. They almost *have* to find something for me."

"Oh, Kent." Margaret picks his hand off the table and kisses his fingers, and Kent thinks maybe he really can pull off a miracle.

As he walks through the lobby toward the garish hotel bar, Kent wonders if the fans will even recognize him. It's an eighties party, and he's wearing a feathered blond wig and sequined pants. But when he steps into the swirl of pointing fans, of reality stars high-fiving over rounds of shots—"Dude, I loved you on your season!" "I loved you on *your* season!"—he once again feels the old show pony inside him shake its mane.

There is an order to this chaos, like the physics of a tropical storm. At the fringes of the party are the casual fans. They shift uncomfortably, not totally sure why they're here, nudging each other as each passing reality contestant enters the fray. Past them is a circle of superfans. These people show up at every event and have formed a community that exists like bees pollinating a flowerbed. Some of them Kent recognizes from his days on the circuit over a decade ago. They have come prepared, with high-priced photo gear that will capture the evening in HD and push it out across social media. Finally, at the eye of the party, at the bar, are the bulk of contestants themselves, feeding off the attention from the fans and each other. For six months while their seasons aired, they were celebrities, and then suddenly they weren't.

A tentative fan approaches him. "Excuse me, Kent? Can I get a selfie?"

"Of course!" His mouth smiles into the flashing phone as his eyes scour the crowded bar for Billy Phillips. "Would you ever go on *Endure*?" Kent asks.

"*Me?*" The fan chuckles, delighted with the idea. "I get grouchy when I miss lunch."

"You could do it," Kent says. "If you believe in yourself, you can accomplish anything."

He sees Billy Phillips across the room. He's wearing a leather vest like Billy Idol, and his hair is dyed blond and spiked. He's chatting with two young girls with dark mascara, both dressed in black. They look like the backup dancers in a Robert Palmer video. Kent shoulders his way through the crowd, smiling for selfies.

"Kent!" Billy Phillips screams into his face. "Kent Duvall! The legend!" It's only 7 p.m., but Billy Phillips is already wildly drunk.

"Billy. It's such an—"

"You're a beast," Billy says. "Dude, when you—man, I still remember how—Woooo!" He raises his drink into the sky as if he's clinking glasses with God.

"Sorry to interrupt." Kent is used to the antic energy of reality TV contestants, but Billy Phillips is drawing his power from a purer source. He remembers an old photo that went around the Internet, from Billy's pre-wealth days. Overweight, fully bald at twenty-three. Now he has a personal trainer, a private chef, probably an on-staff hair replacement surgeon personally harvesting follicles from a high school's worth of teenage boys. He looks like a werewolf on the Atkins diet. Kent says, "I just wanted to talk to you about—"

"Hold that thought." Billy leans in close and stage-whispers to Kent. "I think I'm going to have a threesome with these girls." The Robert Palmer girls shift in place. They can clearly hear him but seem not to care.

"I'd love to grab a moment," Kent says. "Just to talk about—"

"I am fucked up, man. But tomorrow. I'm peacing out after the group dinner. But I would be honored. Let's sit together. Dinner with the legend. I can't believe it. Dude. You are a *beast*." Billy fist bumps Kent, hugs him, looks him in the eyes, and fist bumps him again.

"I'll be there," Kent says. "And listen, a word of advice."

"Hit me."

"Don't hook up with fans. It's taboo."

"I think you may not have heard me," Billy says. "I said *threesome*."

"Think about it. You sleep with a fan, and that's going to be on every chat board on the Internet."

"So what?" Billy asks.

Kent has no answer for that. So what? There was a code. It just wasn't done. So what? It was so obviously bad that it didn't bear explaining. So what? Kent twists his wedding ring and walks away.

He sits down at a table with a group of former contestants—a grave digger, an astronaut, a school bus driver, and a foxy boxer.

"Well well," the grave digger says. "Look who's come out of retirement."

"Doing some pre-gaming for *All Stars*?" asks the astronaut.

"They're doing an *All Stars*?" Kent asks. "Like actually?"

"Oh ho, Mr. Coy." The foxy boxer smiles.

"First round of calls went out last week," says the school bus-driver.

"Is there going to be a second round?" Kent asks.

"Smile for a picture," shouts a fan. With barely a ripple, the five pivot, smile, and turn back to each other.

"I'll make a pre-game deal," says the foxy boxer. "But I already have a side-deal with Carl."

"Carl?" says the astronaut. "There's no way they'll cast Carl. His confessionals are shit."

"Fans *love* Carl," says the foxy boxer. She points across the room, where a mob has surrounded a six-foot-four goliath in full camouflage, with a huge tangled beard that looks like it might be the winter home to a family of woodland creatures. "What a slut," says the foxy boxer.

The subject of *All Stars* makes the show pony tug against its bit. It worries Kent that he hasn't heard anything. No early calls, no rumors. Not that he would even want to do the show again, he thinks. These people spend their lives waiting to redeem their past failures on an *All Stars* season, but he hadn't done anything wrong. He'd won.

Still, the idea that they would cast *Carl*.

And what would going back even do to his legacy? When the fans look at him, they see that slow-motion shot of him beating his chest, his hair feathering around him in the sun. Could forty-four-year-old Kent—balding, sagging Kent—ever live up to that? But what if he could? What a story that would be. And think of the fans. Not that he needs the attention, but it could be great for his speeches. He could sell out auditoriums again . . .

No. Because ten years from now, he'd be right back here, with even less hair. Margaret's right, he thinks. These events are all the same. But Kent has dinner tomorrow with Billy Phillips. He's a *beast*. He's a *legend*. He'll redeem all that wasted time. He texts Margaret: *spoke to billy, getting dinner tomorrow*. She sends him back three hearts. *My babe*, she writes. *I'm proud of you*.

He heads to the bar for a drink. A cute blond is standing next to him. He's noticed her eyeing him all evening.

Ashley something. She was the first person off the show this season—a beverage marketer or pharmaceutical sales representative. She had volunteered for her team in the gross insects challenge, he remembers, and then panicked when they poured tarantulas on her. Was a tarantula even an insect? There'd been an on-screen chyron, #tarantulafreakout. Now she's looking around the room with that familiar first boot expression, half desperate to be recognized, half certain that she doesn't deserve to be.

461

"Hi," he says. "Ashley, right?"

"Oh my god, you know who I am. Kent Duvall knows who I am!" Ashley's wearing a spandex leotard with pink wristbands. She looks like she just stepped off the cover of a Jazzercise VHS. "I am literally dying right now. I'm such a fan!"

"Don't say that. You're one of *us* now."

"I remember watching you win when I was eight years old!"

Kent refuses to do the math.

A thin man with a skin disorder wearing a Megadeth T-shirt is standing a few feet away taking pictures of them on his Nikon and smiling secretively to himself. It's not clear if the T-shirt is part of a costume or if the man simply hasn't bothered to change clothes since 1988.

"Smile for the camera!" Kent says. He grips Ashley by the shoulder and gives a loopy, exaggerated grin. The fan takes the smile as an invitation and closes the distance.

"I want to shake your hand," he says to Kent, barely registering Ashley.

"You can do that." Kent offers his right hand, keeping the left one around Ashley's shoulder. Hanging loosely. Casually. Two pals. It's not like Kent's looking to hook up, but he has always enjoyed the occasional innocent flirtation. It's as if by his physical proximity to Ashley he's maintaining not a set of options, exactly, but a set of possibilities.

"Man, when you—when you caught that shark with a spear," the fan says. "I couldn't believe it. I said to my wife, someday I'm going to meet him and shake his hand."

"Dreams really do come true," Kent says. He never caught a shark with a spear. The man is confusing him with some other contestant, possibly on some other show.

"Sure enough," says the man. "I'm Travis."

"I'm Kent. This is Ashley."

"I know who you are!" Megadeth says to Kent. He hardly glances at Ashley. "I'd like to buy you a shot, Kent."

"Only if you buy Ashley one too."

Megadeth leans in to the bartender and orders three lemon drops.

"Lemon drops?" Kent asks. "Are we sorority girls?"

Megadeth stammers a response, and Kent's heart squeezes in pity. "Just kidding," he says. This is how he is supposed to feel. In control. Extending pity. Bestowing grace.

"What should we toast to?" Kent asks.

Megadeth is speechless, still flush with embarrassment over the lemon drop debacle.

"How about to sharks?" Kent offers. "Because they don't stop moving till—"

"Till Kent kills 'em!" Megadeth exclaims. "To sharks!" The three clink glasses and down the shots. The sweet and sour liquid puckers Kent's mouth.

"It was great meeting you," he says to Megadeth, and with a firm handshake he ends the conversation. Megadeth walks away, and Kent whispers to Ashley, "Should we get a non-sorority-girl drink?"

The night speeds up. He's signing autographs, posing with groups of other contestants. There are more shots. A shy fan approaches and asks him to autograph a photo, and he autographs her forehead. He performs karaoke with the survivalist from *Naked and Afraid,* belting out "We Are the Champions" in a trilling falsetto as he struts across the stage.

He is walking outside with Ashley to the hotel pool. The air smells of chlorine, and the sliver of moon at the pool bottom looks like he could scoop it up into his hands. Ashley leads him to the far end, away from the crowd. They sit on the diving board. She's asking him about the other contestants she's met that night, and Kent is eviscerating them one by one. He's so drunk that his guilt at this series of small betrayals is far down inside him, like the pulse of his heart in his toe. The foxy boxer buys her Twitter followers. The astronaut tried to kill himself. Carl's only a millionaire if you're counting STDs.

"You know what I hate the most?" Kent's face is numb from the booze. It's like speaking through an ice-cream cake shaped in his image. "People make these judgments based on this edited show. But that's not the *real me*. Sometimes I feel like the fans just expect so much—and I hate that I'm letting them down."

"You? You're *Kent Duvall*." Ashley breathes. "I was only out there for four days. I was barely even on the show. Nobody here knows who I am. When the fans do talk to me, it's almost, like, out of pity."

"Hey. Those first four days are the *hardest*. You were there as much as anybody. You starved. You slept in the dirt. You shivered in the cold."

"I'm not even scared of tarantulas," she says, as if picking up an argument that was already in progress, one that has been in progress for many months. "It was just that coffin. It was so *hot*. You lose control for one second, and then for the rest of your life, you're hashtag tarantula freakout."

"Nobody thinks that about you," he says, though in fact that is exactly what he remembers about her. The show did a slow-motion zoom on her face, frozen in Pompeian terror. Kent wasn't sure if the high-pitched shrieks were hers or a sound effect added in post.

"I'm *not* one of these ditsy girls," Ashley is saying. "I grew up on a ranch. Did you know I built our shelter? Me. A girl. But they didn't show *that*. If you're blond, and you freak out, then . . ." Ashley shakes her head and looks up at Kent. "If I ever get a second chance, I've been practicing."

"Practicing?" A ranch girl. He can see something rural about her now, notes the muscles in her forearms that definitely aren't from spin class or cardio boot camp.

"With the tarantulas. I go down to the pet store. The owner's a friend. He lets them crawl on my face." She shudders, despite her practice. "Do you think they'd call me for an *All Stars?* People say I'm a memorable first boot. I heard they might do a season that's all first boots."

"You'd be a *lock*," he says. "You're exactly who they want. Someone who has a big story inside them, who just needs a second chance."

The way she gazes at him reminds him of the way girls used to look at him, when his season just finished airing. He met Margaret at one of his gigs, in line at a cafeteria. "Who are *you?*" she asked, in a "why should I give a shit" way. At the time he found her irresistibly alluring, a cold breeze as he was swaddled in his blanket of praise. But that chill wind kept blowing even as his blanket frayed. She doesn't really have to drink day-old coffee, he thinks now. She's punishing herself. To punish him.

"Do you want to see my boobs?" Ashley asks.

Suddenly Kent feels old and paternal. Is this what the young people do now? Just show their breasts? Oh, Ashley, he thinks. You do not want to show me your boobs. But he can see the neediness blaring from her eyes. She needs validation—*Kent Duvall's* validation. If he refuses, she'll feel rejected. How could he do that to poor Ashley? Really the only decent thing for him to do is to look at her boobs.

"It's a hard offer to turn down." Nobody can accuse him of *asking*. He's simply not *refusing*.

Ashley pulls down her top, and there are her breasts.

"Very nice," he says, trying to maintain eye contact.

"That's all?" she asks.

No. That's not all. They are gorgeous breasts. Is there such a thing as the reverse of a memento mori? Something that makes you believe in

464

possibilities that transcend time? That no matter how much his own skin sags, no matter how far his hairline recedes, somewhere in the world there will be perfect breasts like Ashley's? He realizes he is staring, and just to relieve the awkwardness of the moment—really just for Ashley's sake—Kent leans down and kisses her.

The pounding that he thought was coming from inside his skull is in fact coming from his hotel door. Kent staggers across the room. Standing in the hallway is a small woman with pancake makeup and a bouffant hairdo.

"We're all *waiting.*"

He recognizes that cowbell.

"Waiting for me?" Kent is struggling to get his bearings. Last night is a series of disconnected images, like a flip book out of order.

"On the bus. The reason you're here?" Gita Seuss leans in close. "The reason I am paying you $1,500 instead of donating that to the *children?*"

"Children?" A clue. OK. So the charity has something to do with children.

"Let's go."

"Could I have a moment of privacy?"

"Now."

He's still wearing his sequined pants. Gita Seuss stands there watching while he slips on a T-shirt from his duffel. His mouth tastes of dead weasel, and he makes a feint to grab his toothbrush, but she thrusts herself into the open bathroom doorway.

"*Now,*" she says again.

He opens the minibar and takes a tiny bottle of vodka.

"You're going to pay for that," Gita says, with genuine loathing.

"I know." He chugs the vodka and tosses the empty bottle into the trash.

Gita Seuss grabs his hand and pulls him shuffling out of the hotel toward a yellow school bus that is idling in the parking lot. "I don't know why it's so difficult for you people," she says. "I work so hard to do a little good, but give someone an ounce of fame, and suddenly they're better than everyone else." The bus smells of exhaust and vinyl seating. They're all sitting there, crammed into the tiny benches: fifty-seven glaring, hungover, former reality television contestants. At the back of the bus, Billy Phillips is chattering to the foxy boxer, as high octane as a revving motorcycle. Ashley scoots to the side of her bench, making room, but Kent can't even look at her.

"Plant your ass," Gita Seuss says, and he sits down in the open seat.

"Hey," Ashley says.

"Hey." Kent angles his feet away from her, into the aisle. There's a rip in the seat in front of him, and tufts of foam, yellow as an aging cheese, push outward from the vinyl. He deserves to feel awful, he thinks. This is his penance. As the bus pulls out of the parking lot, Kent forces himself to think of Margaret. To remember the time they went sledding at India Point Park, the two of them in down jackets, cramming onto one child-sized plastic orange disk. On their first run, they hit a bump sideways and flipped, tumbling over each other down the icy hill. Kent panicked as he pulled her out of a snowdrift. Would she be injured? Or worse, furious? But when she surfaced, Margaret was laughing so hard that he couldn't tell her tears from the melting snow.

He would learn that there was nothing Margaret found funnier than wipeouts. "Diggers," she called them. He'd seen her at her desk, contorted over a YouTube video of people falling off rope swings. Ski fails, inner tube flips. Margaret was a connoisseur. And when it was herself taking a digger, that was the funniest of all. He remembers when she tripped over her own two feet walking out their front door and cut her knee on the brick porch so badly that she needed stitches. She couldn't stop laughing, even as the blood soaked her socks. But the first time Kent saw her overcome with glee was in that snow bank, and he forces himself to think about her laughing, crying face.

As the bus's diesel engine throbs beneath him, however, the blurry mental Polaroids of last night start to saturate. And as Kent is dragging the sled up the hill for their second run, Margaret heckling the other sledders, there's the slalom of Ashley's hip. And on the second run, as Kent pulls up the sled's wobbly edge, trying to steer back toward the same bump, hoping to wipe out in the same way, there's Ashley on the edge of the hotel bed, wearing only one sock and both pink wristbands. And a new feeling starts to surge upward, much, much worse than the guilt. Kent starts to feel aroused. He focuses on the seat in front of him, pressing his finger into the rip, forcing the foam back inside.

The bus takes them to an outdoor mall that borders a manmade lake, where a group of volunteers herds the contestants toward three rows of long tables. Kent's grateful just to be led, to be liberated for a moment from the weight of his consciousness. In front of each seat is a placard with the contestant's name, their reality show, and how well they did. It must be a thousand degrees. Heat warps the air. In the distance, a line of fans stretches into infinity. Each has paid $30 or $50 to receive

466

a poster with the pictures of the different contestants. They will progress through the gauntlet of tables collecting autographs. Kent can hardly believe anyone would wait for two hours in this obscene heat to receive scribbled names on commemorative posters. He wishes he cared about anything as much as these people care about former reality TV contestants.

Gita Seuss blows a whistle, and the press of fans files in. The contestants are arranged in order of their show's season, so Kent is near the front. Fans approach the table and hand him their posters, and he scrawls *Kent Duvall, winner,* above his face. The picture is the same shot of him smiling into the starry future that is framed in the Memorabilia Room. Some of the fans want a selfie. They lean across the table, and he puts his hand around their shoulders and smiles into their phones. He can feel them shaking beneath his hand like frightened rabbits. They make small talk. "Would you ever do the show?" he asks. "*Me?*" They chuckle. "I get grouchy when I miss lunch!"

An hour into the event, and the line of fans still blurs into the horizon. Kent's head is pounding when a man thrusts the poster into his hands and says, "Can you sign it, 'To sharks'?"

The phrase is vaguely familiar, like a jingle from a long-ago commercial. Kent looks up. Standing above him is a man in a Megadeth T-shirt. Oh yes. This guy. He can't remember the guy's name, but he does remember the horrible skin condition, the flaky nodules that hang off his face.

"To sharks," the man says again, like it's their private joke.

"Oh hey," Kent says. "To sharks."

"That was a fun night," Megadeth says.

"Hell yeah."

"Check out these pics. You're in a bunch of them."

Megadeth leans over the table and presents Kent the viewfinder of his Nikon. He clicks through a recreation of Kent's previous evening. "There's you and Ashley at the bar. That's you singing karaoke. That's you signing an autograph. That's you and Ashley at the pool. That's another of you at the pool." Kent's breath catches in his chest. You can clearly see in the second picture that Ashley's top has been pulled down. In the next, their foreheads are almost pressed together. "Here's you and Ashley kissing." Megadeth keeps narrating as if these pictures that could destroy Kent's life are of purely anthropological interest. "That's you and Ashley leaving the bar." There's no menace in the man's voice. Just description.

Kent can sense the line shifting behind Megadeth, annoyed fans jostling in the heat.

"Wait, go back." Kent's voice is hoarse.

"Go back?" Megadeth asks.

"Scroll back," Kent says, but what really he means is *go back* in time, flip backwards through the camera's pictures so that the night can end in that first loopy grin.

"Sir, there is a *line*," the woman behind Megadeth says.

"I paid my $30," Megadeth says to the woman. "I'm going to take my turn."

"I paid my $30 just like you," the woman says. "Your turn doesn't get to last all day."

"Sorry, ma'am." Kent grabs Megadeth and pulls him away from the tables, toward the artificial lake. The stagnant water stinks, green algae scumming its surface. The lake is clogged with discarded debris from the mall patrons—a Starbucks cup, food wrappers, the plastic packaging from a Barbie. "I'm going to lose my place," Megadeth objects. "I want to get Carl—"

"I need you to delete those pictures."

Megadeth takes a step back in horror. "Delete them? I can't do that."

"Why not?"

"I've got to upload them. The whole reason I come to these events is to document them for my followers."

Kent feels his headache pushing out from the center of his skull. Little black specks start to polka dot his vision. "I'll pay you back for your entrance fee. How much was it? $30? I'll pay you $100. I'll pay you $500."

"It's not about *money*." Megadeth looks offended. "My followers are counting on me."

"Okay, not all the pictures. Just delete the ones of me and Ashley." Kent leans in close and holds up his ring finger with its scratched gold band. "I have a wife."

"I have a social media account," Megadeth counters.

"If you post this picture, my wife will *leave me*. Please. Don't ruin my life over a picture."

"My followers are expecting me to document this event. What kind of person would I be if I deleted this just because it's inconvenient for you? Just another corrupt liar."

Kent stares at Megadeth. In his muddled hangover, he must be missing something. "Are you fucking with me?"

"Do you know the reason I like *Endure?*" Megadeth asks. "Because it's pure. No tricks. No compromises. Just man against the wild."

Wonderful. He's being held hostage by a lunatic. Kent doesn't think of himself as a romantic person, but now the romantic notions are flowing out of him. "Please. My wife—Margaret—she's the best thing that ever happened to me. My whole life has just been looking for people to *like* me, but Margaret, she *loves* me. Even in spite of—in spite of—me. We have a nice life together. It could be a nice life. I'm trying to make it a nice life. That's why I'm here, to—"

Megadeth is unmoved.

"Is there anything I can do?" Kent begs. "What if we—trade?"

Megadeth takes a deep breath, as though the prospect that something might weigh against his fidelity to his social media account has never occurred to him. "Wow. A trade."

"Yes! A trade. You wouldn't be deleting the pictures. We'd be trading. You'd be giving me the photos, and in exchange, I would be doing something for you. A trade."

Back at the tables, Kent sees the woman from the line talking to Gita Seuss.

"Well, the kiddos are big fans," Megadeth says. "Not of you. You're before their time. But of the show. You could come to dinner at my house tonight."

"Tonight?" Tonight is dinner with Billy Phillips. "Tonight's no good. I could do tomorrow?" His mind is spinning. He can reschedule his flight. It's not like he has work. He'll make up some excuse to tell Margaret—

"Nuh-uh," Megadeth says. "First it's tomorrow night. Then tomorrow something comes up, and it's next week, and by the time you finally come over, none of my followers will even care about the pictures anymore."

Gita Seuss is storming toward him.

"Okay," Kent says, the show pony spooking and rearing. "Tonight."

"Travis didn't tell us anybody would be coming home with him." Shockingly, Mrs. Megadeth looks like a normal human—a careworn mom of two, but with bright blue eyes and an A-line dress that might have been purchased within the past year. What does this woman think of her husband spending his nights playing paparazzi with reality contestants? She bustles around the kitchen preparing roast chicken while a towheaded little boy sets the table. Kent swanned in here like an honored guest, but this is a functioning family unit he could only dream of. The house is filled with homey touches. Family photos taped to the refrigerator. Inspirational slogans carved on wood blocks. *Bless this house with love and laughter. Always remember you are braver than you think you are. A perfect marriage is just two imperfect people who refuse to give up on each other.* A little girl peeks shyly from behind a door. She has inherited Megadeth's skin condition, and Kent's heart breaks for her road ahead.

"How did you and, um, Travis meet?" Kent asks Mrs. Megadeth over dinner.

"Ol' Travis here swept me off my feet in the dance hall. You never seen such footwork, though you might not believe it to look at him." Mrs. Megadeth beams at her husband.

"Aww, he doesn't care about all that. Kent, tell the kiddos about that shark you killed," prompts Megadeth.

Kent can see the pride Megadeth takes in bringing him here, and he does not want to correct him in front of his beaming wife and adoring children. So he makes up a story about a shark. Everyone on the island was starving, he says, so hungry they couldn't move. Even though it was a stormy day, Kent knew he had to do something. He waded into the water with his spear to go fishing. That was when he saw a dorsal fin cut through the waves. It was a giant—not a Great White, but close. The creature was coming right for him. He raised his spear up into the air and—

"No," Megadeth says. "That's not how I remember it."

"No?" Kent says. "Maybe it was edited differently on TV."

"Don't tell me what I saw with my own two eyes," Megadeth says.

Kent glances at his watch. It's 7 p.m. If he hustles, he can still make dinner with Billy Phillips. "This was so delicious. But I really should be heading—"

"You know what we'd like?" Mrs. Megadeth says. "We want you to face off against Travis. Mano a mano."

"You want us to . . . fight?"

The entire family cracks up. "Not *real* fighting," Mrs. Megadeth says. "Wii boxing."

This seems almost more bizarre, but Megadeth gives him a look that says *remember our deal.* So Kent follows the family into the next room, where a sixty-five-inch TV dominates a carpeted living room full of overstuffed brown leather couches. Megadeth hands him a white plastic remote, and before Kent knows it, two digital avatars are facing off in a ring, and a cartoon announcer yells, "Fight!"

"What do I do?" Kent asks.

"You ever boxed before?" asks Megadeth. "Just like that."

Gripping the white dongle, Kent throws a tentative jab and watches his digital avatar swing its fist into a digital Megadeth.

"Ya got me!" Megadeth says. "You ready?"

They fight. Kent stands before the family's TV, jabbing with his left arm, shifting his hips into right crosses, pivoting for his hooks. He connects with a few good punches, but Megadeth just makes tiny motions of his hand. He knows exactly the way to angle the dongle for maximum impact, and while Kent is wearing himself out dodging and weaving around the tan carpet, Megadeth barely moves. Before long, Kent's avatar is KO'd.

"You did it, baby!" shouts Mrs. Megadeth. "You KO'd Kent Duvall!"

"You can do better than that," Megadeth says. "Rematch."

"I really should be getting back," Kent says. It is 7:30. It's not too late.

"Best of three," Megadeth says, with a look.

Kent glances at his phone. There's a text from Margaret: *How's dinner with Billy?* she wants to know. *An unexpected struggle,* he writes back. Then he takes up the Wii boxing dongle. The announcer shouts, "Fight!" This time Kent doesn't even try to dodge or counterpunch. He takes a dive. He lets Megadeth e-pummel him. Within seconds, his avatar is on the mat.

"Well, there it is. You won," says Kent. "Thank you again so much for—"

"You can't just get KO'd in ten seconds,' says the wife. "You killed a shark."

"Don't be such a lump," says the little boy.

"Lump!" repeats the little girl, giggling.

"You said best of three," Kent says. "You won, and I'm going back to the hotel."

"You have to *try,*" Megadeth says. "Now it's best of five."

The next round, Kent is angry. He made one stupid mistake, and now he's trapped here for eternity? Watching his one shot at a decent life slip away? Rage fills him, and he flails and jabs with his whole body. To his amazement, it works. Megadeth is on the ropes. The digital crowd goes wild.

"Beat his ass!" laughs Mrs. Megadeth.

Kent dances across the living room as though it were the arena of his life, punching and dodging. Yes, he is going to e-fight his way out of here. He is going to knock out Megadeth and storm out the door. Kent is taken by a wild physical joy. He will meet Billy Phillips, he will get a job in sales, he will go home to his wife. He made a mistake, but he has learned from it, and isn't that all you can ask? Megadeth's health meter is heading to zero. One more good punch and he'll be finished.

But as Kent winds up a haymaker, Megadeth flicks his wrist. Megadeth has only been toying with him. A massive uppercut sends Kent's digitized head thudding to the mat.

Kent's shirt is soaked with sweat by the time he leaves the Megadeths'. Travis went six undefeated rounds, and this pummeling was followed by Mrs. Megadeth and then both children. It's 10 p.m. when his taxi arrives at the hotel.

The first person he sees is Gita Seuss, who is standing by the hotel door. "Have you seen Billy?" Kent asks. "Billy Phillips?"

She looks at him like he's covered in open sores. "Billy Phillips left hours ago, and I think you could learn a few—"

Kent turns and walks away from her, toward the bar.

"This is your last year!" Gita Seuss shouts after him. "You'll never come to this event again!"

He laughs at the absurdity of the threat. He's failed at the one positive thing that was supposed to come from this weekend, but at least he's salvaged things with Margaret. He sits down at the bar and orders a Jack neat. Next to him is a professional poker player, and as Kent drinks the whiskey, to take the edge off, she explains to him why the fluoride in water is a government plot. He's comforted by the familiar lunacy. He will stay here tonight, having ridiculous conversations like this, and tomorrow he will gratefully return to his normal life.

"Have you seen this?"

Ashley is standing behind him, holding her phone up to his face. Her browser is open to a Reddit thread: "Did Kent Duvall and Ashley March hook up at the Alabama Event?" He grabs the phone. There's a zoomed-in picture of him and Ashley on the diving board. The image is grainy and pixelated, but it's clearly them. Ashley's top is pulled down. Did Megadeth upload the photo anyway? No, Kent is sure that would go against the man's insane moral code. And the pictures are far too low-resolution for Megadeth's pricey Nikon.

"Who took this?" he rasps.

Ashley shrugs and gestures around them. There are hundreds of fans attending this event, uploading thousands of pictures. Among those thousands, some enterprising sleuth has zoomed in on the extreme background of just one.

"Can you believe that someone made a thread about us?" Ashley is showing concern, trying to disguise her delight. "Do you think casting looks at this stuff? I mean, maybe they'd cast us together on *All Stars?*"

In the picture, Ashley is looking over her shoulder, right into the crowd. She knew, Kent thinks. His phone buzzes in his pocket. He orders a shot of Jack, but the phone is buzzing; it won't stop buzzing.

"Hello?" He's in the bathroom, whispering into his cell phone.

"I'm so *embarrassed*," Margaret says. "Do you know three people have already sent me the link to your little escapade?"

"I didn't *ask* her to. She just—"

"The worst part is, I thought better of you. Not that you wouldn't cheat. Obviously I'm not that naïve. I just figured if you ever did, you'd show a little fucking discretion. On a diving board, Kent? Why not yell *cannonball* and do it in midair?"

"I didn't know about the cameras." He knows as he says this that it's the weakest excuse in the history of human infidelity.

"You didn't know about the cameras?" She laughs, a short, staccato sound like stabbing an ice block. "*You* didn't know about the cameras?"

She's still laughing when she hangs up the phone, probably will laugh all evening at the sublime digger of their marriage. Kent staggers back to the bar, back to his whiskey. *Did* he know? He can't even consider it. Tomorrow he will think about his life, but tomorrow is a lifetime away. For now he is here, doing shots. The bar smells of beer and sweat. He is making alliances with the foxy boxer, and the grave digger, and the astronaut, and Carl. Now he is signing autographs, clinking glasses. The lights in the room are far too bright. Ashley is chattering to him about *All Stars*, but Ashley was yesterday's adventure. Now he is taking a selfie with a group of fans. He sees himself in the phone screen, a forty-four-year-old bald man with a gut, his nose crimson, dark bags hanging under his eyes as he presses his flushed cheek against a giddy teen. *That is me*, he knows. Now he sees one of the Robert Palmer girls, and now he is buying her a drink.

Nominated by Becky Hagenston, One Story

POSTCARDS TO M.*

by ALLISON BENIS WHITE

from KENYON REVIEW

That you have grown still enough to write to.
Or to be left alone—to be left alone.
A few hours from here, a field of poppies so red I want to be cut.
Stain the seams, tear myself apart.

That place so close to the end of a song.
In the pause, just afterward, the silence rushing in.
Here is my mind, here is my mind (tilted into my hands).
What kind of loneliness is this, kissing every finger?

To your lost room: all pictures of wildflowers.
To your lost room: honey poured on your tongue by someone you
    love.
Silence, thick as frosting, in my mouth.
Then the music of your name.

A place to tell you something, to tell myself.
I tried to call you in the dream but I could not dial correctly.
I could not die correctly.
In a dark-gold dress, the madness has gone quiet.

A memory of your face as radiant anxiety.
Opening a series of boxes, and inside the last, smallest one, a
    pearl.

What things did you imagine to cool your mind?
Even if it is to die, it is beautiful to decide.

In the window, my face trapped in light.
A cutout woman in a cutout dress, cutting out her paper death.
What is there to feel now that would matter?
Here: wish you were.

° After Hari sasakis "Phone of The Wind." (a glass phone booth he built on a hilltop to cell a
dead loved one)

Nominated by David Hernandez

THINGS I DIDN'T DO WITH THIS BODY & THINGS I DID

by AMANDA GUNN

from LANA TURNER

1

I didn't bear a child with it, bear a drunk friend's arm around its shoulders, bear it over a fence in one go, bear it from Harlem to Wall Street by foot, run it until it vomited, run it until it vibrated with joy, lean it long against a redwood it had hiked to, lay it on the earth beneath the aurora borealis, march it white-laced until it wed, march it in an uprising for a killed Black man, march it to war until it was dead, bear a lover eager on its spine, bear it back to its natal soil, bear it to the lake's center under the swift awesome power of its legs. Bear witness: I did not make its child. I didn't bear it to the home it asked me for. Instead, as if by stumbling, as if by walking backward even, as if the beginning & not the end held the drum & cymbal & jazz bands,

2

I bore three lovers in its mouth, bore a blow to its cheek, bore the snap & drag of the Atlantic at high tide, bared its breasts on that beach, scored its ankle with a knife twelve thin times, bored into the white underflesh of its thigh, bore its scars, bore tattoos to cover its scars, bore hot wax where it was tenderest, bore on its face a heavy, comely face, bore smoke deep in its tissues, bore the soft, bore the love of its family, withheld from it embraces, withheld from it a decent meal, bore love for the boy who refused it, bore the death of the boy who didn't, bore the weight it

476

made from the pills I had handed it, bore its joints' irreparable ache, bore the turned sweet smell beneath its breast, taught water to bear it so I could rest, bore its sloughings, bore its swellings, bore its manifold solitudes, and on the rare, keen nights it stayed with me, I bore its bright fragrant solitary intolerable pleasure.

Nominated by Mary Kuryla

SPECIAL MENTION

(The editors also wish to mention the following important works published by small presses last year. Listings are in no particular order.)

NON FICTION

Julia Koets—Someone will Remember Us (Southern Indiana Review)
Elena Passarello—Death Sentence (Brevity)
Zachary Fine— Life Studies (The Point)
Michelle Battiste—The Planning, the Chair, The Ash (Gettysburg Review)
Susanne Paola Antonetta—Commensals (Georgia Review)
Michael McCallister—Off-Grid (Michigan Quarterly)
Leo Rios—Vagabond (Georgia Review)
Lois Parshley—Cold War, Hot Mess (Virginia Quarterly)
Hanh Hoang—Bedtime Stories From Vietnam (New England Review)
Ricardo Frasso Jaramillo—Omayra (In Other Words) (The Rumpus)
Debbie Urbanski—Inheritance (The Sun)
Lacy M. Johnson—What Slime Knows (Orion)
Catherine Jagoe—Finding The Springs (Water-Stone)
Yi Shun Lai—My Father Reads A Poem To Me (Brevity)
Morgan Talty—The Unintelligible (Georgia Review)
Joni Tevis—Suffer The Lilies (Brink)
Sarah Curtis—The Ghosts of Lubbock (Colorado Review)
Linda Hall—Three Books, Two Hats, And An Essay Survival Plan (Salmagundi)
Alice Mattison—As My Vision Deteriorates, Every Word Counts (Electric Literature)
Katie Moulton—The Middle (Sewanee Review)

Patricia Hampl—It's Come to this (America Scholar)

Thomas Dai—Driving Days (New England Review)

Anna Leahy—Ordinary Pandemonium (Mississippi Review)

Margret Ann Thomas—Gun Bubbles (Creative Nonfiction)

Jan Shoemaker—Nest (River Teeth)

Wendy S. Walters—After The Father (Bomb)

Edward Hirsch—Anthony Hecht: "More Light! More Light!" (Hudson Review)

Melissa Febos—The Wild, Sublime Body (Yale Review)

Robert Stewart—The Ride (Blast)

Aimee Nezhukumatathil—Potoo (Missisippi Review)

Franny Choi—Imitation Games (Gulf Coast)

James Brown—Leaving Las Vegas (River Teeth)

Kim McClarin—On White Violence, Black Survival, And Learning How to Shoot (The Sun)

Jacob M. Appel—Guilty Bystanders (Briar Cliff Review)

Roz Spafford—Life As We Knew It (About Place Journal)

Jeannette Cooperman—Not With A Whimper But With A Bang (Common Reader)

Hilma Wolitzer—The Great Escape (Electric Literature)

Joyce Zonana—The Hungry Artist (Hudson Review)

Padgett Powell—Eff The Classics (Book Post)

George Hutchinson—Remembering The Peace Corps (Raritan Review)

Andre Dubus III—Ghost Dogs (The Sun)

Jen Silverman—The Dissenters (Gettysburg Review)

Elizabeth Benedict—Covid Diary (Salmagundi)

Liz Rose Shulman—The Rubber Band (Another Chicago Magazine)

Nafis Shafizadeh—Koestler And Me (Ploughshares)

Judith Nies—A Real American Story (Arrowsmith)

Andrew Furman—Quarantine (Prairie Schooner)

John Griswold—Of Baldness And Fathers (Common Reader)

Chris Dennis—A Series of Rooms Occupied by Ghislaine Maxwell (Granta)

FICTION

Alegra Hyde—Mercy (Crazyhorse)

Daisy Hernandez—Soursop (Iowa Review)

Adam T. Weinstein—A Brief History of Bauska. . . . (FC2)

Lauren Pruneski—Mama, Mama (Southern Review)

Marian Crotty—What Kind Of Person (Iowa Review)

Jesutofunmi Omowumi—God Has No Gunmen (Story)

Robert Travieso—Open When Alone (Kenyon Review)

Richard Powers—Saints Hill (Conjunctions)

Judith C. Mitchell—How We Met And What Happened Next
 (The Sun)

Leo Rios—Vagabond (Georgia Review)

Stephanie Anderson—After The Aquifer (Terrain)

Rob Ehle—Bible School (Fiction)

Stefanie Wortman—Milkrush (Laurel Review)

Emily Greenberg—Alternative Facts (Santa Monica Review)

Casey Guerin—What Consumes You (Greensboro Review)

David Nicholson—That's Why Darkies Were Born (Chicago Quarterly
 Review)

Ha Jin—Freedom (Narrative)

Anthony Veasna So—Generational Differences (Zyzzyva)

D.R. MacDonald—Coywolf (Epoch)

Brandon Hobson—A Man Came To Visit Us (Noon)

Cara Blue Adams—At The Gates (Mississippi Review)

Anu Kandikuppa—The Belfort (Colorado Review)

Mesha Maren—We Cannot Yet Call It Failure (Joyland)

Ashton Politanoff—Reflectons From The Redondo Reflex Archives
 (Noon)

Kirstin Valdez Quade—After Hours At The Acacia Park Pool (American
 Short Fiction)

Lydia Conklin—Rainbow Rainbow (Paris Review)

Wendell Berry—A Time and Times and The Dividing of Time
 (Threepenny Review)

Thomas Pierce—Little Eye (Zoetrope)

Lee Conell—My One And Only. . . . (ZYZZYVA)

Jessica Fordham Kidd—Going Blue (Puerto Del Sol)

Anne Ray—Noe Valley (Story)

Mala Gaonkar—Ladakh (American Short Fiction)

Douglas Silver—America America (The Sun)

Taisia Kitaiskaia—Gloria (American Short Fiction)

Tamas Dobozy—Operative O (New Letters)

Elizabeth McCracken—The Get-Go (American Short Fiction)

Claire Luchette—Sugar Island (Ploughshares)

Yohanca Delgado—The Little Widow From The Capital (Paris Review)

Katherine Fallon—Letting The Penguin Out (Agni)

Laura Jamison—Just Her Luck (Scoundrel Time)
Elisa Albert—Mammals (N+1)
Rebecca Gonshak—The Anarchist (Prairie Schooner)
Hurmat Kazmi—Sissies (American Short Fiction)
Tim Conrad—Trivial (Massachusetts Review)
Kristina Gorcheva-Newberry—Poplars (Zoetrope)
Mary Kuryla—Hive (Paris Review)
Jenzo Duque—Papi (Narrative)
Jayne Anne Phillips—A Journey (Conjunctions)
Mike Jeffrey—Blue Boy (Idaho Review)
Michelle Ross—Paula Watt (Witness)
A.D. Nauman—The Cat (Chicago Quarterly Review)
Brittney Corrigan—The Ghost Town Collectives (Terrain)
Sophie Hoss—Summon The Moon (Bomb)
Galen Schram—Tattoos (Bellevue Literary Review)
Jason Brown—Pineland (Missouri Review)
Emma Pattee—Our Last Night In Tulum (Idaho Review)
Scott Pomfret—If Anyone Moves (Ruminate)
Sasha Wiseman—Still Life (Southampton Review)
Fei Sun—Shadow (Mississipi Review)
C.M. Lindley—The Burn (Georgia Review)
Rebecca Kwee—On The Echoing Green (Shenandoah)
Mona Susan Power—Naming Ceremony (Missouri Review)
Akil Kumarasamy—The Healing (Conjunctions)

POETRY

Roselie Moffett—A Prophecy Is Nothing (Narrative)
Yi Won—The Mirror's Dance (World's Lightest Motorcycle Zephyr)
Darius Atefat-Peckham—I Learn A Language I am Afraid To Speak
  (Florida Review)
Ae Hee Lee—Korea: Things To Review Before Landing (Georgia
  Review)
Arien Reed—The Ballad of A Married Trans Man (Florida Review)
Dan Beachy-Quick—Canto X (Kenyon Review)
James Schuyler—A Friend (Court Green)
Gustavo Hernandez—Third Shift (Cultural Daily)
Cecily Parks—Pandemic Parable (Mississippi Review)
Fay Dillof—Two Truths And (Zyzzyva)
Joseph Bathanti—Steady Daylight (The Sun)

Darius Atefat-Peckham—Here's a Love Poem to Persian Carpets.
(Tahoma Literary Review)

Rosanna Alice Boswell—There is something erotic about dressing the
plus-sized mannequin at work (Iron Horse Literary Review)

Ching-in Chen—Flood Fathers (Nombono)

Patricia Clark—Oxygen (Plume)

Doris Ferleger—Uncursing Tourette's (Boomer LitMag)

Eugenia Leigh—Bipolar II Disorder: Second Evaluation (Zuihitsu for
Bianca) (Tahoma Literary Review)

Ada Limón—Forsythia (Virginia Quarterly Review)

James Longenbach—Dorsoduro (The Cortland Review)

Robin Meyers—Diego de Montemay or (Yale Review)

Preeti Vangani—What This Elegy Wants, (Red Wheelbarrow)

Danielle Legros Georges—The Afternoon (Ibbetson Street)

Rena Priest—Remembering Ta Ta at T'am Whiq Sen (Empty Bowl)

Nancy Miller Gomez—Tilt-A-Whirl (New Ohio Review)

Philip B. Williams—The Void (American Poetry Review)

Diane Seuss—from Little Epic (Kenyon Review)

Carl Phillips—Sunlight In Fog (Ploughshares)

Kelly Rowe—In The Garden (New Ohio Review)

Stephanie Chang—Lotus Flower Kingdom (Adroit Journal)

Rosa Alcala—Industrial Sign Language (Georgia Review)

Lynne Thompson—Seeking Paradise (Rust and Moth)

Katie Farris—Why Write Love Poetry in A Burning World. (Beloit
Poetry Journal)

PRESSES FEATURED IN THE PUSHCART PRIZE EDITIONS SINCE 1976

A-Minor
About Place Journal
Abstract Magazine TV
The Account
Adroit Journal
Agni
Ahsahta Press
Ailanthus Press
Alaska Quarterly Review
Alcheringa/Ethnopoetics
Alice James Books
Ambergris
Amelia
American Circus
American Journal of Poetry
American Letters and Commentary
American Literature
American PEN
American Poetry Review
American Scholar
American Short Fiction
The American Voice
Amicus Journal
Amnesty International
Anaesthesia Review
Anhinga Press
Another Chicago Magazine

Antaeus
Antietam Review
Antioch Review
Apalachee Quarterly
Aphra
Aralia Press
The Ark
Arkansas Review
Arroyo
Art angel
Art and Understanding
Arts and Letters
Artword Quarterly
Ascensius Press
Ascent
Ashland Poetry Press
Aspen Leaves
Aspen Poetry Anthology
Assaracus
Assembling
Atlanta Review
Autonomedia
Avocet Press
The Awl
The Baffler
Bakunin
Bare Life

Bat City Review
Bamboo Ridge
Barlenmir House
Barnwood Press
Barrow Street
Bellevue Literary Review
The Bellingham Review
Bellowing Ark
Beloit Poetry Journal
Bennington Review
Bettering America Poetry
Bilingual Review
Birmingham Poetry Review
Black American Literature Forum
Blackbird
Black Renaissance Noire
Black Rooster
Black Scholar
Black Sparrow
Black Warrior Review
Blackwells Press
The Believer
Bloom
Bloomsbury Review
Bloomsday Lit
Blue Cloud Quarterly
Blueline
Blue Unicorn
Blue Wind Press
Bluefish
BOA Editions
Bomb
Bookslinger Editions
Boomer Litmag
Boston Review
Boulevard
Boxspring
Brevity
Briar Cliff Review
Brick
Bridge
Bridges
Brown Journal of Arts
Burning Deck Press

Butcher's Dog
Cafe Review
Caliban
California Quarterly
Callaloo
Calliope
Calliopea Press
Calyx
The Canary
Canto
Capra Press
Carcanet Editions
Caribbean Writer
Carolina Quarterly
Catapult
Caught by The River
Cave Wall
Cedar Rock
Center
Chariton Review
Charnel House
Chattahoochee Review
Chautauqua Literary Journal
Chelsea
Chicago Quarterly Review
Chouteau Review
Chowder Review
Cimarron Review
Cincinnati Review
Cincinnati Poetry Review
City Lights Books
Clarion
Cleveland State Univ. Poetry Ctr.
Clover
Clown War
Codex Journal
CoEvolution Quarterly
Cold Mountain Press
The Collagist
Colorado Review
Columbia: A Magazine of Poetry and Prose
Columbia Poetry Review
The Common
Conduit

486

Confluence Press
Confrontation
Conjunctions
Connecticut Review
Constellations
Copper Canyon Press
Copper Nickel
Cosmic Information Agency
Countermeasures
Counterpoint
Court Green
Crab Orchard Review
Crawl Out Your Window
Crazyhorse
Creative Nonfiction
Crescent Review
Cross Cultural Communications
Cross Currents
Crosstown Books
Crowd
Cue
Cumberland Poetry Review
Curbstone Press
Cutbank
Cypher Books
Dacotah Territory
Daedalus
Dalkey Archive Press
James Dickey Review
Decatur House
December
Denver Quarterly
Desperation Press
Dogwood
Domestic Crude
Doubletake
Dragon Gate Inc.
Dreamworks
Dryad Press
Duck Down Press
Dunes Review
Durak
East River Anthology
Eastern Washington University Press

Ecotone
Egress
El Malpensante
Electric Literature
Eleven Eleven
Ellis Press
Emergence
Empty Bowl
Ep;phany
Epoch
Ergol
Evansville Review
Exquisite Corpse
Faultline
Fence
Fiction
Fiction Collective
Fiction International
Field
Fifth Wednesday Journal
Fine Madness
Firebrand Books
Firelands Art Review
First Intensity
5 A.M.
Five Fingers Review
Five Points Press
Fjords Review
Florida Review
Foglifter
Forklift
The Formalist
Foundry
Four Way Books
Fourth Genre
Fourth River
Fractured Lit
Frontiers: A Journal of Women Studies
Fugue
Gallimaufry
Genre
The Georgia Review
Gettysburg Review
Ghost Dance

Gibbs-Smith

Glimmer Train

Goddard Journal

David Godine, Publisher

Gordon Square

Graham House Press

Grain

Grand Street

Granta

Graywolf Press

Great River Review

Green Mountains Review

Greenfield Review

Greensboro Review

Guardian Press

Gulf Coast

Hanging Loose

Harbour Publishing

Hard Pressed

Harvard Advocate

Harvard Review

Hawaii Pacific Review

Hayden's Ferry Review

Here

Hermitage Press

Heyday

Hills

Hobart

Hole in the Head

Hollyridge Press

Holmgangers Press

Holy Cow!

Home Planet News

Hopkins Review

Hudson Review

Hunger Mountain

Hungry Mind Review

Hysterical Rag

Iamb

Ibbetson Street Press

Icarus

Icon

Idaho Review

Iguana Press

Image

In Character

Indiana Review

Indiana Writes

Indianapolis Review

Intermedia

Intro

Invisible City

Inwood Press

Iowa Review

Ironwood

I-70 Review

Jam To-day

J Journal

The Journal

Jubilat

The Kanchenjunga Press

Kansas Quarterly

Kayak

Kelsey Street Press

Kenyon Review

Kestrel

Kweli Journal

Lake Effect

Lana Turner

Latitudes Press

Laughing Waters Press

Laurel Poetry Collective

Laurel Review

Leap Frog

L'Epervier Press

Liberation

Ligeia

Linquis

Literal Latté

Literary Imagination

The Literary Review

The Little Magazine

Little Patuxent Review

Little Star

Living Hand Press

Living Poets Press

Logbridge-Rhodes

Longreads

Louisville Review
Love's Executive Order
Lowlands Review
LSU Press
Lucille
Lynx House Press
Lyric
The MacGuffin
Magic Circle Press
Malahat Review
Manhattan Review
Manoa
Manroot
Many Mountains Moving
Marlboro Review
Massachusetts Review
McSweeney's
Meridian
Mho & Mho Works
Micah Publications
Michigan Quarterly
Mid-American Review
Milkweed Editions
Milkweed Quarterly
The Minnesota Review
Mississippi Review
Mississippi Valley Review
Missouri Review
Montana Gothic
Montana Review
Montemora
Moon Pie Press
Moon Pony Press
Mount Voices
Mr. Cogito Press
MSS
Mudfish
Mulch Press
Muzzle Magazine
n+1
Nada Press
Narrative
National Poetry Review
Nebraska Poets Calendar

Nebraska Review
Nepantla
Nerve Cowboy
New America
New American Review
New American Writing
The New Criterion
New Delta Review
New Directions
New England Review
New England Review and Bread Loaf
Quarterly
New Issues
New Letters
New Madrid
New Ohio Review
New Orleans Review
New South Books
New Verse News
New Virginia Review
New York Quarterly
New York University Press
Nimrod
9×9 Industries
Ninth Letter
Noon
North American Review
North Atlantic Books
North Dakota Quarterly
North Point Press
Northeastern University Press
Northern Lights
Northwest Review
Notre Dame Review
O. ARS
O. Blk
Obsidian
Obsidian II
Ocho
Oconee Review
October
Ohio Review
Old Crow Review
Ontario Review

Open City

Open Places

Orca Press

Orchises Press

Oregon Humanities

Orion

Other Voices

Oxford American

Oxford Press

Oyez Press

Oyster Boy Review

Painted Bride Quarterly

Painted Hills Review

Palette

Palo Alto Review

Paper Darts

Paris Press

Paris Review

Parkett

Parnassus: Poetry in Review

Partisan Review

Passages North

Paterson Literary Review

Pebble Lake Review

Penca Books

Pentagram

Penumbra Press

Pequod

Persea: An International Review

Perugia Press

Per Contra

Pilot Light

The Pinch

Pipedream Press

Pirene's Fountain

Pitcairn Press

Pitt Magazine

Pleasure Boat Studio

Pleiades

Ploughshares

Plume

Poem-A-Day

Poems & Plays

Poet and Critic

Poet Lore

Poetry

Poetry Atlanta Press

Poetry East

Poetry International

Poetry Ireland Review

Poetry Northwest

Poetry Now

The Point

Post Road

Prairie Schooner

Prelude

Prescott Street Press

Press

Prime Number

Prism

Promise of Learnings

Provincetown Arts

A Public Space

Puerto Del Sol

Purple Passion Press

Quademi Di Yip

Quarry West

The Quarterly

Quarterly West

Quiddity

Radio Silence

Rainbow Press

Raritan: A Quarterly Review

Rattle

Red Cedar Review

Red Clay Books

Red Dust Press

Red Earth Press

Red Hen Press

Reed

Release Press

Republic of Letters

Review of Contemporary Fiction

Revista Chicano-Riqueña

Rhetoric Review

Rhino

Rivendell

River Styx

River Teeth
Rowan Tree Press
Ruminate
Runes
Russian *Samizdat*
Saginaw
Salamander
Salmagundi
San Marcos Press
Santa Monica Review
Sarabande Books
Saturnalia
Sea Pen Press and Paper Mill
Seal Press
Seamark Press
Seattle Review
Second Coming Press
Semiotext(e)
Seneca Review
Seven Days
The Seventies Press
Sewanee Review
The Shade Journal
Shankpainter
Shantih
Shearsman
Sheep Meadow Press
Shenandoah
A Shout In the Street
Sibyl-Child Press
Side Show
Sidereal
Sixth Finch
Slipstream
Small Moon
Smartish Pace
The Smith
Snake Nation Review
Solo
Solo 2
Some
The Sonora Review
Southeast Review
Southern Indiana Review

Southern Poetry Review
Southern Review
Southampton Review
Southwest Review
Speakeasy
Spectrum
Spillway
Spork
The Spirit That Moves Us
St. Andrews Press
St. Brigid Press
Stillhouse Press
Stonecoast
Storm Cellar
Story
Story Quarterly
Streetfare Journal
Stuart Wright, Publisher
Subtropics
Sugar House Review
Sulfur
Summerset Review
The Sun
Sun & Moon Press
Sun Press
Sunstone
Sweet
Sycamore Review
Tab
Tamagawa
Tar River Poetry
Teal Press
Telephone Books
Telescope
Temblor
The Temple
Tendril
Terrain
Terminus
Terrapin Books
Texas Slough
Think
Third Coast
13th Moon

THIS
This Broken Shore
Thorp Springs Press
Three Rivers Press
Threepenny Review
Thrush
Thunder City Press
Thunder's Mouth Press
Tia Chucha Press
Tiger Bark Press
Tikkun
Tin House
Tipton Review
Tombouctou Books
Toothpaste Press
Transatlantic Review
Treelight
Triplopia
TriQuarterly
Truck Press
True Story
Tule Review
Tupelo Review
Turnrow
Tusculum Review
Two Sylvias
Twyckenham Notes
Undine
Unicorn Press
University of Chicago Press
University of Georgia Press
University of Illinois Press
University of Iowa Press
University of Massachusetts Press
University of North Texas Press
University of Pittsburgh Press
University of Wisconsin Press
University Press of New England
Unmuzzled Ox
Unspeakable Visions of the Individual
Vagabond

Vallum
Verse
Verse Wisconsin
Vignette
Virginia Quarterly Review
Volt
The Volta
Wampeter Press
War, Literature & The Arts
Washington Square Review
Washington Writer's Workshop
Water-Stone
Water Table
Wave Books
Waxwing
West Branch
Western Humanities Review
Westigan Review
White Pine Press
Wickwire Press
Wigleaf
Willow Springs
Wilmore City
Witness
Word Beat Press
Word Press
Wordsmith
World Literature Today
WordTemple Press
Wormwood Review
Writers' Forum
Xanadu
Yale Review
Yardbird Reader
Yarrow
Y-Bird
Yes Yes Books
Zeitgeist Press
Zoetrope: All-Story
Zone 3
ZYZZYVA

THE PUSHCART PRIZE FELLOWSHIPS

The Pushcart Prize Fellowships Inc., a 501 (c) (3) nonprofit corporation, is the endowment for The Pushcart Prize. "Members" donated up to $249 each. "Sponsors" gave between $250 and $999. "Benefactors" donated from $1000 to $4,999. "Patrons" donated $5,000 and more. We are very grateful for these donations. Gifts of any amount are welcome. For information write to the Fellowships at PO Box 380, Wainscott, NY 11975.

Alan and Karen Furst
John Gill
Robert Giron
Beth Gutcheon
Doris Grumbach & Sybil Pike
Gwen Head
The Healing Muse
Robin Hemley
Bob Hicok
Hippocampus
Jane Hirshfield
Helen & Frank Houghton
Joseph Hurka
Christian Jara
Diane Johnson
Janklow & Nesbit Asso.
Edmund Keeley
Thomas E. Kennedy
Sydney Lea
Stephen Lesser
Gerald Locklin
Thomas Lux
Markowitz, Fenelon and Bank
Elizabeth McKenzie

McSweeney's
Rick Moody
John Mullen
Joan Murray
Thomas Paine
Barbara and Warren Phillips
Hilda Raz
Stacey Richter
Diane Rudner
Schaffner Family Foundation
Sharasheff—Johnson Fund
Cindy Sherman
Joyce Carol Smith
May Carlton Swope
Andrew Tonkovich
Glyn Vincent
Julia Wendell
Philip White
Diane Williams
Kirby E. Williams
Eleanor Wilner
David Wittman
Richard Wyatt & Irene Eilers

MEMBERS

Anonymous (3)
Stephen Adams
Betty Adcock
Agni
Carolyn Alessio
Dick Allen
Henry H. Allen
John Allman
Lisa Alvarez
Jan Lee Ande
Dr. Russell Anderson
Ralph Angel
Antietam Review
Susan Antolin
Ruth Appelhof
Philip and Marjorie Appleman
Linda Aschbrenner
Renee Ashley
Ausable Press
David Baker
Catherine Barnett
Dorothy Barresi
Barlow Street Press
Jill Bart
Ellen Bass
Judith Baumel
Ann Beattie
Madison Smartt Bell

Beloit Poetry Journal
Pinckney Benedict
Karen Bender
Andre Bernard
Christopher Bernard
Wendell Berry
Linda Bierds
Stacy Bierlein
Big Fiction
Bitter Oleander Press
Mark Blaeuer
John Blondel
Blue Light Press
Carol Bly
BOA Editions
Deborah Bogen
Bomb
Susan Bono
Brain Child
Anthony Brandt
James Breeden
Rosellen Brown
Jane Brox
Andrea Hollander Budy
E. S. Bumas
Richard Burgin
Skylar H. Burris
David Caligiuri

Kathy Callaway
Bonnie Jo Campbell
Janine Canan
Henry Carlile
Carrick Publishing
Fran Castan
Mary Casey
Chelsea Associates
Marianne Cherry
Phillis M. Choyke
Lucinda Clark
Suzanne Cleary
Linda Coleman
Martha Collins
Ted Conklin
Joan Connor
J. Cooper
John Copenhaver
Dan Corrie
Pam Cothey
Lisa Couturier
Tricia Currans-Sheehan
Jim Daniels
Daniel & Daniel
Jerry Danielson
Ed David
Josephine David
Thadious Davis
Michael Denison
Maija Devine
Sharon Dilworth
Edward DiMaio
Kent Dixon
A.C. Dorset
Jack Driscoll
Wendy Druce
Penny Dunning
John Duncklee
Nancy Ebert
Elaine Edelman
Renee Edison & Don Kaplan
Nancy Edwards
Ekphrasis Press
M.D. Elevitch
Elizabeth Ellen
Entrekin Foundation
Failbetter.com
Irvin Faust
Elliot Figman
Tom Filer
Carol and Laueme Firth
Finishing Line Press
Susan Firer
Nick Flynn
Starkey Flythe Jr.

Peter Fogo
Linda Foster
Fourth Genre
Alice Friman
John Fulton
Fugue
Alice Fulton
Alan Furst
Eugene Garber
Frank X. Gaspar
A Gathering of the Tribes
Reginald Gibbons
Emily Fox Gordon
Philip Graham
Eamon Grennan
Myrna Goodman
Ginko Tree Press
Jessica Graustain
Lee Meitzen Grue
Habit of Rainy Nights
Rachel Hadas
Susan Hahn
Meredith Hall
Harp Strings
Jeffrey Harrison
Clarinda Harriss
Lois Marie Harrod
Healing Muse
Tim Hedges
Michele Helm
Alex Henderson
Lily Henderson
Daniel Henry
Neva Herington
Lou Hertz
Stephen Herz
William Heyen
Bob Hicok
R. C. Hildebrandt
Kathleen Hill
Lee Hinton
Jane Hirshfield
Hippocampus Magazin
Edward Hoagland
Daniel Hoffman
Doug Holder
Richard Holinger
Rochelle L. Holt
Richard M. Huber
Brigid Hughes
Lynne Hugo
Karla Huston
1–70 Review
Iliya's Honey
Susan Indigo

Mark Irwin

Beverly A. Jackson

Richard Jackson

Christian Jara

David Jauss

Marilyn Johnston

Alice Jones

Journal of New Jersey Poets

Robert Kalich

Sophia Kartsonis

Julia Kasdorf

Miriam Polli Katsikis

Meg Kearney

Celine Keating

Brigit Kelly

John Kistner

Judith Kitchen

Ron Koertge

Stephen Kopel

Peter Krass

David Kresh

Maxine Kumin

Valerie Laken

Babs Lakey

Linda Lancione

Maxine Landis

Lane Larson

Dorianne Laux & Joseph Millar

Sydney Lea

Stephen Lesser

Donald Lev

Dana Levin

Live Mag!

Gerald Locklin

Rachel Loden

Radomir Luza, Jr.

William Lychack

Annette Lynch

Elzabeth MacKieman

Elizabeth Macklin

Leah Maines

Mark Manalang

Norma Marder

Jack Marshall

Michael Martone

Tara L. Masih

Dan Masterson

Peter Matthiessen

Maria Matthiessen

Alice Mattison

Tracy Mayor

Robert McBrearty

Jane McCafferty

Rebecca McClanahan

Bob McCrane

Jo McDougall

Sandy McIntosh

James McKean

Roberta Mendel

Didi Menendez

Barbara Milton

Alexander Mindt

Mississippi Review

Nancy Mitchell

Martin Mitchell

Roger Mitchell

Jewell Mogan

Patricia Monaghan

Jim Moore

James Morse

William Mulvihill

Nami Mun

Joan Murray

Carol Muske-Dukes

Edward Mycue

Deirdre Neilen

W. Dale Nelson

New Michigan Press

Jean Nordhaus

Celeste Ng

Christiana Norcross

Ontario Review Foundation

Daniel Orozco

Other Voices

Paris Review

Alan Michael Parker

Ellen Parker

Veronica Patterson

David Pearce, M.D.

Robert Phillips

Donald Platt

Plain View Press

Valerie Polichar

Pool

Horatio Potter

Jeffrey & Priscilla Potter

C.E. Poverman

Marcia Preston

Eric Puchner

Osiris

Tony Quagliano

Quill & Parchment

Barbara Quinn

Randy Rader

Juliana Rew

Belle Randall

Martha Rhodes

Nancy Richard

Stacey Richter

James Reiss

Katrina Roberts
Judith R. Robinson
Jessica Roeder
Martin Rosner
Kay Ryan
Sy Safransky
Brian Salchert
James Salter
Sherod Santos
Ellen Sargent
R.A. Sasaki
Valerie Sayers
Maxine Scates
Alice Schell
Dennis & Loretta Schmitz
Grace Schulman
Helen Schulman
Philip Schultz
Shenandoah
Peggy Shinner
Lydia Ship
Vivian Shipley
Joan Silver
Skyline
John E. Smeleer
Raymond J. Smith
Joyce Carol Smith
Philip St. Clair
Lorraine Standish
Maureen Stanton
Michael Steinberg
Sybil Steinberg
Jody Stewart
Barbara Stone
Storyteller Magazine
Bill & Pat Strachan
Raymond Strom
Julie Suk
Summerset Review
Sun Publishing
Sweet Annie Press
Katherine Taylor
Pamela Taylor
Elaine Terranova
Susan Terris
Marcelle Thiebaux
Robert Thomas

Andrew Tonkovich
Pauls Toutonghi
Juanita Torrence-Thompson
William Trowbridge
Martin Tucker
Umbrella Factory Press
Under The Sun
Universal Table
Upstreet
Jeannette Valentine
Victoria Valentine
Christine Van Winkle
Hans Vandebovenkamp
Elizabeth Veach
Tino Villanueva
Maryfrances Wagner
William & Jeanne Wagner
BJ Ward
Susan O. Warner
Rosanna Warren
Margareta Waterman
Michael Waters
Stuart Watson
Sandi Weinberg
Andrew Wainstein
Dr. Henny Wenkart
Jason Wesco
West Meadow Press
Susan Wheeler
When Women Waken
Dara Wier
Ellen Wilbur
Galen Williams
Diane Williams
Marie Sheppard Williams
Eleanor Wilner
Irene Wilson
Steven Wingate
Sandra Wisenberg
Wings Press
Robert Witt
David Wittman
Margot Wizansky
Matt Yurdana
Christina Zawadiwsky
Sander Zulauf
ZYZZYVA

CONTRIBUTING SMALL PRESSES FOR PUSHCART PRIZE XLVII

(These presses made nominations for this edition.)

(The following small presses made nominations for this edition)

A&U Magazine, 21-17 41st St., #3, Astoria, NY 11105

About Place Journal, Black Earth Inst., Box 424, Black Earth, WI 53515-0424

AbstractMagazineTV, 124 E. Johnson St., Norman, OK 73069

Abyss & Apex, 116 Tennyson Dr., Lexington, SC 29073

Acorn, 115 Connifer Ln, Walnut Creek, CA 94598

ADI Magazine, Jeyasundaram, 101 Martini Dr., Richmond Hill, ON L4S, 2S5, Canada

Adirondack Review, PO Box 147, Gouverneur, NY 13642

The Adroit Journal, 1223 Westover Rd., Stamford, CT 06902

Aeolus House, PO Box 53031, 10 Royal Orchard Blvd, Thornhill ON L3T 3CD, Canada

Afternoon Visitor, Brady, 1226D Rochester Ave., Iowa City, IA 52245

Agni Magazine, Boston Univ., 236 Bay State Rd., Boston, MA 02215

Airlie Press, PO Box 68441, Portland, OR 97268

Air/Light, English Dept., USC, 3501 Trousdale Pkwy, Los Angeles, CA 90089-0354

Alaska Quarterly, ESH 208, 3211 Providence Dr., Anchorage, AK 99508

Alba Publishing, PO Box 266, Uxbridge UB9 5NX, UK

Alien Buddha Press, 501 Bushy Creek Rd., Woodruff, SC 29388

Allium Journal, Columbia College, 600 So. Michigan Ave., Chicago, IL 60605

Alternate Route, Starr, 741 Katydid Ct., Martinez, CA 94553-2221

Alternating Current, PO Box 270921, Louisville, CO 80027

Always Crashing, 1401 N. St. Clair, #3A, Pittsburgh, PA 15206

American Journal of Poetry, 375 Greenyard Dr., #A, Ballwin, MO 63011

American Poetry Review, 1906 Rittenhouse Sq., Philadelphia, PA 19103

American Short Fiction, 109 West Johanna St., Austin, TX 78704

And I Thought Ladies, 1521 Ritchie Hwy, #401, Arnold, MD 21012

Animal Heart Press, Gordon, 300 Long Shoals Rd., #17-O, Arden, NC 28704-7764

Another Chicago Magazine, 1301 W. Byron St., Chicago, IL 60613

Appalachia Journal, Woodside, 41 Bridge St., Deep River, CT 06417

Appalachian Heritage, Shepherd Univ., PO Box 5000, Shepherdstown, WV 25443

Appalachian Review, Berea College, CPO 2166, Berea, KY 40404

Apparition Literary, Robinson, 1220 Johnson Dr., #81, Ventura, CA 93003

Apple Valley Review, 88 South 3rd St., #336, San José, CA 95113

Apricity Press, Mason-Reader, 3279 Coraly Ave., Eugene, OR 97402

Aquarius Press, PO Box 23096, Detroit, MI 48223-0096

Arachne Press, 100 Grierson Rd., London SE23 1NX, UK

Ariel Publishing, Lamilki, 2720 W. Rascher Ave., 2W, Chicago, IL 60625

Ariel's Dream, Valdez, 1206 E. Fox Chase Dr., Round Lake Beach, IL 60073

Arion Press, 1802 Hays St., The Presidio, San Francisco, CA 94129

Arizona Authors, 1119 E. LeMarche Ave., Phoenix, AZ 85022

Arkana, UCA, Thompson Hall 324, 201 Donaghey Ave., Conway, AR 72035

Arkansas International, UAR, Kimpel Hall 333, Fayetteville, AR 72701

Arrowsmith Press, 11 Chestnut St., Medford, MA 02155

Arts & Letters, CBX 89, Georgia College, Milledgeville, GA 31061-0490

As It Ought To Be, 5312 Denny Ave., #6, North Hollywood, CA 91601

Aster(ix), Cruz, English Dept, 5th flr, 4200 Fifth Ave., Pittsburgh, PA 15260

Atherton Review, 2824 Buckpass, Mariposa, CA 95338

Atticus Review, Cafaro, 13034 N. Mimosa Dr, Fountain Hills, AZ 85268

Augur Magazine, 102-3444 Keele St., Toronto, ON M3J 1L8, Canada

Aunt Cloe, Mann, 2259 Sutton St. SE, Atlanta, GA 30317

Autofocus Literary, Wheaton, 3711 March Ave., Orlando, FL 32806

Autumn Sky Poetry Daily, 5263 Arctic Circle, Emmaus, PA 18049

Awakened Voices, 4001 No. Ravenswood Ave., #204-C, Chicago, IL 60613

Awakenings, 4001 N. Ravenswood Ave., #204-C, Chicago, IL 60613

Awst Press, PO Box 49163, Austin, TX 78765

The B'K, 1635 Cook St., #214, Denver, CO 80206

Balance of Seven, 917 Stone Trail Dr., Plano, TX 75023-7109

Baltimore Review, 6514 Maplewood Rd., Baltimore, MD 21212

Bamboo Dart Press, 112 Harvard Ave., #65, Claremont, CA 91711

Bare Life Review, PO Box 352, Lagunitas, CA 94938

Bat City Review, Univ. Texas, 2 University St., B5000, Austin, TX 78712

Bay to Ocean Journal, Eastern Shores Writers, PO Box 1773, Easton, MD 21601

Bayou Magazine, UNO-English, 2000 Lake Shore Dr., New Orleans, LA 70148

Bear Review, 4211 Holmes St., Kansas City, MO 64110

Bell Press, 202-1622 Frances St., Vancouver, BC V5L 1Z4, Canada

Bellevue Literary Review, 149 East 23rd St., #1516, New York, NY 10010

Bellingham Review, MS 9053, Western Washington Univ., Bellingham, WA 98225

Belmont Story Review, 1900 Belmont Blvd., Nashville, IN 37212-3757

Beloit Poetry Journal, PO Box 1450, Windham, ME 04062

Bennington Review, Turner, 999 Hart St. #2, Brooklyn, NY 11237

Better Than Starbucks, PO Box 673, Mayo, FL 32066

BeZine, Dickel, 9 Shalom Yehuda, Apt 7, 9339511, Jerusalem, Israel

BHC Press, 885 Penniman #5505, Plymouth, MI 48170

Big Bend Literary, 22813 Fm 170, Terlingua, TX 79852

BigCityLIt, Cappelluti, 85 Creek Rd., Middlebury, VT 05753

Big Other, 1840 W. 3rd St., Brooklyn, NY 11223

Big Windows, 2012 Marra Dr., Ann Arbor, MI 48103-6186

Bird Brain Publishing, 7640 Ridgeway Ave., Evansville, IN 47715

Birdseed, Jai, 3 Blu Harbor Blvd., #551, Redwood City, CA 94063

Birmingham Poetry Review, English, UAB, Birmingham, AL 35294-0110

The Bitchin' Kitsch, 1635 Cook St., #214, Denver, CO 80206

Bitter Southerner, PO Box 1611, Athens, GA 30603

BkMk Press, 5 W 3rd St., Parkville, MO 64152-3707

Black Bomb, 50 Jarrett St., Asheville, NC 28806

Black Bough Poetry, 18 Hendrefoilan Rd., Tycoch, Swansea, SA29LS, UK

Black Lawrence Press, Goettel, 279 Claremont Ave., Mt. Vernon, NY 10552-3305

Blackbird, VCU, English, PO Box 843082, Richmond, VA 23284-3082

Blank Spaces, 282906 Normanby/Bentinck Townline, Durham ON NOG 1R0, Canada

Blink-Ink, P.O. Box 5, North Branford, CT 06471

Blood Orange Review, W.S.U., English, Box 645020, Pullman, WA 99164-5020

Bloodroot Literary, Mosteirin, 71 Baker Hill Rd., Lyme, NH 03768

Blue Heron Review, N66W38350 Deer Creek Ct., Oconomowoc, WI 53066

Blue Horse Press, 5403 Sunnyview St., Torrance, CA 90505

Blue Jade Press, 517 Sylvester Dr., Vineland, NJ 08360

Blue Light Press, PO Box 150300, San Rafael, CA 94915

Blue Unicorn, 13 Jefferson Ave., San Rafael, CA 94903

BOA Editions, 250 N. Goodman St., #306, Rochester, NY 14607

Bodega Magazine, 451 Court St., #3R, Brooklyn, NY 11231

The Boiler, 1118 Bernard St., Denton, TX 76201

Bomb, 80 Hanson Place, #703, Brooklyn, NY 11217-1506

Book Post, 107 Bank St., New York, NY 10014

Boomer Lit, 4509 Beard Ave So., Minneapolis, MN 55410

Booth, 4600 Sunset Ave., Indianapolis, IN 46208

Borda Books, 19 E. Isla St., Santa Barbara, CA 93101

Border Crossing, Creative Writing, 650 W. Easterday Ave., Sault Ste. Marie, MI 49783

Bottom Dog Press, PO Box 425, Huron, OH 44839

Boulevard, 6614 Clayton Rd., Box 325, Richmond Heights, MO 63117

Box Turtle Press, Hoffman, 184 Franklin St., New York, NY 10013

Braided Way, 8916 Shank Rd., Litchfield, OH 44253

Briar Cliff Review, 3303 Rebecca St., Sioux City, IA 51104-2100

Brick Road Poetry Press, 341 Lee Rd. 553, Phenix City, AL 36867

Bright Flash Literary Review, 12520 Caswell Ave., Los Angeles, CA 90066

Brilliant Flash Fiction, 4201 Corbett Dr., #343, Fort Collins, CO 80525

Brink Literary Journal, 450 Hwy 1 W, #126, Iowa City, IA 52246

Broadkill Review, 25624 E. Main, Onley, VA 23418

Broadsided Press, PO Box 24, Provincetown, MA 02657

Broadstone Books, 418 Ann St., Frankfort, KY 40601-1929

Bull City Press, 1217 Odyssey Dr., Durham, NC 27713-1772

Bullshit Lit, 735 Oxford St., Houston, TX 77007

Burial Day Books, Pelayo, 4417 W. Montana, Chicago, IL 60639

Burningword Literary Journal, PO Box 6215, Kokomo, IN 46904-6215

C & R Press, 500 W. 4th St., #201-C, Winston-Salem, NC 27101

California State Poetry Society, Trochimczyk, PO Box 7126, Orange CA 92863

Canned Magazine, 6 Keari Lane, South Burlington, VT 05403

Capsule Stories, PO Box 11762, Clayton, MO 63105

Carve Magazine, PO Box 701510, Dallas, TX 75370

Cast of Wonders, Bailey, 521 River Ave, Providence, RI 02908

Catamaran, 1050 River St., #118, Santa Cruz, CA 95060

Catapult, Wilson, 234 Sullivan Pl., Brooklyn, NY 11225

Central Avenue Publishing, 396-5148 Ladner Trunk Rd., Delta BC V4K 5B6, Canada

Červená Barva Press, PO Box 440357, W. Somerville, MA 02144

Chautauqua, UNC-W, Creative Writing, 601 S. College Rd., Wilmington, NC 28403

Cheap Pop, Russell, 801 O St., #260, Lincoln, NE 68508

Cherry Tree, Washington College, 300 Washington Ave., Chestertown, MD 21620

Chestnut Review, 114 Honness Ln, Ithaca, NY 14850

Chicago Quarterly, S. Haider, 517 Sherman Ave., Evanston, IL 60202

Chiron Publications, PO Box 19690, Asheville, NC 28815

Chiron Review, 522 E. South Ave., St. John, KS 67576-2212

Choeofpleirn Press, 1424 Frankin St., Leavenworth, KS 66048

Cholla Needles, 6732 Conejo Ave., Joshua Tree, CA 92252

Cimarron Review, English, 205 Morrill, OSU, Stillwater, OK 74078

Cincinnati Review, English, PO Box 210069, Cincinnati, OH 45221-0069

Circling Rivers, PO Box 8291, Richmond, VA 23226

Cirque Press, 3157 Bettle's Bay Loop, Anchorage, AK 99515

City Lights, 261 Columbus Ave., San Francisco, CA 94133

Coachella Review, UCR Palm Desert, 75080 Frank Sinatra Dr., Palm Desert, CA 92211

Coal City Review, English Dept., University of Kansas, Lawrence, KS 66045

Coastal Shelf, 3306 Country Club Dr, Grand Prairie, TX 75052

Coffin Bell Journal, 225 N. Ogden St., Buffalo, NY 14206

Cold Moon, Jacobson, 405 S. Jefferson Way, Indianola, IA 50125

Colorado Review, CSU, English, Fort Collins, CO 80523-9105

The Common, Frost Library, Amherst College, Amherst, MA 01002

The Common Reader, Washington & Lee, CB 1098, 1 Brookings Dr, St. Louis, MO 63130-4899

Complete Sentence, J. Thayer, 59 Lorene Ave., Athens, OH 45701

Comstock Review, 4956 St. John Dr., Syracuse, NY 13215

Concho River Review, ASU Station #10894, San Angelo TX 76909-0894

Concision Poetry Journal, 1971 9th St., White Bear Lake, MN 55110

Conjunctions, Bard College, Annandale, NY 12504-5000

Connecticut Literary Anthology, CCSU English, 1615 Stanley St., New Britain, CT 06050

Connecticut River Review, 9 Edmund Pl, West Hartford, CT 06119

Concrete Desert Review, 37500 Cook St., Palm Desert, CA 92211

Constellations, 127 Lake View Ave., Cambridge, MA 02138-3366

Contrary Journal, S. Beers, 615 NW 6th St., Pendleton, OR 97801-1317

Copper Nickel, Wayne Miller, UC-D, English - CB 175, PO Box 173364, Denver, CO 80217-3364

Copperfield Review, Allard, 2654 W. Horizon Ridge Pkwy, #B5-364, Henderson, NV 89052

Court Green, English, Columbia College, 600 Michigan Ave., Chicago, IL 60605

Crab Creek Review, 633 4th Ave. W, #304, Seattle, WA 98119

Craft, 70 SW Century Dr., Ste. 100442, Bend, OR 97702

Crannóg Magazine, 6 San Antonio Park, Salthill, Galway, Ireland

Crayne Books, 905 NE 80th Ave., Portland, OR 97213

Crazyhorse, College of Charleston, 66 George St., Charleston, SC 29424

Cream City Review, UW-M, PO Box 413, Milwaukee, WI 53201

Creative Nonfiction, 607 College Ave., Pittsburgh, PA 15232-1700

Creature Publishing, 91 Clifton Pl, Ste. 1D, Brooklyn, NY 11238

Cultural Daily, 3330 S. Peck Ave., #14, San Pedro, CA 90731

Cutbank, Univ. of Montana, English, LA 133, MST410, Missoula, MT 59812

Cutleaf, Lesmeister, 922 Pleasant Ave., Decorah, IA 52101

Cutthroat, A Journal of the Arts, 5401 N. Cresta Loma Dr., Tucson, AZ 85704

Dead Skunk, 915 E. Chestnut St., #1, Jeffersonville, IN 47130
Decadent Review, Sorauerstr. 9A, 10997, Germany
december, P.O. Box 16130, St. Louis, MO 63105-0830
Decolonial Passage, PO Box 35238, Los Angeles, CA 90035
Deep Wild, 2309 Broadway, Grand Junction, CO 81507
Delmarva Review, PO Box 544, St. Michaels, MD 21663
Denver Quarterly, English, Univ. of Denver, 495 Sturgis Hall, Denver, CO
    80208
Deuxmers, PO Box 440, Waimanalo, HI 96795
Devil's Party Press, PO Box 491, Milton, DE 19968
The Dewdrop, V. Able, 2417 Laura Lane, Mountain View, CA 94043
Dialogist, Loruss, 925 Leroy S., Ferndale, MI 48220-3114
Diode Editions, PO Box 5585, Richmond, VA 23220
Digging Press, 130 W. Pleasant Ave., #307, Maywood, NJ 07607
Discover New Art, Ste.100442, 70 SW Century Dr, Bend, OR 97702-3557
DMQ Review, 16393 Bonnie Lane, Los Gatos, CA 95032
Dope Fiend Daily, 301 Regency Dr., Deer Park, TX 77536
Doubleback Review, 52671 Santa Monica Dr, Granger, IN 46530
Dragonfly, 87 Colonial Village, Amherst, MA 01002
Dread Machine, 43 Lexington Rd., Avon, CT 06004
Dream Pop Press, PO Box 2793, Roanoke, VA 24001
Dribble Drabble Review, 43 Twelve Oaks Dr., Murphysboro, IL 62966
Driftwood Press, 14737 Montoro Dr., Austin, TX 78728
Drunk Monkeys, 252 N Cordova St., Burbank, CA 91505
Dryland, Padilla, 2014 ½ E. Cesar E. Chavez Ave., Los Angeles, CA 90033

EastOver Press, Legmeister, 922 Pleasant Ave., Decorah, IA 52101
Eco Theo Review, Johns, 2225 Lane Rd., Greensboro, NC 27408-3415
8th and Atlas Publishing, M. deParis, 911 Walnut St., Winston-Salem, NC 27101
86 Logic, 3621 30th St., New York, NY 11106
Ekphrastic Review, 1505-1085 Steeles Ave. W, North York, M2R 2T1, Canada
Elder Mountain, MSU-English, 128 Garfield, West Plains, MO 65775
Electric Literature, 147 Prince St., Brooklyn, NY 11201
ELJ Editions, PO Box 815, Washingtonville, NY 10992
The Elephants, 1624 11th Ave. SW, Olympia, WA 98502
11th Floor Books, Ivan Mistrik, Ozvoldikova 4,841 02 Bratislava, Slovakia
Emerge Literary Journal, PO Box 815, Washingtonville, NY 10992
Emerson Review, Emerson College, 120 Boylston St., Boston, MA 02116
Epiphany, 71 Bedford St., New York, NY 10014
Epoch, 251 Goldwin Smith Hall, Cornell University, Ithaca NY 14853
Epoch Press, North Woodlea, Garelochhead, Helensburgh G84 0EG, Scotland

Escape Pod, Bailey, 521 River Ave., Providence, RI 02908

Etcetera Poetry, Naughton, 312 Pennsylvania St., #2, Buffalo, NY 14201

EX Ophidia Press, 919 2nd Ave. W., #407, Seattle, WA 98119

EX/POST, 1054 Wild Dunes Way, Johns Creek, GA 30097

Exit 13, PO Box 423, Fanwood, NJ 07023

Exponent II, 13 Hunting St., #1, Cambridge, MA 02141

Exposition Review, 1958 S. Beverly Glen Blvd., Los Angeles, CA 90025

Evening Street Press & Review, 2881 Wright St., Sacramento, CA 95821

The Fabulist Magazine, 1377 5th Ave., San Francisco, CA 94122

failbetter, 2022 Grove Ave., Richmond, VA 23220

Fairfield Scribes Press, McBain-Ahern, 1510 Stratfield Rd., Fairfield, CT 06825

Fantasy Magazine, Sorg c/o Locus, 655 13th St., #100, Oakland, CA 94612

Farmer-ish, 302 Davis Rd., Eddington, ME 04428

Fatal Flaw, 122 E. 17th St., #3F, New York, NY 10003

Feels Blind Literary, 2121 Miller Ave., Richmond, VA 23222

Fiction, City College of NY, English, Convent Ave at 138th St., New York, NY 10031

Fiction International, SDSU, English, 5500 Campanile Dr. San Diego, CA 92182-6020

Fictional Passage, 5 Hollow Lane, Lexington, MA 02420

Final Thursday, 815 State St., Cedar Falls, IA 50613

Fine Print Press, PO Box 64711, Baton Rouge, LA 70896

Finishing Line Press, POB 1626, Georgetown, KY 40324

First Matter Press, 221 SE 15th Ave., Portland, OR 97214

Five Points, Georgia State Univ, Box 3999, Atlanta, GA 30302

518 Publishing. 1647 Spring Ave E., Wynantskill, NY 12198

Five South, 1850 Industrial St., #714, Los Angeles, CA 90021

Flapper Press, 10061 Riverside Dr., #115, Toluca Lake, CA 91602

Flash Back Fiction, Jendrzejewski, 2 Pearce Close, Cambridge, CB3 9LY, UK

Flash Flood, Jendrzejewski, 2 Pearce Close, Cambridge CB3 9LY UK

Flash Frontier, 35 Sutherland St., Dunedin 9016, New Zealand

Flash Frog, 1010 16th St., #311, San Francisco, CA 94107

Fledging Rag, 1838 Edenwald Lane, Lancaster, PA 17601

FllK//Books, Greene, 3929 E. Via Estrella, Phoenix, AZ 85028

Floating Opera, Hasenheide 9, Berlin, BE 10999, Germany

Florida Review, English, PO Box 161346, Orlando, FL 32816

Flourishing/Florescence, Guidelight Prod., PO Box 233, San Luis Rey, CA 92068

Flying Island, Indiana Writers, 1125 E. Brookside Ave., B-25, Indianapolis, IN 46202

Flying South, 546 Old Birch Creek Rd., McLeansville, NC 27301

Flypaper Lit, J. David, 9919 Biddulph Rd., Brooklyn, OH 44144

Foglifter, Flynn-Goodlett, 633 33rd St., Richmond, CA 94804

Foothill Poetry Journal, 160 E. 10th St., B2/B3, Claremont, CA 91711-5909

The Foreign Service Journal, 2101 Street NW, Washington, DC 20037

Forge, 4018 Bayview Ave., San Mateo, CA 94403-4310

Four Way Books, 11 Jay St., #4, New York, NY 10013-2847

Fourteen Hills, SFSU-Creative Writing, 1600 Holloway Ave., San Francisco, CA 94132

Fourth Genre, 434 Farm Lane, Rm 235, MSU, East Lansing, MI 48824

Friendly City Books, 118 5th St N, Columbus, MS 39701-4522

From the Farther Trees, Hollow, 3209 Allerton Cir, #A, Greensboro, NC 27409

Frontier Poetry, Roark, 753 S. Detroit St., #2, Los Angeles, CA 90036

Fruit Bat Press, 3840 N. Drake Ave., #2, Chicago, IL 60618

Galileo Press, 3222 Rocking Horse In, Aiken, SC 29801

Gallaudet University Press, 800 Florida Ave. NE, Washington, DC 20002-3695

Galleywinter Poetry, 2778 Elizabeth Pl., Lebanon, OR 97355

Gargoyle, Peabody, 3829 13th St. N., Arlington, VA 22201

Gathering Space, 57 Montague St., #9H, Brooklyn, NY 11201

Gemini Magazine, PO Box 1485, Onset, MA 02558

Georgia Review, 706A Main Library, Univ. of Georgia, Athens, GA 30602-9009

Gettysburg Review, Gettysburg College, Box 2446, Gettysburg, PA 17325

Ghost Parachute, 617 N. Hyer Ave., #4, Orlando, FL 32803

Gigantic Sequins, 4610 Skyline Dr., Anniston, AL 36206

Ginninderra Press, PO Box 3461, Port Adelaide 5015, South Australia

Gival Press, PO Box 3812, Arlington, VA 22203

Glass Lyre Press, PO Box 2693, Glenview, IL 60025

Glassworks, 260 Victoria St., Glassboro, NJ 08028

Gnashing Teeth, PO Box 143, Rockport, TX 78381-0143

Golden Foothills Press, 1438 Atchison St., Pasadena, CA 91104

Golden Square Review, 10429 Baltic Rd., Cleveland, OH 44102

Good Life Review, 13910 N. 192nd St., Bennington, NE 68007

Good River Review, Spalding Univ., 851 S. Fourth St., Louisville, KY 40203

Graft Poetry, Frizingley Hall, Frizinghall Rd., Bradford BD4 4LD, UK

Grand Canyon Press, 90 West Cottage Lane, Tempe, AZ 85282

Granta, 12 Addison Ave., Holland Park, London W11 4QR, UK

The Gravity of the Thing, 17028 SE Rhone St., Portland, OR 97236

Grayson Books, PO Box 270549, West Hartford, CT 06127

great weather for MEDIA, 515 Broadway, #2B, New York, NY 10012

Green Linden Press, 208 Broad St South, Grinnell, IA 50112

Greenbelt News Review, 15 Crescent Rd., #100, Greenbelt, MO 20770-1887

Greenpoint Press, Salzberg, 200 Riverside Blvd, Ste. 32E, New York, NY 10069

Greensboro Review, 3302 MHRA Bldg., UNC, Greensboro, NC 27402-6170

Green Writers Press, 34 Miller Rd., W. Brattleboro, VT 05301
Guernica, Khatry, 527 Ronalds St., #6, Iowa City, IA 52245
Guesthouse, 1106 E. Washinton St., Iowa City, IA 52245
Gulf Coast Journal, English, University of Houston, Houston, TX 77204-3013
Gyroscope Review, PO Box 1989, Gillette, WY 82717-1989

Halfway Down the Stairs, Roberts, 6425 164th St., Chippewa Falls, WI 54729
Hamby Stern Publishing, 241 SW 64th Ct., Miami Beach, FL 33144-3149
Harpur Palate, English, B.U., PO Box 6000, Binghamton, NY 13902
The Harvard Advocate, 21 South St., Cambridge, MA 02138
Harvard Review, Lamont Library, Harvard Univ., Cambridge, MA 02138
HauntedMTL Press, PO Box 2291, Eagle River, WI 54521
Hayden's Ferry Review, ASU, P.O. Box 875002, Tempe, AZ 85287-5002
Hedgehog Review, Univ. of Virginia, PO Box 400816, Charlottesville, VA 22904
Helix Literary Magazine, 1615 Stanley St., New Britain, CT 06050
Hennepin Review, 2355 Fairview Ave., Box 229, Roseville, MN 55113
HerStry, 2520 N. Pierce St., #4, Milwaukee, WI 53212
Hex Publishers, PO Box 298, Erie, CO 80516
Highland Park Poetry, 1690 Midland Ave., Highland Park, IL 60035
Hinterland Press, Entertainment Center, Univ. East Anglia, Norwich NR4
    7TJ, UK
Hippocampus, 210 W. Grant St., #104, Lancaster, PA 17603
Hobart, 2228 Glencoe Hills Dr., #4, Ann Arbor, MI 48108
Hole in the Head Review, 85 Forbes Ln, Windham, ME 04062
The Hollins Critic, Hollins University, Box 9538, Roanoke, VA 24020
Honeyguide, 60 Avalon Cr., Smithtown, NY 11787
Hong Kong Review, 2306 Prosper Commercial Bldg, 9 Yin Chong St., Kowloon,
    Hong Kong
Hoot Review, 4534 Osage Ave., C-102, Philadelphia, PA, 19143
The Hopper, 4935 Twin Lakes Rd., #36, Boulder, CO 80301
Hub City Press, 200 Ezell St., Spartanburg, SC 29306
The Hudson Review, 33 West 67th St., New York, NY 10023
Hyades, 71 Balmoral Rd., Kellyville, NSW, Australia
Hypertext, c/o Rice, 1821 W. Melrose St., Chicago, IL 60657
Hypocrite Reader, Wheeler, 653 10th St., Oakland, CA 94607

I-70 Review, 5021 S. Tierney Dr., Independence, MO 64055-6930
iamb, 57 Thorpe Gardens, Alton, Hampshire GU34 2BQ, UK
Ibbetson Street Press, 25 School Street, Somerville, MA 02143
Ice Box, UAF-English, PO Box 755720, Fairbanks, AK 99775
Icefloe Press, 30 Kensington Place, Toronto, ON M5T 2K4, Canada
Idaho Review, BSU-Creative Writing, 1910 University Dr., Boise, ID 83725-
    1545

IHRAF Publishes Literary Journal, International Human Rights Art Festival, 4142 73rd St., #5M, Queens, NY 11377

Ilanot Review, 35 Bauli St., #6, Tel Aviv 6291776, Israel

Illuminated Press, 6011 Sirrine Rd., Trumansburg, NY 14886

Illuminations, CC-English, 66 George St., Charleston, SC 29424

Image, 3307 Third Avenue West, Seattle, WA 98119

Indie Blu(e), 1714 Woodmere Way, Havertown, PA 19083

Inked in Gray, 1428 S. Crossbow Ct., Chandler, AZ 85286

Inner Child Press International, 202 Wiltree Ct., State College, PA 16801

Intima Journal, 36 N. Moore St., #4W, New York, NY 10013

Inverted Syntax, PO Box 2044, Longmont CO 80502

Invisible City, USF, Kalmanovitz Hall, Rm 302, 2130 Fulton St., San Francisco, CA 94117

Iowa Poetry Association, Baszczynski, 16096 320th Way, Earlham, IA 50072

The Iowa Review, 308 EPB., Iowa City, IA 52242

Iron Horse, Patterson, English, MS 43091, Texas Tech Univ., Lubbock, TX 79423

Irreantum, Jepson, 115 Ramona Ave., El Cerrito, CA 94530

Iskanchi Magazine, 165 So Pleasant Grove Blvd., #46, Pleasant Grove, UT 84062

Italian American Journal, Terrone, 3556 77th St., #31, Jackson Hts, NY 11372-4588

J Journal, English, 619 West 54th St., 7th Fl, New York, NY 10019

Jacar Press, 6617 Deerview Trail, Durham, NC 27712

Jabberwock Review, MSU, PO Box E, Mississippi State, MS 39762

James Dickey Review, Reinhardt U., 7300 Reinhardt Cir, Waleska, GA 30183-2981

Janice Beetle Books, 8 Birch Lane, Florence, MA 01062

Janus Literary, Leagra, PO Box 881, Garner, NC 27529

Jelly Bucket, Eastern Kentucky Univ., English/Theater, Mattox 101, 521 Lancaster Ave., Richmond, KY 40475

Jelly Fish Review, C. James, 533K the 18th Residence, Taman Rasuna RT16/RW1 Menteng Atas, Kota Iak Sel 12960, Indonesia

Jerry Jazz, 2538 NE 32nd Ave., Portland, OR 97212

Jersey Devil Press, 1826 Avon Rd. SW, Roanoke, VA 24015

Jet Fuel, Muench, 1508 W. Erie St., #3, Chicago, IL 60642

Johns Hopkins University Press, 2715 No. Charles St., Baltimore, MD 21218-4363

The Journal, OSU - English, 164 Annie & John Glenn Ave., Columbus, OH 43210

Juked, 108 New Mark Esplanade, Rockville, MD 20850

JuxtaProse, 4430 Aster St., Springfield, OR 97478

Kallisto Gaia Press, 1801 E 51st St., #365-246, Austin, TX 78723
Kelsay Books, 502 S. 1040 E, #A119, American Fork, UT 84003
Kelsey Review, MCCC, 1200 Old Trenton Rd., West Windsor, NJ 08550
Kenyon Review, Finn House, 102 W. Wiggin St., Gambier, OH 43022-9623
Kepler Production, 915 Chapel Dr., Bountiful, UT 84010
Kestrel, Fairmont State Univ., Humanities - 2640, Fairmont, WV 26554
Khalis House Publishing, 84 Mcmahon Dr., Newmains, ML2 9BS, Scotland, UK
Khôra Magazine, 510 SW 3rd Ave., #101, Portland, OR 97204
Kissing Dynamite, C. Taylor, POB 662, Scotch Plains, NJ 07076
Kitty Wang's, Mambo Academy, PO Box 5, North Branford, CT 06471
Kore Press Institute, PO Box 42315, Tucson, AZ 85733
Kweli Journal, POB 693, New York, NY 10021

La Traductière, 22 rue saint Amand, 75015 Paris, France
La Vague, 7809 Estancia St., Carlsbad, CA 92009
Lake Effect, Humanities, 4951 College Drive, Erie, PA 16563-1501
Laksa Media, PO Box 57060, Calgary, AB, T1Y 5T4, Canada
Lamar University Literary Press, PO Box 10023, Beaumont, TX 77710
Lamplit Underground, 2301 West Anderson Hwy, #102-2, Austin, TX 78757
Lascaux Review, 3155 Pebble Beach Dr., #10, Conway, AR 72034
Laughing Ronin Press, PO Box 234, Owensboro, KY 42303
Laurel Review, NWMSU, 800 University Dr., Marysville, MO 64468
Lavender Review, 4 Corley Loop, Eureka Springs, AR 72632
Leavings Literary Magazine, 1929 Karen Ln, Tallahassee, FL 32304
Ledgetop Publishing, PO Box 105, Richmond, MA 01254-0105
Leon Literary Review, 2 Saint Paul St., #404, Brookline, MA 02446
LEX/Literary Excellence, Lamilki, 2720 W. Rascher Ave., #2W, Chicago, IL
    60625
Ligeia Magazine, Wagner, 7802 Chevalier Ct., Severn, MD 21144
Light, 1515 Highland Ave., Rochester, NY 14618
Lily Poetry Review, Cleary, 223 Winter St., Whitman, MA 02382
Limp Wrist, 520 NE 28th St., #708, Wilton Manors, FL 33305
The Lincoln Review, English, University of Lincoln, Brayford Way, Brayford
    Pool, Lincoln LN6 7TS, UK
Line of Advance, 2126 W. Armitage, #3, Chicago, IL 60647
Lips, 141 Madison Ave., Clifton, NJ 07011
The Literary Hatchet, 345 Charlotte White Rd., Westport, MA 02790
LitMag, c/o Berley, 23 Ferris Lane, Bedford, NY 10506
Livingston Press, Stn 22, Univ. West Alabama, Livingston, AL 35470
Loch Raven Review, 1306 Providence Rd., Towson, MD 21286
Long Day Press, 61 Carmine St., #A-C, New York, NY 10014
Longleaf Review, Trott, 463 Sconticut Neck Rd., Fairhaven, MA 02719
Longridge Editors, 325 W. Colonial Hwy, Hamilton, VA 20158

Los Angeles Review of Books, 6671 Sunset Blvd., #1521, Los Angeles, CA 90028

Lost Balloon, 1402 Highland Ave., Berwyn, IL 60402

Lost Boys Press, PO Box 1178, Higley, AZ 85236

Lost Horse Press, 1025 So. Garry Rd., Liberty Lake, WA 99019

Lothlorien Poetry Journal, Strider Marcus Jones, 7 Baptist Walk, Hinckley Leics LE10, IPR, England

Loving Healing Press, 5145 Pontiac Trail, Ann Arbor, MI 48105-9238

Lucky Jefferson, 221 W. Harrison St., Chicago, IL 60607

Lowestoft Chronicle, 1925 Massachusetts Ave, #8, Cambridge, MA 02140

The MacGuffin, 18600 Haggerty Rd., Livonia, MI 48152-2696

MacQueen's Quinterly, PO Box 2322, Kernersville, NC 27285

Mad Zebra Press, 51 Larry Drive, Monmouth, ME 04259

Madville Publishing, PO Box 358, Lake Dallas, TX 75065

Main Street Rag Publishing, POB 690100, Charlotte, NC 28227

Maine Review, 1000 River Rd., Dresden, ME 04342

Manhattan Review, 440 Riverside Dr., #38, New York, NY 10027

Mannison Press, 5805 Caldera Ridge Dr., Lithia, FL 33547

Mantle Poetry, c/o Jackson, 4422 Milgate St., Pittsburgh, PA 15224

The Margins, Asian American Writers, 112 W. 27th St., Ste. 600, New York, NY 10001

Massachusetts Review, Photo Lab 309, 211 Hicks Way, U-Mass, Amhgerst, MA, 01003

matchbook, 333 Harvard St., #5, Cambridge, MA 02139

Meadowlark, PO Box 333, Emporia, KS 66801

Mercer University Press, 1501 Mercer University Dr., Macon, GA 31207-1515

Meridian, U. of VA, PO Box 400145, Charlottesville, VA 22904-4145

Michigan Quarterly Review, 3277 Angell Hall, 435 S. State St., Ann Arbor, MI 48109-1003

Middle Creek Publishing, 9167 Mountain Park Rd., Beulah, CO 81023

Midway Journal, Pennel, 2603 Ashton Crt., Endicott, NY 13760

Midwest Quarterly, PSU, 44 Grubbs, 1701 South Broadway, Pittsburg, KS 66762

Midwest Review, Wisconsin Univ., 5125 Pepin Pl. Madison, WI 53705

Mighty Fine, Brink Literacy Project, 13999 County Rd 102, Elbert, CO 80106

Milk Candy Review, Ulrich, 3145 Grelch Ln, Billings, MT 59105

Minerva Rising Press, 17717 Circle Pond Court, Boca Raton, FL 33496

The Minnesota Review, Hockman, 3036 Redbud St., Culpeper, VA 22701

Minola Review, 669-A Crawford St., Toronto, ON M6G 3K1, Canada

Minutes Before Six, 2784 Homestead Rd. #301, Santa Clara, CA 95051

Minyan Magazine, Marlow, 7683 Cross Village Dr., Germantown, TN 38183

Mississippi Review, USM, 118 College Dr., #5144, Hattiesburg, MS 39406-0001

Missouri Review, 453 MeReynolds Hall, UMO, Columbia MO 65211

Mizna, 2446 University Ave. W., #115, Saint Paul, MN 55114

Mobius, Journal of Social Change, 149 Talmadge, Madison, WI 53704

Mock Turtle Zine, Birdsall, 276 Ashley Ct., Beavercreek, OH 45434

Modern Haiku, PO Box 1570, Santa Rosa Beach, FL 32459

Modern Language Studies, Susquehanna Univ., English, 514 University Ave., Selinsgrove, PA 17870-1164

Molecule, Carver, 12 Hawthorne Blvd, Salem, MA 01970

Mom Egg Review, POB 9037, Bardonia, NY 10954

Months to Years, Louwers, 54 Enchanted View Cir, Fishersville, VA 22939

Moon City, English, MSU, 901 So National Ave., Springfield, MO 65897

Moon Park Review, PO Box 87, Dundee, NY 14837

Moon Pie Press, 16 Walton St., Westbrook, ME 04092

Moon Tide Press, 6709 Washington Ave., #9297, Whittier, CA 90608

Moonpath Press, PO Box 445, Tillamook, OR 97141-0445

Moonrise Press, PO Box 4288, Sunland, CA 91041-4288

Mount Hope, Roger Williams Univ., 1 Old Ferry Rd., GHH20, Bristol, RI 02809

Mud Season, O'Bern, 103 Bradford Dr, Coatesville, PA 19320

Muddy River Poetry Review, 15 Eliot St., Chestnut Hill, MA 02467

Muse-Pie Press, 73 Pennington Ave., Passaic, NJ 07055

MUTHA Magazine, 304 18th St, Brooklyn, NY 11215

Muzzle Magazine, S. Edwards, 107 Shaftsbury Rd., Clemson, SC 29631

N+1, 68 Jay St (H405) Brooklyn, NY 11201

Narrative, 668 Riverside Dr., #56, New York, NY 10031

National Flash Fiction Day, Jendrzejewski, 2 Pearce Close, Cambridge, CB3 9LY, UK

Naugatuck River Review, 45 Highland Ave., #2, Westfield, MA 01085

Negative Capability Press, 150 Du Rhu Dr., #2202, Mobile, AL 36608

New England Review, Middlebury College, Middlebury, VT 05753

New English Review, Mallock, 305 Chippewa Cir., Nashville, TN 37221-4018

New Flash Fiction, 210 W. Lincoln Ave., Indianola, IA 50125

New Letters, 5101 Rockhill Rd., Kansas City, MO 64110-2499

New Lit Salon Press, 513 Vista on the Lake, Carmel, NY 10512

New Ohio Review, Ohio Uuniversity, 201 Ellis Hall, Athens, OH 45701

New Orleans Review, Campus Box 195, Loyola Univ., New Orleans, LA 70118

New Pop Lit, 2074 17th St., Wyandotte, MI 48192

New Territory Magazine, K. Foster, 304 N. 8th St., Oskaloosa, IA 52577

New Verse News, Greenlot Sambandha M-32, Kec. Mengwi, Kab. Badung, Munggu, Bali 80351, Indonesia

Newfound Journal, Eppinger, 636 Chatham Rd., Somerdale, NJ 08083

Next Page Press, 118 Inslee, San Antonio, TX 78209

Night Heron Books, 69 W. Hanover Ave, Morris Plains, NJ 07950

Night Picnic Press, PO Box 3819, New York, NY 10163-3819

Nightboat Books, 310 Nassau Ave., #205, Brooklyn, NY 11222-3813

Ninth Letter, English, 608 S. Wright St., Urbana, IL 61801

No Contact Mag, 1001 E. Byrd St., #6730, Richmond, VA 23219

No Wasted Ink, 18543 Yorba Linda Blvd, #111, Yorba Linda, CA 92886-4135

Nodin Press, 5114 Cedar Lake Rd., Minneapolis, MN 55416

Nombono, A. L. Hope, 343 East 3rd St., Corning, NY 14830

Noon, 1392 Madison Ave., PMB 298, New York, NY 10029

North American Review, Univ. Northern Iowa, Cedar Falls, IA 50614-0516

North Carolina Literary Review, ECU Mailstop 555 English, Greenville, NC 27858-4353

Northampton House Press, 7018 Wildflower Lane, Franktown, VA 23354-2504

Northwest Review, Nelson, 7060 SE 13th Ave., Portland, OR 97202

Not a Pipe Publishing, PO Box 184, Independence, OR 97351

Novel Slices, 136 Muriel St., Ithaca, NY 14850

Nowhere Magazine, 252 Charles Hommel Rd., Saugerties, NY 12477

Nuala Ni Chonchúir, 10 Mont Pleasant Ave., Ballinasloe H53 R970, Co. Galway, Ireland

null pointer press, 86 Silver Sage Cres., Winnipeg MB R3X 0K2, Canada

Obsidian, Illinois State Univ., Box 4241, Normal, IL 61790

Off Assignment, Lescure, 1725 17th St. NW, #214, Washington, DC 20009

The Offing, PO Box 220020, Brooklyn, NY 11222

Okay Donkey, 3756 Bagley Ave., #206, Los Angeles, CA 90034

On the Sea Wall, R. Slate, PO Box 179, Chilmark, MA 02535-9800

One Art, M. Danowsky, 219 Sugartown Rd., #J-304, Wayne, PA 19087

orangepeel, 2144 Ravenglass Place, Apt. F, Raleigh, NC 27612

One Story, 232 3rd St., #A108, Brooklyn, NY 11215

Orca, 6516 112th Street Ct., Gig Harbor, WA 98332

Oregon Humanities, 921 SW Washington St., Ste. 150, Portland, OR 97205

Origami Poems Project, 1948 Shore View Dr., Indialantic, FL 32903

Orion, 1 Short St., Ste. 3, Northampton, MA 01060

Orion's Belt Magazine, 157 W. 105th St., #4ER, New York, NY 10025

Ornithopter Press, 37 E. Merwick Ct, Princeton, NJ 08540

Osiris, 106 Meadow Lane, Greenfield, MA 01301

the other side of hope, Plasatis, 8 Kaymar Court, Chorley Old Rd., Bolton BL1 6BA, UK

Owl Light News, 5584 Canadice Lake Rd., Springwater, NY 14560

Oxford American, PO Box 3235, Little Rock, AR 72203-3235

Oyedrum, 1725 Toomey Rd. #200, Austin, TX 78704

Oyster River Pages, 1 Greenwood Ave., Glen Burnie, MO 21061

P. R. A. Publishing, PO Box 211701, Martinez, GA 30917

Pacific Pulse Press, Tomey, 5921 Waterford Bluff Ln, #1418, Raleigh, NC 27612

Paddler Press, 124 Parcells Cres., Peterborough, ON K9K 2R2, Canada

Paloma Press, 110 28th Ave., San Mateo, CA 94403

Pangyrus Lit Mag, Harris, 79 JFK St., #B202, Cambridge MA 02138

Paranoid Tree Press, 3317 Pillsbury Ave S., Minneapolis, MN 55408

Pareidolia Press, Marienburger Str. 30, Hinterhaus, 10405 Berlin, Germany

Paris Dispatch, Montes, 608 W. Beech Ave., McAllen, TX 78501

The Paris Review, 544 West 27th St., 3rd fl, New York, NY 10001

Parliament Literary Journal, 1111 Central Ave, Highland Park, NJ 08904

Passages North, English, NMU, 1401 Presque Isle Ave., Marquette, MI 49855-5363

Passengers Journal, 3046 43rd Ave W, Seattle, WA 98199

Pastel Pastoral, Geering, 3209 Allerton Cir., #A, Greensboro, NC 27409

Peach Magazine, Maier, 123 Westminster Ave., Syracuse, NY 13210

Peauxdunque Review, 4609 Page Dr., Metairie, LA 70003

Pembroke Magazine, P.O. Box 1510, Pembroke, NC 28372-1510

Pen Women Press, 15 Fairway Dr., Novato, CA 94949

Peregrine Press, PO Box 685, Damariscotta, ME 04543

Perennial Press, M. Giovina, 2801 Turk Blvd., #103, San Francisco, CA 94118

Perugia Press, PO Box 60364, Florence, MA 01062

Philadelphia Stories, Rodriguez, 10 Sycamore Ct., Media, PA 19063

Phoebe, GMU, MSN 2C5, The Hub 1201, 4400 University Place, Fairfax, VA 22030

Pigeonholes, 5823 16 Avenue, Delta, BC V4L 1G8, Canada

The Pinch, UM-English, 435 Patterson Hall, Memphis, TN 38152

Pithead Chapel, Magowan, 113 Elsie St., San Francisco, CA 94110

Plain View Press, 1101 W. 34th St, #404, Austin, TX 78705

Planet Scumm, 26 NE 76th Ave., #B, Portland, OR 97213

Planetesimal Press, 157 Adelaide St. W., #175, Toronto, ON M5H 4E7, Canada

Pleiades, UCMO, English, Martin 336, Warrensburg, MO 64093-5214

Plough, 151 Bowne Dr., PO Box 398, Walden, NY 12586

Ploughshares, Emerson College, 120 Boylston St., Boston, MA 02116-4624

Plume, 740 17th Avenue N, Saint Petersburg, FL 33704

PodCastle, Bailey, 521 River Ave., Providence, RI 02908

Poet Lore, 4508 Walsh St., Bethesda, MD 20815

Poetica, 900 Granby St., #122, Norfolk, VA 23510

Poetry Box, 3300 NW 185th Ave., #382, Portland, OR 97229

Poetry Magazine, 61 West Superior St., Chicago, IL 60654

Poetry Online, Dobbs, 2715 30th Ave. So., Minneapolis, MN 55406

Poetry Pea, Hellstrasse 1 B, 8127 Forch, Switzerland

Poetry South, 1100 College St., MUW-1634, Columbus, MS 39701

Poets Wear Prada, Hoffman, 533 Bloomfield St., 2nd floor, Hoboken, NJ 07030

Poiesis, W. The Trees, 1013 West Sixth St., #2, Bloomington, IN 47404

The Point, 30 N. LaSalle St., Ste. 2240, Chicago, IL 60602

Ponder Review, 1100 College St., MUW-1634, Columbus, MS 39701

Popnoir, 1851 Oneida Crt., Windsor, ON N8Y 1S9, Canada

Porcupine Literary, Grieco, 3009 N. Edison St., Arlington, VA 22207

Porter House Review, English, Texas State Univ., 601 University Dr., San Marcos, TX 78666

Posit, 245 Sullivan St. #8-A, New York, NY 10012

Post Grad Journal, 163 Remsen St., #4, Brooklyn, NY 11201

Post Road, Boston College, English, 140 Commonwealth Ave., Chestnut Hill, MA 02467

Potomac Review, 51 Mannakee St., MT/212, Rockville, MD 20850

Potter's Grove Press, 8307 E. State Route 69, #25803, Prescott Valley, AZ 86312

Prairie Journal Trust, 28 Crowfoot Terr. NW, PO Box 68073, Calgary, AB, T3G 3N8, Canada

Pratik, Barnstone, 13501 Earlham Dr., Whittier, CA 90608

Presence Journal, 65 Clark Ave., Bloomfield, NJ 07003

Press 53, 560 N. Trade St., Ste. 103, Winston-Salem, NC 27101-2937

Psaltery & Lyre, 4917 E. Oregon St., Bellingham, WA 98226

A Public Space, 323 Dean St., Brooklyn, NY 11217

Puerto Del Sol, NMSU, PO Box 30001, MSC 3E, Las Cruces, NM 88003

Pulp Literature Press, 21955 16th Ave., Langley, BC, V2Z 1K5, Canada

Puritan, 65 Watergarden Dr., #305, Mississauga, ON L5R 0G9, Canada

Purple Wall Stories, 1206 Capuchino, Burlingame, CA 94010

Quarter After Eight, Walsh, 359 Ellis Hall, Ohio University, Athens, OH 45701

Quarterly West, Univ. of Utah, English/LNCO 3500, 255 S. Central Campus Dr., Salt Lake City, UT 84112-9109

Quartet, Blaskey, 10613 N. Union Church Rd., Lincoln, DE 19960

Queerlings, S. Tait, 8 Belgrave Rd., Bingley, West Yorkshire BD16 4NB, UK

Quiet Lightning, 256 40th Street Way, Oakland, CA 94611

Quill and Parchment, 2357 Merrywood Dr., Los Angeles, CA 90046

Rabid Oak, 8916 Duncanson Dr., Bakersfield, CA 93311

The Racket, Sanders, 2045 Grahn Dr., Santa Rosa, CA 95404

Radar Poetry, 19 Coniston Ct., Princeton, NJ 08540

Raritan, Rutgers, 31 Mine St., New Brunswick, NJ 08901

Rat's Ass Review, 309 Chimney Ridge, Perkinsville, VT 05151

Rattle, 12411 Ventura Blvd., Studio City, CA 91604

Raven Chronicles, 15528 12th Ave. NE, Shoreline, WA 98155

Rebel Satori Press, 84 Carolyn Ct., Arabi, LA 70032–1955

Reckon Review, PO Box 1280, Flat Rock, NC 28731

Red Fez, 3811 NE Third Court, #G-208, Renton, WA 98056

Red Rock Review, 6375 W. Charleston Blvd., Las Vegas, NV 89146

Red Wheelbarrow, DeAnza College-English, 21250 Stevens Creek Blvd, Cupertino, CA 95014

Redactions, 182 Nantucket Dr., Apt. U, Clarksville, TN 37040

Redfern Ink, 219 Cummins St., Franklin, TN 37064

Redwood Press, 6101 Gushee St., PO Box 411, Felton, CA 95018

Relief Journal, Taylor Univ-English 236 W. Reade Ave, Upland, IN 46989

Repsouls, 4712 E. 2nd St., #239, Long Beach, Ca 90803

Reservoir Road, 1295 Beacon St., #884, Brookline, MA 02446

Reunion: The Dallas Review, Univ. Texas, PO Box 830688, Richardson, TX 75080

Revolute Literary, Randolph College, 2500 Rivermont Ave., Lynchburg, VA 24504

Rhino, PO Box 591, Evanston, IL 60204

Ridgeway Press, English Dept., Wayne State Univ., Detroit, MI 48202

Rinky Dink Press, 15552 N. 156th Ln, Surprise, AZ 85374

Rivanna Review, 807 Montrose Ave., Charlottesville, VA 22902

River Heron Review, PO Box 543, New Hope, PA 18938

River Mouth Review, 2023 E. Sims Way, #364, Port Townsend, WA 98368

River Styx, 3301 Washington Ave., #2C, Saint Louis, MO 63103

River Teeth, English, BSU, 2000 W. University Ave., Muncie, IN 47306

Rivercliff Books, 15 Meeting Grove Ln, Norwalk, CT 06850

Roanoke Review, 221 College Lane, Salem, VA 24153

Rockford Review, PO Box 858, Rockford, IL 61105

Roi Fainéant Press, 3247 Evergreen Hills Dr., #1, Macedon, NY 14502

Room, PO Box 46160, Stn. D, Vancouver, BC V6J 5G5, Canada

Rose L. Cirigliano Studio, 320 East 42nd St., #1507, New York, NY 10017

Ruminate, 2723 SE 115th Ave., Portland, OR 97266

The Rumpus, PO Box 2230, Falls Church, VA 22042

The Rupture, 2206 W. Broadway Ave., Spokane, WA 99201

Rust + Moth, 4470 S. Lemay Ave., #1108, Fort Collins, CO 80525

Rye Whiskey Review, 301 Regency Dr., Deer Park, TX 77536

Sad Girl Press, PO Box 39032, Harewood Mail PO, Nanaimo, BC, V9R 1Po, Canada

Sagging Meniscus Press, 115 Claremont Ave., Montclair, NJ 07042

Salamander, Suffolk U., English, 8 Ashburton Pl., Boston, MA 02108

Salmagundi, Skidmore College, 815 N. Broadway, Saratoga Springs, NY 12866

Salt Hill Journal, English, 100 University Ave., 401 Hall of Languages, Syracuse, NY 13244

Sancho Panza Literary, 16 Carleton Rd., West Hartford, CT 06107

Santa Clara Review, Benson 16, 400 El Camino Real, Santa Clara, CA 95053

Santa Fe Literary Review, 6401 Richards Ave., Santa Fe, NM 87508

Santa Monica Review, 1900 Pico Blvd., Santa Monica, CA 90405

SAPIENS magazine, 530 Creekwood Trl, Black Hawk, CO 80422

Saranac Review, SUNY Plattsburg, 101 Broad St., Plattsburgh, NY 12901

Saturnalia Books, 105 Woodside Rd., Ardmore, PA 19003

Scarlet Tanager Books, Day, 1057 Walker Ave., Oakland, CA 94610

Schuylkill Valley Journal, Danowsky, 219 Sugartown Rd., #J-304, Wayne, PA 19087

Sci-Fi Lampoon, Treiber, 18624 Orlando Rd., Fort Myers, FL 33967

Science Fiction and Fantasy Poetry Assoc., PO Box 1563, Alameda, CA 94501

Scotland Street Press, 100 Willowbrae Ave., Edinburgh EH8 7HU, Scotland

Scoundrel Time, 6106 Harvard Ave., #396, Glen Echo, MD 20812

Scribble, Johnson, 7137 Cedar Hollow Circle, Bradenton, FL 34203

Scribendi, UNM-Honors College, MSC06 3890, 1 University of New Mexico, Albuquerque, NM 87131

Sequoyah Cherokee River Journal, 6143 River Hills Circle, Southside, AL 35907

Seven Kitchens Press, 2547 Losantiville Ave., Cincinnati, OH 45237

Severance Magazine, 117 Lenape Dr., Milford, PA 18337

Sewanee Review, 735 University Ave., Sewanee, TN 37383

ShabdAaweg Review and Press, P. Srivastava, #14-15, 10 Pari Dedap Walk, Tanamera Crest 486062, Singapore

Shark Reef, Hammer, 90 Buck Way, Coupeville, WA 98239

Sheila-Na-Gig, 203 Meadowlark Rd., Russell, KY 41160

Shenandoah, Payne Hall, W&L Univ., Lexington, VA 24450

The Shore Poetry, 843 Johnson Rd., Salisbury, MD 21804

Shoutflower, 1162 S. 10th St., #3F, Philadelphia, PA 19147

sight for sight books, 1395 Barber Dr., Eugene, OR 97405

Silver Pen, 9841 Hickory Lane, St. John, IN 46373

Silverfish Review, PO Box 3541, Eugene, OR 97403

Simple Simons Press, 521 Park Ave., Elyria, OH 44035

Sinister Wisdom, 2333 McIntosh Rd., Dover, FL 33527-5980

Sinking City, 9375 SW 77th Ave, #4025, Miami, FL 33156

Sixteen Rivers Press, PO Box 640663, San Francisco, CA 94164-0663

Sky Island Journal, 1434 Sherwin Ave., Eau Claire, WI 54701

Slag Glass City, Borich, English Dept., DePaul Univ., 2315 N. Kenmore Ave., Chicago, IL 60614

St. Rooster Books, Murr, 241 W. Walnut St., Oneida, NY 13421

Sleet Magazine, 1846 Bohland Ave., St. Paul, MN 55116-1906

Slippery Elm, Univ. of Findlay, 1000 N. Main St., Box 1615, Findlay, OH 45840

Slipstream, Box 2071, Niagara Falls, NY 14301

Smartish Pace, 2221 Lake Ave., Baltimore, MD 21213

Smokelong Quarterly, Allen, 2127 Kidd Rd., Nolensville, TN 37135

Snarl, 512 Rockledge Road C4, Lawrence, KS 66049

So to Speak, MSN 2C5, The Hub Rm 120, 4400 University Dr., Fairfax, VA 22030

Sonic Boom, R. Smith, 753 Stanford White Way, Middletown, DE 19709

South Dakota Review, USD-English, 414 East Clark St., Vermillion, SD 57069-2390

Soflopojo, O'Mara, 1014 Green Pine Blvd., #E-1, West Palm Beach, FL 33409

The Southampton Review, 239 Montauk Hwy., Southampton, NY 11968

Southeast Review, English, FSU, Williams Bldg. 205, Tallahassee, FL 32306

Southern Humanities Review, 9088 Haley Center, Auburn Univ., Auburn, AL 36849-5202

Southern Indiana Review, USI, Orr Center #2009, 8600 University Blvd., Evansville, IN 47712

Southwest Review, PO Box 750374, Dallas, TX 75275-0374

Sparked, 3306 Country Club Dr., Grand Prairie, TX 75052

Spartan, 18218 29th Ave. NE, Lake Forest Park, WA 98155

Spectacle Magazine, Wash U -English, 1 Brookings Dr., St. Louis, MO 63130

Speculative Nonfiction, Lemos, PO Box 15, South Lancaster, MA 01561

Speculatively Queer, 7511 Greenwood Ave. N, #4108, Seattle, WA 98103

Spit Fire Review, Harris, 1219 Ansley Ln., Mentone, CA 92359-9610

Split Lip Magazine, 409 E. Cherry St., Walla Walla, WA 99362

Split This Rock, 1301 Connecticut Ave. NW, #600, Washington, DC 20036

Spoon River Poetry, ISU, Campus Box 4241, Normal, IL 61790

Squares & Rebels, PO Box 3941, Minneapolis, MN 55403-0941

Stackfreed Press, 634 North A St., Elwood, IN 46036

Stairwell Books, 161 Lowther St., York, YO31 7LZ, UK

Stanchion, 609 E. 11th St., #4B, New York, NY 10009

Star 82 Review, PO Box 8106, Berkeley, CA 94707

Star*Line, 61871 29 Palms Hwy, Joshua Tree, CA 92252

Starship Sloane Publishing, 603 Splitrock St., Round Rock, TX 78681

Steel Toe Books, 500 W 4th St., Ste 201-C, Winston-Salem, NC 27101-2782

Still, 89 W. Chestnut St., Williamsburg, KY 40769

Stonecoast Review, DeGroat, 13 Barker St., Jay, ME 04239

Storm Cellar, c/o Goodney, 601 E. Washington St., #4, Greencastle, IN 46135

Storm of Blue Press, 127 Barrington Oaks Ridge, Roswell, GA 30075-4773

Story, 312 E. Kelso Rd., Columbus, OH 43202

Storybrink, Sean, 61 Harris Ave., Albany, NY 12208

Strange Horizons, PO Box 1693, Dubuque, IA 52004-1693

Streetlight Magazine, 56 Pine Hill Lane, Norwood, VA 24581

Sugar House Review, PO Box 13, Cedar City, UT 84721

The Summerset Review, 25 Summerset Dr., Smithtown, NY 11787

The Sun, 107 North Roberson St., Chapel Hill, NC 27516

Sundial, Murphy, 5932 Valley Forge Dr., Coopersburg, PA 18036

Sundog Lit, 607 W. Edwards Ave., Houghton, MI 49931

Sunlight Press, 3924 E Quail Ave., Phoenix, AZ 85050

Superpresent, 3130 Pemberton Walk, Houston, TX 77025

Susurrus Magazine, 205 W. Montgomery Xrd, #608, Savannah, GA 31406

Sweet: A Literary Confection, 83 Carolyn Lane, Delaware, OH 43015

SWWIM Every Day, 301 NE 86th St., El Portal, FL 33138

Sycamore Review, Purdue - English, 500 Oval Dr., West Lafayette, IN 47907

Synkroniciti, 7603 Rock Falls Ct., Houston, TX 77095

TAB Journal, Chapman University, 1 University Dr., Orange, CA 92866

Tahoma Literary Review, PO Box 924, Mercer Island, WA 98040

Tar River Poetry, ECU, MS 159, East 5th St., Greenville, NC 27858-4353

Taurean Horn Press, PO Box 526, Petaluma, CA 94952-0526

Temple Talk, PO Box 147, Tenafly, NJ 07670

Terrain.org, P.O. Box 41484, Tucson, AZ 85717

Terrapin Books, 4 Midvale Ave., West Caldwell, NJ 07006

Territory, 415 Ronalds St., Iowa City, IA 52245

Terror House, 30 N. Goulds St., Ste. N, Sheridan, WY 82801

Texas Review Press, Box 2146, Huntsville, TX 77341-2146

Thimble, 218 Larry Dr., Duncanville, TX 75137

Thirty West Publishing House, thirtywestph(at)gmail.com, PA

This Broken Shore, 15 Sandspring Dr., Eatontown, NJ 07724

3: A Taos Press, P.O. Box 370627, Denver, CO 80237

3 Elements Review, Collins, 198 Valley View Rd., Manchester, CT 06040

300 Days of Sun, H. Lang-Cassera, Nevada State College, 1300 Nevada State
    Dr. DAW 126, Henderson, NV 89002

Three Rooms Press, 243 Bleecker St., #3, New York, NY 10014

Threepenny Review, PO Box 9131, Berkeley, CA 94709

Thrush Poetry Journal, 889 Lower Mountain Dr., Effort, PA 18330

Tia Chucha Press, PO Box 328, San Fernando, CA 91341

Tiferet Journal, 211 Dryden Rd., Bernardsville, NJ 07924

Timber Journal, UC Boulder, 226 UCB, Hellems 101, Boulder, CO 80309

Tiny Spoon, PO Box 1304, Denver, CO 80201

Tiny Wren Lit, 99 Tabilore Loop, Delaware, OH 43015

Tipton Poetry Journal, 642 Jackson St., Brownsburg, IN 46112

TL;DR Press, 213 Heady Lane, Fishers, IN 46038

Toad Hall Editions, Stein, 757 Shore Rd., Northport, ME 04849

Tolsun Books, 7 E. Aspen Ave., #1, Flagstaff, AZ 86001

trampset, PO Box 668, Youngsville, NY 12791

Transformations Press, 35 Essex St., Wenham, MA 01984

Transit Lounge Publishing, Scott, 95 Stephen St., Yarravill VIC 3013, Australia

Trio House Press, 2191 High Rigger Place, Fernandina Beach, FL 32304

TriQuarterly, English, University Hall 215, 1897 Sheridan Rd., Evanston, IL 60208

TulipTree Review, PO Box 133, Seymour, MO 65746

Tusculum Review, 60 Shiloh Rd., PO Box 5113, Greenville, TN 37745

Two Sylvias Press, PO Box 1524, Kingston, WA 98346

Umbrella Factory, A. ILacqua, 838 Lincoln St., Longmont, CO 80501

Unbound Edition, 1270 Caroline St. NE, #D120, Atlanta, GA 30307-2954

Uncharted Magazine, 518 Nancy St., Warsaw, IN 46580

Uncle B. Publications, 510 Blue Ridge Rd., Indianapolis, IN 46208

Under the Gum Tree, PO Box 5394, Sacramento, CA 95817

Under the Sun, PO Box 332, Cookeville, TN 38503

Understory, K. Barrett, Mt. St. Vincent Univ., 166 Bedford Hwy, Halifax, NS B3M 2J6, Canada

Undertow Publications, 1905 Faylee Crescent, Pickering, ON L1V 2T3, Canada

University of Alabama Press, Box 870380, Tuscaloosa, AL 35487

University of Arizona Press, 1510 E. University Blvd., Tucson, AZ 85721

University of Wisconsin Press, 728 State St., #443, Madison, WI 53706

Unlimited Literature, Alexander, 9001 Golf Rd., #8H, Des Plaines, IL 60016

V Press, Dale, PO Box 554, Greer, SC 29650

Valley Voices, MVSU 7242, 14000 Hwy 82 W., Itta Bena, MS 38941-1400

Varient Literature, 204 S. 4th St., Mebane, NC 27302

Variety Pack, Benjamin, 208 North St., Buffalo, NY 14201

Veliz Books, PO Box 961273, El Paso, TX 79996

Versification Zine, 2248 River Oaks Dr., West Columbia, TX 77486

Vertvolta Press, 3614 California Ave SW, #236, Seattle, WA 98116-3780

Vestal Review, Galef, 65 Edgemont Rd., Montclair, NJ 07042-2304

Vincent Brothers Review, 8502 Seawell School Rd, Chapel Hill, NC 27516-9245

Virginia Quarterly Review, 5 Boar's Head Ln, PO Box 400223, Charlottesville, VA 22904-4223

Volume Poetry, Gilmore, 55 Clifton Pl., #1, Brooklyn, NY 11238

The Waking, Nelson, 701 Aztec Dr., #B, Ft. Collins, CO 805211

Wandering Aengus, PO Box 334, Eastsound, WA 98245

warning lines, 206 Bodkin St., Pittsburgh, PA 15226

Washington Writers' Publishing House, 2814 5th St. NE, Washington, DC 20017

Water-Stone Review, MS A1730, 1536 Hewitt Ave., St. Paul, MN 55104-1284

Waters Edge Press, 615 South Pier Dr., Sheboygan, WI 53081

Watershed Review, 400 West First St., Chico, CA 95929

Waterwheel Review, Smith, 52 Grey Rocks Rd., Wilton, CT 06897

West Branch, Stadler Center, 1 Dent Dr., Lewisburg, PA 17837

The West Review, 994 Overlook Rd., Berkeley, CA 94708

West Trade Review, 801 W. Trade St., Charlotte, NC 28202

Whale Road Review, 3900 Lomaland Dr., San Diego, CA 92106

Whiptail Journal, Lehmann, 134 White Birch Dr., Guilford, CT 06437

Whistling Shade, 1495 Midway Pkwy, St. Paul, MN 55108

The Whitefish Review, 708 Lupfer Ave., Whitefish, MT 59937

Wigleaf, MU-English, 114 Tate Hall, Columbia, MO 65211

Willamette Writers, 5331 SW Macadam Ave., #258, PMB 215, Portland, OR 97239

Willow Springs, 601 E. Riverside Ave., #400, Spokane, WA 99202

Willows Wept Review, 17517 County Road 455, Montverde, FL 34756

The Windsor Review, 401 Sunset Ave., Windsor, ON N9B 3P4, Canada

Winnow, 131 Green Meadow Ct, Washington, PA 15301

Wisconsin People & Ideas, Wisconsin Academy, 1922 University Ave., Madison, WI 53726

WMG Publishing, PO Box 269, Lincoln City, OR 97367

Woodhall Press, 81 Old Saugatuck Rd., Norwalk, CT 06855

The Worcester Review, PO Box 804, Worcester, MA 01613

Wordrunner eChapbooks, PO Box 613, Petaluma, CA 94953

Words & Sports, 2228 Glencoe Hills Dr., #4, Ann Arbor, MI 48108

World Literature Today, 630 Parrington Oval, #110, Norman, OK 73019-4033

World Stage Press, 2702 W. Florence Ave., Los Angeles, CA 90043

World Weaver Press, PO Box 21924, Albuquerque, NM 87154-1924

Worple Press, Sycamore Cottage, Church Common, Snape, Suffolk 1P17 1QL, UK

Woven Tale Press, PO Box 2533, Setauket, NY 11733

Wrath-Bearing Tree, 8550 Cirrus Ct., Colorado Springs, CO 80920

Writing Disorder, PO Box 3067, Ventura, CA 93006

Wrongdoing, Ph 18-650 Sheppard Ave E., North York, ON M2K 3E4, Canada

Yale Review, 250 Church St., 4th flr, New Haven, CT 06510

Yalobusha Review, Graduate Writing, Univ. of Mississippi, University, MS 38677

Yellow Arrow Publishing, PO Box 102, Baltimore, MD 21057
Yellow Medicine Review, SMSU, 1501 State St., Marshall, MN 56258

Zephyr Press, 400 Bason Dr., Las Cruces, NM 88005
Zig Zag Lit Mag, 42 Munsill Ave., #E, Bristol, VT 05443
Zoetrope: All Story, 916 Kearny St., San Francisco, CA 94133
ZYZZYVA, 57 Post St., Ste. 708, San Francisco, CA 94104

CONTRIBUTORS' NOTES

JAMAICA BALDWIN's first book, *Bone Language*, will be published by Yes Yes Books in 2023. She studies at the University of Nebraska.

ELLEN BASS is the author of three recent books from Copper Canyon. This is her fourth Pushcart Prize.

MICHELLE BOISSEAU died in 2017. She was the author of several books of poetry and a Contributing Editor at *New Letters*.

KATHRYN BRATT-PFOTENHAUER, a student at Syracuse University, will publish a chapbook, *Small Geometries*, next year.

SAM CHA was born in Korea. His chapbook, *American Carnage*, is available from Portable Press.

MARIANNE CHAN is the author of *All Heathens* (Sarabande Books, 2020).

JENNIFER CHANG is the poetry editor of *New England Review* and the author of books from The University of Georgia Press and Alice James Books.

LEILA CHATTI is the author of the poetry collection *Deluge*. (Copper Canyon Press, 2020) which won the Levis Reading Prize.

KIM CHINQUEE is often called "the Queen of Flash Fiction."

ELAINE HSIEH CHOU's debut novel, *Disorientation*, is forthcoming from Penguin Press.

GINA CHUNG is the author of the novel *Sea Change* and the short story collection *Green Frog*, both from Vintage.

NANCY CONNORS' most recent work has appeared in *failbetter*, *Compressed* and *The Phare*.

ROBERT CORDING has published nine books of poems, most recently *Without My Asking*.

DOUG CRANDELL's recent book is the novel *They're Calling You Home.*

STEVEN ESPADA DAWSON is the son of a Mexican immigrant and is the incoming Halls Poetry Fellow at the University of Wisconsin.

DANIELLE CANDINA DEULEN is the author of a memoir and two poetry collections. She teaches at Georgia State University.

MAGGIE DIETZ is the author of two poetry collections and teaches at the University of Massachusetts.

RITA DOVE was the United States Poet Laureate from 1993–1995. This is her fourth Pushcart Prize selection.

SHANGYANG FANG comes from Chengdu, China. He is a Stegner Fellow at Stanford and the author of a poetry collection, *Burying the Mountain.*

KATIE FARRIS' most recent book is just out from Alice James Books. She lives in Atlanta, GA.

STEPHEN FISHBACH is a former TV executive and speech writer. *To Sharks* is his first published fiction.

MARCELA FEUNTES teaches writing at Texas A&M University. She is at work on her first novel.

THAISA FRANK's fifth book of fiction, *Enchantment* (Counterpoint, 2012), was selected for "Best Books" by the *San Francisco Chronicle.* She lives in Oakland, CA.

JEAN GARNETT is an editor at Little, Brown.

MOLLY GILES is the author of three story collections and the novel *Iron Shoes.*

GAIL GODWIN is the acclaimed author of numerous novels and two story collections. She has also published two volumes of her journals. She lives in Woodstock, NY.

AMANDA GUNN is a Stegner Fellow at Stanford. Her debut poetry collection is forthcoming from Copper Canyon Press.

BANZELMAN GURET's work is appearing in *Chicago Quarterly Review, New Delta Review* and *South Carolina Review.*

DEBRA GWARTNEY's first memoir, *Live Through This*, was a finalist for The National Book Critics Circle Award. She won her first Pushcart Prize last year.

JANICE N. HARRINGTON is the author of several books and teaches at the University of Illinois.

LE VAN D. HAWKINS is a Chicago based writer, poet, and performance artist. He is working on *What Men Do*, a memoir.

JAY HOPLER's *Green Squall* won the Yale Younger Poets Award in 2006. He taught at the University of Florida. He died in June, 2022.

BRIONNE JANAE is the author of *Blessed Are the Peacemakers* (2022) which won the Cave Canem Prize. She is co-host of the podcast "The Slave Is Gone."

ILYA KAMINSKY is a USSR-born, Ukrainian-Russian-Jewish-American poet, critic, translator and professor. In 2019, the BBC named Kaminsky among "12 Artists who changed the world".

VICTORIA LANCELOTTA is the author of a story collection and the novels, *Far* and *Coeurs Blesses.*

DORIANNE LAUX's most recent collection is *Only As the Day Is Long: New and Selected Poems* (W.W. Norton). She is Chancellor of The American Academy of Poets.

ADA LIMÓN is the author of six books of poetry and won the National Book Critics Circle Award For Poetry. Her new book is just out from Milkweed.

NICOLE GRAEV LIPSON's essays have appeared in *Creative Non-Fiction, Forth Genre, The Hudson Review* and *Alaska Quarterly Review.* She lives in Massachusetts.

WHITNEY LEE is a Maternal Fetal Medicine Physician. She lives in Chicago with her family.

LISA LOW's debut chapbook, *Crown for the Girl Inside*, is forthcoming from Yes Yes Books.

SANAM MAHLOUDJI's debut novel *The Persians* is forthcoming from Scribner and 4th Estate in the UK. She lives in London.

SALLY WEN MAO is the author of three collections of poetry, most recently *The Kingdom of Surfaces* (Graywolf, 2023).

DANIEL MASON won the Joyce Carol Oates Prize For Fiction. He is the author of three novels and a story collection from Little, Brown.

ALICE McDERMOTT's eighth novel, *The Ninth Hour,* was published by FSG in 2017. She won The National Book Award For Fiction in 1998. She teaches at Johns Hopkins University.

KAMILAH AISHA MOON was the author of *Starshine & Clay* (Four Way Books) and other acclaimed collections.

JEB LOY NICHOLS lives off the grid in Wales. His latest book is *Suzanne and Gertrude. Knock Turn* is due soon.

IDRA NOVEY teaches at Princeton. Her new novel, *Take What You Need,* is forthcoming in 2023.

D. NURKSE's most recent book is *Country of Strangers: New and Selected Poems* (Knopf, 2022)

JULIA PAUL is a poet and an attorney. Her collection, *Shook*, is published by Grayson Books.

ROGER REEVES is the author of *King and Me*. His most recent book is *Best Barbarian: Poems* (Norton).

ALEYNA RENTZ is a recent MFA graduate from Johns Hopkins University and is the senior fiction reader for *Salamander*.

ELIZABETH ROBINSON is the author of twelve books of poetry, most recently *Counter Part*.

MARY RUEFLE is the author of *Dunce* (Wave Books, 2019), and a finalist for the 2020 Pulitzer Prize, The National Book Award and The National Book Critics Circle Citation.

KAREN RUSSELL has won four previous Pushcart Prizes. Among her awards is a MacArthur Foundation "Genius Grant" in 2013.

JOSEPH SIGURDSON lives in a cabin in rural Alaska. He debut novel, *Buffalo Dope*, was published by Thirty West Publishing House in 2021.

JEN SILVERMAN's debut novel, *We Play Ourselves*, was published in 2021.

BENNETT SIMS is the author of two books from Two Dollar Radio. He teaches fiction at the University of Iowa.

KATE OSANA SIMONIAN is an Armenian-Australian writer of essays and fiction. She has finished her first novel, *Singleton*.

ANTHONY VASNA SO (1992-2020) won the National Book Critics Circle John Leonard Award.

BRANDON TAYLOR is the author of the short story collection *Filthy Animals* and the novel *Real Life*, shortlisted for the 2020 Booker Prize.

ELIZABETH TALLENT is the author of a novel and four story collections. She teaches writing at Stanford.

JONI TEVIS is the author of two books of essays, both from Milkweed Editions. She teaches at Furman University in Greenville, SC.

KATRINA VANDENBERG is the author of *The Alphabet Not Unlike the World* and *Atlas*.

SAM HERSCHEL WEIN's third chapbook is forthcoming from Porkbelly Press.

ALLISON BENIS WHITE is the author most recently of *The Wendys* (Four Way Books, 2020). She has received honors from The Poetry Society of America, Academy of American Poets, Poets & Writers and others.

ISAAC YUEN's work can be found in *Orion, Pleiades, Gulf Coast* and other publications.

INDEX

The following is a listing in alphabetical order by author's last name of works reprinted in the *Pushcart Prize* editions since 1976.

530

535

561

567